D0095408

**BY SCOTT SIGLER**

**THE GENERATIONS TRILOGY**

*Alive*

*Alight*

*Alone*

**NOVELS**

*Infected* (Infected Trilogy Book I)

*Contagious* (Infected Trilogy Book II)

*Ancestor*

*Nocturnal*

*Pandemic* (Infected Trilogy Book III)

**GALACTIC FOOTBALL LEAGUE SERIES**

*The Rookie*

*The Starter*

*The All-Pro*

*The MVP*

*The Champion*

**GFL NOVELLAS**

*The Reporter*

*The Detective*

*Title Fight*

**SHORT STORY COLLECTIONS**

*Blood Is Red*

*Bones Are White*

# ALONE

# ALONE

BOOK THREE OF THE GENERATIONS TRILOGY

## SCOTT SIGLER

DEL REY

NEW YORK

*Alone* is a work of fiction. Names, places, characters, and incidents either are the product of the author's imagination or are used fictitiously. Any resemblance to actual persons, living or dead, events, or locales is entirely coincidental.

Published in the United States by Del Rey, an imprint of Random House, a division of Penguin Random House LLC, New York.

DEL REY and the HOUSE colophon are registered trademarks of Penguin Random House LLC.

Library of Congress Cataloging-in-Publication Data
Name: Sigler, Scott, author.
Title: Alone / Scott Sigler.
Description: First Edition. | New York : Del Rey, [2017] | Series: The generations trilogy ; 3
Identifiers: LCCN 2016033771 (print) | LCCN 2016040149 (ebook) |
ISBN 9780553393194 (hardback) | ISBN 9780553393200 (ebook)
Subjects: | GSAFD: Science fiction.
Classification: LCC PS3619.I4725 A792 2017 (print) | LCC PS3619.I4725 (ebook)
| DDC 813/.6—dc23
LC record available at lccn.loc.gov/2016033771

Printed in the United States of America on acid-free paper

randomhousebooks.com

2 4 6 8 9 7 5 3 1

First Edition

Book design by Caroline Cunningham

For Shannon. The world is a bit darker without you in it.

I miss you.

# THE BIRTHDAY CHILDREN

Italics=deceased

| EM'S GROUP | |
|---|---|
| ◎ | B. Aramovsky |
| ○ | K. Bello, M. Savage |
| ◑ | *K. O'Malley* |
| ✪ | *J. Yong* |
| ✪ | T. Spingate |
| ⊕ | |

| BISHOP'S GROUP | |
|---|---|
| ◎ | |
| ○ | R. Cabral, M. D'souza, *J. Harris*, O. Ingolfsson, Y. Johnson, E. Okereke |
| ◑ | G. Borjigin, Q. Opkick |
| ✪ | Y. Bawden, R. Bishop, *U. Coyotl, T. El-Saffani*, T. El-Saffani, Q. Farrar, *S. Latu, W. Visca* |
| ✪ | *G. Beckett*, X. Gaston |
| ⊕ | K. Smith |

| XOLOTL KIDS | |
|---|---|
| ◎ | B. Walezak |
| ○ | D. Abbink, G. Abrams, W. Alves, R. Andreasson, R. Ansel, A. Aucciello, K. Baardwijk, M. Bardsley, S. Bohner, R. Broz, V. Buffone, H. Chowdhury, A. Csonka, *D. Doyle,* L. Esser, K. Grosser, N. Harman, M. Hoffman, P. Howland, E. Jahoda, K. Jepson, W. Kysely, *E. Lestrange,* U. Marshall, L. Maus, D. McBride, G. Mehmet, R. Pecora, *I. Perreault,* A. Poole, F. Pope, J. Queen, Y. Raske, J. Rigby, T. Romagnoli, D. Roth, M. Savona, A. Schoettmer, I. Sharman, V. Sherazi, E. Simonis, G. Snider, D. Szwarc, Z. Taylor, A. Tittensor, J. Tosetti, I. Tosto, M. Traverso, P. Van Kane, G. Vincent, L. Wieck, *J. York* |
| ◑ | *J. Abrantes, T. Aeschelman,* L. Bariso, H. Bemba, N. Derrickson, T. Schuster |
| ✪ | V. Abdul, O. Afoyalan, *E. Argyris,* T. Arkema, H. Blaha, C. Boesch, U. Brankovich, K. Brown, P. Bruhn, *W. Cadotte, B. Cody,* I. Darzi, P. Değirmenci, *N. Derrickson,* A. Dreesens, I. Fields, D. Giroux, N. Holub, H. Horn, D. Hornick, P. Horvat, C. Hrabe, M. Krejci, *S. Kysely,* E. Loncar, B. Marija, F. Metharom, V. Metharom, *R. Mohammed,* V. Muller, S. Myska, J. Olson, C. Pokorny, S. Radic, I. Resnik, S. Schovajsa, *J. Thorn,* C. Tosi, A. Uzun, *M. Vendi,* Q. Wakefield, S. Xanth |
| ✪ | M. Cathcart, C. Kalle, A. Nevins, N. Peura, B. Zubiri |
| ⊕ | L. Pokano, F. Yilmaz |

## SHUTTLE KIDS

A. Aaltink, P. Abbink, V. Agim, J. Aiolfi, Z. Akinyi, C. Albert, A. Almog, E. Aloísio, A. Amsel, M. Andrews, Í. Angerona, H. Anima, A. Antónia, I. Antonizius, C. Anxo, A. Apollodoros, K. Armbruster, J. Asta, S. Attar, B. Babirye, J. Bartram, K. Benson, V. Bernhard, G. Bjarne, M. Blanco, X. Bobbi, S. Bohumír, K. Bousaid, O. Boyce, V. Breindel, B. Bureau, A. Carlota, O. Charmchi, T. Chinwe, T. Church, T. Cindi, K. Costello, H. Dalibor, C. Danailov, A. Danica, B. Danielle, X. De Campo, P. De Felippis, R. De Witte, F. Doretea, R. Dykstra, S. Eadburg, F. Eccleston, H. Einarsson, K. El-Amin, C. Eld, D. Érica, V. Erikanos, D. Esparza, F. Estera, H. Fabian, C. Fehér, M. Ferrari, V. Filipov, S. Fortunato, S. Frank, H. Gerben, C. Gilbert, P. Glietezzia, W. Golanz, D. Grieve, I. Hachilinski, E. Haig, D. Hallman, B. Hanley, H. Harald, N. Hasenkamp, A. Heimirsson, E. Hinog, L. Höfler, A. Hornik, A. Hovanesian, L. Iakovu, N. Adoha, T. Iona, I. Jonkheer, P. Ivanov, M. Jäger, S. Jeffers, A. Jelena, T. Jolånka, J. Joris, C. Júlia, E. Jurre, T. Juvenal, F. Kamala, A. Kay, K. Klavdiya, E. Kowalcyzk, M. Lagunov, R. Lan, N. Leary, M. Leblanc, J. Lei, A. Livia, É. Llorenç, B. Lunete, L. Lyudmyla, A. Machado, S. Machán, N. Malley, X. Merckx, S. Metharom, Z. Min, H. Min-Jun, C. Miron, S. Morgan, C. Nauer, M. Nicolson, J. Nikole, N. Nilsson, K. Nogah, T. Oberto, S. Ochoa, O. Oliver, A. Oluwatoyin, N. Ophelia, Y. Pajari, G. Pandev, C. Pavia, L. Peak, N. Pemphero, N. Poindexter, A. Potenza, C. Quintana, J. Rhee, J. Royston, Z. Salut, H. Salvay, W. Scarpa, K. Schlusser, H. Schwenke, D. Shemaiah, A. Shepherd, K. Siet, A. Sigurosson, E. Skye, A. Sniegowski, P. Spini, G. Stabile, N. Taalay, E. Tabitha, J. Tawfeek, M. Tesar, S. Uidhir, E. Vaccaro, S. Van Der Beek, O. Vanev, B. Vasilyev, Y. Vibius, L. Vincent, C. Wasylyna, D. Weekes, R. Williams, S. Winona, K. Yancy, C. Yazhu, Y. Yeriyahu, J. Zénaïde, B. Zheng, J. Zinat, T. Zola, P. Zuleika

# PART I

## HOME AND HEARTH

# ONE

A stabbing pain jolts me awake.

My neck . . . the needle, the *snake* . . .

No, not a stab. A poke . . . a poke of cold metal. I lift my head, look around. My silver bracelet. I wear it over the sleeve of my black coveralls, its wide ring circling my right forearm just below my elbow—I must have rolled over in my sleep, laid my neck on the long point that extends from the flat ring down to just behind the back of my wrist.

I'm cold. I'm wet. It's raining again. Correction: it's raining *still*. I was sleeping on the tiny metal deck of a spider cockpit, other people crammed in around me. My thigh is numb—I rolled over onto the combat knife I always have strapped to my leg.

So tired. As uncomfortable as I am, I just want to go back to sleep.

A boy's voice: "Em, wake up."

Victor Muller, part of my spider's three-person crew.

"D'souza spotted them," he says. "She's coming."

That wakes me up for real. If Maria is coming, maybe it's time to fight.

*Finally.*

I sit up. Muscles, cramped and stiff. My cold skin feels like it's made of half-dry clay. Our black coveralls are good at keeping us warm, but in the jungle the dampness always finds a way in.

Ten days of this. Ten days of hiding, without fire or heat, without a hot meal, eating prepackaged food and raw jungle plants. Ten days since I bathed—I want a shower almost as much as I want to catch the Belligerents. I want to lie on my couch, Bishop's arms around me as I watch the jungle from afar, not from within it.

I miss him. I miss his eyes, his hair and his smile. I miss the very smell of him. If we're able to force our enemy to battle—and that is a very big *if*—I might be hurt in the fighting. Possibly even killed. Before I left, he told me he loves me.

Did I tell him the same thing?

I think I did. Yes, I must have.

*You would have told O'Malley, and you know it.*

Well, hello, Annoying Little Voice. How nice of you to show up now.

Annoying Little Voice always wants me to second-guess myself, to doubt my decisions. It always seems to think things would be better *now* if they'd gone a different way *then*. If I'd made different choices. If I'd had stronger self-control. I hate that damn voice.

Wiping the last of the sleep from my eyes, I reach up and grab the armored ridge that surrounds the cockpit. I stand, slowly, careful to not jostle the branches that hide our position.

The twin moons of Omeyocan—one bluish, one maroon—shine through sparse cloud cover. In the daytime, this jungle is bright with yellow leaves, brown tree trunks and long blue vine stems. At night, everything is a blue-purple shade of gray. The plants gleam with wetness.

Spingate still insists on calling our machines "pentapods," but no one listens to her about that. To us, they are *spiders*. Five-legged, yes, but spiders all the same. The machines are meant for a two-person crew: driver and cannon operator. We use them with crews of three, adding one person who can fire with whatever weapon they have at hand. Three makes for close quarters. The cockpit is open-air. No glowing holograms here—all the controls are manual, built to last a thousand years, to take a real beating and keep on working. A waist-high, horseshoe-shaped armored ridge surrounds the cockpit, protects us from bullets and musket balls. The ends of the horseshoe blend into the cockpit's rear wall, which comes up to my sternum. If I stand straight, I can rest my arms on the spider's sloping back and fire my bracelet at whatever is behind us.

We've repainted the spiders to cover up centuries of superficial damage. Each one has black numbers on the sides (ours is 05), while most of the shell is dark yellow with jagged stripes of brown and blue—the colors of the jungle. When the machines work correctly, they blend in well. Of course, they're all a couple of centuries old, so they don't work correctly all that much. Parts often clatter and gears frequently grind, making unmistakable noise. We do our best to fix those problems when they come up.

There are two legs in front, two on the sides—one each below where the armored ridge blends into the back wall—and one leg in the rear. The three-jointed legs all end in hard, sharp points, which can slice right through any enemy unfortunate enough to be in our way.

I ride in the cockpit's right side. Yoshiko Bawden, the driver, is on my left, in the middle. She's a tall, muscular circle-star who thinks it's funny to make fake burp sounds. When she's not being crude, though, she is a fierce warrior. She's always kept her black hair shaved down. Before we began this campaign, she had some of her fellow circle-stars tattoo the word KILLER on the right side of her head. She has a pitchfork strapped across her back and a bracelet on her right arm over her coveralls. She used to use an axe, like Bishop does, but she prefers the pitch-fork for jungle fighting. I have known her almost since I first woke up. I'm so grateful to have her as part of my crew.

"Little" Victor Muller is on Bawden's left, where he mans the beam-cannon. He's not little anymore, though. When the circle-star came out of his coffin, I was a bit taller than he was. Now my eyes come up to his chin. He's added muscle as well. He's not as thick as Bishop, probably never will be. Victor has the same wiry frame my friend Coyotl had—long, lean, athletic. Victor wears a bracelet on his right arm. In his hands, he holds a spear. Not *my* spear, of course, but one that looks close to it. A repeat-ing rifle is slung over his back, black barrel and the black loop lever that lets him reload it with a flick of his hand gleaming from a recent cleaning and oiling. Victor has become one of our best warriors, almost as skilled as Farrar, Bishop and Bawden, who are all fully grown.

I am brave enough to fight, but I'm not stupid—I want people in my crew who can protect me. I'd rather have Bishop instead of Victor, of course, but right now it's more important to our people that Bishop remains back in Uchmal.

The lower half of our spider is buried in the jungle floor, the upper half covered in branches and vines. Sometimes you hunt your enemy—but only if you can find them. When you can't, your best bet is to set a trap and hope your enemy falls into it.

It looks like they finally have.

A light rustling from the jungle in front of us. I see what looks like a thick, yellowish snake rise from the underbrush and move toward us. The furry snake ends in wicked, hooked pincers that can snap together so hard they'll damn near cut a person in two.

A few meters away, the full animal rises up from the underbrush. A year ago, the sight of this predator would have scared me half to death. Now? It only scares me a quarter of the way.

When I first saw these creatures, I didn't have the memories or words to describe them. It's still hard. Different people have remembered different things at different times, filling my head with images of animals that Matilda only read about in books. The heavy body of a bear. The thick trunk of an elephant. Below where the trunk connects to the head is a piranha's dagger-toothed mouth. Claws of a tiger. All of it covered in brown-striped yellow fur. Heavy plates of mottled yellow bone on its chest. Three beady black eyes in a line on each side of the head, which is also plated in yellow bone.

On the back of this beast, on a saddle made of tough leather, sits Maria D'souza, a fellow "empty."

She took to calling the big predators *hurukans*. We're not sure where that word comes from, but as soon as any of us heard it, we agreed it was the perfect name.

"Hail, Em," Maria says. *"Guthana, Yalani."*

Maria greets me first in English, then in the Springer language. She always wants the Springer fighters in her squad to know I am in charge—*Yalani* means "leader."

"Hail, Maria," I say. "You've found them?"

She nods. "The Belligerents are coming from the east, closing in on the cornfield. I have the Creepers circling behind them to cut off any escape. Barkah and his infantry battalion are positioned to the north as a reserve, per your orders."

*Cornfield* sounds a bit grand for our sickly crop, but we have invested countless hours getting it to grow.

"How many Belligerents?" I ask.

"Maybe a hundred," Maria says. "All on foot. No cavalry of any kind."

"Excellent. Where do you want us?"

Maria points north.

"Straight ahead, *Yalani*. My squad will attack from the southwest. When you strike, we'll be on your left flank."

Atop the 650-kilo hurukan she calls Fenrir, Maria is a striking figure. She wears cloth strips of yellow, green and blue, just like the Springer warriors. Vine juice and dirt cover her brown skin, helping her blend into the jungle. She has a half-dozen knives strapped to her body and a repeating rifle slung across her back. When the violence began months ago, I offered her one of our precious bracelets. She declined. She chooses to use the same weapon as the Springers in her cavalry squads.

The snake-wolves are the top predators of this world. As far as we can tell, they kill and eat everything they see. That included the Springers. Then came Maria, who somehow learned how to not only capture the beasts, but *tame* them as well. She's trained others to do the same.

Mounted atop her monster, Maria D'souza has become a death goddess of the jungle. She has killed more enemy soldiers than anyone. Except for Farrar, of course, but that's why we used him as bait.

We used to think Barkah controlled all the Springers on Omeyocan. We were wrong. There are four main tribes that we know of. Barkah's tribe, the Malbinti, claims the areas around Uchmal. The Khochin are far to the south of our city. The Podakra are just a day's ride to the west. The largest tribe of all, the Galanak, fill the jungle to the northeast.

"Belligerents" is what we've come to call the Springers that attack us at every turn. We haven't taken any alive yet, but based on the clothing of those we killed in battle they have members from all four known tribes, *including* the Malbinti. Barkah doesn't know why some of his people joined them.

The Belligerents don't have uniforms, but they do have one unifying element. In addition to the jungle rags of blue, yellow and green, they all wear at least one bit of red.

Red—the same color as the robes Aramovsky wore, as the robes in the carvings on the Observatory.

In the past few months, the Belligerents have been burning our crops, attacking us when we go outside the walls. Whatever their reasons, the Belligerents are aggressive and trying to kill my people.

I can't allow that to continue.

"Get into position," I say to Maria. "We attack immediately."

Maria and Fenrir vanish into the jungle with barely a sound. How something that big can move so quietly, I have no idea.

"Finally," Bawden says. "Those bug-eyed bastards can't escape this time."

I give her a short glance. Bawden was close with J. York, a circle boy who was killed by Belligerents a few months ago. Bawden wants revenge. Too many of my people want revenge.

"Our allies are also *bug-eyed bastards*," I say. "Do you forget that? Or do you want to cuss at the people who are fighting on our side?"

Bawden answers with only a belch, which makes Victor laugh.

I'll never understand circle-stars.

"Clear away the brush," I say. "We go now."

Victor and Bawden toss aside our cover of branches. My spear is held by a bracket mounted on the cockpit's rear wall. I yank the spear free, then raise it high and circle it in the air—the signal for my platoon to move out. Branches rustle around us as two other spider crews clear them away and prepare to leave. A dozen young circle-stars silently rise up from hidden places in the underbrush. They wear black coveralls, like me, but are wrapped in vines, their faces and hair smeared with dark mud. They make ready to march, make ready to fight.

Including me, my platoon has twenty-one humans: nine on spiderback, twelve on foot. Maria's squad—"D'souza's Demons"—has three snake-wolves and their riders, along with eighteen Springers on foot. Squad Two—called "the Creepers" and led by Lahfah, Barkah's mate—has the same numbers as D'souza's Demons. That means we'll attack with a combination of sixty-three troops, three spiders and six snake-wolves. We're slightly outnumbered, but technology is on our side. And in reserve, we have two hundred Springers led by Barkah himself. I almost feel sorry for the Belligerents we're about to attack.

Almost.

"Bawden, lead us out."

She does. Our spider rises up, the cockpit now four meters above the jungle floor. Mud drips down from the dented yellow shell and the black *05* painted on either side.

We march to battle.


The Belligerents like to hit and run. They never fight in the open. When they started attacking our people, our crops, Barkah's patrols and his new city of Schechak, we would ride our spiders out from Uchmal to fight them. But as fast as the spiders are, by the time we reached the conflict the Belligerents had already melted into the jungle, leaving bodies and carnage behind.

Just over a year ago, Aramovsky led our people to war with Barkah's father, the former Springer king. The battle was brief but bloody. Barkah and I brought our two peoples together. We made peace. While some hatred and distrust remained between our two races, we worked hard to coexist, to learn from each other so that both cultures could flourish and grow.

Other than a few scuffles, there was little trouble.

But six months ago, that started to change.

Barkah's people started to confront us. Verbally at first, then arguments turned to fistfights. Then knife fights. My people—and Barkah's—started getting hurt. Barkah and I both punished the aggressors, trying to set an example that hate would not be tolerated.

It's not just the Springers who are changing. My people have grown steadily angrier. More vocal about making Uchmal "human-only," about driving *all* Springers out of the jungle around our city. Whenever I hear this talk, I shut it down—as do Bishop, Borjigin and many others—but these hateful feelings are gaining momentum.

We initially blamed our own increased hostility on the stress and anxiety caused by three starships closing in on Omeyocan. The first of those will reach orbit any day now, Spingate tells me. We don't know what these aliens want. We don't know where they came from. We have to assume they're coming to kill us, bringing death just as our *Xolotl* brought death to the Springers.

Now, however, I don't think the approaching starships are the reason for these troubles. As a people, our attitudes have shifted too far, too fast—and the presence of those ships wouldn't explain why the Springers have become more violent. I'm at a loss to explain what is happening to all of us.

Before the Birthday Children arrived, all Springers lived underground. It was the only way they survived the endless attacks of roaming spiders, machines still following commands given to them centuries ago. Since Barkah and I made peace—and since I stopped the spiders from ravaging the countryside—most of his tribe now lives in Schechak, the first aboveground city his species has had in at least two hundred years.

As more Springers move into that city, they have abandoned the underground villages and endless tunnels surrounding Uchmal. The Belligerents have made good use of these hidey-holes. Once the terrorists are out of sight, it's nearly impossible to find them again.

That's why we had to stay hidden for days, suffering through the pouring rain, freezing our butts off—so we could catch them aboveground. We have to hit them with force before they can slither beneath the surface like the worms they are.

It frustrates me to no end that we spend so much time trying to defeat the Belligerents. Three alien ships are coming to Omeyocan, which means the beings already on this planet should be working together to create a common defense. But instead, we fight among ourselves. Diplomacy is complicated; fighting is simple. I guiltily admit to myself that part of me— a *big* part—is excited this battle has come. Maybe we can eliminate our enemy, then Barkah and I can concentrate our energies on the larger threat yet to come.

The Annoying Little Voice creeps up again: *It's too late for that. If you were a better leader, you'd have unified everyone already.* I smile to myself as I put that voice in its place, lock it into the shadowy back room of my mind—something I seem to be able to do only when it's time to fight.

Bawden guides our spider through the jungle. Behind us are two more spiders and a dozen tireless young circle-stars armed with bracelets, rifles and their handheld weapon of choice. Somewhere off to my left, D'souza's Demons are moving in as well.

I smell smoke: our corn crop, burning.

The Belligerents have eluded me for months, but now they've taken the bait.

*We have them.*

I rotate my right hand sharply left, then right, the hard twitch that activates my bracelet. I feel a vibration as the weapon powers up. The white stone at the base of its long point starts to glow with a soft light.

"Bawden, keep moving forward, quietly," I say. "Victor, get ready, see if we can take out their lookouts before they sound a warning."

I didn't think the corn crop was enough bait by itself, so I ordered Farrar to build a small outpost right in the middle of the field. The presence of the outpost means that the Belligerents have to bring a larger force if they want to destroy it. But the outpost isn't the real bait—Farrar is.

Among Barkah's tribe and the Belligerents both, Farrar has come to be known as *meh ahn nahak*. Loosely translated, it means "the digger of graves." Many jungle battles result in hand-to-hand combat, where Farrar is deadly with his preferred weapon—a long-handled shovel sharpened to a razor's edge. He's almost as big as Bishop, and his skin is nearly as black as that of the Grownups. Even from a distance, Farrar is an instantly recognizable figure. I had hoped his presence might be too much for our enemy to resist.

That meant, though, putting him and his squad of five young circle-stars in significant danger. This is war, and those are the chances a leader has to take to catch an enemy that refuses to stand and fight. Now that the trap has been sprung, all Farrar and his squad have to do is hunker down and survive the next few minutes.

Our spider quietly steps through the underbrush, a stalking

predator worthy of its namesake. Victor rolls out his neck, loosening up for the coming battle. He unslings his rifle, raises the stock to his shoulder and scans the jungle. His bracelet is a more powerful weapon, but he can fire eight rifle rounds in the time it takes the bracelet to recharge for a second shot.

The rifles are made in Schechak's new factories. At first, the Springers used muskets against us. Muskets have to be reloaded after every shot, while the more accurate rifles can fire ten times before reloading. Victor is probably our best marksman, although Maria is close—she can hit a bull's-eye from fifty meters away while the hurukan beneath her tears through the jungle at a full gallop.

Me? I'll stick with the bracelet. Rifles kick too much. They hurt my shoulder.

"Coming up on the clearing," Bawden says.

I raise my spear, point it right, then left, telling the trailing spiders to fan out. Spider 04 goes right, 02 goes left.

The crescent-shaped clearing. The same place where Aramovsky led my people against the Springers. That battle created too many corpses on both sides for us to completely forgive each other. That's why I chose the clearing as a site to grow crops. I hoped that if we could turn a place of death into a cradle of life, the memories of that battle might fade a bit faster. It seemed to work for those first six months. Now the Belligerents constantly attack our crops. They don't want the field of death to grow over—*hate* is the only crop they want to harvest.

Filtering through the jungle, I hear the unmistakable sounds of war. Rifle fire, echoing musket reports, the telltale hiss of bracelet beams lashing out.

The battle has begun.

"Bawden," I say, "take us to full speed!"

I grip the armored ridge with one hand. We lurch forward,

the need for silence forgotten. I duck down to avoid the branches and snagging vines that slap against the metal shell. The two flanking spiders will match our speed. We'll pull ahead of our foot soldiers, but I don't have a choice—if we don't close quickly, the Belligerents could either escape or overrun Farrar and his squad.

Through the dark jungle, I see the bright glow of flames. Our spider bursts from the trees and into the clearing. Our carefully tended field of corn is a sea of writhing orange.

We've surprised several Belligerents. At the sight of our powerful machines, they flee, flames silhouetting their graceful movements. Strong legs launch the Springers in powerful leaps, long tails trailing behind to balance out their thick bodies. Firelight reflects off their three eyes. Wide toad-mouths bark out what might be commands, might be screams of panic.

Victor slings his rifle and grasps the cannon controls. I wish we didn't have to use this horrible weapon, but the Belligerents are destroying our crops, attacking us, *killing* us.

I duck down, so that only my head and shoulders are above the protective ridge. I straighten my bracelet arm, find a target, and give the order.

"Fire!"

I flick my fingers forward. A beam of white light lances out from my bracelet's long point, ripping toward the closest Belligerent—I miss.

Victor does not. The cannon's beam is larger than mine, glows so bright it seems to dim the flames. The beam hits a leaping Springer, blasting the living creature into a hundred bits of smoking meat and bone.

Beam-cannon fire lashes out from my left and right, tearing up thick chunks of dirt. Flaming corn spins away in pinwheeling clouds of sparks.

I hear the terrified, pain-filled screams of our enemy.

But I also hear muskets boom and rifles crack, see cones of flame flicking from the dark, there one second, then gone the next. One of those cones flares up just to my right: I pivot in place, as Bishop showed me, squaring my shoulders toward the target. At first I see nothing but smoke and flame, then movement, a hopping Springer silhouetted against burning corn.

I fire.

White light catches the Springer in midair. Over the roar of the flames and the bursts of weapons fire, I hear it shriek in the split second before it is torn in half.

This is not the first time I've killed.

It won't be the last.

The few Belligerents we can see realize they are cut off from the jungle. They scatter along the edge of the flames, rushing to my left. Big mistake. I hear the growling howls of snake-wolves, then D'souza's Demons rip from the darkness and into the flickering light. She stands in her saddle, rifle tight to her shoulder, her knees bending in time with her mount's galloping stride. She fires: I see a Springer go down.

Her mount overruns a fleeing Belligerent. The snake trunk snaps forward. Pincers slam shut on the poor creature, bony points punching through cloth and flesh. The trunk curls up, raising the Springer high before whipping it down so fast that bones shatter on impact.

Bawden slows our spider. We stop at the edge of the blazing corn crop. I see narrow paths through the flames. The Belligerents cleared space before they set the fires, giving themselves a way to escape where our cavalry could not follow. Smart. But this time, we are smarter.

Far off to my right, I hear rifle fire and hurukan roars echoing over the flames.

"Lahfah's Creepers," Victor says. "The Belligerents must have fled and run right into them."

Bawden unslings her rifle, sights down the barrel and slowly turns left, then right, looking for a target.

"Bastards," she says. "I hope they all die. Em, some of them could be hiding in the flames. Let me go into those paths and root them out."

I don't want any more death if it can be avoided.

"Stay in the spider," I say. "If we see any Belligerents, try to capture them. A prisoner is more valuable than a corpse."

From the north, we hear distant rifle cracks. That's Barkah's battalion. The Belligerents fled in all directions, and in all directions we were waiting for them.

Our corn burns. There's no putting out this fire. It would have been better to catch the Belligerents before they set this blaze, but the large crop was part of the bait. When you want something bad enough in life, you have to make sacrifices to get it.

"Movement," Victor says as he swings the cannon to bear.

I look, see a Springer hop out from the fire. Its jungle rags are smoldering; its three yellow eyes are wide with fear. Its skin is mostly red—it is so young the purple coloration that marks a teenager has barely begun to set in. A child soldier. But a strip of red cloth tied around each arm tells me this "child" is our enemy.

"Hold your fire," I snap at Victor. To the Springer, I shout: *"Gaintox!"*

I know very little of the Springer language, but I made sure I learned their word for "surrender."

The Springer panics, rushes back into the burning cornfield, instantly vanishing behind shimmering flames.

*"I'll kill it,"* Bawden shouts as she leaps over the ledge.

I instinctively reach out to grab her, to stop her, but my fingers clutch only empty air.

Victor tilts the spider cannon up, a reaction to keep from accidentally shooting the circle-star woman who hits the ground running. In an instant, he's over the ridge and chasing her, rifle slung, both hands on his spear.

The circle-stars move so fast I feel like I'm in slow motion. Spear in one hand, I swing over the rail, then descend the built-in ladder rungs. Circle-stars can leap out of the cockpit and not kill themselves, but I'm not engineered for war like they are.

I hear shouts from the other spider crews, and from the circle-star infantry behind me that is finally reaching the clearing, yet there is no time to wait.

What is Bawden doing? She's never disobeyed an order before. This isn't like her at all.

I rush into the flames after my people. The narrow path twists and turns through the tall burning corn—I'm instantly lost in a maze of fire. Heat bakes my face and hands, stings my eyes.

Through the shimmering haze, I see Bawden in a small open space where the fire has mostly burned down. She's smiling, pitchfork in hand as she and the yellow-eyed Springer child soldier circle each other, each step kicking up fresh ash. The Belligerent holds a hatchet in its two-fingered hand. Bawden is at least twice as large as her terrified foe.

From another path, two more Belligerents rush in, the rags tied around their bodies smoldering with small flames. They hold muskets tipped with long bayonets—the sharp metal shimmers with reflected firelight. The hammers of their muskets are not cocked back; the weapons are empty. The Springers are either out of ammo or haven't had time to reload.

I aim my bracelet, but don't shoot. My eyes are watering and the heat makes everything shimmer madly—I might hit Bawden. I sprint toward her.

Outnumbered three to one, Bawden attacks. She roars, jabs

with the pitchfork. The young Springer flinches in terror, turns away—the sharp pitchfork tines plunge into its back. Before she can pull it free, the second Springer's bayonet pierces her shoulder. Bawden screams in pain, but grabs the musket barrel—she and her foe struggle for the weapon.

Just as I enter the small space, the third Springer comes straight at me, long hopping steps closing the distance. I raise my arm and flick my fingers. A beam of white light shoots out . . .

. . . and *misses*.

The Springer ducked down and to the left.

The bracelet needs a moment to recharge, something the Springer seems to know.

"*Yalani, nahnaw,*" it growls: *Kill their leader.*

It recognizes me.

My enemy lunges forward, bayonet point driving at my belly. I sidestep, sweeping the spear in front of me, knocking the musket aside.

Everything happens so fast. I have a moment to strike, but I hesitate and that moment vanishes. The Springer's wide mouth curls into a very humanlike, hateful snarl.

Bawden screams again. A snap-glance: the second Springer's bayonet is buried in her thigh.

We are all so close together, two humans and three Springers, walled in by a circle of flame, locked in a fight to the death.

The burning corn seems to blast apart—Victor bursts into view, startling all of us. Flaming cinders and sparks cling to his black coveralls. A vision of fire and rage, he steps forward and thrusts his spear—the blade punches deep into the guts of Bawden's attacker. Without a pause he yanks the weapon free and stabs it home again.

A flicker of movement in the corner of my eye is the only

warning I get, but it is enough. My attacker thrusts again, driving the bayonet at my face. I flinch and turn: the point slashes my cheek.

Then Victor is there, closing the short distance with two fast steps. The Belligerent turns to face him, but three eyes take in Victor's bracelet point, aimed right at the wide mouth.

*"Gaintox,"* Victor says, loud but calm. His stare is steel. His arm and fist are rock-still.

The Springer tosses the musket aside, then kneels in the ash.

The small child soldier, the red-skinned one, lies still, eyes wide open and unmoving. It's dead. The third rolls in the dirt, hands on its belly, thick fingers smeared with blue blood. I wish I couldn't hear its wail of pain and fear, but there is no shutting that out.

The fires are fading fast. Tall young corn quickly becomes ankle-high embers.

I hear no more gunfire.

This fight is over.

# TWO

orning dawns on Omeyocan. Blurds buzz through air that smells of wetness and mud.

My spider marches on.

Victor drives. Bawden lies on the small deck at our feet, asleep. We stabilized her wounds. Her injuries are bad, but not life-threatening—she'll be all right once we get her into Smith's medical coffins.

We have a guest crammed into the cockpit with us: none other than Barkah, the Springer king. He's on my left, pressed in between me and Bawden. I smell the burned-toast scent that has become so common I almost never notice it unless I'm very near a member of his species.

Gone are the jungle-colored rags he wore when we first met. His orange jacket is smooth and wrinkle-free, dotted with intricate patterns of colored glass. I think the orange clashes with his reddish-purple skin, but we've found that Springers' taste in fashion is far different from ours.

Barkah lost his middle eye in our fight with Matilda and her Grownups. He wears a patch over it: orange, made from the same fabric as his coat. The two eyes that remain are a pretty shade of emerald green.

An intricate copper plate hangs from his thick neck. The Springer equivalent of a crown, it marks him as royalty. The polished metal gleams in the reddish morning sun. *Everything* about Barkah now seems polished. He is so different from when I first met him in the jungle.

This road, too, is different from when I first saw it. It was a footpath through the trees and vines, so narrow you felt leaves brush against you on both sides. Now it is wide, cleared of plants. The surface is an uneven mishmash of dirt, stone, gravel and flat bits of broken buildings. While it is a far cry from the highways of Matilda's memories, this is the greatest road Omeyocan's jungle has seen in at least two centuries.

Trees rise up on either side, as do the shattered, vine-covered buildings of the once-massive Springer city. The ruins are vast. No matter how much progress we make, they will be here for centuries to come.

My spider marches in a long column made up of the two other spiders in my platoon, our circle-star infantry, D'souza's snake-wolves, and Farrar's squad, which has a place of honor directly behind Barkah and me. A few of Farrar's circle-stars suffered wounds when the Belligerents attacked, but our trap closed so quickly that they didn't have to fight for long.

Shockingly, we didn't lose a single person. Luck? Superior tactics? Superior weapons? I don't really care which, I'm just happy that we don't have to dig yet another grave.

Barkah's foot soldiers march with us as well, two long lines that flank the fifteen Belligerents who survived the battle. Each prisoner wears one of those telltale strips of red cloth some-where on its body. Most of the prisoners are wounded.

I glance at Victor. His face and hands are dotted with burns. Our coveralls are flameproof—another legacy left by the Grownups—but there was no protection for his exposed skin. Some of the dirty-blond hair on the right side of his head is gone, replaced by a red and black burn. It looks painful. If it is, Victor shows no sign.

He fought flawlessly. Fast and efficient, no wasted movement. He killed one Springer, yes, but took a prisoner, as I requested. Not only can he fight, he follows orders. Unlike Bawden. She ignored my commands, almost got herself killed, almost got *me* killed. It's just not like her.

I'll let Bishop figure out what to do about her actions. He's in charge of our "military," what little of it there is.

*Bishop*. I haven't seen him in over a week. I can't wait to see him again.

Victor notices me looking his way.

He smiles. "You were amazing, Em."

I laugh. "Me? You should have seen yourself."

"You were in danger," he says. "I'd do anything to protect you. Anything."

To protect me, Bawden . . . everyone, probably. Victor is a circle-star, born to defend us all.

"Are you excited to see Zubiri?" I ask. "It's been ten days since you two were together."

He shrugs, looks forward. "I suppose. She's nice, but I think I enjoyed being in the jungle with you more."

Maybe he's still excited from the battle. I've seen the way Victor and Zubiri adore each other. Once the thrill of the fight has worn off, I know he'll be ready to spend some time with her.

But the love lives of my people aren't important at the moment. We fought, we won, and now I need to focus on bigger issues.

I turn to Barkah. "I'll ask you again—what's going to happen to the captured Belligerents?"

He snorts, indicating his disgust. The Springers have some very humanlike mannerisms. Or is it that we humans have Springer-like mannerisms?

"*They traitors,*" he says. "*They earn punish.*"

A Springer's wide mouth and thick throat can make more sounds than we can. Chirps and clicks, growls and glassy tones, as well as most of the noises that go into our human words. When Barkah addresses a crowd, his words boom with volume and power. But when he speaks one-on-one, his voice sounds coarse, like spilled gravel.

Barkah has learned English at a frightening pace. Even though he doesn't have all the words right and has trouble forming sentences, he can carry on full conversations. His grammar is off, but I understand his tone—when he says the word "punish," he's *excited*.

"If you kill them, we won't know if there are more," I say. "Or where they're hiding."

Barkah laughs, a sound that always reminds me of a boot heel grinding broken glass against stone.

"*What they know, I know. They talk.*" He frowns, knowing he missed a word. He glances at me. "*They* will *talk.*"

We ride on in silence.

Barkah has changed. A year ago he tricked me. His friendship was a ruse, a way for him to kill his father and become king. I knew then to never trust Barkah. I still don't, but he's proven to be a good leader for his people. He led them aboveground. He ordered this new city to be built. When he negotiated with me about human-Springer relations, he was always firm, but fair.

Then the fighting between our peoples flared up again.

Since the Belligerents started attacking, I feel like Barkah has become . . . *meaner*. I suspect the biggest reason we haven't taken prisoners so far is because his troops are merciless. Maybe even cruel.

I don't know what is going to happen to these captured Belligerents. Nothing good, I am sure. I want to take them back with me, put them in the Observatory's prison cells. There, at least, they would be fed and we could heal their wounds.

But that choice isn't mine to make.

I've already tried to pressure Barkah into turning the prisoners over to us. That made him angry. *Very* angry. Right now our two species are cooperating. At least the ones under his control are. If he was to turn his people against us, join with the remaining Belligerents—or even other tribes—and attack Uchmal? We'd be outnumbered at least a thousand to one.

I don't dare risk our uneasy truce. When it comes to the Springers, what Barkah wants, Barkah gets.

We are entering the small Springer city. Barkah hops up on the spider's back, waves Lahfah forward to join us. He is the king and, even though she lives in Uchmal with us, she is his queen—he wants his people in the city to see the royal couple arrive together.

A hurukan trots up beside us, Lahfah atop it. Even though we fought together, she's been deep in the jungle with her platoon and hasn't talked to me in days. When our eyes meet, she lets out an oh-so-familiar bellowing laugh that sounds like the tinkling of broken glass.

I killed a living, thinking being only a few hours ago. We buried eighty-three enemy bodies. One of my own almost died. Those things hang heavy on my heart, to be sure, but to lay eyes on my friend makes me all smiles.

"*Hem,*" Lahfah says. She is as delighted to see me as I am to see her. "*Face good?*"

"I am fine. Thank you for asking, Lahfah."

Lahfah has trouble understanding the difference between the words *you* and *face*. They seem to mean the same thing to her.

She tried to greet me in my language. I try to do the same for her.

"*Nin yawap tallik ginj?*"

Lahfah screams with delight. Looks like I said it right for once. How about that? It's only taken me a year to learn how to say the equivalent of "Do you feel well?" Barkah can converse with any of my people, while the best I can do is manage a few pleasantries with his.

Barkah barks a single, harsh syllable. Lahfah stops laughing. She's obeying his command, but doesn't look the least bit upset at his tone. She's used to it. In that way, their relationship reminds me of the way Spingate treats Gaston.

Part of what makes Barkah an effective leader is knowing what looks impressive. Coming into the city after a successful battle, with prisoners in tow, riding side by side with the human leader on a human war machine? For Springers, it's hard to get more impressive than that.

That's why he insisted my troops ride with him into Schechak. He's the king, but not *everyone's* king. The Belligerents are proof of that. Some of his own subjects are among the Belligerent dead and captured.

The wide road we're on runs through Schechak and then straight on to Uchmal. Such a contrast between the two cities.

Uchmal's vine-covered walls rise high, an intimidating message of strength and accomplishment. In comparison, the Springer city seems like little more than an overpopulated frontier town.

Some of Schechak's six-sided buildings are new, made from rocks and chunks of ancient buildings mortared together with concrete and even dried mud. Most buildings, though, are repaired ruins. Every building is topped with a pointed, six-sided thatch roof woven from the blue stems of jungle vines. The smaller buildings are houses or shops. Larger buildings have brick smokestacks rising up from the sides. These are the Springers' new factories, where they weave fabric, cut cloth, forge metal, hammer out tools and weapons or process food.

A year ago, the land that is now Schechak was nothing more than ancient ruins. Springers continue to migrate here from all across Omeyocan. Borjigin tells me that Schechak's current population is already over five thousand. In another year, how many Springers will live here, only a short march from our own city gate?

The wide road leads through the city. Springers are gathered on either side, packed in deep. They cheer, a crazy yell that sounds a bit too much like Matilda's memories of croaking toads. Springers lean from the windows of the six-sided brown buildings. Many sit on the blue roofs. All welcome their victorious king back from battle. Music blares, several instruments and several songs all fighting against each other for dominance.

Whenever I visit Schechak, vendors are hawking everything you can think of. This time is no exception. Fabric, clothes, furniture, food, polished glass, raw metal . . . it's all for sale. I see vendors in the crowd waving beautiful woven tapestries and detailed paintings, wood and stone carvings so lovely they take my breath away. I've traded for many pieces of Springer art that decorate my house. Maybe my people will learn how to make art, but if so that will be many years in the future. For now, the Birthday Children have more than enough real work to keep us busy.

Barkah plays to the crowd. Instead of waving at his people, which humans would do, he tilts his head up in a quick jerky motion. It always makes me think he's having trouble swallowing something.

A flash of movement overhead makes me flinch. A rock, but not thrown my way. It crashes into the head of a marching Belligerent prisoner, makes the already wounded Springer stumble. More rocks fly out, as do rotten fruit, garbage, sticks and clumps of dirt, hitting and splattering the prisoners.

I wait for the Springer guards on either side to stop the assault. They don't. I look to Barkah, knowing he won't let this shameful act continue.

He doesn't say anything. He stares straight ahead, thrusting his chin up and out at his loving subjects.

"Your *Highness*," I say, and this time it's my tone that carries the meaning, "I remind you, again, that I want to talk to these prisoners. Will any of them still be alive when I come back in a few days?"

Barkah looks at me. His green eyes are piercing, intelligent, calculating.

"*Some will live,*" he says.

At the city center, the road bends slightly left. When we make that turn, I see a wooden framework, so new some of the lumber sparkles with fresh sap. It's like a small building without sides. No . . . it's a *stage*.

At the center of that stage, two thick poles stick up, joined together by a long crossbeam. From the crossbeam hangs six ropes, each ending in a noose.

Matilda's memories flash, define what I see, and I'm horrified: I am looking at a gallows.

I grab the shoulder of Barkah's fancy orange coat.

"You're going to *execute* them?"

Barkah looks at me, then at my hand. I'm suddenly aware that we're surrounded by thousands of his people. Three spiders, a few snake-wolves and a dozen circle-stars are a dangerous force, but in the middle of the Springer city we would be overwhelmed in seconds.

I let go of his coat, smooth out the fresh wrinkles. I smile warmly at him for the benefit of his watching people.

"Execute," I say quietly. "Prisoners . . . *nahnaw?*"

He looks forward.

*"Some will live,"* he says again.

I feel a chill inside. It stuns me that I once thought of Barkah as my friend, that we were like-minded individuals. I sought peace—he sought only power. He used me then. He uses me now. He will hang some of the prisoners, make an example of them, show his people what happens if they cross his will.

"You can't kill them," I say. "They surrendered."

His two good eyes blink slowly. His chin juts out, brings cheers from his subjects.

*"Not your laws,"* he says. *"Not your culture."*

He's being pleasant enough, but his message is clear. Unless I want to start a war, there is nothing I can do. Does respecting another culture mean standing by idly while prisoners are tortured and murdered?

"Barkah, we're leaving," I say. "We have to return to Uchmal. Victor, stop and lower."

Victor stops the spider. The machine lowers until the metal belly clangs against the broken road. Maybe Barkah thought I would drop him off on his gallows, so his people could see how the humans serve him so well, but now they can watch him get out and walk.

I know the Springer king well enough to see he's not pleased with me. He hops down the street to the gallows as his subjects croak their approval.

"Victor," I say, "take us home."

# THREE

The Birthday Children march home.

Three five-legged machines, yellow and brown, ridden by teenagers in dirty black coveralls. Six snake-wolves—massive, tawny predators ridden by humans and Springers clothed only in strips of fabric that help them fade into the foliage. On foot, some two dozen rifle-carrying Springers, also wearing jungle rags. Finally, guarding our rear, young humans wearing black coveralls and wrapped in vines, rifles slung over their shoulders. Some of them carry farm tools they use in battle. That strange tradition was born from our initial lack of weapons, yet has persisted long after we were able to arm everyone with spears and knives.

Most of the Springers who fought with us stayed in Schechak. The ones still with us are mostly from D'souza's units, but a few dozen of Barkah's soldiers live inside Uchmal's circular walls, side by side with humans.

In total, our city houses about two hundred Springers. Most are civilians, teenage purples and young reds, studying math, science, medicine and engineering. We also have a handful of purple-blue adults as well as a few pure-blue elderly, who teach us about native plants and animals, the seasons and how to survive them, the places that are rich in metals and minerals, Springer culture and history . . . all the knowledge of Omeyocan passed down from generation to generation over the centuries.

Uchmal's vine-covered walls loom before us, much taller than the trees of the jungle ruins. We filled in the holes that Barkah's people used to crawl under the walls. We rebuilt the Water Gate that blocks anyone from entering the city via the river flowing in from the jungle. Our gates are always closed, always locked from the inside. Hundreds of thousands of Springers live in the jungle ruins around us—we can be friendly, yes, but we also have to be careful.

The most important repair, though, was to several ancient tower cannons. Borjigin and his engineers have fixed four of them so far. These weapons possess terrifying power. As our bracelets are to Springer muskets, the tower cannons are to our bracelets. If the Belligerents—or any other Springer tribe, for that matter, *including* Barkah's—ever try to assault our city, the tower cannons will blast them to bits.

Even from outside the walls, I see the massive Observatory rising up from the city center. It is the biggest building in Uchmal. I wonder if it might be the biggest building in all of existence, the biggest that has ever been. It is so tall its shadow stretches beyond the wall and into the jungle.

The road ends at the East Gate. Towers, built into the wall, rise up on either side. One tower flashes with a gleam of reddish light—the morning sun reflecting off a long, silver tower cannon.

"We should be close enough," Victor says. "Try using the jewel?"

I sigh. "Jewels haven't worked in a while."

"I could try, if you like," he says. "Can I do that for you?"

He's got that look on his face again—so eager to do something for me.

I pull out a communication jewel from one of my many pockets and hand it over. He nestles it into his ear and taps it twice.

"This is Victor Muller, calling to the East Gate, over?" He waits. I see him squint, trying to listen. "Sorry, can't understand you. Say again?"

We found the jewels in an Observatory storeroom. They don't have much range, but from this distance we used to be able to communicate jewel-to-jewel with someone at the gate. Lately, the devices haven't been working that well. No one knows why.

The East Gate is the same one we went through the first time we left Uchmal to see what the jungle held in store for us. As we approach, the massive metal doors slowly swing outward. They are oiled now and open smoothly, without the piercing metal screeches they once made.

Barkah had thousands of Springers waiting to welcome him home. We have only five humans—two halves, along with three circles.

Borjigin is one of the halves. In the past year, he's grown taller and even more handsome. He spends most of his time outside, fixing things, which has tanned his skin and sun-bleached the long black hair he wears in a knot atop his head. In one hand he holds his messageboard, the little flat computer he's never without.

He is one of many who have put away their tough black coveralls in favor of actual clothes. He wears blue pants and a long-sleeved orange shirt. The shirt's color is so close to that of Barkah's jacket I assume both garments were made in the same place. Borjigin wears the same shoes as I do, though, as almost everyone does—tough black boots left for us by the Grownups.

Standing with him is Tina Schuster, one of our three young halves. She also holds a messageboard, but wears something very new for my people—a dress. The white cloth fits her nicely, ripples in the same slight breeze that caresses her long blond curls.

Dresses seem so strange. So impractical. Tina is all arms and legs, still growing into her body, but the dress looks pretty on her. I wonder how I would look in one. Would I like it?

More importantly, would Bishop?

As Victor drives our spider through the gate, he points to his ear and shouts down at Borjigin.

"When are you going to fix these stupid jewels?"

Borjigin frowns. "As soon as we figure out what's wrong with them. It's not just the jewels"—he holds up the messageboard—"these won't connect with the Observatory computer unless we're right next to the building. We're working on it." He glances up and down the column entering the city, a worried look on his face. "Where's Bawden?"

I point toward my feet, where Bawden lies hidden behind the spider's thick metal ridge.

"She's down here, wounded but stable."

Borjigin touches his cheek, mimicking where the bayonet point sliced me.

"That's a nasty cut," he says.

My fingertips trace the spot, draw forth a slight sting. I'd forgotten about the wound. Maybe I'm so used to being hurt by now that I don't think anything of it.

"Doc Smith is waiting at the Observatory, ready to tend to the wounded," Borjigin says. "What other casualties do we have?"

I shrug. "Other than Bawden, just a few minor wounds."

Borjigin smiles in amazement, both pleased and surprised.

"*No one* died? Did the Belligerents run away or something?"

"They tried," Victor says before I can answer. "But Em's plan worked perfectly! Fifteen Springers captured, another eighty-three killed. They burned the corn crop, though."

Borjigin shakes his head. Schuster taps something on her messageboard, perhaps a little too hard. The engineers have worked tirelessly on our food and water supply. Not a week seems to go by without the Belligerents destroying something we need for survival. Perhaps now, after our victory, that will change.

Food is our biggest long-term problem. While we *can* eat native Omeyocan plants and animals, they don't give us the nutrition we need. If that was all there was for us to eat, we wouldn't starve right away, but eventually we *would* starve. Most of our diet comes from prepackaged food the Grownups sent down centuries ago. Those stores were poisoned by the mold, but vine-root juice kills the mold and neutralizes the toxin. There is enough packaged food to last us years. If we don't find another solution, we'll be in trouble when that supply runs out.

The Observatory held several chambers full of carefully preserved seeds from our "home" system—wherever that is—but no instructions on how to make the plants survive Omeyocan's animal and insect pests, or flourish among this alien water, soil and air. The gears have been working hard to turn those seeds into crops. We've had little success so far. The cornfield was the closest we've come to an actual harvest, so of course Borjigin and Schuster are angry.

I really like Borjigin. He has a brilliant mind for managing this city, and when it comes to working with machines he is the best on this planet. He's everything a half should be—but he's not *my* half. I would give anything for O'Malley to be here waiting for me instead.

Today, like every day of my life, I miss that boy with all my heart.

"I'll take Bawden straight to Doc Smith," I say. "You close the gate and make sure everyone gets food, water and rest, all right?"

Borjigin nods. "Oh, and Bishop called an all-hands meeting. Everyone is to report to the Grand Hall in an hour."

Maybe Bishop wants a group debriefing or something. I'll worry about that later. Right now I need to get my friend to the hospital.

"Victor," I say, "take us to the Observatory."

"Yes, ma'am."

The spider quickly speeds up. Pointy metal feet *clack-clack-clack* against the street's flat stones.

Our city has changed so much. We've cleared away vines and repaired buildings. Ziggurats rise up on both sides of the wide street, as do square and rectangular structures. Borjigin tells us this place was made to hold three million people. Perhaps even more. We'll never clear away *all* the plant growth—that would take forever—but the areas that we use have been restored to their original grandeur.

So much progress. We have a long way to go and the work will never end, at least not in our lifetimes, but I am so proud of what we've accomplished.

We pass the Spider Nest, the huge ship that originally brought the spiders and the construction machines down from the *Xolotl*. We cleared away the vines that hid the ship's silver hull. It will never fly again—too many holes and the engines have long since rusted to junk—but now it gleams and shimmers with reflected sunlight.

As our spider races by, I see machines going in and out of the Nest: a truck carrying a load of excavated dirt and rocks; a spider wobbling madly on two damaged legs; a long four-legged machine that we use to cut down trees and bring back logs.

We pass a side street that Kalle, the gear primarily responsible for our food research, has turned into a garden to grow experimental crops. She has dozens of small plots like this spread across the city. This one holds turnips, I think. Like the corn, these plants don't look good. The leaves are shriveling, turning brown. Stems sag slightly, as if the plants can never quite get enough water.

The best-looking part of this small plot is Kalle's "scarecrow." It's a pressure suit from the shuttle that would supposedly let people go outside—into the blackness of *space*, if you can believe it—and fix problems on the shuttle's hull. The pressure suit is tied to a cross. It's supposed to scare away blurds that like to nibble the plants. Judging from the chewed up leaves, I don't think it works very well.

We approach the open space where Huan Chowdhury works. He's our budding archaeologist. Uchmal was built upon the ruins of a destroyed Springer city, which itself was built on top of yet another city built by yet another race of aliens—the Vellen—who appear to be gone for good. Digging through the layers can tell us about those that came before us.

Huan started his work by going down the open shaft in the Observatory's Control Room, where O'Malley and so many others died. That shaft is surrounded by a red metal wall. We've come to call it "the Well," because it looks like one. Huan studied the layers of the shaft for a few days, even found a natural tunnel complex at the bottom, but said it felt "too spooky" down there and refused to explore any further. He asked me if we could knock down a small building instead, so he could excavate below the foundation and continue his research. I approved—he's been digging in this spot ever since.

Huan's job is to learn all he can, see if he can identify why at least three races came to this very spot and at least three more are on the way. We have many mysteries to solve, but right now that is the most pressing one.

He sees our spider. He waves as we pass by. Victor and I wave back. Huan has brown skin and a bright smile. He's *always* smiling.

I am so proud of him. He isn't a gear, like Spingate and the other scientists, and he isn't a half, like Borjigin and the other city managers. Huan is a circle—like me. He was bred to know nothing, to do what he was told. He was bred to be a slave. And yet here he is, doing an important job, quickly becoming our expert on the subject. Whenever one of my people goes beyond the duties expected of their caste, I know there is hope for our future.

Unlike the jungle roads, Uchmal's ancient streets are straight and smooth. We named the big east-west road Yong Boulevard, after the first of us to die on the *Xolotl*. The north-south road is named Latu Way. Both roads lead to one place: the Observatory.

Even after over a year of living in this city, I'm still stunned by the size of this towering ziggurat. Many of us live inside. It has thousands of rooms, as well as our hospital, storerooms, prison and the all-important Control Room. The thirty-layered Observatory offers more space than we could ever need. Borjigin tells me it could house two hundred thousand people with ease, a city within a city. The Observatory is so large that we haven't fully explored it—to this day, we're still finding new rooms and the interesting things left inside of them.

Wide streets surround the Observatory. We've cleared them of plants. Borjigin insisted on that, saying that a fire could spread across the vines that cover almost everything in this city. He wanted to make sure such a blaze wouldn't reach the Observatory. Flames couldn't really hurt the building, of course—it's a mountain of stone—but the project gave the shuttle kids something to do. It took them over a month to complete the work. I have to admit, it does look very nice to see the vine-covered Observatory surrounded by neat, clean streets.

Our shuttle sits in the wide plaza just south of the Observatory. Gaston and Opkick have spent countless hours working on the shuttle's computer, trying to see if there's any history in the system's memory. So far, nothing. They discovered the shuttle has a name, though—*Ximbal,* which apparently means "to journey" in some ancient language. It's unlikely *Ximbal* will ever move from this spot, because we used the last of the fuel in its tanks to get it here. Unless we learn how to make more, *Ximbal* will never fly again.

Most of our people are on the plaza, working. Many wear black coveralls, but more than a few wear colorful clothes: shirts, pants, jackets and dresses made by the Springer factories. I see a spider—number 01, Bishop's spider—sitting idle, along with a few small wheeled vehicles and a hulking, beat-up black truck we've nicknamed Big Pig. The truck's front end kind of resembles a pig's snout. Big Pig's flatbed is surrounded by thick metal walls, and each of its black wheels is taller than I am.

Before we reach the plaza, Victor brings our spider to a stop.

"Em, do you want to visit the memorial? I'll take Bawden to Doctor Smith."

The memorial. The twisted metal X where we buried the remains of those who died in the Observatory fire. Victor is asking if I want to visit O'Malley's grave. It's been too long since I've been there, but there's much to do. The dead can wait a little longer.

"No, thank you. Take us in."

Victor parks the spider by the Observatory's main entrance. This entrance was once sealed up tight and obscured by thick vines.

As big as the ziggurat is, we've found only two other ways in. When we shut all three doors, the place is impregnable. We've laid in large supplies of food and water. That's why I make everyone live either inside the Observatory or close to it—if the Springers were to break through Uchmal's gates, all of my people can shelter inside for months, if not years. Borjigin installed Springer war horns across the city, a system he calls the "emergency warning system." If that goes off, everyone is trained to run for the Observatory.

My people are walking in and out of the building. They look like tiny insects scurrying around a huge hive.

Opkick walks toward us, messageboard in her hand. She's followed by Kenzie Smith, our circle-cross doctor. Okereke and Kishor Jepson, both circles, follow along carrying a metal stretcher. Opkick is pregnant. Her swollen belly strains her white shirt. I've only been gone ten days, but she looks much bigger than the last time I saw her.

"Hail, Em," she says. "The boys will get Bawden down after Doctor Smith takes a look at her."

I wearily descend the ladder. Smith reaches for the first rung to start up, looks at me, then grabs my jaw. She doesn't do it hard, but her grip is firm—this is Smith's way, to move a body however she likes, to see what she wants to see, never asking for permission.

"This cut is bad," she says. "Go to the hospital, tell Francine to fix you up."

"I will. Just take care of Bawden first."

Smith gives my shoulder a quick squeeze, then scrambles up

the rungs. That's the closest she'll ever come to showing me real emotion, I suppose, so I'll take it.

Opkick, on the other hand, has no problem expressing herself. She hugs me tight. I hug back, careful of her belly.

"The baby isn't going to break, Em."

I laugh, embarrassed. "I know, but you're so much bigger!"

She smiles wide, rubs her free hand across her stomach.

"Smith says it will be any day now. We're so excited."

Okereke is grinning, and with good reason—he's the father. He's short, but thick with muscle. He has the darkest skin of any of our people.

Smith climbs down from the spider, rubbing a hand through her brown hair.

"It's safe to move Bawden," she says. "Put her on the stretcher, but do it gently."

Okereke and Jepson scramble up. Victor helps them gently lower Bawden, who is still asleep. They put her on the stretcher and carry her into the Observatory.

"It was close," Smith says to me. "If that puncture wound in her shoulder had gone a bit lower, it would have pierced her lung. She wouldn't have made it back alive. Why did you get so close to the enemy? Is something wrong with all those guns you adore so much?"

I'm exhausted. I'm not about to explain my strategy or what went wrong.

"Just take care of the wounded, all right?"

Smith stares for a moment, not hiding her contempt. She thinks proper leadership would mean we don't fight at all. When we do, for whatever reason, she always thinks the fault is mine.

"Get your face looked at," she says. "Don't wait or it could get infected."

She walks into the Observatory.

Victor drops down, laughing lightly.

"Not exactly a hero's welcome, Em."

I shrug. It never is.

"Forget her," he says. "We *won*. Everyone worked well together. No one died. I'm lucky to serve under you."

He puts his right hand on my left shoulder, the circle-star's gesture of respect. I do the same to him, and look up at his dirty face.

"You did well," I say. "If not for you, Bawden would be dead. I might be, too. I'll tell Bishop personally."

At the mention of Bishop's name, Victor's smile fades.

"You're going to see him right away, aren't you."

A statement, not a question.

"I am. Aren't you going to see Zubiri?"

Victor shrugs. "Sooner or later. Don't forget that Borjigin told us to go to the Grand Hall. I'll see you there."

With that, he jogs into the Observatory, spear in hand, slung rifle jostling on his back.

A few months ago, it was all I could do to keep him from running off to see Zubiri every chance he got. I wonder if something happened between them.

Love. It's a mystery to me.

I start to think of Bishop, but it's O'Malley's face that comes to mind. I must visit his grave soon, tell him all about the battle.

But first, I need to have someone fix up my cut.

# FOUR

The hospital is busy. It's in the Observatory's second layer. Everything here is white: the pedestals, the cabinets, the walls, the floor and the coffins—sixty-six of them, to be exact, laid out side by side in two rows of thirty-three each.

Smith, Lucky Pokano and Francine Yilmaz—our three circle-crosses—are hard at work fixing the cuts and scrapes suffered during the battle. Ten circle-stars are being treated. So are seven Springers; our docs have gotten good at fixing them up as well.

Smith stands at a pedestal next to a closed coffin that holds Bawden. Lucky is working on Farrar, who had a long cut on his arm. Farrar hid the wound from everyone, like he always seems to do.

Francine leans in close to my face, dabbing at my cut with something that stings.

"Three hours in a med-chamber will fix you right up," she says. "No scar at all."

The circle-crosses call them med-chambers. The rest of us still call them *coffins*. Finding new words for things doesn't change what they actually are.

"Just stitch it up," I say. "I've got work to do."

Francine sighs. She's tiny. She's barely grown at all since we landed. She's filled out some, though, and has a woman's curves. She has the cutest little nose. Long black lashes frame her big, dark eyes. The Grownups dressed us like dolls—Francine actually looks like one.

"Em, all your scars . . . we can get rid of those. You'd be so much prettier without them."

I smile at her. She means well, but she doesn't understand me. My scars are *mine*. Each one makes me look a little bit different from Matilda's ideal vision. In the faraway crawl spaces of my thoughts, I hope that if Matilda ever does overwrite me, she will hate her own face because of all the damage I have done to it.

"Thank you," I say. "I appreciate your concern. Now stitch me up."

Francine does as she's told. Fourteen quick, efficient stitches on my cheek and she's finished.

I thank her again, then walk over to Smith. Icons and lines float above the pedestal in front of her, information I now know represents heart rate, blood pressure, temperature, oxygen saturation and a few other things.

"How is Bawden?" I ask.

"She needs two days in there," Smith says. "Three, tops, and she'll be as good as new. Then you can take her out into the jungle again and see if you can get her properly killed instead of just horribly wounded."

Smith annoys me, but I understand her. Her job is to repair people, to save lives. My job is to protect people, but sometimes the only way to do that is to kill those that would harm us. When evil comes, you can't always talk to it—sometimes it must be destroyed. That's why there are people like Bawden, Victor, Bishop, me, D'souza . . . when real danger comes, people like Smith stay behind us.

"I wish we didn't have to fight," I say, trying to reason with Smith for the hundredth time. "I wish no one attacked us, I wish the jungle was nicer, I wish air tasted like candy and we all got to sleep on a bed of pretty flowers."

I try to reason with her, sure, but I don't try *hard*.

Smith snorts. "One of these days you're going to bring me someone I can't fix. Then we'll see how funny it is."

"You think I *like* this? I hate fighting."

She glances at me. Her mouth twists into a rueful grin.

"No, you don't *like* it—you *revel* in it." She points to my cheek. "You revere it so much you want to show it off. I was made to heal. You? You were made to kill. You are death."

The voice of the boy I love comes from behind me.

"Someone has to be death," Bishop says. "That's how civilization works. What you can't defend will eventually be taken away from you."

Smith rolls her eyes. "If the two of you don't mind, I've got lives to save."

She turns her attention back to her pedestal display. Maybe I'm the leader of my people, but I've just been dismissed.

I leave the hospital. I hear Bishop walking behind me, but I don't turn to look at him. I walk down the stone hall and descend a flight of stairs before I stop.

We're alone.

Now I turn. I haven't seen his face in ten days. That tightly curled blond hair. Those dark-yellow eyes, lovely but bleary from lack of sleep. As tired as he looks, his smile still steals the air from my lungs.

"I missed you, Bishop."

His hands slide around my waist. He lifts me as if I weigh nothing at all. I throw my arms around his thick neck. His lips on mine: warm, eager, wanting. Maybe the kiss lasts for a second, maybe it lasts for an hour.

He sets me down.

"And I missed you."

His hand on my face, his thumb gently tracing my latest badge of bravery. His eyes swim with a mixture of worry and pride.

"Looks like I almost lost you."

I touch the hand that is touching my face. "Never. You'll never lose me."

*Not like I lost O'Malley . . .*

"I still think it's bad strategy for you to go out and fight," he says. "You're our leader. If the blade that made that cut had struck true, you'd be dead."

He's proud of me, yes, but this particular argument he will never let go.

"I can't ask others to do what I won't do myself. And it went well. If it wasn't for Bawden rushing into the fight, no one in my platoon would have been hurt at all."

Bishop's face wrinkles with surprise.

"Bawden? But she's so reliable."

I shake my head. "She lost it. She jumped out of the spider, screaming that she wanted to kill. She ran into a burning cornfield without any support. Victor and I had to go in after her."

Bishop rubs his chin. I hear his callused hands scraping against his blond stubble.

"That's happening more and more," he says. "Our discipline seems to be fading. I'm worried about it."

I nod. I am, too.

"Still, she can't act like that," Bishop says. "It's unacceptable. I'll speak with her."

I wouldn't want to be in her shoes when that happens. Among the circle-stars, disobeying orders is a heavy sin.

"And what about *Victor*? How did he do?"

The way Bishop said Victor's name . . . with a touch of anger? There seems to be a growing rivalry between the pair. Bishop prides himself on being our best fighter, so I guess it's no surprise, considering how skilled Victor is becoming at all things involving war.

"He was amazing," I say. "He saved Bawden's life. Probably mine as well. He captured two Belligerents, killed another."

Bishop's jaw muscles twitch. He nods.

"Where are the prisoners now?"

I describe what I saw in the Springer city, how Barkah acted. Bishop's face clouds over with anger.

"It's dishonorable to kill captives," he says.

"I know. I tried to bring the prisoners with us, but Barkah wouldn't listen. The way he's been acting lately . . . I couldn't risk a confrontation when we were so heavily outnumbered."

Bishop nods slowly. "The Springers are acting more violent, *we're* acting more violent, the Belligerents gather out of nowhere to attack us . . . I don't understand what's going on."

I take his hand. "We'll figure it out. You look exhausted—anything big happen while I was gone?"

Just as it was important for people to see me lead the attack on the Belligerents, it was important for people to know Bishop can run things if anything happens to me. That's why I left him in charge.

"Only the biggest thing there is," he says. "Spingate said the first alien ship is approaching orbit, or something like that."

We have no idea where it came from. We have no idea what's inside of it.

"I'll go see her right now," I say. "Anything else?"

He looks away.

"Bello tried suicide again. She somehow managed to chip off a piece of her cell wall, used it to cut her wrists."

That damn woman. Why does she have to be so much trouble?

The Springers kill their prisoners—our prisoner tries to kill herself.

"I'll go talk to her," I say.

Bishop gives me that look, the one that says *I told you this would happen.*

"If she succeeds on the next try, any information she has dies with her."

I feel my anger flare. "For the last time, we are *not* going to torture her."

His eyes narrow. "She's the only one who knows why those ships are coming. Now the first one is here. This is *necessary.*"

I rub at my temples. This is giving me a headache.

"No torture, Bishop."

"You always listen to Spingate," he says. "She agrees with me that it's the right thing to do."

"*No!* All right? No torture, and that's final. Don't ask again."

He grunts, then nods.

It isn't just Spingate and Bishop—many people think we should get the information out of Bello by . . . wait, what's the phrase people use to justify this disgusting concept? Oh, yes: *by any means necessary.*

While I'm in charge, that will never happen.

"I'll talk to Bello first, then Spin," I say. "Then I need some sleep. Will I see you at our house later tonight?"

*Our house.* His and mine. The thought of a night in our place, where I don't have to think about any of this, where I can just be with him . . . it lifts my mood.

Bishop smiles, shakes his head.

"You can't go home yet. Borjigin called that meeting."

"Borjigin said *you* called the meeting."

He blinks a few times.

"Oh, that's right. I called it."

"What's it about? I just got back from a battle. I'm exhausted—I don't want to sit in some damn meeting right now."

"You're going," Bishop says. "You'll understand when you get there. Go to the Grand Hall after you see Spingate. Just do it, Em, it's important."

He kisses me again. When he finally walks away, I feel like part of me goes with him.

Tonight I will allow myself time to relax. Now, though, there is much work still to do.

Spingate's lab is below me. Our prison cells are above.

I head up the steps.

# FIVE

I stand with a metal tray in my hands. Warmth billows out from between the iron bars of Korrynn Bello's cell.

She's naked, lying on a straw mat on the floor. Two months ago, she tried to hang herself with her blankets, tying them together and looping them over the thick wooden support beam that runs across the ceiling. One month ago, she tried to strangle herself with her coveralls. We don't have enough people to watch her all the time, so we had to take away anything she could use to hurt herself. That includes clothes, which is why we keep it so warm in her cell.

She knows I'm here. She won't look up at me. Her frizzy blond hair hides her face. Her skin is so pale.

"Bishop told me what you did," I say.

My tone is harsh. As my people struggle and sacrifice, fight to build a new culture, to *survive,* this selfish woman tries to take her own life instead of helping us. I do have some sympathy for her—just not very much.

"Kill me," she says. Her voice is a low moan, a whisper of the pain that crawls up from deep in her soul. "That's what you're good at, isn't it, Em? Killing?"

She's trying to make me angry. I won't let her.

"I brought you tea."

"Stop calling it that. Sholtag isn't *tea*. Real tea is amazing. You'll never know what it tastes like."

Of all the things she complains about—and there are too many things to count—she mentions a lack of tea more than any other.

"It's better than nothing," I say.

Finally, she looks up at me. This thousand-year-old thing wears the face and body of my dead friend. Her nose is slightly crooked. Her left eyelid droops, always a little lower than her right. The imperfections of her face are mementos of my rage, when I flew out of control on the shuttle and beat her nearly to death.

Just looking at her is an endless reminder of why I work so hard to stay calm. I can hurt people. I am capable of evil.

She glances at the tray. "*Two* cups? You must want to talk."

I nod.

Korrynn sighs. She stands and walks to the bars. She reaches through and takes one of the paper cups.

She stares at it. "I don't deserve at least a ceramic mug?"

"We both know what you'd use that for."

"But it gets cold so fast."

"Then drink quickly."

I take the other cup and set the metal tray on the stone floor, making sure it's well out of her reach.

We found the paper cups in one of the Observatory's countless storerooms. I take a sip of sholtag. It tastes like wood. Not in a bad way, though. Wood and mint. The Springers drink this all the time. At first I hated it, but I've come to like it.

"Disgusting," she says after taking a sip. She shrugs. "At least it's warm. Thank you." She glances at the palm-plate just outside her cell, on my side of the bars. "Now that we've had a nice drink, how about you let me go for a walk?"

All I have to do is press my hand to the plate. Spingate programmed the prison cell doors to open only for me, Bishop or Borjigin. But now is not the time for a casual stroll.

"The first alien ship is almost here," I say. "Stop playing games, Korrynn. Tell me why the *Xolotl* came to Omeyocan."

I used to call her Bello, which I hated, because that was the name of my friend. At some point, she asked me to call her by her first name. I should be careful what I wish for—calling her Korrynn makes this monster seem like a real person.

She's not. She is one of *them*.

"You know my demands," she says. "Until I get what I want, I won't tell you anything. I'm sure you fixed the antenna. I'm *sure* of it."

Other than carefully supervised walks—where her hands remained shackled for fear she might try to grab a guard's knife or gun—Korrynn has spent every moment of the last year in this cell. In all that time, she has refused to give us the information we need so badly.

"I've always told you the truth about the antenna," I say. "We're trying to fix it, trying very hard. But that doesn't matter anymore. Didn't you hear me? The alien ship is here. Tell me what I need to know, so I can protect us."

She shrugs. "Then find another way to reach the *Xolotl*. Until I can speak with my friends, I won't tell you a godsdamned thing."

Korrynn Bello lifts one hand, palm out toward me so I can see the long, angry cuts on her wrist.

"You're running out of time," she says. "Sooner or later, I'll find a way to kill myself. Or maybe before I can, the aliens will attack and do it for me. If you want what I know, find a way."

I tried to not let her make me mad, but like every time before this one, I failed.

Korrynn Bello knows why the *Xolotl* came to this spot. Whatever that reason is, I assume it's the same thing that drew the Springers, the alien ship almost in orbit, and the two alien ships still on the way.

There are more mysteries she could solve for us. What happened on the *Xolotl* that left so many people dead? Was Matilda really responsible for all those dismembered bodies? Who erased *Ximbal*'s memory, and the memory of Ometeotl, the Control Room's powerful computer?

But Korrynn refuses to talk until she can speak with her friends.

Until she can speak with Matilda.

"I promise you, I'm doing everything I can to fix that antenna," I say. "Please . . . tell me why the *Xolotl* came here. What is it about this place that makes people want to kill and destroy?"

She takes a long sip of sholtag.

"Until I get what I want, you'll never know," she says. "Gods, I am so alone."

And there it is, the phrase she always repeats, the one that sends me into a fury.

"You don't have to be lonely! I've told you that you can be one of us. All you have to do is tell me what you know!"

"You don't understand," she says. "You can't. You are all

children. *Babies*. I need my people. It was never supposed to be this way."

Gods, she makes me so *angry*.

"Some of the others want to torture you to get the information."

Those words slip out before I realize I'm saying them. I yelled at Bishop for bringing it up, yet here I am, letting my anger take over, using torture as a threat.

She glances at my legs, at the knife strapped to my right thigh. Damn—I meant to come here unarmed, but the knife is always on me and I forgot about it.

But Korrynn isn't threatened, by my words or by the knife. She laughs.

"You think you can beat it out of me? Little girl, you don't even know what *real* pain is. Being transformed is worse than anything. Worse than the rod. Worse than when you assaulted me in the shuttle. Worse than when Spingate elbowed me after you stabbed Yong. Worse than when I cut myself, when I tried to hang myself. You want to torture me? Go ahead—I'm tougher than *all* of you."

My skin prickles with goosebumps. My anger disappears.

"What did you just say?"

She casually takes another sip.

"I said I'm tougher than all of you."

"No," I say, shaking my head. "Before that. About when Yong got stabbed."

Korrynn nods. "Yes, when I grabbed Spingate to try and get her off Yong, and she threw her arm back and elbowed me in the face. I don't think she meant . . . meant to . . ."

The naked girl/woman blinks.

She touches her mouth, so lightly, in the spot where Spingate's elbow connected. It connected with that mouth—but not that *person*.

"You weren't there," I say. "That was *our* Bello."

Our Bello, who was overwritten shortly after that. The creature that took over her mind shouldn't have any recollection of that moment.

*This* Bello, this overwritten thing, she's suddenly confused. She shakes her head lightly.

"No, I . . . well, I don't know what I was saying. I must be thinking of when you beat me on the shuttle. Yes, that's it."

When O'Malley was overwritten, his brain, his soul, everything that made him *him* was supposed to be gone forever. But when I stabbed him, when he was dying in my arms, he smiled at me. He thanked me. In that brief instant, my O'Malley was still in there.

And if Korrynn remembers the moment of Yong's death, maybe my Bello isn't completely gone.

Brewer said the longer we were awake, making our own memories, the less chance the overwrite would work. I've been awake far longer than Bello or O'Malley was—if Matilda ever catches me, tries to overwrite me, what would happen?

Korrynn sets her cup on the floor. She lies on the mattress, turns her back to me.

"I'm tired," she says. "Go away."

I can't stand to look at her anymore. Such a selfish, hateful little creature.

"If this is what a thousand years of life would get me, I hope I die at a hundred."

She rolls over onto one elbow, and smiles at me. When she does, I see the dark space of two missing teeth—another memento of when I attacked her. She refuses to have them fixed.

"The aliens are finally here," she says. "Which means you'll die *far* sooner than that."

Her words send a chill up my spine, crank my anger to new heights.

I walk away, wondering how the person I keep naked and alone in a prison cell continues to have the upper hand.

# SIX

The Observatory is the heart of Uchmal.

The Control Room is the heart of the Observatory.

Ometeotl, the living computer, is the heart of the Control Room.

*"Welcome back, Empress Savage."*

I have barely set one foot in this room and I am already annoyed.

"I've told you to use *my* name, not hers," I say, louder than I normally would, because I'm speaking to the *room*, not a person, and for some reason it always feels like I need to shout to be heard.

*"As you wish,"* Ometeotl answers. *"Welcome back, Em. You have been missed."*

Maybe the computer hidden within these stone walls thinks so, but apparently no one else here does. The people in this room barely notice my arrival.

This is the place where O'Malley was overwritten. The place where I killed him. The place I killed Old Bishop. Other people died here, too: several brave Springers, Old Dr. Smith, the overwritten Coyotl and a few Grownups whose names we will never know. This was a place of flame and smoke, bullets and blood, hatchets and hate. But as with so many other things on Omeyocan, we have changed its form.

The room once held golden coffins designed to wipe out our minds and replace them with the minds of the Grownups. We removed those coffins. In the space where those little death factories stood, we erected a dozen pedestals that are used for education. We cleaned the walls and ceiling, scrubbed away the char and soot. We painted everything bright white, painted over the mural showing human sacrifice. We removed the twisted metal X where the overwriting process happened.

We turned a temple of evil into a classroom where humans and Springers alike learn how to make a better world.

In a way, we overwrote this room. Take *that,* Matilda.

Every one of those dozen pedestals is in use, yet the students barely give me a glance. They seem . . . upset. Maybe Spingate's lessons are more demanding than usual.

In the center of the room sits the Well, a waist-high red metal wall that encircles the dirt shaft leading down to a power cell. Etched on that wall, the carbon symbol: an outer ring with four dots, an inner ring with two dots, and a solid circle at the center.

That same symbol is at the very top of the Observatory. It was also atop the ruined church where Spingate and I first talked to Barkah. In the past year, we've learned it's the symbol of a forgotten Springer religion. We don't know what the symbol meant to Matilda and the builders of Uchmal, or why the race she tried to exterminate would have already been using it before the *Xolotl* arrived.

Symbols. So important to the Grownups that they embedded

them on our foreheads: the double-ring, SPIRIT, representing religion; the gear, MIND, our scientists; the half-circle, STRUCTURE, the engineers who build machines and make this city run; the circle-crosses of HEALTH, our doctors and teachers; our soldiers, our circle-stars, aptly named MIGHT.

And, of course, the empty circles. SERVICE. Slaves.

But what does the carbon symbol mean to the church?

At the back of the room is a wide, waist-high platform with six more pedestals. On the platform stand Theresa Spingate and Xander Gaston—my two closest friends—and Halim Horn, Spingate's top assistant.

Halim is unique among us: a circle-star that doesn't like to fight. The other circle-stars look down on him for that. Even Bishop. Bishop sees no problem with other symbols wanting to fight *alongside* the circle-stars, but one of his own wanting to be anything *other* than a warrior? To him, that is a betrayal of their birthright.

But it doesn't matter what Bishop thinks about it. Out of our 275 people, we have only *seven* gears. That's seven scientists to handle almost all of our needs. Halim's desire and ability to help Spingate frees her from some things she'd consider to be drudge work.

Halim hides his circle-star symbol behind a white strip of cloth he's tied around his head. On that headband, he's stitched a new symbol: an empty circle, like mine, but with a diagonal slash through it, the ends of the line protruding just past the circle's outer edge. He says the symbol is called an "empty set." It represents his lack of belief in our symbols. I don't think he should be ashamed of who he is, or trade one symbol for another, but that is how he identifies and I have no issue with it.

Spingate and Gaston look exhausted. They *always* do. They

work long, hard hours. They're the only ones who make *me* feel lazy. And having a baby, I gather, doesn't exactly help them get more sleep.

Gaston scratches absently at his thick black beard. He won't admit it, but I'm convinced he grew it to annoy Bishop. Bishop's best effort to grow a beard resulted in a thin scrabble that looks like he glued sparse bits of hurukan fur to his cheeks. He's annoyed someone so much smaller than he can do something he can't.

As if Ramses Bishop needs facial hair to show how "manly" he is.

Gaston's hands work glowing images floating above a pedestal. A cloth sling runs from his left shoulder down to his right hip. Nestled inside the cloth is a lump of noisy (and often smelly) delight known as Kevin Spingate-Gaston.

They named their baby after my O'Malley.

Theresa is also lugging about a baby, but this one is still inside her. She's six months pregnant with their second child. Yet here she is, working away.

"Hello, Spin."

She looks up from her pedestal, seems confused by my face for a moment.

"Oh. Hello, Em. You're back."

Is she glaring at me?

"Spin, are you okay?"

She blinks rapidly, then gives her head a little shake. The confusion seems to clear.

"I'm fine. Come up and join us, please."

I step up onto the platform. I walk to Gaston first.

"Hey," he says. His hands and eyes remain fixed on the pedestal display, but he turns his body so I can get at the baby.

"Wow, Xander, I didn't know you missed me so much."

He grunts once. I pull little Kevin free of the sling and Gaston returns his full attention to his work.

Kevin is so *clean*. So soft. I love the way he smells—except when his diaper needs to be changed, of course. He has Spingate's eyes, Gaston's nose and chin. Without a doubt, though, the thing I love the most about this child's face is his little forehead.

Because Kevin has no symbol.

He is the first human on Omeyocan without one. He has no legacy of slavery or dominance, of being a have or a have-not. He has no memories of what he's *supposed* to be, of a life that others have planned for him. When he grows up, Kevin Spingate-Gaston can choose whatever path he likes.

That makes him a symbol unto himself: a symbol of what this planet can be, what our people can be.

I turn slightly, for some reason showing the baby to Spingate as if she's never seen the boy before.

"He's so wonderful," I say. "He's perfect."

Finally, she smiles. There is the beauty that is my best friend.

"Thank you," she says. "He's growing so quickly."

He is at that. I've only been gone ten days but it feels like the baby has doubled in weight. I bounce him up and down a little. His mouth opens in a toothless grin that is the spitting image of his mother's. She gently pets his head, brushing aside his thin red hair.

"Spin, you and Xander seem a little angry," I say. "Is everything all right?"

"You mean besides the fact that we have three alien ships above us, Zubiri can't get the optical telescope to work correctly, and we have an antenna that won't let us communicate with the *Xolotl*, which we need to do if Bello is going to tell us anything about why all these ships—including ours—came to Omeyocan?"

Her words mirror my own frustration.

"Yes. Besides that."

Her nose crinkles as she thinks.

"I don't know." She speaks quietly, so that only I can hear. "I just feel more . . . *aggressive* lately. I've yelled at Xander for no reason a couple of times. He was a good sport about it at first. He tried to be patient with me, but a couple of days ago he started yelling back. We're getting mad at each other and we don't know why." She nods toward the students down on the floor, working away on their lessons. "Them, too. They're so grumpy. We've all been working so hard. I guess the pressure of the approaching ships is getting to us."

It's that, and more. Much more. The way Bawden acted. The Belligerents gathering to attack us. The way Barkah has changed. I am gifted at solving puzzles no one else can figure out, but for this, I'm at a loss. I push those thoughts away to the back of my mind. Most often, that's where the pieces come together, when I'm not really thinking about them.

"There's something else," Spingate says, her voice a tight whisper. "I've been having nightmares."

"What about?"

She starts to speak, then stops. She looks at little Kevin for a moment, then shakes her head.

"Never mind," she says. "It's nothing. I'm just not sleeping well is all."

Whatever the dreams were, they disturbed her. I know this girl almost as well as I know myself; when she's ready to talk to me, she will. Until then, getting any information out of Theresa Spingate is like trying to get blood from a stone.

But *do* I know her? She's changed. The Spingate I thought I knew would have *never* thought torture was acceptable.

"Well, I hope everyone feels better soon," I say. Then, loud enough for everyone to hear: "What's going on with the alien ship?"

Spingate looks at Halim. "Put it on the main display."

He nods, works the glowing controls floating above his pedestal. The air above the red well flares to life. Spingate and I stand together, waiting. Gaston joins us. Without a word, he gently takes Kevin from my arms and nestles the baby back into the sling.

The image forms. I've seen it so many times in the last six months. A small sphere of blue and yellow and brown represents Omeyocan, our planet. Hovering above it is a red dot labeled *Xolotl*—our ship of nightmares that traveled over a thousand years to get here.

Then there are the three unknowns. A blue dot represents the first alien ship. When we discovered it, Ometeotl labeled it *Beta-One*. Gaston didn't like that generic name, said he wanted his enemies to have a "face," whatever that means. He renamed it *Basilisk*. Farther out, a yellow dot—*Gamma-One*, renamed *Goblin*. And beyond that, a green dot that represents *Delta-One*, renamed *Dragon*.

"The *Basilisk* is thousands of miles from the *Xolotl*, but both ships have a line of sight on Uchmal," Spingate says. "I think the *Basilisk* will settle into final orbit in the next two days. It probably can't safely launch shuttles until then."

Two days. We might be at war in just two days.

"Do we have any way of communicating with it?"

Gaston shakes his head. "Not unless the antenna magically fixes itself. Even if it was repaired, I'm not sure if it would work. Since you left to fight the Belligerents, the electronic interference that's screwed up our communications systems has gotten worse."

I think of the jewels and Borjigin's messageboard problem.

"Could the *Basilisk* be doing that?" I ask. "Or one of the other ships?"

"I don't think so," Gaston says. "Whatever the problem is, it seems to be originating from Omeyocan, not from space."

More bad news. I need the antenna to work so Bello can talk to Matilda. And if war does come, we may need to communicate with the *Xolotl* anyway.

"So even if we fix the antenna," I say, "it won't work because of this interference?"

Spingate shrugs. "Hard to know. The antenna is directly connected to the power plant down in the Well, so a working signal would be exponentially stronger than anything the jewels or the messageboards produce. It might overpower this interference. I've still got Nevins, Peura and Harman working full-time on fixing it. Opkick has been helping them search storage rooms for parts, but so far they haven't been able to repair the damage."

When we first climbed the Observatory's three thousand steps and reached the top layer, we saw a tall stone pillar decorated with our symbols. At that time, we didn't know the pillar housed an antenna meant to let the Observatory communicate with the *Xolotl*. At some point in the two centuries after Uchmal was built, a power surge of some kind damaged the antenna, cutting Matilda off from the spiders and from the construction robots that built this great city.

I stare at the simple blue dot representing the *Basilisk*. The blankness of it tears at me. Because of the radio telescopes spread out across the city and in the jungle I know *where* the alien ships are, but for now we have no idea what they look like.

"How about the repairs to the Goffspear telescope?" I ask. "When will those be complete? I need to see this ship."

"Soon," Gaston says. "Zubiri thinks she's getting closer."

I try to control my anger.

"You've been telling me *soon* for over a year," I say. "Maybe that word means something different to you than it does to me."

His face twists into a snarl. "Then *fix it yourself*. If you know so much, *you* do the godsdamned work!"

I take a step back, shocked at his response.

"*Gaston,*" Spingate snaps, "don't take your frustration out on Em!"

"Oh, it's all right for *you* to be a bastard to *me,* but I can't be one to Em? Sure, *that's* fair."

She points a finger at him. "You shut your stupid mouth. Your attitude makes me *sick.*"

I'm dumbfounded. Since we landed on this planet, these two have been inseparable, their love perfect, patient and kind. Yet here they are screaming at each other.

Gaston takes a step toward her, but before he says anything else little Kevin starts to cry.

The sound shocks Gaston and Spingate out of their sudden burst of anger. Their faces turn red. Spingate steps to Gaston, puts her arms around him. He hugs her back, the baby between them. Comforted in this sudden embrace, Kevin stops crying.

"Maybe you two need a break from work," I say quietly.

Halim comes closer, flashing a disarming grin, hands up as if to say *don't take it out on me* even though he could probably beat all three of us up at the same time.

"Actually, it's time for that meeting in the Grand Hall," he says. "Borjigin said to make sure we weren't late."

Again with the damn meeting?

Spingate runs a hand through her thick red hair. She sighs heavily, as if trying to clear the stress from her body.

"Yes, the meeting," she says. "We should all go now, together."

I point to the blue dot. "This is more important."

"We have at least a day," Gaston says. "If we don't do this meeting now, we might not get to do it at all. I'm told it's very important."

Spingate claps her hands. The students all look up at her.

"Everyone, to the Grand Hall," she says. "Right now."

The students exchange excited looks as they rush out of the room. Does everyone know what this is about except me?

Halim puts his arm around my shoulders.

"Help me out, Em. If you're not on time, Borjigin said he would come down here and yell at me. I'm a delicate soul. I might wither and die."

I can feel the strength in his muscular arm. He is a circle-star, after all.

"You might wither and die," I say. "I find that hard to believe."

"Did I mention how delicate I am? What if I say *pretty please*?"

He smiles wide.

Halim rarely asks for anything. I look at Spingate and Gaston. They're also smiling. Whatever this is, everyone is in on it.

I sigh, and I give in.

"Fine. Let's go."

# SEVEN

The four of us walk toward the Grand Hall. It is the largest room in the Observatory. At least the largest one we've found so far—this place is full of hidden doors and hallways. We're still discovering new areas almost every week.

We've had several all-hands meetings in the Grand Hall. It's quite beautiful. Large marble columns support an arched stone ceiling. There were carvings of torture and human sacrifice, but we covered those with large tapestries made by the Springers.

I like the Hall, but one part of it really bothers me—a raised dais with an obnoxious golden throne. I'm sure that's where Matilda thought she would rule. The left side of the throne has a bracket that holds a ceremonial golden knife, its pommel decorated with a double-ring symbol done in rubies. The right side holds a thin red cane—a working "rod," the torture device used to punish people, especially children. Matilda used an identical rod on me when I was her captive. The *pain*. I shiver involuntarily every time I see the thing, which is why the entire throne is covered in a blanket made of hurukan fur. Out of sight, yes, but not out of mind—we all know the throne is there, a constant reminder of the evil that built this city.

None of us have sat in that throne. None of us ever will.

Spin, Gaston, Halim and I walk down the stone corridor. I hear noise coming from the Grand Hall. Loud conversation. Laughter. And . . . is that *music*?

We reach the entryway. One step inside, and I stop cold.

This huge room is full of people and Springers. So many of us, here, maybe *all* of us.

I think everyone has bathed, even those who fought with me against the Belligerents. Bodies washed, hair combed. Most of my people wear Springer-made clothes instead of the familiar black coveralls.

And our Springers . . . hundreds of them, all dressed up. Long robes of fine cloth, in so many wonderful colors. Hems and collars trimmed in bits of gleaming glass. Buttons of polished metal etched with intricate patterns.

Everyone looks so *nice*.

The music stops.

All heads turn to stare at me.

Gaston starts to clap. Spingate joins him, then Halim . . . then *everyone*.

They are applauding. Applauding *me*.

My face feels hot.

"What's going on?"

Borjigin slides out of the crowd. He wears a new blue outfit, beams with pride and joy. He takes my hand and leads me into the Hall.

"People, let's hear it for our leader! Let's hear it for *Em*!"

They clap harder. They hoot and holler. I see smiles from Bishop, Opkick, the shuttle kids, Victor . . . I must be the only person who wasn't in the know.

"Borjigin," I say, "what is this?"

He pulls me in for a hug. "It's a celebration of your triumph in battle. A way for those of us who did not fight to thank those that did. I had it planned all along as a ceremony, but when you told me we didn't lose *anyone*, I turned it into a party!"

He leads me around the room. There are tables full of food: meats and cheeses, pastries, a whole roasted Omeyocan piggy sitting on a huge silver tray. Candies and treats. Platters full of unwrapped grain bars from our food warehouse. The Springers consider those a delicacy. I see another table topped with a pile of small black circular cookies, also from the storehouse, and standing next to that table, of course, is Farrar. He smiles at me, chewed-up cookies caked on his teeth. He always did have a sweet tooth.

There are exhibits, too. Kalle is behind a pedestal, its glowing display showing some kind of wiggling worm thing. I see three shuttle kids with instruments: one with a harp of some kind, one with a brass trumpet, one with several small drums set up around her. Two displays of paintings—not Springer paintings, I'm shocked to see, but *human* ones. A table where black-haired little Bernice Walezak is talking to a dozen people. She wears white robes, smiles like an angel.

Borjigin sweeps his arms wide, a gesture that includes the band, the people, the food, the exhibits . . . everything.

"Important things happened while you were gone," he says. "And there were some things happening while you were here, but you were too busy to notice. I wanted to take a moment and bring all of these things together, so you could see that you're fighting for far more than just survival. Art, science . . . this is the culture we're all building together. Building because of *you*, Em. Because of your leadership."

All this attention, all focused on me. I'm grateful, but I hate it.

Borjigin finally seems to notice how uncomfortable I am. He looks at the people gathered around.

"We have about an hour," he calls out. "Then most of us need to get back to work. Eat, drink, learn and enjoy!"

The crowd applauds again, maybe this time more for him than for me, then they return to what they were doing. The music starts up. The room fills with the sounds of conversation.

I'm used to being the center of attention, but not like this. I'm embarrassed. I'm also very touched.

"Borjigin, you shouldn't have done this."

He laughs. "You never ask for anything for yourself, so I took it upon myself to show you how much we appreciate what you do. This celebration isn't just for you, of course—take a look at your soldiers."

Victor is tearing into a plate overstuffed with steaming piggy meat. A bandage covers the burn wound on his head. He's eating and laughing, talking to Louise Bariso, one of our halves. Bawden is in a wheelchair. The plate on her lap holds a small roasted animal. I recognize it—the same animal Visca found right before he was killed. How I miss him. Maria and Lahfah are laughing and dancing together in front of the little band, along with a young circle-star girl named Ines Darzi. They've all traded in their dirty jungle rags for long scarves of all colors that flow in time with their movements.

The people who fought with me, human and Springer alike . . . just a few hours ago they were putting their lives on the line. Now they are playing, laughing, enjoying this moment like there is no tomorrow. With the *Basilisk* coming in, maybe there *isn't* a tomorrow. They should have fun while they can.

We all should.

Borjigin is clapping in time with the band.

"They're wonderful," I say.

"The Springers made the harp," Borjigin says. "We found the trumpet and the drums in a storage room. Tama, Robert and Karen have been practicing their instruments for weeks."

Tama Church, Robert Williams and Karen Benson are all circles. I had no idea our people could be musicians.

I point to the paintings.

"And those?"

"Axel uses paint provided by the Springers," Borjigin says. "Crystal uses charcoal. They were both hiding their art away, like they thought it would get them into trouble or something."

I shake my head. Axel Shepherd and Crystal Gilbert—both shuttle kids. And, both circles.

"You said there were important discoveries?"

Borjigin takes my hand and leads me to Kalle's pedestal. She waves everyone away so she can focus solely on me. She has such a sweet smile. Unfortunately, what usually comes out of her mouth is anything but sweet.

"Sorry those godsdamned jungle rats burned our crops," she says.

I can't even guess how many hours she invested in developing that cornfield. I don't blame her for being angry, but at the same time I don't need her racism.

"Kalle, we have *guests*," I say. "Can you mind your language, please?"

She huffs, then glances at Lahfah and a few other Springers.

"It's just a word, Em," she says, but not as loud. "Words can't hurt you."

"They can't? Tell that to those who died in Aramovsky's war. Besides, the Springers aren't *rats*."

"Close enough for my taste."

"You've never even seen a rat."

She laughs. "But I remember what they look like. Don't you?"

I do. I didn't at first, but when some people started calling the Springers *jungle rats*, I looked it up on one of the Observatory's pedestals. Once I saw it, I "remembered" it, meaning that Matilda knew about rats when she was a little girl. The only memories that are truly *mine* are the ones that came after I woke up in my coffin, in the dark, screaming and fighting for my life.

"I'm glad you beat them," Kalle says. Her tone is slightly more respectful. "Did you kill them all?"

"No, not all."

"Too bad."

I don't bother telling her that those who survived will probably all die at the hands of Barkah.

She waves her hands above the pedestal. An image sparkles to life—it's the purple vine root. We use its juice to neutralize the toxic mold that makes all food on this planet poisonous.

"I finally had a breakthrough with this thing," she says. "Magnify."

The image zooms in on one spot of the root as if we are plunging into it at high speed. What looked like smooth skin is actually marked with tight wrinkles. We dive further, *through* those wrinkles, into the flesh itself. Tiny dots appear, which grow into irregular cubes packed in together.

"Those cubes are plant cells," Kalle says. "Increase magnification."

The cubes seem to expand. I see that there are dots in the middle of each one, something at the center of the cell. Then I see movement—something long and thin, sliding *between* the cubes.

I point at it. "What is that?"

"It's a microorganism. I first saw them months ago, but assumed they were just a pest of some kind. My recent experiments, however, show that the worms secrete a manganese compound that kills the mold and neutralizes the mold's toxin."

Borjigin nudges me.

"Told you things happened while you were gone," he says.

I stare at the image while my brain catches up with what Kalle just said. I don't understand all her words, but I think I get her meaning.

"So it's not root-juice that makes our food safe to eat," I say, "it's *worm* juice?"

Kalle nods. "A disgusting yet accurate way to describe it, sure."

"Does this worm thing eat the root?"

"No," she says. "I believe the worms eat waste from the plant cells. Without the worms, in fact, I think the roots would die, killing the vines. Do you know what the word *symbiotic* means?"

I shake my head.

"It means that two or more organisms are interdependent. Sometimes it means two species live in close association that may be—but is not necessarily—beneficial to each other. What we have with the roots and the worms is called *obligate symbiosis*. Do you know what that means?"

She's really starting to annoy me.

"Obviously I don't."

She shrugs. "Who can tell with you? You're always so full of surprises. *Obligate symbiosis* means the two species can't survive without each other. Without the worms, the vines die. Without the vines, the worms die."

Borjigin is excited, and getting impatient.

"Tell her the best part," he says.

Kalle points at the image. Her fingertip touches the worm, sending up a little cloud of multicolored sparkles.

"I think I can modify the worms so they become symbiotic with our corn," she says. "And our turnips, and all of our crops. The mold isn't just toxic to us, it's toxic to the plants the Grownups sent down here. That's why everything we grow looks so sickly. If I can get the worms to live symbiotically with our crops, we'll be able to grow our own food."

Despite the unknown threat orbiting us high above, despite the dangers lurking in the jungle, for the first time we have real hope at *permanent* survival on Omeyocan.

"How long will it take to make it work?"

Kalle shrugs. "I couldn't say. Years, maybe. From what I've learned so far, I'm sure I can do it, but it's going to take a shucking long-ass time."

Borjigin frowns at her.

"Kalle, language. You know Em doesn't like that."

She grins at him. "They're just words."

Maybe they are, but I've had enough. I can only take Kalle in small bits.

I walk to the paintings, admire the work. It's really quite impressive. My people can make *art*. I wouldn't have known if I hadn't seen it with my own eyes.

Walezak is leading a few people in prayer. I'm not crazy about religion, but I do notice her robes are white—not red, like Aramovsky wore. Her message sounds peaceful and positive.

I glance at Borjigin.

"You left Aramovsky in his cell, right? And Bello?"

He nods. "I wouldn't remove either of them without your permission. You know that." He looks around the room. "Aside from them, the only ones missing are Zubiri and Okereke. No one could find them. They knew about the party. Zubiri was looking for parts for the Goffspear—maybe she found another hidden room."

I'm glad at least someone is still working.

"Make sure Aramovsky and Bello get some of this food," I say. "But no—"

"No plate or utensils for Bello, I know," Borjigin says. "I'll see to it."

I get a plate. The piggy is delicious. Farrar gives me some cookies for desert. He is all smiles and laughter. Everyone is having so much fun. Yes, the alien ship is close. In a couple of days, we could all be at war. That's what makes this happy moment even more precious.

This is what we are fighting for.

Someone pushes through the people on my right. It's Zubiri.

"I found something," she says.

The brilliant gear has grown. She's almost as tall as I am. Zubiri is still young, but her beauty already rivals that of Spingate. Dark-brown skin, darker eyes. Her black hair is a soft, curly cloud. She is one of the few who prefer the same outfit we were born in: white button-down shirt and a plaid skirt. We found thousands of those outfits in Observatory storerooms, in all sizes—her clothes fit perfectly.

For all her beauty, though, there is no hiding the damage this world has done to her. Her left sleeve is rolled up and pinned closed just above her elbow. She lost the arm in Aramovsky's war. Smith has done wonders repairing Zubiri's ruined face and broken teeth, but the girl will never get her arm back.

"Hi, Zubiri," I say. I tilt my head toward Victor. "Are you and your boyfriend going to dance?"

She starts to shake her head, stops when she glances at Victor. He doesn't seem to notice she's there. Her eyes cloud over for a moment, shimmer with wetness, then Zubiri finishes that paused shake of the head.

"No time for that," she says. "I've found something very important. I need you, Spingate and Gaston to come with me. Right now."

Zubiri is worried. And maybe more than a little afraid.

I glance at Borjigin, not wanting to spoil his party.

He sighs. "Well, I got you to enjoy thirty minutes of fun, which is better than nothing. Go, I'll get everyone back to work in a little bit."

I stand on tiptoe and kiss his cheek.

"Thank you," I say. "I really mean it."

And with that, I gather up Spingate and Gaston.

We follow Zubiri out of the Grand Hall.

# EIGHT

From the outside, the size of the Observatory boggles the imagination. It's a thirty-layer ziggurat. Each layer has a hundred steps. Each step is as high as my knee. Standing next to this building, we feel like gnats. Standing atop it, it feels like you can see the entire world.

From the inside, the Observatory seems somehow even bigger. The hallways twist and turn, sometimes in random directions. We've had people get lost not just for a few minutes or a few hours, but for *days*. Ometeotl is able to provide some maps, but—like so many other things the computer should know—much of its memory about the Observatory has been erased. Opkick set up strict rules about who can go where, when, and with whom, just to make sure someone doesn't vanish for good. She's been trying to estimate how many hallways there are, how far they go, and she's still not sure. Many rooms await behind hidden doors—there is much here we have yet to discover.

So it doesn't surprise me that Spingate and I have followed Zubiri for thirty minutes through the stone hallways, and we still haven't reached her new discovery. Gaston went back to the Control Room, worried that if he's not paying constant attention to the alien ship it might somehow do something we're not ready for.

Zubiri won't talk to me as we walk. I've asked four times what's this about; every time she opens her mouth to speak, she seems to choke on the word. She's not crying, but it's easy to see she's biting back heartbreak—heartbreak she thinks *I* caused.

What did Victor say to her?

So I follow her. I'm exhausted and I still haven't changed out of the clothes I wore for ten days in the jungle. I *smell*. I want to go home. But Zubiri has long since earned our respect. If she needs me to see this now, then I see it now.

We're on the tenth layer. We turn a corner and I see Okereke standing halfway down the hall. He's been waiting here this whole time? No, not waiting—*guarding*.

Zubiri walks up to him, stops.

"Open it," she says.

Okereke nods. He presses a small discoloration in the stone wall. Something clicks. A horizontal chunk of stone pops open. In the space behind it, a row of black symbols on a white background: circle, circle-star, double-ring, circle-cross, half-circle and gear. Okereke taps these in a pattern, so fast I can't follow it.

A wide, hidden stone door swings open without a sound. I wonder how many hundreds of times people have walked right past it, not realizing it was there.

Zubiri enters the room. Spingate and I follow her. Okereke remains outside.

On the far side of the small room is a green metal rack. On that rack, at waist height, are five wide spaces. The first space on my left is empty. The next four are filled with gleaming, golden, six-sided objects. Matilda's memories flashfire the shape—like a *pencil*, but flat on both ends. They are big enough for me to fit inside if I tucked up tight. The rack was clearly designed specifically to hold these objects.

There is no dust on the golden surfaces. No dust in this room, either. The door must have stayed sealed shut for centuries until Zubiri figured out how to open it a few hours ago.

Spingate seems to recognize these things. Whatever they are, they frighten her. She stares at the golden objects as if she knows what they are, but speaking their name out loud would somehow bring a nightmare to life

The two smartest people I know are quaking in their boots.

"Enough of this," I say. "What are these things?"

Being in the presence of these objects seems to chase away Zubiri's heartbreak. Most of it, anyway. Whatever Victor said to hurt her, it pales in comparison to this new reality.

"I've been working on the telescope nonstop," Zubiri says. "Crawling around inside of it, trying to figure out why we can't see out of it. The computer memory was wiped, that's why we don't understand how it works, why we have to figure it out for ourselves."

She's anxious, upset, apologizing for something that I already know, something that isn't her fault.

"No one is mad at you," I say softly. "Just tell me what these are."

She takes a deep breath, continues.

"There is a hatch at the base of the telescope. We've been trying for months to get it open, but the access panel is complicated. The telescope is a delicate instrument—you can't just bang on it with hammers, you know."

My patience is running out. "We know. Go on."

Zubiri takes a deep breath, then continues. "Today, Okereke

finally got that hatch open. He did it by entering a pattern sequence he's been working on. He's good with patterns, better than you'd expect from a circle."

Spingate doesn't seem to notice Zubiri's inadvertent insult. I notice it, of course, but for once I don't care—I want to know what this is all about.

"I crawled inside the hatch," Zubiri says. "I thought I would be looking up at a lens of some kind, because I knew I was in the biggest, longest part of the telescope. But there isn't a lens. The end of the telescope . . . it's open. Like the barrel of a gun. And the interior of the barrel isn't round, it's six-sided. Hexagonal. A barrel just a little bit wider"—she nods toward the golden objects—"than one of those."

I can't believe what I'm hearing.

"Zubiri, are you telling me these pencil-shaped things are some kind of giant *bullets*?"

She nods. She's shivering. She's that scared.

"Inside the hatch door, I saw some numbers. I found Opkick. She's been trying to understand the Grownups' cataloging system, why they number doors the way they do, why some rooms are hidden, that kind of thing. She told me the numbers from inside the hatch probably coordinated with the tenth layer, northwest corner. Okereke and I were very excited, so we started searching. That's why we missed your party—I'm sorry about that."

"It's fine," I say. Like I give a damn about the party right now.

"Okereke and I searched the halls," she says. "We found that hidden panel. He entered the same sequence there that he used to get the hatch open, and here we are."

Objects that might be bullets . . . bullets bigger than my whole body.

I step closer to the rack, stand in front of the giant pencil piece that fills the second space from the left. I notice something below the object, on the rack itself. A small plate with engraved letters. It reminds me of the plaque that decorated the foot of my birth-coffin, the one that told me my name. But this small plaque doesn't show a single letter, a period, then a name—it shows a name, then a number.

"*Goff*," I say, letting my fingertip trace the hard edges of the engraved letters. "And the number 2."

I look at the plaque under the first space, the empty one. It reads *Goff 1*.

The three to my right read *Goff 3, Goff 4* and *Goff 5*.

And then it hits me. I think of the weapon I carry with me almost everywhere, our symbol of power and leadership.

It hits Spingate, too.

"*Goffspear*," she says. "It's not one word. It's two. *Goff* . . . and *spear*."

Zubiri nods.

"The telescope isn't just for seeing," she says. "It's for *targeting*. I think the telescope is a weapons system designed to fire these hexagonal objects. I think we've been wrong about the Observatory all along. It's not some cultural center or temple—I think this place was built to destroy spaceships."

# NINE

**M**y house. My favorite place.

Uchmal is large enough to house three million people. Considering that there are only 275 of us, plus around 200 Springers, there isn't much competition when it comes to picking out a home.

Bishop wanted to live in the Observatory. It's "safe," he likes to say. Maybe so, but that place has no windows—I've spent enough of my life locked up in confined places. And I *need* to be away from the Observatory, at least some of the time. I accept my role as leader, but that doesn't mean the constant demands don't wear me down.

I chose the top floor of a small, four-layer ziggurat. It faces the wide road of Yong Boulevard. We're close enough to the Observatory that I can run there in minutes, or be there in seconds if I'm on spiderback.

My house's outside walls are stone panels that swing out easily on hidden hinges. I leave all four sides open most of the time, even when it's cold. I hate feeling enclosed. I want to see, I need to *breathe*.

I've filled the place with handmade Springer furniture, carvings, rugs, tapestries and brightly colored paintings. I got all of it in exchange for a backpack full of grain bars. Springers can't seem to get enough of those tasty treats. I think of the party— I'll have to get some paintings from Crystal and Axel in here next.

My house is just tall enough that I can see past Uchmal's circular walls. Far to the west, the endless jungle ruins of Omeyocan are a constant reminder of both the destruction my progenitors caused and this planet's untamed beauty. To the north and south, the long expanse of buildings and ziggurats. To the east is the Observatory, massive and ever present. Halfway between it and us is Visca's Spire, a tall black obelisk that stretches toward the sky. We named it after the first casualty in our conflict with the Springers. The Spire has elevators, but they don't work. Sometimes people will take the twenty flights of stairs to the top just for the view.

My favorite couch faces to the west. During the rare times Bishop and I are both home, we often sit there, together. Even if it's raining out, we can cuddle up, stay dry, and just stare out at the glory of Omeyocan.

Which is what we are doing right now. His arm is around me. My head is on his chest. We watch the red sun setting over the yellow jungle. We haven't been alone together in ten days. The last of my strength went into—finally—taking a hot shower. We both want something more than a cuddle, but neither of us has the energy to do anything about it.

So the couch it is. And honestly? I couldn't be happier. Clean hair, clean skin, clean coveralls, and I feel like a different person.

Right now I'm not "the leader." I'm not *"Yalani."* I'm just a girl listening to a boy's beating heart.

"I missed you," Bishop says. "And I'm so pooped."

"Me too. To both."

Far off in the jungle, animals chirp and hoot and howl. At this distance, the sounds merge into a soft song. If I wasn't soaking up every last second with Bishop, filing it away in case this violent place takes him away from me, I would have nodded off long ago.

He turns his head, kisses my hair.

"That's amazing news about the Goff Spear," he says. "Does Zubiri think she can get it to work?"

"She says she needs a few days. She's afraid to try, though. The Goff Spear rounds are nuclear weapons. If something goes wrong, she's worried they might destroy the Observatory."

We stare up at the stars. Gaston says one of the twinkling lights out there is the *Basilisk,* but I don't know which one.

Even though my body is finally relaxing, I can't make my mind do the same. It is full of swirling puzzle pieces: the way people are getting mad at each other, the Belligerent attacks, Barkah's change in behavior, aliens in orbit, spaceship-killing bullets . . . somehow these things connect. I hope I figure out how everything fits together before it's too late.

"Em, what do you want?"

The question strikes me as odd.

"Right now, just this," I say. "Just to be with you."

"That's not what I mean. All the work we're doing. I know it will go on for our lifetimes, but you work harder than anyone else. Do you always want to be the leader?"

"No," I say, instantly. "I do it because it has to be done. I want to build up a stable society, then I want to let someone else take over. I just want to be a normal person."

Bishop laughs. "I don't think you're capable of that."

"Jerk."

He laughs again, pets my hair.

"You're so . . . *driven*," he says. "When you stop being leader, all that energy has to go somewhere. What do you want to do then?"

I realize I've never really thought about that. And yet, seeing those circles at the party, making *art*, creating things that would have never existed without their specific mind, their specific vision . . .

Something pops into my head.

"I think I want to be a writer."

"You mean make up stories?"

I close my eyes, sink a little deeper into him.

"Maybe. Or maybe I'll write about real things. Like the history of our people. It's so hard on us, not knowing our past. If I write, maybe Kevin and other children can know what we went through."

He pauses for a moment. I feel him nod.

"That's beautiful," he says. "I hope you can do that."

I love the sound of his voice. There's a burr in it, a huskiness that is just *male*. Usually gender doesn't matter to me. I could give a damn what kind of parts you have, as long as you can do your job. But that's when I am working. In the precious few minutes when I am not, I love that Bishop is everything a man should be.

He clears his throat in the way he does when he's trying to find the right words. My heart sinks—I know what he's going to say before he says it, and it's not something I want to talk about, not tonight.

"You defeated the Belligerents," he says. "You promised me that once they were beaten, we could talk about starting a family."

I'm already so tired, and he somehow finds a way to make me more so.

"We don't know if they're gone for good."

"You're stalling again," he says. "If you don't want a family with me, Em, why don't you just say so."

*Because I'm afraid that if I say that, you won't want to be with me anymore.*

"Please, Bishop—there's an alien ship coming. Can we talk about this some other time?"

He backs off. He always does. He wants children. I think it's too early for that. And, to be honest, I'm not even sure I *want* children. At all.

"You haven't told me much about the battle," he says, changing the subject. "Do you want to talk about it?"

I think of the Springer being torn apart by my bracelet beam.

"It was hard being out there for so long," I say. "I was always so wet. And *cold.*"

I feel him stir.

"Did Victor try and keep you warm?"

Again, that name said with a hint of anger, a touch of disgust.

"What do you mean *did he try to keep me warm*? We all froze our asses off out there. Why would he . . ."

I suddenly feel so stupid. I sit up.

"You think there's something going on between Victor and me?"

Bishop doesn't answer. I can feel the tension in his body.

"There's not," I say. "Victor is a good soldier. He's reliable. But he's just a boy—you're my man."

That seems to relax him somewhat.

"Well, it might be good to tell Victor the same thing."

"What are you talking about? I said I don't like him that way."

"No, but *he* likes *you* that way."

"That's ridiculous."

"He has a crush on you, Em. Everyone sees it but you."

I think about the things Victor said to me. And how he doesn't seem interested in Zubiri anymore. Could Bishop be right? The very thought embarrasses me.

"Well, I'm not interested in him."

"Even though you said he was *amazing?*"

"He fought well, all right? Stop reading into it."

Maybe this is residue from his budding rivalry with the boy. Or . . . maybe the "rivalry" isn't about who is a better warrior— maybe it's about *me*.

I put my head back on Bishop's chest.

"I don't want to talk about it anymore," I say.

I feel him nod.

"Fair enough," he says. "Something else I want to discuss, anyway. For the next battle, you need to let me fight. I was made for war, Em. You're made for greater things."

I don't mention what I was actually "made" for. I'm a circle. I was made to be a slave.

Bishop is just poking me now, bringing up things we've already talked about. Many times. Why can't he just relax with me?

"I needed you here so everyone could see you, watch you manage things while I'm gone," I say. "We have to think about our long-term survival as a people. If anything happens to me, you—"

"Nothing is going to happen to you."

I hear his heartbeat quicken. In combat, he stays remarkably calm and efficient. Alone with me, though, is the only time he lets his guard down, lets his emotions show.

"I know you feel that way," I say. "But Omeyocan is a place of death. Since we landed, we've lost twenty-one people."

I let that number sink in. It's a reminder to him that death could take any of us, at any time.

And probably will.

"If I die, you have to lead," I say. "Or if you don't want to lead, help the person that does. This isn't about me or you—it's about our people. Barkah needs to see me out there, in the battles, taking risks. He has to know I'm not like his father, that I won't sit back and let others fight for me."

Maybe that's the real reason behind my decision to lead our troops into battle. Barkah has thousands of subjects. Regardless of our weapons and technology, I know full well that if he thinks we're weak, he might be able to wipe us out with numbers alone.

Bishop hates that he can't fight. *Hates* it. But like all of us, he does what must be done.

We stare out into the jungle for a long while before he speaks again.

"I have to tell you something. When you were gone, I had trouble sleeping."

"Awwww, you missed me that much?"

"More than you could ever know, but it wasn't that. I . . . if I tell you this, will you promise not to tell anyone else?"

That gets my attention. If there's one thing that defines Ramses Bishop, it's that he doesn't care what anyone thinks.

"Of course," I say. "Anything you tell me in confidence stays with me, forever."

He hesitates. I wait. When it comes to actions, Bishop moves without hesitation, with speed that is simply shocking. When it comes to strategy—or to emotions—it takes him a little longer to know his mind.

"The first few nights you were gone, I slept fine," he says. "But then something changed. I started having nightmares."

We're not together every night, but when we are, he sleeps like the dead. I've never known him to have a nightmare.

Spingate never had them, either.

His voice is a thin whisper. "I was scared, but not because of something else. I was scared of *me*, because I hurt someone."

A shiver ripples across my skin. Just like the shiver I felt when I saw Spingate and Gaston yelling at each other. I know Bishop better than I know myself. I love him, and he is good to me, but I can never, *ever* forget how dangerous he can be.

I sit up again, stare at him. "Who did you hurt?"

He looks down. He won't meet my eyes.

"Victor," he says. "I . . . I killed him."

"What, like an accident? Or a training duel?"

Bishop makes us do combat training every day. We often use real weapons. Sometimes, people get hurt, but experiencing danger is a necessary part of being able to fight efficiently when your life is on the line. Duels are a huge part of that training— one-on-one battles with blunted spears or other weapons.

He still won't look at me.

"Not a duel," he says. "I came up from behind him. I stalked him. I murdered him."

For the briefest moment, I feel an overpowering urge to stand and run. Aside from the snake-wolves, Bishop is the deadliest creature on this planet. Then the urge passes, and I feel ridiculous for being afraid of him.

"It was just a dream," I say.

He nods.

"But it felt so real. I woke up in the middle of it, right after I ran him through. I was screaming. Not from fear, Em . . . I was screaming with joy."

My people are getting more violent. My people are having

nightmares. A sense of dread takes root in my chest. It lies there, twitching, wiggling.

I reach out, caress his cheek.

"It was just a dream," I say again.

But was it?

I nuzzle into him. I feel his hand on my head, stroking my long black hair. I lose myself in that sensation. As big and powerful as Bishop is, this dealer of death has a touch so tender it makes me melt.

I swear, it makes me want to purr.

Like O'Malley's kitten.

The kitten he had to strangle.

My special, perfect moment evaporates.

They made O'Malley's progenitor kill his own kitten, just to prove something that didn't need to be proved. Down here we all work so closely together toward our common goal that sometimes I forget just how awful our species can be.

Bishop's regular breathing tells me he's fallen asleep. Lying on the couch, in the steady hum of my planet, I'm able to let go of disturbing thoughts. I breathe in deeply through my nose. I smell Bishop. I smell the jungle.

My fear slips away, and sleep takes me.

# TEN

Rain hammers so hard the jungle leaves moan in pain.

Omeyocan's twin moons glare down.

The rain transforms the yellow jungle to red. It's not water that pours from the sky—it's *blood.*

"Look what you've done, Em."

That voice.

*J. Yong.*

He's curled up in a ball on the floor of a *Xolotl* hallway, his blood mixing with the endless gray dust to make crimson slush. Red stains his white shirt where I stabbed him in the belly. He rolls from side to side, but his eyes never leave mine.

"Look what you've done," he says.

"I'm sorry! I didn't mean it!"

I know that's a lie.

Yong cries out. His cry becomes a squeal, because he's not Yong, he's a pig—the pig I killed in the Garden.

"Look what you've done, Em," the pig says.

Blood sprays from its slashed throat, a crimson gusher that coats the green grass.

"But I had to," I say. "You were in pain."

The pig's head tilts back, the cut I made widening until the head comes off and tumbles across a nighttime jungle floor. It rolls to a stop—now it's a Grownup's coal-black head wearing the metal and glass mask they use to breathe Omeyocan's air.

"Look what you've done," Old Visca says.

I want to turn away. I can't.

"You were going to shoot my friend," I say. "You were going to murder Barkah. I had to kill you, I had no choice!"

The head is a head one second, a huge Grownup the next. Coal-black skin is cratered, cracked and smoking, because this thing was ripped to shreds and now has been put back together.

"There is always a choice," Old Bishop says. "*Look what you've done!*"

His words are thunder, a concussion that echoes through the city, bounces off ancient stone walls.

The fissures in his body flare with white fire, and once again he is torn to pieces, but each piece moves as if it is a living animal, grows arms and legs and vibrating blurd wings, crawls and scurries and flies back together in a self-assembling puzzle of gore that becomes a Springer . . .

"You murdered me," it says. "Look what you've done."

It's the one I shot in the battle with the Belligerents. When I killed it, I didn't think I saw details, but I was wrong—I would recognize this being anywhere.

"Look what you've done," it says again.

"I had to!" I'm crying. I never cry. My voice is the voice of a weakling, someone who begs. "I'm so sorry, I *had to*."

The Springer's two-fingered hands slide to its belly, grab the spear sticking out of it. Blue blood sprays out, mixing with the ankle-deep red dust-slush at its feet.

"Look what you've done to me, Em."

Now it is Ponalla, the Springer I killed in the jungle.

"The *first* Springer you killed," Ponalla says. "There were more. Look what you've done to *us.*"

Ponalla stands in a field of carnage. Blood rain pours down. All around me are the twisted, ravaged bodies of Springers and humans, shattered remains of ruined spiders. Smoke and fire and flesh and bone.

"Your fault," Ponalla says. "You could have stopped all of it, if you were stronger."

*"Aramovsky did this, not me!"*

My words come out as cracked little things, as worthless and ineffective as my leadership.

Leadership. The spear in Ponalla's belly . . . it's *mine*. I need it to stop this nightmare.

I grab the spear shaft, but it's not a spear anymore. It's the handle of a knife, thick with jewels and slick with blood.

*Red* blood.

A knife buried in yet another belly, the belly of a boy wearing black coveralls.

No.

No, I can't take this, I will go insane and I will never wake up *I will never wake up I don't want to see this I don't want to re-member!*

"Look what you've done," Kevin O'Malley says.

The stone walls shake around us, the stone floor trembles beneath. His head is in my lap. He smiles up at me with pure love, which makes it even worse. I killed him, but he was *still in there.*

"Look what you've done to me, Em."

I want to tell him I love him, that I will *always* love him and that I'm so sorry, that I didn't know he was still in there, but I suddenly can't even hear my own words. Everything is a roar. The world shudders around us.

His hands reach up, grip my shoulders.

"Wake up, Em," O'Malley says. "Wake up."

His fingers curl in, squeeze hard enough to hurt. He doesn't know his own strength.

Just like Bishop.

"Wake up."

O'Malley shakes me. The world roars louder, and then he vanishes into the darkness of a fading dream.

# ELEVEN

"**E**m, *wake up!*"

My eyes snap open. Bishop, hovering over me, shaking me, fingertips digging into my soft flesh like iron claws. He lets go but the shaking doesn't stop.

A long, low, droning howl, rising and falling, echoing off every building. Borjigin's emergency warning siren.

Another sound, an explosion, its roar so loud I wince, so loud it *hurts*, makes my inner ear flutter like something is kicking it.

"We're under attack," Bishop says, his voice level and spooky-calm. "Move."

I've fallen off the couch. The floor trembles beneath me. Earthquake? But he said we're under attack. . . .

The tremble subsides. I stand. My house is falling apart. The ceiling leaks streams of dust. Deep cracks line my once-smooth walls, like lightning frozen in stone.

Bishop runs to the stairs, but I don't follow him. I have to see what's happening. I sprint to our east balcony and look out.

Uchmal is ablaze.

A dozen fires burn high, illuminating clouds of billowing smoke and dust. Fire makes shadows dance, as if the surrounding buildings are lit up from a dozen tiny suns that have settled on our streets. A ten-layer ziggurat a few blocks down has crumbled like it was stomped on by a giant boot, the peak smashed in, one tiered edge standing thin and tall like a broken brown tooth. The vines that covered the ziggurat are ablaze, leaves burning bright, heat making the long stems twist as if the fresh ruin is carpeted in a blanket of writhing fire-snakes.

We're under attack? The Springers don't have weapons that can do this . . . do they?

Up above, blazing lights . . . long-tailed comets scorch the night sky, plummeting down to strike my city.

I don't know what I'm seeing, exactly, but the source of this destruction becomes suddenly obvious—the alien ship is bombarding us.

One of those comets streaks directly toward me, louder than all the others, a thunder-scream that freezes me where I stand. The fireball smashes into a ziggurat across the street, erupts in an explosion that shuts my eyes, that throws my arm in front of my face before the boiling breath of an angry giant blows me backward. I slam into a table, knocking it over as I spill across the stone floor.

Searing pain on my left shoulder. I slap at it with my right hand even as I lurch to my feet, off-balance. Flames flare: the table is ablaze. Bits of the ceiling break free and drop down. My paintings and tapestries wriggle with fire. The floor trembles so fiercely I can barely stay on my feet.

I dash to my bedroom, jam my feet into boots.

Bishop rushes in, hunched over against the crumbling stone ceiling, arm near his face to protect against the heat and flame.

"Em, come on!"

I follow him through our burning house. Down stone stairs: one flight, then another, then another.

We are out on the street. My city burns. Flames reach up from craters and the husks of smashed buildings. I hear screams, both human and Springer, echoing through the night. The warning siren wails. Above us, tongues of fire streak down to hammer the ground.

Bishop points eastward.

"The Observatory, it's not being attacked."

I see that he's right. The mammoth structure rises up, blocking out the stars, yet it is free of flame. Surely that won't last. Our attackers are raining fire down all around us—they can't possibly miss the biggest building on this planet.

"We need to run for the jungle," I say. "The city's being destroyed!"

"Stick to your emergency plan." Bishop's voice is calm and resonant. "The Observatory is big enough that it can probably survive the impacts."

My plan was to protect us against a Springer attack, not a barrage from space. Most of my people live in the Observatory, so they'll already be there. Those that don't are trained to head for it at the first sound of the siren.

But with comets blazing down, with buildings collapsing, I think of the Observatory crumbling, of being buried beneath a mountain of stone. My breath seizes up. I will not die in the dark, *I will not*. The jungle, the open spaces, that's where we need to be.

I see two people lurch out of a crumbling building. Young circle-stars. Kai Brown, that's his name, and the girl is Ines Darzi. Brown wears black coveralls, while Darzi—one of

D'souza's Demons—is still decked out in the fancy scarves she wore at the party. They stop, kneel by an unconscious girl sprawled out on the rubble.

The girl is hurt. There will be more wounded. In the Observatory's hospital, Kenzie can help them. And if we run to the jungle, we have no central rallying point. My people will be spread out, disorganized . . . defenseless.

We will stick to the plan.

I point to the kids. "Let's help them."

Bishop is much faster than I am. He reaches the wounded girl before I'm even halfway there, scoops her up and throws her over his shoulder.

Darzi's face is badly burned, but her eyes are clear and she is not afraid. A silver bracelet is on her right arm, long point aimed at the ground. The bracelet's crystal glows white, ready to unleash its deadly energy. Brown hovers near, a Springer-made hatchet in his hand.

"Stay with me," I tell them, and we run down the wide Yong Boulevard toward the towering Observatory.

Others join us in our mad rush, stumbling out of buildings or crawling from the rubble. One moment there are the five of us, the next seven, the next ten. Still the comets streak down like swords of flame, punishing our city.

A roar far louder than the others, that thunder-scream telling me a comet is plummeting toward us.

"*Down,*" Bishop screams, and we throw ourselves to the flat stones as a fireball punches into the street not a hundred strides ahead of us. Wind-driven flame washes over our backs. Something smashes into my chin. Rubble showers down around me, hammers into me.

The world goes silent.

For a moment, I can't hear anything. Then, a high-pitched

ringing. Sounds fade back in: the heaving roar of tall flames, the crack and crumble of collapsing stone, the coughing and cries of my people.

We are close to the Observatory, but not close enough.

A pillar of fire rises high into the night sky. Visca Spire is ablaze. A comet took a chunk out of it on the way down. The tower shudders, then something breaks in the middle—the top half tilts sideways, trailing a long arc of orange and red flame. It smashes across the width of Yong Boulevard in a cloud of smoke and ash and hot stone, completely blocking our path.

"Everyone, *up*," Bishop screams. "Grab the wounded, we'll go around!"

It should be me shouting to my people, leading them on, but I have no air in my lungs. Bishop will get us to safety.

I see a girl to my right, struggling to rise. Fancy rags smolder, dance with bits of fire. It's Darzi. I throw myself on her, smothering the flames, then I grab her and pull her up.

"On your feet!"

She wobbles once, but I catch her, steady her, then she's standing on her own power. Blood pours down her face. Her left arm hangs limply. She coughs, then moves to help someone else up.

I see a boy lying facedown across a pile of broken brick. I rush to him, boots slipping on the loose rubble. I fall twice before I reach him. At the back of his head is a knot of white, a tied headband—it's Halim Horn.

I kneel and grab him, turn him over to scream at him to *get up*, to *run* . . .

. . . but he will never do either of those things, not ever again.

Halim's lower jaw is gone, the place where it once was now a void of ragged red flesh and broken bone. His throat, too, is missing—I can see the bones of his neck. His head . . . it's barely attached to his body.

Dead eyes stare out.

Eyes that look exactly like they did in the Observatory: brown, wide, still wet, but now lifeless, hollow, empty.

A glob of red spreads across his white headband.

A hand, pulling at my coveralls. Darzi, screaming at me to move, screaming at me just the way I screamed at her a few moments ago.

I distantly hear another crushing impact, feel the faint caress of billowing heat.

Halim is gone. The boy who didn't want to fight, who wanted to be a scientist, now he is nothing but meat. His dreams will forever go unfulfilled.

*I will find who did this . . . I will find them and I will slaughter them.*

I stand. Fire all around us. Our world is ablaze. Flame rises up from ziggurats, dances in the streets, whips and whirs with the blowing wind. We have to move, but to where?

Bishop runs to my side. He still has the girl over his right shoulder, and now a boy over his left. The two limp bodies look like toys.

"Em, help me find a safe way through the fire."

Again that dauntless calm. Bishop is iron, cold and hard. His steadiness soothes my fear and rage.

The fires are closing in. Heat bakes us, grows hotter by the second. I don't see a way clear. Smoke sears my lungs, stings my eyes. We'll be cooked alive.

A new noise, coming from the far side of the crumbled, burning spire that blocks the street. Through the shimmering heat, I see something approaching.

Something *big*.

I recognize the new noise: an engine.

The remnants of Visca Spire billow outward, broken bricks

tumbling and flame-kissed stones spinning as the fire is pierced by a moving wall of metal.

Trailing flames from its strange front end, Big Pig thunders across the rubble. It slows suddenly—huge black tires squealing and sliding on broken stone—then shudders to a halt.

The driver's door opens.

"Everyone, *come on,*" Victor screams at us. "Go go go!"

People rush for the truck. I push Darzi toward it, then grab at Brown, who is slow to rise. His leg is broken. I throw him over my own shoulders in a fireman's carry, the way Bawden taught me to do.

Bishop is next to me, urging me on, his steps strong and sure despite his double-shouldered burden.

The heat hammers at us, tries to drain the life from our very bodies.

Then Victor is there, pulling Brown from my shoulders. Coughing madly, I stagger toward the back of the truck, no longer sure of what's happening around me. Someone lifts me. Hands pull me up. I wipe tears from my stinging eyes. I'm in the truck's big bed, which is full of dirt and people. Darzi, Brown, Bishop, people from my neighborhood, others Victor must have rescued along the way.

Zubiri is here, her white shirt filthy from the dirt and the smoke. She has a thick leather bag over her shoulder, and from it she pulls out clean white bandages. She ties off wounds, not with Smith's delicate touch, but rather with an urgency born of desperation. She's coughing hard, not even bothering to cover her mouth as she moves from wounded person to wounded person.

The truck lurches. We grab for the sides, for each other, for anything that will let us hold on as Victor turns it sharply.

I grip the top of the truck bed's wall, pull myself up to look over. Fires all around. They aren't spreading, though, and some are already dying out. The vines are damp from the rains. If they had been dry, Uchmal would be a sea of flame.

The truck hits something in the road, bounces over it roughly enough to make me lose my grip. I fall back to the dirt. All around me, the lurching ride makes people struggle to maintain their balance.

Zubiri crawls across the dirt toward me.

"Em, you're cut," she says. She pulls a white bandage from her bag and presses it to my jaw. "Hold this tight, keep the pressure on it."

In a daze, I reach up to do what she says, then realize I'm already holding something in that hand. Something soft. In a distant, dreamy state, I look to see what it is.

A strip of bloodstained white cloth.

Halim's headband, embroidered with the null-set symbol.

I feel the truck slow sharply, again hear the screeching of tires. We stop. The heat is gone. Cool night air caresses me, soothes my scorched skin. The Observatory—it looms over us. If we can get inside, maybe we'll survive to see the sun rise again.

People call to me. Hands gently pull me to my feet, then lower me to the ground. Someone slides under my arm, helps me walk.

There is no fire here.

The Observatory's vines dance with shadows cast by the flames we've left behind.

# TWELVE

The circle-crosses patch up our wounds until the attack stops. We don't know if it will start up again, so those of us who can walk rush from the Observatory and into the nighttime streets.

Usually, I lead. Sometimes in violent situations, Bishop takes over. Now, it is neither of us—Borjigin tells everyone what to do.

He is on spiderback, messageboard in hand. While Kenzie tended the wounded, Borjigin was making a list of who is missing and where they live. He assigns people to dig, to carry water to workers, to call out for the missing by name, to use spiders and trucks to move rubble.

Most of the fires have already burned out. The city is made of stone and brick. What wood and cloth there is—furniture, doorframes, things like that—is already consumed.

Everywhere, the smell of smoke. Of scorched stone. And another scent I know all too well, one that I had hoped I would never know again: the smell of burned flesh.

A few of the Springers who live in Uchmal are here with us.

The rest are digging madly in a nearby area, as that's where most of them lived. As bad as my neighborhood looks, I'm told theirs is even worse.

I don't see Maria anywhere. If she's dead . . .

Borjigin assigns me to a crew with Farrar and a young gear named Milton Cathcart. Farrar swings a pickaxe to break up the stones of a collapsed entrance. Milton and I shovel away the broken chunks as fast as Farrar makes them. Milton works hard, but babbles the entire time, saying that the comet-missiles were probably big rocks "superheated" from punching through the atmosphere. He uses words like "potential energy" and "giga-jewels." I don't know what those things mean. I keep shoveling.

I hear a murmur of alarm, people shouting that we're under attack again. A Springer war horn echoes through the city—and this one isn't from our emergency system.

Bishop shouts commands, telling us to form lines and set up firing positions. People scramble to take cover. I hear the rattle of rifles being cocked, barrels bracing on heavy stone, mutters of "Springer backstabbers" and "godsdamned jungle rats."

Are the Belligerents attacking? We're at our weakest, this would be the ideal time for them to strike, but how could they have gotten through the gates?

Far down the wide, straight swath that is Yong Boulevard, toward the Observatory, I see movement through the swirling smoke. Springers, *hundreds* of them, marching in a tight formation. Flat carts rolling on wooden wheels. Some of the carts have wooden frameworks on top. At first I think they are the trebuchets the Springers used in the Battle of the Crescent-Shaped Clearing to hurl boulders at our spiders, but these frameworks don't look the same.

Something big quickly moves from the back of the column to

the front . . . *two* somethings. I can't make them out . . . hurukans? Yes, hurukans, with riders. One rider carries a flag that waves slightly in the wind.

But the Belligerents don't have hurukans, at least not that we've seen.

All around me, my people settle in for this unexpected fight. Those who have bracelets and rifles take aim. Those who don't hunker down and clutch tight to axes, knives, hatchets, spears and other weapons, ready to rush forward on command.

*Spears* . . . I don't have my spear. It was in my house. I am without our symbol of leadership.

A short gust of wind clears the smoke for an instant, and in that instant I see the hurukans and their riders—it's Maria, atop Fenrir, and Lahfah atop her mount. Riding behind Lahfah, carrying the flag . . . it's Barkah.

I drop my shovel. I step out into the street, feet crunching on rocks and cinders.

Bishop screams at me to take cover. I raise my hand toward him, palm out, silently telling him to leave me be.

Maria must have opened the gates, let the Malbinti soldiers in.

Barkah has one arm around Lahfah's waist. He's wearing a long blue coat with silver trim, finery that seems out of place amid this wreckage.

His flag . . . it's white.

Just like the one I carried the first time I met him.

"Bishop," I say, "tell everyone to hold their fire."

Bishop barks orders. My people slowly rise from cover, their weapons pointed at the ground.

Barkah slides off Lahfah's hurukan. He hops toward me, stops just a few steps away. At least two hundred Springer soldiers stretch down the street behind him. He sets the flagpole butt on the broken stone street. The white fabric flutters slightly.

He coughs from the smoke. I know his moods, his expressions. He's holding back rage, but there is also anguish and sympathy swirling within him.

*"Hem . . . we help?"*

I nod. Perhaps I will never fully understand this alien, but right now he is exactly what we need. I put my right hand on his thin left shoulder.

"Thank you," I say. Then, I look for Borjigin, see him on his spider, and shout up to him.

"Barkah and his people are here to help us—tell them what to do."

# THIRTEEN

We don't bury our dead.

We burn them.

After the fight in the Observatory where O'Malley, Coyotl and others died, and the fire that reduced them all to ashes, we've chosen funeral pyres as the way we say goodbye.

We gather around a bomb crater not that far from where my home stood. Okereke covered the bottom of the crater in a neat layer of logs and kindling. Our nine fallen friends lie on top, side by side, shoulder to shoulder.

I wish I had my spear.

Humans and Springers alike line the crater's edge. Barkah is here, dressed in fine regalia. Lahfah is next to him—she's *filthy*, covered in soot and ash.

The Springers who died in the attack have been taken out of the city, to be buried in the jungle. Barkah's people have their traditions, we have ours.

Walezak is giving a nice little speech. Something about the glory of dying in the service of your fellow citizens. I have a feeling similar speeches have been given for thousands of years, maybe as far back as humanity goes. The living can make it all sound heroic and magical, because the dead can't argue. Anyway, I'm not really listening. I have one line to deliver, so I pay just enough attention that I don't miss my cue.

Walezak is so small, yet she delivers her speech with volume, conviction. She stands there in white robes, a lit torch in one hand held up high.

"So we bid you farewell," she says. "And we say *thank you* for being part of our lives."

All heads turn to me. My cue, I almost missed it.

"May the gods welcome them home."

My people echo my words: *"May the gods welcome them home."*

Walezak tosses the torch into the crater.

Borjigin has been experimenting with what he calls *accelerants,* a too-fancy word for "things that burn really fast." When the torch hits, flames *whoosh* up instantly, making all of us take a step back.

*"Sorry,"* Borjigin calls out.

I look around, but the burst of flame didn't hurt anyone.

In the pit, Birthday Children bodies burn. When they are reduced to ash, circles will fill in this hole. We'll put up some kind of memorial, as we did with the melted X that marks the resting place of O'Malley's ashes and the ashes of those who died with him.

I'm done here.

Some people ride spiders or other vehicles back to the Observatory.

I think I'll walk.

I'd rather be alone for a little while.

# FOURTEEN

Our world has descended into chaos. I can't shake the feeling that I'm missing something, something that makes these puzzle pieces fit. No one I talk to has answers.

But there is one person I haven't spoken to yet. I haven't spoken to him in a long time.

There are twelve cells in our jail, set in two facing rows of six each. Stone walls, iron bars. No windows. We use these cells as punishment for various crimes. Most people serve only a few days here, sometimes a few weeks. All except for our two permanent guests—Korrynn, and her former partner in deceit, Aramovsky.

I have to walk past her cell to get to his. She's asleep, or at least pretending to be. I'm not here to talk to her anyway. Aramovsky's cell is on the same side of the hall as hers. They can't see each other, but they're close enough to talk if she ever chooses to do so. She rarely does.

I stop at his cell.

"Hello, Aramovsky."

He's lying on his bed, arm over his eyes. At the sound of my voice, he sits up instantly.

"Em. Walezak told me about the attack. Did we lose anyone?"

Walezak is the only person who visits him for anything other than delivering food. One double-ring providing emotional comfort to another.

Aramovsky has changed so much since we put him in here. The hatemonger who started a war claims to have seen the error of his ways. He says he wants to make amends for what he's done. He seems sincere about that, but I will never trust this man.

Because of Aramovsky, O'Malley is dead.

Yes, I am the one who drove a knife into Kevin's belly, but that never would have happened if Aramovsky hadn't betrayed us. Aramovsky made a deal with Matilda; in exchange for power, he sold us out.

"Nine," I say.

Nine people, gone. We're down to 266 survivors. The deaths crush me. I am the leader; this loss of life is my fault.

"Nine *humans*, that is," I say. "Because I'm sure you won't be the least bit upset by the fifteen Springers who also died in the attack."

He winces, as if those words sting. He's always been a great actor.

"I take no joy in their deaths," he says. "The Springers are our friends."

I don't bother telling him that Barkah's efforts saved human lives. His soldiers attacked the rubble, clearing it away far faster than we could have done on our own. The carts were cranes, which Borjigin used to stabilize damaged walls long enough to rescue two of our people who were buried in the wreckage. On our own, we wouldn't have reached them in time. And then there's the obvious fact that we were devastated by the attack—Barkah could have easily wiped us out for good. Instead, he helped us in our time of need.

Aramovsky stands and walks toward me. He grips the vertical bars of his cell, leans his face closer. He's not wearing a shirt. He's as tall as he was when we first woke—maybe even a little taller—but his skinny days are long gone. There isn't much to do in his cell, so he exercises constantly: push-ups, sit-ups, stretching, things like that. Muscles ripple beneath his dark skin.

"Em, I know you told me not to ask you anymore, but I have to. When can I get out of here?"

He's in this cell for two reasons. The first is for the things he did. The second is because if his Springer "friends" get their hands on him, they will chop him into tiny pieces.

"Not now," I say. "It's not safe."

He sags a little. How is it possible I feel bad for Aramovsky? It's his fault O'Malley is dead. And Coyotl. And Beckett. And the fourteen kids who died in the Battle of the Crescent-Shaped Clearing. And the hundreds of Springers who died there as well. So much blood on Aramovsky's hands, yes, but to be stuck in this stone cell for over a year? If it was me in there, I wonder if I would be positive and optimistic, like him, or if I'd try to kill myself, like Bello.

"I want your thoughts on our situation," I say.

"Of course," he says instantly. "Anything to help."

I tell him about the bombardment, about the other two ships that will be here soon. I tell him about the Belligerents and Barkah's inconsistent behavior. I tell him about how Spingate and Gaston act toward each other, about her nightmare, and Bishop's—and mine.

Before I know it, I am telling Aramovsky *everything*. The

words pour out of me. He might already know much of this from Walezak's visits, but I don't care—saying it all out loud is a relief. Hearing my own words helps me mentally catalog the vast problems we face.

He listens attentively, nodding occasionally, asking small clarifying questions. He's always been a good listener. It's part of what helped him come to power.

When I finish, his eyes crinkle in thought.

"I know you don't want to hear it," he says, "but this is the influence of the God of Blood."

I want to kick myself. Why did I think this superstitious fool might have real answers?

"The same God of Blood that stood by when we put you in this cell for a year? Doesn't sound like he has all that much power."

Aramovsky shakes his head. "It doesn't care about me. It doesn't want to protect anyone. It creates chaos, Em. It wants hate. It wants its namesake—it wants blood."

*Chaos.* The same word I was thinking when I came here.

"So the God of Blood *told* you to start a war?"

I say it snarkily, trying to anger him, but he doesn't take the bait. He stares at me, solemn and grim.

"It doesn't work like that. The God of Blood is a trickster. It doesn't *speak* to you, it shapes your emotions. Only after you defeated me did I see what I had done, did I see how my envy of you grew to become bitter jealousy. Only after I was in this cell did I see how hate slowly took me over, guided everything I did. Now I am constantly on guard against its deceptions, its influence. I've learned how to fight it when it tries to manipulate me. You say our people are acting more violent? Then be careful, Em. I know you don't think the God of Blood is real, but I assure you, it is. I succumbed to it. Others will, too."

I don't believe in gods, yet Aramovsky's words stir fear deep inside me. He believes what he's saying, every last word.

I think of how the Belligerents suddenly gathered together, individuals from several tribes joining to try and drive us out of Uchmal. Their species against ours.

Is that so different from Aramovsky's war?

"You hated the Springers," I say. "Why? Why did you want to kill them?"

He shrugs. "Because they were different from us."

There is no shame in those words. I can see he no longer feels that way about the Springers, yet he shares his reason for starting a war as if it were no more important than talking about the weather—he's simply stating a fact.

"Thank you for the talk," I say.

"Did it help?"

"No."

But maybe it did, a little. I don't know why.

"Em, if the aliens attack again, I volunteer to help fight. I don't want to die in here knowing that I didn't make up for the awful things I did."

"You *can't* make up for them."

Those words hit him hard.

"At least let me try," he says. "Please. Every war needs cannon fodder, right? Better that I die than someone who doesn't deserve it."

The pain in his eyes. He hates himself. He wants to be better.

No. I trusted him once. He betrayed me. I will never trust him again.

Aramovsky is in prison, and there he will stay.

# FIFTEEN

My wounds are bandaged. So are Bishop's. He hurt his leg in one of the explosions. He didn't show pain or let it slow him down, which is no surprise.

I've gathered my council. These are the people that I most rely upon. Bishop, of course, because we are at war and he speaks for the circle-stars. Spingate and Gaston, because they are the only ones who can tell us what happened. Zubiri, because she is smarter than everyone else. Borjigin, because he runs our city, and during last night's attack he proved himself as a leader beyond any doubt. Barkah, because he represents his tribe of Springers. He and Lahfah are going to stay in Uchmal for a few days, be part of our strategy sessions. His tribe is allied with ours, after all, and we have been attacked.

We're gathered in the Observatory's Control Room. We stand around the Well's waist-high red wall. A glowing hologram of Omeyocan floats above it, complete with the colored dots that represent the *Xolotl* and the alien ships.

"*Goblin* and *Dragon* have sped up," Gaston says. "They accelerated significantly after the *Basilisk*'s attack. *Goblin* will probably be here in a day, the *Dragon* maybe the day after that."

Not the news anyone wanted to hear. We thought we had months before we'd have to worry about those ships.

Gaston clears his throat, stands straight and rigid. He stares at a space somewhere above my head.

"The bombing is my fault," he says. "The *Basilisk* wasn't close enough to safely launch shuttles, still isn't, but I didn't account for kinetic bombardment. It's a lot easier to launch rocks than it is to launch personnel. I should have prepared us for that. I did not. I failed."

His head is back and his chest is out, not in pride, but in acceptance. He's trying to take the blame. His stance is the stance of a man who refuses to make excuses.

As if he could be to blame—I'm the leader, not him. The *failure* is all mine.

"You're not the only one who should have thought of it," I say. "If I had asked you if it was possible the ship might bomb us, would you have accounted for it then?"

He seems suddenly unsure. He was ready to bear all the responsibility, not pass it off on someone else. Xander Gaston is a good person.

"Answer me," I say.

He nods. "I might have, yes."

"You *would* have," Bishop says. "Yes, you should have thought they would bomb us. Em should have thought of it, too, and I *definitely* should have thought of it. I didn't. There's nothing we can do about that now. Assigning blame doesn't bring back the dead."

Spingate reaches out and takes Gaston's hand.

"That battle is over," she says. "Time to get ready for the next one."

Gaston's rigid posture breaks. He slumps, so much so he nearly collapses. He was ready to be chastised, to be punished—not forgiven.

Spingate is correct—time to move on and prepare for whatever comes next.

"Borjigin," I say, "update us on the wounded."

He consults his messageboard.

"Eleven people left in the hospital," he says. "All will be out by tomorrow, except for Delilah Szwarc, who will be in there for a few days. Smith had to amputate her leg."

I can't help but glance at Zubiri's missing arm. Some wounds are beyond even the medical miracles left to us by the Grownups.

"We're still gathering information on damage to the city," Borjigin says. "Looks like sixty-six impacts, total. Most were in the residential area. The Spider Nest took a hit, but the maintenance and repair machinery inside is still functioning. We got lucky there. One of the meteors struck our main food warehouse. It was destroyed. Food supply isn't a major concern, though, as we'd already set up secondary warehouses as a contingency against war or natural disasters. We've still got at least a year's worth of rations, which I'll further subdivide and store in many places across the city."

The puzzle pieces spin in my head. The aliens hit the Spider Nest and the food warehouse. Important buildings.

"Gaston," I say, "is there any way they could know what we had in the Spider Nest and the food warehouse?"

He purses his lips, thinking.

"Depends on their technology," he says. "We know the Spider Nest can't fly, but they might not know that. It's easily identifiable as an orbital-capable ship. Could be the reason they targeted it, to take out a potential spacecraft we could use to attack them."

"But they didn't target *Ximbal*," Bishop says. "No craters anywhere near our shuttle."

Gaston nods. "Right. And the food warehouse is a stone building, like thousands of others in Uchmal. I don't think they could have known what was in there. The food warehouse is big, sure, but larger buildings went unscathed."

The puzzle pieces spin faster.

"Could the aliens see *us*?" I ask. "Where people go?"

"Probably," Gaston says. "Even with really good optics, though, we'd be very tiny, with no detail. Kind of like if you stood on a tall ladder and looked down at an ant hive."

*Ants.* We've never seen those ourselves, but we know them from our progenitors' memories. It's hard to see individual ants . . . they kind of blend together. But a bunch of them, moving in the same direction, that makes ant *trails* far easier to see than the individual ants themselves.

"People use the Spider Nest and the food warehouse all the time," I say. "And there were people walking to and from the residential areas. Maybe the *Basilisk* chose its targets based on foot traffic, assuming the busiest places were the most important?"

"Except they didn't hit the Observatory," Spingate says. "It has more traffic than any other building."

She's right.

"So much for my theory," I say.

"*Hypothesis,*" Spingate says.

I glare at her, annoyed. "What?"

"A *hypothesis* is an attempt to explain something. A *theory* is what happens when you test the hypothesis and confirm it is accurate."

Gaston rubs hard at his face. "Theresa, must you be such an annoying know-it-all?"

She snarls, is about to yell at him, but I cut her off.

"There was *no* damage to the Observatory?"

Borjigin shakes his head. "Not a scratch."

The puzzle pieces refuse to fit. My frustration builds. What am I missing?

"There's only one reason to not target the Observatory," Bishop says. "They don't want to destroy it—they want to capture it. To do that, they need to land troops. We'll have to fight them in the streets."

"Or shoot them down," Gaston says. He looks at Borjigin. "How many tower cannons are operational?"

"Four," Borjigin says. "But we were working on two more that might be salvaged."

Gaston shrinks down the map, showing us the whole city. "We can mount them equidistant around the wall. That gives us the best chance at hitting incoming landing craft, no matter which direction they come from."

Bishop rubs his hands together. "Gaston's right, Em. We need those last two cannons online."

"Make it happen, Borjigin," I say. "Take whoever and whatever you need."

He nods. "I'll get it done."

"There's something else strange about the bombs," Spingate says. "I sent Cathcart out to collect data on crater depths as well as the distance impact debris was thrown. The biggest crater was just over three meters deep. I won't go into the math right now, but based on the explosive power we observed, that indicates the impact of an object about twenty-five centimeters in diameter, assuming it was something about the density of iron. Ometeotl, show the animation I made."

A flash from the blue dot representing the *Basilisk;* a pale blue line streaks away from it.

"We think the alien projectiles were rocks or metal of varying density layers," Spingate says. "When these balls hit the atmosphere, they started to burn up." The streaking blue object turns white. Tiny flames flare up, leave a growing tail behind it. "The atmosphere slowed them some. Most meteors break up while still descending. These did not."

As the white streak descends, the display of Uchmal zooms in closer. In seconds, we're looking at a wide area around Visca Spire. The streak hits nearby, causing a billowing explosion of fire. A shock wave races out, rippling the street stones and hammering nearby buildings. A smoldering crater marks the impact site.

Spingate arches her back, making her belly stretch out a bit farther. She sighs with fatigue. She's still got three months to go, but I get the impression carrying a whole extra person inside of you can wear a girl out.

"Here's what I don't get," she says. "If the aliens had used bigger projectiles, they would have done exponentially more damage. I mean, a projectile just *twice* the size would have destroyed dozens of city blocks and made craters over six meters deep. Why didn't they use bigger projectiles? Why did they go easy on us?"

"*Easy?*" Bishop can't believe what she just said. "Twenty-four of us died."

His count includes both the human and Springer deaths. That bit of respect isn't lost on Barkah.

"*Easy* was the wrong word," Spingate says. "What I mean is, why didn't we have far more casualties? If the aliens really wanted to wipe out Uchmal and everyone in it, all they had to do was throw bigger rocks."

I feel a familiar buzz at the back of my head. The size of the rocks . . . it's one of the missing pieces I need. I know I don't have enough information to see the big picture, not yet, but four things stand out: *the shuttle, the Observatory, shallow craters, they only attacked parts of the city where we go the most.*

I look to Barkah.

"Did any meteors hit Schechak?"

*"No hits,"* he says. *"No in city, no in jungle."*

The aliens weren't attacking the *planet* . . . they were specifically attacking *Uchmal.* But why do that and not hit the Observatory? Why wouldn't they attack Uchmal's largest building, where most of our people live and work?

I stare at the map. What am I missing? I need to get up high, as high as I can, and see if my eyes can show me something this map can't.

"Everyone, get back to your jobs," I say. "I'm going to the peak."

# SIXTEEN

I climb the circular metal steps that take me to the Observatory's top layer. The walls glow soft white around me. Just above, I see a bit of the sky, mostly hidden by a large stone slab supported by four golden poles.

When we first climbed the Observatory's three thousand steps, that slab was flush with the Observatory's top layer. The slab supported a tall pillar decorated with Bishop-sized symbols of the Grownups: circle at top, then circle-star, double-ring, circle-cross, half-circle and gear. Aramovsky pressed his hand to a palm print inside that gear: the platform rose up on those poles, revealing this staircase that led down into the gargantuan building.

I feel the morning heat even before I finish the climb. Maybe two hours until the reddish sun is directly overhead, and already the day is the hottest we've had in weeks. I step between the golden poles and onto the top plateau. The first thing I notice is the large carbon symbol engraved across the stone beneath my feet. I always notice it, because O'Malley was the first of us to see it. Even though we still don't know its full significance, it always makes me think of him.

This spot truly is the top of our world. I can see forever. The sweltering sun bakes mist from the yellow jungle ruins. The tallest trees look like grass. Uchmal's city walls and buildings are like a child's toys.

Snow-capped mountains rise up to the west. To the north, the lake that feeds the river flowing into our city. To the northeast, the crescent-shaped clearing where Aramovsky fought the Springer king, where I defeated the Belligerents. The clearing has a black smudge in the center—the remnants of Kalle's cornfield.

All of it, from north to west to south to east and back again . . . this is my home.

The lake . . .

Sometimes when I see that blue surface, I have the tiniest bit of Matilda memory. A red canoe. My grampa, smiling, laughing. It should be a happy memory, but it isn't. It bothers me.

I push the splinter of memory away and walk to the plateau's edge. Far below, I see the plaza, a thumbnail-sized tan square. On it, *Ximbal* is a tiny gleam of silver. No damage to the shuttle or the plaza. If I believed in the gods, I'd thank them for that miracle. Although, if gods *were* real, then I'd have to ask them why they let the attack happen in the first place. The best "miracle" would be no attack at all, wouldn't it?

The area all around the Observatory is untouched. Beyond that, though, I see the attack's carnage.

Beautiful Uchmal, the stone city built for the Birthday Children, is pockmarked and ravaged. The residential area is ripped apart like fresh-turned farmland. Bits of buildings stick up like cracked brown bones. Rings of black surround each crater, where flames were hot enough to dry out the wet vines and set them ablaze. The slightest breeze stirs blackened ash into tiny, spinning whirlwinds.

Down there, nine of us died.

Down there, a flying stone ripped away Halim's throat.

Down there, somewhere, is my spear.

*I want it.*

Maybe the wood shaft burned up. Maybe the blade melted. I don't care. I will find it. Even if it is a melted lump of metal, I will have Borjigin hammer it into a new weapon—a weapon I swear I will use on the aliens who did this to us.

Matilda destroyed the Springer city. She killed thousands. Maybe millions. I know that if there really are gods, if there is justice, her descendants might have to pay for her crimes. I know this, yet I don't care; the Birthday Children did *nothing* to deserve such punishment. We are not responsible for the actions of those who came before us. If we must suffer for our own sins, so be it, but we will not give up our blood for crimes committed by others.

Something about the bomb craters bothers me.

*Why didn't they attack the Observatory?*

If the aliens destroyed the places where we walked the most, congregated the most, why wouldn't they hit the place where most of us live? It makes no sense.

I look up at the stone slab. A rope ladder dangles from it. I climb. When I reach the top, I see three boys lying on their backs, eyes closed. Nevins and Peura are gears, scientists like Spingate and Zubiri. Harman is a circle. Like me. I've spent a little time with him. For lack of a better way to say it, he just isn't very smart. He's here to help the other two, to be their assistant.

Nevins couldn't be more skinny, while Peura has steadily gained weight since he awoke. Both boys have straight black hair and chocolate-brown skin. If it wasn't for the difference in their bodies, they could be mistaken for brothers. Harman is already taller than I am, thick with muscle. When he's full grown, he'll be a red-haired giant, bigger than Farrar, maybe even bigger than Bishop. The poor boy burns so easily, though— he's going to be feeling the effects of this little nap all over his small nose and freckled face.

The thick pillar lies on its side. When I first saw it, I thought it was stone. I was wrong. It's some man-made material—tough and strong, but hollow.

The contents of the pillar are spread about the slab: bits and pieces of disassembled machinery. Those bits once made an antenna capable of communicating with the stars. Some of the parts are shiny, almost new, but many are melted blobs. Tangles of colored wires are spread out like spilled wax. This collection of pieces is a puzzle, yes, but not the kind of puzzle I could ever solve.

"Having a good nap, boys?"

They lurch to their feet so fast I'm surprised they don't pee themselves. They look terrified, as if I am a hurukan and not a girl that is barely taller than any of them.

"Em," Harman says. "I . . . we . . . there was thinking and we . . . and you . . ."

He's stammering nonsense. Not the smartest of the three, but at least he had the courage to actually speak.

"I need this antenna fixed," I say. "*Now*, not later, not after you've had a nice rest."

They look at each other, frightened anew.

"But Grandmaster Spingate told you," Nevins said. "She said she did. We can't fix it. We *can't*."

I point to the spot where they were just lying.

"So you think you can just go to sleep instead? People are dying, you lazy fools!"

They shrivel in place, shoulders hunched, eyes cast down. Maybe they'd *rather* have a hurukan sneak up on them than face me when I'm angry.

"We were trying to think," Peura says. He has a communication jewel in his left ear. His voice is thin and light, little different from the wind that usually whips across this tiny plateau. "Zubiri told us to do that from time to time. To stop and just *think*. We've done everything we know how to do, Em. Some of the parts are broken for good. It's just . . . well . . . some things can't be fixed."

I think of Halim. He was broken, too. His parts could not be fixed.

Yelling at these boys isn't going to magically make them smarter.

"So you were thinking," I say, lowering my voice, making it softer. "Did you think of anything?"

The three of them shake their heads as if they are one body.

"We need help," Peura says. "Can Zubiri help us for a while?"

If the telescope really is a weapon, I can't spare Zubiri from that project, not even for an instant.

"I guess you better lie back down for a while and think some more," I say. "I don't care what Spingate told you. Zubiri is busy. *You three* need to fix this antenna. Everyone's lives depend on it."

I don't know if that last part is true or not. Reaching the *Xolotl* and letting Bello talk to her friends might make a difference; it might not. If it could possibly help our survival, though, these boys must find a way.

There is always a solution. *Always*.

"Get back to work," I say.

I turn toward the rope ladder, then pause. The cityscape seems to shift. The buildings are already tiny bumps to my eyes, yet they change, they blend together into a shapeless brown mass.

*The craters . . .*

How could I have not seen it right away?

The shape isn't perfect, but now that I've seen it I can't *un*see it: a wide circle with the plaza at dead center.

The meteor attack didn't avoid a specific building . . . it avoided an *area*.

Peura rushes to me, tugs on my sleeve. He's holding his left pointer finger against his communication jewel in his ear, as if he has to focus hard to understand what he's hearing.

"Spingate wants you in the Control Room," he says. "Zubiri fixed the telescope!"

# SEVENTEEN

The elevator stops. I step out into a Control Room alive with activity. A glowing image of the Observatory hovers above the Well. It's an image I've seen a hundred times, but there is something new: halfway up each side, on the ninety-degree corners, are glowing orange dots.

Spingate, Zubiri and Gaston are standing on the platform. Spin adjusts her sling; little Kevin is fussing, crying softly. Spin whispers something comforting, but the baby doesn't stop.

I quickly walk past the students at their pedestals. No lessons today—each display shows some part of the Observatory. I catch glimpses of a weapon I have not seen before, boxy and tan with a long black barrel sticking out of it. No, *six* barrels, all bunched together.

I step onto the platform. Spingate looks up from her work. She's afraid; something has disturbed her right down to her core.

"Zubiri did it," she says. "Or Ometeotl did, because of the attack—Zubiri isn't sure yet. The telescope is working—we have visuals on the alien ships. *All* of them."

Her words hang in the air. I glance at Zubiri. She nods slightly. I've waited months for this—we all have.

I point to the floating Observatory.

"Then why are you showing that instead of our enemies?"

"The attack activated systems we didn't know existed," Gaston says. "Those orange dots are antimissile batteries. Opkick and the halves are examining them now, seeing if any of them still work. If the aliens bombard us again, we might be able to hit their meteors before they impact, break them up so they don't cause as much damage."

I feel a rush of mixed emotions—hope and excitement that we might be able to defend ourselves against the next strike, anger that these systems sat idle while nine of my people died.

"Why didn't they activate during the attack?"

"*I did not know they existed, Empress.*" Ometeotl's voice echoes through the room. "*The orbital bombardment overrode some of the programming blocks that were put into my system long ago.*"

I'd give anything to find out who screwed up the computer's memory. I don't believe in torture, but for that person? I might make an exception.

"All right," I say. "Show me our enemy."

"You need to see the *Xolotl* first," Gaston says to me. "Theresa, put it up on the main display."

He isn't asking Spingate, he's *commanding* her. In *Ximbal*'s cockpit, where his authority is unquestioned, this is what he sounds like. I've never heard him use that tone with her anywhere else. She obeys instantly.

"On main display," she says.

The air above the Well sparkles to life. Multicolored flecks gather and glow, swell to blobs, then shrink, rush together and take shape.

A cylinder.

Copper in color, pitted, scratched and gouged all along its length.

I think of the drawing Spingate made in the dust, so long ago, when she said we had walked in a circle.

The part of the cylinder facing Omeyocan ends in a flat, squashed cartoon face surrounded by a ring of small images I can't quite make out. It reminds me of the Mictlan symbol stitched into our black coveralls and our red ties. Just past the cartoon face, a tiny tube sticks out of the cylinder, ending in a small sphere. The sphere is barely a speck compared to the *Xolotl*'s massive size, yet I know what it must be: the Crystal Ball, the place where we first learned we were on a spaceship and not in an endless dungeon.

At the cylinder's far end, a slightly smaller cylinder juts out, points away from the planet. This section is a mishmash of pipes and machinery, gray and silver and teal tapering to a narrow black cone.

Gaston steps off the platform and walks to the Well. He hops onto the red wall, walks around its flat, narrow top with the grace of a circle-star.

"This is where we were when we woke up," he says, pointing to a section of the *Xolotl* near the Crystal Ball. The area he indicates is small, barely more than the tip of the huge ship. He then points to the middle of the copper-colored tube.

"We have no idea what's in here," he says. "That's the part the Grownups sealed off. The part past the end of the Garden, perhaps."

He reaches out, grabbing the image of the *Xolotl*, rotating it. He spreads his hands, making a section bigger. I see a long, deepening groove that ends in a flat gray door that would open like a set of huge jaws.

"Landing bay," he says. "Inside that door is where our shuttle was. And this"—he runs his fingers across the gray, silver and teal section, lets them linger on the tapering black cone—"is the *Xolotl*'s main engine. This is what brought us here."

His voice is full of awe. Aramovsky has his gods, Gaston has this.

"They trained me to command that ship," he says. "Now that I've actually seen it, Em, so much of my training is flooding back. Just like with *Ximbal*. I had to show you that to show you this—put the *Basilisk* on the display."

The *Xolotl* blinks out.

The air above the Well sparkles. An image coalesces . . . it's the same image I was just looking at.

"You put the *Xolotl* up again," I say.

Gaston shakes his head. "Look at the colors."

What is he talking about? It's the *Xolotl*. The long, copper-colored cylinder, the section with machinery and pipes, the tapering engine cone, the . . .

The section with the machinery, the pipes . . . the colors are different. Gleaming, dark reds. Cobalt blues. And the front of the ship, the flat, circular end that points toward Omeyocan, it doesn't have the squashed cartoon face . . . the front of this ship is gray. On that gray disc, in thick, black lines, are the two rings and seven dots of the carbon symbol.

I glance at the Well wall, knowing a matching symbol is etched into it—black on red instead of black on gray.

"The two ships are almost the same," I say.

Zubiri steps off the platform, slowly walks to the Well. She stares up at the image, her wide-eyed face bathed in reflected light.

"Our ship and the *Basilisk* came from completely different

areas of space," she says. "Millions of light-years apart, yet they look like almost identical designs. How can that be?"

Spingate and Gaston say nothing. They don't know, either.

"Maybe it's a coincidence," I say.

Zubiri shakes her head. "Impossible. Theresa, please show her."

"Putting *Gamma-One* on the display," Spingate says.

*Gamma-One*. The *Goblin*.

The *Basilisk* fuzzes out.

This image that replaces it is smaller, perhaps because the *Goblin* is farther away from us. It is not quite as detailed as the first two, but there is no mistaking what I see: a thick, copper-colored cylinder, a smaller section sticking out the back, tapering to a black engine cone. The *Goblin*'s circular front is deep green, semi-translucent like glass. Etched on it in yellow lines is a curling symbol with thornlike points. I don't know what that symbol is.

"Now show me the *Dragon*," Gaston says. Standing atop the red wall, fists on his hips, silhouetted in the display's light, he looks so commanding. He reminds me of Bishop. He reminds me of *me*.

The image blurs, fuzzes, crystallizes, becomes clear. The smallest of the four ships I've seen so far is the least detailed, yet there is zero doubt—the *Dragon* looks like the *Goblin*, which looks like the *Basilisk*, which looks like our *Xolotl*.

The *Dragon*'s flat circular front is pure white. No symbol. The part tapering away from the copper-colored cylinder's far end is also white. The black engine cone looks identical.

"They're *all* the same," I mutter. "Different colors, but basically the same ship."

"*Grandmaster Spingate*," the room says. "*New contact detected. Labeling it Epsilon-One.*"

My heart sinks, weighed down by a sense of defeat, a feeling that no matter what we do we will eventually lose.

Zubiri turns her back to the red wall. She sags slowly, sits on her heels. She starts to cry.

"It will never end," she says. "Never."

"Silence on the bridge," Gaston snaps.

The sharpness of his voice startles me. Zubiri as well—she stops crying, looks up at him in confused surprise.

I don't know what a "bridge" is, but Gaston seems to think he's in one.

"Show me the new contact," he says. "Global model, and in scale."

*"Processing, Captain Xander."*

The image of white-fronted *Dragon* dissipates in an angry shower of sparkles. Those sparkles rush together to form the familiar blue, green and brown orb that is Omeyocan. Big at first, wider than the width of the Well, but the planet shrinks as if we're flying away from it. I see the *Xolotl,* now highlighted in glowing red, then the *Basilisk,* highlighted in glowing blue. As the planet shrinks, those ships quickly become nothing more than colored dots.

Omeyocan reduces to the size of Gaston's chest. The two moons blur into view, then shrink in time with the planet.

A green dot appears: the *Goblin.* When our planet is the size of Gaston's head, I see a white dot—the *Dragon.*

When Omeyocan is as tiny as Gaston's eyeball, I see a fifth colored light. This one is purple.

*"The purple dot represents Epsilon-One, Captain,"* the room says.

Gaston stares. "We'll call it the *Eel.* Show me the *Eel*'s projected time to arrival in orbit."

A long, curved purple line appears, connecting the new dot to Omeyocan.

*"At current rate of speed and factoring in deceleration, the* Eel *will reach orbit in fifteen months, ten days, Captain Xander."*

Gaston's shoulders sag. His veneer of leadership fades away.

One of Matilda's school lessons flares to life in my thoughts. They taught her about *solar systems.* Planets and their moons, all orbiting around a central star. That's what this display reminds me of, except the "star" is Omeyocan, and the "planets" are alien ships.

Alien ships coming to destroy us.

Zubiri's cheeks gleam with tears, reflect the colored lights of this horrible reality.

"We're in hell," she says. "Ship after ship after ship . . . they will keep coming. We'll never beat them all."

A high-pitched wail comes from the walls and ceiling.

*"Alert, Captain Xander—incoming projectile fire from the* Basilisk."

Gaston hops off the Well and runs to join Spingate on the platform.

"Show me," he says as he slides to a stop at the pedestal next to hers. Spingate's hands are already moving, grabbing floating images of light, moving them, twisting them.

*"Attack-level magnification,"* Ometeotl says.

The glowing display of Omeyocan swells like we are plummeting toward the planet. We don't see the entire orb anymore, just a curve of it. At the center, so small I barely recognize the huge city wall, I make out Uchmal and the surrounding jungle. High up above, the tiny blue dot of the *Basilisk.* Thread-thin blue lines reach out from it, streaking down toward our city.

"How many projectiles in the first salvo?" Gaston asks, his hands moving just as furiously as Spingate's.

"*Seventeen,*" Ometeotl answers. "*Time to first impact, thirteen minutes and seven seconds.*"

"Are the missile-defense batteries active?"

"*Chancellor Borjigin confirms three of the four batteries are functioning, Captain. I have full control of physical systems. Targeting and tracking system active.*"

"Fire at will," Gaston says. "Shoot the godsdamned things down."

"*As you command, Captain. I will initiate automated defense fire as soon as the projectiles enter the stratosphere.*"

Spingate's hands are a blur of light and color. I have no idea what she's doing. I feel stupid and useless.

"Batteries one, two and four active," she says. "A total of thirty-one combined antimissile bursts available. That's not enough . . . should we only target the projectiles aimed at the Observatory?"

Gaston snarls, thinks for a moment. I can almost see the anger simmering inside of him.

"If we only protect the Observatory, they might figure out we're low on ammo," he says, talking out loud as he works through the problem.

There are no easy answers here—for once, I'm glad the decision is not mine to make.

"The *Basilisk* is close enough to safely launch landing craft," Gaston says. "But it hasn't yet. We have to assume that's coming, make sure we can shoot down at least some of those ships. Ometeotl, target the first twenty projectiles, regardless of where they are aimed. Save the last eleven antimissile bursts for incoming aircraft only. If the Observatory or *Ximbal* are directly targeted, use those reserve rounds."

*"Affirmative, Captain."*

He's making an impossible choice, protecting our people and our only working spaceship, possibly at the expense of being able to shoot down the alien ground troops. I could jump in, I could tell him what to do, but in all honesty, he knows more about air combat than I ever will. I trust him.

Gaston glances at Spingate. "Battery three, the one that doesn't work, are there any rounds in there?"

Spingate moves icons. "Another twelve rounds."

"That gives us a little more breathing room," Gaston says. "Ometeotl, tell Borjigin to have people evenly distribute the ammunition from battery three to the other batteries."

Zubiri starts crying again. Maybe she's a genius scientist, but right now she looks like a terrified little thirteen-year-old girl.

Twelve minutes until the streaks of fire split our sky and shatter our city.

Twelve minutes . . .

"Zubiri," I say, "the telescope is working—does that mean the Goff Spear works? Can we shoot it?"

She looks up at me, eyes wet and wide.

"I haven't verified that yet. The Goff rounds are nuclear weapons—without testing, we can't take a chance that they might malfunction and detonate inside the Observatory."

*"A second enemy salvo has launched,"* Ometeotl calls out. *"Seventeen additional projectiles, time of impact estimated at twenty-one minutes, fourteen seconds. Total incoming projectiles—thirty-four."*

Gaston points at Zubiri. While she looks like a little girl, he suddenly looks like a grown man.

"Load the Goff Spear," he growls. *"Immediately."*

She shakes her head, screams back at him in a broken voice.

old you, I haven't had time to test it! For all I know, it
low up instead of launching. It could kill us all!"

ton looks at me, nods once, returns to his mad work
the pedestal. I'm the leader of our people, but with that
glance I realize that in here, *he* is in charge, and he has just
n me orders.

I walk to Zubiri and haul her to her feet.

"Let's go," I say. "We're loading that weapon."

# EIGHTEEN

'm breathing so hard from sprinting here. I feel the Observatory shudder. Our antimissile batteries, shooting at yet another incoming meteor. I marvel at weapons so powerful that just firing them can shake this man-made mountain of stone.

Zubiri isn't breathing as hard as I am—for a scientist, she's in better shape than I would have thought.

"Lock it down," she says to Okereke. "Johnson, use those clamps on top, make sure they're secure."

We're in the room with the Goff Spear rounds. The golden hexagonal chunk known as Goff 2 lies in the strange cart. It fits perfectly, like an egg in an egg carton. Okereke and Johnson fasten a hinged bracket down on top. They close clamps, tighten screws. The cart's solidity, the padding, the tight fit, the springs that support the wheels—the Grownups didn't want the hexagonal object jostled in any way.

I think of what Zubiri said ten minutes ago in the Control Room: *For all I know, it could blow up instead of launching. It could kill us all.*

We can cower in our stone mountain and hope we aren't hit, just like the Springers hid in their underground cities. Or we can take our chances and fight.

*Attack, attack, when in doubt, always attack.*

Sometimes the voice of my father is wrong. This is not one of those times.

"Move faster," I say. *"Move!"*

Okereke, Johnson, Ingolfsson and a younger circle boy named Daniel Roth roll the cart down the hallway. Okereke is singing a song; the circles' steps land in time to the beat.

The cart has a long handle with four handholds. There is no motor on it, nothing like the engines that drive the spiders or the trucks. I wonder if the Grownups wanted to make sure people had to really *think* about using this weapon. Is that why the rounds are so far from the telescope? Is this weapon so horrible that they wanted to make sure people had more time to consider if it should be used at all?

Up ahead, Opkick is standing in front of an open elevator I haven't seen before. This one is wider than the one that leads down to the Control Room—just wide enough for the cart that carries the Goff round.

"That elevator leads to the loading chamber," Zubiri says. "Only a few minutes now."

She's jogging behind the cart, next to me.

The floor beneath us shudders again—another round fired in our defense, or an enemy meteor punching home?

Opkick waves madly for us to hurry. She has her messageboard pinned under her armpit, and a hand cupped under her pregnant belly.

"Come on," she calls out. "You're slowing down!"

Her words give the circles new energy. Okereke increases the song's rhythm. The circles increase their pace to match.

We're almost to the elevator when the building shakes again, but far harder this time. Dust trails down from the ceiling. I see a tiny bit of the wall's surface chip free and fall to the floor. The cart's wheels run over it, crushing it to powder.

The elevator opens to a place I haven't seen before.

For some reason, I expected a big, sprawling room, like the landing bay up on the *Xolotl*. This room is cramped. No wasted space. Just wide enough to roll the cart in.

Heavy, curved, gleaming metal brackets—not gold, but a similar color, perhaps it's brass—support the bottom of a large cylinder made of the same material. The cylinder angles up steeply, through a channel cut into the Observatory's stone. It really does look like the barrel of a massive rifle.

The floor here is steel. The walls, too, at least where we can see them; equipment I don't recognize covers everything. Flashing lights, knobs and switches, levers as long as my arm. Two pedestals are active, images already swirling above them.

Zubiri pushes past me.

"Stay out of the way," she says. "Okereke, open it. The rest of you, unfasten the brackets and get ready to load the round, but don't do *anything else* until I tell you to."

Okereke steps to a round hatch mounted on the side of the massive gun barrel. At the center of the hatch, a panel with our familiar symbols. He taps out a pattern; I hear the loud clank of bolts sliding free. He grabs a handle and leans back hard. It takes all his strength to pull the hatch open. Most doors in this building open effortlessly. Some even open on their own. Okereke's struggle is yet another reminder from the Grownups: *Are you sure you want to fire this weapon?*

Zubiri climbs through the open hatch. She moves well despite her missing arm, but her motions are still awkward. She looks around, craning her head this way and that. Unseen lights play off her dark-brown skin. She flips white switches, turns black dials.

"It's ready," she says. She crawls out, steps to me and takes my hand. Her fingers are warm. They squeeze in time with her words.

"Em, *please*. We shouldn't do this. My progenitor wasn't trained to operate this weapon. If I get something wrong, the bomb could blow up right here or it could jam in the barrel. It's been at least *two centuries* since this equipment was checked. The aliens haven't attacked the Observatory—we're safe here for now."

Zubiri isn't a warrior. I am. I don't know why the *Basilisk* hasn't hit the Observatory yet, but when it does we will be done for. I don't care if using this weapon is risky—we need to stop these attackers while we still can, before they launch shuttles of their own and invade.

"Load it," I say. "Right now."

She doesn't want to. She does anyway, telling Okereke and the others exactly what to do.

I leave the cramped space and sprint for the Control Room.

By the time I rejoin Spingate and Gaston, I'm exhausted, soaked in sweat.

I rush to join Spingate on the platform. "What's our status?"

"Five defensive rounds left," she says. "Not counting the eleven Gaston is keeping in reserve."

For once, she isn't wearing her sling. Joandra Rigby wears it instead. She's a circle who sometimes works as Kevin's babysitter, when both Spingate and Gaston really need to focus on their work. Joandra is down on the floor, holding little Kevin in her arms. His crying screech is impossible to ignore.

Gaston stands by the Well's red wall. His outstretched arms are bathed in light, dozens of glowing symbols floating on or near his hands. He's looking up at a mix of images: a top-down map of Uchmal with flashing red circles; live scenes of broken and burning ziggurats; meteors streaking down followed by their long orange tails of fire; the *Basilisk,* tinged in blue, and far away from it, the *Xolotl,* tinged in red.

He looks down at me. "What's the status on the Goff Spear?"

"They were loading it when I left," I say. "It should be ready by now."

"We're in bad shape," he says. "We've stopped a lot of incoming rounds, but several got through. Impacts all over the city."

*"Grandmaster Zubiri reports that the Goff cannon is ready to fire."* Ometeotl's words give me hope. *"The* Xolotl *and the* Basilisk *are both in range."*

On the display of Omeyocan, the blue and red dots flash rapidly.

"Target the *Basilisk,*" Gaston says.

His voice reminds me of Bishop's when we're in combat. The two boys are so different, yet when lives are on the line both of them are calm and reliable.

On the hovering display, the *Basilisk*'s blue light pulses faster.

*"Target solution confirmed, Captain."*

"Then hit that bastard," Gaston says. "Fire!"

Nothing happens. I feel the room vibrate.

"Four defensive rounds left," Spingate calls out. "After that we'll need to use our eleven-round reserve."

"Ometeotl, I said *fire*," Gaston says. He's not so calm anymore. "Shoot the damn weapon!"

*"Of the people present in this room, only Empress Savage may authorize firing of the Goff Spear."*

Gaston stares down at me, his eyes wide with rage and his upper lip curled into a wicked snarl. He looks like a madman.

"Tell it to shoot, Em! *Kill them!*"

I start to do just that, an automatic reaction to the chaos unfolding around us, but I pause. Yet again, Zubiri's words rip through my thoughts. If the Goff Spear malfunctions, will I cause all of our deaths?

The room shudders. Cracks appear in the walls. Trails of dust puff down from the ceiling.

"That was close," Spingate says, looking at her pedestal display. "Only a few blocks from the Observatory."

We didn't attack the *Basilisk*. It attacked us. The aliens inside that ship started this fight.

If it's war they want, they messed with the wrong girl.

I have a spear, and I will use it.

"Ometeotl," I say, "fire the weapon."

*"By your command, Empress Savage."*

The floor, walls and ceiling thrum. They pulse like the heart of a planet-sized stone giant. A buzzing sound drowns out everything except for baby Kevin's piercing wail. My hair stands on end. I feel the vibration in my bones, in my teeth.

There is a whooshing sensation, as if the room's air is sucked out for a split second, then rushes back in. My eardrums flutter in complaint.

The thrumming stops.

The display above the shaft changes. Gaston's multiple scenes vanish, replaced by the lone image of the *Basilisk*.

From Uchmal, a long red streak flashes toward it. At the head of that streak, a metal ball that sizzles and bubbles and shimmers with godlike energy.

It seems to take forever for the red streak to close the distance.

The *Basilisk* fires weapons at the ball, to no apparent effect. The massive ship starts to move, but it is far too slow, far too late.

The red streak punches into the *Basilisk*'s copper hull.

I have a moment to think *That didn't work,* then the enemy ship's hull starts to swell. Another childhood memory of Matilda's: pork sausages on my father's grill, heating and swelling until the skin splits and bubbling meat pushes through. The *Basilisk*'s copper hull *tears*—flashing red energy pulses out, somehow solid and gas and liquid all at once, curling like the dissolving tentacles of some demon monster.

The copper hull snaps in the middle: the ship breaks in two. The halves slowly spin for a moment, then they, too, break up, shattering into a hundred pieces.

Only moments ago, there was a ship with who knows how many living souls aboard. Now, there is a cloud of wreckage.

"Gods," Spingate says. Her voice is a whisper, but I hear it clearly.

Kevin stops crying.

"Ometeotl," Gaston says, "status report."

The room's dispassionate voice confirms my fears.

*"The* Basilisk *is destroyed. No escape ships detected. Entire crew presumed to be dead. Enemy salvos one and two have either impacted or were destroyed in flight. No incoming projectiles remain."*

Gaston shakes a fist at the shattered ship.

"I hope it *hurt*." His voice is hoarse with bloodlust. "I hope your last moments were full of panic and terror, you gods-damned bastards!"

I think of the room that holds the Goff Spear rounds. One was missing. I wonder if what we saw just now happened before, in the two centuries before we arrived, to some other alien ship that we will never know about.

I stare at the display, at the spreading wreckage. How many intelligent beings just died at my command? Yes, they bombed us, but how many of them had no choice in that matter? How many of them had nothing to do with this war, nothing to do with the decision to attack?

How many civilians did I just kill?

An arm around my shoulder. It's Spingate.

"You had to," she says. "We didn't have any choice."

She always seems to know what I'm thinking. I resist for a moment, then let her pull me in.

As she hugs me, rubs at my back, I see Joandra holding little Kevin, jostling him lightly to comfort him.

Babies.

When the *Basilisk* blew up, were there families?

Were there babies?

If there were, now they are dead.

I have killed them all.

*I am the wind . . . I am death.*

# NINETEEN

There is one final meteor shower. Everyone comes out to watch.

We find ourselves in a world of flame: Uchmal burns around us, while high above the wreckage of the *Basilisk* rains down, a thousand streams of blazing light that scar the nighttime sky.

Humans and Springers ascend the Observatory steps. Hundreds of us, climbing together, as if taking step after step is some kind of quiet ritual celebrating our mutual survival.

Some stop after only a few layers. Some make it only halfway. Some of us, like me, march steadily upward. I have never felt this tired. My soul feels dead.

Ten layers climbed.

Then twenty.

At twenty-five, the vines are stunted things. Past twenty-six, we're too high for the vines to grow at all. I don't stop until I've climbed all thirty layers—*three thousand* steps—watching my city burn as I go.

The day's high heat was the worst thing that could have hap-

pened to us. Steady sunlight dried out the vines that have clung
to Uchmal's buildings for centuries. The results are tragic. All
around and below us, the black night is turned to day by spreading flame. Fire follows the vines that cover almost everything,
jumping from yellow leaf to yellow leaf, from blue stem to blue
stem, from tree to tree, sheathing every ziggurat and building in
a shimmering cascade of blazing orange.

The Observatory is isolated from the fire, it seems, thanks to
the project that cleared plants and dead leaves from the plaza
and the surrounding streets. I think of how I argued with Borjigin, told him that was a waste of energy. I'm grateful he kept
bothering me until I gave in.

Those who made the climb with me stand at the pinnacle of a
mountain island rising high from a sea of fire. It's not just
Uchmal—beyond our circular walls, parts of the jungle burn as
well. Not as intensely, though. Perhaps the ground there holds
water longer than our stone streets, slowing the blaze. I hope the
Springers out in the jungle are safe. We have no word from
Schechak. Barkah and Lahfah were with us in Uchmal when this
attack began. They have no idea what's happening in their city,
and they won't know until the fires burn out. Right now, the
Observatory is the only safe place.

High above, the *Basilisk*'s remains continue to rain down.
The flaming pieces break apart as they fall, creating showers of
smaller glowing trails. Spingate told me most pieces will burn up
completely before hitting the ground. I watch them with an insane mixture of emotions: primitive satisfaction that I have
killed those who tried to kill us; anguish that I have taken lives,
maybe *thousands* of them; fear that the fires below will not stop,
that they will spread across the planet, turning everything to
ash; a haunting sense of failure I couldn't find a way to end this
without violence.

There are about thirty people and maybe ten Springers on the Observatory's top layer. Bishop is up here, as are Borjigin and Bawden, Lahfah and Barkah.

I was wary of Barkah's ambition, but not any more. He had the perfect opportunity to destroy us—he chose to help us instead. My tribe and his are bound together now, temporarily united by the presence of a third that wants all of us dead. For now, at least, the fates of our two peoples seem intertwined.

The Springer king hops closer to me.

*"Hem, tragedy,"* he says. *"Why?"*

*Why.* The question I need answered more than any other. Why did the *Basilisk* come here? Why did the other ships? Why did the Springers?

Why did the Grownups?

"I don't know. I wish I did."

I look into his two good eyes. Those green orbs are filled with rage and sorrow. He's silhouetted by the burning horizon.

*"Underdirt,"* he says. *"If we go underdirt, you with us."*

The words are slightly off, but my heart breaks with their meaning. If he and his people have to return to their subterranean villages and towns, Barkah is inviting us to go with them. He's offering my people shelter.

"Thank you," I say. I point at the long flames streaking the sky. "The attackers are dead. *Nahnaw.* We destroyed that ship."

He points straight up, to the stars.

*"Two more come,"* he says. *"Tomorrow, will prepare underdirt."*

Three more, actually, although *Epsilon-One*—the *Eel*—is more than a year away. *Goblin* and *Dragon* will be here in days. Every ship that has come to Omeyocan has brought a cargo of war. There is no reason to think the next two will do anything different.

I see a boy on the far side of the top layer, facing north. Huan Chowdhury. He made the climb.

*Why?* Barkah asked. Why have so many races come to this planet? That is the most important question right now. That is the missing piece of the puzzle.

Huan has spent a year digging, studying. He might be the only person who can venture a guess.

I sit down next to him. Our legs dangle over the edge, heels bouncing against the top layer's stone sides. The fire has spread to the northern part of Uchmal. Buildings seem to shiver beneath a living sheen of flame.

"It's horrible," I say.

Huan jumps a little. He didn't notice me sit down.

"It is," he says. "Just horrible."

Huan and I are both Birthday Children, which means we're basically the same age even though I'm physically six or seven years older than he is. He always seems to be smiling, but he's not smiling now—fear makes him look like a different person.

"There are three more ships coming," I say. I'm sure he already knows. News spreads fast here. "Plus us, and the Springers."

"And the Vellen," he says.

*Vellen* is the Springer name for the race that came before them. Strange, one-eyed creatures with backward-folded legs, a middle set of arms and a second set of smaller arms that grew from the sides of their heads.

"And the Vellen," I agree. "That's seven races. I need to know why you think they came to Omeyocan."

He shakes his head. "I don't know, Em. I'm just a circle."

I nod. "So am I."

He glances at me, checking to see if I'm having fun at his expense. I'm not.

"But you're our leader," he says.

I point to my forehead symbol. He knows it's there, looks anyway. Maybe he forgets that I'm an *empty*, just like him. Sometimes I do, too.

He starts to talk, stops. I see in him what I see in so many circles: self-doubt.

"Go ahead, Huan. A bad guess is better than no guess at all."

He gazes out at the sea of fire.

"I don't think the races came here on their own," he says. "I think they were drawn here. Maybe . . . *lured* here. There's something about this place that calls to the races. I feel it. Do you?"

I do. I felt it when I was in the Crystal Ball and saw Omeyocan for the first time.

"This feeling, or call or whatever it is," Huan says, "I think it creates a desire to not only possess Omeyocan, but also make sure no other race can have it. That's why the Springers wiped out the Vellen. That's why the Grownups tried to wipe out the Springers."

He points up, to the rain of fire slashing our skies.

"That's why the *Basilisk* attacked us. That's why the *Goblin* will attack us next."

Huan's words don't solve the puzzle, but they rearrange some of the pieces. That buzz in the back of my brain again. I feel like I almost have it. *Almost.*

"The Grownups traveled for over a thousand years to get here," I say. "Who knows how long the other races traveled. If everyone came because they were called . . . who did the calling?"

Huan shrugs. "Nothing I've found tells me why the Vellen came. Or the Springers." He shivers, rubs at his shoulders the way Bello used to do when she was afraid. "I don't know why I came up here. This building feels spooky."

*Spooky.* He said the same thing about the Well shaft in the Control Room, where he started his archaeological project.

So many races coming to this place . . .

Races that slaughter each other . . .

The *Basilisk* bombed us, but it didn't target the Observatory . . .

The puzzle pieces stop spinning. They click home. They *fit.*

At least seven races aiming for the same place, but that *place* isn't actually Omeyocan. It isn't Uchmal. It isn't the Observatory.

It's the very ground the Observatory is built upon.

"Go back to the Well shaft in the Control Room," I say. "Start digging there again, immediately."

His head snaps toward me.

"No," he says. "That place scares me."

I gesture to the burning city. "Scares you worse than this?" I gesture to the stars. "Worse than the other ships coming to destroy us?"

He starts to nod, then half shakes his head. He doesn't know how to react.

"It's not a request," I say. "It's an order."

I see the terror in his eyes.

"*Please,* Em. I don't want to. There's something wrong down there."

"So find out what that *wrong* is. Our lives might depend on it."

He holds my stare for a few moments, then gives up and looks away. He'll do what he's told. I won't give him any other choice.

"Huan, go be someplace else," says a voice behind us.

It's Spingate. She's standing over us. Huan takes advantage of the chance to escape, scurries away.

"You start at dawn," I call after him. "Be there or I'll come find you."

Spingate sits in Huan's place. She does so carefully, cradling her swollen belly with one hand.

"We need answers," she says.

I nod. As if I needed a gear to tell me that.

Spingate seems distant, cold. There's no hint of the warmth that was once as much a part of her as her red hair.

"We know who has those answers," she says. "Bello is one of *them*. She knows why the *Xolotl* came here."

I can't stop my annoyed sigh. "I've asked her so many times I'm sick of it."

"Then stop asking. *Make* her tell you."

Her eyes bore into me, insistent, almost commanding. I feel my heart tearing into a thousand pieces. It's bad enough when Bishop asks for this. Not Spin, too . . . *not her.*

"You think we should torture Bello," I say quietly.

She shrugs. "If that's how you want to phrase it."

My temper flares, but I control it.

"I *phrase* it like that because that's what it's *called*. We won't stoop to torture, Spin. We're better than that. We're civilized."

Expressionless, she turns her attention to the burning city.

"You don't understand," she says. "I'm a mother. You're not. We were lucky tonight. The *Goblin* will arrive soon, and when it does, that luck might run out. They could hit us harder than the *Basilisk* did. My son could die. My unborn child could die. *Everyone* could die. Why? Because of your precious honor?"

I rarely cry, but the way her words carve at my soul I'm surprised I don't cry now.

"Honor has nothing to do with it. Torturing people is *wrong*."

She slowly shakes her head.

"I hope your version of right and wrong doesn't wind up killing my family."

She stands, heads to the plateau's edge. She starts down the wide stone stairs, opting for the three-thousand-step descent instead of taking the elevator.

A flashfire of memory. A flash, and a fizzle. Matilda knew Spingate. Brewer told me that before, but this is different. I *feel* it this time. I can't place the memory . . . an image of Theresa Spingate being . . . *cruel.*

Something about that intangible memory makes me wonder—if Bello was a gear, not a circle, would Theresa still be willing to torture her? Or is it only because Bello is an *empty?*

I stand, brush off my legs and butt. The wind has increased. A swirling gray snowstorm of ash filters up from the sprawling fire.

The ash looks just like the *Xolotl's* endless dust.

# PART II

## SIGNALS AND SILENCE

# TWENTY

I circle left, Bawden circles right.

Our boots press into the fine white sand of our training circle. We point wooden practice spears at each other.

"This isn't dance class," Bishop calls out.

He wants us to attack. I've sparred with Bawden enough to know she's blindingly fast with a block and counterattack. I'm trying to figure out her footwork, wait for the right moment to strike.

All around us I hear the *clack-clack* of spears and farm tools bouncing off each other or thudding into bodies.

After we destroyed the *Basilisk,* the *Goblin* slowed its approach, stopped, then moved a little farther *away* from Omeyocan. We've shown what we can do, and the ship reacted accordingly.

Still, we've prepared hard. Our weapons are cleaned, loaded or charged. We've set up primary plans for responding to any landing craft. Barkah and Lahfah have returned to Schechak.

In short, we are as ready as we can be. If we're attacked, we don't know when we might be outside again. Bishop insisted on one last training session here on the plaza, so we might enjoy the sunshine while we still can.

I agreed, but not for his reasons. I've been so busy running here and there, answering endless questions, pushing Huan to keep exploring the shaft, and seeing to a thousand other things that can't happen at all without *my* input . . . I'm frustrated. I want the release that hard training brings; I want to forget, just for a few moments, the endless pressure we're all under.

In other words, I want to *hit* something.

Bawden finally thrusts. I parry, blocking her attack. She grins.

"Come at me, little empty," she says. "Prove you're a real warrior."

"Taunts won't work, sweetheart," I answer as I circle. "Your mouth says such mean things, but your eyes tell me how much you love me."

Bawden laughs—when she does I snap out a knee strike. She barely blocks it.

Hardness settles into her eyes.

Farrar, our other trainer for the day, shouts at us. "Didn't Bishop tell you you're not dancing? Finish your foe, *now*."

I think I have her timing. I thrust at her face. She ducks and spins. I've fought her before, know she'll sweep my legs as she completes that spin, so I jump before she does—her spear's wooden blade whizzes harmlessly beneath my feet. I land and lunge in the same motion before she can bring her spear up to defend, put my blade behind her feet and throw my shoulder into her chest.

Bawden falls hard on her back, air whuffing out of her lungs.

My wooden spear tip is at her throat. She freezes.

"Point, Savage," Farrar says. "Way to be predictable, Bawden."

She glares up at him. "I won two out of three!"

"Which will look nice on your gravestone."

Bawden slaps the sand in frustration. I guess it's not as fun when she loses. I offer my hand. She takes it and I pull her to her feet.

"Rotate partners," Bishop calls out.

There are six sand-filled circles at the plaza's edge. This is where we train. We practice with spears, blunt knives, rifles with dull bayonets, and whatever random things Farrar brings— sticks, broken bits of masonry . . . even rocks. Once he made us fight with belts. Belts *hurt*.

The main thing we do, though, is spar. One-on-one, two-on-one, on our feet, from our backs, one arm tied down as if we were wounded, you name it. These are the skills that will keep us alive in combat.

"Lucky," Bawden says. "I'll kick your ass next time, Savage."

"Looking forward to it."

With that, we both move to the circles on our respective rights.

I find myself facing Victor Muller.

Inside, I cringe. I've *never* beaten him.

He's shaved his head. The medical coffins healed his scalp burns, but he was left with a big missing patch of hair so he cut it all off. His locks were beautiful, yet somehow he looks even *better* with nothing but stubble.

Victor smiles at me, wide and genuine and a little awkward, and I'm suddenly reminded that Bishop thinks this boy has a crush on me.

"Bow and begin," Bishop calls to everyone.

Victor and I bow. I grip my spear, hunting for a weakness in the boy's stance. There isn't one.

He lunges and thrusts. I parry. His spear whirls so fast I don't even see his second strike—the wooden blade presses into the side of my neck.

"Point," he says. "Your hair looks nice today, Em."

My hair's in a tightly braided ponytail, just like always.

"You tell Zubiri her hair looks nice?"

He shrugs. "Haven't seen her. She's very busy."

We return to our starting spots. Victor is so *fast*. Beating him seems impossible. But there has to be a way. There is always a way.

We bow. This time I don't wait—I lunge, feinting at Victor's head before sweeping at his thighs.

He doesn't buy the feint at all, doesn't even move. He blocks my clumsy strike. I start to back away, but he thrusts at my eyes. I blink before I realize I'm doing it, feel his foot behind my heel. I'm falling, but his move tells me where his leg is. I surprise myself with my speed, jam the butt of my spear into his kneecap.

I feel the *thonk* of impact, hear him yelp in pain.

I hit the ground and roll to my feet.

As soon as I'm up, his spear shaft smacks into my chest, drives me backward. I stumble, then his fist drives into my stomach so hard it lifts me off my feet. I drop my spear, land awkwardly on my hands and knees.

Victor's wooden blade touches the side of my neck.

"Point," he says. He smiles wide, extends his hand. "Nice shot to my knee! You're getting so much better, you—"

Bishop levels him with a flying tackle.

The two boys spill into the next circle over, knocking those combatants aside.

Bishop lands on top. He drives an elbow into Victor's mouth—a tooth arcs away.

*"You don't touch her,"* Bishop screams, the roar of a mindless animal.

He rears back for another strike. Before it lands, Bawden rushes in, drives the butt of her spear into Bishop's forehead. The *thonk* echoes across the plaza.

Inside of me, rage explodes.

I stand, step and throw in a perfect motion—my spear closes the short distance in an instant. The wooden point bounces hard off Bawden's sternum. She cries out, crumples to the ground.

Victor staggers to his feet, blood pouring from his snarling mouth. Just as Bishop rises, Victor tackles him, driving them both to the sand again.

In an instant, our disciplined training session erupts into a melee. Kids grab each other, cursing, punching and kicking. Blood and spit flies.

Farrar wades into the carnage, tossing people aside like so much trash. It takes him only seconds to break up the fights.

All but one.

Bishop is straddling Victor, hands locked around the smaller boy's throat. Farrar grabs Bishop, throws him face-first onto the sand before locking a thick arm around Bishop's neck.

"Stop fighting," Farrar growls.

My brain doesn't seem to work. What just happened to me? To *all* of us?

Despite the weight of Farrar on his back, Ramses Bishop struggles to rise.

"I'll *kill* that little bastard!"

I rush to them, grab a handful of Bishop's blond hair and force him to look at me.

"Bishop, *stop*! Victor and I had a fair fight!"

He seems confused for a moment. He stops struggling. I see realization wash over his face.

Farrar looks at me, questioning, as if this might be a trick.

"Let him up," I say.

Farrar does.

Bishop stands, wipes sand from his face.

None of us know what to do.

Victor is on his hands and knees, coughing, spitting blood. Bawden rolls from side to side, hands still covering her chest.

I threw a practice spear, but I didn't think about that. If I'd held the real thing, I'd have done exactly the same—the blade would have punched through her sternum and pierced her heart.

Bawden attacked my man: I instantly wanted her dead.

I see someone hurrying toward us from the Observatory. It's Joandra Rigby, little Kevin clutched in her arms. Even from a distance, I see she's nearly in a panic.

"Everyone," I say, "get back to the Observatory, now. Get Bawden and Victor to Doctor Smith."

Joandra reaches us, chest heaving.

"Em, Gaston wants you, right now! He said the *Dragon* is attacking the *Goblin*!"

# TWENTY-ONE

Bishop and I rush into the Control Room. We ran here as fast as we could, neither of us discussing what just happened. He had no right to attack Victor like that. I was hit, yes, but getting hit is part of training. The way Bishop reacted, the way *I* reacted when Bawden tried to stop him . . . I'm disturbed to my core.

The Control Room is abuzz. Gaston is up on the main platform. The smaller pedestals are all filled—he's put people to work analyzing the information we're getting from the telescope. Bariso and Schuster are there, as is Henry Bemba, three halves delegating tasks to the collection of circles and even a few Springers.

Schuster is wearing black coveralls, like the rest of us. No dress. We're well past the time for wearing anything but clothes suitable for war.

Above the Well, I see two *Xolotl*-shaped ships. One is the yellow-tinged *Goblin*, with its yellow curved-thorn symbol on the circular front. The other is the green-tinged *Dragon*. Tiny green dots are heading away from the *Dragon* and moving toward the *Goblin.*

Bishop and I join Gaston on the platform.

He glances at us, then back at the display above his pedestal.

"Damn, Bishop," he says. "What happened to your head?"

The spot where Bawden hit him is already swelling, a big red bump with a circle in the middle the exact diameter of a spear shaft.

"Never mind that," I say. "What's going on? Where's Spin?"

"She's sick," Gaston says. "She could barely stand. Must be from the baby. She can't do anything about what's happening between these ships, so I told her to go lie down."

Spingate is *always* in the Control Room. It feels odd here without her. But considering the way she talked to me on top of the Observatory, maybe it's for the best that I don't see her now.

"The *Goblin* was moving away from Omeyocan," Gaston says. "It wasn't leaving, just making sure it was out of Goff Spear range. That brought it closer to the *Dragon. Dragon* recently changed course and headed straight for the *Goblin*—now the *Dragon* appears to be attacking it with smaller ships."

The swarm of green dots reminds me of blurds buzzing over the river's surface.

I pull my braid around over my right shoulder, stroke it nervously.

"I don't see the *Xolotl*," I say. "Where is it?"

"Matilda apparently doesn't want any part of this," Gaston says. "The *Xolotl* is beyond the horizon; we can't even see it right now."

Joandra Rigby enters the Control Room. She's not as fast as Bishop and I, especially when lugging around a baby. She sits on the platform's edge, tries to regain her breath.

On the display, I see something moving on the *Goblin*. It's the landing bay doors—which must be huge but look tiny in relation to the massive ship—opening like the jaws of a monster.

"Defensive action," Gaston says. "*Goblin* launching fighters of her own."

A swarm of yellow dots slides out of the landing bay and heads to meet the oncoming green cloud. The yellow dots seem slower than the wave they fly out to meet. Slower, and fewer.

Midway between the two great starships, the green and yellow swarms collide. Two half-solid masses become a single yellow-green cloud that sparks and flashes and flickers. It takes me a moment to realize the combined cloud is thinning—lights of both colors are blinking out.

A strand of green, maybe five dots in all, rips from the roiling cloud and heads straight at the yellow-tinged *Goblin*.

"*Dragon*'s fighters already control the combat zone," Gaston says. "They're sending a few units to strafe the *Goblin*."

I glance at Bishop. He notices my look, meets my eyes, shrugs, goes back to watching the display. He knows war, yes, but not this kind—space is Gaston's domain.

The five green dots spread out and attack the *Goblin* from five different angles, a predator's claw clutching down on its prey. Lights flicker across the *Goblin*'s surface.

"That's counterfire," Gaston says. "*Goblin* gunners trying to shoot down the incoming *Dragon* fighters."

One of the *Dragon*'s green specks disappears. Then another. Flashes of orange blossom on the *Goblin*, and this time it's not from counterfire—the *Dragon*'s fighters are landing big, explosive hits. Another green dot vanishes. I think that the *Goblin* might survive this assault, then I glance back to the roiling cloud—it is now almost completely green.

"*Dragon*'s fighters are clearly better than the *Goblin*'s," Gaston says. He sounds worried.

In seconds, the last few yellow dots blink out, leaving only green. The remaining *Dragon* fighters close on the yellow-tinged *Goblin*. Counterfire isn't even half of what it was to begin with—the *Dragon*'s fighters are taking out the *Goblin*'s guns.

"*Numerous breaches on the* Goblin*'s hull,*" Ometeotl calls out. "*The* Dragon *is launching a second wave.*"

Six new green dots leave the *Dragon* and head straight for the *Goblin*. These new dots are fatter, thicker.

"I think those are boarding craft," Gaston says. "The *Dragon*'s crew doesn't want to destroy the *Goblin*, they want to capture it. Ometeotl, give me more detail."

"*Detail is at maximum, Captain Xander.*"

He mumbles something under his breath, a curse word that would have gotten him severely beaten when we were in school.

The fat dots reach the *Goblin,* land on the long, tapering part that sticks out the back.

"The boarders will try to breach that hull," Gaston says. "If they do, it will be hand-to-hand fighting against the *Goblin*'s crew."

We watch for a long time. The *Goblin*'s counterfire flickers diminish further, then cease completely.

I imagine a desperate battle of knives and guns and energy blasts, a battle fought between two unknown species.

More killing—and we still don't know the reason for it.

"*The* Goblin *is changing course,*" Ometeotl calls out.

The besieged ship starts moving toward the *Dragon*. I don't know why I pick sides, but I hope the *Goblin* attacks. Maybe both ships will be destroyed.

When it gets closer to the *Dragon,* the *Goblin* slows, then stops.

It doesn't attack.

The two mother ships sit side by side, round front ends facing toward my planet.

"Captured," Bishop says.

Gaston nods. "Looks that way."

Was the *Goblin* going to attack us, like the *Basilisk* did? If so, is it possible that the *Dragon* took out that threat as a gesture of good faith, because those aliens want to be our allies?

I wish that were true, but it seems unlikely. We don't know what this brief battle means for us. I have a feeling we won't have to wait long to find out.

Little Kevin wakes up, lets out a happy squeal. The sound is like a trigger that releases our pent-up stress. Not all of it, but enough that I relax a little. If a baby can . . .

Wait . . . something is wrong.

Kevin. When Spingate isn't working, Kevin is *always* with her.

Spingate isn't here.

But I am. She would have known I'd be here for this.

*Bello* . . .

Without another word, I sprint for the elevator.

# TWENTY-TWO

The moment I step through the door into the cell block, I hear Aramovsky shouting for help.

I see him at the end of the hall, his face pressed between the bars, one arm waving madly.

"Em, *stop Spingate!* The God of Blood has her!"

I slide to a halt in front of Bello's cell, the soles of my boots skidding across the stone floor.

A naked Korrynn Bello hangs from the ceiling support beam by a rope tied tight around her wrists. Her toes dangle just above the stone floor.

Theresa Spingate stands in front of her. Flecks of blood dot Spingate's face. In her hand is a thin cane—the rod from the Grand Hall throne. It's smeared with thick blood, a red identical to that of the cane itself.

Bello's head hangs down, thin blond hair half-hiding a left eye that is already swollen shut. She spins slightly from left to right, the rope creaking in time. Her lower lip is split and ragged. Blood trails from the lip, from a gash on her forehead, from her horribly broken nose, down her cheeks, under her chin and down her too-white body, a path of crimson that drips from her toes into a puddle on the stone floor.

*... plop ... plop ... plop ...*

I press my hand to the palm-plate—the cell door won't open. Spingate reprogrammed it.

"Theresa, open this door!"

She looks at me, but I'm not sure it's me that she sees. Her eyes are wide, her teeth are bared. Her hand is a white-knuckled talon gripping the red rod. I remember Matilda using that device on me, the searing agony it caused every time she touched it to my body.

Spingate is my best friend, the person I know better than anyone—with her face twisted up like that, she is almost unrecognizable.

*The God of Blood has her. . . .*

"Bello must talk," she says. "She hasn't yet, but she will."

There's cold-blooded anger in Spingate's words, but also a trembling of doubt. Maybe she thought torture would be easy.

"Spin, open this godsdamned cell, *right now!*"

Her voice holds doubt; mine does not. My words are roaring muskets firing at close range.

She glances at Bello.

"Bello will break. She'll tell us what she knows. She *has* to. Why don't you understand?"

My best friend is talking, but it's not really *her*. Theresa is a puppet, controlled by an invisible entity, by pure evil.

"Something is affecting us all," I say. "Something is *changing* us. Listen to me—we don't torture people. We're not like the Grownups!"

Spingate didn't just use the rod to shock, she *beat* Bello with it. Severely. And still Bello wouldn't talk. How can a woman

who is so weak she cries from loneliness resist this kind of physical punishment?

I realize Bello isn't spinning anymore.

She isn't moving at all.

The drip-drip of blood falling from her toes is slowing.

. . . *plop* . . .

. . . *plop* . . .

I have to get in there.

"Spin, if she hasn't talked yet, she's not going to. Her will is
too strong. Please open the door. *Please!*"

Spingate's face furrows in confusion.

"My children, Em." Her voice is thin, distant. "I need to protect them. Bello knows why the aliens are here. While she stays
silent, our people die. Don't you see? My son could be next."

I point to Bello. "Spin, *look* at her."

Spingate does.

"You're doing this for your children," I say. "What if it
works? What if torture becomes accepted in our culture, part of
who we are. Imagine our world ten years from now—then imagine that it's *Kevin* hanging by his wrists, that someone is hitting
him with the rod, over and over and over again."

Spingate stares. She blinks. That blankness washes over her,
the same one I saw on Bishop's face after he attacked Victor.

"Imagine it's your son," I say. "Bleeding. *Screaming.*"

Spingate looks at the red rod in her hand like she doesn't
know how it got there. A drop of blood falls from the end, splats
against the cell floor.

She looks at me. Horror twists her face—horror brought on
by realization.

"Em . . . what did I just do?"

She drops the rod. It clatters against the stone. She shuffles to the cell bars, reaches through and presses her hand to the palm-plate. When she takes her hand away, it leaves smeared fingerprints of blood.

The door lock clicks.

I yank it open and rush inside. I draw my knife from the sheath on my thigh and slash the rope. Bello drops like a bag of meat, like she has no bones.

She hits the floor. She doesn't move.

I rush to her. I slice the ropes from her wrists, then sheathe my knife. I feel her face: it's cool to the touch.

I press my ear to her chest: no heartbeat.

I lay her flat on her back, put my hands on her sternum and drive them down, once, twice, three times, just like Smith showed us to do. I press my mouth to Bello's and breathe out hard.

She doesn't respond.

I do chest compressions again, again push air into her lungs.

She doesn't respond.

Over and over I do this, feeling the rage building inside me, sensing my soul eroding, flaking away—how could my best friend *beat a woman to death*?

Hands on my shoulders. A man's hands.

"Let me try," Aramovsky says.

Spingate let him out.

I fall to my butt, get out of his way.

Aramovsky's chest compressions are stronger, his larger lungs force in more air than mine ever could. He is methodical, pumping away, desperate to save Bello.

Still she doesn't respond.

A sheen of sweat breaks out on Aramovsky's dark skin. Of course it does—it's hot in this cell, and he's working so hard.

*She's not moving.*

I start to crawl backward, wanting to get away from the body. . . .

My hand comes down on something round—the rod.

"Come on," Aramovsky hisses as he keeps pumping. "Come on, Bello, *fight!*"

I hear crying, and for a moment my heart surges with hope, because that's what Bello does, *cry,* until I realize it's not her—it's Spingate.

She's standing in the open cell doorway. Tears streak her blood-flecked face. Her lower lip quivers.

Really? *Now* she feels bad?

I pick up the rod.

Aramovsky sits back, wipes sweat from his forehead with the back of his hand.

"It's no use," he says. "Bello is dead."

I feel myself nodding as I stand.

"Of course she is," I say. "Because this godsdamned *gear* killed her."

I step toward Spingate. She stares at me, shakes her head.

"Em, I . . . I didn't mean . . ."

"Yes, you did, you bitch," I say, then I jam the rod tip into her neck.

Spingate's body convulses. She makes a strange gurgling sound.

"Yes, you did," I say, and I pull the rod away.

She collapses backward into the space between the rows of cells, her arms wrapped protectively around her round belly.

"Yes, you *did.*" I step out of the cell, touch the rod to her cheek. She convulses anew, that strange sound coming from deep in her throat. Her face wrinkles tight in agony. Her splayed fingers stretch out, half-curled, grabbing at nothing.

I'm going to kill this bitch. Her and her unborn baby, which will probably turn out just as evil as she is. Spingate tortures circles? She *murders* my kind? I'll show her. I press the rod harder against her face, use it to pin her head against the stone floor.

A blur of motion: the rod is ripped from my grasp.

I turn to face Aramovsky. Sheened in sweat, he holds the rod in his right hand.

"The God of Blood has you," he says. "Fight it."

I draw my knife. The images on the Observatory walls, of double-rings torturing people, burning them, *skinning* them. Aramovsky, who started a war, who sent me out to die. He should have killed me when he had the chance.

"*Fight it,* Em," he says, snarling out the words. "You are the strongest of us, don't let it control you."

I drop into a fighting stance, looking for a way past the rod he holds.

Aramovsky tosses the rod into the cell.

He puts his hands to his sides. He closes his eyes.

"Kill me if you must," he says. "But if you do, the God of Blood will own you forever."

I see the veins in his neck pulsing beneath his skin.

One slash of my blade will open up those veins. Aramovsky's blood will spray everywhere.

Just like the pig's did.

It will flow and puddle.

Just like Yong's did.

*The God of Blood has you.* . . .

I blink. I hear nothing. All I see is a defenseless man standing before me.

My knife clatters against the stone floor.

I glance at Spingate. She's curled up on the floor, shaking, drooling blood.

I glance at Bello. Naked. Lifeless. *Dead*.

Aramovsky opens his eyes.

"Now you know, Em" he says. "Now you know what it's like."

# TWENTY-THREE

Bishop and I can do nothing but stand and watch. One of us usually leads, but right now the fate of our people relies on Giles Borjigin.

We're atop a wall tower. A thick stone battlement runs along the outside edge of the circular floor. The battlement is taller than I am, but there are notches cut into it so people can look out. To the north, I see the river snaking off through the jungle ruins, slicing between the canyon of trees rising up on either side. To the south, I can see all of Uchmal—blackened, burned, coated in ash.

Opkick is up here, with us, as are five filthy circles awaiting their next task. Two of the circles, Elisa Hinog and Kurt Armbruster, have been trained to fire the cannon and will make sure it's working properly.

We can't spare circle-stars to crew the wall cannons, as we need them in the city streets, battling with rifle and spear and spider. Halves, gears and circle-crosses have important jobs to do when the fighting begins; we can't spare them, either.

What we *can* spare—as always—are circles.

The circles up here are filthy because they've spent all morning raising a five-meter-high dirt ramp against the city side of the tower.

Up that ramp walks a metal giant.

Borjigin is inside, piloting the massive, two-legged, fifteen-meter-tall construction machine that we found in the Spider Nest, the same giant that he turned into a war machine at Aramovsky's command. In that battle, I ordered Spingate to fire shuttle missiles at the giant, which caused the death of the four people inside.

I remember their names: Abrantes, Cadotte, Aeschelman, Cody.

They burned alive. Because of me.

I feel Bishop's hand on my shoulder, squeezing, reassuring.

"Are you thinking about when we stopped Aramovsky?"

I nod.

"You did what you had to do," he says quietly. "It was war."

Using the word *war* frames my decisions, but it doesn't justify them.

We watch the giant machine continue up the ramp.

"I don't think that's an excuse," I say. "Spingate did what she thought she had to do—she's a murderer because of it, not a hero."

Bishop shakes his head. "Whatever Spingate is, her mind is too valuable to waste away in prison. You need to let her out and put her back to work."

"She tortured a human being to death," I say. "She'll stay where I put her."

Which is in a cell, right next to Aramovsky's.

Aramovsky claims something took Theresa over, fanned the

flames of her deepest fears, somehow *forced* one of the smartest people I know to listen to her most primitive, hateful instincts.

She killed Bello. Spingate will be punished—she is responsible for her actions.

*But you felt it, didn't you? You felt the God of Blood. You could have killed Spingate just as easily as Spingate killed Bello, killed Spingate and her unborn baby . . .*

No, there's a difference. I *didn't* kill. But is that only because Aramovsky was there to interfere?

I glance at Bishop. He went into a rage and almost killed Victor. If Victor had died, would I have put Bishop in a cell?

If I'd been holding a real spear instead of a practice one, Bawden would be dead—would I have put *myself* in jail? Would I have let someone else put me in there?

"You're being stupid," Bishop says. "This isn't the time for your morals if those morals get in the way of our survival. Spingate is special. Her mind is irreplaceable. What's more important—the accidental death of an enemy, or the deaths of our people that might occur because she's locked up instead of being in the Control Room where she belongs?"

I don't know the right answer to his question.

Spingate has always been among the most reliable of the Birthday Children. Smart, self-sacrificing, dedicated. Honorable. The fact that she, of all people, did what she did? It intensifies the sense of anger and dismay spreading through our people.

Spingate. Bishop. *Me.* The fight on the training ground. The Belligerents. Barkah and his prisoner.

Is something really making us all do evil things?

Or are we all just evil to begin with?

"Here we go," Bishop says, nodding toward the giant. "We better get clear."

We press our backs against the curved battlement wall, making space for Opkick and the circles to work.

Borjigin spent months rebuilding his giant, using tubes, wires and other parts I don't understand from the hundreds of dead machines rusting away in the Spider Nest. He even painted over the giant's scorched metal frame, turning it from fire-smudge black to a light blue dotted with bright bits of steel. Cables and cords of green and black snake through the framework. The left arm ends in a bright blue, three-fingered pincer. The right ends in a scoop shovel big enough for five people to stand in comfortably. Right now, though, it holds today's prize—a long wall cannon, silvery metal blazing reddish in the afternoon sun.

Opkick shouts instructions to Borjigin. The scoop rises above the battlements. The three-fingered pincer gently lifts the cannon from the scoop and sets it down in the center of the tower. Opkick barks commands to the circles, who scramble to fasten the cannon to bolts mounted in the stone.

"That's the last one," Bishop says. "I hope they're enough."

The wall surrounding Uchmal has sixty-four towers. Once upon a time, Borjigin tells me, every tower had a cannon. Out of all of those, he and the other halves were able to cobble together enough parts to make six working weapons. He's spaced these evenly around the wall. If the city was a clock face and due north was twelve o'clock, we have cannons at 1, 3, 5, 7, 9 and 11. We're standing in the one o'clock tower. The three o'clock tower is the one above the East Gate, and so on.

"Use the signal flags," I say. "Tell the Observatory the cannon is in place."

Bishop pulls an orange handheld flag from inside his coveralls: he steps to the tower's south edge and moves the flags in a simple pattern.

Twenty blocks away, someone atop a four-story ziggurat

waves a much larger orange flag, mimicking Bishop's pattern. Moments later, I can just make out a third orange flag, another twenty blocks closer to the city center.

"It works," Bishop says. "Good. Between the flags and the horns, we'll be fine."

We've given up on the communication jewels. They don't work at all now, not even close to the Observatory. Borjigin still doesn't know what's causing the interference, and he doesn't have time to figure it out.

If the aliens land and we have a ground war, our combat units need to communicate with each other. Bawden came up with the idea of using signal flags to relay messages through the city. Lahfah brought us more war horns—we'll also use those to coordinate troop movements, just like the Springers do in the jungle.

Centuries ago, this city had a huge arsenal with which to defend itself, but time is the great destroyer. Machines and weapons went untended. Rust ate metal. Delicate parts corroded. Synthetic materials broke down.

Other than bracelets, rifles, spears, knives and farm tools, we don't have much: the Observatory's automated defense, six tower cannons, seven spiders, four heavy trucks converted from hauling dirt to hauling infantry, the Big Pig and some small unarmored vehicles.

And, of course, the Goff Spear and its three remaining rounds.

We have four platoons of human soldiers. I lead one platoon. Bishop, Farrar and young Darzi lead the others. A platoon consists of three spiders—each with a crew of three—and twelve infantry.

*Infantry*. That's a funny word. It's supposed to mean trained soldiers. We have circle-stars, yes, who have programmed memories and fighting skills, but most of them are physically only thirteen years old. They are children with guns. And we don't even have enough of them, so each platoon is rounded out with a handful of circles. Shuttle kids, mostly, also physically thirteen years old, but any combat training they've received has come in the last six months.

We have help from Barkah. Four companies of his Malbinti warriors are hidden throughout the city. Two hundred soldiers in each company, armed with rifles and muskets. Inside our own walls, armed Springers now outnumber us over three to one. A risk, yes, but if Bishop is right and the aliens land ground troops, it's a risk worth taking.

There are more of Barkah's forces out in the jungle ruins, ready to defend Schechak. Eight companies organized into two battalions, sixteen hundred warriors ready to fight whatever comes their way. Assisting them are the hurukan squads: D'souza's Demons and Lahfah's Creepers. The snake-wolves are best suited for jungle warfare, so that's where they are stationed unless things really get out of hand here in Uchmal.

If our new enemy lands among the trees, they are in for a serious fight.

A long wail, rising and falling, reaches across the city—the emergency warning siren.

Did the people in the Control Room detect incoming ships?

Everyone atop the tower looks to the sky, searching this way and that. My heart races. We've prepared as best we can, but we're not ready.

I hear it before I see it; the distant roar of a rocket echoing across the jungle canopy. Something about that sound is oddly familiar. Is it one of those "fighters" from the *Dragon*? Or, worse, a swarm of them?

Bishop points north. "There!"

Far out at the horizon, I see a black dot.

Bishop shouts at the circles installing the silver cannon.

"Get that weapon online! Right now!"

Other wall cannons might have an angle, but it's flying straight at us—our tower will have the best shot.

It comes in low, skimming the yellow treetops. The noisy ship trails a thick, roiling cloud of black.

Wait, the sound of that rocket . . . how do I know that sound?

"Cannon is online," Opkick shouts.

Bishop points at Elisa and Kurt.

"Man your weapon!"

They're shuttle kids. Barely thirteen years old. They looked shocked. They have trained and trained, but this isn't a drill. This is real.

Elisa sits in a metal chair mounted on the cannon's right side. She pulls a targeting rig close to her face, starts working the controls. Kurt steps to the weapon's left side, where he'll monitor a dozen different settings.

The enemy ship is coming in low, fast and loud.

The white crystal atop the silver cannon begins to glow.

A blazing white beam fires from our left, coming from the eleven o'clock tower. It misses the incoming ship, leaves a shimmering reverse-image streamer dancing across my vision. I see a small fireball rise up from the jungle, where the beam touched down.

Now I realize why the ship is flying at tree level—it's below the top of the city wall, meaning most of our cannons can't get a line of sight on it.

Just one ship . . . why just *one*?

"Weapon charged," Kurt shouts. His voice breaks on *charged*. He's so young he's still in puberty. He sounds as scared as he looks.

"Targeting," Elisa says. She's shaking.

Icons flash on her display: an image of the ship, a crosshairs lined up on it. That ship . . . it's larger in the targeting display, I can make out details I can't with my naked eye.

It's not sleek, as I expected . . . it's black, and it's . . .

. . . it's *lumpy.*

It's the same ship that brought Bello down a year ago, that took Matilda and Old Gaston back up to the *Xolotl.*

*"Stop,"* I scream as I rush at Elisa, yank her hands away from the controls. I turn to Bishop. "That ship is *ours!* Signal all batteries to cease fire!"

He doesn't second-guess me, even for an instant. He faces south, starts making sharp signals with his flag.

A beam of light lashes out from the southeast, from the three o'clock tower. This beam grazes the lumpy ship's back, lashing up a splattering wave of molten metal. The ship starts to tremble. It dips down into the trees, vanishes for a second, then arcs back up above the canopy in an eruption of leaves and vines.

The shuddering ship struggles to rise—it's not going to make it over the vine-covered wall.

I grip the slot in the battlements, pouring my will into that ship.

*Climb. Climb, dammit!*

It's going to smash into the wall just to our right. It climbs. I wince as it reaches the wall—the ship's belly grinds against the stone edge and bounces over, trailing a cloud of pulverized stone, spinning vine leaves and billowing smoke.

The lumpy ship tilts hard right and drops toward the wide, north/south street that is Latu Way. It whizzes by blackened stone buildings on either side. Cones of fire shoot out from all over the lumpy ship, fluttering and flickering in an effort to keep it level. It slows dramatically as the already-ruined undercarriage slams into the street with an ear-splitting spray of sparks. Metal grinds against stone.

The ship slides to a stop some twenty-five blocks south of our position.

A massive shadow above my head makes me duck. The huge scoop-shovel of Borjigin's giant touches down on the battlement's floor with barely a clank. In the giant's "head," through light blue bars and a slot cut into metal plating, I see Borjigin's face.

"Em, *get in*," he shouts. "Let's go!"

Bishop and I scramble into the scoop. Borjigin lifts it clear. The giant machine turns. Long strides take it down the earthen ramp and onto Latu Way. Each thundering step makes the big machine tremble, rattling us in the scoop. Bishop and I hold on tight as big legs chew up the distance.

I flick my wrist left and then right. Bishop does the same. Our bracelets glow with the promise of death.

We reach the ship in minutes. It's twisted and broken. It will clearly never fly again, but it's mostly in one piece. Thin smoke curls up from a dozen tiny tears and cracks. The nose cone is badly dented.

Bishop waves at Borjigin to get his attention, then points to the ground. A hatch opens on the back of the giant's head. There is a long ladder running down the giant's spine, but Borjigin ignores it—with agility I would have never expected from him, he balance-walks along the giant's shoulder and down its arm toward us. He jumps into the scoop, then waves at someone still inside the chest.

"Put us down!"

A whir of machinery, the hiss of hydraulics.

The scoop hits the ground. We scramble out onto the street.

The lumpy black ship seems much bigger up close. Eight to ten people would fit inside it comfortably.

Bishop runs to the nose cone, looks through a crack.

"I think there's someone moving in there!"

Borjigin sprints to the side of the ship, finds a door just behind the cockpit. The door is badly bent and refuses to open enough for him to enter. Bishop and I join in—the three of us yank and yank until the door pops opens with a shriek of complaining metal.

I scramble into the ship's shadows, Bishop at my heels. Sunlight filters through cracks in the hull, lighting up beams of swirling smoke.

A black form falls out of the pilot's seat.

It's a Grownup, gnarled and thin, wearing the metal frame and clear mask that lets its kind breathe on Omeyocan. I can't make out the face through all this smoke.

I aim my bracelet. Bishop does the same.

The Grownup is trembling, coughing so hard its thin body shudders. Its skinny legs are twisted, misshapen and limp.

It lifts its head.

A sunbeam finds its way through the cracked hull to light up the Grownup's visor and the face behind it. Two bulbous red eyes look at me, eyes that whirl with a soft, red glow.

"Little Savage," it says between violent coughs. "Do be a . . . be a sweetie, and . . . don't kill me a second time."

It's Brewer. I can't believe it.

I lower my arm. "What are you doing here?"

He raises a trembling coal-black arm, points a bone-thin finger behind Bishop and me.

"Beware the Cherished who bears gifts," he says. "Or who gifts bears with chairs that itch."

Bishop and I both turn and look deeper into the ruined lumpy ship. Through the swirling sunbeam smoke, I see a long shape, thick straps holding it tight against gray foam padding.

I recognize the shape.

"You've got to be kidding me," I say.

Bishop looks from the shape to me, then back to the shape again.

"What is it?"

I saw something like it up on top of the Observatory, only that one was broken up into a hundred pieces. This one? This one is new. This one is *whole*.

"It's an antenna," I say. "Brewer brought us an antenna."

# TWENTY-FOUR

'm in the hospital. Kenzie Smith and I stand next to a closed white coffin. Inside it, Brewer.

"He's in bad shape," Kenzie says. "His left side took the brunt of it—broken tibia, fibula broken in *three* places, fractured femur, broken hip bone. A couple of cracked ribs for good measure, although I've never seen ribs like his before. Whatever they did to make Grownups live for so long changed their bodies immensely."

Brewer passed out as soon as we tried to move him. I'll never forget his scream of pain. Bishop used his signal flags to call for vehicles and medical help.

Nevins, Peura and Harman rushed to the crash site almost as fast as Kenzie did. Once Brewer was safely away, they crawled into the lumpy ship, excited beyond any level of self-control. They *oohed* and *aahed* over the antenna, squealed with delight at finally understanding where a few of their mystery parts were supposed to go. Some bits broke in the crash, but the boys are confident that between the new and the old they now have enough working pieces to make a functioning antenna.

"How long until he's out of there?" I ask Kenzie.

"Depends on if you want him on his feet or in a wheelchair. That hip will take weeks in the med-chamber, if I can heal him at all. His bones are so brittle."

"I don't care if he can walk, as long as he can talk."

He risked his life to deliver the antenna. Why? Can he tell us why the *Xolotl* came to Omeyocan? Can he tell us why the alien ships are here?

"There's something else," Kenzie says. "He's dying."

"Of course he's dying, he's a thousand godsdamned years old."

She shakes her head. "He's got small-cell carcinoma. It's metastasized."

Kenzie stares at me for a moment, all solemn, waiting for a response.

I shrug. "I don't know what that means."

She waves her hand over the top of the white pedestal next to the coffin. An image sparkles to life: the outline of a thin man, legs together, hands at his sides. The image is white. His chest is dotted with spots of deep green. There are spots of green all over him, including his head.

"He has lung cancer," she says. "And it has spread to his lymph nodes, his liver, his bones . . . his brain. He must be in excruciating pain."

I look at the white coffin, as if I can suddenly see through it to the gnarled, ancient man inside. I think back to when I first spoke to him, up on the *Xolotl*.

"Lung cancer," I say. "Would that make you cough?"

"At his stage, yes. A lot."

"So cure him. The coffins can fix that, right?"

Kenzie shakes her head. "Med-chambers can do a lot, but many conditions are beyond the technology."

Zubiri's arm. Delilah's leg. Some things can't be healed.

"How long until he dies?"

Kenzie thinks this over for a moment, runs a hand through her hair.

"Based on what I know, what I see, he should have been dead a year ago. I honestly don't know how he's still alive. He can't have more than a few weeks left. A few days, probably."

If he dies before he can tell us why he came . . .

"Fix what you can as fast as you can," I say. "Then wake him up."

I turn to leave.

"Wait," Kenzie says. "I need to talk to you about Spingate. She's extremely upset."

My jaw tightens. "She's a murderer. Her feelings are not important to me right now."

"You won't let her see her own child. It's killing her."

"Which means the baby is safe," I say.

Kenzie rubs her eyes. "Theresa wouldn't hurt little Kevin."

"And I wouldn't have thought she could hurt Bello, either."

This is taking a toll on Kenzie, draining her. She looks at me with an expression I've become all too familiar with—she wants this to make sense. She wants answers.

Answers that I don't have.

"Theresa is the sweetest person I know," Kenzie said. "How could she have done that to Bello?"

"I don't know," I say.

Kenzie glances at the lines of coffins. She shivers.

"What's happening to us, Em? When is this going to stop?"

I've never seen her this distraught.

"I have no idea," I say. "I'm doing the best I can."

She forces a smile. "I know. But please, reconsider not letting Spin see her baby. All right?"

I think of Bello, hanging by her wrists, and Spingate, holding the bloody rod. Was that really a one-time thing, or could it happen again?

"I'll think about it," I say.

Kenzie looks off, nods, then goes back to work on the pedestal display next to Brewer's coffin.

# TWENTY-FIVE

We're atop the Observatory.

Dawn sets the sky aglow.

Brewer sits in a wheelchair, blanket over his legs, staring out at Omeyocan's endless expanse. A strong breeze sweeps clouds of vine ash across the city, makes Gaston's black locks flutter, pulls a few tickling strands of hair free from my braid.

Gaston, Bishop, Aramovsky, Kenzie Smith and I are here with Brewer. Kenzie insisted on coming so she could keep an eye on her patient. I brought Aramovsky because he knows religion, which I suspect is at the root of everything we face. And because I think he may have stopped me from killing Spingate. I was that lost in my rage. I'm not about to set him free, but I think he's earned some time out of his cell.

Gaston won't look anyone in the eye. He's deeply ashamed of Spingate's hateful act. I think he feels responsible, somehow, as if it's his fault he let her out of his sight.

I stare at Brewer, try to sort through my feelings. He's horrifying to behold; gnarled, wrinkled and spindly, the embodiment of the evil that's been done to us. But he is also the person who protected us, spent centuries keeping us from being erased. Without him, we might never have awoken at all, let alone escaped the *Xolotl*.

Looking at him now, though, in person, not over some pedestal connection, I finally see the *real* B. Brewer—an ancient, broken man staring out at the lost dream of his life.

Bishop carried the wheelchair up the spiral staircase with Brewer still in it. Bishop moved as gently as he could, but with each step Brewer let out a little whimper. A broken hip must be an awful thing. We asked Brewer several times if he wanted to stop. He didn't.

Because more than anything else, he wanted to see the planet that had been promised to him so long ago.

His eyes are bigger than ours, rounder. They stick out slightly from his head, almost touching the clear mask that covers his face. Combined with the fleshy folds that hang where his nose and mouth should be, the Grownups look hideous.

"I waited twelve centuries for this view," he says. "Give or take a century."

His voice is soft, muffled by the mask. The mask filters out the poisons from Omeyocan's air. Poisons for *him*. We're different— we were created to live here.

"Or take," he says. "Take a flake and cake a rake."

I glance at Bishop. He's pulling slightly at his lower lip, staring at Brewer, a worried look on his face. I understand how he feels. Up on the *Xolotl*, I wondered if Brewer was crazy. Now I'm sure of it. Since Kenzie let Brewer out of the hospital coffin, the man has been babbling, repeating words, making nonsensical rhymes.

On the slab above and behind us, we hear Nevins, Peura and Harman installing the new antenna. The irony digs at me—we tried desperately to fix the antenna so Bello could talk to the *Xolotl*, and now that she's dead the *Xolotl* has sent us an antenna.

If Spingate had waited just one more day, Bello would still be alive.

Soon, Peura tells me, we'll be able to talk to the *Xolotl*. I'm hoping for that, yes, but for much more—if we can reach the *Goblin* or the *Dragon*, maybe we can communicate with those aliens before it is too late.

Maybe I can make peace instead of war.

Until the boys get the antenna working, though, this crazy, ancient man is our only connection to the bigger picture.

"So *dirty*," Brewer says. "Dirty dirty gurty city."

Was Uchmal supposed to be his paradise? He endured centuries of pain to reach this place.

"It's not as bad as it looks," I say. "Most of the buildings are fine. Only the vines burned."

Huge craters dotting the city contradict my words.

"Grungy mungy," Brewer says.

I glance to the sky. It's an involuntary tic now—whenever I'm outside I look up, wondering when the next attack will come.

Before we brought Brewer up here, Gaston told me both the *Goblin* and the *Dragon* had passed below the horizon, out of sight of our radio telescope. We don't know where those ships are. They might be landing troops on the far side of the planet for all we know. But if they do that, those troops will have to march or fly thousands of miles to reach us. Bishop says that's not strategically sound. He thinks they'll land closer, if not in the city itself—which means we'll soon see those ships again.

"Brewer," I say, "you asked us to bring you up here. Now we need you to focus and answer some questions. Can you do that?"

"Do not speak to me as if I am the child, girl. Respect your elders who are also the same age as you but not really. Ask and ye shall receive bereave conceive."

I take a breath, steady myself. So many questions. That we might finally get answers nearly overwhelms me. I'll focus on the most important questions first.

"Why did you bring the antenna?"

"Because you asked me to."

I glance at Kenzie.

"You mean *Matilda* asked you to," she says softly to Brewer. "Yes?"

Brewer coughs. "Potato, tomahto, vibrato."

He's working *with* Matilda now? The ship she used to escape Omeyocan is the same one he came down in, so that much adds up.

I step to the right side of Brewer's wheelchair, squat down on my heels.

"You kept Matilda and the others from overwriting us. You were her enemy. Why are you working with her now?"

He looks down at me. His red eyes seem strange . . . kind of unfocused, clouded.

"I know why *you* want that girl, Matilda, but we could be the last humans in existence," he says. "We *must* keep the children alive. We must help them against the aliens. I remember how to fly—I'll take the spare antenna down to them."

He's looking right at me, but he thinks I'm *her*. Does he not know where he is?

*The last humans in existence.* Just mad babbling? He's crazy, but the way he said it doesn't *feel* like mad babbling. In all this time, I've never really thought about where other people might be—it's just been *us*.

We can't be the only ones. Can we?

"Brewer, you already flew down to Omeyocan," I say. I gesture to the horizon. "Just look."

He stares at me for a few seconds, then gazes out over the jungle.

"Beautiful," he says. "Did you know I waited twelve centuries for this view?"

I stand, huddle with Kenzie, Bishop, Gaston and Aramovsky.

"Damn, Smith," Gaston says. "Could you have drugged this loser up any more?"

"Be quiet," Kenzie snaps. The wind whips at her brown hair. "You don't know a damn thing about medicine, Gaston. I don't think this behavior is from the painkillers. Not all of it, anyway. I think Brewer is senile."

*Senile.* I know that can happen to old people, and Brewer is over a *thousand* years old. Whatever was done to make him live this long, his body and his brain are finally wearing out.

I again squat by his side. I don't want to touch him, but I take his hand anyway. My skin crawls, as if I'm picking up a fist-sized centipede. His grip is weak. His gnarled skin is cold.

He squeezes my hand, gives it a little reassuring shake.

"It's all right, Matilda, I'll go," he says. "With what happened last time, they'll kill you as soon as they see you. They'll kill any Cherished on sight. Except me, maybe. I'm the only one Little Savage might spare."

Brewer thinks he's talking to Matilda, but he's right—I do want to kill her. If I'd done that when I first had the chance, O'Malley would still be alive.

Frustration bubbles up within me. This isn't *fair,* godsdammit. Bello wouldn't talk and now she's dead. Brewer came down and now he's senile?

Aramovsky leans close to me, whispers.

"If he thinks you're Matilda, pretend to be Matilda. Get as much information as you can."

Aramovsky's voice: so calm, so steady. It's actually kind of soothing.

*Pretend to be Matilda.* I'll give it a try.

"Brewer, tell me what the antenna will do for them again?"

"The children are under siege," he says. "If we can reach them, we can help the whelps with orbital observation."

He waves his free hand like he's dismissing some annoying comment.

"Yes-yes-yes in a dress, I know I destroyed the antenna in the first place, but you had that coming. Now isn't the time for quibbles *or* nibbles. If humanity is to survive, this must be done."

He sabotaged the original antenna? Why? Another mystery to solve, but one for later.

"Eyes in the sky," Bishop says, excited by this concept. "If we face ground troops, knowing where they are is critical."

This time it's Gaston who whispers to me.

"Find out why the *Xolotl* won't fight. If Matilda wants to keep you alive, the best way is to destroy those trying to kill you. Why doesn't she engage?"

This would be so much easier if Brewer knew where he was, perhaps *when* he was. I think of a way to phrase the question.

"We should just destroy those other ships," I say. "Don't you agree?"

The ancient creature laughs—a harsh, wet cough cuts the laugh short. Bits of gray paste splatter against the inside of his visor.

Brewer's head lolls back. His eyes scrunch tight. Painkillers or not, he's clearly fighting against horrific agony.

He takes a moment to gather himself, then answers.

"Destroy them with what? The six decrepit Macanas Vick that Tick Tick wastes his time with?"

*Macanas . . . Vick Tick Tick . . .* he's talking nonsense.

"Macanas," Aramovsky says, almost shouting the word. He's wide-eyed, immersed in a flashfire moment. "Those are . . . I know those. They're fighter craft, interceptors, made for space combat."

The name means nothing to me, but Brewer nods.

"I monitored the fighter battle between those two mother ships," he says. "Our Macanas are completely outclassed, if they work at all. *Destroy those other ships,* you say. Somehow, Matilda, you still don't appreciate what that last battle did to the *Xolotl.* I mean, it only happened *two centuries* ago, so maybe you haven't had time to process it."

I again glance to the sky, feel that imaginary clock ticking down. Something drew those ships here. That same something must have drawn *us.*

I ask the most important question there is

"Why did we come to Omeyocan?"

He slowly turns his head to look at me.

"The prophecy," he says. "The Founder said the scourge is coming. We're going where Tlaloc wants us to be. I'm not like you, Matilda—I was *born* into the church. When the ship leaves, my father says I have to be on it. I don't have a choice."

Now he thinks the *Xolotl* hasn't even started its original journey? Maybe looking at my face, the young face of Matilda Savage, is confusing him further.

And . . . he said he didn't have a choice? I'd assumed the Grownups were the cause of everything, that it was their decision to make this journey. Could it be they had no more control over their destiny than we did?

Aramovsky steps to the wheelchair, squats down on the side opposite me. He stares at Brewer like Brewer is the only thing that exists.

"You said you were born into the church. What church?"

Aramovsky doesn't sound calm anymore. He's agitated, as if he's on the verge of remembering something very important.

Brewer looks at Aramovsky. The bulbous red eyes narrow.

"You're playing with me, Boris."

*B. Aramovsky* . . . the *B* is for *Boris*.

Aramovsky grips the chair's wheel, squeezes hard.

"Tell me, Brewer. Right now. *What church?*"

"*The* church, of course," Brewer says. "The Church of Mictlan."

The moment those words leave his mouth, my memories flashfire, make connections that have been right in front of me all along. *The Church of Mictlan*. The symbol on our red ties, stitched into our black coveralls. The squashed-face symbol on the *Xolotl*'s round, flat front.

"Our clothes were school uniforms," I say. "Our classes, our training . . . *all* of us were in the Church of Mictlan."

I've mocked Aramovsky for his religion, called him a fool, but it turns out religion is what brought us here in the first place. Is he the fool, or am I?

"How many people were in the church?" Aramovsky asks, both eager and astonished.

Brewer squints one red eye, thinking.

"The Founder claims a million at the cotillion in dresses of vermilion," he says. "But there's a reason the ship will only take forty thousand, because that's all there is. Don't argue with me, Boris—you take the religious history courses far too seriously. Sometimes you don't use your own brain."

*Forty thousand?* The Birthday Children are not even three hundred strong—forty thousand on the *Xolotl* seems like an unimaginable amount.

"You mentioned *the scourge*," Bishop says. "I can . . . I can almost remember that. What is it?"

"The Abernessia," Brewer says. "They are coming. The Founder told us so. They bring hellfire and damnation, a pestilence to punish humanity. But when they reach Solomon, we'll be long gone."

*Solomon . . .*

Another flashfire rips through me, through all of us.

We were little kids, eight years old, taking a shuttle from a planet—from Solomon, our *home*—up to the *Xolotl*. Solomon, burning behind us, alien warships raining fire down upon it. Cities wiped out. Millions of people dying.

And I . . . I was crying. *Screaming.* I look at Gaston. He was there with me. So was Aramovsky. And Spingate and O'Malley . . . Okadigbo and Yong and . . . and *Brewer*.

B. Brewer's coffin. The emaciated little boy inside, skin dried taut to the skull. Repressed memories flesh out that face, bring hair back to life, reincarnate a mischievous smile, an infectious laugh. I look at the wrinkled, ancient thing sitting in the wheelchair.

"We were *friends*," I say, breathless. "We all took classes together. We played together."

Brewer nods, and when he does I see the Grownup and the child in the same body.

"We are a *lacha*," he says. "Twelve that will have immortality together, as the Founder foretells, as Tlaloc promises. I am sorry, Matilda—to be Okadigbo's attendant forever and ever? How horrible. Bello has it rough with Theresa, but you have to admit nobody is as awful as Okadigbo."

He laughs. He coughs. He settles into his chair.

The wind sends yellow waves across the jungle canopy.

What is *Tlaloc*? I still don't know, but one word Brewer said resonates—*lacha*. It means "twelve." Twelve coffins in our room. Twelve people who were together since childhood.

It never occurred to me there was a specific reason we woke up in the same room. I don't remember the details, but my progenitor's connection to Brewer is far deeper than I knew.

Brewer pats my hand.

"But honestly, Matilda, you need to stop making goo-goo eyes at Kevey-Wehvey. It's silly for you to think you can be with him."

Kevey-Wehvey . . . *Kevin*.

O'Malley was in our *lacha*. Could I have been in love with Kevin O'Malley since I was just a little girl?

"Why is it silly?" I ask.

Bishop puts his hand on my shoulder. "Em, we need to focus on the important things right now."

I slap his hand away, glare up at him. "Stay *out* of this, Bishop."

I shouldn't care about some schoolgirl crush a thousand years gone, but I can't help it. I do everything for everyone else, all the time. This is for *me*. I'm a woman without a past—I want my history back.

I squeeze Brewer's hand. "Why is it silly? Tell me."

He sighs. "Silly nilly billy willy. Kevin is above your station! Are you looking for yet another reason for Okadigbo to be mean to you? You're my best friend in all the ship, Matilda, but your father and I agree on this."

His words wash over me like a wave of ice-cold water, shatter me, break free new flashfires in an assault of emotions; when I first woke up in my coffin, when I thought it was my twelfth birthday, I was afraid I'd be late for school, that my mother would punish me for that.

Because when I was twelve, I lived with her.

But our ship fled Solomon when I was *eight*.

"My parents . . . they were on the *Xolotl*?"

Brewer nods.

My breath catches. The universe condenses to a single point the size and shape of Brewer's ancient face.

"Are my parents still alive?"

He blinks, confused.

"Of course not," he says. "Don't be stupid, Matilda."

I move to the front of his chair, lean in close, my hands gripping the handrails.

"Brewer, listen to me. I am not Matilda. I'm *Em*. I need you in the here and now. You flew a ship from the *Xolotl* down to Omeyocan. Don't you remember? *Please.*"

Out of the corner of my eye, I see Kenzie shaking her head.

"You can't just will him out of it," she says. "That's not how senility works."

But this time, it *does* work. Brewer blinks. His eyes focus on me.

"Oh dear," he says. "It happened again."

The disgusting folds of flesh where his mouth should be . . . they're trembling. He's upset. He's *scared*.

"My intellect is all I have left," he says. "And it's fading. Slipping away, just like my life did. Do you know what that's like?"

Does he want sympathy from me? From *me*, who never had a life at all, let alone one that could slip away?

I feel sorry for him. I hate him. I want to help him. I want to kill him.

Brewer tries to lean away from me, but he can't; he's trapped in this chair. I hover over him, a cat poised above a helpless mouse.

I grip his left forearm. Harder than I intend, I think, because he flinches.

"*You* lived this long," I say, my words simmering with anger. "As did Matilda. So why couldn't my parents?"

Brewer relaxes slightly. "Ah, I see said the blind man. Little Savage, your mother and father were *vassals*. Only the Cherished were chosen for rebirth."

Deep down, I knew my parents were gone, and yet I can't stop sadness from crushing me. I should have been smarter—I shouldn't have *hoped*. They've been dead for a millennium and more. The only way I will ever know them is through Matilda's memories.

And I have so few of those.

"You said you and my father agreed about Kevin. You talked to my dad?"

"Of course," Brewer says. "After we departed, he took you, me and Bello to services in the Flatland every Sunday."

My life already seemed so cruel. Now I learn that this madman knew my father, yet I never will.

"I remember sitting on my father's lap," I say. "He didn't have a circle on his head." Another bit of that memory flutters to the surface. "Come to think of it, I didn't have one, either."

Brewer raises a trembling hand to wipe his wet mouth-folds, but his visor blocks it.

"That recollection must be from when you were very young," he says. "The church assigns our stations on our sixth birthday."

Aramovsky's fingertips drift to his forehead, trace the symbol there. Gaston and Bishop do the same with theirs, an automatic reaction.

I was assigned my "station"—my circle, my *empty*—at the age of *six*? I was marked as a slave before I had any understanding of how life works.

"So my father wasn't in the church, then?"

"He was," Brewer says. "Vassals are the lowest level. They don't get stations. I suppose we might think of them as *regular people*."

Aramovsky drops to his butt. He's staring off, shaking his head. It's all too much for him. I understand, because it's all too much for me.

"The vassals were slaves," he says. "Like the circles?"

Brewer tries to wipe his mouth again, hits his visor again.

"So long ago," he says. "Hard to remember. Empties were slaves, yes, but far above vassals. Empties are the Cherished just as much as I am."

He raises his arm, looks at it.

"We Cherished did *this* to ourselves. We cheated death, kept it at bay so we could survive the journey and be rewarded in paradise with our new bodies."

*The centuries have not been kind to the Cherished,* Brewer once said. He was talking about his withered body. The Cherished created us—their *receptacles*—to house their consciousnesses so they could be young again.

Gaston has been quiet so long I forgot he was here. Finally, he speaks.

"The trip from Solomon to Omeyocan took centuries, as you're so damn fond of repeating. If the Grownups were modified to survive the trip, how did the vassals survive?"

Brewer laughs, and this time, at least, he avoids that awful cough.

"Xander-dander, smart in the air and dumb on the ground, as always. The vassals didn't survive. They grew old. They died."

The horrifying images of the *Xolotl* flash through my thoughts. Severed arms, piles of skulls, stacks of bodies, and . . . babies.

*Babies.*

"Families," I say. "The vassals had families?"

Brewer nods. "The birds and the bees if you please. Many people had children. Even some of the Cherished did. Don't you remember your own daughter?"

I take a step back, shake my head. He thinks I'm Matilda again. And Matilda had a child? *I* had a child?

I feel Bishop's stare. He's *smiling.* A warm smile, one of love— one of hope.

"Children," Brewer says. "That's why most vassals joined the church, really. On Solomon, those people had no future. Their children would have lived short, brutish lives, just like they did. The Founder promised safety, education—hope for a better tomorrow. And when her prediction about the scourge started to come true, believers flooded in. People came from all over human space. New Rodina, Capizzi Seven, Tower, Madhava, the Quyth Orbital Stations . . . even Earth. So many cultures came to join."

Aramovsky lies flat on his back. He stares straight up at the sky.

"But the trip here took centuries," he says. "The vassals had to know their children wouldn't even *see* Omeyocan. Neither would their grandchildren, and so on."

"Hundreds of thousands of people were born and died on that ship without knowing anything *but* the ship," Brewer says. "Over thirty generations that saw neither Solomon nor Omeyocan."

My life is far from perfect, but I have to wonder if I have it better than those people did. What would it be like to be born on a ship, to grow up and one day realize that you would live your whole life within its hull? To know that by the time the *Xolotl* reached Omeyocan, you would be five, six, ten, *twenty* generations back, completely forgotten.

It would fill me with rage.

Puzzle pieces click together.

"They rebelled," I say. "The vassals wanted receptacles. They wanted the same transformation the Grownups had, so they could live to see Omeyocan."

Brewer folds his spindly fingers together.

"Some of them, yes. They mutinied because they didn't know their place in life. They wanted the same privileges as we Cherished. But you knew that, Matilda. You fed on that selfish desire, used it to become the rebellion's leader. To this day, I still don't know if you actually thought they were in the right, or you just wanted to seize power. And your *blasphemy* when you won, making new Cherished and promising them they would live side by side with us on Omeyocan. Disgusting."

Gaston glances at me. "That must be why some of us woke up with bigger bodies. The new batch, the ones who woke up with twelve-year-old bodies and not just twelve-year-old minds, their growth began after the rebellion, when the *Xolotl* had already been traveling for centuries."

"Correct," Brewer says. "The original *lachas* incubated for far too long, but the rebels' timing was just about right."

I realize I'm caught up in the moment. I want to hear everything, but I've let myself be distracted away from the information we desperately need.

"All the ships that came here look the same," I say. "How did the Church of Mictlan get the *Xolotl*?"

Brewer looks at me—I see his eyes cloud over.

"Ships? What other ships?"

*No,* I will not let him slip away.

I reach to grab his arm again, but before I can, Kenzie grabs mine.

"Em, *stop it,*" she says. "He needs rest."

Rest? Is she insane? I'll—

From the pillar platform come the excited shouts of three teenage boys.

Peura leans out over the edge, looks down at us. His chubby face is electric.

"It's working! I sent a test ping, just two short bursts of static followed by two long bursts. We got the same message back. Em, the *Xolotl* can hear us!"

And then, the city moans—the emergency siren.

*No, not now, NOT NOW!*

Gaston grabs my arm.

"Let Theresa out of her cell, *now*. I need her in the Control Room with me."

He sprints for the spiral staircase that leads to the elevator.

Nevins, Harman and Peura scramble down the rope ladder. They must have hit a switch, because the slab is already slowly lowering on its gold pillars.

Bishop scoops up Brewer's chair. Aramovsky and Kenzie walk with him, hands out, hovering to catch Brewer if Bishop stumbles, but Bishop does not.

I'm the last one down. As I descend the metal stairs, the slab closes above me, sealing out both the morning's light and most of the emergency siren's haunting drone.

That sound means only one thing: one of the alien ships is closing to attack range.

# TWENTY-SIX

I took Aramovsky back to his cell. He argued, said he wanted to go out and fight with everyone else, but I reminded him we would be fighting side by side with the Springers, and that they would probably kill him on sight.

When I put him in, I let Spingate out. She'd heard the alert horns, knew why I was there. We didn't say a word to each other.

Bishop is in the streets, getting our units into position. If the aliens land troops, we need to be ready.

Harman and Nevins stayed in the spiral stairwell below the antenna pillar. If the aliens attack the pillar, they are willing to rush out and make repairs.

Gaston is once again in his favorite spot, standing atop the Well wall.

Above the Well, the glowing display of Omeyocan, slowly spinning. A yellow dot comes slowly closer—the *Goblin*.

"No sign of the *Dragon*," Spingate calls out. "Or the *Xolotl*."

Gaston huffs. "Big surprise. As usual, when a fight comes, our progenitors are nowhere to be found."

Spingate is on the platform. Her belly, swollen. *I would have killed her and the baby both.* Milton Cathcart is with her, his eyes fixed on the icons floating above his pedestal. He's assumed Halim's duties, I suppose. Spingate has little Kevin in her sling. In a back corner of the room, Joandra Rigby leans against the wall, arms crossed. She's glaring at Spingate, glaring with pure venom.

Joandra, too? Is there anyone not turning into a horrible person?

I'm down on the floor, standing with Peura at a student pedestal. He's trying to reach the *Xolotl*.

"Ometeotl," Gaston calls out, "do we have a targeting solution?"

*"Not yet, Captain Xander. The* Goblin *is not yet in range. ETA to firing solution, forty-two seconds. Grandmaster Zubiri reports that the Goff Spear is loaded and ready to fire."*

A red ring appears on the display, the image of Omeyocan at its center.

"That red line is the Goff Spear's outer range. Once the *Goblin* crosses it, we can destroy it."

The yellow dot is coming closer. It looks like we have a few minutes before it reaches the red line. I don't want this battle to end the same way as the last. I'm hoping the *Xolotl* can help us somehow.

Peura's hands are covered in light. He's moving glowing icons, working the controls. I wish I knew what he was doing so I could assist—I feel so helpless.

He shakes his head. "The *Xolotl* isn't responding to pings, or anything else. I think it's beyond the horizon."

"Because it's *gone*," Gaston calls out. "Didn't you hear me? Those cowardly bastards ran away as soon as the *Goblin* started approaching. Matilda wants nothing to do with a space battle."

Matilda wants me to live, but not so badly that she's willing to fight those that attack us. Why am I not surprised?

We're on our own.

We've *always* been on our own.

Movement by Gaston's feet draws my attention—a black rope, looped over the Well's edge. I hadn't noticed it before. From inside the Well comes Huan Chowdhury's voice.

"Gaston, get out of the way!"

Gaston looks down into the shaft.

"You okay, Huan?"

"*Get out of the damned way or I swear I will stab you in the balls!*"

"I'll take that as a *no*," Gaston says, then walks a few steps along the circular top, his attention again returning to the display above him.

I squeeze Peura's shoulder. "Keep trying," I say, and walk to the Well.

Huan Chowdhury climbs up the rope, climbs up *fast*. He falls more than swings over, lands hard on the floor. I take a knee next to him.

"You're trembling," I say. "Did you see something down there?"

He's in a fetal position, shaking hands close to his chin. He wears a canvas climbing harness over his black coveralls. Every inch of him is covered in dirt and mud. His big teeth chatter. Not from the temperature, from fear.

"Huan!" I give his shoulders a shake. "I don't have time for this! What did you see?"

"Didn't . . . didn't see anything. Just felt something, down there with me."

He's acting like this because he got spooked?

I grab his harness, use it to sit him up. I thump his back against the Well wall, maybe a little too hard. People like me face down guns and hatchets, fight the *real* enemy, while people like Huan cower at shadows? Whatever he has to tell me, it better be good.

"You didn't see anything," I say. "Tell me what you *felt,* then."

"Been going through the tunnels." He's talking slowly, forcing his words through quivering lips. "End of the tunnel . . . wasn't hard dirt . . . I was able to push through it into another tunnel complex, one I hadn't seen before. It's *wet.* Wet and warm"—his eyes lock onto mine—"it felt like *breath.*"

My bottled-up anger swells, it pushes, looking for a way out.

"And that's it? You felt a warm draft and you panicked?"

He shakes his head hard. "No, it was more than that, I . . . I heard a voice. It was my mother. She said *Don't be afraid.*"

His mother? She's probably been dead as long as my mother has. Could he have heard Springers? They were in the Observatory long before we were. Maybe there's another way into those tunnels. But no, if it was Springers, there's no way Huan could mistake them for his own mother. He must have imagined it.

"Forget the voice," I say. "Did you actually *see* anything?"

He shakes his head again. "No. I was too scared, I ran."

He missed his godsdamned mommy. I needed this idiot boy to find information critical to our survival, and all he can do is piss his pants because he's afraid of shadows? What would he do if he ever faced *real* danger?

I yank Huan to his feet, shove him toward the door.

"Get out of my sight, you coward."

Still trembling from the fear of what he saw down there—and, perhaps, his fear of *me*—Huan sprints out of the Control Room.

"*Goblin* approaching firing range," Gaston says. "Em, if you're done intimidating little kids, think maybe we can focus on the alien race that's trying to kill us?"

The yellow dot of the *Goblin* creeps closer to the red line. When it gets there, I will give the order to fire—thousands of intelligent beings will die. It is an order I do not want to give.

There has to be another way.

I run back to Peura. The boy is still trying. He's on the verge of hyperventilating.

"You can't reach what isn't there," I say. "Instead, can you use the antenna to talk to the alien ship?"

"I . . . I don't know. I'll try."

"Don't bother," Gaston says. "We'll blow that ship out of the sky before they can launch an attack. Besides, they're aliens—even if we can reach their ship we can't communicate with them."

Gaston doesn't even want to try to stop this battle from happening? That's not like him. Or rather, that's not like the Gaston I used to know. Is this really how he wants to be, or is this unknown anger affecting him like it affected Bishop and Spingate?

Like it affected *me*.

I lean in close to Peura. "Don't worry about Gaston. Just try, all right?"

He nods, and once again his hands are a glowing blur.

On the big display above the Well, the *Goblin* has almost reached the red line.

"Ometeotl," Gaston says, "show me the *Goblin*'s probable maximum firing distance, and also maximum probable distance from which it can launch atmospheric-capable craft."

Two more lines appear. A purple one—marked MISSILE ZONE—appears a bit inside the red one that signifies Goff Spear's outer range. A blue line—marked LAUNCH DISTANCE—is farther inside the purple.

Gaston reaches out and touches the purple line, his fingers kicking up multicolored sparkles. He turns to look down at me.

"If the *Goblin* gets here, they can start firing. We don't know if they'll ignore the Observatory like the *Basilisk* did."

"Peura, *hurry*," I say quietly. "We have to talk to them now!"

He looks at me, wide-eyed, shaking his head. Stupid Em—this kid's nerves are shot, pressuring him isn't going to help.

"Take a breath and keep trying," I say, forcing myself to sound calm. "Just do your best."

Peura nods and gets back to work. I see sweat beading on his forehead, wetting his black hair.

"*The* Goblin *is entering Goff Spear range,*" the room calls out.

On the display, the glowing yellow dot touches the red line.

"Em, we're ready," Gaston says. "Give the command to fire."

I close my eyes. I don't believe in gods—I don't even believe the God of Blood is real and I *felt* it compel me to do violence—but for the first time I pray, pray to a god I know nothing about.

*Tlaloc, please, help us—please don't make me murder thousands, make them talk to us.*

There is no answer.

"Em, stop screwing around," Gaston says. "The *Goblin* is almost in missile-launch range."

I open my eyes. Sure enough, the yellow dot is past the red line and approaching the purple one.

"I'm sure I reached them," Peura says. "I'm sure of it. No response." He looks at me, shaking his head. "Em, I *know* they received our signal. If they wanted to reach us, they could."

Gaston glares down at me. "Em, *give the godsdamned order to fire!*"

The *Goblin* is almost to the purple line.

Every race that's come here has come to kill. The race populating the *Dragon* seems to control the *Goblin,* and even if they didn't, why would either race be any different from the Vellen, Springers and humans? These aliens are coming because of the same signal that brought us.

I tried to communicate. They didn't respond.

If I wait, my people die.

*Kill your enemies and you are forever free. . . .*

"Ometeotl," I say, "fire the Goff Spear."

The room thrums, pulses. I hear that buzzing sound, drowning out all other noise. Like before, my hair stands on end, my teeth and bones vibrate.

The room's air is sucked out and rushes back in.

The noise ceases, as does the thrumming vibration.

A red streak flashes out from Uchmal toward the *Goblin.*

"Increase magnification on target ship," Gaston says.

The display above him changes. We see the *Goblin*'s green front, the yellow symbol etched there. I realize that I will never get a chance to know what that symbol means.

The wait is agonizing. The red streak draws closer. It seems an eternity before our weapon connects. The *Goblin* swells, swells, swells . . . then rips apart.

"*Target destroyed,*" the room says.

Cathcart and Peura whoop with joy. Gaston shakes his fist at the image of the ship breaking into a hundred pieces.

But something is wrong. . . .

"*Possible contact,*" Ometeotl says. "*Significant interference from the detonation. There may be a solid mass beyond it.*"

"Oh no," Gaston says. "Ometeotl, tell Zubiri to reload the

Goff Spear, right now! And ask her how long until we can fire again!"

Spingate takes a reactive step back from her pedestal. Her arms wrap protectively around little Kevin.

"What's happening?" I ask.

No one answers.

I walk to the Well wall and look up at Gaston.

"Gaston, what is it?"

He points to the wreckage of the *Goblin*.

"The *Dragon*," he says. "We couldn't see it because it was in the blind spot behind the *Goblin*."

Through the cloud of wreckage, I see the *Dragon*'s plain white flat front coming closer.

Our radio telescope's waves radiate out in an ever-expanding sphere—when that sphere hit the *Goblin*, anything behind the ship was invisible to us.

The evil of what I just witnessed . . .

"They used the *Goblin* as a screen," I say. "They knew full well we would destroy it. They sacrificed thousands of lives to get closer to us."

"Zoom out," Gaston says.

The image above him changes: Omeyocan, the blue LAUNCH DISTANCE line, beyond that the purple MISSILE ZONE line, the red line of the Goff Spear's outer range.

The *Dragon*'s green dot passes through the red line.

"*Grandmaster Zubiri is reloading,*" Ometeotl says. "*Eight minutes, twelve seconds before the Goff Spear can fire again.*"

"Gods," Spingate says. "That's not enough time."

We watched, transfixed, as the green dot passes through the purple MISSILE ZONE line.

And keeps going, without firing any weapons.

I understand their strategy—the *Dragon* is going to launch

landing craft, then retreat out of our range before we can destroy it. They will try, anyway—they don't know how long it will take us to reload. Whatever race is on that ship, it's a race that is willing to gamble.

The *Dragon* closes in on the purple line.

"Ometeotl," I say, "do you acknowledge my absolute authority?"

*"Yes, Empress Savage."*

"Then I transfer authorization to fire the Goff Spear to Captain Xander Gaston."

*"Order understood and implemented, Empress Savage."*

The green dot reaches the purple line.

As soon as it does, dozens of tiny green dots fly away from it.

*"Ships launched,"* Ometeotl says. *"Twenty-one small fighter craft and six larger craft—most likely transports. Approximately seventeen minutes until they reach Uchmal."*

I can do no more here.

"Gaston, don't activate the antimissile batteries until you get my signal, understand?"

He nods without looking at me. "I know the plan, Em. And if I get a shot at *Dragon,* I'll kill it. Now get out there and kick some ass."

Is this the last time I will see him? The last time I will see Theresa?

I look to the platform. Theresa's eyes meet mine.

"I believe in you," she says. "Please come back to us."

I hope I do.

Without another word, I leave to join my troops.

# TWENTY-SEVEN

I rush from the Observatory into the morning light. Beneath the *Ximbal*'s wings, Bishop waits with two dozen members of our army. Humans and Springers both. These are the squad leaders who will soon rush to their units and give the final commands.

Uchmal is about to become a battleground.

High above, Omeyocan's atmosphere eats up the *Goblin*'s pieces. That ship traveled an unknown, impossible distance to bring its people here. Now it is nothing but streaks of burning metal.

I've wiped out another race.

Em Savage: bringer of extinction.

Our emergency siren fills the air, but already another sound is fighting it for dominance—the echoing roar of approaching aircraft.

Far off to the west, high in the sky, I see a cluster of tiny black dots.

We don't have long.

I sprint across the plaza to our shuttle. The squad leaders part, close in behind me as I stand next to Bishop.

I face my fellow soldiers. Sunlight glints off muskets and rifles, bayonets and knives, hatchets and long-pointed bracelets, farm tools and spears. Farrar is stone-faced. The younger circlestars look excited but worried. They might soon be fighting for their lives. I wish Maria was here, but her unit is out in the jungle.

Oddly, I feel no doubts about the coming battle. We will not back down. We will not run and hide.

I was born a circle. A slave. Now I am a leader. A warrior. A general.

I am a killer, and it is time to kill.

"We didn't ask for this fight," I say to my soldiers. "The antenna is working. We tried to contact the *Goblin,* talk to whoever or *what*ever is on that ship—we were ignored."

My soldiers exchange glances. They're scared, of course, but now they think this fight might have been avoided if only the enemy had spoken with me. That makes my soldiers *mad.*

Good. Anger is better than fear.

I pound my fist against my chest, three times, punctuating my words.

"Let . . . them . . . *come*! We are ready. We, who have sweated here, bled here, *died* here. We who have been here for centuries, and we who were *created* for this planet."

The Springers who understand my words translate for those who do not. Heads nod. Faces tighten with commitment, with the hard knowledge that war has come to our doorstep.

"Remember our strategy," I say. "We know this city, they do not. Use upper floors to your advantage. Enter a building, identify your exits, then find windows and fire down upon your enemy. When they come up to get you, melt away and do it again. *Remember the signals*—horns and flags both. Once the fighting starts, things will break down. You'll have to think for yourselves. You—"

"*Hem!*"

The single, hoarse syllable cuts me off.

I turn. Lahfah is mounted on her galloping hurukan, a handful of Springers hopping along behind. All of them are filthy, their jungle rags so covered in ash that wisps of the stuff trail along behind them.

She's supposed to be out in the jungle. I start to get angry, wonder what she's doing here, then she raises her hand high—she's holding a spear.

*My* spear.

Lahfah brings the hurukan to a halt a few steps away. She dismounts, offers me the spear. The shaft is lightly charred in a few places, but still looks solid. And the blade . . . it's undamaged. The edge catches a glint of red sun, and I know that Lahfah just sharpened it.

I take the weapon. Char instantly blackens my fingers and palms, but I don't care—I have my spear.

How long has she been searching the ruins for this?

She knows what the spear means to me, to all of us. With it comes belief—I was ready to fight, now I'm ready to *win*.

"Thank you," I say.

"War," she answers. From the mouths of Springers or humans, it seems, that word sounds identical.

From a pocket of my coveralls, I pull out a strip of white cloth streaked with dried blood. I tie it around my head. My soldiers stare at it, take in Halim Horn's null-set symbol.

"Today, we are not Springers," I say. "We are not humans. We are not circles, circle-stars or anything else. We, *all of us,* we are the people of Omeyocan."

I raise the spear. This piece of wood and metal that has come to symbolize so much to both races. Every eye stares up at it, draws strength from it.

"Today, we will fight for what is *ours*," I say. "Why will we win? Because *we live here!* To your positions!"

For a moment, the combined battle cry of two peoples drowns out the incoming rockets' roar, then my soldiers rush to their assigned places.

Victor and I crouch on a fifth-floor balcony in the southwest quadrant. We're high enough up that I can see over the walls. I watch the incoming ships streaking in from the west above the jungle canopy—twenty-one thin fighters that are all sharp angles and points, and six fat troopships packed with enemy soldiers.

The ships are almost in range of our tower cannons.

Bawden is on the ground floor with our spider, hidden from view.

In buildings to the north and southeast of me, lookouts in balconies stay low, watching my every move. They're waiting to relay my signals.

The roar of the incoming ships is so loud there is almost no point in talking—I'd have to scream in Victor's ear to be heard at all.

Our towers open fire.

Bright white cannon beams lace the sky. One of the smaller enemy ships explodes in a cloud of reddish-orange flame. The wrecked vessel tumbles down and disappears into the yellow jungle.

Unlike Brewer's lumpy ship, the fighters shoot back. They pulse with amber flashes, give birth to tiny missiles trailing long cones of gray smoke.

Those missiles close the distance in seconds. Two of them smack into the five o'clock tower, *boom, boom*. The top of the tower vanishes in a billowing fireball, thick chunks of stone spin away in all directions.

I know who was manning that gun: Isaac Hachilinski and Cassie Nauer. Two shuttle kids. Two circles. They lived barely a year, and now they are gone.

The wave of attacking ships passes over the wall. Another fighter explodes. A tower beam lances through one of the fat troopships—trailing flame, it plummets into a ten-layered ziggurat.

Missiles snake into the seven o'clock tower. The fireball sends stone flying, launches the silvery cannon—now twisted and warped—whirling end over end into the city, where it crashes into a soot-caked building.

Joannes Tosetti and Liselot Wieck. Dead.

We've already lost two towers. The fighters roar above me, a swarm of death heading for the center of the city. I can wait no more.

I lean toward Victor, hold up one finger.

He stands and waves his orange flag: down-left-down-up-left. The north lookout sees this. She stands, faces the Observatory, then uses her own flag to mimic Victor's sequence.

As enemy fighters bank and swerve above Uchmal, flag waver after flag waver quickly relays the simple message back to Gaston and Spingate, safe in the Control Room's depths.

Halfway up the Observatory, long black antimissile barrels slide out of hidden slots.

Our mountain of stone becomes a giant monster swatting at the gnats buzzing through the sky. The air fills with crisscrossing streaks of missile smoke, white tower cannon beams and the ragged red flashes of the antimissile batteries.

Fighters explode, one after another.

South of my building, a fat troopship angles toward a wide street. One second it is flying smoothly, descending to unload whatever it carries, the next a stream of red fire reaches out from the Observatory's southwest corner. The troopship erupts into a thousand flaming pieces, a deadly hail of bouncing metal that scatters in all directions.

When this battle began, only fifteen of the Observatory's antimissile rounds remained. I knew waiting to use those might cost us tower cannons, but we had to make sure the enemy ships were so close they couldn't be missed, we had to make every antimissile round count. That strategy resulted in the deaths of at least four of my people—in a way, I sacrificed them to lure the enemy in.

I am a killer. That is who I am.

That choice may haunt my dreams later, but for now it seems to have worked. The surviving fighters point their noses straight up and accelerate on columns of flame; they must be heading back to the *Dragon*. I count only ten of them—we destroyed the rest.

Victor thumps me on the back. "Em, it worked! The skies are clear!"

Springer horns sound from the southeast. Three long notes, then two short, then two long—the alert signal for ground fighting.

At least one troopship landed.

We've knocked their ships out of the sky, but the battle isn't over.

Now the fight moves to the streets.

# TWENTY-EIGHT

Bawden guides our spider through the streets. Victor grips the cannon controls. My bracelet hums with the promise of death.

This won't be like the battle with the Belligerents. They were dangerous enough with their muskets and bayonets, but this time our enemy came from the stars.

What weapons will we face?

My squad's other two spiders crawl along behind us, our circle-star infantry behind them.

Up ahead, rifle and musket fire echoes through the streets, off tall stone buildings darkened by fire and dusted with ash. I hear the crackling sizzle of bracelet beams, the *whuff* of spider cannons, shouts of rage . . . and screams.

Screams of wounded humans and Springers. A third kind as well. This kind chitters. It clicks. It hums.

The screams of our enemy.

And, above it all, far off in the distance, the low rumbling of rockets. I look up, search, but the skies above Uchmal remain clear.

The sound of battle grows louder. We're closing in. I can *smell* it, too, the stench of gunpowder and burning machines.

Bawden turns a corner.

The street is partially blocked by the wreck of a sleek fighter craft. Thick black smoke billows from its shattered shell. Part of the fighter remains stuck in a building three stories up, smoldering with unseen fire.

Next to the wreck lie two dead bodies—one human, one Springer, both with horrific, gaping wounds of mangled flesh and splintered bone. They died so recently that their blood still spreads, red swirling with blue, both mixing with the street's ash, dirt and gravel. I don't recognize the Springer. The human is facedown, thankfully—one less name I have to know right now.

Bawden drives past the wreck and the bodies, stops the spider at the next intersection, just close enough for me to look around the corner.

Two blocks down the street, a troopship. Where our shuttle is streamlined, silver and sleek, the alien ship is thick, segmented and spiny. Its dark gray color eats up the morning sun. Unknown symbols on its hull gleam in rich shades of violet.

Like maggots spilling forth from a rotten fruit, enemy soldiers scurry around the troopship, looking for cover against blistering rifle, musket and bracelet fire that pours down from buildings on either side of the street. The enemy soldiers move fast. I can't quite make out what they look like, because their colors shift and swirl, matching those of the street or building or ship or wreckage around them.

The aliens return fire. Their bulky black rifles stutter with orange muzzle flashes, bullets ripping fist-sized chunks from the stone walls around the windows.

I see something moving on top of the troopship—an armored turret with a stubby barrel. It reminds me of our tower cannons. The barrel lets loose a gout of flame and a deafening boom; down the street, a third-floor balcony erupts in a blossom of fire and stone, and I know that more of my people are dead.

The enemy ship . . . it looks undamaged. If it landed, can it take off again? Can it fly?

I grab Victor.

"When we charge, *don't hit the ship*. We're going to capture it. See if you can take out its cannon up on top."

I lean out over the armored ridge and shout back to the rest of our squad. The other two spiders are close behind, the circle-stars crouched around their legs.

"We're going in! Spiders, protect our flanks, and *do not* target the enemy landing craft. Circle-stars, follow us in. The enemy has camouflage armor that lets them hide easily. That will make them hard to find if they escape, so make sure none of them do!"

I slide back into the spider's protected cockpit, knowing that some of my circle-stars are going to die today.

*Attack, attack, when in doubt, always attack.*

I draw a deep breath, feel my lungs expand. I take a fraction of a second to center myself. These could be my last moments of life. If I die, I want to die a good death.

It's time.

My held breath erupts as a roaring battle cry.

"Bawden, *chaaaaaaaarge!*"

I duck low and hold on tight as our war machine turns the corner and hurtles toward the enemy. Bullets hammer against the metal spider, *ping-ping-ping*, so many hitting so fast it sounds like a musical instrument. Behind us, my circle-stars fire rifles and bracelets between our spiders' legs.

My heart kicks so hard each beat makes my vision twitch. My mouth tastes like sand. It will only take seconds to reach the enemy, yet each instant drags out for eternity.

*I don't want to get shot, I don't want to die. . . .*

Victor fires the cannon—the troopship's turret explodes in a thousand pieces.

A roaring boom: our spider tilts hard left. I slam into Bawden, but hang on. The spider levels out, each step a lurch that tosses me forward, then back, but we keep advancing.

I rise up just enough to aim my bracelet.

A frozen moment, a blur of images. An alien close ahead, armor shifting from tan to black to brown to ash-gray, the colors of the city. Limbs that are too long, joints too small. A dancer's graceful fluidity. Spikes and curving protrusions—part of the armor, or part of the creature beneath? Black rifle firing, muzzle flashes lighting up the alien like an orange strobe light.

I flick my fingers forward.

My bracelet's beam blinds me for an instant. By the time I can see again, the alien is no more. I've reduced that elegant creature to splatters of flesh, spinning bits of armor and a fading mist of yellow blood.

The sounds of war and death: relentless, unforgiving. Rifles, muskets, bracelets, beam cannons, the *rat-tat-tat-tat* of alien weapons, explosions, roaring fire, screams of agony. I'm terrified beyond measure, waiting for a bit of metal to punch through me and end my short life.

Victor fires the spider cannon again. The beam slices into the street, turning paving rocks into a blurring cloud of stone shrapnel, sending a pair of aliens spinning through the air.

The armored aliens rush forward to meet our charge. They

should be retreating into the buildings, finding places to hide and fight from cover. They have better weapons, yes, but we outnumber them and hold higher ground—their behavior makes no sense.

Bullets ricochet off the spider's armor.

I fire again, killing another enemy soldier just as their charge meets ours.

Our spider's front leg slashes down, long metal claw impaling an alien, punching through color-shifting armor as if it were paper. The alien's click-hum-chitter scream of death is awful, a sound I know will never fully leave my ears.

We're through their charge and closing in on the troopship. Behind me I hear the battle cry of my young circle-stars as they meet the line of armored aliens. Rifles fire, knives slash, spears thrust. People die. The air splits with a numbing howl of war so horrific the God of Blood must be dancing to its tune.

The landing craft's rear end is open, a monster's maw with a wide ramp serving as the tongue. At the top of the ramp, two aliens fire away at us.

"Bawden, drive us inside!"

The lurching spider pivots as she obeys.

Victor unslings his rifle. He crouches low, his body mostly protected by the spider's ridge. His legs bend with each lurching movement, keeping his head and chest impossibly level. He fires the rifle, flicks the black loop lever beneath it forward with a *clack* that reloads the weapon, fires again, his movements fast and sure.

One of the aliens falls from the ramp.

I mimic Victor's stance. I hold my spear tight in my left hand, raise my right arm, aim at the alien and fire. My shot goes wide, hits somewhere inside the landing craft.

Bawden's lips curl back into a primitive snarl—our spider

scurries up the ramp and into the fat bug-ship. Open sky gives way to gray ceiling.

The last alien leaps into the cockpit, smashing into all of us and knocking me hard against the armored ridge. Victor grapples with it, the alien's armor a swirling pattern of cockpit, black coveralls and Victor's face.

Bawden is between me and the alien. She draws her knife and thrusts—the blade skids off color-shifting armor. I drop my spear and lunge over her, grab the alien's arm. It twists, trying to throw me off. Victor snatches his rifle up from the spider's metal deck, jams the barrel under the creature's chin—*bang*clack*bang*clack*bang,* three bullets rip through the helmet.

The dead alien falls into Bawden, who stumbles into me and knocks me backward. I tumble over the spider's armored ridge.

The back of my head slams against metal.

Everything swirls around me . . . I try to rise . . . I can't . . . blackness drags me under.

# TWENTY-NINE

Odors engulf me: antiseptic, wet charcoal, scorched stone, blood, smoke, grease . . . burning flesh. This is what pain smells like, what *death* smells like.

And *damn*, does my head hurt.

I'm still in the landing craft, sitting on a crate of some kind. Kenzie Smith is stitching a gash on the back of my head.

I was out for a while, apparently. By the time she woke me up, the battle was over.

Bishop could be alive, dead, injured . . . I haven't heard from his unit.

The inside of this alien ship looks strange, but the design is obvious in concept: it was built to carry hundreds of tightly packed troops from one place to another, with little thought given to comfort. Everything is the same flat, dark gray as the outside.

The spider is still in here. Seeing it crammed into this tight space, I'm even more impressed with Bawden's driving skills. I wonder if the dead alien remains in the cockpit where Victor killed it.

The spider hull bears hundreds of new dents, yellow and brown paint dotted with gleaming spots where bullets hit home. The leg closest to me is badly bent, metal torn apart on its top segment. I hope Borjigin can fix the damage quickly and get 05 back into service.

"Finished," Kenzie says. I feel a sting as she wipes at the newly stitched cut. She walks around in front of me. Her fingertips gently turn my head this way and that. Every motion feels like a sledgehammer thudding into my brain.

"Your skull is thick," she says. "Usually, that's the cause of many problems, but in this case it helps."

She's making a joke. That means I'm all right.

Something flies over the spider's armored ridge and clanks against the metal floor. The something rolls once, stops when it hits my foot. It's the alien's helmet, with three gore-smeared bullet holes in the top. No swirling colors now, it's just a dull shade of gray.

Kalle's head peeks over the spider's ridge.

"Em, come up and see this!"

I start to rise. Kenzie puts a hand on my shoulder.

"You can go when I'm *finished*," she says.

I knock her hand away and stand. The sudden movement makes my throbbing head flush with new pain.

"I'm good for now," I say. "I'll see you in the Observatory later."

Kenzie huffs.

"You never listen to the people you *need* to listen to," she says. "Thick skull indeed. I should have tended to the seriously wounded first, but here I thought I should take care of our *leader* before anyone else. Silly me."

With that, she picks up a big bag of medical supplies and trudges down the ramp, out of the ship.

I watch her go with a sense of longing—I should have asked for a painkiller. My head hurts so bad I can barely think.

"*Em!*" Kalle's shout echoes off the troopship's walls, makes me wince. "I said get up here!"

I press my fingertips to my temples. I look up at the tiny tooth-girl. She smiles and vanishes behind the ridge.

The fact that she's here at all tells me we control the city. That's good, but there's still much to do. I need a casualty report. What's our ammunition situation? Did we take any prisoners?

I need to get out there and see what's going on. But when I do, I'll learn how many of my people died. I just can't handle that yet. Seeing what Kalle has to show me will delay that news for a few moments.

Slowly, I climb the spider's rungs and slide over the ridge into the cockpit. The dead alien lies in a fingertip-thick pool of thick yellow fluid. Kalle is kneeling in the stuff; it's all over her black coveralls, her hands, even her face.

She grins up at me.

"Isn't this amazing?"

The alien's armor lies scattered about. Kalle removed all of it. The once-graceful creature is now nothing but a pile of dead flesh.

Its skin looks stiff. Maybe *shell* is a better term than *skin*. I've never seen a color like this. Some of the jungle's brighter flowers might come close to it. Matilda's memories call up a name: *fuchsia*. The color is so bright and beautiful—it seems out of place on an unmoving corpse.

Two arms, two legs and a head, but any similarity to humans ends there. The legs and arms have three sections, not two, and they're *thin;* my arms are to this creature's what Bishop's are to mine. The alien's joints seem so small they might break at the slightest movement.

Narrow chest, a waist so tiny I could wrap my hands around it with forefingers and thumbs touching. Standing up, this creature must be a whole head taller than me, but I would outweigh it by quite a bit.

The spikes I saw weren't a part of the armor, they came *through* it. The spikes are long and delicate, like curved rose thorns that jut out of the alien's arms and shoulders.

Matilda's memories fire. The narrow joints, the shiny shell, the long curves. There's only one thing in her past that even remotely resembles this creature. That insect, stinging her—stinging *me*—when she was only four years old. The burning sensation . . . the fear.

"It kind of looks like a Solomon wasp," I say.

Kalle stops her work, looks the corpse up and down.

"A little bit," she says. "Better nickname than *jungle rat,* I'll give you that."

I don't have the energy to yell at her.

Compared to this willowy form, our human bodies are thick and brutish. Victor's bullets mangled the top of the alien's head, but I can still make out a face. At least I *think* it's a face. Long and thin. A slate-blue ridge runs down the middle.

I point down at two thick bumps halfway up the face, one on either side of the ridge.

"Are those eyes?"

Kalle nods. She uses her finger and thumb to pry one open. Beneath the lids is a corn-silk-yellow eye. Other than the color, the eye looks so much like a human's that I lean away in an unconscious reaction of horror and surprise.

I expect the eye to move, to focus, to see me.

It won't, of course—not unless these things can live with the tops of their heads blown apart.

Kalle lets go. The lids slowly close.

First the Springers, now this. Life—*intelligent* life—must come in many, many forms. What did the aliens on the *Basilisk* look like? We will never know.

I leave Kalle to her gruesome work. I'm shaken to my core. That creature . . . so *beautiful,* yet it came here to kill us.

I walk down the ramp. The stench of war hits me anew. Long curls of smoke drift in from some unseen fire. Dead wasp-aliens litter the ground. There are Springer bodies, too. And, of course, the fallen of my own people. A circle's face stares out blankly. I recognize him—*I. Tosto.* Strange first name, what was it? Oh yes: *Iseult.*

Iseult has a hole in his chest the size of my fist.

My platoon's other two spiders are heavily dented, but it looks like they didn't take any serious damage.

Our wounded—human and Springer both—are laid out all over the place. Kenzie and Pokano bark out orders to tend to this cut, that broken arm. Victor, Bawden and the other circle-stars jump to obey, to help their fellow soldiers.

Tina Schuster scurries from person to person—dead and alive alike. She's doing a head count. Soon she'll give me that casualty report. Maybe my brain will stop throbbing by the time she does. I hope so, because when I see that report, my heart will hurt far more than my head ever could.

Behind me, I hear the metal feet of a spider coming down the street. My three are accounted for, which means this one is from another platoon. I start to turn, but I freeze.

The spider has to be from Bishop's unit.

What if he's not in it?

What if it's someone come to tell me he's gone?

I've lost O'Malley . . . I can't lose Bishop, too.

The spider stops behind me.

I force myself to look.

Bishop stands alone in the cockpit, smiling at me.

Relief hits me so hard it buckles my knees. It's all I can do to keep from collapsing.

He swings a leg over the ridge and drops down. My sense of command and responsibility vanish as I run to him, throw my arms around his neck. He squeezes me tight, so tight I can't breathe, but I don't *want* to breathe, I want him to hold me like this forever so I know he's real and he's *alive* and he's *mine*.

Bishop steps back. He places his right arm on my shoulder. I place mine on his.

"Hail, Em."

"Hail, Bishop."

He's as happy to see me alive as I am to see him, but there is work to be done.

"Three troopships landed inside the city walls," he says. "One was heavily damaged. Barkah's Springers got to that one first. They took no prisoners. My unit found the other troopship. We had them surrounded, but they kept fighting. It's almost like the aliens didn't want to live at all, like they came here to die."

Just like the ones I fought. There is something to that, something I need to figure out quickly.

"Was the landing ship damaged in the fight?"

He shakes his head. "Not much. I figured if it landed, it could fly, so I charged it on foot, killed the two aliens inside and captured it." He pats my shoulder, gives me an admiring grin. "I sure wish *I'd* been smart enough to drive a spider inside of it."

I see the pride on his face. It makes me feel good.

We didn't plan to capture any ships, but under fire he and I had the same instinct. Now we have two troopships. Can we learn to fly them? Or do they have fuel that would work with *Ximbal*'s engines? If either answer is yes, our new enemy has made a critical mistake.

"What about the *Dragon*?" I ask.

"Gaston sent a runner with news. It was out of range by the time the Goff Spear was ready to fire again. We can't hit it, but at least we won the day. We're victorious."

I glance around, take in our casualties.

This is victory?

"There's something else," Bishop says. "Gaston's runner also had a message from the hospital—it's Brewer. His end is near, and he wants to see you."

# THIRTY

The hospital has never been this full.

Most of the white coffins are closed, wounded circles, circle-stars and Springers inside. I still don't have casualty numbers, but the battle cost us dearly.

Smith, Yilmaz and Pokano try to be everywhere at once, constantly checking dozens of wounded. The three of them must be exhausted, but they fight on, show no signs of slowing.

I sit in a chair next to an open coffin at the room's far end, away from the bustle. Inside the coffin: Brewer. The pedestal display beeps in time with the slow beat of his heart.

The time for questions has passed. This is about him now.

"Of all the people I'd want by my side when I die," he says, "you're last on the list."

Kenzie told me there's nothing left that can be done.

B. Brewer is in his last moments. Yilmaz gave him drugs to take away most of his pain. Considering he's spent an eternity in agony, that's a blessing.

His mask is gone. A thin, clear tube runs into the fleshy folds where his mouth should be.

"If you'd like someone else, I'll get them for you," I say. "Suit yourself."

His wrinkled body jiggles with laughter, the bone-scraping-bone sound I remember all too well, but there is something new in it. This is *real* laughter, the kind made from joy—not from sarcasm.

"Oh, my-my-my," he says. "Did you hear that, Mattie? An actual laugh. And it didn't even hurt."

His voice is soft, weak. He knows he is dying, yet he seems to enjoy these final moments. To suffer for so long, then to be free of pain . . . that must be like heaven itself.

He called me *Mattie*. A small part of me remembers that name—that's what he called Matilda when they were little. When they were childhood friends.

He again thinks I'm her. If that's who he wants at his side, I'll play along as best I can.

"I'm sorry for everything," I say. "I know that doesn't help, but I am."

He stares at me for a moment. His big red eyes are fading to pink.

"Do you know why you're the last person on that list, Mattie? Because everyone else on that list has been dead for a long, long time."

He raises one thin, gnarled hand toward me. I take it, hold it gently, afraid I might break him. His skin feels paper-thin. Only a trace of warmth remains.

"Where did we go wrong?" he asks. "We did what we were told. We obeyed. We served. Why didn't we get the reward that was promised to us?"

His words dig at my soul. He never had a choice. And because he stood up to Matilda—for reasons I still don't understand—he lost his chance to be reborn.

"Because people lie," I say. "They tell us what we'd like to hear so they can get what they want."

His other hand rises up, pats my knuckles.

"At least I got to see Omeyocan," he says. "So many did not."

I hear his heartbeat slowing.

"I wish there was something I could do," I say.

He gently pulls his hand away.

"There is . . . one thing," he says. His voice is so soft now I have to lean close to hear him.

"Anything, Brewer. Anything at all."

Color briefly flares back into his eyes. "Tell me it was worth it. Tell me all the pain, the sacrifice . . . the *loneliness* . . . tell me it was worth it. Tell me my life *mattered*."

People lie, yes, but this time, at least, I can tell the honest truth.

"You saved us," I say. "Yes, your life matters, because you used it to give life to others. The Birthday Children will never forget what you've done. They will never forget *you*."

For an instant, the red eyes sharpen. They see me, recognize me.

He doesn't have a mouth, but I think he's smiling.

The eyes fade from red to pink.

The heartbeat changes from a slow beep to a flat, unwavering tone.

Brewer's eyes turn white.

He is gone.

# THIRTY-ONE

We gather around a crater to say goodbye once again.

It's a bigger crater than last time, because we have more bodies.

Three rows of them this time.

In all, we have seventy-two dead: Brewer, eight young circle-stars, nine circles, fifty-four Springers, lined up shoulder to shoulder in no particular order. Brewer lies at the center of the middle row. Coal-black, withered and gnarled, he's flanked on one side by a circle-star boy of thirteen, and on the other by a Springer missing part of her head.

The Malbinti usually bury their dead, but not this time. Barkah insisted that his soldiers fell fighting for Uchmal, so they should be memorialized as people from Uchmal are. They fought together, they died together, they will burn together.

It's a touching sentiment, further cementing the bonds between his people and mine.

Humans and Springers line the crater's edge. Barkah already

gave his speech. Now Walezak is giving hers, the ceremonial funeral torch held high.

I wonder how many more of these mass burials we'll have.

Considering there are only 249 Birthday Children left, there won't be that many before we're all gone.

"So we say goodbye," Walezak says. "And we say *thank you* for being part of our lives."

This time I don't miss my cue, but I no longer give a damn about words that came from some meaningless religion. With everyone watching, I walk to Walezak and take the torch from her hand.

"You will not be forgotten," I say. "Those responsible for your deaths will pay. I swear it."

I toss the torch into the crater.

Flames catch instantly, a *whoof* that engulfs the corpses as one. Borjigin seems to have his accelerants under control. That's good, at least—we need every weapon we can get.

# THIRTY-TWO

The *Dragon* has again vanished beyond the horizon.

Bishop is in charge of redistributing our troops, filling in gaps left by casualties. Borjigin is repairing our spiders, Opkick is distributing ammunition, and so on. It's a team effort, really.

Except that right now, the effort doesn't involve me.

I sit in my room in the Observatory, sharpening my spear. I'm waiting for Peura to come get me. The *Xolotl* is in range again. He assured me that it won't be long until he makes contact.

Right now, I want to be alone. I need a few minutes to think about our situation.

My personal things were destroyed when my home collapsed. This room contains a straw mattress made by the Springers, one extra pair of boots, two extra black coveralls, and my weapons.

We are at war—what other possessions do I need?

Just one: the white pedestal that stands in the corner, waiting to be activated.

I run the sharpening stone along the blade, as Coyotl once

showed me. The sound of stone on metal is comforting. This is something I can control.

I miss Coyotl. I miss so many people.

The Wasps launched six landing craft. Each one held 666 enemy soldiers—an invading army of almost four thousand. Half of them died when their ships were shot down by tower cannons or the Observatory's antimissile defenses.

Two craft landed successfully. One crash-landed. Schuster counted a total of 1,612 alien troops that made it out of those ships.

We killed them all.

Bishop and Farrar are raving that we "only" lost seventy-one soldiers, are elated about a "kill ratio" of almost twenty-three to one. They're sad for our losses, of course, but at their core they're built for war; they accept that every battle brings casualties.

Which is part of why I want to be alone. The fact that Bishop is *excited* about our "major victory," as he calls it, disgusts me. The battle had an effect I didn't see coming: my people seem much calmer. The tension and the increased need for violence have eased away. That in itself disturbs me, as if our desire for blood is quenched.

For now, anyway. I have a feeling that desire will build up again, and soon.

I need answers. Brewer is gone—I must get those answers from someone else.

From someone I never wanted to speak to again.

A knock on my door.

"Come in."

The door opens. Peura enters. His lips are horribly chapped. He's been chewing on them, a nervous tic. Poor kid is a wreck.

"The *Xolotl* is in range," he says.

I stand. I think of putting the spear in a corner, but change my mind—for this conversation, I'd rather hold it.

"Connect me," I say.

We step to the pedestal. He waves his hands over the flat top. Glowing symbols appear. He moves them, turns them, then steps back. His hands grip each other, squeeze so hard the fingers look bleach-white.

"It's ready," he says. "Just tap the pedestal, and it will call the *Xolotl*. I don't know who will answer, or if anyone will answer at all. Do you want me to stay and make sure it works?"

"No. Stand in the hallway, please. Close enough I can call you if I need you."

He leaves, closes the door behind himself.

I tap the pedestal. Sparkles of color flare to life, a glimmering, shining cloud that appears out of nowhere. The sparkles immediately coalesce into a gray shape that darkens, then turns black.

It is the head and shoulders of a Grownup.

A Grownup with one eye.

Matilda.

"Thank the gods," she says. "You're still intact."

Genuine relief in her voice, but those words—not *you're alive*, but rather, *you're intact*. To her I am not a person, I am an object. A vessel to be filled.

Her good eye whirls with intensity, with blatant hunger for my mind, my body, my life. The other eye is covered by a hard, shiny piece of white plastic. That's the eye I ruined when we fought.

The very sight of her makes my skin crawl.

"Yes, I'm *intact*, no thanks to you. You fled when the *Goblin* came close. You're the same coward you have always been."

"Oh, *please*," Matilda says. "Our ship has already been through one battle, darling-dear, which was one too many. Or did you think the vessel that brought those hopping vermin simply dropped them off and then flew away?"

That explains why we've never seen any sign of a Springer mother ship. The Grownups must have destroyed it about the same time they bombed the Springer city.

"So you can't help us," I say. "You can't help defend this planet you've spent your too-long life pursuing?"

"We're trying to build a tanker ship. If we can deliver fuel to the shuttle, you can come up here, out of danger."

The laugh that escapes me sounds like that of an insane woman.

"*Out of danger?* How in hell's name do you think me walking into the viper's nest, coming *to you,* puts me out of danger? You, who sent a senile old man to do your dirty work, want me to come up there and, what . . . *trust* you?"

She waves a hand, dismissing my words.

"Brewer doesn't have a receptacle. His brain is rotting away. He's useless."

"And now he's gone."

She pauses.

"Brewer is dead?"

"He is," I say. "Natural causes."

She sent him here, knowing his days were numbered, but his passing seems to catch her unawares, as if reality suddenly doesn't match how she thought she'd feel.

"It's irrelevant," Matilda says. "He's lucky that I gave him a final way to serve and didn't have someone slice his throat."

I feel a mad grin spread across my face.

"You would have someone else do it, because you've never done your own dirty work, right? You don't know what it's like to put that knife in, to twist it, to watch someone die at your hand."

Her spindly fingers curl into a shaking fist.

"*Who do you think you are?* I *made* you! You are *nothing.* You don't *exist*! Did you take *my body* out to fight the invaders?"

I lean close to her image, so close that if we were actually face-to-face the spit of my scream would splatter against her good eye and plastic patch both.

"You're godsdamned right I did! I led my people. I'm willing to die for them, if need be—unlike *you,* you sniveling coward!"

Her twisted knot of a fist becomes a frail finger aimed at my face, jabs out and hits my forehead in splashes of multicolored sparkles.

"You put my perfect body at risk defeating that little token force! I've waited *twelve centuries* for that body, you horrible little worthless *bitch*!"

Matilda vibrates like a leaf in a tree. Spit hangs from her mouth-folds. Her one red eye blazes so bright it lights up the gnarled black skin around it.

I was just as furious as she was, but my fury was blasted clean away by two words.

"*Token force?* What does that mean?"

She leans back. She wipes the wetness from her mouth-folds. The glow of her eye returns to normal.

"It means the ships that landed in Uchmal were a diversion, you stupid infant. They screened your radio telescopes from seeing the *real* force, which they landed a few hundred kilometers to the northeast, well beyond the ruins of the vermin city."

She's lying. She has to be. We *won.* But . . . during the battle . . .

"The other rockets I heard. I thought those were an echo."

"They were not," Matilda says. "There's some kind of interference coming from Omeyocan that is screwing with our sensors, so we don't have exact numbers, but Gaston thinks at least twenty troop transports landed."

Gaston. *Her* Gaston, the one she fled the planet with.

Wait . . . *twenty*? No, it would be twenty-*one*, another gods-damned multiple of three, I know it, and if those troopships are the same size as the ones that landed in our streets, that would be a force of . . .

"Fourteen thousand." The words leak out of me, little more than a whine of escaping air. "They landed *fourteen thousand* troops?"

"So it appears," Matilda says.

"Why didn't they just land with the others? Those numbers would have overwhelmed us."

"Because they didn't know what your defenses were," Matilda says. "Basic strategy, darling-dear—send a probing force to find out what your enemy has and how they will react."

I think of the Wasps we fought in the streets of Uchmal. Even when outnumbered and outgunned, they didn't run for cover. They fought hard, yes, but they fought like they knew they were going to die. Their behavior now makes sense—they were on a suicide mission. They were a sacrifice to hold our attention, to tie us up and keep us from seeing the real threat.

Now that threat is safely on Omeyocan. Even with Barkah's army, we're outnumbered five to one. The Wasps have better weapons, better armor . . . how can we possibly defeat them?

"Tell me where they are," I say.

"Why, so you can go get my body destroyed? I don't think so. And I couldn't tell you if I wanted to. We detected their launch and were able to roughly extrapolate their landing area, but that is all. Thanks to that interference, we can't see anything on the planet. We don't know where the bastards are."

We need to find the Wasps and find them *now*. We have to

gather information on our enemy. I can send Maria. No, I'll go with her. I have to see for myself what we face.

I will do that, but I don't know when I might talk to Matilda again. There are things I *must* know.

"Tell me why you came here," I say. "The church, all of you. Dad, Mom . . . why did people come here?"

"Didn't you ask Brewer?"

"I'm asking *you*. Just tell me. Give me this one thing."

She stares at me. A gnarled hand reaches up, lifts the hard eye patch and tosses it away. She's going to tell me, but the price is looking at what I've done to her, at the ragged hole where her eye used to be.

"We came because of the Founder's prophecy," she says. "I met her once. Do you remember that?"

I shake my head.

"The first time I entered the Mictlan compound. I didn't speak to her, I only saw her. As ancient as she was, she was just mesmerizing. So much *power*. The Founder heard the call from Tlaloc, then built the church up from nothing."

That name again: *Tlaloc*. Is it a real thing?

"The call for what?" I ask. "To come to Omeyocan?"

"That and so much more. The call foretold the Abernessia invasion, gave us the location of Omeyocan and the schematics for the ark that would take us there."

Wait . . . she said "schematics." . . . that word means plans, blueprints. . . .

"The *Xolotl* . . . the church didn't design it?"

"The ship jumped between *galaxies,* darling-dear. Beyond any technology known to man. Only the word of the gods could bring such a miracle."

I thought gods were made up, but something sent a call across the universe, a call that drew my people here. Did that call radiate out from Omeyocan like the signals from our radio telescope? If so, that signal spread equally in all directions . . . it must have hit other races.

The call contained *schematics* . . .

Which is why all the ships look the same.

My tongue feels swollen. My stomach roils. Humans were called here; so were the other races—called here by *something on this planet.*

"The alien ships look exactly like the *Xolotl,*" I say. "Is that what the Springer ship looked like?"

Matilda nods.

Religion brought us here. Did religion bring the other races as well? Do the ships orbiting our planet have their own "founders" who sent thousands of their kind here to fight and die?

"That *call* your church is based upon, the call wasn't just for humans," I say. "The other races heard it, too. That's why all the ships look the same."

Matilda laughs. "Did you figure that out yourself, darling-dear? As the Founder foretold, paradise is promised, but never *given*. Paradise must be earned with blood and sacrifice."

She knew this was a planet of endless war. When did she learn this—before the *Xolotl* departed, or at some point during the journey? Did Brewer know? Did *all* the Grownups?

There is so much more to learn, but I'm wasting time. Somewhere in the jungle, our enemy gathers.

"I have to leave," I say. "I'm giving orders that none of my people are to talk to you or anyone on the *Xolotl.* I don't trust you, Matilda."

"Don't go into the jungle," she says. "Please, Em, don't go out there."

Now she uses my name?

"I have to go. That's what a leader does."

Matilda shakes her head.

"We might be able to send fuel down to you in six days. Just don't . . . you can't . . . all . . ."

Her image is fuzzing out in bursts of colored static.

". . . they're trying—" she says, then her image puffs away.

Did something go wrong with the broadcast?

The air above the pedestal again flares to life.

But it's not Matilda.

It's a man.

Not a blackened, gnarled Grownup—an *adult* man. Older than me, yes, but the way we're supposed to get old.

His image crystallizes. His smile is one of pure joy, total amazement.

"I can't believe it," he says. "It's you."

His long black hair is tied up in a topknot. I see a few strands of gray in there. Small wrinkles line his eyes. Something comforting about looking at his face.

He wears a blue robe tied over one shoulder, simple but clean, with folds that seem very precise. The word *toga* pops into my head. Around his neck hangs a thin steel necklace dotted with bits of colored glass.

"It's *you*," he says again, laughing.

"You know me?"

"Well, I know *of* you. Victor was right. I can't believe it! You're Matilda Savage."

He says her name with reverence. I am not her and I will never be her, but I can explain that later. If there *is* a later.

"And who are you?"

"My name is Marcus."

He pauses, looks down. I see his hands—he's counting on his fingertips. I hear him mumbling something over and over.

*Eight, eight, eight, eight . . .*

No, he's not saying *eight* . . . he's saying *great*.

"I think I need maybe thirty-five *great*s." he says. "Hard to say for sure."

He smiles, warm and wide.

"I'm Marcus Savage, your great-great-great—and then some—grandson."

# THIRTY-THREE

**B**rewer told us the *Xolotl* was built to house thousands of people.

*Babies . . .*

Generation after generation after generation.

"You're a vassal," I say.

Still smiling, Marcus shakes his head.

"Our ancestors were, yes, but that word doesn't apply anymore. The New People are free people."

Vassals had children. So did some of the Cherished.

Matilda's daughter that Brewer spoke of . . . could she have had kids of her own? Could Marcus Savage be my actual flesh and blood?

Do I have family after all?

"I'm not Matilda. I'm *Em*."

"Well, of course," Marcus says. "Victor told me."

That name stops me cold. I feel like I'm being pummeled senseless with words and concepts, a flurry of strikes coming so fast I can't parry or duck.

"Victor . . . *Muller?*"

Marcus nods. "Would you like to talk to him?"

I stare blankly. I don't know how to react, I don't know what to think.

Marcus takes a step to his left.

A Grownup steps into view.

"Hello, Em. That is the name you prefer, is it not?"

"Sure. That's fine."

The gnarled creature shakes its head slowly.

"So *young.*" His voice is raspy, like that of all the Grownups, but there is a strange tone to it. . . . he sounds . . . *happy?*

I'm looking at the ancient version of the boy in my spider crew. This Grownup, "Old Victor," he has the same gnarled skin of Matilda and Brewer, but it's lined with dozens of gray streaks—scars. They crisscross his arms and shoulders, mark his face. Some of the scars are ragged, like bolts of lightning forever frozen in time, but others are intricate patterns—carefully planned designs, not the remnants of random wounds.

On his wrinkled black forehead, the ragged gray lines form a circle-star.

"I haven't seen you like this in centuries," he says. "You are so beautiful. And your hair . . . has it really been a *thousand years* since I touched it?"

A shudder washes through me. That this *thing* would ever touch me fills me with disgust.

This is all too much.

"I don't understand what's happening," I say.

"We knew Brewer took an antenna down to you," Old Victor says. "We've been waiting for you to use it. When you did, we cut into the broadcast signal."

"So you're not working with Matilda?"

Marcus laughs. "Hardly."

"I was on her side once," Old Victor says. He holds up a hand, turns it, showing me the gnarled skin. "I won the right to do *this* to my body. So did many who fought for her. But I saw the error of my ways and have fought against her ever since."

I adjust my grip on my spear. I suddenly feel like an idiot, standing here holding it, posturing with it. I want to be in the jungle, with Maria. I want to *fight*. Fighting is simple. This? I don't even know what "this" is.

"The *New People*," I say. "How many of you are there?"

"Five thousand, three hundred and sixty-four," Marcus says without a moment's hesitation. "Including the child that was born yesterday."

Over *five thousand* people are still living on the ship?

"Not possible," I say. "We didn't see any adults like you when we were on the *Xolotl*."

Marcus holds his hands shoulder-width apart, like someone showing the size of a fish he caught. "Say the *Xolotl* is this big." He shortens the space between his hands until they are almost together. "You saw only *this* much of it."

"Brewer controlled the abandoned section in the prow," Old Victor says. "That's where you were. Matilda controls the middle section, which includes the bridge. We control everything beyond that. Until you took the shuttle, we didn't even know there were any receptacles left onboard."

I open my mouth to ask him about his own receptacle, then stop. If he's telling the truth, there's a possibility he doesn't know about our Victor. Maybe that's safer.

I suddenly want Spingate here with me, to explain this. The size of the *Xolotl* is already beyond my ability to imagine.

"But five thousand people . . . how can you feed that many?"

Marcus laughs. It's a delightful sound. I think he laughs often. "The *Xolotl* originally supported eight times that many," he says. "Feeding five thousand isn't hard. Many fields and orchards have died out, but more than enough remain. And we get meat from cattle, chickens and pigs."

Pigs. The same kind that killed Latu, no doubt. One pig was enough to feed twenty of my people. And Brewer showed us images: hundreds of cows in pastures, *thousands* of chickens in cages.

The Wasp troopships we captured. Gaston is trying to learn their controls. Zubiri is studying the fuel they carry, seeing if she can convert it for *Ximbal*'s use. If either of them succeed, could we fly back to the *Xolotl* and bring some of those animals down here? Could we raise herds of our own?

I'm getting ahead of myself again. If we can't defeat the Wasp army, what's the point of bringing down livestock?

*Five thousand people . . .*

"We're at war," I say. "We need help. This city is big enough for all of you, for a *hundred times* your number. Help us fight and we can—"

Marcus holds up a hand, stopping me in mid-sentence.

"Em, the New People can't survive on Omeyocan. You're modified to breathe the air—we're not."

Marcus and his kind weren't "created," like I was. They are susceptible to the same poisons that can kill the Grownups.

But still, so many people . . .

"The Grownups—I mean *the Cherished*—they can survive down here for a time with masks. Could you use masks and help us fight? What weapons do you have? We need spiders, bracelets, cannons . . . anything you've got."

Old Victor shakes his head. "There are few weapons aboard. And no ships left with which to deliver them."

"But Brewer said there were fighter craft."

"There are," the Grownup says. "But they are interceptors, made for space only. They can't fly in atmosphere. I'm sorry—we can't help you."

I had a momentary flicker of hope: more soldiers, more weapons. Old Victor's words extinguish that flame, leave me even more dejected than before.

"Then we have nothing to discuss. I have a war to win."

"You *can't* win," Old Victor says. "We know about the second wave of troopships. You need to find a way to come back up here and leave Omeyocan behind."

Marcus smiles. "We will welcome you with open arms."

Leave Omeyocan?

Wait a second . . . that's what Matilda wants, too.

I finally contact her, refuse her demands, and these two just so happen to "cut in" to her signal?

My anger flares, instant and overwhelming.

"You're working with Matilda."

Marcus shakes his head. "No, of course we aren't! We just don't want to see you get killed!"

"Omeyocan is my *home*." My voice rings with hate, drips with violence. "We've bled for it, *died* for it. How dare you suggest we abandon our birthright!"

"Yes, you have bled." Old Victor's tone is that of a soldier who has seen much. "Yes, you have died—if you stay, you will continue to do so. Even if you beat this ground army, another alien ship is coming. More may come after that. I believe this war is not meant to be won, it is meant to be continuous."

His words echo my own fears. We can win the next battle and still lose the war. And if we win *this* war, will there just be another? We're running out of equipment. There aren't even 250 of us left—we're running out of *people*.

"Tell me why the ships come here," I say. "Why all this war, this killing?"

Old Victor's shriveled shoulders shrug.

"The scriptures ordained that the promised land would not be given—it had to be earned with blood and sacrifice. That was the message that the Founder received from Tlaloc. The alien races obviously received the same message."

Tlaloc, the mysterious "god" that called the races here.

Blood and sacrifice . . .

. . . god . . .

. . . blood . . .

The God of Blood. If this Tlaloc is real, could it be the God of Blood that manipulated Aramovsky, that enraged Bishop, that caused Spingate to murder Bello, that almost made me kill Spingate? I *felt* it, guiding me, pushing me. How long can I deny it is a real thing?

"The killing won't stop," Old Victor says. "Find a way to escape while you still can."

No. This is a trick, and I will not fall for it.

"You want me to leave the place I was *made for*, and come up there so you can hand me over to someone whose sole purpose in life is to wipe me from existence? No thanks. You bastards created us specifically to live on Omeyocan. This planet breathes in our very bones. We'll beat the Wasps. We will survive."

Old Victor's red eyes seem to dull a little. He sags in place. He's getting tired.

"Omeyocan is a place of forever war. I beg you, Em, believe me."

"If this planet is so awful, then why don't you take the *Xolotl* and run away?"

"Matilda's power is weakened, but she still controls the bridge," Old Victor says. "That means she controls where the

*Xolotl* goes. She doesn't just want you, Em, she wants Omeyo-can. She wants what was promised to her. Bring your people up here, together we can overthrow her and we can finally leave."

Ah . . . could that be the *real* reason they want us to come up? They want us to fight their battles for them.

I wish Brewer were still here. Maybe he could tell me if Victor is genuine. But without Brewer, there's no way to know.

"You're either a liar working for Matilda, or a coward who fears her," I say. "Either way, we're not going anywhere."

I'm suddenly grateful I hold the spear after all. I thump the butt against the floor.

"We will defend our home."

I don't wait for them to spew more lies. I go into the hall and tell Peura to break the connection, to make sure no one but me contacts that ship.

I tell him what will happen to him if he disobeys me.

From the terrified look on his face, I know he will not.

I leave him to his work and set out to find Maria.

# THIRTY-FOUR

D'Souza's Demons and Lahfah's Creepers gather on the plaza. Six snake-wolves—three from each platoon—stand idly by, pincers picking up unwrapped grain bars from a pile and popping them into their wide mouths. They love that food even more than the Springers do, it seems. It keeps the mounts calm as their riders talk to me and Barkah.

We stand over a beautiful, hand-drawn leather map spread out on the plaza tiles. The map has Uchmal at its center. It's not as detailed as the electronic maps, of course, but we can carry this one with us into the jungle. Barkah drew it. He has so many talents.

Maria makes a sweeping gesture that takes in the areas to the south and the west.

"The Khochin and Podakra tribes live here, so we won't run into them," she says. She taps a spot just north of Uchmal. "This is Schechak. We're going around that." Finally, she taps a spot far to the northeast, beyond the area drawn on the map. "This is all Galanak territory. We're looking for the Wasps, but we have to be careful—the Galanak hate the Malbinti."

Lahfah, Barkah and the two other Springers present all spit on the ground. The Malbinti is Barkah's tribe—they hate the Galanak right back.

"So we stay *quiet*," Maria says. "Stick to your grid pattern. There is no excuse for you to miss our scheduled rendezvous. If you don't show up, the rest of us will assume you're dead and look in your assigned grid for the enemy. We have an *enormous* area to cover. Everyone understand?"

Human heads nod, Springer tails slap against the plaza tiles.

"And *do not* engage," I say. "If you're attacked, *run*. Our mission is to find out what the Wasps have, not to kill them one or two at a time, understand?"

Nods and slaps.

"I'll ride with Maria," I say. "I'm in command, but if she gives an order, you all follow it without question. Let's go."

The riders walk to their mounts for a final check of harnesses and gear.

Barkah hops to Lahfah. He doesn't want her to leave, to put herself at risk, but he understands what's at stake. Besides, if he tells her not to go, she'll go anyway, and that will make him look bad.

Barkah is exceptional at not looking bad.

He's wearing a violet coat decorated with blue glass beads. He's taken to painting his tail in streaks of orange and blue, which somehow makes him seem even more regal.

Lahfah, on the other hand, wears jungle rags, with knives and hatchets stuffed into her belt. Barkah looks like a king. His queen looks like a killer.

The two of them nuzzle close. They intertwine their tails.

They press closed eyes together. That's the Springer version of kissing.

I wish I had someone to kiss *me* goodbye, but Bishop doesn't want to talk to me. He's furious I'm joining the scouting mission. He says my leadership is too valuable to risk, that I should stay behind Uchmal's walls.

He's right. I know he is, but I have to get out of here. I need the open spaces.

I tried to leave Bishop in charge—he declined. He has too much to do prepping for the city defenses.

So, while I'm gone, Borjigin is our leader.

I walk to Maria and Fenrir. She's stroking his tawny flank, cooing to him like he's a housecat and not a 640-kilo apex predator with pincers that could snap her head clean off.

"Come pet him," Maria says.

"I'd really rather not."

"You're going to be on his back for days," she says. "Maybe weeks. I hope you understand just how *much* jungle is out there."

"Of course I understand."

I don't, really. I just visit the jungle—Maria *lives* out there.

She takes my right hand and presses it against Fenrir. The beast stirs slightly—I try to pull away, but Maria is stronger than I am and she keeps my hand on the beast's fur.

Fenrir is . . . *warm*. He's dirty—and oh my *gods* does he stink—but his fur is soft.

"Don't flinch," Maria says.

I start to ask *why,* then see movement on my left—razor-sharp barbed pincers hover inches from my face.

I stay very, very still.

Between the pincers are Fenrir's little pink nostrils. They open

and close, open and close—then they bump against my forehead.

"He likes you," Maria says.

When the thick snake trunk moves the pincers away, I sneak
a hand down to my privates to make sure I didn't pee myself.

"Eyes up," Maria says. "The murderer is coming."

Sure enough, Spingate is walking our way.

I stride toward her. I miss her desperately, and at the same
time don't want to see her at all. She knows how angry I am; she
wouldn't have come if she didn't have critical information to
share.

When we're a meter apart, we both stop.

"Make it quick," I say.

She's scant steps away, yet we seem as distant as Omeyocan is
from the *Xolotl*. Theresa Spingate was my closest friend. Now
she is a stranger to me.

"Gaston has figured out most of the troopship controls," she
says. "He thinks he'll do a test-flight tomorrow morning. And
good news from Zubiri as well. She and Henry Bemba are building a processor that will convert troopship fuel into a form that
works with *Ximbal*'s engines."

"How long will that take?"

"Zubiri estimates a day or two, she's not sure."

Could that work be completed before the Wasp army gets
here? The shuttle has weaponry—when the Wasps attack, we'll
need that firepower.

Or, we could fly *Ximbal* up to the *Xolotl*, evacuate the city . . .

I shake my head, hard. We are *not* leaving our home.

Spingate glances over my shoulder at Maria and Fenrir.

"Bishop told me you were going," she says. "I didn't believe
him. He loves you, you know. You two should have children."

"I don't need relationship advice from you. Or advice of any kind."

She looks down. My tone is a rebuke. I know her well enough to understand that she didn't come here just to tell me about the troopships and Zubiri's experiment.

Her hand absently rubs at her belly.

"Em, you have to understand . . . I didn't want to hurt Bello."

Her voice wavers. She's still trying to come to grips with what she's done.

"You didn't just *hurt* her," I say. "You *murdered* her."

Spin lets out a breath as if I just kicked her in the stomach.

This is gutting her, and I'm glad. She tortured a woman to death—I *want* my words to hurt.

"I couldn't have known Brewer would bring an antenna down the next day," she says. "Lives were at stake, Em. I had to—"

"How much fuel will we have when Zubiri is finished?"

My words are sharp, biting. I don't care about her excuses. I only care about facts.

She looks off, wipes at her eyes.

"Some will be lost in the conversion process, but there should be enough to fill the *Ximbal*'s main tank. We're taking it from the crashed troopship, so that won't affect the fuel supply of the two working craft."

If Gaston can fly the ships we captured, that would give us three working aircraft. I could quickly move our people to multiple areas. I could move Barkah's troops, too. The ruins, the deep jungle . . . if we can find our enemy, we might be able to flank them, or even hit them from behind.

Spingate is staring at me. I feel a stab of guilt for being so cruel to her—she's *haunted* by what she did in that jail cell. If I was really her friend, wouldn't I be there for her instead of making it worse?

She misses what the two of us have lost.

So do I. So much.

No . . . *no!* I will not feel this way. It's not like she broke up with Gaston and needs comfort—Spingate tortured Bello to death.

*And you would have done the same to Spin if Aramovsky hadn't stopped you . . . you would have done* WORSE. . . .

Maybe I'm wrong for acting this way, but that doesn't matter right now—I need to find our enemy.

"You told me what you came to tell me," I say. "Anything else?"

Her eyes glisten with tears that don't quite fall.

"No. Nothing else."

I turn away, but her voice stops me.

"You don't understand," she says, her tone biting and aggressive. "You *can't.* Not until you have children of your own."

She storms off toward the Observatory.

Whatever signal left this place, whatever "the call" really was, I wish I could go back in time and stop it from happening. Omeyocan is a place of hatred, of death, and . . .

. . . the signal . . .

. . . *the call* . . .

Puzzle pieces spin, circle, rotate, flip, all trying to fit together. . . .

The Church of Mictlan, founded to build the *Xolotl,* to bring people to this planet. The other races receiving the same signal, using the same schematics to build ships that look almost exactly like ours . . .

The way the Wasps fought . . . they didn't care about taking cover, they came right at us. They should have run. They should have surrendered. Instead, they fought like their own lives weren't important, like they were sacrificing themselves for something greater . . .

Aramovsky used religion to start a war, to make people *want* to kill.

I look at the Observatory.

So much damage to Uchmal . . . but no damage to that massive building.

Or to the area around it . . .

*The signal . . . the call . . .*

The pieces finally click together.

Two attacks from two different races, yet no damage in this particular spot?

The aliens didn't attack the Observatory because the call, the signal, it came from the Observatory itself.

Or, rather, from whatever lies *beneath* it.

# THIRTY-FIVE

A pair of flashlights illuminate the narrow tunnel.

There are no ceiling supports of wood or stone. These tunnels weren't engineered, they weren't made by flowing water.

This is the kind of tunnel an animal would make.

Something *dug* this.

I sent D'Souza's Demons and Lahfah's Creepers on the scouting mission—but told Lahfah herself to wait for me. Once I'm done with Huan, she will take me north. We know the rendezvous points for the check-ins, so as sprawling and vast as the jungle is, we should be able to connect with Maria.

Unless the Wasps get her first.

"Huan, I don't give a damn if you're afraid—keep moving."

If only I was as brave as I sound. There's something about this tunnel . . . something *wrong*.

Huan Chowdhury glares back at me. My climbing harness matches his. The rigs' metal loops secure us to ropes when the inclines are too steep to walk, or when they drop straight down. I'm filthy, he's filthy.

"You better watch your ass, Em. You get lost down here"—he smiles, rests his hand on the handle of the knife in his belt—"and they might never find you ever again."

The growl in his voice . . . is he threatening me? I didn't bring my spear—it's too cramped down here for it—but I have a knife, too, and I know how to use it.

*Test me, little boy, and I'll add one more kill to my list. . . .*

I stop walking. What kind of a thought was that? You don't *kill* someone for words. And Huan's thinly veiled threat . . . that's not like him at all.

Whatever release we gained with the fight against the Wasps, it's gone.

Because the God of Blood is in us.

"Huan, we both need to relax," I say. "The violent urges are coming back. Do you feel them?"

He glares at me, suspecting I am trying to trick him. Then he rubs his eyes. His face scrunches up.

"Yeah," he says. He grabs his chest, fingertips digging into straps and black canvas. "In here . . . I'm so angry and I don't know why."

I've felt this thirst for violence before. Strong in the jungle. Stronger in the city. Stronger still in the Observatory, and strongest in the Control Room.

But in these tunnels, it's even worse.

There is something evil down here. The source of all the hate and anger . . . we're closing in on it.

Whatever it is, could it also be the thing that called so many races across the stars?

And it's not just anger this time . . . there is also *fear*. My body screams at me to *get out* of this place, to just *run*.

I will not run. I will not give in.

"You were right," I say to Huan. "It is spooky down here. *Damn* spooky."

He looks at me doubtfully. "Are you mocking me again?"

I shake my head. "No, and I'm sorry I did before. It's terrifying down here. I should have believed you. We all should have."

I see the anger melt from his face. In that moment, Huan isn't a little boy anymore—he's a man finally getting the respect he deserves.

"Thank you," he says.

Something unspoken passes between us. Whatever must be done down here, Huan and I will do it together.

We continue on. At the tunnel's end, there is a Huan-sized dark shadow in the muddy wall.

"That was the spot I told you about," he says. "I was able to push through into a new tunnel. A few meters farther in, there's a bend to the right. That's where I heard the voice."

He doesn't want to continue. Neither do I.

But we have to.

I slip through the muddy opening into a larger tunnel. Huan hesitates, then follows.

It's hotter in here. Hotter and more humid, just like Huan said.

And then I feel it, just barely—a push/pull of air, soft, repetitive, insistent.

As if something was breathing.

I'm so afraid it's hard to think. It's like an entity is in my heart and head, *making* me afraid the same way I would make a puppet dance.

"Huan, I'm really sorry I called you a coward."

He nods, a simple movement that tells me I'm forgiven. I believe him now, that's all that matters to him.

We continue on. The soles of our boots squish in mud. Our flashlight beams play off of water slowly dripping from the ceiling and thin rivulets running down the walls.

Up ahead of Huan, I see the tunnel bend sharply to the right.

Huan points with a shaking hand.

"That's where I heard her," he whispers. "That's where I heard my mom."

We have to go on, but I can't bring myself to take another step forward.

Then I hear it—a soft human voice echoing off the wet dirt walls.

"*Don't be afraid. . . .*"

Not a woman's voice . . . a man's.

My body trembles. I want to run away, but my feet have frozen solid to the tunnel floor.

"Don't be afraid," the voice says again, closer now. "I'm right around the corner. I'll approach slowly."

The voice of an older man. It sounds a little like Marcus.

I grab Huan's arm.

"You said it sounded like your mom!"

He's shaking his head, nonstop.

"It *did*! I swear it did!"

"Don't be afraid," the man says a third time. "I'll step around the corner now."

He does.

It's a man. Old*er* but not *old*. Jeans and a blue button-down shirt.

Black hair.

Black mustache.

Matilda's memories are sparse, scattered and mostly fuzzy. Very few of them burn so clear they are real to me, like I experienced that moment myself.

One of those memories has come to life.

A memory of being a little girl, crying, sitting on a man's lap.

I stare at that man now.

A single word escapes my tight throat.

"Daddy?"

# THIRTY-SIX

He can't be real. He *can't*.

My father smiles.

"Hello, peanut."

His words crush me, steal the strength from my limbs. I lean against the tunnel wall to stop myself from falling.

*Peanut.*

That's what he used to call me. Call Matilda. Call *us*.

I know he's not *my* dad. Matilda was born—I *hatched*. In the deep fiber of my being, though, she and I are the same person. Which means no matter what this thing is, I feel a connection to him so powerful and so real it doesn't matter who came from where.

This is my father.

Am I imagining this?

"Huan," I say, "what do you see?"

"A man." Huan sounds almost as shocked as I am. "A black-haired man with a mustache."

"You've done well, peanut," my father says. "We know that

many of you died on the journey here. That is to be expected. Only the strong survive, and only the strongest merge."

This is madness.

"You're dead," I say, my voice cracking on the words. "You've been dead for a thousand years."

That smile . . . so warm, so loving.

"Think of me as an echo. An echo of a concerned parent, if you will, perhaps no different than the memory in your thoughts that lets me take this form."

This is a memory? I don't understand.

"Can you read my mind?"

"Not in the way you mean," he says. "I drew from your experiences to find a form that is important to you."

He can't read my mind, but he can read my memories? I don't know how those things are different.

He is anguish and heartbreak dragged from my past and sculpted into reality. My *father*. So many times I've wished I could meet him. Now here he is, but he's not real. Whatever this thing is, it is cruel.

A tiny part of me is glad I'm not looking at an "echo" of O'Malley. I don't know if I could take that.

Maybe this thing would have chosen my mother, but I don't remember what she looks like. I don't know her face.

Am I going insane? This whirlwind of emotions

*—love and hate and terror and killing rage—*

whips at me, makes it hard to see, impossible to think.

*"Em,"* Huan whispers. *"Em, say something."*

My fingers flex on the handle of my knife.

Have to focus . . . I'm here for answers.

"My people received a signal," I say. "Very long ago."

My father shrugs. *"Long* is a relative term, peanut."

*"Don't call me that!"* I draw my knife, shake it at him even

though I'm not sure if there's anything really there that I can cut. "Did you send that signal, or not?"

"I did. But not for myself. As I told you, I'm an echo. I'm not real. You know one like me. . . . his name is . . . ah, now I have it—his name is Ometeotl."

The Observatory computer.

"You're a *machine*," Huan says. "A godsdamned robot?"

My father glances to the tunnel ceiling, a painfully natural, *human* expression—he's thinking over Huan's words.

"No, not a machine, but perhaps *robot* is close. I am a small piece of a sentient, biological organism."

He smooths his mustache. He does this because I remember my father doing the same thing.

But . . . why *my* father?

"You take a form only I know," I say. "Were you Huan's mother before?"

My father nods. "I was. Now you are both here, and of the two of you, peanut, I sense you're the natural leader—you are the stronger one."

He isn't talking about physical strength. He can look into our thoughts. Or, perhaps, into whatever passes for our *souls*. I don't know what lies in Huan's heart, but I know the blackness that buzzes within mine.

"Stronger," I say. "To you, that means *more violent,* doesn't it?"

My father's smile widens.

"Violence and strength are the same thing. In all the history of all the worlds before this one, and in all the history of all the worlds yet to come, the violent *always* win. Those who are capable of committing violence, or getting others to commit violence for them, or who build systems that create mass violence, more *efficient* violence—those beings eliminate the opposition and, therefore, create the future."

He's spouting some kind of philosophy. I don't care about that.

"The signal wasn't for you," I say. "So who was it for?"

He beckons us to follow him.

"Come. I will show you."

He wants to take us deeper into this place of hate and fear.

I want to run away. I want to be with my friends, touch their faces, hear their voices, celebrate all that is *real* and *solid* and *true*.

But if I don't get answers, those friends could die.

And I realize something ironic, something twisted and dark— I never met my real father, but I often feel his spirit within me.

He would expect me to be brave, to follow through.

*If you run, your enemies will hunt you.*

I will not run.

I sheathe my knife. "Lead on. Show me who did this to us."

Huan glances at me, that guarded look again in his eyes. He hears the barely controlled rage in my voice. I've been hurt before, badly, but this is different—something has *invaded* me, forced its way into the most private place anyone can have.

And that something is going to pay.

My false father leads us into the tunnel on the right. A few meters farther is a narrow opening on our left.

"Do not be afraid of what you see next," he says. "This could be the destiny of your people."

He walks through the opening.

Huan and I follow, into a small cavern. Two flashlights aren't nearly enough to light up the whole space.

Our beams play against something large, something with the satiny gleam of dull metal.

Metal . . . that *moves*.

# THIRTY-SEVEN

"Tlaloc," Huan whispers. "What is this?"

Something unrecognizable fills this cavern, presses against the ceiling and walls. It's *bigger* than the cavern, with much of its bulk hidden by darkness, dirt and mud. I can't see all of this thing, but it has to be massive, maybe as large as five shuttles laid end to end.

Matilda's memories flashfire, try to match words to what my eyes take in.

Some of those words are for real animals: *whale . . . eel . . . hanash . . . lamprey . . . centipede . . . Rewall . . . Lisa's cardon . . .*

Other names represent creatures of legend, things that never existed at all: *Jörmungandrm . . . Quetzalcoatl . . . death worm . . . Bakunawa . . .*

Then her memories lock onto something repulsive and disgusting, something that's so close to what I see I can't possibly call it by any other name.

*Grub.*

A gleaming copper color instead of translucent white. If there is a head, I can't see it. All I see is the long body wedged into the mud slimed across it. The Grub is as much a *part* of this cavern as it is inside of it. The thing twitches, wriggles, sending undulations down its length in trembling waves of fat. I see things fluttering beneath the copper skin, see the coursing pulse of barely visible liquid that can only be its blood.

My father steps toward this . . . this *leviathan* . . . and I realize that his boots leave no footprints in the mud. He's not real. He's just an image, projected onto the ground before us, or directly into our minds, I don't know.

"This is the reason you're here," he says. "This is the next generation of my kind. One species, and *only* one, will merge with it, complete the cycle. I sent a call across the universe, inviting any who heard it to come and compete for this ultimate blessing."

"You're wrong," Huan says. "I remember sermons from school, from church . . . we were destined to find the promised land. But that thing isn't *land*. And the other ships that came here, the other races—how could they respond to the same call that brought us when we all speak different languages?"

My false father nods as if to say *That's an excellent question.*

"Our race first rose to the stars five hundred million years ago," he says. "Our ability to communicate with any intelligent species is too complex for you to understand, but I will try to explain. There are commonalities in the mental processes of sentient creatures. Certain energies generated from conscious, intelligent thought have similar patterns." He gestures to himself. "I'm using those patterns now to create this image. I have also used such patterns to appear in different forms."

One moment he is my father, the next he is a Vellen, like the statues I saw in the Springer church. My height, the one big eye, the backward-folded legs, the larger middle set of arms just above the hips, the thin arms coming out the sides of the head, ending in delicate hands.

The strange creature speaks with my father's voice: "*This* race landed and built a city above this spot, but they could not defend themselves."

The form shifts again, becomes a green-eyed Springer wearing beautiful clothes of purple trimmed with silver lace and dotted with real jewels—not bits of melted glass. No Springer has clothing this fine, not even Barkah.

"This race destroyed the first, even stood where you stand right now."

The Springer shifts back to the form of my father.

"Sadly for them, they were not strong enough to survive *your* race's arrival. The closer my child comes to rising, the more powerful the urge to compete for his love."

When we first lived here, we had problems with the Springers, yes, but nothing Barkah and I couldn't handle. About six months ago, things got worse. Then the Belligerents came. Were they somehow drawn toward Uchmal by this *urge to compete?* And in the past few days, incidents of violence amongst my people—the fight on the training ground, Spingate torturing Bello, me almost killing Spingate . . .

I don't understand how this can be, but the facts seem obvious; the Grub is doing something to our heads. It is the cause of the hate and violence that's tearing us apart.

"Now a new race has landed," False Father says. "You will destroy them or they will destroy you. Or perhaps the Springers that you stupidly allow to live will be the ones who wipe you out. When my child rises, we shall see who is there to merge with him."

Huan's hand moves to his belt, rests on the handle of his knife.

"Huan, *don't*," I say.

"He's making us fight each other," Huan says. "Like animals."

False Father nods. "Trials determine the strong. For a species as primitive as yours, to merge with us is the ultimate gift. Your kind rules planets—our kind rules space itself."

"*Merge,*" I say. "What does that mean?"

"When my child rises, he will be weak. Defenseless. The strongest species will protect him until he can protect himself, then be a part of him when he leaves this planet."

Huan's nose wrinkles in confusion. "Leave? You mean on a ship?"

False Father shakes his head.

"Our kind do not need ships. We move through space as easily as you walk on land. But the nature of our biology requires that smaller, intelligent organisms merge with us, tend to us from the inside. Together, my child and the winning species will explore the stars, see the wonders of the universe. And someday, the descendants of that species will be there when my child breeds. On some distant planet in some other galaxy, my child will lay its three eggs, just as I did."

My dad died over a thousand years ago. The thing that looks exactly like him turns slightly, gazes lovingly at the giant, coppery Grub.

"An echo of my child will send out a call of its own. That call will reach intelligent races, who will build new ships. They will travel to that planet. They will compete against each other. The strongest will survive, and will join with my grandchild."

Huan's grip tightens on the knife handle.

"So your squirming, jiggling baby doesn't need a ship, it *is* a ship," he says. "We'd be, what . . . its crew?"

False Father thinks on this for a moment.

"Merging is far more than that," he says. "Once my child travels to the stars, he will not be able to live without you. And you will change, too, to where you cannot live without him. He will protect you from the vastness of space. In return, you tend to his needs."

Two species that can't survive without each other.

Just like the tiny organisms that live in the vine roots.

That's what we would be to this massive thing: *worms*. We would be a part of it. It would be a part of us.

*Symbiotes*.

Huan adjusts his stance. His boots make sucking sounds in the mud.

"So you want us to be *babysitters*?" he says. "You're so powerful you can draw all these races and make them fight, but you can't protect your babies?"

"As it is with any intelligent race," False Father says. "Can the newborn human babies protect themselves?"

I think of little Kevin, soft, helpless. If left on his own, he would quickly die.

"Our parents protect us," I say. "Most of our parents do, anyway. But not you—you abandon your children?"

"Our ancestors reached the stars and stayed, but at a price. When our kind leaves a planet, our bodies change permanently. We retain the ability to survive planetside only long enough to deposit our three eggs and"—he gestures to himself—"leave an echo which can send a call and communicate with those that answer it. After we lay eggs, we undergo a final change and we become too delicate to survive in heavy gravity. We end our lives as creatures of the cosmos, seeing all the beauty we can before we pass on."

"You're like insects," Huan says. He points to the Grub.

"That's some kind of larva, right? It will change, like a maggot turning into a fly. Your species is nothing but damned *bugs*."

False Father spreads his hands.

"Our kind has survived half a billion years. We have watched hundreds of races like yours evolve, flourish, reach the stars, then fade and die out. After humanity has vanished from history, my kind will still be spreading across the universe, finding new worlds and merging with new races."

Wait . . . what he said . . .

"You said *three* eggs." I point to the wriggling monstrosity. "There's two more of those?"

"They hatch one at a time," False Father says. "The next two are buried deeper. When this child leaves the planet, the next child will hatch, develop and eventually rise."

"Multiples of three," Huan says, his voice dreamy, distant. "Everything is multiples of three . . ."

Three eggs. My *lacha*—my *twelve*. The coffins on *Ximbal*, 168 of them. The Church of Mictlan references multiples of three over and over again. And it's not just us: six Wasp troopships, 666 soldiers in each one, twenty-one troopships landing somewhere in the jungle.

I wonder if the cultures aboard the *Basilisk* and the *Goblin* celebrated the same number.

"The signal," I say. "The call you sent out. Did it contain this information? Did our Founder really understand what was waiting for us here?"

"Impossible to know," False Father answers. "An infinite number of races has interpreted an infinite number of calls an infinite number of ways. I can communicate directly with you because you're here, because you are close enough that I can sense and interpret your thought patterns. Exoplanets are far too distant for that. We can only send, we can't receive, we can't communicate. The signal we broadcast has two parts. My part is mathematical—ship designs, galactic location and more. The second part of the signal comes from my child, a nonlinguistic impulse our kind has sent out for over half a billion years— a primitive, basic urge to *come,* to *fight,* to *join,* to *love.* To *serve.*"

Maybe the Founder knew what awaited us here, maybe not. She clearly understood, though, that other races would come to this location, that there would be a brutal war. She prepared for it—when we were just children, Okadigbo was trained to use the Goff Spear.

"Why humanity?" I ask. "Why the Springers? The Vellen and the other races?"

"My kind evolved on a planet similar to this one. So did the first race that joined with our kind. As adults we travel the stars, but our"—he smiles at Huan—"our *larvae* and *pupae,* they need oxygen, they need gravity. The call included this planet's atmospheric composition—the races that could survive here came. Finding new races to merge with us is part of why we have spread so far and survived for so long, but those races must be able to survive inside our skin as did the first race. That is why those that join with us must be a carbon-based, oxygen-breathing species."

Carbon. The symbol on the Well wall. On the Springer church. On the *Basilisk's* flat prow. The symbol was part of the signal that went out across the stars. Some races, including my own, made that image part of a new religion, a religion dedicated to obeying the call of a powerful being.

Of . . . of a *god.*

Tlaloc. The God of Blood. It's real. And it's right in front of me.

I look at the Grub. This glistening nightmare is what makes us want to fight, want to kill. This is what is making us *hate*. Maybe it only magnifies the natural urges we have inside of us, but if this thing wasn't here would Spingate have killed Bello? Would the Belligerents have come at all?

It's been down here the whole time.

That's why the other races didn't bomb the Observatory—because they knew, or maybe *sensed* is a better word, that their god lived down here. That must be part of the signal the Grub sends out.

"So what happens now?" I ask. "Do you expect us to just . . . what . . . come down here and climb in? What if we choose not to do that?"

False Father smiles at me.

"My child has been growing stronger. You've felt it. Soon, it will rise, and when it does, every sentient being around will be *compelled* to protect it."

I want to believe that isn't possible, but look what has already happened. Six races have reached Omeyocan. A seventh is on the way. Who knows how many more are coming? There is a power here beyond comprehension. Maybe it's advanced technology, maybe it's something else, but if this species has existed for half a billion years it is because their strategy *works*.

I thought gods didn't exist.

I was wrong.

"What if more than one race is *worthy*?" I ask. "We're working closely with the Springers. Your *child* tried to make us kill each other—it failed."

"Your two races have already fought," my false father says. "Multiple times. Do you think that was a coincidence? You've overcome the urge for now, which is a testament to your strength. When my child rises, however, those urges will become irresistible. The races will fight. One race will win, the others will be eliminated."

His words chill me. If he's right, not even Barkah and I will be able to keep our people apart. And if we fight each other, there is no way we can defeat the Wasps.

We're doomed.

I thought the Grownups were evil, but they're pawns. Just like we are. The Cherished, the Springers, the Wasps . . . we've all been manipulated and drawn in by a lie so massive it spans *galaxies,* maybe even the universe itself.

We were brought here to fight to the death, for the privilege of being *worms.*

The hiss of a knife sliding out of a sheath.

Huan rushes at the Grub. Screaming, spitting, Huan raises his blade and drives it down.

A *crack* of energy louder than any gunshot makes my body vibrate.

Huan is flung backward. He splashes into the thick mud next to me, slides to a stop.

I kneel beside him. His body is trembling so hard his teeth rattle. Smoke rises up from his face and hands, which smolder with fresh burns.

"Huan! Are you all right?"

A stupid thing to say. He's hurt bad.

I look up at my father. If he was real, I would gut him.

"My child protected himself," he says. "Your friend is lucky to be alive—that was a fraction of my child's power. The next attacker will not be as fortunate."

"You said it couldn't defend itself!"

He smooths his mustache. "Not against all attacks, no."

Fury fills me, *encases* me. I want to *hurt* . . . I want to *murder.*

I drag Huan to his feet. He's shaking so bad he can barely stand.

"Can you walk if I help you?"

Grimacing, he nods.

Supporting his weight, I turn my back on the Grub and the Echo.

"Good luck," False Father calls after me. "My child will soon rise. If you are strong, if you are *smart,* you will kill the Springers before that happens, because when it does, they will come to kill you."

I stop and turn, careful not to drop Huan. I look at the image of the man that raised my progenitor.

"Don't worry, *Father*—I promise you I'll strike first."

And I will. But not against the Springers.

Whatever it takes, I'll find a way to destroy the thing responsible for all of this.

I will kill the God of Blood.

# THIRTY-EIGHT

I stand next to the throne in the Grand Hall. Huan is with me. We look down at the faces of my people.

So much to tell them. So little time.

Huan leans against the throne because he can't stand on his own. Physically weak but mentally strong, he refuses to go to the hospital until this is done. He grits his teeth against the pain.

I tell everyone about my talk with Matilda. I tell them of Old Victor, somehow manage to not look at our Victor when I do so. I tell them about Marcus and the five thousand vassal descendants. I leave off the strange fact that he's *my* descendant, because that's not important right now. I tell them there are no weapons on the *Xolotl* for us, how we can't count on any help from our mother ship.

I talk about the tunnels. The Echo. The signal.

Then, I tell them about the Grub. The size of it, how it's making us violent . . . how we're supposed to fight to the death so one race can *merge* with it. How it might soon rise.

Faces stare back. Incredulous. Afraid. Disbelieving. And more than a few, *angry*. At me, for telling the truth?

Maria and her squad are scouting, and a few cannon crews are in the towers serving as lookouts, but the rest of my people are here. Bishop, Kalle, Bawden, Farrar, Borjigin, Kenzie, Schuster . . . everyone. I even had Aramovsky brought down from his cell, although I hope that doesn't turn out to be a mistake.

The Springer residents of Uchmal are here, too, although I notice they aren't mixed in with us like they were before. They're clustered closer to Barkah and Lahfah. The distrust between our peoples is growing once again.

"That's it," I say, finishing my tale. "That's what we saw."

For almost a minute, there is only silence.

Walezak is the first to speak.

She steps forward from the crowd. "You're a *liar*."

Huan points to the burns on his face. "Look what it did to me. Em speaks the truth."

Walezak's lip curls into a hateful sneer.

"You did that to yourself! Or you had Em do it to you! The gods called us here. *The gods,* not some imaginary monster that supposedly has to be born on a planet and then lives *in space.* That's ridiculous!"

Kalle steps forward, calm as can be.

"There are some parallels to the amphibian life cycle," she says. "Like toads, for example—eggs and tadpoles can only live in water, while adults of most species spend their lives on land. If the organism Em found does begin life on a planet, then lives out in the void, I suppose we'd classify it as an *astro*phibian."

Walezak stares at Kalle like Kalle is speaking a different language.

"Granted, it would have to be an extremely complex life

cycle," Kalle says. "But that kind of drastic physical change isn't that dissimilar from what insects or blurds go through. Like a caterpillar becoming a moth. If what this *Echo* told Em and Huan is true, the creature begins as an egg. When it hatches, it becomes a larva—the form it is now. Sometime after it rises, it must metamorphize into a form that can leave the planet. Let's call that form a *nymph*. Maybe it has a couple of nymph stages, actually—a *protonymph* that leaves the planet, then a *deutero-nymph* that lays eggs. After that it changes again, into the final, nonbreeding adult form."

Spingate steps out of the crowd. Her breathing is ragged.

"Em said it's *making* us do things," she says to Kalle. "Is that even possible?"

Kalle nods. "Definitely. Some parasites can change the behavior of their hosts, force them to do things that seem crazy. Maybe this Grub's larval phase is parasitic, making the races fight to determine a dominant species, and then, when it's a nymph, it becomes symbiotic."

Tears trickle down Spingate's face, but she stands tall and stiff. Watching how this news strikes her, it rips my heart into pieces. She's been hammered down by the guilt of killing Bello; it must be wrenching to hear that maybe, just *maybe*, it wasn't entirely her fault.

"But *how*?" she says. "How could that thing control us?"

"Maybe some kind of alteration to our neurochemistry," Kalle answers. "For all we know, it could be releasing spores that infect us, change the way we think and act. Or more likely, it's some mechanism far beyond our understanding. Em said the Echo claims its species is five hundred million years old. That's *two thousand* times longer than humans have even existed. I mean, the Grub's species could have evolved some form of control we don't know about, or they could have engineered this ability into their own offspring—like how the Grownups engineered us to survive on Omeyocan when they can't survive here themselves."

Kalle is just guessing. That's clear to me, clear to everyone. But the matter-of-fact way she describes the possibilities—combined with what Huan and I saw—erodes disbelief.

And if anyone should believe in intelligent life being modified, if not created from scratch, it is the Birthday Children.

Someone begins to cry. I can't see who.

"But the church," Borjigin says. "I don't remember much of it, but . . . how could the church be steered wrong like that?"

Still leaning against the throne for support, Huan shakes his fist.

"Because it was a *trick*!" His words bounce off the room's stone walls. "Our religion is a *fake*. Don't you get it? The thing below our feet sent a signal, and when the Founder got that signal she founded the church. She made a religion so she could control people!"

Everyone starts yelling at Huan, or at each other. The Grand Hall is awash in fury and confusion.

Bishop steps out from the crowd. The crowd immediately quiets down.

"Whatever this *Grub* is, we have to kill it," he says. "If it's making us do bad things, we must destroy it."

Farrar shakes his head. "We don't dare. Just because we've seen it doesn't mean it's not really a god. Look what it did to Huan. If that was just a warning, what happens if we make an organized attack against it? I don't like the idea of making a god mad."

He has a point. If I send people down there, they might die, and right now we can't afford to lose anyone. I'm caught between two threats: the Grub rising and the Wasp army. Because

284        SCOTT SIGLER

of the Grub, I should get my people out of Uchmal, but we can't abandon the Goff Spear, not with the *Dragon* still up there. And the city has walls, cannons on those walls—this is the best place to defend against the Wasps.

Now Aramovsky shuffles forward, hunched over as if the weight of his past actions is too much to bear.

"We have to face facts," he says. "It's not a real god. And Huan is right. Our church . . . it's all make-believe."

No one speaks. Not even Walezak. Everyone in this room knows of Aramovsky's devotion to religion. To hear him say such things is almost as jarring as me talking about the creature below the Observatory in the first place.

"We can argue all we like, but look into your hearts," he says. "Look at where we are, what's happened to us. Everything Em describes matches what we've seen with our own eyes. The church . . . the Founder made it up."

Someone else starts to cry. I don't blame them—I almost want to cry myself. Even though I know what's happening, the way Aramovsky talks makes everything seem more real.

The Birthday Children never had a choice.

And those that didn't give us a choice, they themselves were duped.

I've never felt so hopeless.

Bawden steps out of the crowd. She stares at her feet.

"But that means our parents were tricked," she says. "*Everyone* in the church was tricked. How can that be?"

Aramovsky finally stands straight, addresses everyone with just a hint of his former vocal power.

"Because the Founder needed to build a ship," he says. "For that, she needed people. *Lots* of people. And money. I don't pretend to know the details, but I can't deny the truth any longer— the Founder invented a religion so people would follow her blindly, do what she needed them to do. And people fell for it. *Thousands* of them."

A heavy mood settles on the Grand Hall. Heads hang. My people don't know what to make of any of this. Neither do I. We are in the eye of a storm of madness, trying to comprehend a power that is beyond anything we could know.

The Grub is a problem we *must* solve, but as shocking as it seems, right now it is not our biggest problem.

"No one is to enter those tunnels," I say. "We'll deal with the Grub as soon as we can. For now, everyone keep preparing the city defenses. Lahfah, let's go, we have to ride hard to catch up with Maria."

Bishop gawks at me in disbelief.

"You can't leave. We have to deal with this, right now."

"It will wait," I say. "If we don't find out what the Wasps are bringing against us, we might not live long enough to deal with the Grub at all."

And on top of that, I just need to *go*. I need the jungle around me. I need to be free of this place.

I raise my spear and thump it on the stone dais. The reverberating *thunk* draws all eyes to me.

"I'm leaving, immediately. Borjigin, while I'm gone, you're in command. Bishop, Farrar, Bawden, if *anyone* tries to go down into the Well, you are to put them in a jail cell. Do you understand?"

"We understand," Farrar and Bawden say in unison.

Bishop glares at me for a moment. I glare back. I won't give in to what he wants. The church might be fake, but the Wasps are real. We can argue about what the past means after we secure our future, and the only way to do that is to know what's coming.

Finally, Bishop nods.

"I understand," he says. "What about Aramovsky? Put him back in his cell?"

I look at Aramovsky. He's a beaten man. His religion took us to war. His religion caused so many to die. And now he knows, finally and for certain, that his religion was a lie.

"He's spent enough time in jail," I say. "Put him to work."

I descend the dais steps and head for the exit. Lahfah joins me.

I hope we find Maria before we find the Wasps.

# PART III

## VIOLENCE AND VISIONS

# THIRTY-NINE

ahfah and I left near dusk. We rode through the night. The twin moons lit our way as we passed through seemingly endless, overgrown ruins of hexagonal buildings. The sun was just beginning to climb when we finally entered untouched jungle. As big as Uchmal is, it is but a dot in the sprawling expanse of the former Springer city, which is itself but a speck in the infinite jungle.

It took all of the next day to reach the rendezvous point, where we connected with Maria and the other hurukan riders. They hadn't found the enemy yet, but they'd seen a big column of smoke on the distant horizon. I gave everyone a quick update on what Huan and I found. No arguments from the riders, no debate—they're not ignoring my shattering news, but they know that if you don't pay full attention to the jungle, the jungle can kill you.

So can the Galanak.

So can the Wasps.

We'll worry about the fake church when we get back. For now, we focus on the dangerous task at hand.

I ride with Maria on Fenrir. I want Lahfah with me, too, so I changed up the two squads. Demons, Creepers . . . none of that matters right now. Nedelka Holub, a circle-star girl, rounds out our squad. We're riding northeast, toward where Maria saw the smoke. The other three riders head due north, working their grids.

Fenrir streaks through the jungle, powerful and silent. I hold tight around Maria's waist so I don't slide off and crash into the underbrush.

Our way seems perpetually blocked by thick trees, dense bushes and dangling vines, yet the hurukan slides past all of it as if the yellow plants and brown trunks are mist, as insubstantial as the projected image of my father. I've taken hundreds of spiderback rides through the jungle, but there is a huge difference between riding a machine and being on the back of a powerful predator.

Lahfah is off to our left, flashing in and out of the jungle's cover. Nedelka is somewhere on our right. I hope she's keeping up.

*The Grub* . . . I saw it, yet I can still scarcely believe it. What are we going to do? Huan could have died. We could send people down with guns, but my instincts tell me that will get them killed. My false father said the Grub couldn't defend itself, but it did.

No . . . he said it couldn't defend itself *against all attacks.*

What did that mean?

Fenrir cuts sharply left, banking around a thick stump caked with blue moss, and my butt slides to the right. I start to slip, but Maria reaches behind her and shoves me back into place. She's so *strong*. A year in the jungle, a year taming these beasts . . . it has made her a different person.

She talks to me over her shoulder.

"You loosened your grip. Did your mind wander?"

I'm embarrassed, but I tell the truth. "It did."

"Pay attention. Hold on tighter. You're not going to break me. If you fall off and die, Bishop will have my head."

I do as I'm told. We're just riding, but it feels good to hold Maria tight.

The jungle envelops me. She's right, I need to focus. And unlike an all-powerful alien baby, this is something I can actually control: *war*. Our enemy is out here somewhere.

Maria leans back, pulls on the reins. Fenrir instantly slows— I can't believe something so big can stop so quickly, so smoothly. Up ahead, Lahfah and her mount silently slip through a pair of wide yellow leaves and come toward us. The muscles of Lahfah's mount ripple beneath its tawny fur. The long trunk is raised high. I can see its pink nostrils flaring open and closed.

D'souza sniffs the air.

"We're close," she says.

I inhale deeply. It's faint, but I smell it, too—the unforgettable odor of burned Springer flesh.

Lahfah's lithe mount stops next to ours. Nedelka and her hurukan melt out of the jungle without a sound, join us.

*"Smoke smell old,"* Lahfah says quietly. *"Fire dead?"*

We scan the trees above us, but there is no trace of smoke.

"The fire must have burned out," Maria says. "But if we can still smell it, we can find it. Spread out. Stay in visual distance."

She leans forward, scratches the side of Fenrir's furry head. The snake trunk curls back toward her. Even though Maria said the beast "likes" me, I can't help but flinch away from those lethal pincers.

"Fenrir, my lovely," Maria says. "Do you smell that? Smell?"

The little nostrils on the trunk's end open and close, open and close. The pincers clack together twice—Maria has taught it that *one* means "no," and *two* means "yes." These animals are not only big and lethal, they are *smart*.

"Good boy," she says, then sits up. "Em, you better hold on for real this time."

I wrap my arms tight around her stomach. Not that long ago, Maria D'souza was just a circle—an "empty," like me. She taught herself the Springer language. She tamed these huge animals. She became a strong leader. I love Bishop with all my heart and respect his abilities as our greatest warrior, but Maria D'souza is my hero.

She snaps the reins.

"Fenrir, *seek!*"

And with that, the beast plunges through the jungle.

# FORTY

Since I awoke in my coffin, I've seen so many horrors.

But nothing like this.

The four of us stand side by side at the edge of a burned-out Springer village. A small stream runs through the center. Seven or eight bodies are piled up in that stream like a log jam. Water flows up and around the corpses, carrying with it streaks of blue blood and clumps of ash.

Thin wisps of smoke curl from blackened boards and timbers. Even ten strides away, even though the fire has been out for hours, we still feel the heat.

I don't know if the wooden buildings were built after Barkah and I made peace, or if this place is far enough away from Uch-mal's spiders that these Springers never had to live below ground. I don't think it matters. The village is *broken:* burned-out huts, smashed pottery, scattered muskets and hatchets.

And bodies. So many bodies . . .

Most of the corpses smolder, blackened and scorched by the same fires that leveled this place. The smell of charred flesh is so strong that I press my mouth against my inner elbow, try to breathe through the thick fabric of my coveralls.

Some of the bodies are whole. Others are in pieces, blown apart by bullets or hacked up by blades. A few are smashed into bloody piles of flesh and clothing—something *big* ran them over. Wide, parallel, ankle-deep trenches run through dirt, mud, burned wood, even the bodies themselves.

"Are those truck tracks?" Maria asks. "Like maybe they have a Big Pig?"

No one answers her.

All the colors of the Springers are represented among the corpses: blue adults, purple teenagers, red children. Some of the corpses are so small I could hold them with one hand.

These were civilians. This wasn't a battle—it was a slaughter.

Lahfah speaks in Springer. Maria and Nedelka listen closely. I'm the only one here not fluent in that language.

"What did she say?" I ask Maria.

"She said this is the work of . . . the best translation is *barbarians*. Lahfah has experienced war. Even before we came, the Springer tribes fought with each other. She's never seen anything like this. She says it's like the stories handed down from her ancestors about the destruction of their big city."

From when Matilda's machines attacked. From when my kind came from the sky and wiped out everything they could find, murdering thousands.

Now the Wasps are doing the same thing.

If they'll do it to the Springers, they'll do it to us.

It's easy to see where the attack came from. The tracks stretch northeast into the jungle. Trees were cut down—long fallen trunks stretch away from either side of the path; squat stumps lie between the parallel tracks.

And it's easy to see where they went: southwest, toward Uchmal.

Nedelka's hurukan stirs, tries to turn back to the jungle. She snaps on the reins, keeps her mount in place.

"We should head back to Uchmal," she says, her voice quavering. "This is horrible."

Maria looks at me, waits for my orders.

"We have to know what we're up against," I say. "Follow them."

# FORTY-ONE

We don't know exactly how many troopships landed, but we do know they carried more than just soldiers.

A year ago, I was with O'Malley. Aramovsky had won the election and become leader. He'd taken my spear. He'd sent me out—alone—to talk to the Springers, hoping I would fail, hoping I would die. O'Malley snuck away from the others, risked his life to be by my side.

O'Malley wasn't a fighter. He wasn't good in the jungle. He had nothing to offer other than his love.

I miss him so much.

He was with me when we felt the ground shaking, when I climbed the tallest tree I could find and saw the long lines of the advancing Springer army. That sight made me feel like my people had no hope.

I am again high up in a tree, looking out at an army—but this time, the enemy I see is far more terrifying.

Nedelka is on the other side of this ridge, watching our

mounts. Maria and Lahfah are in the tree with me. The tree is halfway up a steep hill, not at the top, where we'd be more visible against the backdrop of a darkening sky.

Because if we're seen, we're dead.

Utter destruction marches through the valley below us. Six huge armored vehicles roll along in a single-file column, their flat treads leaving the now-familiar parallel tracks. They are terrifying machines, much larger than our spiders. And so *loud;* we heard them long before we got close, which let us move off their trail and through the jungle so we weren't seen by rear scouts. The rolling hulks are painted in irregular stripes of yellow and brown. Each of them has a cannon mounted on an armored turret, long barrel pointing forward like the stinger of a deadly insect.

"I think I know what those are," Maria says. "Tranks. No . . . *tanks.*"

The lead vehicle has a horizontal saw mounted on its front. The column of tanks weaves around the biggest trunks, but most of the trees are simply mown down.

Far to the left and right of the tanks are machines similar to our spiders, also painted in jagged streaks of yellow and brown. These are fatter, though, with eight long legs instead of five.

Maria points to the one closest to us.

"Em, do you remember what a *tick* looks like?"

The word stirs up Matilda's memories. The eight-legged machines do look a bit like those nasty insects.

We count twelve "ticks." Four groups of three: one group far out front, a group on either side, and a group in the rear.

Behind the tanks are six lightly armored trucks, similar to Big Pig. These look like they are made to carry cargo more than fight—food, weapons and ammunition, I assume.

Each truck tows something that disturbs me deeply—the biggest cannons I've ever seen. The black barrels are long and thick. They strike me as oversized rifles or muskets—I'm guessing they fire projectiles instead of energy. *Big* projectiles, by the looks of things.

Tanks, supplies, artillery . . . and infantry. Wasp foot soldiers seem to fill the valley below me, their armor blending with the vines and trees. If they weren't moving, I'm not sure I'd see them at all. They carry deadly rifles like the ones we faced in the city battle. A few of them carry thicker, fatter rifles that are as big as the soldiers themselves.

"So *many*," Maria whispers. "Lahfah, what's your count of their infantry?"

I think Maria forgot to speak in Springer, but Lahfah answers quickly.

*"Thousand eight,"* she says. She rubs at her middle eye, then corrects herself: *"Eight thousand. That how said?"*

I nod. "That's how you say it, yes."

When Matilda told me of the Wasp troopships landing in the jungle, I estimated some fourteen thousand enemy soldiers. Obviously the trucks, tanks, ticks and cannons took up much of the available space on those craft, but still . . . *eight thousand* foot soldiers. Even with Barkah's troops, we're outnumbered three to one.

And then there's the fighter craft that flew back up to their mother ship. When the ground troops attack Uchmal, I know those fighters will be there.

"How long will it take us to get back to Uchmal?" I ask.

Maria breathes deep, considering. She says something in Springer to Lahfah, who thinks before replying. Maria nods.

"The snake-wolves are getting some rest now," she says.

"We'll have to take breaks on the way back, but if we push hard we can reach Uchmal by this time tomorrow."

I nod toward the enemy force.

"And them?"

Maria stares down into the valley. The tanks roll along. The troops march through the jungle.

"They have numbers, but that costs them speed," she says. "If they keep moving at the pace we see now, they'll reach Uchmal in two days."

Which means we'll have just one day to prepare.

A *single godsdamned day* to prepare against tanks, troops and cannons, but at least we have that day. That doesn't make strategic sense to me—why didn't they land closer and hit us before we could get ready?

A Springer horn echoes from the north, in the jungle on the far side of the marching army.

From the southwest, in front of the advancing Wasp army, a second war horn answers the first.

My blood runs cold.

"*Galanak,*" Lahfah says. "*Tribe attacking.*"

The Galanak. The largest Springer tribe we know of. That village we saw was probably in their territory.

The Wasps react. They shout at each other in their piercing clicking tongue. Orders of some kind. The tanks stop. The infantry spreads out, making a wide circle around the trucks. The troop movements are uncoordinated, as if many of the soldiers are unsure of how they are supposed to act. Wasps with copper streaks on their shoulder armor scream at the confused ones, push them in the right direction.

"They're new to this," Maria says. "Like our circles were when we first started training them to fight."

The tick groups rush into the jungle, eight legs a blur as they vanish among the dark trees and thick underbrush.

The southwest horn sounds again, closer this time.

The tanks spread out, creating space between them. Turrets pivot to point toward the threats in front of them and on their right flank.

The Wasps obviously have better weapons and equipment, but as a whole they are uncoordinated and slow to respond.

Matilda's words come back to me: *Find out what your enemy has and how they will react.*

I watch. I learn. I *memorize*. Seeing how the Wasps respond to this threat is a huge stroke of luck. If I know their strategies, maybe I can find holes in them.

Both horns bellow again, followed by a sound I know all too well—a guttural war cry from thousands of Springers. Louder than the one I heard in the crescent-shaped clearing a year ago. This Springer army must be far larger than the one we faced.

A massive volley of musket fire; muzzle flashes in the heavy jungle cover reveal a long line of Springers spread through the underbrush. A few Wasp soldiers fall. A few others panic and run away. The copper-striped leaders grab them, hit them, throw them back toward their units—or just shoot them as a warning to the others.

"*Galanak yinilah nahnaw,*" Lahfah says.

I glance at Maria.

"Death-revenge," Maria says. "The Galanak tribe wants payback for the village."

"How many soldiers do the Galanak have?"

Maria translates for Lahfah.

"*Thousand fifteen,*" the Springer queen says, then corrects herself. "*Fifteen thousand soldiers. They all come.*"

I hear another musket volley. More movement, as if the jungle itself has come to life and is slithering toward Wasp soldiers that take cover and form rough lines of their own.

The Galanak outnumber the Wasps. Fifteen thousand Springers are closing in, giving me a surge of hope that the Wasp invasion might be routed right here, right now.

Then the tanks open fire.

Deafening echoes flood the valley. I instinctively move to cover my ears, almost fall, grab at branches to stop myself from tumbling down.

Fireballs erupt in the Springer lines. Trees shatter. Bits of vines soar into the air. In those brief flashes of light, I see Springers torn apart, ravaged bodies spinning away in all directions. Between detonations, I hear the screams of the terrified, the wounded and the dying.

The tanks pour it on, blasting huge, flaming holes in the tortured jungle.

Another war horn sounds: three short blasts, a pause, three short blasts.

The Springers that can still move rise and flee.

Blurs of machinery tear through the darkening jungle, rush past the crackling flames. The ticks are giving chase. Their weapons flash staccato bursts that shred flesh and wood alike.

Then, a different kind of scream—the Wasp foot soldiers rise from cover and shout as one as they move into the jungle after their attackers. When they pass fallen Springers, they shoot them repeatedly or draw long knives and hack at them, over and over again. The wounded Springers cry out. I don't need to understand their language to know they're begging for mercy.

They get none.

The armored aliens slaughter them.

Sounds of battle fade, not so much from distance as from the obvious fact that there's no one left to kill.

Maria, Lahfah and I stay perfectly still in our tree, stunned into silence. The battle lasted only a few minutes, tearing the heart out of the jungle. Fallen trees. Broken stumps. Burning vines. Smoldering craters. And everywhere . . . *bodies*.

"Thousands," I say, ever so softly lest these killers hear us. "There were *thousands* of Springers."

"And they were waiting," Maria says. "Springers chose the ground, had the position they wanted. And they still didn't stand a chance."

Lahfah says nothing. She's making a strange noise—the Springer equivalent of crying.

The Wasp troops are inexperienced. They won with greater firepower, not greater discipline. Now I understand why they landed so far from Uchmal. They needed enough distance to make sure we couldn't hit them as they unloaded, but there was a bigger reason—the Wasp soldiers don't have combat experience. Before this army hits our well-defended walls, before these soldiers face my battle-hardened people, the Wasp commanders want their troops prepared to face enemy fire and to know what it's like to kill.

They *wanted* the Springers to attack.

When we fought the Wasps in Uchmal, we outnumbered them.

When the next battle comes, *we* will be outnumbered.

We will be outgunned.

The *Xolotl* can't help us.

No one can.

I close my eyes, lean my forehead against the tree's rough bark.

*Reality is what it is whether we like it or not.*

The reality is we can't win this war.

I have always searched for ways to keep my people alive.

Now there is only one way left.

I know what needs to be done, but I can't do it without the help of my partner, my friend, my lover—I must talk to Bishop.

"Let's get back to Uchmal," I say. "As fast as we can."

# FORTY-TWO

The sun is setting when we reach Uchmal. This time it's not just Borjigin waiting for us at the city gate—thankfully, Bishop is there as well, standing tall in spider 01.

I slide off Fenrir and run to him, he hops down from the spider and runs to me. He takes me in his arms. For one sweet moment, we're not leaders, we're not soldiers—we are a boy who desperately missed his girl, and a girl who desperately missed her boy. We hold each other in full view of Borjigin, Maria, Nedelka and Lahfah, and we don't care.

I'm filthy and exhausted from the long, hard ride. I smell like Fenrir. But there's no time to clean up, no time to rest.

"The Wasp army is coming," I say to Bishop. "I need to talk to you, in private. Right now. Let's take your spider."

He runs a hand over my dirty hair, pulls me in for another fast, desperate hug.

"As you wish," he says, and walks to the machine.

Maria slides off Fenrir, leans close to me and whispers: "I wish he was taking *me* for a little private time."

Our world is ending, yet I can't help the blood rising to my cheeks.

"It's not like that!"

Maria grins at me. "Too bad. It *should* be like that."

Yes, it should, but there isn't enough time.

"Please take Lahfah and find Barkah for me," I say. "Tell him I need to talk to him in my room, alone, in one hour. It's important."

Her smile fades a bit. She gives me a *what is this about?* look, but she doesn't question me.

"I'll take care of it," she says, then kisses my cheek. "Now go see your boy."

I run to join Bishop.


The waterfall's roar fills my ears. White mist crashes down, lit up by Omeyocan's twin moons. Blurds zip in and out of the spray. I wonder if they are playing.

"*Now* can you tell me what this is about?" Bishop asks. "We don't have time for dramatic nonsense. Why did you ask me to come here?"

We're standing in the spider's cockpit. As we drove from the gate to the waterfall, I told him about the Wasp army, the battle, how outnumbered we are. He's anxious to get back to our people and start planning for Uchmal's defense. But before that, I will say what must be said.

"We're here because this is where we first kissed. Where we first saw a spider. It was here that everything changed for us— and it's here that everything will change again."

Bishop shakes his head in exasperation. I'm clearly trying his patience.

"Em, I love you, but you're playing games. Every second matters. Get on with it."

I take his hands in mine.

"We can't beat their army," I say. "We have to leave."

Bishop thinks for a moment, choosing his words carefully.

"That might be the best strategy. If those cannons you saw have a greater range than ours, they can sit back and hammer the towers. The Observatory's antimissile batteries are almost out of ammo. If we lose the tower cannons, the Wasps can march right in or land troops anywhere they like. Maybe you're right—we take everyone to the ruins, go underground with Barkah. Then we fight a guerrilla campaign. We hit them where we want, when we want."

"Like the Belligerents did? We wiped them out, remember?"

That stops him for a moment.

"We're smarter than they were," he says. "Barkah's people hid from the automated spiders for *centuries*. We can hide from the Wasps the same way."

I shake my head.

"That's not the life I want our people to live. When I said *we need to leave,* I didn't mean leave Uchmal. We need to return to the *Xolotl.*"

His eyes narrow in confusion.

"But you said there's no weapons on that ship. All the *Xolotl* has to offer is a few old fighter craft. What would be the purpose of going up there?"

He is a warrior through and through, bred to defend his people. The thought of running is so contrary to who he is that he can't even process what I'm telling him.

This will be hard for him to hear. Almost as hard as it is for me to say.

"The purpose would be to leave Omeyocan. For good. I'm giving the order to abandon the planet."

Even this simple statement takes him a few moments to comprehend. I watch his face change from loving to guarded.

"But this is our home."

I shake my head. "It never really was. This place is poison."

His eyes narrow with anger.

"This world is *ours*. We've fought for it. We were made for it. We can't leave."

I put my hands on his shoulders.

"We leave or we die, Bishop. You have to see that."

He flinches away as if he suddenly can't stand my touch. That move was a reaction, he didn't think about it at all, yet it makes my heart drop.

"I can't believe you want to give up. You? Em Savage? Miss *if you run your enemies will find you*? You've gotten us through worse! You overcame Aramovsky's lies. You stopped the Springer war. You're the reason we escaped the *Xolotl* in the first place. That place was *hell,* and now you want to take us back?"

His voice is rising. He's never yelled at me before, not even once.

"The Wasps have weapons we can't beat." I keep my voice level. I don't want to aggravate him further. "And there's another alien ship coming, remember? The Wasps won't be the last enemy we face. But that doesn't matter—the Grub is driving people crazy. It's made us hate each other, fight each other. It's made us *kill* each other."

"Spingate was weak," he says.

"When you strangled Victor, was that just weakness?"

"He *hit* you!"

"In a training session," I say. "In a fair fight, the way he's done a hundred times before. You almost killed him! You attacked him from behind, like a coward."

Bishop leans back as if I'd just slapped him.

"I am no coward."

"No, you're not. You're also not a murderer, but on the training ground you almost were. And if I'd had my normal spear close by, Bawden would be dead. That's the Grub's influence. If it can make you and me give in to rage, what do you think it will do to the others when its power grows?"

He crosses his arms.

"Then we kill it now, before it gets stronger."

"We *don't* . . . *have* . . . *time*! The Wasps will be here tomorrow. The Grub could rise at any moment, and when it does, I don't think any of us will be able to resist. I saw it, I *felt* it. When it rises, we won't just be fighting the Wasps, we'll be fighting the Springers, too. And we'll be fighting each other."

"If anyone comes at me, I will *destroy them*!" His face twists into something primitive and hateful. He snarls, slams a fist against the cockpit's back wall. "I've killed before and I will kill again! Do you hear me? And if you try and stop me, Em, I swear to the God of Blood that *I will kill you*!"

His words hang in the air like the waterfall's mist.

I stand very still, say nothing.

Bishop blinks. He's confused. His hateful face grows slack. His cheeks flush bright red.

"Em, I'm . . . I don't know . . . I didn't mean to say that."

I force myself to take his hands again.

"It's all right," I say softly. "That's what the Grub does to us. It makes us hate. Maybe you didn't like Victor to begin with, but you *love* me—you just threatened my life. Now do you understand?"

He looks at the waterfall, refuses to meet my eyes. Maybe the Grub is affecting him, but Ramses Bishop doesn't believe in excuses; he said the words, which means he's at fault for saying them.

"We have a way out," I say. "Did Zubiri tell you how long until our shuttle is fueled?"

Bishop nods. "She thinks tomorrow around midnight."

It's just past sunset now. Maria thinks the Wasps will be here around this time tomorrow—midnight will be too late. I know Zubiri and Gaston are working as fast as they can. We'll have to find a way to slow the Wasps down.

"What about the captured troopships?"

"Sooner than the shuttle," he says. "Nevins is scheduled to do the first test flight tomorrow at noon, Cathcart right after that. Then they have hull integrity checks, or something like that."

He continues to stare at the waterfall.

"Bishop, look at me."

I reach for his face, to cup it, to hold it—with a sharp wave of his arm, he slaps my hands away.

Tears in his eyes. He feels betrayed. The person he loves is asking him to abandon everything he stands for.

"If you want to run, coward, then *run*," he says. "Take your godsdamned shuttle and leave. I will stay. I will *fight*."

I knew it would come to this. He won't be the only one that feels this way. Bishop is an icon among us—if he stays, many will follow his lead. As a people, we must not be divided. Despite Bishop's bravery, despite his skill as a warrior, despite his dedication to protecting our home against anyone and everyone, if he stays, he will die.

And so will those who stay because of him.

That I will not allow.

"Bishop . . . do you love me?"

The words crack his anger, but don't destroy it.

"You know I do. Don't dare use that against me."

I already feel like a villain, because I *am* manipulating him, but I need him on my side no matter what it takes.

"Staying is suicide," I say. "For you, for anyone who won't leave. If you love me, Bishop, if you *truly* love me, then trust in me."

Physically, Bishop is the strongest of us. But this isn't a test of physical strength—this is a test of will. When it comes to that, I am more powerful than anyone.

"We're going to take control of the *Xolotl*," I say. "If we have to kill Matilda and her people to do that, then so be it."

He finally looks at me. "What about the descendants of the vassals? Will we have to kill them as well?"

I thought Old Victor and Marcus were in league with Matilda, but now I believe that was the God of Blood warping my thoughts. If we have to fight them, we will, but I hope we don't have to.

"They told me they want us there," I say. "Together, we can make a new culture."

If I want Bishop on my side, I must be merciless. I must use every weapon I have. I hate myself for this, but lives depend on it.

"A new culture," I say. "Not just for you and me . . . for our children as well."

He lets out a half breath. He's stunned. He stares at me with his yellowish eyes . . . those big, soulful eyes.

"Children," he says. "Do you mean it?"

I reach out, slowly, and take his hand, expecting him to slap it away again. He does not. He's the most powerful man I know, yet now his hands are limp, almost lifeless. When I slide my fingers between his, they barely flex at all.

"Do this for me," I say softly. "Our people need to see that you and I are unified."

His fingers curl around mine. His eyes narrow, his jaw clenches. He nods.

"I support you, Em. Now and forever. When you announce your plan, I'll be at your side."

I have him. This is the right thing to do, and yet inside I feel so utterly *wrong*. I don't know if I want children. If we make it out of this alive and I choose against having kids with Bishop, will he ever forgive me?

I don't know.

What I do know is that the dead can't forgive anyone.

I will keep Bishop alive.

Him, and as many of my people as I can.

"We have to go," I say. "As soon as we're back, call a general meeting. I want everyone in the Grand Hall, even the tower crews. Man the cannons with Springers until the meeting is done."

Bishop nods. He guides the spider toward the Observatory.

I look back at the waterfall. I watch our special place fade into the distance, knowing that I will never see it again.

# FORTY-THREE

My people are gathering in the Grand Hall. I stand alone in my sparse room, practicing spear forms. Before I tell the Birthday Children what comes next, there is someone I must speak to first.

*"Hem?"*

Barkah stands in my open door.

"Come in, please."

I realize I don't have any chairs. There is nowhere for us to sit.

Tension between our peoples is growing again, yet he came alone, as I asked. No bodyguards. This is a sign of Barkah's trust in me.

Trust that I am about to betray.

Not that long ago, he and I stopped a war. We saved lives. Now I will ask him to put those lives at risk, and to make an impossible decision—a decision I would not know how to make myself.

He wears new clothes. Long purple robes that fall just short of the floor, trimmed in yellow and green patterns. His copper necklace gleams. There are smears of red and gold above and below his eyes. His eye patch matches that color combination. He and I are both leaders, yes, but we're very different—the worse things get on our planet, the more time he spends on his appearance.

He already knows much. The Grub. The rising that could be just days away. The two additional eggs. The new ship that is a little over a year out. The fact that more ships will probably come after that. Lahfah will have informed him about the marching Wasp army.

Now I add to that list of bad news.

"Barkah, we're leaving the planet. All of my people will fit in our shuttle. We are returning to the ship that brought us here. We have enemies there, enemies that will fight us. And someday we'll need to colonize a new planet. That means we need to take our weapons with us, our bracelets, our rifles, even the spiders. We will leave tomorrow, before the Wasps arrive, so they can't damage our shuttle. Do you understand?"

His two good eyes lock on mine. I'm again surprised at how much they look like ours. Similar shape, yes, but it's not that— there is an intelligence that bubbles within. It isn't like looking into the eyes of an animal. With any Springer, there is a *connection,* an understanding that we are more than our urges and instincts. I think of my false father, what he said about intelligent beings having similar patterns of thought. I think of the Wasp I killed—if I had managed to capture it, would looking into its eyes have given me the same feeling of connection I get from looking into Barkah's?

The Springer king takes a long time to respond. I wait.

When he speaks, I hear anguish in his voice.

*"We fight, together,"* he says. *"We win, together."*

He thought we were unified, our peoples fighting for the same thing. We were. Things change.

"There is no way to win. If we stay, my people will die."

I don't know if he understands all of my words. From the look in his eyes, though, he gets my meaning.

Barkah nods.

That is not something the Springers do. He learned that gesture from us. He does understand, and also accepts his new reality—his strongest ally will not be here to help him anymore.

Telling him that was hard, but it's nothing compared to the news I give him next.

"The ship we're traveling to was made to hold forty thousand of us. There are only five thousand people on it now. We captured two Wasp troopships. Each one carried six hundred and sixty-six armored troops, but if we pack tight, each could carry a thousand Albonden. If you want, we can take two thousand of your people with us. We can take *you* with us."

I don't speak much Springer, but I know what they call themselves: *Albonden.*

Two centuries ago, the Albonden ruled this planet. They lived in a city so large it dwarfed Uchmal. Springers numbered in the millions, at least, perhaps *tens* of millions. Matilda shattered that civilization, slaughtered the Springers, drove the survivors underground to live like insects in the dirt. Perhaps the Springers will go underground again and survive, just as they did with us, but I doubt it.

If the Wasps don't wipe the Springers out for good, the next race to arrive will. Or the race after that. Taking two thousand of his people with me is the least I can do to make good on a debt inflicted by my progenitor, a debt I could never begin to fully repay.

Barkah takes only a few moments to make his decision.

*"Will send two thousand with you,"* he says. *"Lahfah say enemy arrive sundown tomorrow. You leave sooner?"*

Now for the final piece of my request.

"Our shuttle won't be ready in time. We need to delay the enemy advance long enough to prep all three ships and to safely load your people. We'll attack the Wasps at noon, try to slow them down. Will you fight with us?"

This time his decision is instant.

He offers his hand, another behavior he picked up to better communicate with us. Three fingers, not five, but biological differences don't matter—he knows what the gesture means to me.

I take his offered hand, squeeze it tight. He squeezes mine.

*"We fight,"* he says. *"Together. One last time."*

I pull him close, hug him. I know he should stay with his people, lead them, but I don't care—I'm selfish and I want my friend to live.

"Come with us, Barkah. This planet is doomed."

He holds me tight.

*"Will think on it,"* he says. *"Now, we prepare for war."*

With that, he leaves.

I've told him what his people face, and what decision I've made.

Now it is time to tell mine.

# FORTY-FOUR

My people have gathered in the Grand Hall.

All 249 of them, all armed and ready for war.

Another forty-seven faces should be here, but their bodies belong to Omeyocan.

Bishop and I pulled Gaston, Smith, Spingate, Borjigin and Maria aside. I told them of my decision. All but Maria instantly agreed. Spingate and Gaston are eager to leave this world behind—they long for somewhere safe to raise their children. I think Kenzie understands Omeyocan is a place of death, and she's tired of watching people die. As for Borjigin? I can't say his reasons—maybe he sees his Coyotl everywhere he looks, like I still see my O'Malley.

Maria didn't agree, but she didn't object, either. She loves it here. She could survive in the jungle indefinitely. She could live on her own, or with the Springers. I think that she wants to stay, but she believes in my leadership so strongly she supports my decisions even if it means doing something she doesn't want to do.

I stand on the dais, next to the throne, flanked by my five closest friends. Our symbols aren't supposed to matter, but that's wishful thinking—symbols *always* matter. The people standing by my side are our most respected gears, circle-star, half and circle-cross.

I have no double-ring up here with me. There are only two of that symbol anyway. Walezak glares at me constantly, blames me for turning people against the gods. Aramovsky is lucky to be out of his cell at all; I'm not about to give him a place of honor.

I face the rest of our people. They are on the floor, gathered in a semicircle. The smaller kids, like Zubiri and Kalle, sit cross-legged; taller kids stand behind them. The tallest of us—Farrar, Bawden, Aramovsky, Victor, Okereke and the other adults—look over their heads.

Everyone waits for me to speak. A year ago, I wondered why they listened to me at all. I don't wonder anymore. I'm the one who leads by example. I'm the one who fights from the front.

I'm the one willing to make the hard choices.

And no choice is harder than this.

"We are in great danger," I say. My words echo off the Grand Hall's stone walls and vaulted ceiling. "Greater than ever before."

Even though I'm sure the gossip has already spread, I quickly cover our tactical situation with the Wasp army. I remind everyone of the Grub and what it's doing to us. I remind them that another ship is coming, and that more may follow.

I speak the hard truth: if we stay, we might never be free of violence.

"That is reality," I say. "I know it's hard to hear, *impossible* to hear, but reality is what it is whether we like it or not."

I see sadness, anguish, fear. More than anything else, I see *anger*. So much of it that I don't want to tell them what comes next.

But I must.

I take a deep breath and deliver the hardest news of all.

"Our dream of paradise is dead. That is why we are leaving. *Ximbal* should be fully fueled by sunset tomorrow. When it is, we're abandoning Omeyocan and returning to the *Xolotl*. We will take control of that ship and leave this world behind."

Stunned silence. Some people still look angry, but most look confused, as if I'd spoken Springer instead of English.

Farrar raises a hand.

"How long do we stay out in space?" he asks. "When do we come back?"

Heads nod. The question was on everyone's mind.

I clear my throat. No backing down now.

"I'm afraid I didn't make myself clear. We're leaving Omeyocan behind *forever*. We will travel the stars in search of a new home."

Confusion fades. On some faces, relief—those people would rather take their chances out among the stars than stay in this terrifying place. On other faces, disbelief . . . even *betrayal*.

Plenty of us, perhaps a third of our number, clearly do not approve of my decision. I don't care. I'm saving their lives.

Victor gently pushes through the kids in front of him, steps over the first row. He thumps his spear butt against the stone floor. Its sharp blade points up to the vaulted ceiling.

"My home is here," he says. "I will not leave."

Kalle stands up next to him.

"I'm not leaving, either. I can't even believe you mean what you're saying, Em. We can beat them."

More than a few murmurs of agreement.

"It's not just the Wasps," I say. "It's not just our difficulties

with the Springers. It's not just that more races might come here
to fight us." I point down to the ground. "Below us is a creature
of pure evil. It's making us want to fight, to kill each other. We're
leaving as soon as the *Ximbal* is fueled and Gaston finishes
teaching Nevins and Cathcart how to pilot the Wasp troopships."

Kalle tilts her head. "And why would we need the troopships?
If we decide to leave, wouldn't all of us fit in *Ximbal*?"

"Because two thousand Springers are coming with us."

Tempers erupt. People are yelling at me, shouting obscenities.
Some because they don't want to leave Omeyocan. Of those that
do, many can't stand the thought of taking another race with us.
I underestimated how quickly my people could forget about
Barkah's help after the first meteor attack. It's the Grub, affecting us all, playing on primitive emotions of self-preservation, of
hate.

If only the shuttle was ready right now. The longer we wait,
the more likely we are to erupt into violence with each other.

I raise my spear and I shout.

*"Be . . . quiet!"*

The grumbling dies down. This scene has played out several
times since we arrived—I will talk and they will listen. I only
need to stay in charge a little bit longer. Once everyone is on the
*Xolotl,* once we take control, they will see that leaving Omeyocan was the right decision. If they want a new leader after that?
So be it. In truth, I'm tired of being in charge—I could use a
rest.

"There is more than enough room on the *Xolotl* for all of us,"
I say. "And there are five thousand people like us up there—little
kids, teenagers, adults, old men and old women. They have invited us to join them. We will be part of a much larger community, a community that has already survived on that ship for

*twelve hundred* years. That's longer than Uchmal has existed. Longer than the Springer city that came before it. The people we will be joining, they know how to survive."

The vassal descendants were an abstract thought before. Now that we might join them, the idea of stability, of being with more people than we knew existed, it has an undeniable appeal. On some faces, I see anger and frustration shift toward hope.

Bawden steps forward.

"What about Matilda and the Grownups that control the ship? And what if my progenitor is alive?"

"We are *taking* that ship, by force," I say. "I'm not going to lie to you and tell you I have it all figured out, because I don't. But know this—the *Xolotl* will be ours. Anyone who tries to stop us will be dealt with. And I won't allow any of you to live under constant threat, so if your progenitor is still alive, your progenitor will be dealt with."

In my head, *dealt with* means *executed*. We're not the ones who created life so that it could be overwritten, so that the creators could live forever no matter what the cost. Any progenitor that would harm us must be killed.

Including Matilda.

*Especially* Matilda.

"The Wasps might reach Uchmal before *Ximbal* is ready to leave," I say. "We're going to have to slow the Wasps down. Your individual unit leaders will go over your duties soon. For now, take thirty minutes and pack anything you want to take with you on the shuttle. You're allowed to keep anything that fits in one standard backpack, and that is *all* you can keep."

Victor takes two steps closer to the dais.

"I'm not packing anything," he says. "Because I'm not leaving."

I'd hoped there wouldn't be trouble. That was naïve of me.

"You're going," I say. "Everyone is. That's an order."

He shakes his head. "If you're leaving, then you are not my leader. I refuse your order."

Bishop points a finger at him. "Shut your mouth, Muller. The decision has been made. We don't have time to debate."

"There is no debate," Victor says. He does not sound angry—he sounds resolved.

I have to get through to him.

"I can't let anyone stay behind," I say. "Anyone who stays will die, don't you understand that?"

He adjusts his grip on his spear.

"That's what you think will happen. You are making the decision you think is best, but that decision is not best for me. I will fight for Omeyocan, or I will die here."

Another murmur rolls through the crowd, a murmur of surprise and support.

For a moment, I think Victor chose those words to mock me, to parrot something I said before we first stepped off *Ximbal* onto our new world—*The Birthday Children will survive on Omeyocan, or the Birthday Children will die here.* Then I remember properly; Victor can't be mocking me, because I never actually said those words out loud.

I only *thought* them.

He and I are so very much alike.

"No one stays behind," I say, letting my volume rise. "Everyone is getting on the *Ximbal,* and that is final."

Victor nods, as if he expected me to say that.

"You are making the coward's decision," he says. "I challenge your leadership."

Bishop starts forward. I grab at his arm, expecting him to

stop, but he shakes me off with barely a shrug. He strides down the dais steps, stands nose-to-nose with Victor.

People near them back away, giving the two circle-stars room.

"We don't have time for a vote, you idiot," Bishop says. "The enemy is almost at our gates. Em has made her decision and that decision is *final*."

Victor shakes his head. "She doesn't decide for me. If your girlfriend wants to abandon our home, then she is no leader of mine."

Bishop snarls and reaches for Victor's throat.

Victor moves faster than I've ever seen a human being move. He steps back, and in a fraction of a second the tip of his spear is at Bishop's throat.

Bishop freezes, a shocked look on his face.

"Not this time," Victor says. "This time I don't have my back turned."

He's going to kill my Bishop.

Without thinking, I sharply rotate my hand right, then left, activating my bracelet.

"*Don't,*" Victor snaps, his voice still calm but now much louder. "Raise that arm, Em, and I'll slice his throat before you can fire."

The Grand Hall is still. No one moves. All Victor needs to do is give his spear one slight push.

The anger that vanished from Bishop's face seeps back in.

"Put it down," he says. "Put it down and let's settle this, one-on-one."

Victor slowly shakes his head. "Instead of me putting mine down, how about you pick up yours? No practice spears this time—we use the real thing. If you win, I do what Em says. If I win, I decide what's best for me, and you let everyone else decide what's best for them."

A *duel*? Is that what he's suggesting?

"Stop this," I say. "Put the godsdamned spear *down*, right now. We don't settle our differences by killing each other over them."

Victor's eyes don't leave Bishop. Neither does his spearpoint.

I've had enough of this. I step toward them.

"Victor, I'm warning you for the last time, you—"

Bishop raises a hand, not toward Victor, but toward me.

"Stay out of this, Em," Bishop says, his words a low growl. "This little pup wants to meet me in the circle? I accept his challenge."

Victor takes a step back. Bishop smiles at him.

All around, heads nod. Murmurs of approval, a tone of excitement, eager expressions.

My people *want* this fight. Do they hope one of the boys will die?

"This is madness," I say. "Don't you all see? The Grub is messing with our heads. We don't solve problems by fighting. This isn't *us*!"

Bishop heads for the exit. He's on his way to the plaza, to the sand-filled training circles.

Victor gives me a sidelong glance.

"People do solve problems by fighting," he says. "It's called *war*. This isn't any different."

With that, he follows Bishop, and everyone follows him, hungry to see blood spilled. Even Maria and Borjigin rush out.

I said *no* and it didn't make a difference. My words are suddenly meaningless.

In seconds, I am left standing with only Gaston and Spingate.

What do I do now?

The feeling of hopelessness drives through me. Everything is falling apart at the last moment.

"We have to stop this fight," Spingate says.

I shake my head. "We can't."

But maybe I can stop them from killing each other.

We head for the training ground.

# FORTY-FIVE

An army of bloodthirsty alien warriors is bearing down on us, and my people watch two of our own fight. If I give orders for everyone to return to their posts, those orders will be ignored—my leadership will be even further compromised.

I can do nothing but watch, just like everyone else.

The night is clear. No clouds. Omeyocan's twin moons blaze down. A few people brought torches. Flickering firelight illuminates the training pit sand, reflects off razor-sharp spearheads. Bishop and Victor circle each other, legs bent, spear tips out in front of them. Bishop is bigger than the younger boy, but the way Victor *moves:* lithe, smooth, no wasted energy.

Victor is a great fighter. I have fought both against him and side by side with him. I know how fast he is. Someday, perhaps in a few years, he could be the best of us, even better than Farrar and Bishop.

Today is not that day.

I just hope Bishop doesn't accidentally kill him.

They warily move around the training circle's edge, booted

feet pressing into the sand. People are packed in around them, only a few steps away from the circle, so close that if either fighter is knocked out of the ring the crowd will be able to push them right back in again.

The faces of my people, twisted by bloodlust. They lean forward, grab at each other, shake fists and shout for the fight to begin. Has the Grub done this to us, made something in our minds that did not exist before? Maybe. Or is this desire to see violence something that has always been there, just below the surface, hiding among our orderly society?

Bishop takes a short step forward and thrusts. Victor parries it with a clack of wood on wood.

The crowd screams in glee.

Bishop's feet are wide, his knees bent. He keeps a low center of gravity, just as he taught me to do. Victor's weight rides on the balls of his feet. His head dips a little with each of Bishop's steps—he's trying to lock in the bigger boy's timing.

Bishop shoots forward, thrusts at Victor's chest. Victor dodges left; the blade hisses by. Bishop instantly adjusts, flicks his blade up at Victor's face—a reaction so fast I barely see it—but the younger warrior is even faster. He leans back, avoiding the slash even as his own spearpoint slices through Bishop's shoulder, trailing blood behind it.

The crowd roars like a wild animal.

Bishop winces as he bounces away, again circles to his left.

Victor presses the attack, lunging forward and thrusting at Bishop's heart. Bishop moves to parry, but the thrust is a feint—in a blur of motion, Victor angles his spear down. The tip slashes through the coveralls of Bishop's right thigh.

The duel has lasted only a few seconds, yet Bishop's blood drips from a pair of wounds, red streaks that stain the white sand.

Victor isn't just *fast*, his speed is *blinding*.

My people scream so loud. They love what they see. They want more.

This can't be happening. Bishop is hurt, bleeding . . . could he really *lose*?

The younger boy dashes in again, forcing Bishop to move right. Bishop puts all his weight on his wounded leg; he winces and stumbles. Victor strikes, squatting low and sweeping the spear along the ground. The shaft cracks into Bishop's ankle—he falls, hands outstretched, his spear skidding away.

Bishop lands on his hands and knees, kicking up a spray of sand. Before that sand arcs back down, Victor has closed the distance.

He thrusts at Bishop's neck.

Everything stops.

I'm paralyzed, waiting for a gush of blood to paint the sand crimson.

But there is no gush, just a tiny bead of red where the point of Victor's blade presses into the side of Bishop's neck.

Bishop doesn't move.

The crowd is silent.

I'm speechless. *Thought*less. Everyone is.

Victor Muller beat the unbeatable.

"Yield," the boy says.

His message is simple and unmistakable. Just as his fighting style radiates efficiency, so too does this final action. There is no doubt what will happen if Bishop tries to rise.

Someone breaks the silence with a guttural shout: *"Kill him!"*

The crowd surges back to life, howling with rage and delight.

Bishop remains still. Only his eyes move, flicking to the spear that lies in the sand just an arm's reach away.

*Kill him!* the people scream, over and over, *Kill him!* I'm stunned to see those calling for Bishop's death include Farrar, Bawden, Kalle, Borjigin . . . Maria.

The Grub is warping even the strongest of us.

Bishop fought for these people, bled for them, protected them. He has been our pillar, strong and unbreakable, but just like that, they want to see his blood spilled onto the sand.

Victor's hands tighten on his spear shaft.

I step to the edge of the circle.

"Bishop, yield," I say.

When he doesn't respond, I scream it: *"Yield!"*

He looks at me. I can see it in his eyes—he can't believe he lost. The blade did not slice into his belly, but he's gutted just the same.

"I yield," he says.

The crowd screams for his blood anyway.

Victor takes a step back, thumps the butt of his spear into the sand. Emotion finally overwhelms him. His face wrinkles with disgust—not at Bishop, but rather at the crowd.

"All of you, *shut your godsdamned mouths!*"

His words are a slap across hundreds of faces. They stare at him, dumbly. A wave washes over them, reality crashing in. They finally understand what they sounded like, how they howled for the blood of a man who would have given his life for any of them.

My people are ashamed of themselves.

The Grub has power over us, yes, but not *complete* power.

Maybe there is still time.

Farrar and Bawden drag Bishop from the sand. Kenzie kneels by him, goes to work on his wounds.

Victor raises his spear.

"We're at war. The normal rules don't apply. No vote, no debate—I defeated Em's champion, that makes *me* the leader."

I wouldn't have thought I could be shocked to my core again, yet with those simple words, I am.

To my disbelief, heads nod.

This is how we function now? Just like that, the best fighter is our leader?

"The shuttle goes nowhere," Victor says. He speaks to all of us, but stares straight at me. "You will not take that weapon away from us."

This cannot happen. I won't allow it.

"I'm taking *Ximbal*," I say. "And *everyone* is coming with me. I don't care if you defeated Bishop, Victor, you're coming, too. We're all leaving this place together."

"You will not take the troopships, either," Victor says, as if I hadn't spoken at all. "We need everything we've got to beat the Wasps. Don't bother arguing, Em—we don't have time for it. I'm the leader now. You will do what I say."

A word pops into my head, something from Matilda's childhood. Something my father used to say. Something I would have never even thought of saying for fear of the rod.

"Victor, that is pure *bullshit*."

I hear people gasp. They look at each other, wondering if they just heard me right. We've been on our own for over a year with no adults, no Grownups, we have fought and died, remade this city in our image, and yet one bad word can stun people? The beatings they must have given us all when we were little to make us petrified of a few simple words . . .

Victor shakes his head. "Cursing won't make a difference."

"No, it won't," I say. "But violence will." I look around at the crowd. "That's what you all love now, isn't it? Violence? *Blood?*" I tap my temple. "Have you all become so simpleminded that some evil thing beneath our city can change who you are, how you think? We are stronger than this!"

Victor strides toward me. He stops a few steps away, his eyes narrowed more with annoyance than fury.

"This is over," he says. He holds out his hand. "I'm the leader now. Give me your spear."

His works perfectly fine, as we've just witnessed, but mine is different. Charred, chipped and beat up, it remains our symbol of leadership. If Victor takes it, then this is truly over. And if that happens, his actions will condemn my people to death.

I step to the training circle's edge. I spin my spear once, twice, then slam the butt into the sand.

"You want my spear, little boy? Then *take* it from me."

His eyes squint in doubt.

"Em, are you serious? Are you challenging me?"

I turn in place, looking at this crowd of people who are so easily manipulated.

"Would you all like that?" I ask them. "Would you enjoy seeing Victor and me duel, because you're so *entertained* by pain, by death?"

Some of them hold my gaze, but most look down. I'm magnifying their shame. Victor's words cracked the God of Blood's hold on them—my words are shattering it into a million pieces.

"Em, don't be stupid," Victor says. "I just beat Bishop and there isn't a scratch on me."

I hold out my right hand palm-up, curl my fingers in three times.

"You want scratches? Come get some."

A hint of betrayal in his eyes. And then, I remember his crush. Was the fight against Bishop just for leadership . . . or, in Victor's mind, was it also for *me*?

Maybe he thought he would rule, and I would be happily by his side.

He thought wrong.

"Make your choice," I say. "Get in the circle, or shut your mouth and do what you're told."

His expression hardens.

"The enemy is coming," he says. "We don't have time for more duels. If you insist on this challenge, I have no choice but to make an example of you."

I spit into the sand.

"You talk too much, Victor. Let's settle this."

# FORTY-SIX

I take off my boots. I want to feel the sand between my toes. It is cool and soft.

The shaft of my spear is charred and cracked, but still solid. This weapon has seen me through hard times. I need it to see me through one more.

Spingate pushes through the crowd, steps into the training circle. Dancing torchlight makes her red hair shimmer.

"This is *crazy*," she says. "Single combat isn't how we pick leaders! We can have another vote."

She doesn't think I can win. No one does.

Victor gives his spear a spin to the right, then to the left.

"Isn't time for a vote," he says. "This last fight, then no more. Anyone who challenges me after this will be put to death."

He's so confident. Barely more than a boy, but the way he fights, the way he *speaks* . . . it's almost as if he's destined to be a leader. Is Old Victor proof of that?

If leadership is Victor's destiny, that destiny will have to wait.

"Spin," I say, "get out of the circle."

She does, shaking her head in both disgust and despair. Gaston takes her hand.

"Em, don't do this," he says. "You're going to get killed. This is ridiculous."

Other people chime in. Some murmur I have no right to challenge Victor at all, that Bishop's loss settled things. I don't care—I'm getting my people off this planet.

If violence rules, then I will rule by violence.

I nod at Victor. "You ready?"

He nods back. "May the best fighter win. I'll try to go easy on you."

Victor is committed to this course of action, but he clearly doesn't want to fight me.

Something I can and will use against him . . .

If we'd dueled a week ago, he would have easily defeated me—he's too fast, too strong. But in that week, I won a battle only to learn I'd lost the war. I learned about *diversions.*

I dart forward, thrust for his heart.

Victor dances right—my blade slices empty air, I'm too top-heavy, off-balance. I stumble, use my weapon to stop myself from falling—the spear tip sinks deep into the sand.

Before I can pull it free, Victor's blade streaks for my throat. I twist left—his thrust misses me by a hair.

He steps back, a small smile lifting the corners of his mouth.

"Nice speed," he says. "You're fast, but not fast enough."

*You hurt my man, now I'll hurt you in more ways than one. . . .*

"I love you," I say.

The words are so quiet I don't know if he hears them, but he sees them on my lips. From the way his eyes widen, I know he understands what I said. The words are like a slap to his face, stunning him for just an instant.

My spear blade is still buried in the sand. I lift and flick at the same time, launching a streak of tiny white grains straight into Victor's face.

The move is so subtle and quick he doesn't have time to duck or even blink. For an instant, his fighting form is forgotten as he twists his head away, lets go of the spear with one hand to rub at his tightly scrunched eyes. He quickly realizes his mistake, again grips the shaft with both hands and points his spear to the last place he saw me—but I've already moved to my right.

I slash down, slicing across the back of his hand. Blood spills out, streaming red jewels that sparkle in the torchlight before they hit the white sand, bead up in grainy clumps.

*You tried to take what is mine, now you will pay with your life.* . . .

Squinting and blinking, Victor pivots, swings wildly. I easily block the strike and step in fast, erasing the distance between us. I twist my hips and turn my shoulders, transferring strength and momentum into my weapon—my spear butt comes up in a sharp arc that hits Victor in the balls so hard it lifts him off his feet.

He grunts, stumbles. That shot would have dropped most boys, but, half bent over, he shuffles backward, still trying to defend himself. He's squinting, looking for me, trying to blink the sand out of his eyes.

The lust for brutality courses through me. I don't fight it—it fills me with strength, with pure *power.*

*I'll end you, I'll* KILL *you.* . . .

I close in for the finish.

Victor somehow recovers enough to plant his feet and thrust forward, spearpoint driving toward my guts, but the shot to his groin has slowed him. I slip past his blade, slam my right knee into his stomach: he doubles over, air whuffing out of his lungs.

He can't see—now he can't breathe.

I drive my elbow into his nose; I hear and feel it *snap*.

Victor falls to his side. His spear rolls away. His hands flounder in the air, as if they can't decide between rubbing his eyes, clutching his broken nose, holding his balls or stemming the blood gushing from his slashed hand.

Victor Muller is defenseless.

And now he'll pay for what he's done.

"You thought you could take what is mine," I say. "You thought *wrong*."

He raises his bloody, shaking hand toward me. "I yield!"

I laugh. *"I don't care!"*

Will I slash his legs and arms, watch him bleed out, crying, begging for mercy? Or stab him through his throat, so I can see the look in his eyes as he dies the same way he tried to kill Bishop? Or should I make him go slowly, with a deep, *deep* gut wound, so he can try to stuff his own intestines back into his belly?

A blade in the belly . . .

The same way I killed Yong.

That makes me pause, but only for a moment. Yong attacked me. He deserved to die. So does Victor—I *hate* him, I want to hear him *scream*.

I raise my spear.

Spingate calmly steps between us.

"Don't kill a defenseless person," she says. "It will haunt you forever. Trust me, I know."

I should kill her, too, kill them *both*.

"This is what the Grub wants." She taps her temple. "The God of Blood is corrupting you, it's doing to you what it did to me."

*The Grub . . .*

Yes, it's affecting me. Why shouldn't it? The Grub is *guiding* me, guiding me toward my true self.

Victor lies there, helpless. Just one stab to his belly . . .

Yes, the *belly,* the same way I killed Yong.

*The same way I killed O'Malley.*

My temper vanishes, leaving a void that is filled by a rush of cold reality.

Victor is in a fetal position, wounded hand still upstretched toward me, blood pattering down to the sand. His nose is broken and bleeding. He can barely see.

He's defenseless.

He *surrendered.*

And I was going to murder him, because of that thing with the wet metallic skin, the disgusting blob wriggling beneath the dirt, the abomination that wants us to *hate.*

I lower the spear.

Spingate's eyes brim with tears.

"You did it," she says. "You did what I couldn't."

She wishes she'd been stronger. I see it in her, see her desperate desire to take it all back.

But she can't.

Spin stepped in front of me knowing exactly what could have happened. I look around, realize that no one else did a damn thing. Even Bishop stayed quiet, didn't yell at me to stop—only Theresa acted.

My best friend risked her life to save my soul.

I drop my spear. I grab Spingate, hug her as tight as I can.

"Thank you," I say. "Thank you."

I let her go, kneel next to Victor.

His eyes still blinking madly and watering from sand, he looks at me with a clear mix of admiration and disbelief.

"You defeated me."

"I had to."

His voice drops to a whisper.

"When you said . . . said that you . . ."

Even as beat up as he is, there is hope in his voice, hope that I meant those three magic words: *I love you.*

"I lied," I say. "I had to get you off guard."

That admission hurts him far worse than the physical damage. He can't hide his need for me, not anymore, but he recovers almost instantly. Victor somehow finds the strength to make his blood-smeared lips smile.

"We're at war," he says. "Winning matters. *How* you win does not. I'm yours, Em. Where you lead, I will follow."

Then Kenzie is there, gently pushing me aside.

Okereke and other circles bring stretchers, take Victor and Bishop away.

I look at my people. I slowly turn in place to take in those who gleefully watched us fight like mad beasts.

It shouldn't have happened like this, but it did. I will not let this moment go to waste.

"Anyone else question my right to lead?"

Hundreds of heads slowly shake from side to side.

"Good. Let's get to work."

# FORTY-SEVEN

I hold our strategy meeting in the *Ximbal*'s pilothouse. The walls appear clear, showing us the Observatory and people rushing about the plaza in the reddish glow of the rising sun.

With me are Bishop, Maria, Gaston, Zubiri, Barkah, Lahfah and, yes, Spingate. We've all worked through the night, preparing for the upcoming battle. They look as exhausted as I feel.

Bishop wears only shorts. He's on crutches. Bandages are wrapped around his shoulder and thigh. Kenzie says he needs another hour in the med-chamber. He won't be at a hundred percent, but he'll be ready to fight.

We stand around a waist-high, glowing disc of a map. On it, Uchmal is no bigger than a button, and Schechak, just to the north, is but a pin. Both sit within an area the size of a dinner plate that represents the jungle ruins of the ancient Springer city. Beyond the ruins, a huge area of land that includes the valley where I saw the Wasp army. Small words float above shaded areas marking the Springer tribes: *Malbinti, Khochin, Galanak, Podakra.*

Eleven columns of smoke dot the Galanak territory, making a zigzag line that points roughly toward Uchmal and Schechak. At the end of that line, a red dot flashes—the location of the Wasp army, just confirmed by Malbinti scouts.

Gaston points to one of the smoke columns.

"That's the village D'souza's Demons found. Some of the other fires were reported by the second hurukan unit, and the rest are close enough that we can see them from the top of the Observatory."

The second unit found villages that looked just like the one Lahfah, Maria and I saw.

"*Galanak, nahnaw,*" Barkah says.

The destruction has upset him, shaken him so much he doesn't bother with English. He speaks quickly to Maria. She listens, solemnly nods, then translates.

"Barkah says the Wasps destroyed most of the large Galanak towns. Combined with the routing of the Galanak army, he thinks that tribe is almost completely wiped out. The word he uses for all this best translates to *apocalypse.*"

The Wasps are clearly coming for us, but they're slaughtering any Springers they find along the way. This isn't war—this is extermination.

"How long until the Wasps reach us?" I ask.

Maria studies the map. She chews at her lower lip.

"Looks like they've sped up," she says. "A lot. At their current pace, I'm afraid they'll be here a couple of hours before sunset."

Gaston crosses his arms, shakes his head. "Way too soon. *Ximbal* won't be fully fueled for at least three hours after that."

And here I didn't think things could get any worse. We'll be too late. Unless . . .

"Maybe we don't need a full tank," I say. "How long to load just enough to get us to the *Xolotl*?"

Gaston stares at me like I just said the dumbest thing anyone has ever spoken.

"Um, that's a really, *really* bad idea, all right? That doesn't account for any contingencies, or if we can't actually board the *Xolotl* and have to come back down. We need a full tank."

Maria points to the red dot on the map.

"I hate to ruin the story for you, Gaston, but here's how it ends—the Wasps take over Uchmal. Period. We can't beat them. If we don't evacuate before they get here, you, Spingate, your baby and everyone you know will be chopped up into little pieces. *Coming back* is the least of our worries."

Gaston sneers at her. He looks at the gathered faces, perhaps expecting someone to back him up. No one does. Not even Spingate.

"We're out of options," she says to him. She speaks softly, patiently. "If we produce the minimum fuel needed to reach the *Xolotl*, how long will that take?"

He rubs at his face. I'm sure there are all kinds of worst-case scenarios rolling through his head, but Spin summed it up perfectly—we're out of options.

"Sunset, at the earliest," Gaston says. "And that's not me being difficult, that's physics. We can only convert the fuel at a fixed rate. The process can't be rushed."

I bang my spear butt lightly on the floor, twice, to make sure I have everyone's attention.

"I know that isn't what any of us wanted to hear," I say. "But we spent all night planning a delaying strategy. That strategy *will work*. It has to. We need to make sure the Wasps don't reach Uchmal until after the sun sets. We have to slow them down, *and* leave enough time for us to get back to the shuttle. Got it?"

Everyone nods. Everyone except the Springer king. He stares at the map.

"Barkah," I say, "they're going to do to Schechak what they did to the Galanak villages. You need to evacuate everyone."

Maria starts to translate, Barkah waves her off. He understood what I said.

We stay quiet, give him time to think.

He turns to Lahfah, rattles off a fast, sharp sentence in Springer. I recognize a few words—he's asking his queen if she agrees with Maria and me that the approaching army is truly unbeatable.

Lahfah doesn't hesitate. She speaks softly, quickly. No laughter in her voice now.

Barkah again stares at the map.

Finally, he looks at me.

"*Malbinti march south,*" he says. "*Abandon Schechak, immediately.*"

If all goes well, my people will be gone from this planet in a few hours. We can't help the Malbinti against the Wasps. I wish them well.

Bishop takes over. He maps out our plan to use our spiders as fast attackers, to position our soldiers in small ambush groups to pick away at the incoming troops from multiple directions. Maria's hurukans will serve as fast-moving decoys—if all goes well, the Wasps will think there are two dozen of them, not just the six we have. Borjigin's machines will quickly ferry troops around the jungle to flank the Wasps, something Bishop calls a "force multiplier." Barkah points to the areas on the map where he can bring his larger numbers to bear.

They cover many angles, but the map itself draws my focus away from the conversation.

The valley . . . how the Wasps moved through it . . . how they spread out when the Springers attacked, but before that they were in a more concentrated formation . . .

"The Goff Spear," I say, blurting out the words so loud everyone stares at me. "Zubiri, is there any way to aim the Goff Spear at the Wasp army?"

If she holds any animosity toward me for her troubles with Victor, she doesn't show it.

"The Goff Spear is built to fire at orbital craft," she says. "We can't aim at a ground target. Besides, these are very particular weapons, designed to penetrate the extremely thick armor of the *Basilisk* or the *Xolotl,* but the part that goes *boom* is a nuclear warhead—we definitely don't want them going off down here."

My frustration flares. We have a weapon that can destroy massive spaceships, but we can't use it to win this battle?

"What about the rounds themselves?" Spingate asks. "Can they be rigged to explode on their own?"

Zubiri huffs. "Didn't I just tell you it fires *nukes?*"

"Answer Spingate's question," I say. "Can you rig them?"

The one-armed girl glares at me, but she nods.

"It would take me about eight hours, I think, to modify it. Let me show you why this is a horrible idea. *Ximbal,* show damage radius of a Goff round detonation, centered on the estimated position of where the Wasp army will be in eight hours."

The flashing red dot moves much closer to Uchmal, becomes the center of an orange circle, which itself is surrounded by a larger gray circle.

Schechak is at the edge of the orange circle.

Uchmal is inside the gray.

"The explosion would produce a massive fireball," Zubiri says. "Every living thing inside the orange circle would be burned alive. The gray area represents what's called a *shock wave*. The walls of Uchmal would likely crumble. All but the biggest buildings would collapse. And then there's the fallout, which, depending on wind direction and speed, would poison a thousand-kilometer-long, two-hundred-kilometer-wide swath of jungle for decades to come. Any creature inside that area in the first few hours after detonation would likely die within weeks from radiation."

She crosses her arms, glares at all of us. "Any questions?"

There are none. My friends look at the map, stunned by the destructive power at our hands.

But I'm not stunned; I feel pieces fall into place.

The *Basilisk*'s assault, ignoring the area around the Observatory . . .

My false father, saying the Grub could defend itself but not against *all* attacks . . .

He meant attacks like this.

"A nuke could have wiped the Springer city off the map, but Matilda didn't use nukes," I say. "If the *Basilisk* used nukes, they could have taken us out easily. They didn't. The Echo's signal, it must include some kind of absolute command to not use big bombs that could hurt the Grub."

Has Matilda known about the Grub all along, or did she obey the call's commands the same way the *Basilisk*'s crew did?

I made a promise to myself, that I would kill the God of Blood. The nuke would do that. But it doesn't matter. We clearly can't use a weapon that would kill us, too. Unless . . .

"A *timer*," I say. "The Grub is drawing the Wasps to Uchmal. If we could set some kind of timer, we could have the nuke go off after we leave—we could wipe out the Grub *and* the Wasps at the same time."

Zubiri shakes her head. "With that weird electrical interference going on around here, there is no way I would trust a timer. The thing could go off before we leave, or not at all. Same thing with any kind of remote detonation—we can't risk it."

It feels like an answer is so close. Frustration creeping in, filling me up.

Gaston smacks his fist into his hand, so loud it startles everyone.

"*Impact,*" he says. "Our shuttle takes off vertically. What if we make some kind of simple bomb rack, rig the nuke to detonate on impact. We go straight up, *way* up, so when we drop it we have enough time to get clear. Then, bang—dead Wasps, dead Grub." He glances at Zubiri. "Could you engineer it to detonate on impact?"

Everyone stares at the young woman who has already lost an arm to war. She seems to shrink under our combined gaze.

"I could," she says in a voice almost too quiet to hear. "But there's no time to engineer any kind of guidance system. All we could do is drop it, let it fall on its own. For the shuttle to have enough time to get clear, we'd have to drop from a high altitude. Even a slight wind could push the nuke off-target. I'm pretty sure that if the Grub is within the orange zone, we'll kill it, but the shockwave zone? I don't think so, it's too far underground."

Bishop nods with excitement. "But if it does work, we destroy the Wasps and the Grub, then we land somewhere else on the planet. We start over."

"*No,*" Spingate says before I can respond. "Without the Goff Spear, we can't stop future races from landing. Even if we kill the Grub, the call has already been sent—at least one additional ship is coming. Maybe more. It's not like those ships will just turn around and go home. For all we know, the next race will scour the planet to wipe out competition, a larger version of what the Wasps are doing now."

She's right. Killing the Grub won't make this planet safe. Our only real chance for survival is to leave Omeyocan behind.

I make my decision.

"Zubiri, get to work on converting the rounds as bombs. Give Gaston the information he needs so he can have the bomb rack built."

"*Hem, no.*" It's Barkah. He's still staring at the map, at the massive zone of destruction if we detonate the nuke. "*My people will die.*"

"Then you better tell them to march south as fast as they can go," I say. "The Wasps have already slaughtered thousands of Springers. Once we leave, they're going to keep coming after you. As horrible as this bomb is, it might kill enough of them and their equipment that your survivors have a chance to go on, instead of being hunted down and slaughtered."

He looks from the map to me. I wait for him to answer, although it doesn't really matter what he says. I will do what must be done.

Finally, sadly, he nods. "*Kill them,*" he says. "*Kill them all.*"

We are unified. I take a deep breath, hold it, let it out slow.

"We have our mission," I say. "Now let's slow these bastards down."

# FORTY-EIGHT

It's late morning. We have only a few hours left. I walk around the plaza, shouting encouragement to my people. They place their backpacks on a scale, one at a time under Tina Schuster's watchful eye, then stack them in neat piles. She's carefully tracking the weight allowance Gaston has given her.

At the *Ximbal*'s rear is a half-rusted tanker truck. A black hose leads from it into an open door in the *Ximbal*'s underside. Louise Bariso and Noam Peura are in charge of loading the fuel.

"How much longer?" I ask them.

Peura checks something on a messageboard.

"Five hours," he says.

Five hours. Can we give him that much time? Maria and her hurukans are scouting the jungle, trying to find the invading army.

Across the plaza are the two captured troopships. Through their cockpit windows, I see Cathcart in one, Nevins in the other, preparing for the flight. Thirteen-year-old boys, each responsible for the lives of a thousand Springers.

Throngs of Springers are gathered around the troopships, panicked crowds jostling for their place, pushing at burly Springer soldiers who are trying, desperately, to keep the boarding process orderly. Scattered piles of belongings litter the ground—things the refugees wanted to bring with them, but there simply isn't room for anything other than the clothes on their backs. Red children, purple teens, blue adults. I notice that none of the refugees have the deep-blue skin of elders. I suppose that makes sense. This could be the future of Barkah's entire race—he won't send those that would live only a few more years. I can't imagine how difficult it was for him to choose the scant few of his kind that will leave Omeyocan behind.

Barkah is among them, shouting in his native tongue, directing traffic. Maybe this is only a fraction of his people, but two thousand panicked Springers makes for a grand swirl of chaos.

I jog to him. He has on yet another new coat, this one emerald green and trimmed with polished bits of steel. It covers him from thick neck down to his big feet.

*"Hem. How long?"*

How long until the shuttle is ready to depart. "Five hours."

He glances at the troopships, at his panic-stricken people, then back at me.

*"That is enough."*

"If their fighters don't attack before then, sure. Are your units in position?"

He nods. His battalions are already in the jungle. Those soldiers will not be coming with us—they will fight until we retreat for the evacuation, then head south to join the rest of the refugees fleeing Schechak.

Our forces are ready: twenty-four hundred Malbinti warriors, seven spiders, all twenty-seven remaining circle-stars, a hundred young circles, and one big surprise.

I hear something, to the north . . .

Faint, distant, but undeniable—the far-off, echoing scream of Wasp fighter craft.

"*Hem, they come,*" Barkah says.

I shout to Schuster, tell her it's time to deploy our forces. She barks orders in turn. In seconds, I hear the deep thrum of a truck's engine.

I turn to Barkah. "Are you ready?"

He shouts something I don't understand. Three of his biggest bodyguards hop out of the crowd of Springers, accompanied by a young red female carrying an embroidered pillow. Barkah takes off his necklace, the symbol of his office, and sets it on the pillow.

Barkah slides out of his emerald-green coat. His arms and chest are tied up in the yellow, blue and green rags of Springer jungle camouflage. The female takes his coat, bows and hops away.

One of the bodyguards hands Barkah a leather equipment belt. The Springer king buckles it on, takes a hatchet and a knife from another bodyguard and jams the weapons into the belt. The final bodyguard hands my alien friend one of our long-pointed silver bracelets.

Barkah slides the bracelet onto his forearm. He twitches his hand right, then left. I see the bracelet's white crystal start to glow.

Finally, the Springer king takes off his embroidered, jeweled eye patch and tosses it aside. From a pouch on his belt, he pulls out another and ties it in place. This patch is plain gray. Stitched on it, in heavy black thread, is a null-set symbol.

Gone is the regal king with his fancy clothes. Before me I see the warrior I first met in the jungle, the brave soul that killed a hurukan with spear, musket and hatchet.

He's not sitting back this time: he's here to fight.

*"Ready, Hem. You?"*

From a pocket, I pull out Halim's bloodstained headband. I tie it around my head, aware as ever that it hides my circle.

Belching smoke, Big Pig rolls to a stop next to us. The heavy vehicle will carry us to our jungle battleground. Dozens of troops—Springer and human both—hang over the thick metal walls, slapping them in a primal rhythm. The Springers wear jungle rags. The humans wear black coveralls, with yellow-leafed blue vines tied around their chests, arms and legs. A thick paste of mud and ash covers the exposed skin of both races.

Two different species, yet every single soldier in that truck wears a headband decorated with the null-set symbol. Some are neatly stitched. Others, crudely done with paint. A few are inked in blood.

I wish there was an afterlife, so Halim could look down and see the impact of his small gesture.

Today, we are all truly one people.

I climb into the truck. Barkah and his bodyguards scramble up behind me.

Big Pig's engine rumbles—we drive off to war.

# FORTY-NINE

am deep in the jungle ruins. Perhaps a hundred people of Omeyocan—Springer and human both—surround me. The jungle canopy arcs above, life-giving vines hanging down. No blurds here, no piggies, no animals of any kind, because wildlife seems to have the good sense to clear the hell out.

If only we could be as smart.

Big Pig dropped me and mine off, then carried Barkah to his own regiment. Far north, we hear Springer war horns, volley fire from rifles and muskets, the deadly bark of Wasp machine guns and the thundering echo of tanks letting off round after round. Barkah has engaged the enemy, but we have no idea how he's doing.

My unit waits for me to speak. Eyes of many colors look at me with fear, excitement and anger. *Always* anger. I am not so foolish to think our newly unified sense of purpose comes only because we now have a common enemy—the God of Blood drives us to fight, and fight we will.

"The Wasps are coming," I say. "Our scouts estimate they'll be at the walls of Uchmal in two hours. Our ships will be ready to leave in four, so we *must* slow them down."

I turn as I talk, looking every single being in the eye, a technique I learned from Aramovsky. These soldiers' thoughts swirl with rage and hatred, both from the Grub's influence and because their home is being invaded. I need to connect with them, make sure they understand I'm *here,* fighting by their side.

I still don't know why I became the leader, but I have learned what a leader must do.

"They have better weapons, but we know the jungle," I say. "We'll use that to our advantage. We get close, hit them hard, then fall back and lure them into our trap. Our goal is to take out as many tanks as we can, understand?"

Heads nod. Springer tails thump against the ground.

Tanks are the enemy's lead element. If we let them roll right in, they'll blow open the city gates and cruise down our streets with infantry close behind. If we attack the tanks, the Wasps will react to defend those tanks. That, we hope, will tie up their ground troops and slow their cannons, keeping them from moving into firing range until our evacuation is complete.

We know they still have the troopships that brought them here. We haven't seen those yet, don't know where they are. All we can do is hope they fear our tower cannons and hold their troopships in reserve.

"Keep fighting until we hear the retreat signal—three long blasts in a row," I say. "When that sounds, all human troops return to the plaza, *fast*. All Springers, leave the battlefield. Head south to join your people. Everyone understand?"

Nods and thumps. Focused eyes. Determined faces.

The Springers here with us will not leave the planet. They

know they are quite possibly fighting for the future of their species. And I know that if we drop the nuke, they probably won't have enough time to make it out of the blast radius. We might only have this one chance to destroy the Wasp army—I will sacrifice thousands of my allies so that millions of them can survive.

If I am very, *very* lucky, these are choices I will have to live with the rest of my days.

I raise my spear.

"Today, we are not Springers. We are not humans. We are *all* from Omeyocan. We fight as one. Rely on each other, and kill as many of those bastards as you can!"

My warriors raise muskets, rifles and spears. A brief, unified bark of solidarity, then the crowd breaks up as they move to their assigned positions.

I jog toward my spider. Good old 05. The holes have been patched, the leg repaired, the shiny dents painted over. Victor and Bawden wait in the cockpit. Victor's hand is bandaged, as is his nose—there wasn't time to heal him correctly.

The three of us are a good team. I hope we all make it.

Next to the spider is Maria, sitting astride the furry, smelly bulk of Fenrir. She smiles the wicked smile of someone who is gifted at war and knows war is about to begin.

"Hail, Em," she says. "That was quite the fancy speech."

"Oh, come on, Maria—you don't use flowery words when your squad is going into battle?"

She shakes her head. "We don't talk. We just kill."

I wonder if Maria will survive the next four hours. I hope so. I hope so very much.

I hand my spear up to Victor, then climb aboard. I'm about to give the order to move out when Maria calls up to me.

"Em, one question?"

I nod.

"I like Bishop," she says. "If you die today, can I date him?"

I laugh. "Don't hold your breath, sugar. I'll be on the shuttle with him in a few hours."

"Or if Bishop dies," Victor says to me, "can I date *you*?"

I don't know if I should be angry or offended—his charming grin erases either possibility. I cut him up, yet still he smiles at me.

Bawden rolls her eyes.

"If we're done talking about our love lives, can we please go fight now?"

I push my spear into its bracket on the cockpit's rear wall, give the shaft a quick shake to make sure it's held firmly, then face forward.

"Take us out, half-speed," I say.

Number 05 crawls through the jungle.


Our careful strategy has already fallen apart.

Maria quietly led us toward the Wasp column, only to run headlong into three of their ticks. Our grand plan to attack instantly turned into running for our lives.

Bawden drives our spider full out, the armored hull bouncing off tree trunks as often as it goes around them. Two ticks scramble through the trees behind us, banking in and out of cover, their rapid-fire guns shredding wood and leaves. Bullets smack into our spider's armor, make the metal ring like a musical instrument.

I can't see Maria anywhere.

Victor pops up from the cover of our cockpit and fires his rifle over the spider's back, eight shots in three seconds, then drops down again. He reloads, hands a blur.

Ahead and to the right, I see a red flag waving from high in the branches—a Springer is up there, hidden among the vines and yellow leaves.

At least part of our plan is back on.

I grab Bawden's shoulder, point to the flag.

"I'm on it," she says, "hold tight!"

Victor and I both grip the armored ridge as Bawden turns the spider hard toward the wide space below the flag—between two thick tree trucks.

The lead tick is right behind us, guns pounding away at our armor.

The moment we pass below the flag, a Springer yells. I lean over the side to look back as hidden ropes are pulled tight— a net rises between the trees. The tick tries to turn, but it's too late. The eight-legged machine flies into the net. Anchoring ropes snap taut. The tick's nose slams hard into the jungle floor. The machine bounces once, spinning, smashes down in a cloud of dead leaves.

Springers hop out of the underbrush, rifles and muskets and hatchets ready to go to work.

I see two lightly armored Wasps slowly crawl from the ruined tick. Just before Bawden turns sharply and I lose sight, the Springers close in on them.

A hail of bullets rings off our spider, makes me drop down behind the cockpit's cover. Victor pops up, emptying the rifle in a blur.

"*There,*" Bawden shouts. "The tanks!"

Through the thick underbrush, I see one, a hulking block of camouflaged metal with that thick barrel jutting forth like a spear. In our mad, directionless escape from ticks, we found our target. Now for the real test—can we lure them away?

"Lighting the smoke," I say, then pull the pin on the thick canisters Borjigin mounted in the cockpit. With a *whuff* of compressed air, the skull-sized container inside shoots high, punching through the canopy before bursting in a cloud of purple smoke.

"Oh *shit-balls,*" Bawden screams, and I'm almost thrown overboard as she turns our spider hard left. Out the right side, I see what she saw—hundreds of Wasp foot soldiers rushing through the underbrush toward us.

Bullets rake us from the left; the other pursuing tick. I lean forward, out in front of Bawden—the tick banks sharply just before I flick my fingers forward, and my beam vanishes harmlessly into the jungle.

Fire from the Wasp infantry pings madly off our spider, forcing Victor and me back down into the cockpit's cover.

"They're chasing us," he says.

Bawden throws him a fast glare. "Wow, Vic, I would have never known."

"Just *drive,* dammit," I say. "Get us to the target point."

We don't have many spiders—Bishop guessed the Wasps probably know that. In fact, we based our whole strategy around that guess. If the Wasps are smart, they know taking out our mechanized units will give them a permanent advantage. We can only hope they want that so bad we can use it against them.

Another musical burst of big bullets hammers into 05's rear. The tick is behind us again, firing away.

Our spider's smooth movement suddenly changes to a lurching shudder, as if someone is rocking it hard side to side.

"*Leg damage,*" Bawden calls out. "I have to take that leg offline. Victor, help me!"

They flip switches, twist knobs, turn dials. While they work, I pop up and fire bracelet blasts over the spider's back, keeping the tick from closing in on us.

The lurching lessens.

"As good as it's going to get," Bawden says. "Hang on!"

As if I could do anything else.

Our spider rips through the jungle. We're hit with a hail of gunfire so concentrated that even Victor won't pop up to return fire. Bullets shred branches and trunks, tear the leaves around us, a swarm of invisible insects chewing the jungle to tiny bits.

Even over the unending gunfire, I hear the tank cannon's roar.

Ahead of us, a fireball erupts, showering us with dirt and mud. I feel a dozen piercing stings on my face and hands. We're moving too fast to avoid it—Bawden drives us straight through the blaze. It singes my skin, but we're through it almost instantly. I look at my hands: big splinters jut out of them, shreds of a tree blasted apart by the tank's powerful round. A glance at Bawden and Victor—their faces bleed from a dozen small cuts.

We're hurt, but the tank is following us . . . our plan is working.

Movement to the right: the tick, again trying to flank us. I flick my fingers forward—this time my beam connects, glances off the tick's armor. It banks away, working the trees and underbrush for cover.

Another tank round erupts near us, then another, and another, each detonation a hard kick to my ears. Concussion waves hammer my body. The air fills with dirt and dust and mud and smoke. Grit in my eyes, my mouth.

It's not just one tank following us . . . it's at least *three*.

The explosions smack our spider side to side, but somehow Bawden keeps the machine from tumbling.

*"Trouble ahead,"* she shouts.

In front of us, the jungle flashes with a long line of rapid-fire bursts—camouflaged Wasp soldiers, dug in and ready.

We were so close to the target point, but now we're cut off from Barkah's troops and from Borjigin's surprise.

"Screw it," Bawden says. "Do or die, you sonsabitches!"

The crazy girl maxes out our speed.

I hit the deck. So does Victor. Bawden squats as low as she can. Bullets smack into the cockpit, ricochet around. A sting in my shoulder, a burn on my leg. Victor cries out.

The roar of gunfire gets closer, louder, then starts to fade—Bawden punched through their lines.

We slow slightly. Blue smoke up ahead; we've reached the target zone.

Gunfire continues to hammer the spider. No wonder these machines dominated the Springers for two centuries. The Wasp bullets damage it, but can't destroy it—simple musket balls would do almost nothing at all to this armor.

Something inside the spider clanks. The machine stumbles, slows to half-speed.

*"Bawden,"* I scream, *"get us moving!"*

She kneels, pulls open a hatch and drops into the spider's guts. "Victor, drive! Em, keep them off us!"

Over the loud-as-hell tanks rumbling along in pursuit, I hear the roar of a tick engine. It's coming, but I can't tell from where.

A war cry of clicks and chirps—the Wasp infantry is advancing on us.

A tank round detonates just to our right, so close I feel the heat. Debris showers us.

And we're *still* slowing down.

"Where the hell is Borjigin?" Victor shouts. "He's supposed to be here!"

We did *our* job—Borjigin isn't here to do his. We're taking fire from all sides. If we get out of the slowing spider, we'll be dead before we hit the ground.

Is this how it ends?

I lie back on the cockpit deck. I look up into the jungle canopy. Yellow leaves, brown branches and tree trunks, blue vine stems. Through the foliage, the dappled late afternoon sky. A few clouds. Far above, Omeyocan's twin moons are just starting to show themselves.

This is a good place to die.

I hope we gave Gaston enough time.

Then, something massive blocks out the sky.

The tallest trees shudder. Long prongs of bright-blue metal push them aside. As easily as a child stepping through tall grass, Borjigin's giant machine steps through the trees, steps *over* us. Huge steel feet smash down, one after another, as it marches toward the oncoming tanks.

The constant hail of bullets switches from us to the giant.

I'm up in an instant, peeking over the back of the spider. The pursuing tick is still streaking toward us, but the sudden appearance of Borjigin's giant sends the Wasp infantry fleeing into the trees.

Our spider grinds to a halt.

"Victor," I say, taking aim at the oncoming tick, "signal to Barkah's troops to close in!"

As a disciplined unit, the Wasp foot soldiers seemed unbeatable—now they're scattered in the deep jungle, where Springers have fought for centuries.

The tick driver finally sees Borjigin's beast, slows and starts to turn away from the monstrosity. It's not shooting at our spider anymore—I finally have two seconds to line up a clean shot.

My bracelet beam blazes out, splashes off the tick's armored cockpit. I don't know if I hit anything inside, but the eight-legged machine stumbles awkwardly. It rights itself—just as a giant bright blue foot crushes through the branches and smashes down on the tick so hard the ground trembles.

A hail of bullets makes us duck down again. Victor pops up, firing fast. I join him, shooting bracelet blasts at a squad of Wasp infantry rushing toward us, led by a big one with copper-striped shoulders. The soldiers move from tree to tree, weaving in and out, firing all the way. This squad isn't like the ones that ran screaming into the jungle. These might be properly trained soldiers—the Wasps' version of circle-stars.

Victor's fire drops one Wasp, my beams drop a second.

I kneel low, look into the open hatch. Bawden is jammed in among the machinery, using her knife to chisel away at some cracked ceramic piece.

"Bawden, if you don't get this thing moving, we're *dead*!"

"Almost got it," she says, and keeps chipping.

*"Here they come,"* Victor screams.

I hear something climbing up the side of the spider. I yank my spear from its bracket, lean out and drive the blade into a Wasp's armored face. The point punches through its helmet, knocking the soldier off the rungs.

Another Wasp leaps onto the spider's sloped front, one hand holding the armored ridge, the other aiming its heavy rifle at me. Victor kicks out hard, his boot smashes into the Wasp's chest—it fires as it falls back, but the bullets go wide.

A third Wasp lands in the middle of the cockpit, pistol in hand. Before it can fire, Victor tackles it, knocking it into me.

All three of us fall to the cockpit deck.

I can't reach my spear.

I draw my knife, wrap an arm around the Wasp's head and saw at the armor covering its throat.

The Wasp clicks and hisses, trying to bring its pistol to bear on Victor, who growls and grunts, holds the Wasp's wrist in a death grip.

We are animals fighting for life.

A flash of yellow whips in from above. Pincers snap shut. The alien is on top of me one moment, yanked high the next.

I scramble to my knees. Maria and Fenrir are next to us; she's firing her rifle, Fenrir is stuffing the Wasp into his mouth, chomping madly with his thick piranha teeth. Two more mounted hurukans rush out of the jungle. Pincers snap. Riders fire. Blood flies. The Wasps fight back, but Maria's huge beasts are too fast, too vicious—in moments, the enemy breaks and runs, scattering in all directions. Around us, a dozen Wasps lie dead, as do one of the hurukans and its Springer rider.

Maria and Fenrir stay beside our spider. The last hurukan, ridden by a howling Nedelka Holub, gives chase.

A tree falls, broken down by a tank that rolls over the stump and rumbles along the trunk, smashing flat the rattling branches and shaking leaves. Two tanks follow behind, a single-file column of destruction.

Borjigin's giant moves to attack.

The lead tank's cannon belches out a roaring cone of flame.

The shell detonates in the metal giant's right shoulder. The arm with the huge scoop comes free with a ringing *snap,* falls, smashes into the jungle floor.

I think everyone inside the giant must be dead, but the machine strides toward the tank.

Smoke billowing from the severed arm, the metal giant's massive pincer-hand reaches out, scoops up the lead tank. I watch, stunned to stillness, as the giant lifts the first tank high and smashes it down on the second.

There is the briefest pause, then both tanks erupt in a cloud of flame that engulfs the surrounding trees and sets them ablaze.

The flames also splash against the giant. Borjigin is driving. He has a crew of three. The fire is already spreading through the massive machine. If I don't do something, the four of them will be burned alive.

"Maria!" I meet her eyes, then point to the ladder that runs up the giant's spine to its hodgepodge head. "Can Fenrir climb up there?"

She leans back, holding the reins, looks up only for a moment before answering me.

"Let's find out." She whips the reins against the beast's back. "Fenrir, *climb*!"

The hurukan rushes at the giant and leaps, powerful legs launching the heavy beast high into the air. The fading sunlight piercing the jungle canopy plays against tawny fur, gleams off the pinkish blood marking a dozen small wounds.

Fenrir's front legs reach out—claws clutch the metal ladder, cling tight even as the snake neck wraps firmly around a broken bit of pipe jutting from the giant's back. Rear legs scramble against metal until they, too, lock on.

"God of Blood," Victor says, breathless. "Look at that."

Maria screams at her mount, urging it higher. One reaching claw after another, Fenrir climbs the burning giant like it is scaling a shaking, flaming tree.

Bawden hops up from the deck, slams the hatch shut behind her.

"We're back in business!"

I point my spear at Borjigin's great machine. "Get us there, now!"

Bawden steers our lurching, wounded Number 05 toward the giant.

The jungle erupts anew as a wave of routed Wasp soldiers rushes past, ignoring us as they flee for their lives. A horde of Springers descends upon them, tearing through the underbrush, dropping down from trees, even swinging in on vines. Guns and muskets fire briefly, then fighting shifts to hand-to-hand. A Wasp draws a long sword that crackles with energy and cleaves an attacking Springer in two. Both halves of the body are still twitching as three more Springers rush in and drag the Wasp down.

Hatchets and axes flash—as good as the color-shifting armor is, it can't stand up to the brutal savagery of these infuriated warriors.

I have never seen such destruction. Two species are fighting for the future of their kind. No one surrenders. No one offers respect to the wounded. There are no deals here, no yielding, only fighting until one side or the other is dead.

Despite the flames licking up the light blue giant, Borjigin moves his monster toward the final tank.

The tank's cannon roars. The shell detonates in the giant's left hip, a billowing explosion of orange flame and black smoke that rips the joint to pieces, sends forth a hail of metal shards that cut down vines, embed in tree trunks, punch through Springers and Wasps alike.

The metal giant sways to the left.

Maria's hurukan loses its grip—clawed feet slip free. High above the forest floor, the big beast swings out, held in place only by the snake neck that is stretched taut to the point of breaking. Maria grips tight to her saddle as the furred body slams into branches, snapping arm-thick wood like kindling. I wait for the beast and my friend both to spin through the jungle to their death. . . . somehow Fenrir hangs on.

Borjigin's giant stumbles, almost falls, but recovers—the machine stands straight.

Maria's mount swings back onto the ladder. Claws grip and *hold*.

Again, the hurukan scrambles higher.

A rectangular chunk of metal erupts from the back of the giant's head, spins through the air to vanish in the jungle. Borjigin climbs out, his coveralls dotted with sticky grease that burns with deep-orange flames. Only one kid, a girl, climbs out after him. They grip handholds, cling tight.

Fenrir reaches them. The long neck coils around the girl, lifts her free. Maria pulls the burning Borjigin onto the saddle behind her.

Fenrir scrambles down the ladder. Long tongues of flame shoot from the giant, making blue paint bubble, singeing Fenrir's bloody fur.

The tank is so close to the giant the long cannon barrel angles up at forty-five degrees. This time, the round erupts dead center in the machine's chest. The billowing fireball forces the hurukan to leap out into the air.

Fenrir slams into the ground—I hear bones break on impact.

The burning wreck of Borjigin's giant tips backward, then topples forward like a falling tree, crashes down on the tank in a whuffing storm of flame.

Something inside the smashed tank explodes, sends streamers of flame so high into the air they arc over the jungle canopy. There is no way the last two crew members of Borjigin's giant could have survived that.

I snatch up my spear. Victor and I are out of the spider, sprinting to our friends. Maria rolls on the ground, holding a shoulder that hangs at a strange angle. Borjigin's leg flops sickeningly. The girl—I recognize her, Sharyl Bohner—is half-trapped beneath Fenrir's bulk. The hurukan kicks, twitches and roars. With every lurch, Sharyl screams in agony.

The beast's death throes are going to kill the girl; I have to finish him.

Fenrir's snake neck finally lies limp. I raise my bracelet to the three black eyes that run down the side of his head and flick my fingers forward—nothing happens.

A shard of metal sticks out of my bracelet's white stone: a piece of shrapnel. Had it hit an inch higher or lower, it would have torn my arm apart.

Victor screams for me to kill the beast. He's got Sharyl's arms, is trying to pull her free.

I grab my spear with both hands. I time Fenrir's lurching, then thrust. The blade slides through an eye and into the head. Fenrir stiffens, spasms . . . falls still.

Bawden slides to a stop next to Victor. Victor's face screws tight with effort as he lifts Fenrir just enough for Bawden to pull Sharyl from beneath the dead animal.

I yank my spear free, grab Maria and drag her toward the spider. Borjigin crawls toward it as well, arm over arm, a look of utter determination etched on his bloody face.

All around us, Springers howl in a victorious battle cry. They've killed the last of the Wasps in this area.

Corpses, everywhere. Smoke rising. Flames crawling up massive tree trunks, twisting through vines. I smell burned flesh and scorched wood.

I smell *blood*.

This is what the Grub wanted.

*Only the strong survive.*

We load our wounded into the spider. It's a tight fit.

A thunderous blast, bigger than anything I've ever felt, showers us with dirt and broken splinters of wood. For a moment, I can't hear, then the sound of roaring flames comes rushing back. Someone grabs me, shakes me.

"Artillery," Victor says. "The Wasps are shelling us!"

Another explosion to our left makes the ground tremble like an earthquake.

I hear Springers screaming.

The Wasp artillery. We got three tanks, but we didn't get their cannons.

I hear the low sounds of Springer horns echoing across the jungle—three long blasts, all in a row.

The sun is setting: we did it.

"Bawden, get us home!"

Our spider jerks to life. Each halting step makes Maria and Borjigin cry out. We can't help them now; they'll have to bear the pain.

Victor shoves something against my chest—it's a Wasp rifle, long and heavy and wicked. He points to a button under the thick barrel.

"That's the trigger. When you press it, hold on *tight*, it's got a hell of a kick. You guard our back—I have to dress Sharyl's wounds or she'll bleed out!"

Bawden pushes the shuddering spider as fast as it will go, a painful pace that hurts us all.

Another explosion, then another, and another. The air fills with flying dirt and a deadly hail of shrapnel.

Over those deafening roars, I hear a familiar rocket-growl coming from the north—Wasp troopships.

They're bringing in their reserves.

# FIFTY

The enemy is close behind.

The setting sun turns sparse clouds into long, ragged red slashes—today, even the sky bleeds.

My people are in full-on retreat, survivors all around us as we rush down the road from the abandoned Schechak toward Uchmal's North Gate. Some of us are barely able to walk; some carry wounded comrades; some stop every few feet to turn and fire back into the jungle ruins. A few don't bother to shoot, and I know why—their rifles are out of ammo, their bracelets are depleted of energy.

Just east of us, the one o'clock tower cannon fires volley after volley into the jungle, trying to take out our unseen pursuers.

Our lurching spider struggles through the tall metal doors. When Bawden finally brings us to a stop, leg joints blow in a burst of sparks. The machine's belly clangs down onto the paving stones.

"No fixing that," Bawden says. "Everyone out!"

Victor leaps to the ground. Bawden lowers Sharyl down to him.

I sling the Wasp rifle, grab my spear and scramble up onto the spider's back.

Big Pig is parked just inside the wall, throaty engine idling. Dozens of wounded lie in its wide bed. A pair of circles sprint to us. Bawden gently lowers Borjigin to their reaching hands.

A block down the street, Springers bustle around five wooden trebuchets. They used these weapons against us in the Battle of the Crescent-Shaped Clearing, but today they're loaded with barrels, not boulders. The launching arms—stripped down tree trunks—are cocked back, ready to fire.

No sign of Bishop or the people in his unit. He knew the plan. If he hasn't made it back by now . . .

So many lives at stake. We can't wait for him.

I face the one o'clock tower and wave both arms over my head, giving them the signal to abandon their position and head for the shuttle. The cannon fires one last burst, then falls quiet.

Victor carries Sharyl to Big Pig; people reach down from the bed, gently pull her in. The two circles load Borjigin in after her. Looks like he's passed out from the pain.

I help Bawden lower Maria to the ground.

Bawden slides under her good shoulder. I slip under her bad, my left hand around her waist, my right holding my spear. I can feel the broken bones grinding inside her.

We move toward Big Pig, but by some unspoken connection, the three of us stop and look back at the spider.

So many fresh bullet holes in the armor I think the machine might be more air than metal. Two legs stand normally, bent at that familiar sharp angle. Two legs are twisted and bent. One is missing altogether.

"Goodbye, Number Five," Bawden says, her voice hoarse from screaming, from smoke.

Maria nods. "And goodbye to you, Fenrir. You were a good boy."

Tears cut trails through the grime on her face. I don't know if she's crying from physical pain, for her hurukan, for leaving Omeyocan, or for the squad member she lost. Probably all of the above.

We help Maria to the truck. Hands reach down to help her up just as the air crackles with a round of rifle fire.

Victor shouts the alert: *"Here they come!"*

Bawden and I sprint for the gate. We slide to a stop, use the tall right-hand door for cover. I drop my spear and unsling the heavy Wasp rifle.

Victor and two circle-stars are at the left-hand door, firing rifles and bracelets.

A tick bursts from the jungle not even fifty meters away, twin guns blazing. It scrambles onto the road and scurries toward our gate. A dozen Wasp foot soldiers fan out behind it, led by a tall one with copper streaks on its shoulder armor.

Bullets spark off the paving stones at our feet, ping off the metal doors.

I aim at the tick, press the button. Recoil smashes the butt against my shoulder, a combination of punches so hard they make me stumble backward.

Our shots hit the armored tick, but they do nothing. It will be on us in seconds. I should have ordered the doors shut when I had the chance.

Then, behind the tick, the jungle erupts again as a spider tears into view. Kai Brown is driving . . . and Ramses Bishop mans the cannon. Behind the spider, a dozen circle-stars and a handful of Springers rush forward to fight.

Bishop's face is a bestial snarl: mouth open, teeth exposed in a primitive roar I can hear even over the gunfire. His face is covered in a mixture of blood, sweat, ash and mud.

He fires the spider cannon. The blast hits the tick in the rear. I see a muffled explosion inside the armored shell, then the machine tumbles, hits the ground and rolls, limp legs flopping.

The copper-striped Wasp commander shouts a click-clack-screech of orders to turn and fight, but his troops are caught in the open with enemy in front and behind.

Victor rises up and screams: *"Charge!"*

He rushes forward armed with only a spear—his rifle is out of ammo, his bracelet drained of power. The two circle-stars with him charge as well, one shooting a rifle on the run, the other armed with nothing but a knife.

I fire the Wasp weapon to give them cover—one round hammers my shoulder, then it does nothing. Empty.

I drop it, grab up my spear and sprint out of the gate, Bawden at my side.

Bishop's spider overruns the enemy. A pointed foot punches through a Wasp soldier, pinning the twitching alien to the dirt.

A burst of machine-gun fire rakes the spider cockpit. Bullets hit Kai Brown in the chest and face: he drops in a cloud of blood. The cannon sparks and starts to smoke—it's ruined.

Some of the Wasps toss their guns aside and draw knives or swords; we're not the only ones who have run out of ammo.

Bishop reaches back, yanks his red axe from its bracket. He roars and leaps from the cockpit, swinging the horrible weapon down—the axe-head drives through a Wasp helmet, splitting the skull within. The creature drops, as limp as if it had never been alive to begin with.

We reach the Wasps at the same time Bishop's circle-stars and Springers do, engulfing the enemy from all sides. Spears and hatchets and axes clash with swords and knives, but the Wasps have no chance. They fall one by one until only the copper-striped leader remains, sword blazing with energy.

It swings at Victor, who angles his body away and jabs his spear through its thin knee. The Wasp tries to swing again, but Bawden leaps and kicks it in the chest, knocking it flat on its back.

Before it can rise, I drive my spear through its neck.

The brave warrior dies on the soil of a foreign planet, far from a home it probably never saw.

My people sprint to the gate. Bishop grabs my waist, tosses me up into his spider. I land, almost slip on Kai Brown's blood. He lies face-up on the cockpit deck, as dead as the alien I just killed.

Bawden and Bishop scramble up the rungs. She takes the driver controls.

Two Springers leap into the cockpit—it's Barkah and Lahfah. Are they evacuating with us?

The Springer king is badly cut, his blue blood mixing with the Wasp yellow that covers him head to toe.

"*Hem,*" he says, then collapses onto the bloody deck. Lahfah kneels by his side.

I can't worry about them right now.

Bawden drives the spider through the gate: the huge doors start to swing shut behind us.

Victor is at the trebuchets with the Springers.

I wave my spear at him. "*Light them up!*"

With a heavy rattle of wood, the five trebuchets launch. The long tree trunks snap high into the air. Attached ropes yank taut, pulling harnesses that swing back, then up, then release their payloads—five barrels sail high over the wall, each trailing a thin line of black smoke.

We don't see them hit, but we hear them: *boom, boom-boom, boom-boom.*

Through the closing gates, I see a wall of fire rise up to engulf the jungle. The flames flare higher than the tallest tree. The intense, instant heat makes thousands of vines writhe in a dying dance.

"Good *gods*," Bawden says. "What was in those barrels?"

"Borjigin's accelerants," Bishop says. "Packed in with chemicals left over from Zubiri's fuel conversion process."

The chemical mix will burn hot enough to set everything around it ablaze, perhaps hot enough to turn the entire jungle into an inferno. Any Wasp foot soldiers—or ticks or tanks—caught in that instant slice of hell are already dying. Those that haven't reached it yet have to either go around or wait for the fire to die down.

That buys us a little more time.

The gate doors slam shut. The people who closed it rush to Big Pig and climb into the bed. Victor and the trebuchet Springers are the last ones in.

Big Pig's driver steers onto Latu Way and drives straight south, toward the Observatory.

Our spider falls in behind it.

Over the growl of Big Pig's engine, I hear a new sound. A high-pitched whistle, growing louder and louder. In the truck's bed, Victor screams at his fellow passengers.

"Artillery, *incoming!*"

The whistle sound grows to a deafening volume. Close behind us, a fireball blossoms from a three-layer ziggurat. Stones spin away, smash into other buildings. Rubble rains down on the streets.

The artillery we couldn't find has found us.

Big Pig picks up speed. The driver pushes the truck hard and fast.

Artillery shells rain down around us, turning our city into a foggy cloud of explosions, fire and smoke, sprays of deadly shrapnel. Buildings shatter. Streets erupt. Flames rise. Ziggurats crumble in upon themselves.

Uchmal has suffered two aerial bombardments so far, but neither compares to this assault. The city that has stood tall for two centuries is finally falling.

A Wasp fighter roars past overhead. A stream of red fire snakes out from the Observatory. The fighter angles up and races off, trailing flame.

If the Wasps only knew how little ammo we had left, they would have swarmed us with their fighters.

Three blocks from the plaza, we pull ahead of the artillery explosions. *The Grub* . . . the Wasps somehow know to not target the area above the Grub.

Big Pig screeches to a halt at the plaza's edge, next to the special cart used to move the Goff Spear rounds. I see the hexagonal rounds mounted under the shuttle's wings. It doesn't look like much is holding them on—I can only hope Zubiri and Gaston know what they're doing.

Bawden stops our spider next to the truck. The trebuchet Springers leap out of Big Pig and hop to us. They help Lahfah lower Barkah down from the spider, help her carry him to the Wasp troopships.

Dozens of people rush to Big Pig to unload the wounded. Bishop and Bawden jump out to help. I see Borjigin put on a stretcher, Okereke carrying Maria in his arms. Kenzie Smith shouts instructions as everyone scrambles up *Ximbal*'s ramp.

A shimmering haze of heat makes the *Ximbal*'s engines look

like they're masked by falling water. The engines of the two Wasp troopships glow red with the promise of power.

All around the plaza, artillery shells hammer down. Buildings that stood for centuries are gone in an instant. A wayward shot strikes the Observatory itself, fifteen layers up, breaking off huge blocks that tumble down the slope in an avalanche of stone.

Over the cries of our dying city, I hear people screaming my name. I look to the shuttle, see Spingate on the metal-grate deck, calling to me, more people around her doing the same.

I'm still standing in the spider's bloody cockpit—I'm the last one left.

I scramble down and sprint for the shuttle. One troop transport is already climbing into the air, slowly driven upward by a column of fire. The second is just starting to lift off.

And then, beneath my feet, the ground *shakes*. Not the hard-hitting thrum of a detonating artillery round . . . this is something more powerful, something much *bigger*.

To my right, a thick slab of plaza stone cracks, tilts upward. It sags back down for a moment, then angles high again. More stone shatters, pushed up from beneath, a miniature mountain growing right before my eyes. From the jagged tip of this new peak, something massive slithers out.

Something *copper*.

The Grub is rising.

My feet hit the *Ximbal*'s ramp—I'm halfway up when the Grub bursts from the plaza. The ground trembles so hard the shuttle *slides*. Metal screeches, twists, warps. The ramp slides beneath me, snaps free and drops away. I manage a desperate leap for the deck. I reach and reach . . . I'm not going to make it—

—Spingate catches my wrist. My hand wraps around hers.

*Ximbal* slowly elevates, cones of flame pushing it straight up.

I hang in the air, my life in Spingate's hand. She lies on her side on the rattling metal deck, her left arm the only thing keeping me from falling to my death.

*Ximbal*'s exterior door is still open. The deck twists and warps beneath Spingate—it's not supposed to be extended while *Ximbal* is flying. Her red hair tosses madly. Her arm is so straight, pulled tight by my weight.

"Spin! *Please* don't drop me!"

Her eyes are closed, her face split by a desperate grimace. Through clenched teeth, she growls out one word.

"*Never!*"

The shuttle continues to climb.

Dangling like a bug on a vine, I don't want to look down—but I can't help myself.

Below me, the undulating Grub squishes its way out, stone and concrete and dirt spilling off its glistening hide. It rears up, a writhing, twisting, wriggling thing still half in the ground—a copper eel, a metallic slug, a nightmare blob, a horrid demon billowing up from hell itself.

The head—if that's what it is—rises high. I see its horror of a mouth gape open: two long, thin jaws, one above the other, like the narrow beak of some nightmare insect.

It *roars,* a sound so concussive it injures the air.

We're far above the shattered plaza, high enough to see much of the city. From the west, Wasps pour down the streets, tanks and ticks and *thousands* of foot soldiers, a wave that would have instantly overwhelmed us.

To the north, Borjigin's fire sends up a thick column of dense black smoke.

To the south, just past the plaza, a pair of troopships set down on the street. Landing ramps lower. Hundreds of Wasp soldiers spill out, armor flashing with the colors of a dying city.

And all across Uchmal, flames rise high, engulfing buildings and ziggurats alike. I thought there was nothing left in the city that could catch fire—I was wrong.

Spingate's grip slips, ever so slightly.

I look up. She's in severe pain, her cheek mashed against the deck's metal grate.

She can't hold me.

The entire deck lurches, bends and suddenly tilts down.

Her grip loosens. I slide. Our fingers lock—it hurts, *so bad,* I'm sure my bones are breaking my muscles are tearing but if I let go I die I fall I die *I must hold on.*

My friend screams in agony, but she fights, she *will not* let me go.

A pair of muscular arms reach out of the open shuttle door, grab at Spingate's belt, at the back of her coveralls—it's Farrar and Bishop. They pull her up, and me along with her.

Wind whipping at my face and hair, I look down one last time.

Beneath us, the Grub crawls free from its huge hole. It wanted us to be worms? It is a worm itself, a thick, fat maggot with stubby legs that are nothing more than cones of wobbling flesh. Muscles ripple through the body, send waves across skin that is already hardening, turning a darker shade of copper.

Wasp soldiers swarm around the leviathan. They are tiny next to it, barely more than specks, but even from this far up I can see that they're dancing.

They're *worshiping* it.

Strong hands lock on my wrist; I'm pulled up like I weigh nothing at all.

Bishop hauls me into the shuttle.

Wind howls around us.

Farrar holds on to the door with both hands as his big boot

hammers down on the deck, once, twice, then with a third powerful kick and a squeal of metal the deck tumbles away.

*Ximbal's* exterior door slides shut.

The wind finally dies out.

Bishop holds me tight.

"Next time," he says, "try and move faster, all right?"

Kenzie is already with us, tending to Spingate—I think her shoulder is dislocated.

Gaston's voice booms throughout the shuttle, telling everyone things are going to get rough, to get into coffins as fast as possible.

I grab Bishop's face, kiss him so hard I hurt my mouth.

"Make sure everyone gets in and holds on tight," I say to him, then I scramble to my feet and rush into the pilothouse.

Gaston stands in the center, bathed in light. Peura is with him. The young gear must be handling the copilot duties that usually fall to Spingate.

The walls are transparent. I can see the city beneath us. The Springer troop transports are close by, the first slightly above and to our left, the second slightly below and behind us. I can see down into the cockpit of the lower one—Cathcart, the pilot, who suddenly looks far older than his thirteen years.

An alert sound screeches, high-pitched and insistent.

I feel the shuttle's rear thrusters kick in. We move forward, fast, the troopships move with us.

No . . . we're going *away* from Uchmal.

"Don't leave until you nuke that godsdamned Grub," I say to Gaston. "Do it now!"

He glances at me. "Em, get out of here and get in a coffin!"

"No way I miss you killing that thing. So *kill* it!"

He shakes his head.

"No can do. We're not high enough yet, and there's a pair of bogeys coming in fast. We have to take them on or we're dead. Peura, take the helm. *Ximbal,* give me targeting and pilothouse crew inertia support."

Around Gaston's head, a complex arrangement of floating icons flares to life.

Three spots in the ceiling suddenly bulge out, extend thin black tentacles. Before I can react, one snakes around my waist and expands, holding me firmly from armpits to upper thighs. The other two tentacles do the same to Gaston and Peura.

"That harness is for high-G maneuvering," Gaston says. "It will keep you from being splattered against the walls. Peura, do you have the damn helm or not?"

"Yessir, I have the helm." Peura's voice cracks on every other word. He's doing his best to stay calm, but he's clearly terrified.

A second piercing alarm makes me jump.

"Proximity alert," Peura says. "Incoming bogeys at six o'clock, twenty degrees down."

Gaston turns in place: the floating icons turn with him.

So much is happening at once. We're almost away, we can't get hit now, we *can't.*

Behind us, I see two flashes coming in fast—Wasp fighters.

"Just let us go," I say quietly. "You win, you can have this whole damn planet."

"Target acquired," Gaston says. "Launch missiles."

The shuttle shudders a familiar shudder, one I felt in the Battle of the Crescent-Shaped Clearing. Four smoke trails shoot toward the incoming fighters.

The fighters flare with staccato flashes—they're firing at us.

"Evasive," Peura says.

*Ximbal* banks so hard to the right that my head and arms flail left. The strange tentacle lifts me at the same time, shifts me a little to absorb some of the harsh move, then brings me right back to where I was.

Gaston was right: without this system, I'd have smashed against the pilothouse walls.

I regain my wits in time to see the smoke trails close in; one fighter erupts in a glorious cloud of fire and metal.

The other loses half a wing; it spins, trailing a corkscrew of smoke.

We did it. We *won*.

And then, fate shatters my moment of elation.

The Wasp fighter spins past us, below us, and slams into the Springer transport, punching into the flat black hull as one piece, ripping out the other side in a dozen. There is no fire, no explosion. The troopship seems to hover in place for a moment—I can see through the cockpit window, see Cathcart's horrified face—then it plummets straight down.

Just like that, in the time it takes to snap my fingers, a thousand refugees are gone.

"Godsdammit," Gaston says. "We were *out*. Gods*damn*it."

The cockpit is quiet for a few moments as we try to come to grips with what just happened.

We escaped the Wasps.

At the same time, we lost many of our own.

We lost Springers.

I don't know if Barkah and Lahfah were on that ship. We may have lost them as well.

Once again, we are victorious. Once again, the price of victory is far too high.

"They're gone," I say. "Now go back and drop our nuke. Kill that thing."

Gaston reaches out, takes my hand.

"We can't. I know how bad you want this, Em, but we burned too much fuel in that dogfight. We don't have enough to do the bomb run and still make it to the *Xolotl*. Remember when I said we needed a full tank?"

I start to weigh our options, to ask if we can kill the Grub and the Wasps and then set down somewhere else, but Gaston isn't giving me that option. He knows better than I what is and isn't possible at this point.

He takes control of the shuttle.

We tilt up, and we head for the stars.

# PART IV

## FLIGHT AND FIGHT

# FIFTY-ONE

Below me, Uchmal gets smaller and smaller, until all details are gone, until it is nothing more than a brown spot with a river running into it, surrounded by jungle. It gets smaller still. Eventually, I can't see the river at all; the city itself vanishes into an ocean of yellow.

I see mountains. I see great plains. I see oceans.

It could have all been ours.

We're in space again.

The Springer troopship is on our right.

I don't want to think. I'm not sure I *can* think.

I feel gravity relax, weightlessness setting in although the mechanical arm keeps me fixed firmly to the pilothouse floor.

Eventually, Gaston brings me back to reality.

"Approaching the *Xolotl*," he says.

It's hard to finally turn my eyes away from what was supposed to be our home, the home of our children and grandchildren, the home of my people for all eternity.

I look forward, to our future, to the next battle we face.

I look upon the *Xolotl*.

Aside from a few variations in color, it looks exactly like the *Basilisk*.

Exactly like the *Goblin*.

Exactly like the *Dragon*.

I wonder at the powers of a being that made so many races abandon their homes. I had no choice in the matter. Nor did my friends. And as much as I hate to admit it, neither did Brewer, Bello, Matilda or any of our progenitors.

The Church of Mictlan existed before any of us were born. The church shaped our lives, controlled us, put us on a path that we could not avoid.

But is that what life is like for everyone? Can a person truly make a life of their own, or can they only continue the culture into which they are born?

"Where is the *Dragon*?" I ask.

"Too far away to stop us," Gaston says. "It appears to be holding its position, well outside Goff Spear range."

The *Xolotl* is a slowly spinning copper cylinder set against an endless black backdrop framed by bright stars. The closer we get, the bigger the ship seems.

Bishop floats into the pilothouse. He pushes off the door, grabs my strange harness and uses it to stand next to me.

"Opkick finished the head count," he says quietly. "Two hundred twenty-five on board."

Which means twenty-four of my people died in the fighting. Or were wounded and couldn't make it back. Or just got lost in the jungle during the battle and had to stand there, helplessly watching *Ximbal* rise in the sky.

I know there is fuel on the *Xolotl*. Matilda said so. But any survivors we may have left behind have no way of contacting us—we can't go back down and search a million square kilometers of jungle for them. The Wasps are waiting there, ready to hit us the instant we go back. The hard truth is that we still have to find a new home, and *Ximbal* is our only way of landing on new planets. I cannot risk this shuttle.

Reality is what it is whether we like it or not—anyone still on Omeyocan is gone forever.

Bishop puts his arm around my shoulders.

He lived up to his word. He gave his support. Now will he expect me to live up to my end of the bargain? Will he expect me to have a family with him?

Do I even *want* a family?

Anyone can make promises—*keeping* them is the hard part.

"The *Xolotl* is beautiful," he says.

He's right; the ship is stunning. Red sunlight plays off the copper hull. Copper, the same color as the Grub's hardened pincers . . . I wonder if there's a connection.

Gaston turns to face me. He's still covered in light, icons and symbols floating around his head.

"Shall I take us to the landing bay?"

I nod.

In minutes, the *Xolotl*'s true size becomes apparent. We are but a dot in comparison. As we get closer, we can't even see the entire ship, just the portion of it that's directly in front of us.

Gaston flies us silently along the endless, rotating hull. The surface is gouged and scratched. There are large craters, as if parts of the hull melted into liquid before cooling back to a solid.

"All that damage," Bishop says. "Gaston, do you think that's from a battle?"

Gaston nods. "Most of it, yes. Probably from when it fought the Springer ship."

We approach something I saw when I was in the Control

Room—a long, deepening groove that ends at massive, flat gray doors.

The landing bay.

Gaston puts the shuttle into a gentle barrel roll, stops the maneuver with the *Xolotl* now above us instead of below. I feel gravity return, a bit stronger than Omeyocan's, holding my feet to the pilothouse floor. The massive ship's rotation appears to slow, then stop. I realize that's because Gaston has the shuttle flying sideways as well as forward—we've matched the *Xolotl*'s rotation. The landing bay is now stationary in front of and above us. It's upside down . . . or is the shuttle upside down? Maybe in space there's no "up" or "down" at all.

"*Ximbal*," Gaston says, "tell the *Xolotl* to kindly open up for us."

Bishop whispers in my ear: "I'll get the circle-stars ready. We have a few rifle rounds left, and our bracelets are recharging."

I can tell by his tone he doesn't want a fight, but if one comes he'll be ready. The last time we were in the landing bay, the Grownups killed El-Saffani, the twins who followed Bishop no matter what he did or said. The twins died because we didn't have good weapons—now we do. If the Grownups bring violence, we'll bring more.

I kiss Bishop's cheek.

"I love you," I say. "Do what has to be done."

He smiles, then gently pushes off, floating toward the pilothouse door.

I wait. I stare at the huge gray doors. They don't open.

"Well, this is rather anticlimactic," Gaston says. "I assume someone on the *Xolotl* controls the doors. Hey, I wonder if I'll see the older me."

Gaston's progenitor flew Matilda back up here. He's still alive as far as we know.

We stare for a few more minutes.

Gaston sighs. "I'm bored. *Ximbal,* broadcast me on the *Xolotl*'s general frequency."

*"Ready to transmit, Captain Xander."*

Gaston squares his shoulders, gives his coveralls a quick tug. The little boy I knew is gone, has been for a long time. Gaston is a grown man. A husband. A father. A leader.

"Attention, *Xolotl.* This is Captain Xander Gaston, requesting permission to board. Open the damn landing bay doors already."

We wait.

A minute passes. Two minutes.

We start to wonder if the *Xolotl* can hear us at all, then the pilothouse's front wall fuzzes with static. The *Xolotl*'s copper hull vanishes from view. Multicolored sparkles appear, brighten, start to coalesce into a shape—a Grownup.

When the image finally crystallizes, it's not Gaston's progenitor we see.

It's mine.

"You've come back to me," Matilda says. "Good girl."

I stare at the image of the one-eyed, hateful creature who created me. To her, I'm nothing but a doll, a vehicle made so she can continue her pathetic life.

She had no right to be the leader of her people, yet that is what she became. I had no right to be the leader of mine, yet that is what *I* became. We are both ruthless and aggressive—no surprise there, since we are the same person.

But Matilda has grown old . . . *ancient*. She won't change her ways. She is a living fossil, stuck in that wrinkled black form forever, while I have matured and learned from my mistakes. I have become more than my creator could ever be.

"I'm no girl," I say. "Not anymore. Open the doors."

This grizzled, nasty *thing* shakes her head.

"And let your little army of uncivilized killers walk right in? I don't think so, darling-dear."

"We have nowhere to go," I say. "Because the *god* that supposedly called you here isn't a god at all. It's a *beast,* Matilda—an alien that has pitted all these races against each other. Did you know that?"

She doesn't answer right away, and in that instant I understand that she didn't know.

"You're a *liar,*" she says.

The intensity carried in that single word.

But I can't lie to her any more than she can lie to me. We both know that, and yet she doesn't believe me. At some level, she's *choosing* not to believe. Maybe this is a truth she can't allow herself to accept, as if accepting it might drive her insane.

Whatever her reason, it doesn't matter right now.

"Open the landing bay doors," I say.

Matilda ignores me. "Little Gaston, turn over control of the shuttle to me. My people will guide it remotely to an access hatch, where the shuttle will dock. Once there, Em, you will come across, alone and unarmed."

I start to refuse her demand outright, to scream at her, but I no longer react from pure emotion. There is information to be gathered first.

"If I comply, will you let the shuttle in?"

She nods. "Of course. I'm not a barbarian."

"And the Springers," I say. "They can come in as well?"

Matilda laughs.

"You think I would let vermin inside this ship? Vermin we almost wiped out when we built our city?"

She doesn't even bother lying to me about the Springers. I'll give her that much, at least.

"So what happens to them?" I ask. "They can't go back down to Omeyocan."

Matilda shrugs her narrow shoulders. "Not my concern. I only care about human lives."

I actually kind of admire her honesty. I can be honest, too.

"Open the doors, Matilda. *Or else.*"

More laughter.

"Such bravado from an infant, from a liar who would betray everything! That shuttle you're on is older than I am. It just went through a battle—it could break down at any moment. All those aboard could be seconds from death. Save your people, Em. Come aboard by yourself and I promise you everyone will be safe."

That agreeable tone of voice. When she wants something, Matilda sounds so reasonable, so nice. But I also hear the hunger within her words. Hunger, and deep concern. She's not lying about the *Ximbal*'s condition—she genuinely thinks it could have a critical malfunction at any moment. And if it does, she's trapped in that awful body forever.

"We have wounded," I say. "While you foam at the mouth, people are dying."

"Then *help* them, darling-dear. Come aboard. Up here, girl, you have no power. The choice is yours to make."

I've had enough.

I turn to Gaston. "How many missiles do you have left?"

"Six," he says, his eyes narrowing in suspicion. "Why?"

"Would that be enough to penetrate the landing bay doors?"

He stares at me like I am mad. By now, I probably am.

"Yes," he says. "But that would destroy the outer doors. We couldn't depressurize, the airlock would be ruined."

"But we *could* land? We would just have to figure out how to get everyone off the shuttle safely. Right?"

He thinks. His face suddenly scrunches, a telltale sign he's having a flashfire moment. His progenitor's knowledge is bubbling to the surface.

"There are emergency measures in the landing bay," he says. "It would take some time, but yes—we can get everyone off safely."

I wait. Matilda heard that exchange; I don't need to tell her what I'll do next.

"Don't threaten me," she says. "I control this ship. I control our *weapons*. If you think you're going to damage the *Xolotl*, you are mistaken. I will blow you out of the sky."

I smile at her.

"Do that, and this body you want so much dies. Which means I *do* have all the power. You can either open the doors or we will blow them open. Gaston, launch missiles in sixty seconds."

He shakes his head no, then his face scrunches again. He's remembering something else.

"*Ximbal,* break contact," he says.

Matilda vanishes.

"Gaston, what are you doing? I had her where I wanted her!"

He waves his hand dismissively.

"You always think you have people where you want them, and that usually ends with blood flying everywhere or something exploding. Listen to me—I think we can open the doors manually, but someone has to go extravehicular."

"Extravehicular?" I'm confused for a moment, then the word registers. "You mean go *outside* . . . in *space*?"

He grins that mischievous grin of his.

"Yeah. Outside. In space. And we better do it fast before *my* progenitor figures out what we're up to."

Through the pilothouse walls, Peura and I watch Xander Gaston float out into space.

He wears a thick pressure suit that covers him from head to toe. Tiny tongues of flame jut from his feet and waist, propelling him forward. He floats down the deepening groove.

*"Approaching the emergency access panel."*

His voice, coming through the pilothouse walls.

"All right," I answer, not knowing what else to say.

It looks like we're hovering above the ship's cratered surface, still as can be, although I know the cylinder—and the shuttle—continues to spin.

Peura glows with light. "I think I remember these lessons. The *Xolotl* has exterior landing bay controls in case anything goes wrong inside."

"What could go wrong inside?"

"Systems breakdown," he says. "Malfunctions, a fire, everyone dying from a gas leak. If no one can open the doors from the inside, you don't want your shuttle crew trapped in space. Emergency external access is a better solution than, say, using missiles to blow the doors apart."

Well well well . . . turns out chubby Noam Peura is a smartass. Who knew?

Gaston reaches the bottom right corner of the sprawling landing bay doors. He's so *small* out there.

Peura moves glowing icons. The wall display changes to a close-up of Gaston.

Gaston opens a copper-colored panel. Beneath it are a pair of parallel rings. No, not rings . . . *handles*. His gloved fingers wrap around them. He plants his booted feet on the copper hull.

*"I hope this works,"* he says.

He pulls. There is a moment's hesitation, resistance, then he leans back—each handle is anchored to a steel cylinder. They slide out, then lock.

*"Oh, who am I kidding,"* Gaston says. *"This is* me *we're talking about—of course it will work."*

He twists both hands inward. The handles and cylinders turn: what was parallel is now a line.

"I think that's it," Peura says. "There will be an emergency signal in the landing bay so anyone inside can get clear before it depressurizes."

We wait.

And then, the massive doors start to slide open.

# FIFTY-TWO

Gaston pilots us into the landing bay, the Springers' troopship at our side. The huge hangar doors shut like jaws clamping tight just before food is swallowed. We opened those doors from the outside, but whoever controls the *Xolotl* closed them behind us.

"They're repressurizing," Gaston says.

Bishop enters the pilothouse, stands next to me. The walls show us the landing bay outside. This is where we escaped. This is where El-Saffani died.

How many more of us will die this day?

We smell of smoke, sweat and blood. We smell of the jungle. We're exhausted from fighting and lack of sleep. We're drained by so many deaths. But our work is not done. Before we can rest, we must take this ship.

We wait.

Equipment racks, machines and various tanks line the landing bay walls. Other than our shuttle and the Springer troopship, though, the large space is empty.

"Pressure equalized," Gaston says.

Which means people can now enter.

But no one does.

"I don't like this," Bishop says.

No movement. This feels wrong. Last time we were here, there were hundreds of Grownups, a shambling nightmarish mass of those who want to erase us.

So now that we've come back, where are they?

"My team is ready," Bishop says. "Farrar, Victor, Darzi and I will go out, with people just inside the *Ximbal*'s door for fire support. Em, I know you want to face danger first, but I insist you stay back. Our people need you now more than ever."

Bruises, splinters, cuts . . . I'm all beat up. Bishop is, too, but he was engineered for nonstop fighting. I wasn't. It isn't the pain so much—I've suffered worse—it's that my body is so depleted it isn't responding fast enough. Until I get some rest, I'm a liability, and we can't afford an iota of weakness.

"All right," I say. "But I'm with the second team giving you cover. And Victor stays with me—his progenitor is out there."

Bishop nods. "I'll take Bawden instead."

"I've finally reached the Springer troopship," Gaston says. He looks relieved. "Barkah and Lahfah are on it. Barkah needed some stitches, but he's all right. He's awake and in command."

My soul sags with relief. Yes, we lost a thousand Springers, but I didn't know them—my friends are still alive.

"Tell Barkah to make sure his people stay put," I say. "We don't need them complicating things."

Gaston nods. "Yes, ma'am."

I turn to Bishop.

"Please be careful."

I stand in the *Ximbal*'s exterior doorway, half-hidden by the bulkhead. I wear a freshly charged bracelet. I don't know whose it was. Several young circle-stars stand with me, including Nedelka Holub, also armed with a bracelet, and Victor, who holds a rifle. We all aim out into the landing bay, ready to shoot anything that threatens our people.

We especially watch the tall, wide doors that open into the rest of the ship. That's where the Grownups came from last time.

*Ximbal*'s deck and ramp are gone. We're high enough above the landing bay floor that Bishop and his team had to hold on to the bottom of the door with their fingers before dropping down.

Bishop, Farrar, Darzi and Bawden spread out through the landing bay. They're still covered in jungle camouflage, skin and hair smeared with mud. Each of them is armed: a bracelet on one arm, white stone glowing. Farrar has his shovel, Bawden her pitchfork, little Darzi a long knife. Bishop, of course, has his red axe, still caked with Wasp blood and bits of yellow flesh.

A heavy clang of metal reverberates through the landing bay—the wide interior door starts to slide open.

Farrar and Darzi rush to different areas, taking cover behind machinery bolted to the walls.

Bawden and Bishop don't hide—they stand tall.

He waves at me to keep everyone where they are. The shuttle's hull is impervious to bracelet beams. If fighting breaks out, my spot is the best position from which to support him and the others.

I snap my wrist left, then right, feel my bracelet power up.

The big metal door rattles on its track. The space beyond is mostly dark, but I see movement.

I aim my bracelet. Victor and those around me take aim as well.

The huge doors open all the way. They stop with an echo of metal that slowly fades.

Finally, those that hide in the shadows step through the door. *Grownups.*

But only two. Behind them, *normal people,* a dozen, armed with knives or clubs. No guns or bracelets. They wear togas similar to what Marcus wore.

Wait . . . Marcus is one of them.

What's going on?

This strange welcoming committee approaches Bishop and Bawden. Old legs, withered bodies, gnarled skin. One of the Grownups can barely walk. He slides his left leg more than lifts it. Each step seems difficult, forced.

"I've got the limping one," I say quietly, and take aim.

"Got the one on the right," Victor says.

The circle-stars with us softly call out their targets.

The two Grownups stop in front of Bishop and Bawden. The taller one says something to Bishop.

Bishop calls to me, his voice echoing through the landing bay: "Em, they want you."

Victor whispers in my ear. "If they even *blink* funny, I'll take them all out."

Regardless of the way Victor vied for power, he believed in me before and he believes in me now.

The circle-stars take my hands and lower me down. Even with their help, it's a big drop—I land on the deck, pleased that I didn't stumble or fall.

I walk to the group, comforted by the bracelet's familiar thrum.

Bishop and Bawden step aside.

I stand face-to-face with the two Grownups.

When you first see Grownups, they all look the same. If you

pay close attention, though, you can tell them apart. The taller of the two, the one that was limping . . . he has white scars all over him, and a white circle-star carved into his black forehead.

"Victor Muller?"

"Correct," he says. His voice is raspy, breathy, *old*. "Welcome aboard."

This could still be a trick. I must be careful.

"Last time we were in this landing bay, we had to fight our way out," I say. "Now you conveniently control it?"

Marcus leans out from behind the Grownups. He's holding a metal pipe in a white-knuckle grip.

"Em, it's all right, Victor is on our side."

"I don't trust him," I say. "And I don't trust *you*, either. So if you're not in charge, keep your mouth shut."

His eyes widen. I think I hurt his feelings.

"Marcus, put the weapon down," Old Victor says. "All of you. If they wanted to fight, you'd be dead already."

Marcus drops the pipe. It clangs against the metal deck. The other normal people with him do the same.

"Yes, we control the landing bay," Old Victor says. "And now most of the ship. We've fought against Matilda for hundreds of years. When she took her best warriors down to Omeyocan, we were finally able to gain territory."

Warriors like Old Bishop, Old Farrar, Coyotl and more. She brought her most loyal and most dangerous followers.

We killed them all.

If Old Victor is telling the truth, Matilda's trip to the planet cost her significantly. She not only lost her inner circle, she lost much of her control aboard this ship. She lost the landing bay? That explains why she wanted us to dock somewhere else.

Serves the bitch right.

"That other ship in orbit, the *Dragon,* it could be coming to attack us," I say. "We need to get the *Xolotl* away from the planet."

"We can't. Matilda and Gaston still control the engines, she . . ."

His voice trails off. He's distracted. He looks over my shoulder, to the shuttle . . . to our Victor.

"Is that . . . is that *me*?"

Longing in that voice. I snap my fingers in front of his red eyes, draw his attention back to me.

"You go near him, you *die*," I say. "Understand?"

The ancient creature nods his disgusting head. "I do. Unlike Matilda, I have no desire to live forever. Death is part of life."

So says the man that's lived for a thousand years.

I get back to the important issue. "How do we capture the bridge so we can leave?"

Old Victor glances at the other Grownup. This one is shorter than him, but a little taller than me.

"Hello, Em," he says. "Welcome aboard."

*That voice* . . .

My stomach drops. The horror of a moment I want to forget floods back . . . blood and dust and tears . . . a young man crying for his mother . . .

"Yong?"

The Grownup nods.

I killed his receptacle, forever ended this man's ability to overwrite, to live on. Right or wrong, my actions have condemned him to a long, slow death.

Does he know what I did?

The red eyes stare.

"I can guess what you're thinking," he says. "Yes, I know it was you."

My bracelet hand curls into a fist, fingers ready to flick forward. The fight is about to begin.

Old Yong raises his hands, gnarled palms facing out.

"I won't hurt you," he says. "So please, don't hurt me."

He has no weapon. Bishop and Bawden are with me. Victor can shoot out both red eyes before the Grownup can even move. We could slaughter these people if we wanted to. They know this, yet here they stand.

I snap my wrist right, then left. There is a small whine as the bracelet powers down.

Old Yong slowly places his right hand on my left shoulder.

"Hail, Em. We're on the same side."

I'm so confused. I killed the younger him, yet he hails me in the circle-star manner, one warrior to another? He hails me with *respect*?

"Matilda and Gaston hold the bridge and the Tactical Command Center," Yong says. "That means they control most of the ship's systems—engines, navigation, weaponry and all external doors, which is why we couldn't open the landing bay for you."

"So let's take the bridge," Bishop says. "And kill her while we're at it."

"We've been trying to do both for hundreds of years." Yong sounds so much like the boy I killed, it's disturbing. "Matilda reset the navigation control codes. We think she's the only one who knows them, so we need her alive. And you have to be on the bridge to use those codes. That place is locked up tight. Not even Brewer could access it. Is he with you?"

I think of the sad old man in the white coffin.

"Dead," I say. "Buried on Omeyocan."

Yong and Old Victor exchange a glance.

"Then he is at peace," Old Victor says. "We haven't seen him in centuries, not since the early days of Matilda's rebellion. His death is irrelevant to our needs—the bridge is untouchable."

Bishop is getting agitated. "Then we'll talk to Matilda, convince her that we need to leave."

Yong shakes his head. His strange mouth-flaps wiggle in time.

"She will *never* leave. Matilda is obsessed—with Em *and* with Omeyocan. She would rather die than leave this place."

There has to be a way. There is always a way.

"We *must* take the bridge," I say. "Just because you haven't been able to do it doesn't mean it can't be done. We bring new eyes to the problem, new ways of thinking."

Yong shrugs. "Fair enough. Our war room is the best place to show you what we're up against."

Marcus finally musters enough courage to step out from behind the Grownups.

"Em, come meet your people," he says. "We've been waiting so long. See the ship, see how we live."

I shake my head. "There's no time for that."

Bishop leans close to me. "A word in private?"

He and I walk closer to the shuttle, out of earshot.

"You should go with Marcus," he says.

"Are you crazy? I don't trust these people."

"Neither do I. That's why you should go. See as much of this ship as possible, figure out if they're telling the truth. If we're going to take *Xolotl*, we need to know if Matilda has allies or if she's as isolated as they say. Farrar and I will work on the attack plan with Old Victor, you learn what you can."

His idea makes sense. Still, I hesitate.

"I don't like splitting up," I say. "It's a risk."

Bishop tilts his head toward the shuttle. "Take our Victor. He'll protect you with his life. Take Barkah and Lahfah as well. The Grownups probably don't know she's an exceptional fighter.

If all of you have charged bracelets, I'm sure you can defend yourselves."

Maybe the *Dragon* won't attack us. Maybe the Wasps are happy with taking Omeyocan. If they do come for us, though, we don't have time to play it safe.

I trust Bishop to come up with the best plan to take the bridge. I'll do as he asks—maybe I'll find another way.

# FIFTY-THREE

There is so much to see. Barkah, Lahfah, Victor and I walk with Marcus and Old Yong.

I also brought Spingate.

She was with me when we first talked to the Springers. I want her with me now. Her arm is in a sling. She winces with every step, but she gladly bears the pain for a chance to see this new wonder. For now, at least, I don't care what Theresa did—she is my friend and I want to share this with her.

Lahfah still looks like she just stepped off the battlefield. Barkah, however, is wearing his emerald-green coat and the necklace, his symbol of office. I wonder how many outfits he packed.

He tries to maintain his regal aura, but he's slowed by his wounds, and he's having a hard time processing what he sees. For him, a ship like this is the stuff of legends. No one he knows has ever seen anything like it. Only in the past year have his people stopped living underground—this must be overwhelming for him.

Lahfah is amazed and doesn't bother to hide it. She makes little noises at each new thing we see—the Springer equivalent of *ooh* and *aah,* I think.

The hallways are similar to what Spin and I saw when we first woke up. *Stone.* Only now does it strike me as odd there's so much stone on a starship.

If I live through this, maybe I'll research the *Xolotl*'s construction when I write the history of our people.

Marcus shows us an orchard. The huge room is identical in size to the Garden where we first ate fruit, where I killed the pig, where Bello was taken. That place was overgrown and wild: bushy trees with dead branches galore; walled pool choked with thick plants and surrounded by waist-high grass; forests so dense you couldn't walk through the underbrush without getting scratched; ceiling lights peppered with dark spots; water spraying out of a broken fountain.

In this orchard, trees grow in regimented rows, not mad tangles. Nothing blocks my view of the massive room's stone walls. Branches are pruned. The fruit looks healthy. The pool is bordered by a long rectangular brick wall, the grass around it is freshly mowed. There are chips and cracks here and there, sure, but those have been neatly patched with concrete or some other substance. The fountain consists of three stacked marble bowls, water spilling from top to middle to bottom. The sound it makes is lovely. And the *light*—the entire ceiling glows soft white. Our Garden was quite dim in comparison.

Perhaps twenty people of all ages are working in the orchard. They wear togas similar to Marcus's, in various colors and patterns. They pick fruit, prune trees, sweep the stone walkway surrounding the pool. When they see me and the others, they stop working.

They stare.

Spin, Victor and I are likely the first outsiders they've ever seen, and it's a safe guess they've never laid eyes on a Springer.

I learn that the orchard's ceiling lights are specifically made for these fruit trees, and that all other crops are grown in a place called "the Flatland." I remember Brewer mentioning that word. I ask Marcus what it is. He says I have to see it to understand it, that we'll finish our tour there.

Marcus and Old Yong show us more.

The "Coop" is lined with racks and racks of cages, each cage holding a black chicken. *Totally* black: beak, feet, eyes, crest . . . even the feathers, which gleam with a purple iridescence.

*Thousands* of chickens.

Barkah looks at one up close, asks me if Springers can eat them. I tell him I think so, but we'll check with Kalle. Lahfah hops up and down with excitement—I think her word for the chickens loosely translates to "fat midnight blurds."

The pigs that killed Latu were black, too. And when we were here before, Brewer showed us a display of all-black cows that are supposedly somewhere on the *Xolotl.*

"Why are all the animals black?" I ask.

"Per the Founder's scriptures," Yong says. "Animals were to have no color."

Spingate and I trade a glance.

"Why no color?" she says. "What's the purpose of that?"

Yong shrugs. "I think I knew, once. It doesn't matter. Hasn't mattered for hundreds of years—these are the animals we have."

The tour continues. This ship is twelve *centuries* old, and it looks it. Neat and clean, mostly, but stone walls are cracked, doors are worn down by the touch of thousands of hands. There are ruts in the stone floors, made over the centuries by countless footsteps. Some rooms are dim, some completely dark.

As we walk, Marcus tells me of the complicated system used

to keep everything alive. Grain grown in the Flatland feeds people, chicken, cattle and pigs. Animal waste—including *human* waste—is used to fertilize the grain fields. Crop leavings and any spoiled food are taken to one of a hundred compost rooms, where worms and insects break the matter down into fertilized soil. There are still huge chambers full of ice frozen even before the *Xolotl* left Solomon, yet all water is recycled.

In centuries past, he tells us, computers and robots managed the recycling of food and water. But after the rebellion, most of those machines eventually broke down. For centuries, these "New People" have dedicated themselves to mastering the system. It's become a religion unto itself, with strict "scriptures" dictating what must be done, when, and how.

This, at least, is a religion I can understand—if the system fails, everyone dies.

As we walk, it hits me that for most of this tour, I don't have that ever-so-slight sensation of going uphill or downhill. Occasionally we turn, and I feel it, but for the most part I don't—that means we're mostly walking along the cylinder's length, traveling deeper into the ship.

Some rooms are massive, full of strange machinery that either doesn't work or hasn't been used for generations. Yong tells us that much of the equipment is only needed when the *Xolotl* is traveling from star to star.

This ship was designed to last a thousand years—a thousand years came and went two centuries ago. Spingate whispers to me that it's no surprise things have broken down. She's shocked the *Xolotl* is still in one piece at all.

That doesn't exactly fill me with confidence, but it does speak to the technical prowess of the Grub species. And, I suppose, to the willpower of the Founder. The ship designs came from the signal, but this marvel was built by people.

Marcus takes us through long corridors: cracked stone walls, worn floors, glowing ceilings, doors made of sliding stone.

We see rooms full of people working on low-tech machines cobbled together from parts of far more complex devices. I'm reminded of the simple Springer factories. People spin yarn, dye fabric, saw lumber, manufacture tools and furniture, process meat and chicken for long-term storage.

In some rooms, we see Grownups side by side with normal people. They, too, are working on simple machines, doing simple tasks.

In every room, though, Grownups and New People alike stop what they're doing and stare at us. Victor stares back, hard, letting the universe know we are not to be messed with. He refuses to sling his rifle, choosing instead to keep it at the ready.

As we walk, we see hundreds of people, yet the ship is so massive it feels like a ghost town.

Spingate seems to sense the same thing.

"You told Em there were over five thousand of you," she says to Marcus. "So where is everyone?"

"In the Flatland." He's obviously proud of that place, says the name with reverence. "We're heading there next."

As we continue down the main corridor, I start to see marks from ancient battles. Chips and gouges in the stone walls, maybe from bullets. Blackened streaks from old fires or explosions. Some doors are cracked so badly that the slabs aren't worth fixing.

Below a particularly evil-looking scorch mark, I see three names engraved into the stone wall.

Jasmine Givens 3461–3484
Steve Wren 3470–3483
Claude Zacanna 3465–3483

"Marcus, who were these people?"

"They died in the rebellion," he says.

Yong runs his black fingers along Steve Wren's name.

"The fighting was awful," he says. "It got so bad there was no time for proper funerals. Where people fell, we chiseled their names, then we ejected their bodies into space."

"What about where we woke up?" Spin asks. "There were bodies all over our area. You didn't eject those."

Yong nods. "Brewer sealed that section off, to protect you. He didn't let anyone in. Not Matilda, not us, not anyone. He was alone for over four hundred years."

All that time. He was more of a hero than I knew.

*Yes, Brewer—your life mattered.*

We keep walking. The names grow more frequent.

One of them stops me cold: *Halim Horn 3445–3484.*

I think of the boy that died in the streets of Uchmal, who wanted to become more than he was. The person who died in this hallway, was it one of Halim's ancestors? Or perhaps even Halim's progenitor? If so, both versions of him are gone forever.

It makes things feel so futile. We fight to survive, we protect our own, we struggle on, and in the end every single one of us will die.

The Grownups wanted immortality. There is no such thing.

"These numbers," I say, gently touching the *3445–3484* next to Halim's name, "what are they?"

Marcus gives me a funny look.

"Are you serious? They're dates. Birth year and the year of death."

Dates . . . *calendars* . . . I realize, yet again, that my lack of a past leaves me missing something important, something basic.

"What year is it now?"

Marcus starts to answer, then stops. He looks off, thinking.

"You know, I'm not sure. Years don't really matter here any-more."

"For you it could be year zero," Yong says. "Start history over if you like. Leave all of this hatred and violence behind."

That's what we've always wanted, really—to start *anew*. But if I am to write about the history of our people, I can't do that without knowing how much time has passed.

"It matters to *us*," Spingate says, reading my mind as always. "What year is it now?"

"It is the year thirty-eight eighty-eight," Yong says.

Halim died on this spot *four centuries* ago. Two hundred years or so before the *Xolotl* even reached Omeyocan, before Uchmal was built.

Marcus seems annoyed at himself that he didn't know what year it was.

"You wanted to make this tour quick," he says. "Shall we continue to the Flatland?"

"No," Yong says. "There is something they must see first."

Another corridor, a short walk "uphill," then a rattling eleva-tor takes us higher. The farther we go, the heavier we feel. When the elevator stops, my legs are already aching with the effort of just standing. We felt this same effect in the Crystal Ball.

Yong leads us into a dusty, wide room made of metal, not stone. A window runs the room's width. Waving cracks in the glass, or whatever the material is, show that the window is easily thicker than I am tall.

Through the window, the grandeur of Omeyocan, surrounded by the void.

Barkah and Lahfah huddle close together. I don't know if they had any external views from inside the troopship—this might be the first time they've seen the blackness of space, or seen their planet from such a distance.

Below our position, the *Xolotl*'s copper cylinder arcs down to either side. There are craters all over it. Directly below us is a long, thick tube, twisted and warped in several places.

"That tube was our primary weapon," Yong says. "A Goff Spear, similar to the one in the Observatory. It was destroyed when the vermin . . ." he glances at Barkah and Lahfah, then back at me. ". . . excuse me, the *Springers*, as you call them, detonated a nuke close by."

Spingate breathes in sharply. "This ship survived a nuclear explosion?"

"Two of them, in fact," Yong says. "Weakened the hull some, destroyed most of our external weaponry. Pretty much all we have left is point defense and some long-range missiles. That's why Gaston wouldn't engage the other ships—with the punishment the *Xolotl* has already taken, he doesn't think we'd last long in a fight."

Gaston—*their* Gaston.

"But the Goff rounds are nukes," I say. "The *Basilisk* and the *Goblin* look just like the *Xolotl*—why were we able to destroy those ships?"

"I'm a soldier, not a scientist." Yong sounds like he's asked the same question himself, many times, and never got an answer he was happy with. "All I know is that the Founder suspected other ships would answer the call. She had a weapon designed to destroy ships built just like the *Xolotl*. The Goff rounds penetrate the thick hull, then explode from the inside."

Zubiri said something similar, that the bombs are nukes but have to go *through* the armor to work.

"Not that it matters," Yong says, tilting his head toward the warped tube. "That was our Goff cannon. It's destroyed. Even if it wasn't, we used up all our rounds against the Springer ship."

Marcus sighs heavily, as if all of this is unimportant.

"Enough with the dead parts of the ship," he says to Yong. "Can I show them the Flatland now?"

There's a whining tone in his voice I don't like very much.

Yong gestures out of the room. "Lead the way, Marcus."

I'm grateful to take the elevator down—maybe *in* is a better word—and give my legs a break. Back in the main corridor, we only walk for a few minutes until, far down the hall, I see a pair of huge stone doors, the biggest I've seen yet.

The closer we get to them, the more engraved names I see. The names become so dense they cover the wall from floor to ceiling, all the way down the corridor.

The slaughter here must have been unimaginable.

We reach the door.

Marcus is all smiles. "Welcome to the Flatland."

The huge stone doors slowly slide apart.

What I see beyond overwhelms me.

My head spins. I must be imagining things. This isn't possible, we're *inside a ship*.

"The cylinder," Spingate says, in utter awe. "It's even bigger than I thought."

Not that long ago, she used her fingertip to draw a picture in the dust, trying to explain how we walked in a straight line yet wound up where we started. I kind of understood, but also kind of didn't.

Now I do.

A vast, sprawling land spreads out before me. In front of us, it looks as flat as flat can be, but the farther out I look, the more I see the *curve*.

I feel like a tiny insect standing inside a hollowed-out log of the largest tree to ever grow on Omeyocan.

Winding roads and paths stretch down the cylinder's length, curve up and away to either side.

Large fenced spaces full of black cows, so far away they are little moving dots.

People riding horses.

Rectangular fields of crops: wheat, corn, tomatoes.

Spin nudges me, points to a nearby field of green plants.

"Those are turnips," she says. "Kalle is going to think she died and went to heaven."

Forest, too, rectangular swaths where the trees are *green,* not yellow.

Sprawling blue lakes.

Clusters of houses—*villages.*

Off to the left, a wooden silo painted red, and next to it, red with white trim, a barn. Around the barn, fenced-in black pigs.

*A farm . . . something about a farm, something important . . .*

Above me, a bright line of energy stretches down the length of this bizarre place. I feel its heat on my face. This line must act as the sun, spreading light across this curved landscape. The line is bright enough that I can't see past it, to where the cylinder's curves meet high above.

Yong laughs at our amazement. His laugh isn't like Brewer's, like the sound of broken bones scraping together, or harsh and evil like Matilda's—Yong's laugh is rich and full of life.

"Welcome home," he says.

Marcus takes a few steps ahead of me, turns, spreads his arms out wide.

"Look at it," he says. "For twelve centuries, the Flatland has sustained our people. The gods provide."

Yes, a "god" provided this. I wonder what Marcus would think if he knew what that god looked like.

If what Brewer says is true, the *Xolotl* once supported over forty thousand. With the New People, the Springers and us, we are at most sixty-five hundred—there is no reason we can't survive here, *flourish* here.

Barkah hops past Marcus. The Springer king gawks at the expansive space. I wonder what's going through his head.

Finally, he turns to look at me.

"*Hem . . . your home?*"

"*Our* home," I say. "For all of us, together."

He goes back to gawking. Lahfah hops out to join him. Their tails intertwine. Together, they stand there, trying to see everything all at once.

Victor puts an arm around me, shakes me out of pure excitement.

"Just *look* at this place! Em, you did it."

He jogs to Barkah and Lahfah. The three of them start dancing together.

*Dancing.*

Spingate takes my hand. Her smile is warm, loving, apologetic.

"Victor is right," she says. "You found a way."

She sounds different. She *looks* different. We are only a few hours separated from our ordeal on the planet, yet the hate, animosity and fear she's carried for weeks has finally drained away.

We may never know why some of us were more susceptible to the Grub's influence than others. All I know is that, finally, I am looking at the girl I knew. The *real* her.

I am looking at Theresa Spingate—my best friend.

"I still have to pay for what I did," she says quietly. "I'll never forgive myself."

I think of how Aramovsky stopped me. Spingate killed Bello—I would have killed Spingate and her baby.

"We'll figure it out," I say. "We can't take back the things we've done. All we can do is move forward and make the best life we can."

I hug her. She hugs me back. I smell like smoke and blood and war. Spin, somehow, still smells clean. We've been through everything together. Maybe she's not her full self, not yet, but once we leave this planet far behind, I know she will be.

I see a horse ride out from a village and gallop fast toward us. On it is a teenage boy wearing a robe like Marcus's, but in black.

Barkah and Lahfah flick their wrists left, then right. White stones glow. Victor takes aim with his rifle.

Yong holds up a hand. "Don't shoot. He's not attacking, he's a runner from Victor. *Our* Victor, I mean. *Old* Victor. Damn, this stuff gets confusing."

"You can say that again," Young Victor says.

The boy reins the horse to a stop before us.

"Victor needs you all at the war room," he says. "The other ship, it's changed course . . . it's coming toward us."

# FIFTY-FOUR

We ride black horses through the corridors. *Horses,* on a starship. It reminds me of being on Fenrir. I feel a pang of loss for that brave animal.

The horses gallop down the hallways, hooves clacking on stone. When people on the *Xolotl* need to get somewhere fast, this is how they do it. Yong quickly explained the ship used to be full of small vehicles and something he called a "tram," but even the replacement parts for those things wore out centuries ago.

Such a strange place the *Xolotl* is.

We ride through a stone door into a larger room. Flags hang above the door. We saw a similar room a year ago, but it was dark and the floor was covered in grease.

Golden pedestals are set up all over the room. There are more Grownups here, as well as people wearing black togas. Teenagers run to us, take the horses' reins, help us down, then lead the animals away.

Three of the pedestals are close together in the center of the room, their displays combined to make an image almost as big as that above the red well.

Old Victor, Bishop, Farrar and Gaston stand around those pedestals, staring up at a glowing Omeyocan, the familiar red dot of the *Xolotl,* and the dreaded green dot that is the *Dragon.* A blue line arcs between the two ships. In the middle of that line, a counter that reads *0:17:34:22.* The last two digits are seconds, ticking down as we watch.

"*Dragon* is on an intercept trajectory with us," Gaston says. "It's coming fast."

"What's the countdown represent?" I ask.

Old Victor adjusts pedestal icons. The image above zooms in on the *Dragon.* It's fuzzy from this distance, but I can make out a long tube mounted on top of the massive copper cylinder.

"They have a Goff Spear," I say.

Gaston nods. "Not exactly like ours, and it's mounted on a different spot on their hull. That means the Grub probably didn't provide that weapon design. Humans came up with it on their own. So did the Wasps. There's no doubt, though—it serves exactly the same purpose ours did. It's a ship-killer."

"The timer represents how long it will take the Wasp ship to reach that weapon's can't-miss range," Old Victor says. "When the timer hits zero, if they fire their Goff Spear, we have no chance of stopping the round from connecting."

Seventeen hours, thirty-four minutes and counting.

I've hated Matilda since I first learned of her existence, but never so much as right now.

"We have to take the bridge," I say.

Bishop slowly shakes his head.

"Her area is sealed off by meter-thick blast doors which are guarded by beam-cannons in armored turrets," he says. "When Old Victor said they'd been trying to get in there for centuries, he wasn't kidding—we couldn't get to Matilda in seventeen *days,* let alone seventeen hours."

He rubs his fingers into his forehead. He's slouching. Bishop is not the kind to easily admit defeat. If he says we don't have enough time to get to Matilda, we don't.

I refuse to accept that. "There has to be another way."

Yong shakes his head. "There isn't. I told you that when you came aboard. Bishop now sees the same thing. You will not get what you want by force. She wants one thing, and one thing only."

Me. She wants *me.*

"No way," Gaston says. "That monster will not get my friend."

I look around the room, desperately hoping someone has an idea, even a bad one. No one does. Not Bishop, not Spingate, not Gaston, not the Grownups. I see rage and frustration, but no answers.

My chest feels tight. It can't end like this. There has to be a way. There *has* to be.

"Then we talk to Matilda again." I point to the green dot. "We need to make her understand what's coming for us."

Yong speaks softly, patiently. "She understands just fine. She's forcing us to decide right now—she gets Em, or everyone dies."

He doesn't sound surprised, or even concerned. Yong is ready for death. Life is just a show to him. No matter how the plot varies, he already knows how the story will end.

"But Matilda will die, too," Spingate says, desperation bleeding from her every pore. "The witch has to know that!"

Old Victor nods. "She knows. Her power base is gone. She only has about thirty people still with her. We control most of the ship. This is the only chance she will ever have to get Em. She's willing to risk death to take it."

I look at the countdown clock: *0:17:32:26*.

"Will the Wasps try to board us?" I ask no one in particular. "Like they did with the *Goblin*?"

Gaston throws up his hands. "Why would they? The *Goblin* was used as a sacrificial lamb so they could launch landing craft. There's no purpose to capturing the *Xolotl*—they'll just blow us out of the sky."

"It doesn't make sense," Spingate says. "Wasps control Omeyocan now. Why even bother with us?"

Someone answers her, but I don't really hear it. As the others talk, I close my eyes, try to get my head around the pieces of this new puzzle. Maybe the Wasps destroy anything they find, no matter where it is. Or maybe the Grub is making them come after us, driving them into a frenzy to satisfy its bloodlust.

The Grub . . .

*It can't defend itself against all attacks,* my false father said.

The Goff Spear cart on the plaza . . .

Several puzzle pieces form in my thoughts, and just as quickly, they snap together, fitting perfectly.

"They know. The Wasps *know* we have nukes."

Conversation stops.

It was my decision that doomed us.

"The Wasps saw what the Goff Spear could do," I say. "The first thing they would have done was search the Observatory for it, see if they could use our weapon against us to take out the *Xolotl*. The cannon is huge, it's not hard to find. They got the hatch open, they saw the hexagonal shape of the barrel. They realized it's the same size and shape as the cart on the plaza. The *empty* cart. It doesn't take a gear to figure out we took Goff Spear rounds with us."

Gaston hangs his head, covers his eyes with his hands.

"It might not even be that complicated," he says. "We had the damn things hanging under our wings. The Wasps on the ground probably saw them. Em is right—it doesn't take much intelligence to figure out what we've got."

Bishop looks confused. "But why does it matter? Why are they coming after us instead of just letting us go?"

"Because the Wasps will do anything to protect the Grub," I say. "If they think we have nukes that could kill the Grub, they'll destroy us to make sure we can't launch them. And they won't let us leave, because we might come back someday. They need to kill us. Right now."

The words sink in. Maybe the Wasps haven't figured out we have nukes and are coming for us anyway, or maybe they are coming *because* of the nukes. There is no way to know.

"Why they're coming doesn't really matter," our Victor says. "We can't outrun them, so we fight. Our ship against theirs."

His progenitor looks at him, red eyes swirling. "The *Xolotl* has been in a battle and taken heavy damage. Their ship has not. That probably gives them a significant firepower advantage. They'll chew us up from a distance, or sit back and launch boarding craft after they take out our point defense."

Brewer's words flare to life: *Destroy them with what? The six decrepit Macanas that Vick Tick Tick wastes his time with?*

Vick Tick Tick . . . *Vic* Tick Tick . . . *Victor.*

"The Macanas," I say. "Can they defend us against attack?"

Old Victor shakes his head, making his mouth-folds flap.

"We have six ancient interceptors left that *might* still fly. We think the Wasps, as you call them, still have eight of their combined atmospheric/exospheric fighters. Any one of their craft is easily a match for three of ours."

I close my eyes. The cold void is reaching out for me, digging in with invisible claws. Our chance is slipping away. We've come through so much . . . *I've* come through so much. This isn't fair.

"We have to repair the *Xolotl*'s Goff Spear," Gaston says. "Borjigin and Zubiri can help."

"We're old, not stupid," Yong says. "Our halves and gears spent decades trying to repair it. Too much of the barrel is warped. The cannon *cannot* be fixed. I'm sorry, but this isn't a movie or a play—there is no convenient third-act rescue that gives us an easy solution. This is real life."

I feel like I'm sinking.

*This isn't fair . . . it isn't fair . . .*

If we fight, we lose.

We can't run, because Matilda controls the ship.

I told her she didn't have any power.

I was wrong—she has *all* the power.

And just like that, I understand that it's over.

I look at Bishop. He looks at me. My question to him is unspoken, yet crystal clear. Some of my friends will understand that what comes next is the only way. Some, like Gaston and Spingate, I imagine, will fight it. But before I commit, I need to know Bishop is with me. I need to know he understands.

I need to know he will be by my side.

As the others talk, I silently wait for Bishop's answer.

He shakes his head, ever so slightly. Then, he closes his eyes. He lowers his head.

He nods.

I turn to Yong. "Can you contact Matilda?"

His red eyes bore into me. "I can."

If my people are to survive, there is only one choice left.

"Then call her," I say. "I'm ready to talk."

# FIFTY-FIVE

stand in a small, dusty room with Xander Gaston and Theresa Spingate. She holds baby Kevin like the universe might come alive at any moment and try to rip him away from her. She ran to get the child, I think, because even if she doesn't accept reality yet a part of her knows this will be the last time he sees me.

There is no furniture in this room. It happened to be close to the room with the pedestals. I absently wonder what this space was once used for. I know what it is used for now—to say good-bye.

I spoke with Matilda. Afterward, I gave everyone specific orders about what would happen next. Bishop didn't argue, even though it was easy to see this is killing him. Gaston threw a fit, insisted that I talk alone with him and Spin. I've never seen him act like this, so angry and frightened at the same time. He all but dragged me here.

He doesn't want to lose his friend.

"It's the only way," I say. "If I don't do this, we don't get the control codes. The Wasps will destroy us."

Gaston burns with fury. If his rage could be channeled into a weapon, we could destroy all who stand against us.

"I won't allow it." He's speaking with the voice he uses in combat, the voice of the *captain,* the voice of a leader who won't be questioned. "Tell her, Theresa."

Spingate is crying. She isn't even bothering to hold it back. Tears line her face, each wet streak tracing where her nose meets her cheek, then flowing to the outside corners of her full lips.

"You can't let Matilda overwrite you," she says. "We've seen what happens. It will be the end of you."

I nod.

"I know. There's no time for debate. It comes down to one person's life against the lives of sixty-five hundred."

Gaston and Spin are canvases painted in anguish. It hurts so much to see their pain. I wish there was something I could say to make them feel better. How strange: I'm the one sacrificing my life, yet I feel the need to console them.

"I forbid it," Gaston says.

I put my hand on his shoulder.

"It's not your choice to make. It's mine."

Spin shakes her head. Her lower lip quivers. Tears drip from her chin, land on little Kevin's nose. She wants to talk me out of it, but she knows me better than anyone ever has—she knows I won't waver from this decision.

"Godsdamned *bullshit!*" Gaston's tears come now, sudden and intense, half-strangling his words. "There's *thousands* of us, and only a handful of them! We have weapons. You said we had to conquer the Grownups and take the ship, so let's do that, *now!*"

I pull him close. I hold him tight.

"I love you," I say to him.

Sobs shake his body. This man can command starships, can

stand firm and orchestrate death on a grand scale, but here he has no power.

"Total *bullshit*," he says. "I don't want you to go."

I pull away. His tears cool on my cheeks.

"Goodbye, Xander. You're a good man. My life is better for having known you."

I move to Theresa. She's slowly shaking her head.

"How did this happen?" she says. "If you want us to fight, Em, we will fight. You are my friend—I would rather die than let you go."

There is steel in Theresa Spingate. I have seen her face down horrors, both alien and human alike. I have seen her stand up for what is right while everyone around her screams at her to shut up, to cave in, to go along with the wrong decision because that's what the crowd wants.

I hold her tight. I feel little Kevin between us, sleeping soundly.

"You are my friend," I say. "You were the first person I saw. I love you more than words can say. You need to let me go, let me do this. For you. For us. For Kevin. For everyone."

I feel like someone is dragging a jagged blade across my heart. I fear the end. I will never see these people again.

Spin reaches up with one hand, cups the back of my head. She pulls me closer.

"We never asked for any of this," she whispers. "Why can't they just leave us alone?"

The *they* she refers to . . . Grownups? Springers? Wasps? All of the above, probably.

"I don't know." Which is the truth. There is so much I don't know, and now I will never get the chance to learn.

I grip Spin's shoulders, hold her firm as I step back. She's shaking. I lean in, kiss her forehead.

"Thank you for everything," I say. "Who knows? Maybe I'll still be in here when it's done."

My hope is a false one. We all know it.

"Goodbye, Em."

Spin steps to Gaston, who is trying his hardest to stand up straight, to not collapse with heartbreak. She puts her arm around his shoulders.

Together, they stand there. A family. Father, mother, son. They represent the future of my kind. *They* are why I am doing this.

I turn my back on my friends and head toward my fate.

# FIFTY-SIX

We meet in the Garden.

Not an "orchard," but rather *the* Garden. It's just as overgrown as when we were last here. The same thick woods where Bello was taken. The same tangled brambles we crawled through to escape. The same sickly-sweet smell of rotting fruit. The glowing ceiling arcing high above seems to have a few more black spots, but maybe that's just my imagination.

This is where we fought the Grownups.

I could have killed Matilda then. I did not. I wanted to be a better person than her.

That decision is about to cost me my life.

She stands near the broken fountain that is nothing more than water burbling up through tall reeds. She's with three wrinkled, coal-black Grownups. Old Gaston is one of them, a bit shorter than she is. I don't recognize the other two.

Bulbous red eyes, whirling with a soft internal light. The nasty mouth-folds, quivering slightly.

All four Grownups wear silver bracelets, white stones already flickering with power.

Her people are armed.

Mine are not. We weren't allowed to bring weapons.

I have brought three people with me as well, all of whom can fight. Bishop, because there is no Grownup waiting for him. Young Victor, because his Grownup is on our side. And Barkah, because as the leader of his people he needs to understand what's happening.

Bishop seems calm, a stone statue covered in skin, but I can see the turmoil in his soul. Victor is more outwardly upset—hands clench into fists, unclench, clench again. Two boys, both covered with dried mud, blood of different colors, both smelling of sweat and smoke and death. The rivalry between them is forgotten. Neither of them wants me to do this, yet both of them obey the orders I have given to not interfere.

Barkah seems to be taking it all in. I'm not sure what he's thinking.

We walk toward Matilda and her people.

The Grownups level their bracelets at us.

"Far enough," Matilda says.

My friends and I stop. El-Saffani tried rushing the Grownups; the Grownups killed them. Even Bishop has to see the futility of attacking. At least I hope he does.

"Let's not waste time talking," Matilda says. "We all know how this ends."

I can't help myself—I have to try one last time.

"You know I'm not lying about the God of Blood," I say. "You *know* we can't lie to each other. Omeyocan isn't the paradise you were promised. It never was."

I can taste the hate pouring off her.

"To think I was such a coward," she says. "To think that I might quit at the first sign of danger. Are you a sad special snow-flake because the God of Blood put obstacles in your path? If you want something and you don't have to fight for it, darling-dear, then it was never worth having in the first place."

I was wrong. She *does* believe me about the Grub. She just doesn't care. Matilda is single-minded, a dauntless force of will.

"At least get the *Xolotl* out of here," I say. "Every second you wait is a second that brings us closer to a fight we can't win."

"You're telling me that as if I didn't already know. Tick-tock, darling-dear—time's a-wasting."

She is regal. Triumphant.

My heart sinks. "You're *horrible*. How can you put your life above the lives of so many others?"

Her one eye swirls.

"Am I putting my life above so many others, or are *you*? Every moment you waste is another moment that barbarian ship comes closer. And why is your non-life so important, anyway? Hundreds of thousands of people dedicated their existence, their fortunes, their *families,* to bring the human race to Omeyocan. It was a struggle, but great struggle is the price of great achieve-ments. I outlasted my enemies. I outlasted Brewer. I outlasted *you*. You have something I want, Em. I have something you want. It's as simple as that."

Victor shakes a fist at her. "You selfish *bitch*. You're going to get us all killed!"

"*Silence,*" Bishop snaps, turning his head slightly toward the younger circle-star. "Obey your orders!"

Old Gaston glances at Matilda, just for a moment, his red eyes briefly betraying emotion. Is there animosity between them?

If I had time, maybe I could exploit that, but time is something I don't have.

"Children, *please*," Matilda says. "Young man, you're hardly the first to call me that name. But by all means, keep running your little mouths. Take as long as you like."

I stare at Matilda. She stares at me.

"Tick-tock," she says.

We are impossibly different. We are exactly the same. Maybe something happened to her that made her this evil. Or maybe something happened to *me* to make me less so.

We'll never know.

To get what she wants, Matilda Savage is willing to let everyone she knows die.

Em Savage is not.

And that is why, in the end, she wins.

"All right," I say. "I'll do it."

Bishop breaks ranks, steps forward. Grownup arms snap up, aim bracelets—I step between the weapons and my man, put a hand on his chest.

He stops. His face is a mask of calculating savagery.

"I'll kill her." His voice is quiet, controlled, which makes it all the more terrifying. "I'll kill them all."

"You promised me you wouldn't try to stop this."

He looks past me, to the Grownups.

"I lied," he says. "I can't lose you. I *won't*."

Victor nods madly, a crazy grin splitting his face. "I'm with you, Bishop. Let's get them."

Barkah stamps a big foot down hard.

"*Stop*," he says. "*Orders!*"

Just the one word, yet it seems to rattle Bishop and Victor both. The two are torn between their hardwired duty to obey their leader and a deep desire to protect me.

I step past Bishop, stand before Victor.

"It's me or it's everyone," I say. "If you want to protect your people, let me go."

He tries to look into my eyes, but he can't. His head drops.

"I'll go with you," he says. "I said I would follow you anywhere. That includes following you into death itself. Please, let me."

I thought his feelings for me were just a crush. Yet one more thing I was wrong about, because I finally understand—Victor Muller is truly in love with me.

"Permission denied." I stand on my tiptoes and kiss his cheek. "You are so brave, Victor. Be brave now. Our people need you."

I stand in front of Bishop. I reach up, put my right hand on his left shoulder. Inside, he's crumbling. He's *shattering*.

"There has to be another way," he says.

The waver in his voice is almost enough to make *me* turn and rush the Grownups. My throat is dry. It hurts to know I will leave him so brokenhearted.

Ramses Bishop is a soldier. He would sacrifice anything for his people. He is a fighter, one who acts through violence, but this time, his violence would solve nothing.

"My decision," I say. "I do this for all of us."

He looks down. He nods. He puts his right hand on my left shoulder.

"Hail, Em. May the gods welcome you home."

I glance at Barkah. We have been foes. We have been friends. In some ways, this alien understands me better than anyone else, Bishop and Spingate included. Barkah knows exactly what is happening. He doesn't try to talk me out of it. He simply nods.

*"Hem. Peace."*

He gets that this isn't just about me. He gets the bigger picture—the lives of his people depend upon my actions.

I throw my arms around Bishop's neck and kiss him one last time, a deep kiss, a *real* kiss. A kiss that I will take with me into oblivion.

As soon as I let go of Bishop, Barkah hops forward and hugs me. I hug him back, smell the strange odor of his skin, the stench of battle that clings to him still.

I push away. I turn to face my killer.

"I have one condition," I say.

Matilda laughs, a hateful sound that makes me want to tear out her other eye and blind her forever.

"*Now* you have a condition? A tad late for that."

"Just one demand, Matilda. If you don't meet it, you'll find out you're not the only Savage who is willing to die to get what she wants."

For the first time, her aura of confidence wavers. There is the briefest moment where she examines me, trying to decide if my will is as strong as I say.

But she knows it is, because my will is her will.

"What's the condition?"

"When we're connected for the overwrite, *before* it begins, you give the navigation command codes to my Gaston."

"Ri*dic*ulous," she says. "You think I would give away my only bargaining chip?"

I shrug. "You don't have a choice. If you want this body, you give me your word. You're old, Matilda. You're frail. If you die in the process, I have to know my sacrifice is worth it."

She stares at me.

"Tick-tock," I say. "Wouldn't it be a shame to get what you want only to have the *Dragon* destroy us anyway? *Tick-tock*."

It feels good to throw those two words back in her face.

"I accept your condition," she says. "Let's go. We're wasting time."

She turns, gestures for me to walk with her.

I take a step, then look back at Bishop one last time. I was never sure if I loved him completely, the way I loved O'Malley. Only now, when I realize I will never see Bishop again, do I realize I love him just as much.

Maybe more.

Why do I only discover my true feelings for people when it is too late to do anything about them?

"Farewell, my love," I say. "I hope you find happiness."

He says nothing. A single tear rolls down his cheek, cutting a wet line through dirt, smoke stains and blood.

Three steps take me to Matilda. Side by side, I let her lead me toward our fate.

# FIFTY-SEVEN

Bars slide from ancient white fabric, lock around my waist, my ankles and my wrists.

My heart kicks. It's hard to breathe.

For some reason, I expected the room where I die to be white, shiny and clean.

I was wrong.

It's no different from the room in which I first awoke. Dingy. Mostly dark due to lights that probably burned out centuries ago. There's dust here. This place smells of mold and death.

Matilda led me out of the Garden, past the spot where I first fought her, where she lost her eye, where Bishop killed Old Aramovsky. Through the darkness, the only light coming from thin lines of color embedded in the floor.

Through stone doors cracked and cratered by ancient explosions.

Past armored turrets with silver barrels that tracked our every step.

Through doors made of steel, not stone.

And finally, to this room, decorated with only two things: a golden coffin and a black X.

The coffin gleams. The white fabric inside is rippled with age, even torn in a few places.

This is where they overwrote Bello. I don't have to be told this to know my friend ended here.

Old Gaston and the others shackle Matilda to the X, locking down her wrists and ankles. They place the black crown on her head.

This is how Kevin O'Malley died.

I stabbed him, yes, but it's time to let that go. I had no way of knowing the boy I loved was still in there. It wasn't my fault. Finally, I accept that.

I hope that I'm wrong about religion. I hope there's an afterlife. I hope Kevin is there, waiting for me.

Golden coffin lids rise up on either side, slide shut and block out all light.

My life will end the same way it began: in darkness.

I am about to be *erased*.

My body will live on. Maybe some shred of my mind, too—O'Malley was still in there; Bello remembered things she couldn't possibly know. Perhaps a tiny piece of Em will exist within Matilda.

A part of me holds on to the hope that this will fail, but only a small part. I have no illusions: the person that I am will cease to exist. Of all the things that make me who I am—a friend, a killer, a leader, a manipulator, a lover—I am also a realist.

And reality is what it is whether we like it or not.

*"Em, can you hear me?"*

Matilda's voice.

Even though it's pitch-black in here, I shut my eyes tight. Do

I really have to listen to her now? Do I have to hear the voice of that horrible bitch?

There must be speakers in this coffin somewhere, hidden in the old white fabric.

*"I know you're listening, darling-dear. Speak with me in your last moments."*

Her words drip with smug satisfaction.

"Go to hell. You disgust me."

*"How rude. We're the same person. You should be happy."*

I want to jam my fingers into my ears but my wrists are locked down. The coffin is old; these bars are new—I can't break them like I did when I first awoke. I want Matilda to shut up, just *shut up,* but I know she will not, not until the gas drags us both down to blackness.

"I should have killed you when I had the chance."

*"Yes, you should have. Compassion is for the weak. Because of your weakness, you end. Because of my strength, I live anew."*

My eyes sting. What . . . *now*? For all the times I couldn't dredge up a single tear, I spend my last few moments crying?

*"You were spectacular, darling-dear. So vicious. It's odd, but you made me proud. It seems fitting that the greatest foe I have ever faced is actually* me.*"*

If that smug, preening, selfish monstrosity is what I could have become, then maybe it's for the best that I end now.

"Time to keep your promise. Release the navigation command codes."

She laughs. *"Don't be silly, foolish girl. You knew I wouldn't give you the codes. Down in your infant heart, you wanted to join with me. Your pathetic little demand was just for show."*

Rage consumes me, but it's hollow, there and gone in an instant. I gambled. I lost. My existence will end to the bitter sound of her self-satisfied cackle.

*"Goodbye, Em. Gaston, I am ready. Begin the process."*

Old Gaston's gravelly voice comes through the hidden speakers: *"No, Matilda—you made a deal."*

I stop breathing. I stare into the darkness.

Matilda isn't laughing anymore.

*"Always the comedian, Admiral. Begin the process. Don't make me angry."*

*"You gave your word,"* he says.

*"Since when does my word matter? We're at war."*

Her voice cracks on the words. She's afraid.

*"It matters now,"* Old Gaston says. *"I've listened to your lies for centuries. Not anymore. Your selfishness has put my descendants at risk."*

*"Your descendants?"* Matilda shrieks her words. *"You mean the bastard child from that whorish version of Theresa and your receptacle? Those aren't your children, Gaston!"*

*"I'll never have children of my own, because I followed you. Give me the code."*

*"You godsdamned, backstabbing cockroach! Start the process or I'll have you skinned alive!"*

*"You gave your word,"* he says. *"Honor it or suffer the slow demise of dying where you are."*

He's calm, methodical, but he's also enjoying this.

*"Fine,"* Matilda says.

She rattles off a string of letters and numbers that is so long I lose track of them by the tenth or eleventh digit.

*"One moment while I verify,"* Old Gaston says.

The codes . . . if they're correct, will he release me? Maybe I won't end after all.

My heart thunders with hope.

I can't think, I dare not think at all. . . .

A few moments later, Old Gaston says, *"Codes confirmed."*

"Let me out of here! Please! We can fly away, we can escape, we can—"

"*I'm sorry,*" he says. "*Matilda gave her word. So did you.*"

With that, I know it's over. He's right. I did give my word.

I smell something. The gas . . .

"*Ah, it begins,*" Matilda says. "*You did well, Em. You did what needed to be done.*"

The creature I hate more than anything in the universe pays me a compliment. I should be repulsed. I'm not. She won, and she is gracious in victory.

I chose this end, but I did it so that others would continue on.

I only lived a single, short year, but—like Brewer—I made a difference.

So groggy . . . I don't know if my eyes are open or if I'm not able to open them at all. . . .

My constant anger, it's gone.

I feel at peace—my existence *mattered*.

As sleep claims me, I smile.

# FIFTY-EIGHT

Ribbons of memory flutter and fly.

I am six years old.

A smell, stinky but welcome . . . old fish.

I am in a boat.

Not a boat, a canoe. It's red.

An old man is with me. He wears blue robes. He has a symbol on his forehead. Not a gear, not a half or a circle; this one is shaped different, like the number eight on its side.

No, wait, I know what that is . . . it's an infinity symbol. A tattoo, faded black on light brown skin.

I'm holding a fishing pole. We're on a lake. I don't see any other boats. Green trees grow on distant shores. The sun shines down, but it's cold. I'm warm enough, though, because I'm also wearing blue robes.

"Knock knock," the man says.

A surge of excitement. This is my grandfather. He loves to tell jokes.

"Who's there?"

"Boo," he says.

"Boo who?"

"Aw, Matilda, don't be sad!"

It takes me a moment to understand. Now I get it—*boohoo*. I laugh a little, then harder. Grampa laughs. A wide smile carves deep troughs in his stubbly face.

Suddenly I am outside the canoe, watching myself and my grampa fishing.

My grampa . . . a man I trusted implicitly.

A man who was supposed to protect me.

"Matilda, can you keep a secret?"

I am looking at *myself,* at an excited face half-hidden by the blue robe's hood. The little girl nods madly.

"Of *course,*" she says, almost shouting it. "Of course I can, Grampa!"

Grampa frowns, across the water. "Oh, I don't know. . . ."

The little girl quickly reels in her line. The lure clacks against the pole's last ring. Droplets on sharp hooks catch the sunlight, sparkle like molten jewels.

"*Please,* Grampa. Tell me!"

His smile fades. There's a distant expression in his eyes.

Something bad is about to happen. The girl doesn't know it yet. I want to shout *Get out of the boat* but I'm not really there.

"You can't tell your mother," Grampa says. "And you can't tell your dad."

The little girl nods harder. So bright-eyed. So innocent. So trusting.

*Jump overboard and swim away!*

"Do you love your dad?" Grampa asks the girl.

"Yes, I love Daddy so much."

Grampa doesn't love Daddy. Daddy is his son-in-law.

"Then this secret is *very* important," Grampa says. "Because if you don't keep it, your daddy will be hurt. Do you want your daddy to get hurt?"

The little girl's smile vanishes. She doesn't understand what's happening.

*Jump in the water it doesn't matter if you drown because death would be better.* . . .

"No, I don't want Daddy to get hurt."

I know what comes next.

I didn't want to remember this. Not ever.

Grampa smiles. Something about that smile makes the little girl lean away. Fear on her face now, fear of the unknown, of a grownup changing the rules.

"Good," he says. "Very good."

He rises, hands on the side of the canoe for balance. The canoe rocks slightly in the water as he moves toward the little girl, a smile on his face, a distant, *wrong* smile.

The scene vanishes. Coldness in my soul. *Deadness.* What he did . . . how could the girl ever recover from that?

It happened to Matilda.

It happened to *me*.

I'm in my bedroom. I'm scared and hurt. My world has shattered. I can't stop seeing Grampa moving toward me, that sick smile on his face.

My parents are in another room, arguing. Either they think I can't hear or they don't care. I came home . . . *after* . . . and told Mommy what happened. She called me a liar. She *slapped* me. Daddy heard and came rushing in. Mommy told me to be quiet, to not tell Daddy anything, but he picked me up, held me, petted my hair. I started crying so hard.

I told him what Grampa did.

My parents scream at each other. Mommy begs Daddy not to leave, says that he'll wind up in jail, or get shot. Daddy throws things, punches walls. Our house *shakes* with his rage.

Mommy believes me now. I can tell. She's crying so loud. I did something wrong—this is my fault. I made her sad. I made Daddy angry.

I hear the comm ring.

Mommy answers. I can't hear what she says.

I hear the chirp of her disconnecting the call.

"It was him," Daddy says. "Was it him?"

Mommy cries some more. "Yes. He . . . he said they had so much fun fishing."

I hear Daddy's fist punch through a wall.

"He was seeing if she told on him," he says. "That bastard, that fucking *bastard* . . . I'll send him straight to hell."

"There's more," Mommy says. Her voice is so soft I can barely hear it. "He said he's enrolling her in the convent. He's sending someone to pick her up tomorrow morning."

The pause is so long I wonder if they've both fallen asleep.

The convent . . . I know that place. We visited there once. It's part of the main church complex where Grampa lives.

My skin feels like ice. I start to shiver. Grampa wants me in the convent so he can be closer to me.

So he can do what he did in the canoe again.

And again.

And again.

Finally, Daddy speaks. He's not yelling anymore. His voice is just as thin and scared as Mommy's.

"We can't let him do that."

"There's no way to stop him," Mommy says. "He's a Mullah—he can do whatever he wants."

"Cardinals outrank him."

"We don't know any Cardinals," Mommy says. "My father runs the church here. You know that. You think some high-ranking church official is going to side with *us*?"

The awful tone in her voice. I'm only a little girl, but I know I'm smarter than most people my age. Smart enough to understand that tone—my mother sounds *helpless*.

But that can't be. My parents know everything. They are the best people in our city, on Solomon, in the entire Purist Nation. They can do anything.

"I'll kill him," my daddy says. "Swear to High One, I'll kill him."

"David, *please,* listen to me—you won't get near him. We have to think of something else. Can we leave tonight? Can we run?"

"And go where? We have no money. If we go to the forest, we'll die. If we go to another town, they'll find us. We'll never get clearance to leave the planet."

More silence.

"There is one place," my daddy says. "The Church of Mictlan. Those are the only walls your father can't reach beyond."

"*Mictlan?* That crazy woman made the whole damn thing up! She cobbled it together from old Earth religions so she could trick people into building that ridiculous ark. Her religion is fake."

"More fake than ours?"

I start to cry. Somehow this has become the thing they always argue about—religion.

"Mictlan is a *cult*," my mother screams. "Our faith is real! We know Stewart led the exodus from Earth! We made the pilgrimage, saw his landing site with our own eyes. High One led Stewart to leave that bed of sin and found the Purist Nation!"

"The same High One that put your father in power?"

Daddy's words are quiet and cold. They bring silence.

When Mommy finally speaks, she's no longer yelling.

"We might never see her again," she says. "We don't know anything about that place. And we can't afford the tuition."

"We can. If we pledge our labor."

"David . . . that's for *life*. We'd work until we die."

"Which is no different than our lives now," Daddy says, his voice rising. "We work every day. We suffer, and for what? For the promise of Heaven? For knowing that our child will lead the same life we did? Your father blocked me from entering the church. There's never been a way out for us. At least this way she'll be safe."

"We don't know that," Mommy says. "No one knows what goes on behind those walls."

"We know what went on in that canoe. We know what will go on if she's enrolled at the convent."

I pull my blankets tighter around me. Are they going to send me away? I shouldn't have said anything, I'm a bad girl, a *stupid* girl, and this is all my fault.

The ribbon of memory flutters. Another one waves in, soft curls sweeping me up, carrying me to a new place.

It's the middle of the night. I don't hear any grav-cars. During the day our town is noisy, but now it is quiet and still.

A metal gate set in walls of stone. I know, somehow, that when I'm older I will see another gate that looks like this one, only much, *much* larger. This is the place the kids at school talk about: the Mictlan compound. It is a church, but not *our* church. My friends' parents say the same things my mother says, that this place is blasphemous, that the lady who founded it can stand up to the Mullahs and Poseks and Cardinals only because she is richer than anyone in the Purist Nation.

I've seen the children of Mictlan around town. They have circular marks on their foreheads. Tooth-girls. Halves. Circle-stars. Most of them have empty circles, though.

Daddy is talking to a man dressed in black.

The gate opens.

The ribbon of existence flutters.

I'm on a bench. Mommy and Daddy are talking to a woman dressed in black. She's *old*, older than any person I have ever seen. She has so many metal parts on her I wonder if she's actually a robot. She frightens me.

Mommy is shaking. Daddy has his arm around her, holding her close. I've never seen them like this before. They've always been strong, the strongest anyone could ever be.

They are not strong now.

"Your contracts are for life," the woman says, a machine making her raspy voice just loud enough to hear. "You serve at my discretion. Your daughter will get an education. She will be safe behind our walls. If you do this, she belongs to us. Do you understand?"

Mommy asks: "Will we be able to see her?"

"Possibly," the machine-woman says. "But not for the first few years. Even then, we make no guarantees. What we're creating here is bigger than you, than her, than any family. The True God calls, and we all answer."

"The ark," my daddy says. "Will she be sent to the ship? Will we?"

The woman's machine voice is cold, uncaring. "That is not your concern. You are not the first parents to come here seeking safety for their sons and daughters. The Purist Church is corrupt beyond belief. They treat women like property. They turn a blind eye to unspeakable child abuse. If you enroll Matilda with us, she will be protected. She will serve a greater purpose. My only regret is that we didn't get her earlier. She's too old for advanced training. However, as she grows and matures, she may have children of her own. Your grandchildren could be doctors, engineers, scientists . . . all things are possible."

My parents look at each other.

"*Too old*," Mommy says to Daddy, wiping at her tears with the back of her hand. "That means our daughter will be a *servant*. I don't care what they call it, we've seen the people with circles on their heads in town, catering to the people with those other symbols. Our daughter will be a servant her whole life."

Daddy twists in his chair, looks at me. He looks for a long time. Then he turns back to Mommy.

"It will be dawn in a few hours," he says. "There are worse things than being a servant."

Mommy hides her face in her hands. Her shoulders shake. She nods.

The machine-lady pushes a small black box across her desk. The box has a hole in it. My daddy slides his thumb into the hole.

A little light on top of the box turns green.

"It is done," the machine-lady says.

The ribbon flutters, but doesn't vanish. It shifts, slightly. I'm sitting on Daddy's lap. I don't know where Mommy is.

Daddy is crying. He's trying to hold it back, to hide it, but I see his tears. I hear the pain in his voice.

"Matilda, I have to send you away. I know you can't understand right now, but you will. The only way I can keep you safe is to hide you. There may come a time when the tooth-girls tell you to do something dangerous, or the double-rings try to hurt you because they know no one will punish them. If that happens, remember—do whatever it takes to survive."

I shake my head. They can't leave me. They are my *parents*.

"I don't want you to go," I say. "Please, Daddy . . . I want to stay with you."

He pets my hair. He smells like soap.

"You're going to be special," he says. "You're going to be one of the Cherished. Doesn't that sound nice?"

I don't know what that word means. If it means I can't be with him, then I hate the word.

"Daddy, *please*."

My words make him wince. For the first time in my life, I realize that words have power. A hard lesson that I will carry with me forever.

He stands, lifting me like I weigh nothing at all, hugs me, then sets me down. A woman in black clothes enters the room. She has a circle mark on her forehead.

Daddy kneels, kisses my cheeks.

"I'll see you again, sweetheart. Do what you're told. This will be hard for you, but I know you can do it. I know you can."

He turns, walks away. I reach for his hand but he's too fast—he's already gone.

My grandfather hurt me. Because of that, I'm losing my mom and my dad.

I've lost everything.

The world wavers and twists, the ribbon of memory shifts into something new.

I am eleven. I smell animal shit. The world is bright, but it's dimmer than real sunlight.

Because I'm on a starship.

A ship that is shaped like a big tube.

There are kids here with me, kids from my *lacha*. Korrynn Bello, with her frizzy blond hair. Little Bashar Brewer, my best friend. He's always looking out for me. Tall Boris Aramovsky, who is so good at chess. Theresa Spingate, so *gorgeous*—I wish I looked like her. Jason Yong, the bully who always sneaks up on me and yanks my braid.

Kevin O'Malley, the boy who is so pretty it sometimes hurts to look at him. All skin and bones, nothing like the man he will become.

And a brown-haired girl with a snotty look on her face.

Nyree Okadigbo.

I *hate* her.

The girls wear white blouses and plaid skirts. The boys, white shirts and black pants. School uniforms. We're forced to wear these. I want to wear pants, but that's not allowed for girls.

"This is so boring," Theresa says. "Like I need to see any of this."

She twirls a finger in her perfect red hair. She's trying to get O'Malley's attention. He's not watching her. Aramovsky is, though.

The world seems to expand around me, the dream-memory taking on detail.

Up above, the long ribbon of light that runs through our world. In front of us, a red wooden building with white trim: a barn. Green grass. Mud and dirt. Black cows. A pen with black pigs. A few chickens—also black—running loose.

A man walks out of the barn. He wears a funny hat. He smiles, that stupid way adults smile at kids they don't know.

"You all are here to see where your food comes from."

Aramovsky lets out a heavy sigh.

"It comes from the cafeteria," he says. "This trip is preposterous."

He's trying hard to look bored. So is Theresa. They're both nervous, though. I've learned that I can tell how people really feel, sometimes when they don't even know themselves.

"We kill animals quickly, with as little pain as we can," the farmer says. "That's the humane way. But it's not a pleasant experience. For some things to live, other things have to die. You understand?"

O'Malley and Bello nod. Okadigbo pretends not to hear. Aramovsky is busy looking at his shoes.

"Today, you'll watch us harvest a pig," the man says. "These are tame animals, but we still have to be careful. A pig is a strong creature. Any animal will fight hard once they realize they're in danger."

Aramovsky sighs again. "Right. Sure. Our pork chops are dangerous. What a stupid blank."

At that last word, Bello shrinks in on herself. *Blank*. It's a bad word, like *empty*.

The farmer is a grown man, much bigger than we are. No symbol on his dirt-smeared forehead. His hands are callused. He's supposed to avert his eyes, defer to the Cherished, but he stares straight at Aramovsky.

"You brats think you know so much. Here's something you don't know. The pig you eat for dinner? If you're not careful, that pig can hurt you. It can *kill* you. A pig will eat anything— grass, dirt, bugs, crops, meat, cloth, wood . . . even *bone*."

Aramovsky doesn't look bored anymore. He's surprised, as am I, that a vassal would talk to us this way.

Okadigbo, though, finally perks up. She loves it when someone challenges her. Or her friends. She lives to put people in their place.

"I guess we don't have to worry about killer pigs," she says. "Since no one in my *lacha* will ever stoop so low as to work on a farm."

The farmer glares at her. Unlike Aramovsky, Okadigbo doesn't back down.

"I suppose not," the farmer says. "Come with me."

He takes us into the barn.

On the way in, Okadigbo stops, stares down at her shoe.

She stepped in shit.

Yong sees this, laughs a cutting laugh.

"Idiot," he says.

Okadigbo looks at me. She smiles.

"Clean off my shoe, Matilda."

My face grows hot. She's doing this in front of O'Malley?

The farmer steps closer. "No need for that nonsense, missies. Just come along."

Okadigbo turns on him, her eyes alive and eager.

"Shut your mouth, *blank*," she says. "Or I'll tell Cardinal Reyez how you were staring at my legs in a way that made me feel funny."

The farmer's eyes go wide.

"I'm sorry," he says. "Very sorry. My apologies, miss."

Okadigbo smiles at me. She lifts her foot.

"Well, empty? Before we watch the little piggy get slaughtered, clean this shit off my boot."

I'm so mad at her. I hate her. I want to see her die.

Brewer grabs a rag off a fence rail.

"I got it, Mattie," he says, smiling as always. "I'll take a sample and use it for my project on animal digestion."

Okadigbo slowly shakes her head.

"If my shoe isn't cleaned, *by Matilda,* then Matilda gets the rod."

Brewer stops in his tracks.

She's done things like this before. If I don't do what she says, she'll tattle. I'll be punished, because I have to do what she says—I *belong* to her.

Bello stares at the ground, hugging her shoulders. Aramovsky grins at me, happy the power structure is back to the way it was before the farmer yelled at him. Kevin O'Malley has no expression at all.

No one will help me.

I reach for Brewer's rag.

"You can use the rag after," Okadigbo says. "To wipe off your hands."

I didn't do anything to her. I didn't say anything to her. Why does she humiliate me like this?

I *hate* her.

I want to see her die.

I want to see *all* the tooth-girls die.

Someday, I will make that happen. I *swear* it. But if I don't do what she says, the priests will hurt me.

I kneel before Nyree Okadigbo. I reach for her boot.

# FIFTY-NINE

A stinging pain jolts me awake.

I reach to slap it away, but my hands won't move. I'm bolted down.

*Of course you're bolted down, stupid—how many times do you have to get "stung" in the neck before you realize it's just a needle?*

It's not a snake biting me in the dark. I'm not trapped, waiting for a monster to come get me . . .

. . . because I *am* the monster.

Aren't I?

No, I'm still me. And I am her.

I am ancient.

I feel *young.*

*It worked:* all my sacrifices, my plotting and planning . . . I have another chance, a chance to live my *own* life and not what others planned for me.

*It worked:* I'm still *me,* I remember waking up trapped in a coffin, meeting Spingate and the others. I remember the walking and the fighting and the laughter.

So many years, so many *centuries*. My memories are fragments of a shattered vase, pieces all over, pieces missing.

Was the human mind ever meant to exist this long? To soak up a millennium's worth of faces, names, places, experiences, feelings, sensations, emotions?

> *It worked:* I beat that silly girl.      *It worked:* I beat that horrid old woman.

My mind . . . it's splitting in two.

Who am I?

I'm Matilda Savage.

*No, I am not no you're not no we're not . . .*

I'm Em.

*That's not who you are Em is gone you're not her . . .*

I am . . . I am no one.

My scream—desperate, piercing, born from a terrified, ancient mind, driven by powerful young lungs.

What is happening to me?

The sound of machinery. My restraints snap away. Light, so bright it's *blinding*.

"Em, calm down."

The one voice I truly need to hear, Spingate, calling to me. I feel her hands on my wrists, firm but comforting.

"It's all right," she says. "You're safe."

*Safe.* That word again. The word of nothing. The word that doesn't exist.

Theresa says I'm safe . . . but . . . but Theresa is dead. I had her killed because she betrayed me. How can she be talking to me now? She is a revenant come to drag me to hell.

I try to fight her but I'm still weak from the process.

The process.

It worked it worked it          It failed it failed it failed . . .
worked . . .

Hands stronger than Theresa's slide under my arms, lift me
up, hold me.
"Em, relax, I have you now."
Ramses.

One lover of many.          The only boy I've been
                            intimate with.

No . . . Ramses is dead. I saw him die . . . I saw *me* kill him,
during the fire in the Observatory . . .
I killed Ramses. So how is he holding me now? And
O'Malley . . .
I killed Kevin.
My soul is tearing to pieces, cracking like the plaza stone
when the Grub rose.

That thing Em saw . . . the          I told you! I told you and you
God of Blood can't be that it        wouldn't listen!
*can't be that.*

The God of Blood has me, *all parts of me,* he's going to punish me for killing O'Malley and Yong, for all the rebels that
died, for the butchery I did to my own people to show everyone on the *Xolotl* that I was the only way into the future, the
way to life itself, punish me for all the Springers I slaughtered,
for the city I destroyed, for the Wasps I shot and burned, for
the—
"Shhhhh," Ramses Bishop says. "I have you now. *Breathe.*"
I breathe.

My panic ebbs. I am not free of fear, but it no longer controls me. I open my eyes, I look upon the face of Ramses Bishop.

He looks *so young.* . . .

"I have you, my love," he says. His words are sweet like chocolate. "I won't let anyone hurt you."

No, he won't hurt me.

It is I who will hurt him.

A little bit at first, because he's young and the young have hope that life will turn out the way they *want* it rather than the way it actually does. Later, I know his hurt will be so much worse, so much more.

Eventually, he will accept things.

For now, though, I have to give him his first taste of pain, the first tiny tear in his big heart.

"I have you, Em," he says. "I'll never let you go again."

"I'm not Em."

His smile fades. Spingate steps into view. The fear that left me must have pounced on her. I see growing despair in her eyes.

"Yes, you are," she says. "Just focus."

I almost feel bad for these two young people, for these . . . *infants.* They are beholden to their emotions, as they will be for many years to come.

Behind them, another face steps into the light. A face that is black, wrinkled and withered.

"Hello, Matilda," Jason Yong says. "I'm so happy to see you again."

His voice drips with malice, but the two children seem oblivious to the threat. Yong wants to kill me. He always has. Ever since the revolt. He's always wanted to be the leader.

No . . . it's not *me* he wants to kill.

"I'm not Matilda," I say.

I assume Yong will think I am lying, because I've lied to him so many times before . . . but from the look on his gnarled face I know he believes me.

He's been my foe for centuries. He and that bastard Victor.

To think that Old Victor and I used to *date*? The Em part of me is aghast at the Matilda part.

"Whoever you are," Yong says, "you have to finish the ritual."

He offers me a ceremonial knife. It's black. The hilt is decorated with two rings of rubies, one inside the other.

O'Malley used a knife just like this to kill the older version of himself.

And I used a knife just like it to kill O'Malley.

*He was still in there. . . .*

Bishop snatches the blade away.

"I'll do it," he says. "Em has been through enough."

Yong reaches for the blade. "She has to do it herself, that's the ritual."

Bishop easily pushes the smaller Grownup away.

"I said *no*. Don't test me, Yong."

Past the foot of my coffin is the black X. A withered, sagging body—*my* body—hangs limply, head down, wrists held by shackles. She's moaning softly.

Not *she . . . me*. Is that what I look like?

No, what I *used* to look like. Now I am Em, I am Me. Matilda is gone.

Not gone, right there, still alive, I am still alive that evil bitch is *still alive* . . .

But not for long.

The ritual must be completed.

I hold out my hand toward Bishop, palm-up.

He stares at it. "Em, don't do this."

"She has to," Yong says.

Spingate grabs my wrist, tries to push it down.

"Em, Bishop is right! We'll vent her into space, you don't have to be the one."

I grab Theresa's wrist with my free hand, and I squeeze. She snarls, thinking she can hold on, thinking she can resist me, but I squeeze tighter until her snarl shifts to a look of surprise, then pain—she lets go with a gasp.

So much *strength* in this body. I haven't felt anything like it in a thousand years.

"The knife," I say to Bishop. "I will do what must be done."

My words sound as cold as the void itself. I want this over with.

Bishop glances at the knife, then at my palm, then he looks me in the eyes.

"It is my right," I say.

He slaps the handle into my palm. My fingers close around it. I feel the weight.

A small, weak voice calls out: *"Help me . . . please."*

Matilda. *Me.*

I walk toward her. My steps are slow and awkward, yet stronger than they have been in a millennium.

Matilda's head is still hung low. She's pulling at her shackles, weakly, making the chains rattle like a sad, small musical instrument.

"Didn't work," she says. "Gaston, dammit, you . . . you screwed it up."

I stop in front of her.

Matilda's pitiful efforts cease—she's looking at my boots.

"No," she says.

She slowly lifts her head. Even this slight motion seems to take everything she's got.

Her one good eye is pink.

I am looking at Matilda. I am looking at myself. I am looking at a monster. I *am* a monster.

"*No*," she says. "I want to live."

She is an old woman. Ancient and twisted. She did what she thought was right. I can't remember all of what happened to her—to us, to *me*—but I know she felt justified in every action.

But was it her, or was it the "God of Blood"? Was she corrupted, just like Aramovsky was? I was Matilda, once—maybe those memories will return someday, maybe I'll know the answer.

"It's not fair," she says. "I want to live."

But even if Matilda was corrupted, she is responsible for the horrible things she did. Aramovsky had to pay. So does she. I touch her cheek—gnarled skin that was mine a few moments ago feels wretched and vile to these young fingers.

What does a thousand years of agony sound like? It sounds like Matilda.

"It didn't work," she says. "Why didn't it work?"

I almost feel bad for her. "It worked well enough. You knew what would happen. You knew one version of you would be chained here, knew that version would end. And you didn't care. So selfish, right to the end."

She finds the last of her strength, shakes her head hard enough to rattle the chains.

"Let me go! If you kill me, you won't get the codes!"

This is beyond confusing. My head spins in a dozen directions. At my core, though, I know she and I can't both exist. I had a chance to kill Matilda once. I let her live—look at the price of that choice.

"You already gave Gaston the codes. Remember?"

Her one eye stares at me. It's redder now; she's slowly regaining her strength.

She should die with a blade in the belly, in agony, like O'Malley did, but I can't bear to cause unnecessary suffering.

It's time to do the humane thing.

I put the point of the blade on her sternum. I expect firm resistance, but the bone beneath the coal-black skin gives a little, as if her skeleton is spongy with rot.

"I want to live," she says.

I nod. "And I want you to die."

The fingers of my right hand curl tighter around the hilt. My left palm cups the pommel. My strong, young arms push the blade forward.

It sinks in slowly, steel vanishing into blackness, blade hissing against skin until the cross guard thumps into her chest.

There is no winner here. No loser. Em earned a chance for her people. Matilda got her young body.

Thick, red-gray blood drips down from Matilda's sternum, splatters onto the floor.

"I hate you," she says.

"I know."

With that, I pull the blade free.

I stand there and watch Matilda Savage bleed to death.

When she stops twitching, I walk back to the golden coffin. Ramses and Theresa stare at me as if I am an alien thing. Yong simply watches, his feelings indiscernible.

"You say you're not Matilda," he says. "And you're not Em, either?"

I shake my head. Bishop and Spingate exchange a glance. It's obvious they wish with all their tender hearts that I will suddenly wake up and declare, *I was wrong, I'm your little friend, I'm Em!*

But that will never happen.

Yong's red eyes swirl. How I hated looking through eyes just like those, the way they let me see so many things and yet made everything different. I hated that body, too—so *ugly*. In the first few centuries, we called our bodies "pain suits," a joke meant to help us cope with the constant state of agony.

But I don't hurt now. Not at all.

It has been so long since I was without pain that being without it, feeling *normal,* seems maddeningly strange.

My memories roil and clash. They combine to make me recall things that I know never happened. Tiny shards of reality, like small islands in an endless haze of gray.

"If you're not Matilda," Yong says, "and you're not Em, then who are you?"

Parts of me are a woman older than even this ship. A woman who has done unspeakable things, who lost friends, who lost lovers. A woman who can't remember the face of her father, because he's been dead a thousand years.

Parts of me are a girl, barely past the age of twelve, who was thrust into a position with demands far beyond her years. A violent girl who fought and clawed, who learned to be devious because that was the only way she and her friends could survive. A girl who would *not* stop, no matter what the odds.

Two identities. Two completely different people.

And yet, both identities are unified in one key area.

Because both did the things that had to be done.

And in that commonality, I coalesce, I unify as the myriad shards meld together, lock into place like the pieces of puzzles that I am so good at solving.

Brewer warned that the longer Em was awake, forming her own memories and mental connections, the less likely the overwrite process would work. O'Malley was still in there. Some of Bello was as well. But Em was her own person for far longer than those two, and her intellect was too well developed to destroy. Instead of being overwritten, she and Matilda *fused*, their identities and experiences amalgamating into one individual.

An altogether new person.

Brewer. My childhood friend. I called him by his first name back then, I called him *Bashar*. He had a name for me as well.

I am not Em.

I am not Matilda.

I am neither—I am both.

I am something new.

"Mattie," I say. "My name is *Mattie*."

Ramses, Theresa and Jason stare at me. The kids are crushed— they think they've lost someone they love. Yong looks . . . not *elated*, exactly, but so *hopeful*. I'm sure he's wondering if I'll unite all the people and lead us against the Wasps.

The multiple parts of me are talking to each other, comparing notes, seeing the connections that everyone else missed, that we *both* missed.

I'm not Em, I'm not Matilda, but one thing has not changed— I will do what must be done.

"Ramses, darling-dear, do something with this knife," I say. "We don't have much time, and I need to plan."

# SIXTY

I stand alone in the Tactical Control Center, watching the clock tick down.

*12:15:26*

*12:15:25*

*12:15:24*

There isn't time for expansive plans or multiple options. I've invited just five people to help me decide what to do, the only five people who really matter for what happens next—Bishop, Borjigin, Zubiri and both Gastons.

Like the rest of the *Xolotl,* the TCC was built twelve centuries ago. Much of the equipment is dark. Lifeless. I wonder how long it's been each piece stopped working, wonder if—somewhere back on the planet Solomon or elsewhere in the universe—entire empires rose and fell during that time.

The room is round, wide enough to hold twenty people easily. Curved wall panels are displays, like those in the shuttle. A quarter of them are blank and black. Others are peppered with dark spots of varying sizes, like the overhead lights in the Garden. A few panels flicker maddeningly. Those that work correctly show images of Omeyocan, the green dot of the *Dragon* following the red dot of the *Xolotl* around the planet's curve, inexorably closing in.

The Wasp ship is faster than ours—it's too late to make a clean getaway. I felt the God of Blood's power. Even if we break orbit and head straight out into space, I know the Wasps will follow us. They will not let an enemy go, risk that enemy coming back sometime in the future.

The Wasps want to wipe us out.

*12:14:59*

*12:14:58*

*12:14:57*

Memories rush back at a breakneck pace. I'm having trouble understanding what happened when, and to whom. The memories of the farm: those were burned into Matilda's thoughts forever, were the spark against the kindling that lit the fires of revolution. The memories of my parents sending me away, though . . . those memories had been mostly lost. Matilda's brain had blocked out what happened in the canoe, and much of what came after.

My mother and father said the Church of Mictlan was a farce? I/Matilda had completely forgotten that. I/she was only six years old at the time. The merging with Em shook up my long-term memory, broke loose things I didn't even know were there.

The Em part of me wondered if something caused Matilda to wind up so "evil." The Em part had no real past, was able to form her personality off of Matilda's core essence without the contamination of the bad things Matilda experienced. If Em was still around, if she knew what I know now, I wonder if that knowledge would answer her question.

All of this—the church, the *Xolotl,* the symbols, the rituals—was began by a coppery worm burrowed deep in the dirt of a distant planet. I can't recall most of the journey from Solomon. I can't even fully recall how the rebellion began. Those memories will return, I feel them surging, reincarnating, but what matters right now is the next twelve hours.

Old Gaston—the "Admiral," as he prefers to be called—was betraying Matilda. Since the debacle on Omeyocan where Old Bishop and the others died, he'd been feeding Yong and Old Victor information. After my overwrite, he opened the doors to let in Spingate, Bishop and Yong.

There was no one left loyal to Matilda and her cause, because Matilda's true cause was *Matilda.* Centuries of dictatorship have worn down the Cherished. They are ready to do whatever they can to keep the human race alive.

*12:13:46*

*12:13:45*

*12:13:44*

Each second is a knife driving through flesh to gouge bone. Our lives, our very existence as a people, are in danger of being snuffed out forever. This is more than just *survival*—for all we know, we're the last of our kind anywhere in the universe.

The doors to the TCC open. Young Gaston comes in first, followed by Zubiri, Borjigin in a wheelchair, then Old Gaston with Bishop right behind him.

I'm sure the Admiral wants to overwrite his younger self, but Bishop will not let that happen. I need both Gastons right now. The Admiral has immeasurable experience and knowledge of the *Xolotl.* Young Gaston thinks faster and he's got firsthand experience fighting the Wasps.

I sent Bishop to round up these people. There has been no formal declaration of leadership, so I make it now.

"I led the Cherished. I led the Birthday Children. Now I lead everyone. There isn't time for debate. There are decisions to be made. I will make them."

Bishop simply nods once.

The Gastons exchange a glance, but say nothing.

Borjigin looks like hell. He's hurting. Not as much as I was every day for centuries, but his pain is no laughing matter. There is no argument left in him.

Zubiri, though, wrinkles her nose as if she just smelled something bad.

"So, you're Matilda in Em's body?"

Such a pretty girl. A shame she lost that arm.

"Call me *Mattie*," I say. "I am neither. I am both. But that doesn't matter right now—I'm in charge, understand?"

She nods, but that nose doesn't unwrinkle. She's less than convinced. I like her.

"We have to act," Young Gaston says. "They're coming for us."

"I agree," says his older version. "If it's going to take a bloodbath, let's get it over with."

It is difficult to see them next to each other. Part of me has known Old Gaston almost my entire existence. *Centuries* of working together, arguing, fighting side by side, killing, watching those we love die. He is the Admiral. He has seen us through countless technical difficulties and disasters that could have wiped us out. Another part of me has known Young Gaston almost my entire existence. The little boy who became a man. He's just as much a warrior as Bishop is, as Em was.

*12:13:01*
*12:13:00*
*12:12:59*

"Admiral," I say, "how long will it take to prep the five fighters for launch?"

"I started that process as soon as you went into the coffin," the gnarled old man says. "Arming, fueling and systems checks are already under way. The fighters have barely been touched in decades. Flight testing revealed multiple failed parts that must be replaced before launch. Some of them have to be fabricated from scratch. Crews need another six hours."

"And is the shuttle fueling as well?"

Young Gaston nods.

He is more perceptive than Bishop. Far more. Young Gaston has no illusions—he knows his dear friend Em is gone forever. Maybe he's already cried enough, or maybe he will cry later. For now, he's pushed his pain aside to focus solely on our problem.

"Well done," I say. "What is the flight time from the *Xolotl* to Uchmal?"

Young Gaston's eyes narrow. He starts to ask *why*, then checks himself.

"Approximately one hour, fifteen minutes," he says. "But remember, the fighters can't fly in atmosphere. Only *Ximbal* can make that trip."

I look at the wall display, take in the position of the *Xolotl,* Uchmal and the *Dragon.*

We have to try. "Borjigin, Zubiri, I need you to build a Goff Spear cannon in the shuttle, and I need it done in nine hours or less."

Borjigin gives his head a little shake. "A Goff Spear cannon. In the shuttle."

"Correct."

He blinks a few times. "I assume to shoot a nuke at the *Dragon*?"

"Correct again."

He blinks faster. "And you want that done in nine hours?"

"If you need me to repeat the whole thing, young man, I will."

"Ridiculous," Zubiri says. "Strapping bombs to the wings is one thing. Engineering a cannon that can fire a round with enough velocity to penetrate that kind of armor is another. *Ximbal* is ancient. You want us to, what . . . to *hack* a twelve-century-old spacecraft? Make it do something for which it was never intended?"

I nod. "If you can't do it, the *Xolotl* will be destroyed, everyone aboard will die, and the human race might go extinct."

They stare at me.

"Wow," Borjigin says. "Not like you're putting pressure on us or anything."

"I prefer reality over pep talks. And *Ximbal* will be going into combat, so make sure your cannon is well armored."

Zubiri holds up her hand palm-out, waves it in a *wait just a minute* gesture.

"The Observatory's Goff Spear cannon was *twice* as long as the entire shuttle. Barrel length determines velocity. If we can find a way to put a launcher in *Ximbal*—and that's a big *if*—the round won't be moving as fast. That means the Wasp mother ship will have more time to shoot it down. I won't explain the math, but it matters. To score a hit, we'd have to fire from very close range."

I was hoping for better news, but I'll take what I can get.

"You make it fire, I'll take care of the distance," I say. "We'll assign every Cherished gear and half not working on the fighters to help you, but *you two are in charge*—make it work or everyone dies. Go get it done."

They trade one more glance, then they hurry out of the TCC.

*12:12:14*
*12:12:13*
*12:12:12*

"Admiral, give me a list of those who have fighter-pilot training."

Through Matilda's memories, I recall how all symbols except circles received extensive training from ages four to ten. Neural programming combined with chemical memory coding and hands-on repetition resulted in hardwired skills. Just like Bishop knew how to perfectly throw a spear without being taught, Kenzie Smith knew how to heal and Borjigin knew how to fix machines, some of our people can fly the Macana fighters—even if they don't know they possess that ability.

Old Gaston calls up a list of seven names. Many of those names trigger partial impressions, snippets of a face or the color of hair, strands of moments we spent together. My head throbs—I can't tell the difference between Matilda's past and Em's.

Aramovsky, B.
Dibaba, Z.
Goldberg, M.
Kalle, C.
Kalle, C.
McWhite, C.
Walezak, B.

Matilda's memories roil like an angry ocean. No circle-stars were trained as pilots. The Founder wanted them ready to defend the *Xolotl* against boarders, or even board other vessels themselves.

Pilots were drawn from SPIRIT, MIND and STRUCTURES. None from HEALTH, because doctors are expected to tend the wounded, and none from SERVICE, because how could a lowly *empty* manage the intricate complexities of a starfighter?

Dibaba, Goldberg and McWhite . . . all Cherished. Matilda knew/knows them well.

Kalle is there twice, once as a Grownup, once as a Birthday Child.

Aramovsky and Walezak: our double-rings doing double duty.

Five fighter craft. Seven potential pilots.

"Young pilots are preferable," the Admiral says. "So much of combat is about reaction time."

I don't think Bernice Walezak can handle the pressure. Any mistake, no matter how small, could spell doom for all of us. I need people strong of mind. People like Kalle—both versions of her, I imagine. Neither will like this assignment, but they don't have any choice.

Is Aramovsky strong enough? He's spent a year in that cell and he didn't crack. He was willing to die to stop me from killing Spingate. This is what he's waited for, a chance to make good on what he did.

"Aramovsky, Kalle—old and young both—McWhite and Goldberg," I say. "Get them whatever refresher training you can come up with on short notice. Prepare Dibaba and Walezak as well. They'll be backups in case anyone washes out."

"Tell me your plan," the Admiral says. "Because if you're going to fly five decrepit Macanas and a hot-rodded shuttle against the *Dragon*'s exceptional fighter craft, we might as well take as many drugs as possible so we're stoned out of our gourds by the time the Wasps blast us to pieces."

Young Gaston nods. "You saw what happened to the *Goblin*'s interceptors. We can't attack the *Dragon* head on."

"We're not going to," I say. "We're flying *Ximbal* to Uchmal. We're going to destroy the Grub."

The Gastons fall silent.

Bishop smiles. "I was hoping you'd say that."

His eyes sparkle. He doesn't believe what's happened to me is permanent. He probably still thinks I'll "get better," that true love is patient, that someday we'll settle down and have a family. The poor kid.

"But that doesn't help us," Young Gaston says. "Even if you kill the thing, we don't know if that will stop the *Dragon* from attacking the *Xolotl*."

"It might stop them, so we're *going* to kill it, but that's not the main goal," I say. "The Grub doesn't fear small weapons, but it does fear big ones. Like nuclear bombs. The Grub makes the species around it *protect* it, like a parent protects a child. I'm convinced the Wasps know we took at least one nuke with us. When *Ximbal* heads toward Uchmal, I think they'll assume the worst-case scenario—that we're going to blow up their new god. I believe the Wasps will scramble all remaining fighters to stop that from happening."

"That's a lot of assumptions," Bishop says.

I nod. "Remember how you felt on the training ground when you attacked Victor from behind? You wanted to protect Em. Imagine feeling that way about the Grub, only a thousand times more powerful."

Bishop looks down. The memory of that moment still disturbs him.

"She's right," he says. "If the Wasps think we're attacking the Grub, they won't take any chances. They'll send everything they've got."

Young Gaston shakes his head. "So what? You just said the

mother ship will attack us regardless. Why risk the shuttle to kill the Grub?"

"We're going to nuke the Grub, because it *needs* to die, but that's not our main goal," I say. "That strike is a functional feint to draw their fighter cover away. Once we destroy the God of Blood, we go full-burn straight up—we'll use *Ximbal* to attack the *Dragon*."

The Admiral gives a slow, dramatic clap. "Well done, Empress. Only about a billion things that could go wrong, but if none of them do, we'll have one shot at taking out their mother ship."

I smile at him. "You have any better ideas, old friend?"

"If I did, I would have said so already. I'm in."

The younger of the Gastons is far from convinced.

"The shuttle has slightly superior thrust in atmosphere, but once the battle moves into space their fighters will tear *Ximbal* apart. And the fighters won't be the *Dragon*'s only defense. Just like the *Xolotl*, it will have onboard gunnery to combat any incoming threats."

I already know that, because the Matilda part of me remembers the battle against the Springer mother ship. The endless salvos of missile fire, both ships shooting down as many missiles as possible but some getting through. Both ships being hammered, over and over again.

"That's why the *Xolotl* will attack," I say. "As soon as the *Dragon*'s fighters engage the shuttle, we change the *Xolotl*'s course and go straight toward the Wasp mother ship. We launch every missile we have, force the *Dragon*'s point-defense batteries to counter that assault. That won't give our shuttle a free pass, but it might tie up their counter fire enough for the shuttle to get close enough for that single shot."

Bishop crosses his arms. "We don't even know if Borjigin can build the Goff Spear cannon in time. If he can, we're putting our faith in an untested weapon. If it fails, we need a boarding party on the shuttle. Maybe we can blast our way in, damage their engines, slow them down long enough for the *Xolotl* to escape."

Young Gaston sighs. "You know that's a suicide mission, right?"

"This whole thing is a suicide mission," I say. "Even if the plan works flawlessly, *Ximbal* probably won't make it back."

All three men nod.

Bishop squares his shoulders, juts out his chin. "I don't care. I'm going. I'd rather die on my feet than on my knees."

"Very dramatic," Old Gaston says. "But don't worry about your feet or your knees—you'll probably die sitting on your ass in a gunnery chair before you even get close."

Twelve centuries old and he still feels the need to make sarcastic comments.

"Bishop is going," I say. "And so am I."

The Matilda half of me screams inside: *Why did we go through all of this, why did I* WIN, *if you're just going to kill us anyway?*

Em wants to live, too.

I don't care about either of them. I am *Mattie*. Mattie will do what must be done.

Young Gaston sighs again, rubs the heels of his hands into his eyes.

"Well, you two aren't going to hog all the glory without me. I'll pilot *Ximbal*."

"No," the Admiral says, "I will."

There's no room for misguided heroics. I need the best person for the job.

"His reaction time is better," I say. "You just told us that mattered."

The Admiral nods. "It does. Experience matters more, as does anything that would cloud the pilot's thoughts at the moment of action."

The old Gaston turns to the young.

"I didn't have kids. I focused only on the mission." He gestures to his withered body. "Then I did this, putting off a family until I reached Omeyocan and got my new body. After seeing what happened to Matilda when she tried to overwrite Em, I know that even if you and I agreed to join, *both* of us would end. Someone new would take our place. I can't ask that of you. Your babies are the children I never had. If this plan succeeds, they need a father. I'll have ensured my line continues. My life will matter. After all this time, it will *finally* matter."

The Admiral's words echo Brewer's. I feel the same. We've spent centuries bound up in a grand lie. This is a chance to do something good, something for others instead of for ourselves. We've lived our lives—it's time for the next generation to live theirs.

Young Gaston stares, dumbfounded, at his creator.

"I thought you would try and kill me. Like Matilda did Em."

I start to remind him I'm still alive, but that's not what he means. He's right—Em Savage is gone forever.

"You thought wrong," the Admiral says. "And besides, I've been at Matilda's side for a millennium. She doesn't get to be the only one to die a glorious death worthy of song and legend. The two of us will go out in a blaze of glory."

"Hey," Bishop says, "what about me?"

Old Gaston glances at him. "I have bad news for you, son. I watched your progenitor grow from a boy into a man. No matter how old you get, you still won't be able to grow a beard worth a crap."

Bishop's eyes dart to Young Gaston, who grins and strokes his thick beard. Bishop's face turns red.

Men—we're all about to die and he still actually cares about who can grow thicker facial hair?

Young Gaston steps closer to the ancient version of himself, puts his right hand on the wrinkled old shoulder.

"Hail, Admiral," he says. "Thank you. I don't know what to say."

For the first time, perhaps the only time, Xander Gaston is humbled.

Old Gaston puts his hand on Young Gaston's shoulder.

"Say the truth, that we're really doing this because *I'm* the best pilot that's ever lived—you'll have to tell your children that you're the *second* best."

"Ah, I see," Young Gaston says. "I thought I might eventually grow out of being an asshole. Good to know that will never happen."

The Admiral actually laughs.

*11:59:37*

*11:59:36*

*11:59:35*

I tell them the rest of the plan.

# SIXTY-ONE

Time waits for no man. Or woman. Or hybrid.

    *2:26:14*

*2:26:13*

*2:26:12*

Beautiful, streamlined *Ximbal* looks like huge children grabbed it, shook it, dented it, then glued on whatever parts they could find. Man-sized ball mounts are crudely embedded on both sides of the ship, just behind and below the cockpit, and also on both sides just in front of the rear engines. Silver cannon barrels stick out of each ball.

Nine hours ago, I put out a ship-wide call: *We will soon be under attack. I need volunteers for a preemptive strike—but know that those who join me will not be coming back.*

There's actually a small chance that we *will* be coming back, but I wanted people who were willing to give their lives for everyone else. I expected a handful of volunteers. I got hundreds.

No time for vetting, for interviews, to establish who would be the best crew. I looked at the amassed Birthday Children, Cherished, New People, Springers, and I trusted my instincts.

Circle-stars will man the new turret guns, and be ready to board the Wasp ship if that's needed. Yong begged me to be part of this. I think he wants to die in battle, as any proper circle-star would. Joining him are Bishop, Bawden and Young Victor. They are our best marksmen, our best fighters, and that means we must have them.

Old Victor asked if he could join. He begged, too, but his body has been failing him for a long time; there is no margin for error, so he stays here.

If boarding is necessary, we also have two Springers with us: one of Barkah's huge bodyguards—a male named Shumalk— and Lahfah.

Barkah tried to stop Lahfah from coming. He's too wounded to join, and even if he wasn't, I'm not sure he'd volunteer. He ordered Lahfah to stay. She refused his order. He then ordered me to not let her come. I ignored him. If Lahfah is willing to do for her people what I am willing to do for mine, then that is her choice to make. Not his. Barkah tried to drag Lahfah away. I had young circle-stars remove him from the landing bay.

On Omeyocan he was king. Here, I am *empress*.

I take orders from no one.

Lahfah and Shumalk will also be part of the damage control team, along with two Cherished, two New People, and me.

The two Cherished are halves who know *Ximbal*'s systems. They both lost their receptacles at the Battle of the Crescent-Shaped Clearing—Abrantes and Aeschelman. Their receptacles died because the Em part of me ordered Spingate to fire missiles at Borjigin's giant. Now the older selves volunteer to die by my side.

War makes strange bedfellows.

The two New People are my "grandson" Marcus and a woman named Benga Basuki. She is a mother of three. She's so committed to the lives of her children she's willing to die for them. I think Marcus volunteered out of some sense of obligation rather than a genuine desire to sacrifice himself for the greater good; he is the leader of the New People, after all. I'd rather not have either of them, but the New People will need their heroes just as will the Birthday Children, the Springers and the Cherished.

I made sure every group is represented. I can't have future generations point to one group and say, *You didn't do your part.* If we win, there will be a memorial to the heroes who undertook this mission—that memorial will show *all* of the *Xolotl*'s cultures.

I don't know a thing about the *Ximbal*'s systems. Neither do Marcus, Benga, Lahfah or Shumalk. We've quickly been taught how to use "weld wands," how to use sealant to fix punctured pressure suits, how to patch holes, how to mend split cables and a handful of other simple tasks.

I am ancient, so jaded I see even full lives as brief flickers of light that snuff out before they've truly begun to burn. Matilda watched thousands die, for her cause and simply from old age. Over and over and over again on the *Xolotl*'s journey, she saw children born, watched them grow, saw them wither, saw them die.

Because of that, I feel little for the people who are going with me. We serve the greater good. It is the smallest member of our crew, though, that draws a pang of sadness. The purpose of this mission is to fire the Goff Spear—for that, Zubiri must be aboard. She is our expert. Borjigin designed the cobbled-together Goff cannon, but he's too wounded to join us.

The final member of our crew is a circle-cross Cherished: Francine Yilmaz. Like the Admiral, she has no desire to over-write her younger self. Like Brewer, she wants her life to matter. That gives us a doctor on board to patch up minor wounds and get people back into the fight.

Turned out Old Kalle's hands shake constantly. She couldn't work the Macana controls, so she's out. Walezak broke down and cried during the refresher course. She can't handle the pres-sure, so we can't use her. Fortunately for us, Zoe Dibaba is ready and eager to fill Old Kalle's seat.

Our five fighter pilots: McWhite, Goldberg and Dibaba, peo-ple I've known for centuries, as well as Aramovsky and young Kalle, people I've known—in a strange way—my entire life.

A few centuries ago, Chris McWhite and Matilda had an in-timate relationship. It only lasted a few years, but we both en-joyed it and parted on good terms. Goldberg is a wonderful poker player. Dibaba was an ally of Brewer—I never liked her, but she's ready to do her part, and for that I accept her as my ally.

Young Kalle glares at me constantly. She doesn't want to risk her life. I'm not giving her a choice. Lucky for her, Gaston thinks the fighter pilots have the best chance of returning alive.

The Admiral will pilot the *Ximbal*. Noam Peura volunteered to be the copilot. He's as scared as ever, his voice cracking on every word, but he's going.

Our last chance at survival: Eight Cherished. Two New Peo-ple. Seven Birthday Children. Two Springers.

And me.

I am the *only* overwritten person. I suppose I am my own culture, a "Hybrid." Yes, that name should work for my last three hours of life.

I think of a quote I once heard: *I will never be old. To me, old age is always fifteen years older than I am.* Perhaps that quote worked for a 60-year-old looking at 75-year-olds—I wonder if it still applies when you turn 1,208?

*Ximbal*'s crew and the fighter pilots gather beneath the shuttle wing for final instructions. I stand there, my helmet under my arm. I should give a rousing speech, but that was Em's role. We either succeed or we die. If people need more motivation than that, I can't help them.

My spear. For the first time, I realize it's still on Omeyocan. I'm not sure where I lost it. It has been with me almost constantly for a year, and I didn't even realize it was gone. I suppose it served its purpose—we no longer need a symbol of leadership. The role is mine until I choose to give it up.

The Admiral quickly reviews the plan. When he tells us to get to our positions, most do.

Aramovsky lingers for a moment, then approaches me.

Like all of us, he wears a thick gray pressure suit. It makes his lanky frame look thicker, more solid. He holds a helmet under his right arm, visor reflecting the *Ximbal*'s lights. He cuts a dashing figure—the hero pilot off to save his race.

"Em, I just wanted to thank you."

Physically, he is on the edge of being a fully grown man. Yet to me, he is beyond young. I am a millennium older than he is.

"My name is *Mattie*. Em is gone."

He pauses, nods.

"You always talked of *gods*," I say. "Now we're going to kill one. You sure you're ready?"

The tiniest sneer curls his upper lip. His eyes sparkle with hunger, a desire for revenge.

"I'm ready. When someone dies, we say, *Let the gods welcome him home*. I wonder what gods say when *they* die."

I reach up and grip his right shoulder. "Kick some ass, Boris."

He smiles, then heads to his fighter.

The Macanas are black, long and sleek. They sit so low I could swing my leg over the side to get into the cockpit. The fighters all bear the scars of an old battle. No wings, just a tube with an engine on one end, a Gatling gun on the other. Six thick poles angle back from behind the cockpit, each ending in a small thruster. Those change the ship's orientation. A rear gunner is supposed to sit behind the pilots, but the rear guns were all cannibalized for parts, even the seats—those spaces now sit empty.

Someone spray-painted a white null-set symbol on the side of each fighter. Drips of paint stretch down like frozen white blood.

I look at *Ximbal*. Sure enough, someone painted the same symbol on the fat black missile mounted under the shuttle's right wing. The Goff round is inside that missile. The nuke has been modified with something called a "chemical timer." Now we can fire the missile in close to make sure it hits, and use the forty-five-second delay to get clear of the blast radius.

I board the shuttle, climbing a ladder that takes the place of the still-missing metal ramp. I walk left, into what was the coffin room. Now it is a mass of thick plates welded in for extra protection. The length of the room has been converted to an ugly-looking contraption made of metal, plastic and, in some places, even wood. The construct holds several fused sections of the *Xolotl*'s ruined Goff Spear. Halves and gears spent six hours in exosuits, cutting free every straight bit of that warped barrel. Borjigin's genius showed itself yet again—he combined several small pieces together to make this weapon.

The Grownup engineers hadn't thought of that possibility. Maybe they are too old to be creative. They were very impressed with Borjigin's ingenuity. They should be.

We haven't test-fired the new cannon, of course. We can't. We don't know if it will work. If it does not, there is no hope.

Past the cannon's rear end is a hastily built metal rack, also covered in patchwork armor. Inside the rack, I can just make out the hexagonal shape of a Goff round.

One round in a missile for the Grub, one in the cannon for the *Dragon*.

Zubiri is working away, busying herself with final adjustments. She wears a thick pressure suit. She doesn't have her helmet on yet—I see tears on her dark-brown cheeks.

I have lived a hundred lifetimes. She has barely begun to live just one.

Together, we will both die today.

Admiral Gaston's voice rings through the shuttle.

*"Gunners, perform final checks, then retract barrels and button up for reentry. Everyone, remember that no battle plan survives contact with the enemy, and contact them we will. Stay calm, solve problems. And may the gods have mercy upon our enemies, because we sure as hell will not."*

His words move me. I'm shocked: as old as I am, I didn't think that was possible. Xander Gaston—the Admiral—has been my friend for twelve centuries. Of course he could find the words to motivate, to inspire, even in the face of death.

*2:17:46*

*2:17:45*

*2:17:44*

It's time to fight.

I head for the pilothouse.

# SIXTY-TWO

*Ximbal* streaks toward Omeyocan.

The first time it came, it brought children desperate to stay alive.

This time, it brings death.

1:01:13

1:01:12

1:01:11

I stand in the pilothouse. My charged bracelet is held in a bracket on the bulkhead wall. On one thigh, strapped over my pressure suit, is the sheathed knife I used on Omeyocan. On the other, my weld wand in its holster. My external pockets are stuffed with small tools, tubes of sealant, sheets of patch material.

Abrantes is on my right. We're assigned to damage control here. He knows engineering. I do not. Which means I—the "empress" of my people—will function merely as his assistant, as an extra set of hands.

In front of us, bathed in light, are the Admiral and Noam Peura. We all wear thick gray pressure suits—unless you look through our clear helmet visors, Birthday Children and Cherished look exactly the same.

All four of us are held firmly by tentacle-arms that extrude from the ceiling.

The pilothouse walls appear transparent. Below us, night falls on the vast yellow, brown and blue spectacle of Omeyocan. One way or another, this will be the last time I set eyes upon the planet that our prophet promised to us thirteen centuries ago.

I've made a decision. If I survive this mission, I'm done being the leader. My memories are returning. Em's dream burns as bright to me as it did to her—I'll write the history of what brought our people here. I think I'll even use a paper and pen. Who knows? Perhaps I'll create a new kind of "holy book." My sins and mistakes can become a source of wisdom for future generations, a how-*not*-to guide of life, if you will.

That's *if* I survive. Which, most likely, I will not.

"*Attention, shuttle. This is the* Xolotl.*"*

The voice comes from the walls. It is Young Gaston.

"*Ximbal* here," the Admiral says. "Descending toward Uchmal to make our run."

"*Be aware,* Dragon *has launched sixteen small craft. Relaying tracking info to your systems now. You're about to hit that electrical interference, so I'll lose contact with you. Good luck.*"

Sixteen fighters. We thought they had only eight. They kept some in reserve. We can only hope those sixteen are all they have left.

Old Gaston glances back at me through the haze of glowing symbols that surround him.

"Looks like your plan worked," he says.

Well, aren't I the smart one?

The interference. From here on out, the *Xolotl* can't reach us, can't warn us of any further threats. That means the *Dragon,* similarly, can't warn the Wasp fighters. At least we hope that's the case, because our entire plan hinges on it.

"They'll close on us before we reach Uchmal," the Admiral says. "We'll have to go through them to hit the Grub. If we survive that dogfight, they should all be chasing us when we go full-burn for the *Dragon.* Do you want to proceed, Empress? This is your last chance to abort the mission."

In truth, I'd love to abort. This hacked-up, ancient bucket of bolts going head-on against sixteen advanced enemy fighters? That's not a positive equation. But we only have this one shot. And we need them behind us anyway for the plan to work.

"Continue as planned," I say.

Old Gaston pushes a floating icon.

"Attention, attention." His voice rings through the shuttle. "Sixteen bogeys incoming, estimated contact, two minutes. Gunners prepare to fire. Damage control crews, get ready."

There's no point in straying from our approach path. We *want* the Wasps to see where we're going. I take a deep breath, try to enjoy the last few minutes of smooth flying.

Abrantes turns to look at me. Red eyes stare at me through his clear visor. His mouth-flaps are wet.

"You know how people always said you were a bitch?"

People have said that. For a long, long time. *Bitch* is what they call you when you won't do what you're told.

I nod.

"You're different now," Abrantes says. "I like you better this way."

With that, he faces forward.

Well, well, well. In my final moments, I've made a new friend.

Past the Admiral, through the pilothouse walls, I can just

make out the city of Uchmal, a distant spot nestled in the blanket of yellow jungle.

"Here they come," Old Gaston says. "Ten o'clock and down."

I look left. Through the darkening sky, sixteen points of light streak toward us.

The Admiral's hands move quickly. He's not as fast as Young Gaston, true, but his movements are confident and sure.

The shuttle shudders. Em's memories tell me we've just fired missiles. Glowing flashes shoot away, trailing smoke tails that quickly fade into the growing blackness.

The Admiral barks last-minute orders.

"Bishop, ignore the lead ships, focus on third and beyond. Yong, I'm going to bank left and down when they pass, so they'll be above you when they come into your arc. Bawden, Victor, hit anything that comes at our rear."

If the circle-stars answer, I don't hear them.

*Ximbal* banks hard, throwing me against my restraints. Abrantes grunts from the strain. A glimpse of a flash as a missile detonates. A new vibration from the floor beneath me as turret guns open fire.

A shudder and a roar. A man's scream. Air rushes in, loud as the angry shout of a god. The transparent wall to the right of Abrantes turns black.

"Pilothouse damage," Peura says, his cracking voice spookily calm. "Savage, Abrantes, please patch holes and repair the display."

He said *please*. We're getting shot to hell, and the boy is polite?

"Hold on to your privates," the Admiral says, then the world whirls as he throws *Ximbal* into a tight, diving spin. The arm that holds me keeps me from flopping around, stops me from smashing into the pilothouse walls.

The shuttle stops spinning—my head does not. I blink, try to get my bearings. Ragged tears in the floor beneath Abrantes, in the wall to his right.

Then I see the hole in his left hand.

Wild winds catch the red-gray stream pouring from his palm, scatter his blood all over the place.

Abrantes pulls sealant from a pouch on his suit, squirts the entire tube into the hole. The expanding foam seals both the suit and the wound.

"Don't just watch, Savage," he says. "Get those holes in the floor!"

He moves to the wall and opens an access panel.

*Ximbal* banks hard left and climbs. The mechanical arm keeps me on my feet, letting my body move a little to diffuse the momentum, then bringing me back to where I just was.

*"Today, Savage,"* Abrantes screams. "Patch those holes!"

I grab my weld wand from its holster. From a big pouch on my chest, I pull a sheet of patch material. The shuttle shudders and vibrates around me: missiles launching, cannons firing, bullets tearing into us. The bottom end of the weld gun is a vibro-blade. It buzzes so fast it looks like a ghost, goes through metal like butter. I slice away ragged shards sticking up from the hole. Bits of metal scatter, thrown in all directions by Old Gaston's mad maneuvers.

Through the hole, the nighttime jungle of Omeyocan streaks by beneath us.

I place the patch over the hole, then run the weld wand's glowing blue tip along the edges. In seconds, the roar of rushing air dies down a little bit.

"Display repaired," Abrantes calls out.

I patch another hole.

*Ximbal* spins violently. Blood rushes to my head. The arm

holds me in place. Something hits us, rattling so hard my arms and legs flop around like those of a rag doll. When I put my feet back down again, they slide in something wet.

In the wall Abrantes just fixed is a hole the size of my chest. Abrantes lies on the floor in two pieces—he's been torn in half. Red eyes stare out. The fingers of his right hand flex and twitch.

"Abrantes," Old Gaston calls out, "my rotational damper is sluggish, fix it."

"He's gone," I say.

The Admiral turns in place, glances at the ravaged body, then again looks out *Ximbal*'s clear front.

"Peura, disengage, repair the damper," he says. "Savage, don't just stand there like an idiot, patch the damn holes!"

"Disengaging," Peura says. The lights covering him blink out. He kneels, opens an access panel.

Abrantes's guts are all over the floor. I kneel, slide a pile of them toward a hole. Swirling wind sucks them out with a *thwooop* of air. I grab a patch and seal up the blood-smeared hole.

The floor display is still working; I can see below us. We're coming in shallow, just above the treetops.

We're rushing toward Uchmal's walls. Far beyond them, the man-made mountain that is the Observatory rises up from the city center.

Two wall towers lash out at us with tongues of stuttering orange—the Wasps have installed their own cannons.

Something explodes to our left, then to our right. *Ximbal* begins to wobble in a way that I know is not good.

We fly over the wall. Beneath us, buildings and streets are a blur. A Wasp fighter flies past, trailing a fluttering cape of red and orange flame. It arcs down, smashes into a ziggurat and erupts in a fireball that quickly fades behind us.

"Starting our run," the Admiral says. "Gunners, keep them busy!"

We're flying north, directly above Latu Way. I can see right up to the plaza and the Observatory beyond it. The Wasps have set bonfires all around the Grub, a spotted ring of flame that casts flickering light upon the cause of countless deaths.

The God of Blood is massive. Wriggling and vile, it's already grown bigger than when we left.

Among the fires, I see tanks, eight-legged ticks, and tiny things moving around—*Wasps*. They surround their god. Are they worshiping it? Waiting for their chance to "merge" with it?

"Zubiri," the Admiral says, "prepare to fire."

I'm close enough that I can hear her voice through his helmet.

*"Armed and ready. Forty-five-second delay to let us get clear."*

That creature destroyed millions of lives—now it will pay the price.

I stand next to Xander. I point my finger forward and down, toward the coppery God of Blood.

"Burn that bastard son of a bitch, Admiral. *Burn it.*"

The Observatory rushes toward us, massive beyond compare. On either side of us, the city shoots past as a haze of black and brown.

"*Ximbal,* upon detonation, set rear pilothouse display to five thousand pulses per second," the Admiral says. "Our Empress would like to watch. Zubiri, release payload, now, now, *now.*"

The shuttle trembles. Everything vibrates, everything *thunders*. The howling wind cranks higher, screams so loud I'm sure the entire ship is about to shatter into a billion shards.

A flash of gold shoots forward, covering a thousand meters in the blink of an eye. I see a cloud of stone powder-puff up from the base of the Observatory's south wall.

The Admiral raises his hands to the ceiling: we tilt up, start climbing.

The extruded arm holds me in place.

I turn to face the pilothouse's back wall, which shows everything behind us as if the rest of the shuttle wasn't even there.

Our main engines blaze full-out. *Ximbal* shudders under the strain.

Fighters angle up behind us, giving chase. Past them, I see the plaza, the Observatory, growing smaller by the second.

Smaller . . .

Smaller . . .

A flash. The pilothouse wall darkens, protecting us against the blinding light.

The explosion happens in the blink of an eye, but the pilothouse screens slow it down for me, play out every millisecond in glorious detail.

A ring of orange flame expands from the Observatory's base, cascades across the plaza, engulfing the Wasps. They pop like a thousand tiny fireworks. The hated tanks are sent flying, melting as they tumble and spin. The ticks become splashes of liquid steel.

The ring of fire swallows the Grub. The coppery monster actually resists the blast of pressure and heat, survives it for the briefest instant, then massive chunks of metallic flesh fly free. Whatever passes for its blood instantly boils into dark-blue jets of steam.

The God of Blood's long jaws tear off, spin away.

Finally, the monster *bursts* as it vanishes in a growing ball of fire.

For a moment, the Observatory actually *rises,* as if it has engines of its own, then the impossible mountain swells and cracks.

The expanding fireball rips it into a million pieces that are swallowed by flame and lost forever.

The bomb's shock wave radiates out, leveling everything around it. In a flash, a hundred buildings disintegrate, their broken remainders scattered outward in a roiling hail of gravel.

Uchmal disintegrates. A fireball soars into the sky, turning night to day.

A sensation of pure satisfaction envelops me.

*The God of Blood is dead.*

I'll never know if the blast also killed the last two eggs. I hope it did.

I turn to face forward, see nothing but stars ahead. Peura is lit up again, back at his copilot duties.

"Accelerating," he says. "Full escape velocity."

The restraining arm holds me in place, but the thrust is so great that I feel my body *flattening*.

The walls blare with a piercing alarm.

"Eight bogeys in pursuit," the Admiral says. "We have enough distance that they won't shoot for fear they'll have to fly through their own bullets. They'll wait to attack until we escape the atmosphere. Rear gunners, hold your fire until they get closer."

We killed half of them. Will that be enough?

The seconds roll by.

The Admiral twists a glowing icon. "Exiting the stratosphere."

The wounded *Ximbal*'s constant shudder starts to taper off. Less air resistance up here, I think.

"Exiting mesosphere," the Admiral says. "Rear gunners, here they come!"

I turn to look at the rear wall. Eight glowing streaks blaze toward us, closing fast. They are directly behind us.

I look forward once again: our trap is springing shut.

Five black blurs dive straight at us.

Just as we couldn't see the Wasp mother ship hiding behind the *Goblin,* our shuttle is directly between our pursuers and the Macanas—the Wasp pilots have no idea our fighters are about to pounce.

The Macanas rip past us so fast I hurt my neck turning to watch them attack. The five craft instantly close on the Wasp fighters, Gatling guns blazing. Our five pass by their eight, leaving behind explosions so rapid and bright I squint against the sudden light.

"Six enemy fighters destroyed," Old Gaston says. "We lost one of ours."

I don't ask who died.

The two remaining Wasp fighters turn and bank, moving into another exchange with our Macanas. The pilothouse wall magnifies action that would otherwise be nothing but tiny lights.

The enemy ships move like they were born and raised in space itself. Our Macanas seem clumsy and awkward in comparison. As the fighters pass by each other, a Macana sparks briefly, then slowly spins toward Omeyocan. I silently wish for it to pull up, to gain control—it does not. If that pilot is still alive, he or she has only minutes to live.

The loss is costly, but it lets our three remaining Macanas get behind a Wasp fighter. A flash of light; the enemy ship breaks up into a hundred pieces.

Now it's three against one.

Our fighters bank and twist, coming at the lone enemy from multiple directions. I hold my breath, watch the Wasp fighter's impossible maneuvering. Another of our fighters sparks, then breaks into tumbling pieces.

In the end, our numbers prove too great. Our last two fighters close in—the final enemy craft glows brightly for a split second before snapping in two, both halves spinning away.

"Enemy bogeys destroyed," the Admiral says.

The pilothouse walls crackle first with static, then the sound of a familiar voice.

"*Macana Four to Ximbal. We should be outside the interference range, do you read me?*"

It's Kalle.

"We read you," the Admiral says.

"*No damage,*" Kalle says. "*Ammo capacity down to sixty percent.*"

"*This is Macana Two, no damage, ammo at seventy percent.*" Aramovsky's voice.

The Em part of me breathes a silent sigh of relief, while the Matilda part grieves a little more—McWhite, Dibaba and Goldberg are all dead.

Peura is panting so hard his breath steams up the inside of his visor. He's terrified.

"Multiple casualties in rear section," he says. "Zubiri reports the Goff launcher is damaged."

"*Dammit,*" Xander says. "Opening up all comms. Savage, get back there and see if you can help."

The metal tentacle-arm releases me, slithers back into the pilothouse ceiling.

I'm weightless. I'd forgotten about that. I turn and clumsily push for the rear wall, bumping into the floating top half of Abrantes as I do. I spin the wheel lock and open the pilothouse door. I kick off the frame, shooting through the corridor to the area that used to be our coffin room.

Benga Basuki has no head. The stump of her neck trails a bobbing stream of shivering red liquid. Old Yilmaz floats lifeless, her suit torn open, ripped red-gray-coated intestines dangling behind her slowly spinning corpse. The air is clouded with detritus: severed limbs, bits of metal, chunks of plastic, splinters of wood, a Springer leg. A stab of panic and loss, wondering if the leg belongs to Lahfah, but I see her trying to patch a head-sized hole in the hull.

Zubiri, Lahfah, Marcus and Aeschelman are cutting and pulling on the twisted remains of the bomb rack. I'm not sure why they bother—the front half of Borjigin's launcher is ripped to shreds. A half-dozen gaping holes in the walls, ceiling and floor reveal stars twinkling against the blackness of space.

Yong, Bishop, Bawden and Victor must still be manning their guns.

Admiral Gaston's voice in my helmet: "We're closing in. The *Xolotl* will be in missile range shortly. As soon as the *Xolotl* engages the *Dragon,* we make our run."

We're so screwed.

"Admiral, this is Savage. The Goff launcher is ruined."

"Then *fix* it! The *Dragon*'s ship-killing cannon will be in can't-miss range in . . . dammit, twenty-three minutes, eleven seconds."

"This thing is *not* going to fire," I say. "Can we attack their cannon? Can Kalle and Aramovsky attack with us?"

"Our weapons are too small to punch through its armor. And we won't get anywhere near it—their point defense will focus on protecting that cannon and their engines. Figure out another solution, fast."

I try to stay calm. All of my parts—Matilda, Em and Mattie—struggle against the fist of stress and anxiety that squeezes tight my soul.

I shoot across the coffin room, grab onto the twisted bomb rack to stop myself. The rack is a mess, but the hexagonal gold bomb itself . . . it looks undamaged.

"Zubiri, will that thing still detonate?"

She wedges herself into a space in the wreckage, leans close to the bomb. She's looking at a readout of some kind.

"Arming computer is fried," she says. "Twenty minutes to fix it. But what difference does it make? The launcher is destroyed."

"It's a *nuke*," I say. "Can't we just get the shuttle close and detonate it?"

"The *Xolotl* survived two proximal nuke strikes," she says. "Goff rounds work because they penetrate the ship's armor, explode from the *inside*. Without the launcher, we can't generate enough velocity to do that. Just setting off the bombs won't stop them."

There has to be a way. *Has* to.

Wait . . . maybe there is . . .

"Admiral, their ship has the same layout as ours, right?"

"From everything we've seen, the ship designs are almost identical."

"So you know where the *Dragon*'s landing bay would be?"

"If it's in the same place as ours, yes."

"The younger version of you opened the *Xolotl*'s landing bay doors from the outside," I say. "You know how the emergency access works?"

"Of *course* I know how that works!"

Even in this dire situation, Xander can be offended? Amazing.

"If it's the same, could one of us open the landing bay doors?"

There is a pause.

"You want to nuke their ship from the inside?"

"Yes. Can you open it or walk someone else through the process?"

He should be the one to do it, but I need him piloting *Ximbal*.

"Yes to both," he says. "That's assuming the access system is identical."

I glance at Zubiri. "Does the landing bay count as *inside* their armor?"

Wide-eyed, she nods.

"Admiral," I say, "as soon as the *Xolotl* engages with missiles, take us to the landing bay."

In a half-destroyed shuttle with the survival of our race on the line, Admiral Xander Gaston starts to laugh.

"You always were a bitch, Savage, which is why I always followed you. Aramovsky, Kalle, on my wings. Gunners, prepare to board—we're going in."

# SIXTY-THREE

'm in the pilothouse, the extruded arm wrapped around my waist and chest.

*0:8:57*

*0:8:56*

*0:8:55*

The Admiral is piloting. Peura is getting ready for his exo-walk. It will be up to him to get us in.

I pull my bracelet from its bracket, slide it up my arm over my pressure suit.

Xander has put the countdown clock in the upper right corner of our helmet displays. When that timer hits zero, the *Dragon*'s version of the Goff Spear will fire—the *Xolotl* will die.

As *Ximbal* closed in on the *Dragon*, I used my remaining patches to pin Abrantes's body to the deck. *Both* pieces of it.

Out in the void of space, two massive starships launch missiles at each other, a crisscross of shooting stars.

The *Xolotl* is tiny, a flickering dot thousands of kilometers away.

The *Dragon* is close; its slowly rotating cylinder takes up most of our view. The smooth copper surface reflects Omeyocan's reddish sun in a burnished gleam. The *Dragon* looks almost new, completely unscarred by battle.

That's about to change.

A volley of *Xolotl* missiles closes in. Most are destroyed by the *Dragon*'s point-defense guns, but some get through, impact with frightening fury, kicking up massive fireballs that spray out expanding clouds of copper shards, leave liquid yellow craters cooling quickly in the void's freezing embrace.

"Landing bay in view," the Admiral says. "Mapping defensive batteries that can hit us when we're close. Aramovsky, Kalle, transferring locations to your targeting systems—take them out."

*"Roger that,"* Kalle calls, her voice tinny and full of static. *"Come on, Boris, let's cook 'em!"*

The two sleek Macanas zip ahead of us, one above, one to our right. I don't know who is in each one.

The *Dragon*'s big gray landing bay doors look *exactly* like ours—will the emergency access panel be in the same place as well?

Defensive batteries fire at us. The pilothouse walls flash as bright as the sun. *Ximbal* shudders, shakes.

"Damage to engine two," the Admiral says, calm as can be. "Shutting it down."

"What does that mean?" I ask. "Are we going to explode?"

"It means we've lost one-third of our thrust. We can still maneuver, but getting back to the *Xolotl* will be tough."

I almost laugh. He thinks we can go back? I assumed there was no chance of that. The thought that we might plant the bomb and leave—that I might actually *survive* in this young body . . .

Beneath us, the *Dragon*'s kilometers-long copper cylinder slowly rotates. Another *Xolotl* missile lands, creating another puddle of molten copper that quickly cools as it slowly rotates away from us.

*Ximbal* vibrates madly. The pilothouse walls start to flicker.

A defensive gun flashes one last time, then erupts in a gout of flame as one of our fighters takes it out.

"Great shooting, Kalle," Old Gaston says. "That was the last battery that can hit us. We're in the clear. Peura, you ready?"

"*Ready,*" a thin voice calls back.

The Admiral maneuvers the shuttle into position, matching the *Dragon*'s rotation just like he did when we reached the *Xolotl*. My feet once again press against the floor—gravity has returned. It seems like we're perfectly still, a copper behemoth floating motionless above our heads.

Close by, a *Xolotl* missile hits and erupts, a here-then-gone flash of orange and spinning bits of metal. The crater's molten center briefly bubbles.

Peura's voice sounds in my helmet.

"*Exiting airlock. Beginning exowalk. Wish me luck, guys.*"

A chorus of *good luck*s answers him.

The pilothouse walls flicker, giving me a staccato vision of a boy in a thick gray pressure suit floating through space. He is alone out there. The hopes of an entire race ride with him.

Peura was beyond brave to volunteer as copilot, but this? Exowalking on an alien ship while missiles explode around us? I wouldn't have thought he had it in him. Sometimes courage is carried by a roar—sometimes it is hidden within a wavering voice.

*Ximbal* trembles continuously now, the shake of a dying animal.

The approach to the landing bay: a deepening groove leading to flat gray doors. It looks exactly like the *Xolotl*'s. Exactly. Peura follows that groove, reaches the bottom corner of the massive doors. The flickering pilothouse display makes him look so close I could reach out and touch him.

Sure enough, there is a copper-colored access panel, right where Young Gaston found one on the *Xolotl*.

Can this uniformity of design be our savior?

Peura opens the panel. Beneath are parallel rings, just like on the *Xolotl*.

*"Activating emergency access,"* he says.

He plants his feet on the copper hull. He pulls the handles back, dragging out their cylinders with them. He twists both handles.

I realize I'm holding my breath. I slowly let it out, and I wait.

The landing bay doors begin to open.

*"I did it,"* Peura screams over the comm. *"It worked!"*

A flash of orange and yellow—a missile detonates between us and Peura. Copper shrapnel blasts outward, rips a dozen new holes in the pilothouse.

I don't move. I wait for the pain to announce that metal shards have punched holes through Em's young body.

"Peura, get your fat ass back in here," the Admiral says. His voice sounds strained, forced. "Engine three is out. We're down to one primary engine. Everyone, double-check your suit integrity—that shrapnel hit us hard."

My helmet would let out an alarm if my suit was breached, but I run my hands across my arms, legs, chest and head anyway, searching for punctures.

I find none.

The Admiral is not as lucky. His left arm hangs limply. I see air jetting from his shoulder, carrying droplets of blood with it.

"Xander, you're hit!"

I pull suit sealant from a pouch and squirt it into the hole.

"We need to see if you have internal bleeding."

He pushes my hands away.

"No time. Peura, are you in the airlock?"

There's no answer.

Through the flickering pilothouse wall, I see a gray-clad body floating out into space, frozen globs of blood trailing along, reflecting sunlight with jewel-like sparkles.

I turn to leave. "I'll bring him back."

"Stay *here*," the Admiral barks, his tone so commanding it stops me cold. "Peura is gone. We're going in."

He moves his hands, wincing at the pain. *Ximbal* heads down the trench.

Maybe dying a good death matters to someone who has lived a thousand years. Peura lived only *one* year. I wonder if he had a chance to kiss someone, or if he died not knowing what that felt like.

The shuttle slides over the still-bubbling crater and into the landing bay.

A rush of déjà vu. This hangar is so much like ours back on the *Xolotl*—arcing metal beams overhead, walls curving down to meet the metal floor. The same, yet different. Different tanks and racks of equipment, two of their lethal fighters half-disassembled. I see a troopship and for a moment hope we might use it to escape, but there is a huge hole melted in its side.

*0:6:01*

*0:6:00*

*0:5:59*

I turn my wrist left, then right, activating my bracelet. I wish I had my spear, but I don't. I draw my knife. My suit's thick gloves make holding it a little awkward.

*Ximbal* lowers. I feel the landing gear clank against the deck.

"We're down," Xander says, his strained words echoing through our ravaged ship. "Boarding party, go!"

# SIXTY-FOUR

leave the pilothouse. Bishop and Victor are at the sliding external door. It looks like Swiss cheese. It won't open all the way. Each man has his gloved fingers hooked around an edge. They yank and lean away from each other, forcing the opening wider.

Not enough room for them to get out, but I'm smaller.

I slide through and jump down. I hear Bishop shout, *"Em, wait,"* then I land. I notice it right away—this gravity is lighter than the *Xolotl's*, than Omeyocan.

I sweep my bracelet arm before me, looking for targets.

There are none.

Any Wasps in here must have had time to get to interior airlocks before the outer doors opened.

The landing bay rattles.

"Wasps are shutting exterior doors," the Admiral says, his voice in my helmet. "We can't stop it. When they close, the bay will repressurize and they'll come pouring in. Zubiri, status?"

*0:5:15*

*0:5:14*

*0:5:13*

"Four minutes to arm," she says. "Then one minute to detonation."

"Cutting it close," the Admiral says. "Any longer and they'll be able to fire their ship-killer at the *Xolotl*. Get it done."

We have five minutes to live. Five minutes to hold off the Wasps. Five damn minutes to keep the *Xolotl* alive.

Bishop and Victor finally force the doors open enough to drop down, drawing my attention to the shuttle, the vehicle that has seen us through so much. It is *shredded*. In several places, I can see right through it to the far side of the landing bay. One wing dips at an angle. The rear is blackened, the metal slagged by what must have been intense fire.

*Ximbal* let us escape Matilda. It kept us alive on Omeyocan. Without it, we couldn't have killed the Grub. We wouldn't be on the precipice of defeating our enemy. It is an inanimate object, yet it hurts to see it so abused.

"Take cover," Bishop calls out. "We caught them by surprise, but they're probably putting on exosuits now. We'll be under attack even before they pressurize the hangar. Bawden, stay with Zubiri and guard the bomb. Aeschelman, stay with the Admiral. Everyone else, grab a weapon and get out here!"

I see an equipment rack packed with heavy metal boxes. I sprint to it. Each step launches me farther than I expect. It's all I can do to stop from falling—I'm moving too fast and slam into the rack. I kneel and take cover as best I can. My heart kicks like a mule. I feel my pulse in my eyes, hear it in my ears.

This is where I will die.

Aramovsky's voice over the commlink, scratchy, hard to understand: *"What's the status? Kalle and I are ready to escort you back."*

"Negative, Aramovsky," the Admiral answers. "Too much damage for us to get back. We're staying here. Go home."

*"Bullshit,"* Aramovsky says instantly. *"We're not leaving you."*

The huge doors clang shut, making the entire hangar reverberate.

"Landing bay repressurizing," the Admiral says. "About two minutes to completion, but some of the internal airlocks are already cycling—we'll have company in less than thirty seconds."

*0:4:22*

*0:4:21*

*0:4:20*

More of my crew drop down from the ravaged shuttle: Yong, Marcus and Lahfah. Lahfah holds a Springer rifle. Yong has a bracelet on his right arm, a sword in his left hand. Marcus is empty-handed; his pistol is still in its holster. Human, Grownup, Springer, yet our gray pressure suits make us look like soldiers in the same army—except for Lahfah's tail, of course.

She hops once, soars high. She lets out a squeak of surprise.

Yong bounds toward a bulkhead that will give him some cover.

"Low grav," he says. *"Fantastic!* What a final fight this will be!"

Marcus stands there, confused.

"Marcus, to me," I call, waving my arm. He sees me, comes running, the suit making his movements clumsy and awkward.

"Mattie, why aren't we leaving? We have to get out of here!"

Through his visor, his face is a wide-eyed, open-mouth visage of panic.

"We're not leaving," I say. I pull his pistol from his holster, shove it against his chest.

He takes it, looks at it like it might sting him. He's not cut out for this. He's going to die here, just like the rest of us. I hope he can take a few Wasps with him.

*0:4:01*

*0:4:00*

*0:3:59*

If the nuke doesn't blow, all of this effort is for nothing.

"Zubiri, we still on track?"

"Almost there," she calls back. "Countdown clock is accurate."

The comm line buzzes with multiple voices.

Yong: "Kill 'em all and let the gods sort 'em out. Let's get some!"

Xander: "Internal airlock doors about to open."

Bishop: "Copy that. *Ximbal's* nose is twelve o'clock for all directional call-outs. We can . . . Airlock opening at ten o'clock! *Here they come!*"

Ten o'clock is to my front left, past the shuttle. I see airlock doors slide open—a half-dozen Wasps pour in, their pressure suits red, not gray, their black rifles raging on full automatic.

Bracelet beams slice into them from several angles. The first two Wasps burst apart before they make it two steps into the hangar. I level my arm and flick my fingers forward, drop another one.

The rational part of me knows these Wasps are descendants of those who built their ship. In that way, they are no different than we are—fighting to stay alive, to protect their own kind. The emotional side of me, though, understands it is us or them, that this race has slaughtered my friends; every time my bracelet beam rips one to wet pieces, delicious satisfaction sweeps through my soul.

"Airlock opening at two o'clock," Yong shouts. "Take them out!"

The hangar devolves into utter chaos. I aim, fire, watch my beams cut down one Wasp after another. Bullets pound into the metal boxes in front of me.

A small metal ball bounces past me, skids out of view, then an explosion rocks me against the rack. Marcus falls to his hands and knees. He's lost his pistol. I don't think he fired a single shot.

Xander's voice roars so loud it distorts my helmet speakers: *"Landing bay fully pressurized, all airlocks opening—here they come!"*

*0:2:24*

*0:2:23*

*0:2:22*

Even through my suit and helmet, I hear doors hiss open, hear the screech-click war cry of Wasps rushing in. Strange heads, stranger clothes, fuchsia bodies. They're not wearing pressure suits. Some have guns, but most hold wrenches, pipes, knives, one is swinging a chair . . . these aren't soldiers, they were just the closest to the landing bay.

I flick my fingers forward, turning one into meat.

Aim, *flick*. Aim, *flick*. Aim, *flick*.

They are an avalanche—too many to stop.

"Eat this, you shit-bug bastards!" The Admiral's voice.

*Ximbal*'s front right cannon turret moves—the thick beam lashes out, slashes through the oncoming wave of Wasps. Body parts fly in all directions, splash yellow blood on the walls, the floor, even the ceiling high above.

Marcus stands, tears off his helmet. He looks around wildly, chest heaving.

"Mattie, get me out of here! *Please!*"

I realize he's beyond the cover of our rack a moment before a bullet punches through his left temple and blows his brains out the right side of his skull.

He drops. Three Wasps rush around the rack. I react instantly. Aim-*flick*: the first Wasp erupts, splashing my visor with gore, but I'm already thrusting with my knife, through the blood-mist, driving the blade deep into the Wasp right behind. The third Wasp wears a red pressure suit, raises a rifle to my face.

I twist as it fires—the bullet burst hammers the metal boxes that protected me. I dive at the Wasp's legs. We both go down, sliding across splattered blood and chunks of flesh.

The Wasp reaches behind its narrow back, pulls a long knife. I thrust, he counters and slashes. I grab the wrist of his knife hand just as he grabs mine.

We roll across the deck, a desperate, primitive fight for life made awkward by the bulky pressure suits.

A massive explosion throws us hard against the rack. Metal boxes fall out, hit my helmet, bang hard against my shoulder. I fight the pain that clouds my thoughts, threatens to drag me into darkness.

"Gaston's dead!" Aeschelman, shouting over the comm. "They hit his gun with a grenade! They're rushing the shuttle, I'm falling back to protect Zubiri!"

Zubiri: "Almost there! Keep them off of me!"

Bishop: "Victor's down!"

I struggle to my knees.

My body won't respond . . . everything is sluggish, half-speed.

In *Ximbal*'s exterior door, Bawden half-hides behind a bullet-riddled bulkhead, one hand jabbing her pitchfork down over and over, the other firing bracelet beams, both weapons tearing into a dozen Wasps trying to climb up and in. I hear her guttural screams of rage . . . she doesn't make words, she gives voice to pure violence.

Yong bounds across the floor toward her—a spray of bullets cuts the ancient circle-star down in mid-leap. He hits the deck, skids to a stop against the landing gear.

He doesn't move.

The Wasp I was fighting rises, slashes at me. I twist away, but the blade slices through my pressure suit and cuts deep into my shoulder. I feel the edge glance off bone.

The pain is overwhelming.

I don't know where my knife is.

It slashes at me again. I fall to my back, barely avoiding a blade that trails a thin arc of my own blood.

The Wasp raises the knife high—a Springer hatchet arcs down, *thunks* through the red pressure suit and into the Wasp's back.

The Wasp twitches once, slumps to the side, hatchet handle sticking up at a strange angle.

Lahfah helps me up, then scoops up a loose Wasp rifle and starts firing away.

The hangar is filled with smoke. Raging flames cast strange shadows, making everything dance with light. Alarms scream. The dead are everywhere.

Movement—I look to the shuttle, see Bishop flying through the air, axe raised overhead, an impossible leap made possible by the lighter gravity. He roars as he comes down, kicking one Wasp away from *Ximbal*'s door, driving the blade down through the head of another. Somehow, he lands next to Bawden, who dies a split second later as bullets trace a tight line from her left hip to her right shoulder.

Aeschelman: "They found a way in!"

Zubiri: "They're coming! Help me, it's not ready yet!"

Bishop vanishes into the shuttle. Behind him, a handful of Wasps finally clamber through the door.

0:1:45

0:1:44

0:1:43

*"Mattie, this is Aramovsky, what's going on?"*

The idiot didn't leave?

"Get out of here, dammit! Get clear!"

*"Screw that. Everyone, find something to hold on to, I'm coming in!"*

My legs are knocked out from under me. The bloody metal floor smacks against my helmet. Spiderweb cracks spread across my visor, make it impossible to see. I grab at the helmet, tear it free. It rolls to the side, stops when it hits Lahfah.

She's lying next to me.

Through her visor, her three eyes are half-lidded, lifeless . . . she's dead.

Barkah will be heartbroken.

Three Wasps step over her body. Not wearing pressure suits. A wrench, an axe . . . only one carries what might be a gun, a small pistol.

Reality slows.

My final seconds stretch out. Time is thick syrup. I savor my last gasping breath, taste my own blood. Even the agony in my shoulder is delicious in its own way, for it is my body warning me of the damage, trying to keep me alive. *Life.* About to end.

A gun barrel presses against my temple.

It has been a good life—a *long* life.

A roar so loud the sound alone shakes me. Screeching metal, every atom in the hangar smashing together.

I'm still alive?

That roar . . . it wasn't the Wasp's gun.

Air moves around me. *All* of the air.

*I'm coming in,* Aramovsky said.

In an instant, time snaps back to normal and brings hell with it.

Wind screams, hits so hard it knocks the Wasps off their feet. A line of small explosions traces through the hangar door, slowly forming a wide circle.

Aramovsky is using his Macana's Gatling gun to cut a large hole in the thick metal—the landing bay is decompressing, *fast.*

Wind howls louder, pushes harder.

One of the Wasps tries to rise—the wind knocks it down, pulls it toward the ravaged door.

The heavy rack . . . its supports are bolted to the deck. I grab the support, hook the elbow of my wounded arm around it.

My helmet starts to roll—I snag it just before it's out of reach.

The second Wasp tumbles across the deck, the wind dragging it toward its death, dragging Lahfah's corpse as well.

A Wasp hand locks down on my ankle.

The ship trembles around me. I look to the landing bay doors just as the last Gatling gun rounds slice through it—the ragged-edged metal circle rips clear as explosive decompression hurls it out into space.

The wind blows so strong the Wasp is actually lifted into the air, its grip on my leg the only thing stopping it from being flung across the landing bay and out that hole.

The alien looks at me. The battle has been madness, a cacophony of sights and sounds and dangers, keeping me from focusing on any one thing. Until now—for the first time I see this race's *living* eyes. The eyes are magenta, with flecks of gold.

They *sparkle.*

Those eyes are perhaps the most beautiful things I have ever seen.

I recognize the emotion within them—the Wasp is terrified.

Not a soldier. A mechanic, perhaps? A craftsman? Is this intelligent being an artist? Does it make music? Have a family?

Its tight grip on my ankle is the only thing stopping it from being launched out into space. The wind batters me. The Wasp's weight adds to my own: the support digs into my elbow, makes my entire arm scream with agony.

I whip the helmet down on the hand that holds my ankle, once, twice, a third time.

Something in the alien's hand breaks.

The magenta eyes look into mine one last time, begging, *pleading* for life.

It wants to live.

So do I.

I bring the helmet down again, and the death grip finally loosens. The Wasp flies through the air. It hits the edge of the jagged hole, spins away, and is gone.

The wind dies out in an instant, easing the pressure on my arm. Internal airlock doors must have closed, cutting the landing bay off from the rest of the ship's air supply.

I can't breathe.

Fighting the pain in my arm, I put the helmet back on my head, lock it into place. Air pours in, oxygen fills my lungs.

The gunfire has stopped. The flames are all out. The smoke is gone. Warning lights continue to flash, but if there are alarms, I can't hear them, because there is no air in here to carry the sound.

*0:1:06*
*0:1:05*
*0:1:04*

The speakers in my helmet still work.

"This is Bishop. I've got Zubiri. Aeschelman's dead. Anyone else left?"

"I'm here," I croak, my voice barely audible even to me.

"Bomb armed," Zubiri says, her voice frail, dripping with pain. "One minute till detonation. Goodbye, everyone. I love you all."

Bishop saved her. Or, more accurately, he saved the bomb—she's going to die anyway.

As is he.

As am I.

And then, something flies through the blood-streaked hole in the hangar bay doors.

A Macana fighter . . .

Long and sleek and black and narrow, with a white null-set symbol spray-painted on the side. Reverse engines fire. It instantly slows to a stop, spins so the nose is pointed toward the hole. Landing gear hits the deck. The engines cut out.

The canopy slides back.

A helmeted pilot stands. A *tall* pilot.

Aramovsky.

I use the last of my strength, force myself to rise.

"Get out of here," I say. "You don't need to die."

He sees me. He leaps out of the cockpit and bounds toward me.

What is he doing? It's too late.

"Forty-five seconds," Zubiri says.

Aramovsky reaches me, throws me over his shoulder. I'm too spent to fight him. I'm cold all over.

He rushes back to the fighter, places me in the empty space where the gunner's chair once sat. I look back to *Ximbal*—Bishop is lowering Zubiri down to a waiting Victor. I thought

Victor was dead, but there he is, stumbling toward me with Zubiri in his arms.

Bishop drops to one knee—he's too weak to stand. He slowly tilts forward, then falls out of the open door and hits the deck headfirst. He rolls once, doesn't move. I see cracks in his visor.

Aramovsky sprints to him. Bishop is larger, but with the lighter gravity Aramovsky scoops him up and carries him with little more effort than he used to carry me.

"Victor," Aramovsky says, "put Zubiri in with Em."

Victor looks at me, at this tiny space.

Through his visor, I see his head shake. "There isn't room!"

"Then *make* room," Aramovsky says. "Just stuff her in there!"

I don't understand what's happening. This fighter is too small for all of us.

Victor dumps Zubiri on top of me. There are frozen bloodstains on his chest and shoulders, the holes filled with sealant foam. His every motion is pure agony.

The boy with the crush, the one who would do anything for me. Right to the bitter end, he is brave and loyal, willing to sacrifice himself for others. My heart swells with respect for what this boy—no, this *man*—has done for our people.

"Thirty," Zubiri says.

Victor grabs me, rolls me on my side. Then he grabs Zubiri, shoves her legs to her chest, puts her in front of me—I am the big spoon, she is the little.

Victor looks down at me; our eyes meet.

"I told you I'd follow you anywhere. It's too late to say it, but I'm in love with you."

He takes a step back.

"Twenty-five." Zubiri can barely speak the words.

Aramovsky is there, shoving Bishop into the pilot seat. There's blood all over Bishop's pressure suit. He isn't moving.

Aramovsky grabs Victor, lifts him and sets him in the pilot seat next to Bishop. The move is fast, definitive—I think Victor is in the cockpit before he realizes what just happened. The younger boy adjusts, tries to make two men fit into a space meant for one.

"Twenty," Zubiri says.

Aramovsky grabs Victor's hand, places it on a black joystick studded with controls.

"Move the stick which way you want to go," Aramovsky says. "Thumb button is thrust. Just get out of here, Kalle will help you the rest of the way."

"*Affirmative,*" comes Kalle's voice, tinny and scratchy from the distance.

"Fifteen seconds," Zubiri says.

Aramovsky reaches into the cockpit and presses a button. The canopy starts to slide forward. He steps back.

No . . . no, what is he doing?

"Get in," I say. "Get in here, *I'm ordering you!*"

He smiles at me. "No room."

The canopy closes.

In my helmet, I hear his last words.

"Find our people a home, Mattie. Victor . . . push the button."

The fighter shudders and shoots forward. The hangar doors rush toward us—we're going to shatter against them—and then we're through the ragged hole, swallowed up by the blackness of space.

Kalle's fighter banks in on our right.

"Seven seconds," Zubiri says.

"*Full throttle,*" Kalle says. "*Now!*"

Zubiri and I are pulled backward as the Macana shoots forward.

"Three seconds," Zubiri says. And then, a last, energetic burst of hate: "I hope you burn in hell."

There is no fireball. There is no roar, no explosion that I can hear. A brief blast of static on the comm, then silence. For a moment, I see light reflected off parts of the fighter.

Then the light fades.

"*Victor,*" Kalle says. "*Bank right. Just keep me at your ten o'clock and I'll get you home, okay?*"

Our fighter banks right.

I'm crammed tight in here, but there's just enough room for me to look out at the *Dragon*.

Or, more accurately, where the *Dragon* used to be.

Now that space is nothing but a cloud of debris, huge chunks and small bits alike spreading out in an ever-expanding, ever-thinning sphere. The massive cylinder is in a thousand pieces. Spinning copper shards the size of Uchmal's buildings reflect the red sun's light.

It is a horrid sight.

It is a spectacular sight.

We've done it.

We have killed our enemy. We are forever free.

"*Victor,*" Kalle says, "*you still with me?*"

I feel cold, *so* cold.

Zubiri twists a little. My arm is over her. She pulls my hand to her chest, clutches it, needing any comfort I can give. I ignore the pain in my shoulder and I hold her tight.

"Yes," Victor grunts. "Still . . . here."

*"Stick with me, kid,"* Kalle says. *"Stay conscious for fifteen minutes and we're home free."*

He says something else, but I don't really hear what it is.

Zubiri in my arms, I finally give in to the cold.

The darkness finally drags me down.

# PART V

## THE UNKNOWN

# SIXTY-FIVE

hear people talking.

The words lull me from a deep sleep.

"I think she's coming to."

Theresa's voice. She always seems to be there when I awake.

My eyes flutter open. I'm in a white coffin. I'm tired of waking up in these things. I'm in a small medical bay. It's warm in here. I feel soft blankets against my skin.

"Welcome back," Theresa says.

She sits by my side, her left hand resting on her round belly. Love in her eyes. A soft smile on her face. She looks tired.

In my mind, there are two Theresa Spingates. The beautiful girl I see before me now, the mother, the wife, the person who sacrificed so much for our people.

And the *other* Theresa.

The one who gave up her lovely face and perfect body to become a blackened, withered creature. The one who became selfish and bitter.

The one who betrayed me.

The one I ordered Bishop to kill.

No . . . *Matilda* gave that order, centuries ago. That wasn't *me*. I am something new.

I try to sit up. My body fails me.

"Take it easy," she says. "You lost a lot of blood. You were under for two days."

Maybe staying in the coffin a little while longer isn't so bad after all.

I nod toward her belly.

"How's the little one?"

Theresa's smile widens.

"Doing great. Kenzie tells me we're having a girl."

The baby . . .

Being pregnant . . .

Matilda had a child. I know only faint wisps of that moment. I wonder if those memories will return, or if they're gone forever.

My daughter . . . her name was Celeste. She had five kids of her own. Celeste didn't want to become Cherished. She wanted nothing to do with it, poisoned my grandchildren against it, against *me*. I watched her grow old. I watched her die. Then my grandchildren, all dying from old age while my wrinkled, transformed body carried on.

"We, um." Theresa looks down, uncomfortable. "We have a name for the baby. If you think it's acceptable."

I'm not sure why I would have any say in it, and . . .

Ah. I think I know.

"Korrynn. You want to name her Korrynn."

Theresa still can't look at me. She nods.

"That's beautiful," I say. "The name and the sentiment both."

Ramses Bishop steps into view. He looks horrible. Crutches

under his arms. Dark circles under his eyes. His skin, paler than normal. There are burns on his face and hands, only partially healed.

"You look like hell," I say.

He smiles. "Speak for yourself."

Even all that damage can't make him ugly. Ramses is a vision: strong, brave, loyal, dedicated. And yet I remember the *other* Bishop, the one Matilda knew. I remember the arguments. I remember the fighting. I remember love, then love dying, becoming hate, then even worse than hate—ambivalence.

Looking at his face, at his expression, I can see he doesn't understand yet. He's playing along, respecting me as Mattie, but he thinks that deep down, I'm still Em. He thinks he'll be patient, that he'll wait for me. He thinks I'll "get better."

He thinks we'll have a family.

I'll have to deal with that soon.

The pain is creeping in. My meds are wearing off. The bruises, the bumps, the stitches . . . I think a rib is broken. It's starting to feel like someone is pouring jagged gravel straight into my brain.

"Some bad news," Ramses says. "The incoming ship, the *Eel*, it has sped up. It will be here in six months. And we've detected two *new* ships heading to Omeyocan. The first will be here in about ten months, the second not long after that."

I close my eyes, rest my head on my pillow. *Three* ships are coming to this planet of endless war.

"Are we still in orbit?"

"The *Xolotl* took extensive missile damage," he says. "It barely survived. Gaston and Borjigin think we'll be ready to depart in another day or two, on your order."

Gaston. He means Young Gaston. *Old* Gaston—my friend of twelve centuries—is gone forever.

The first incoming ship is six months out. That gives us a little time, but we can't wait long. It could come after us just like the *Dragon* did. We need to be long gone before it arrives.

"Any word on the Wasps?"

Theresa nods. "Once you killed the Grub, that signal interference went away. Kalle and Opkick have been using the *Xolotl*'s instruments to observe the planet. Kalle thinks most of the Wasps were killed. Any that survived the explosion are likely dying of radiation poisoning. Uchmal—what's left of it—will be a no-man's-land for decades. Maybe centuries."

The interference is gone. The Grub produced it. Or maybe the Echo did. I don't think it makes a difference. One or the other or both wanted the races to fight up close and personal, where the hate could breed, where the rage could swell. I imagine in any war, you can launch bombs as long as you like, but sooner or later, if you want to take and hold territory, you have to put boots on the ground. Maybe the interference was meant to stop orbital ships from using high-tech targeting to take out small units, even single soldiers one at a time. Maybe it was meant to cause greater confusion, deprive armies of effective communication so chaos would rule and the strongest and most resourceful— not the most technologically developed—would win the day.

The interference persisted until we dropped that nuke.

I knew full well dropping the bomb meant I was poisoning the planet. Still, it's hard to hear that it actually occurred.

"And the Springers we left behind?"

"No sign of them," Ramses says. "Some small smoke trails from campfires far outside the ruins. Barkah thinks any survivors are long gone from the area, faded away into the jungle. He doesn't know where they went. Neither does Kalle or Opkick. Barkah is asking if we can go back for more, but Borjigin says he needs two weeks to synthesize enough fuel for a return trip to the surface."

Theresa leans closer. "Before you consider Barkah's request, I'll remind you the troopship is alien tech that we don't yet know how to maintain. If anything goes wrong, if anything malfunctions, whoever we send will be stuck on Omeyocan—we have no other ships to send. Borjigin and Gaston think it will take us at least a year to build another atmospheric-capable craft."

Two weeks for one trip back to the surface to rescue more Springers, and that's *if* we could even find them. Theresa makes the primary point painfully clear, though—if anything goes wrong, we lose the only ship we have that can take people from the *Xolotl* to the surface of any new planet we find.

I can't risk that. Not for the Springers, not for any of our people who might still be alive down there.

And we can't wait the time it takes to build another ship. The *Xolotl* is a wreck. Our missiles are depleted. We have no ship-killing cannon. All we have is a pair of Macanas, and those don't amount to much of a defense.

Which means if we're still in orbit when the *Eel* arrives, and it's hostile, we're dead.

The situation here is untenable.

Everything points in one direction—*away.*

"What about the Grub eggs? Did we destroy them?"

Theresa shrugs. "Kalle says there's no way of knowing, unless people start having nightmares."

"Or we start killing each other," Ramses adds.

I don't think we'll wait to find out.

Omeyocan has eaten up twelve centuries of my life, the lives of my friends, of our ancestors. Is it our job to make sure those eggs are destroyed?

No. It is not.

The Birthday Children have sacrificed enough. So have the Springers. And the Cherished, for that matter.

We've all known war. It's time to let something else run our lives.

"Tell Gaston to set a course for open space," I say. "Any direction that gives us the clearest path away from the three incoming ships. We are leaving, and we're never coming back."

Theresa glances at Ramses. He looks back at her. He nods. So does she.

It is done.

# SIXTY-SIX

I ask Bishop to meet me in the Crystal Ball.

My body has healed. Mostly. The *Xolotl* has been repaired. Mostly. We are four days into our journey into the great unknown.

Our search for a new home has begun.

I will soon give up my leadership role, but not quite yet. Being the leader carries many burdens. It also carries a few privileges. One such privilege is taking the Crystal Ball as my own. This will be my personal space, my "office," if you will, for years to come.

When I was first here, there was a long-dead body on the metal grate floor, stabbed in the back by the spear that became our symbol of leadership. Quite fitting, when you think about it.

The spear is gone, of course. So is the body. People removed it, cleaned up the stains left by decomposition.

Most of the stains, anyway. In a few spots, the metal is permanently discolored. I think that's good—we should never forget the evil we've done to each other.

Em didn't know who that corpse was.

Matilda did—she set up that murder, watched it happen.

This place was where Bishop, Em, Gaston, Aramovsky and El-Saffani discovered we weren't in some endless dungeon, that we were in a starship, far above the land promised to us.

This was where Em first met Matilda.

Those two women are no more. I remain, a combination of them both.

I sit at a desk Borjigin crafted for me. It's made of gray stone, with the top polished flat as glass. He also found me a lovely chair.

My desktop is clean, uncluttered. The New People made me gifts: a glass inkwell, a quill made from a black chicken feather, and a thick, leather-bound book. The cover is branded with the null-set symbol. The pages are blank, save for the first one, where Barkah drew a beautiful image of Lahfah for me to remember her by.

The only other thing on my desk is a white porcelain cup sitting on a white saucer. Curls of steam slowly rise up from the tea inside.

I pick up the delicate cup and take a sip. I think of Korrynn Bello. She was right about one thing, at least—tea is *much* better than sholtag.

I wish she was here to have a cup with me. I lost her twice: once as Em's Bello, once as Matilda's Korrynn.

Losing friends once is hard enough. It's not fair I have to lose everyone a second time.

I stare out the Crystal Ball's clear walls at an endless sea of stars. In the direction of our current heading, there is nothing but empty space.

Behind us, a fist-sized crescent of yellow, brown and blue. Omeyocan, in shadow because we're heading away from it. I can also see tiny crescents of the planet's two moons, one bluish, one maroon.

Every minute we travel, Omeyocan appears smaller and smaller. Soon I won't see it as color, only as a point of light. Not long after that, I'm told, the *Xolotl*'s physics-altering engines—built from schematics provided by a five-hundred-million-year-old race of spacefaring aliens—will activate, and we will leave this area of the galaxy behind forever.

I hear feet on the ladder that leads down from our ship. I look up. The ladder seems to float there in space, connecting the Ball to a small hole in the *Xolotl*'s copper hull.

Bishop descends.

The hull looks a mess. The *Dragon*'s missile fire left huge craters, forever-frozen splashes in a metal pond. Some of the rings overlap each other.

I feel fortunate those strikes didn't take out the Crystal Ball.

I think of the people we lost on that desperate mission. Lahfah. The Admiral. Peura. Yong. Aeschelman and Abrantes. Yilmaz. Bawden. Marcus and Benga. Shumalk. McWhite, Goldberg and Dibaba.

Aramovsky.

He wanted redemption. He got it. I will make sure future generations know of him. Not just as a hero, but not just as a villain, either. My people need to understand that all of us are capable of change.

We don't have to be bad forever. We can fight our urges. We can *choose* to be good.

Zubiri has "retired" at the tender age of thirteen. She wants nothing to do with engineering or science, and *definitely* nothing to do with weapons and war. Maybe she'll change as she grows older. For now, she's chosen to raise pigs. The New People are teaching her their ways.

Victor is still in a med-chamber, kept unconscious by Kenzie. She says he should have died from his injuries. She's at a loss to explain how he was even conscious, let alone able to pilot that fighter back to the *Xolotl*. A bullet through his liver. Lacerated stomach. Punctured lung. And more. Kenzie tells me it could be months before he's out.

I've made sure Old Victor can't get anywhere near him.

Aside from myself, Zubiri, Victor and Kalle—who is as annoying as she ever was—there is only one other survivor of that mission: Ramses Bishop.

He reaches the bottom of the ladder. I stand to meet him. I take in his blond curls, his dark-yellow eyes. He is all smiles and scabs and scars.

"You look well, Mattie. Beautiful as ever."

I, too, am all scabs and scars, but I have no smile to offer. Even for a woman as old as I, this kind of thing never gets easier.

And yet, it must be done.

"Thank you for coming." I almost ask him what he thinks of the view, of leaving Omeyocan, but I realize that such pleasantries are procrastination, delaying the words that need to be said. Because I don't want to hurt him.

Perhaps there is still a bit of girl left in this ancient woman after all.

He's smiling, yes, but it's mostly empty. Hollow. He is happy to be alive, happy I'm alive, happy our people are safe. But, as I have, he's left a trail of dead friends in his wake. This huge, strong man is no brute. He feels deep loss. He knows great pain. His heart has been shattered over and over.

I am about to shatter it yet again.

"We can't be together," I say. "I am telling you, once and for all, that there is no *us*."

His smile fades. He blinks slowly.

"You . . . you're breaking up with me?"

That's not exactly right. I'm not the person he was with on Omeyocan—that was Em—but I nod anyway.

"I'm sorry," I say. "I don't want to lead you on in any way."

"But . . . *why?*"

"Because I'm over a thousand years old. I have a millennium's worth of memories and wisdom that give me perspective on life. You aren't even *twenty*. You are a man, yes, a great man who has sacrificed endlessly for our people and will continue to do so, but compared to my age you are barely even a child. It would not work. I am doing the right thing by letting you go now."

He stares at me for a few moments. He turns his head, gazes out at the blanket of bright stars.

"It's not fair," he says quietly.

I nod. "I know."

He wipes away a silent tear.

"I did everything I was supposed to do," he says. "I was a good person. A good man. I backed you every step of the way. Even when I knew I shouldn't. I changed who I was to be with you."

I reach out and take his big, scarred hand. I expect him to pull away. He does not. We lock fingers. Through his grip, I sense more of his pain—he desperately doesn't want to let me go. I remember how his hands felt against my skin. That part of me wants him still.

"You *are* a good person," I say. "Just not a good person for me. And I am not a good person for you, because the one you did those things for is gone. I'm not *me* anymore, Ramses."

He hangs his head. Another tear drips down. He sniffs once, then nods.

"I think I knew this was coming. I sensed you were different. I understand, Mattie . . . I just don't want it to be true."

I start to say *Reality is what it is whether we like it or not,* but I stop myself. He doesn't need a lecture. He doesn't need this explained. He is hurting enough without me adding to it by being a know-it-all asshole.

"You look just like her," he says. "I know your scars. I know how you got each and every one of them. Why do you have to look just like her?"

He lifts his head. Tears line his cheeks and he does not care. He is a warrior. He is a hero.

"We were *made* for each other," he says.

I nod. "We were. But we're mismatched in time. I know you'll find someone. You will make some lucky woman on this ship impossibly happy, and you will have your family."

He gives my hand a final squeeze.

Without another word, he climbs the ladder.

I watch him until he vanishes into the ship. Then I sit at my desk and gaze out at the stars.

Twelve centuries of wisdom, of watching people interact, of watching heartbreak and healing, it all tells me Ramses Bishop will be fine. That doesn't diminish his current pain, not in the least, but before he knows it he'll find love again.

Ramses Bishop will be happy.

Will I?

I am 1,208 years old. I have the body of a girl of eighteen. The Cherished are alien to me now, wrinkled black things that reek of a time of war and lies and blood and hatred. The Birthday Children are just that—*children.* The things they find important are mostly meaningless to me, things I left behind centuries ago. A few of the New People are a hundred years old or more, but even they seem like mere infants. Barkah and the Springers are another race entirely, friends but so *different* in the way they think and act.

My memories are coming back now. Although they are still a jumble, pieces are starting to fall into place. My final puzzle—that of my own past—is almost complete.

I open the book. I look at the picture of Lahfah, then flip to the first page.

It's blank.

I dip the quill into the inkwell, and I begin to write.

*I made the sacrifices that needed to be made. For my people, I did what had to be done.*

*Because of that, I am the only one of my kind.*

*My name is Mattie Savage.*

*I am alone.*

# Epilogue

*This is the life of Matilda Savage.*
*This is the life of Em Savage.*
*This is the story of our people, and our continuing*
*journey.*
*And now, we approach a new planet. Will this be the*
*place our next chapter begins? We can only hope.*
*If that happens—when it happens—I will create Volume*
*Two of our history.*
*But for now, Volume One is complete.*

> *July 14, 3892*
> *Signed,*
> *—Mattie Savage—*

I close the leather book.
I sit back in my chair, stare at the well-worn cover.
It's finished. I can't believe it.
*I did it.*

I finished my first book.

I've been alive for twelve centuries. I've accomplished so much. I didn't think I could feel this way again, reel from that rush of accomplishment. As I stare at the book—my constant companion of the last four years—I realize this is among the greatest things I have done.

Footsteps on the ladder. I'm not supposed to be bothered here, which means it can be only one person—the leader of our people.

The Crystal Ball is a disaster. There are food wrappers all over the metal grate floor. Scrolls, both tied up and loose, litter my stone desktop, as do crumbs and smears of meals past. I'm ever grateful we didn't bring ants with us into space, or they would live here for certain.

I've been wearing the same toga for days. For weeks, actually. I'm pretty sure I stink. *Bad.*

Some grand old matron of the human race I turned out to be.

I glance up: two people coming down, not just one.

I sweep as much of the garbage as I can off the desk and into the trash bin at its side, realizing too late the bin is already overflowing—I've made the mess worse.

The leader reaches the bottom of the ladder.

I straighten my toga as best I can.

"Hail, Maria."

Maria D'souza rolls her eyes at me.

"Do you *have* to do that crap, Mattie? We've been over this before—you can just say *hello.*"

She wears a green toga dotted with polished bits of steel. The Springers manufacture most of our clothes now, and usually decorate fabric with bits of polished glass, shaped copper, buttons of gold carved from old storage drives, anything that is colorful and fun. Not Maria, though—the only accent she al-lows is steel, which matches the polished rectangle hanging around her neck.

She chooses steel because that's what weapons are made from. She wants everyone to remember that war may come to us again, and if it does, we need to be ready.

Her forehead circle is gone. Kalle developed a way to surgically remove the symbols. No one has them anymore.

No one except me. I not only kept mine, I had it modified, added a line to it—my null-set symbol is part of who I am.

Maria didn't come alone. Little sandaled feet reach the last rung. The three-year-old boy turns, looks at me and smiles wide.

"Auntie!"

He runs to me and I pull him in for a glorious hug. I tousle his curly blond locks. With his mother's light brown skin and his father's hair and dark-yellow eyes, this boy will soon be a heartbreaker.

"Hello, Walter! Are you behaving?"

He kisses my cheek. When he does, his nose leaves a streak of snot on my skin. I don't even care.

"Ew, Auntie," he says, wrinkling his tiny nose. "Stinky."

I'm twelve centuries old and can still get embarrassed? Stunning how we continue to learn about ourselves.

"Sorry, Walt. I've been too busy to bathe."

He runs to his mother and hangs on her arm. She swings him lightly, absently, as if he's nothing more than a giggling handbag.

Maria nods to the desk. "You finished it?"

"How did you know?"

"I've never seen that book closed before. Well, did you?"

A warm feeling in my chest.

"Yes, I did."

Maria lets out a very unleaderlike squeal. With her free arm, she hugs me, kisses my cheek.

"Congratulations!"

My body stiffens. I can't help it.

"Oh, sorry," Maria says. She takes a step back. "I know you don't like to be touched. I just got so excited for you."

I nod. The moment isn't ruined, but it's become awkward.

Little kids can hold me, hug me, kiss me, but not adults. I don't feel comfortable around adults. The Birthday Children mostly leave me alone here. The Cherished have learned not to bother—I can't seem to exchange anything other than superficial pleasantries with them. The New People are the worst—they *bow* when they see me, treat me like I'm some kind of deity. I hate it.

"I'll make this fast," Maria says. "Three things."

That's her style. She communicates quickly and succinctly, then moves on.

When I stepped down as leader, Ramses didn't want the job. Neither did Theresa or Xander. Borjigin won our first election. He worked very hard and established several new policies that helped improve the ship, but in the end he wanted to focus on building machines and repairing long-broken parts of the *Xolotl*. After his one-year term as Yalani—that's what we call our overall leader—he didn't run for reelection.

Maria has won every election since.

She and Bishop are married. I have seen them together many times. They were happy before the birth of their son, and now are even more so. She is in her third one-year term as Yalani.

Maria visits me more often than anyone else. All decisions are hers to make, but she frequently asks for my counsel.

"Three things," I say. "Go ahead."

"First, Barkah is trying to set up a puppet government again, with him as king."

I'm reminded why I stay away from everyone: a ship full of children and their petty motivations.

"Is this the second time he's tried that?"

"Third," Maria says. "This time he's claiming that since the Springers are a minority, he should have a louder say in government, that their rights are being infringed upon."

"The Springers have *exactly* the same rights as everyone else." I tilt my head backward, indicating the turquoise-colored planet we've been approaching for months. "He's doing it because of that?"

"Of course," Maria says. "I think he's angling for a Springer-only homeland if the planet proves permanently habitable. Anyway, I need you in the next session of Congress to advise against any separationist movements. Will you help?"

I sigh, but I nod. While the Springers love Barkah, they realize Em is the main reason they're alive at all. The Springers don't really understand that I'm not her anymore, but since I look like her, I have significant sway over their general opinion.

"Second thing," Maria says. "You've insisted on keeping our history in that book alone. Now that it's complete, we need it properly recorded for future generations. I'm putting my foot down, Mattie—that book comes with me."

I glance at it. The leather-bound tome has been my only friend for the last four years. I don't want to let it go. But I'm not the leader, and it's not my choice to make.

I pick it up off the desk, feel its familiar weight.

Before I can change my mind, I hand it to Maria.

"Wonderful," she says. "Just one more debt the citizens of this ship owe you."

This is the most talking I've done in months. I feel my skin start to crawl. I just want to be by myself.

"And the third thing?"

"Someone is coming down right after I go up."

I sit in my desk chair.

"Please, Maria. I don't want to talk to anyone."

"Too bad, so sad," she says. "Four years of hiding here is enough, I don't give a damn how many lifetimes you've lived. Listen to me carefully—the person coming down made a choice. There was no coercion. None whatsoever. I conducted the interviews myself, repeatedly. So did Ramses and Theresa."

"What are you talking about?"

"You'll see." Maria kneels, holds the book in front of Walter. "This book is *very* important, honey. Can you hold it tight and not let go?"

A wide-eyed Walter nods solemnly, impressed with this new responsibility. He clutches the book tight to his chest.

Maria scoops the toddler up with one arm.

"Remember, this was a *choice*," she says to me, and she climbs the ladder.

I watch her go. Part of me wants her to stay, but it's useless. Conversation is always stilted, forced. I just have nothing in common with these children.

Maria enters the ship.

Someone else starts down the ladder. A man wearing a black toga. He moves with a certain grace, a certain dignity.

When he reaches the bottom, he turns to face me.

It's Victor Muller.

"Hello, Mattie," he says. "A pleasure to see you again."

Other than a few passing words in Congress when I'm required to speak out against particularly stupid ideas, I haven't spoken with Victor in years. He's matured—I can *sense* it more than see it.

"I'm very tired," I say. "What can I do for you?"

He's become more handsome since we left. There is a scar on his cheek he didn't have repaired. He has the face and body of someone seventeen or eighteen, with well-defined muscles and young skin. I know he and the other soldiers train for combat every day, teaching hundreds of New People and Springers in the ways of war. Victor, clearly, is in excellent shape.

"I thought we might talk," he says.

I rub my eyes. "That's the last thing I want, Victor. Whatever would we talk about?"

"Do you remember when I volunteered to join Matilda's mutiny?"

I stare at him, feel my eyes narrow.

"I do remember. Who told you about it?"

"I didn't need anyone to tell me about it. I was there."

"Don't be ridiculous. That was four hundred years ago, you weren't even . . ."

He can't remember that. He wasn't there . . . his progenitor was.

The young man before me smiles.

"Please, call me *Vic* from now on. *Victor* was someone else. We merged. We are one."

For the first time in years, I wish I had my spear. I stand up, so suddenly filled with rage I'm shaking.

"How could you do that to him? He was just a boy!"

"A boy who *chose* it," he says. "Didn't Maria tell you?"

She did. Her "interviews" . . . those were with Young Victor and Old Victor both.

"You . . . I mean . . . *he* . . . he *wanted* to be overwritten?"

"Such a harsh term," Victor says. "But yes, that part of me wanted it, perhaps even more than the old part did."

I feel a burst of excitement, of *hope*—someone I can talk to, someone who has been through what I've been through.

"But *why?*"

He reaches out slowly, takes my hand. I let him. For once, my skin does not crawl at the touch of someone else.

"Because Young Victor was in love with you," he says. "And while he never told you, so was Old Victor. And now, we both are."

I pull my hand away. I can't believe this is happening.

"You go through that process and you assume you can just come here and, what, that I'm *yours?*"

Victor—*Vic*—laughs.

"As if anyone could make Mattie Savage do anything she didn't want to do. I don't *assume* anything. I'm just a centuries-old man asking a centuries-old woman if she'd like to chat for a bit."

The way he and Em fought together on Omeyocan. The way he and Matilda fought together in the rebellion. Brave. Selfless.

*Both* versions of him.

I remember plunging the knife into Matilda's heart, her fury, her terror. But she was evil incarnate—she deserved it. Vic, the Vic I knew for centuries, did not.

"Old Victor helped us," I say. "He shouldn't have had to die that way."

Vic's smile widens.

"He didn't die. He's still alive."

It takes me a moment to process that.

"But the ritual," I say.

Vic shrugs. "The former young me and the former old me agreed there was no need for it. Everyone saw what happened to you, Mattie. When I . . . sorry, when *he* went to the X, he knew he would live on, as long as his body will allow. We have dinner together every night. We even started a book club."

We're all one people now—there's no need for barbaric executions. So obvious and such a simple decision to make, yet it never occurred to me this was possible.

It's nice to know that as old as I am, there can still be surprises.

Vic walks around the desk. He adjusts his black toga, sits on the desk's front left corner, and stares out at the blue planet.

"Speaking of books, Maria told me you just finished yours. Maybe that means you'd like to take a break. If you want me to leave, I will. But if you'd like to sit with me and talk, I'd like that."

The overwrite—perhaps now more accurately described as *fusing,* I suppose—carried risks. Young Victor knew the person he was would die in the process, cease to exist just as Em ceased to exist. He knew that. He did it anyway.

He did it . . . for *me.*

I shuffle more than walk around the desk. I sit on the front right corner.

"Yes, I'd like to talk," I say. "I'd like that very much."

# ACKNOWLEDGMENTS

Scott would like to thank the following people for their research expertise:

- Dr. Joseph A. Albietz III, M.D.
- Chris Grall, MSG, U.S. Army Special Forces (Ret.)
- J.P. Harvey, Colonel, U.S. Air Force (Ret.)
- Dr. Nicole Gugliucci, Ph.D.
- A Kovacs
- Dr. Phil Plait, Ph.D.
- John Vizcarra

# Past Imperfect

◆

## A personal history of an adventuresome lifetime in and around medicine

*Robert Harlan Moser*

Writers Club Press
New York Lincoln Shanghai

# Past Imperfect
## A personal history of an adventuresome lifetime in and around medicine

Writers Club Press
an imprint of iUniverse, Inc.

For information address:
iUniverse, Inc.
2021 Pine Lake Road, Suite 100
Lincoln, NE 68512
www.iuniverse.com

ISBN: 0-595-26388-7

To my wife, Linda, who saved my life.

# *Contents*

# *Preface*

If Robert Moser had not lived the life he sets down in this memoir, he'd have a hard time inventing it. As fiction, it would seem too picaresque, too filled with wonderful adventure, harrowing moments, travel, romance, eccentric characters, intellectual challenges, and all the rewards and hardships of an extraordinary life in medicine. But Moser has lived it, and his art as a writer keeps pace with his animated life as a doctor. The result is a book that takes a reader into the heart of medicine, and into the heart of a fascinating man.

Moser is a fine storyteller, and he has a stream of great stories to tell. You won't forget his foray as a teenager working on a tramp steamer, and the long night in a San Juan bordello his crewmates arranged for him. Or the months under fire as a field doctor in Korea, and the night when the enemy was a malicious fellow officer. In his later years, as Chief of Medicine at Walter Reed Army Hospital, Moser proved as resourceful in resolving such problems as he had been in Korea, only this time he had to cope with political VIPs demanding special care. At Walter Reed he issued a memorable rule for the care of VIPs known as "Moser's Dictum," asserting: "They will get the same superb treatment as any G.I. on the ward; rank or status does not disqualify anyone from any diagnostic or therapeutic procedure that is medically indicated."

As his dictum suggests, this is the story of a man who could meet life's challenges with courage, grace, wit, and a stubborn streak that helped when all else failed. He needed all those attributes for a life that took many unexpected turns, first in the military, then in private practice and serving medicine at large, as editor of the Journal of the AMA, and as Executive Vice President of the American College of Physicians.

As he retraces his footsteps in this narrative, Moser offers a portrait of medicine itself. He is a dedicated teacher, a devout believer in "evi-

dence-based medicine," and a scourge of practices he considers unscientific and unproven, including many alternative therapies that have become popular right before his dismayed eyes. But he is a critic of his own profession as well, having been a pioneer in writing about the problems of drug side effects, and "iatrogenic" illnesses caused by medical treatments. Moser calls himself a curmudgeon, and he lives up to the billing; his opinions are often as provocative as they are insightful.

Writing about oneself in such depth is always risky, of course, and Moser treats himself with the same even-handedness he accorded those VIPs at Walter Reed. He shows the flaws as well as the virtues that characterize many of the dedicated "workaholic" doctors of his generation. His devotion to medicine sometimes won out over his family's desires and needs, and he writes with empathy about the long, sometimes difficult, and ultimately failed marriage. Of his married life, he writes, "I cannot deny a significant element of selfishness. I think I would not liked being married to me." But he is a lucky man, and his memoir ends with an account of retirement as picaresque as his career, blessed with a romantic and loving remarriage.

This is a lofty book, by a man who has dared to climb the heights of life, and now writes of what there is to see.

Paul Trachtman
Former Science Editor
The Smithsonian

# *Prelude*

The more I read these days the less I am inclined to write. It seems there are many more literate people around than I remember in my youth, and they all write books. Aside from the classicists, who discouraged my childhood hopes for making a living with the pen, my efforts, scientific and otherwise, have all been short, not-necessarily-wonderful stuff. Of course, there are quite a few terrible writers who seem to get published, but I try not to read them (although I suspect I have read the first 50 pages of more bad books than most.) I suspect the urge "to write" by people who really shouldn't, has been abetted by the ease of using a word processor. My only excuse is that I feel a need to record some things about what I think has been a rich, unusually variegated and enjoyable life, before I give it all up.

I suspect that each human being feels he/she has a unique story to tell. Some cynics have said that really it is always the same old story but from different boring perspectives. So I reckon its okay to scribble a bit if one really doesn't care whether people read your stuff (much less publish it). Besides, it relaxes me and I sort of enjoy ruminating old experiences and reflecting on my reactions to the curious world we have created. Who knows, maybe my kids and grandchildren will enjoy it. From the aspect of perspective, I have been toying with my *opus magnum* for about four years, mostly late at night when sleep eludes this geriatric insomniac. "Updating" represents a philosophic as well as temporal problem. Each time I ruminate these pages, I seem to remember new things about old events, and every few months truly original things occur that seem sufficiently worthwhile to append. Sometimes it is tough to sort things out.

I admit some autobiographies have impressed me as hubristic, egocentric exercises. If you have managed to accomplish something truly

worthwhile in life (like discovering relativity or identifying new galaxies or chipping out a Moses), someone else should be moved to document your greatness. But lots of lesser folks have written about their prosaic lives, and no one seems too disturbed. In this ramble I have included real names if I recall them, changed some to avoid embarrassing those still alive (or their offspring), and purposely omitted others. If my candor offends some, well, those of my vintage who are still firing a few synapses can write me a nasty letter. Everything I have written is truth, as I remember it. I have not garnished to increase tension or excitement or color. There was enough of each to eschew embellishment. My chronology may be a trifle sloppy here and there, and I know I tend to wander down collateral "non-autobiographical" byways. (These I will place in parentheses to facilitate a quick pass by a reader stimulated to rush ahead to the next great adventure. I will use "his" as my unisex pronoun; "his/her" is awkward and annoying, and to say "her" would be downright silly and contrary to my chauvinist bias.) Well, it has been over seven decades, so what the hell...

# 1

## *Barely Out of the Shell*

◆

## *(admittedly vague, totally undocumented...)*

Everyone tries to remember his earliest days. It would seem that some view such recollections as a measure of intellectual achievement, the ability to describe adventures that occurred when you were barely nascent. From my reading of many autobiographies, I think most of it is self-delusion or prevarication. For many years I "remembered" being a handsome, tousle-haired tyke perched on my father's shoulder, standing next to my mother in some sort of fruit orchard. But years later I discovered an ancient, dog-eared photograph of that very scene. I must have seen that picture before and then forgotten about it. I think a lot of this sort of thing goes on when one decides to write memoirs.

I do remember early days in Philadelphia before grammar school. Many of these recollections are patchy and a trifle out of focus, but some remain surprisingly crisp. We lived in a row house with a glassed-in porch facing a small grassy park with a steep hill. I remember sledding down the sharp embankment and losing control. I was flung under a park bench and out into the busy street. Miraculously, I escaped unscathed, thoroughly terrified, if not chastened. I was the youngest member of a neighborhood gang, the ultimate novitiate. We were really little kids, and our efforts at mischief were downright cute compared to the deadly wildness of some of today's gang-bangers,

although one of the rites of passage was a bit hairy even by contemporary, street-smart standards. Every new kid was obliged to remain alone in a tiny, dark cul-de-sac in the middle of a nearby railroad tunnel while a steam locomotive thundered by. I still recall this incident with vivid, redolent terror. I was curled-up in the "cave," hands pressed over ears, eyes snapped tight shut. It was all quite horrible; the incredible roar, the stench and sear of white-hot anthracite flinging hissing cinders, and the proximity of tons of hurtling steel. It was interminable—not easy to forget.

Walter was our stern leader-martinet, bigger and older than us foot soldiers. He introduced us to crime. Adjacent to the infamous initiation tunnel was the sprawling Budd plant where most of our fathers worked. (Not mine; at that time he was selling some sort of "self improvement" products. As near as I can remember one of his big winners was a topical lotion that was supposed to make people of color much lighter. This was before he began to practice chiropractic.)

At that time, Budd was primarily manufacturing Pullman cars, but they had just landed a juicy contract to make the dials for the revolutionary new telephones. They would punch out the holes, and the discs were discarded into large bins. Walter had an inspiration. He discovered that if one wedged the disc in a small vice and then filed down the sharp edges, magically it emerged close to the size and weight of a dime. One night we scaled the Budd fence and stole a few hundred of the discarded discs. So we launched a cottage industry. We flooded the neighborhood vending machines with ersatz dimes for several weeks. They worked about half the time, a sufficient frequency to interest the local cops. We soon abandoned the enterprise.

My only other recollection of the Philadelphia years was walking to "Feltonville" grammar school. It must be the strange name that stuck in my mind. It was a stark, unpromising, red-brick edifice (weren't they all?). I must have been in third or fourth grade, since by fifth we were in Baltimore. We lived in a row house just off Roosevelt Boulevard about a mile from the old Sears and Roebuck headquarters build-

ing. The incident: coming home for lunch, I entered the house through the back door and was struck by a singular stench. I followed the dreadful odor to the kitchen where a small pot containing peas had boiled off the water. The peas were scorching. I turned off the gas as mother rushed into the room. Evidently she had been distracted. To my astonishment she insisted that the peas were okay, and she forced me to eat them with some tuna salad and milk. After two mouthfuls of the awful stuff I threw up.

I did not eat peas again for 30 odd years. Ultimately, we became reacquainted through the good offices of my gourmet-cook wife. She had been challenged, and the little darlings were elegantly disguised. Now I even like them, undisguised. (She has not yet managed to turn the trick with turnips, okra, eggplant or Brussels sprouts.) I often wonder if similar well-intended but less-than-thoughtful parental brutishness was what turned me (and several million other kids) off these innocent but less-than-delectable vegetables. Minor childhood traumas that our protective forebrains manage to submerge, tend to leave an intellectual residue—redolent, indistinct, often unremembered.

# 2

## *The Jewish Thing*

✦

### *(reflections about religion and related irreverences…)*

nd then I discovered I was a Jew. (I suspect I would not have been admitted to Walter's Philadelphia gang had they known; it was largely a Polish and Irish Catholic cabal.) It happened a few years later in Baltimore. I sort of always knew I was "one," but I never really understood much about "it" or religion. The Revelation occurred in the fifth grade. In those days, we were in the throes of the Great Depression and my folks were struggling. They were trying to establish my dad's shaky new chiropractic practice, and they were very secretive about being Jewish. (It was yet another time when anti-Semitism was rampant. Sustained economic privation and social unrest have always been the traditional substrate for bad times for Jews.) Also, I think my mother was a closet anti-Semite in those years. My father's family was very Russian Jewish, not quite orthodox but close. My mother held them in great disdain. She was outspokenly hostile to my father's mother who was from the old country. Grandma was obese and ill-kempt and spoke only Yiddish. There was no Grandpa. The whole *mishpokhe* lived in Trenton and ran a small, musty dry goods store. They lived in an apartment over the store. Our visits to them were infrequent and always strained. I never really got to know our many uncles, aunts and cousins on my father's side.

But my mother's *tante* and her family also lived in Trenton, and that was a different kettle of gefilte fish. We saw them more often, but I really **hated** those visits. Aunt Annie was a gray, eternally sad woman with big hair that reminded me of George Washington. Uncle Harry was a gray, eternally sad man. The twin dauqhters, Beatrice and Ethel were in their late 20s, and they were eternally sad. Their great tragedy was the death of an elder daughter of tuberculosis, many years earlier. Apparently she had been the blithe spirit, a gifted artist-pianist. That house had been in unrelenting mourning ever since. All mirrors remained covered, shades always drawn. I never recall the hint of a smile or the tinkle of laughter. It was a cheerless mausoleum, a somber shrine to the departed Saint Ida. And it never changed.

I recall one night when I was obliged to stay there alone overnight, a singular event. It must have been before I started school because I remember being very small and powerless. I don't recall much detail, but for my cold fear. I knew the damned house was haunted. For some inexplicable reason I was sent to sleep in a large room in a large bed, totally alone in absolute blackness! (Was this where the ghostly, sainted sister had died?) I had always slept with a night lamp, but this portentous night my child's pleas went unheeded. I stared into the darkness too frightened to sleep but too stoic to cry. Miraculously, I survived the night to awaken very much alive, unsavaged by the demons. I never needed a light in my room thereafter. But that bizarre outcome may be the only positive thing that ever occurred during my exposure to the Addam's family-like Samachsons of Front Street. I lost contact with both branches of the Trenton family over the years.

Then there was glorious Hester. My mother had two brothers, Lou and Dex. Dex ran a hardware store in Long Branch and disgraced the family by marrying a beautiful, red-haired Catholic woman, Emma. Dex was a sort of bland, chunky, happy guy. I liked Emma; she made wonderful lemonade that always had a hint of vanilla. But mother could not abide her. I never knew why, but it had something to do with her being a *shiksa*. We only visited them once.

Lou was a remarkably handsome entrepreneur. I never really knew what he did; it had something to do with soft drinks. His "business" was always spoken of in adult whispers or in Yiddish (the secret non-kid lingo). In retrospect I think his "soft drink" operation was on the fringes of shady; I suspect he ran a speakeasy. He went bust in the crash of 1929, and they had to sell their elegant house and classy Cadillac. Uncle Lou became a traveling salesman (children's clothing), and they moved to a very modest bungalow a few blocks from the beach in Ventnor. Aunt Ora was the wife: short, dumpy and sobby-weepy. My recollection of Ora was seeing her standing for hours by the front window with moist eyes, lace curtain half pulled aside, waiting for Lou to come home. Later I learned that Uncle Lou had a coterie of lady friends on the road.

Hester was their daughter. She was quite a piece of work. Hester was my age, and I was told we had spent a lot of time together as infants. But I became "aware" of her when she taught me how to play doctor when we were pre-schoolers. Now, at 16, she had matured into an exquisite, voluptuous, raven-tressed beauty. She did some part-time modeling and had legions of boyfriends. Our families enjoyed many home-to-home visits. "Going to the shore" was always a kick. There was no question: Hester **always** excited me, and she knew it. She always seemed to brush past me with a hint of perfume and fleeting pressure from wonderful, fully budded breasts. But a first cousin! One night while I was visiting alone in Ventnor, she crept into my room at about three, slipped out of her chemise, crawled into bed, thrust a soft firm breast in my mouth and straddled me—threading me deep inside her. The rest of her family were all asleep in adjacent rooms. In total silence (not easy) she did a few things I had not experienced in San Juan (*vide infra*). In the morning, still more than dazed, I had some vague concern about insemination (ah, the "good old days" of late innocence!). But I figured she knew what she was about. She must have learned that great stuff somewhere.

Over the succeeding years our lives moved apart, and I did not see her again until she was married and had a daughter. I was on temporary duty at Patrick Air Force Base preparing for a NASA Gemini Mission. I knew that Hester and her family lived in Orlando. Quite by coincidence at breakfast on a Saturday, I heard two army Huey pilots chatting about flying over to Orlando to pick up supplies. They were coming back that night. I asked if I could hitch a ride. I had a bit of difficulty remembering Hester's married name, but finally found their number. I had never met her husband, but he knew of me. Very pleasantly he invited me for dinner. Hester picked me up at the airport in a red Mustang convertible. She had put on a little weight (was it 20 years since That Night?), but her flimsy tank-top and denim shorts exuded sexiness. Her kiss of greeting was distinctly uncousinly. After about a ten minute drive she pulled into a motel and said, "Let's go to bed." I was sorely tempted, but demurred. In those days I was still faithful to my wife, and this situation just didn't feel right. (Casual, wham-bam sex has never held much appeal for me. It's not so much a matter of morality, but rather joy. Rapid sexual gratification always left me unfulfilled; it becomes a perfunctory physiological act, graceless and spiritless. But then, that's me)

Hester did not take rejection well. After a rather strained, dour, Chinese take-out dinner, I opted for a cab to the airport. I never saw her again. I heard she had a sort of hectic life: divorced and remarried a few times. I lost all track of the family; it seemed to be a recurring theme.

Back to the Jewish business. In those grammar school days we rarely attended temple; occasional high holy days were "observed" by fasting or skipping school. But my absence was always on pretext of illness. So for me "Jewishness" was only a vague awareness, something slightly unpleasant that other people didn't like. But I never quite understood "religion." (I am not sure I do today. I have always had a problem with "faith." To me it is belief without data. And I find that impossible to accept. Nor do I believe in the supernatural or UFOs.)

I knew there were Catholics and Protestants (who knew from Muslims, Buddhists, Hindus or Animists?); folks who were somehow different from us, but you could not tell by looking at them. In reflecting about those years, I now appreciate (but not condone) my parents' grave concern about anti-Semitism and how it could cause problems for dad's budding practice. This, plus my mother's undisguised antipathy toward my father's "very Jewish" family, kept us in a religious limbo. It left scars on all of us children; none of us are religious "anything." (And as I have indicated, I am far from convinced that quiet agnosticism should not be the dominant world "faith.")

The portentous fifth grade was the scene of my first realization that "being a Jew" could be a serious problem. It occurred with my favorite teacher, Mrs. Townsend. I was a reasonably bright student and English composition was my best subject. Often I wrote essays for "special credit," and Mrs. Townsend was my ever-encouraging ("someday you will be a writer") English teacher. One pleasant fall day, we were walking home from school together and quite casually she asked me what church I attended. I was puzzled because we did not go to church. I think I said, "We go to temple—occasionally." To this day I can recall the expression of disbelief followed by darkness that swept her countenance. We walked on in stony silence. I was perplexed, then devastated. I hated being a Jew. It was something I had no control over and didn't give a damn about, and here it was causing me pain. I ran home to mother and wept my grief. She gathered me up and told me about 5000 years of noble tradition, of bravery under hardship, of soul and spirit forged in steel, of unswerving tenacity to Judaic tenets. She spoke of generations of prejudice and survival. In retrospect it was a sudden encomium to Judaism, a strange outpouring from a closet anti-Semitic Jew. But I reckon that is the nature of ambivalence.

At the time her rhetoric meant nothing to me. All I understood was that my beloved Mrs. Townsend now despised me because I was Jewish. My next composition was a thoughtfully crafted description of a family trip to Niagara Falls. I thought it was my best work. She gave

me an "F"; I had never received anything but an A plus. She said I had written an incomplete sentence. I blamed it on being Jewish. Later, the same week, the class bully, who was very large and very Polish, called me a "kike" loudly and publicly in the schoolyard. We had a fight, and I took a pretty good licking. I **really** hated being Jewish. (After that fight, I learned to box from an older black man who worked at our house, but the story of the brief and notably undistinguished career of "Johnny Waverly" comes later.)

For many years, I denied my Judaism, as did my brother and sister. But when push came to shove and the form inquired about "religion," I always felt obliged to tell the truth. This noble tenet was badly shaken many years later when I applied to Johns Hopkins medical school. I had an excellent academic record with extra-curricular activities in journalism and sports, and I already had acceptances from Georgetown and Maryland in my pocket. But I really wanted to go to Hopkins. I was interviewed by a gnarly orthopedic surgeon. Within minutes I knew I was in trouble. "Father's a chiropractor, eh?…went to Loyola and Villanova, eh?…and you are…?" I knew his eyes had drifted to the top of the page that inquired about "religion." He made an embarrassed little cough, closed the folder; there were no further comments or questions. "You will hear from us." I never did. I know it all sounds like puerile whining compared to the hell that other Jews have endured through the centuries, but at the time it was a shattering blow.

I never had a bar mitzvah around the traditional thirteenth birthday. But for some reason at age 15, it was decided that I should be confirmed. I was sent to a conservative Hebrew school to prepare for the grand day. The other kids were all veteran Jews, and my ignorance of everything Jewish (and not being rich), set me apart. I thought they were all snobbish wimps; they didn't like me either. The rabbi was a much celebrated liberal intellectual (according to my parents), and there came a mystical time during the ceremony when each candidate for manhood came before the great man and he whispered deathless words of wisdom into your ear. He told me, "You are a follower. You

must listen to others and always do the right thing." Of course, he didn't know me from Adam (Isaac?), and his "words of wisdom" really pissed me off! I was editor of the high school newspaper, president of my class, had been in the National Honor Society for a year, was clean-up hitter on our sandlot baseball team, a Life Scout, had already hiked the Appalachian trail by myself, and was about to spend the summer as a cabin boy on a freighter to Puerto Rico! Follower indeed! None of the other creeps in my confirmation class could hold my coat! I was even less Jewish than before.

So when my brother Ken was applying to Quaker Haverford many years later, I told him to lie about his religion. He was about to be graduated from high school with the highest grade point average ever attained in the history of that institution, and I knew he could win a splendid scholarship. So he became a Presbyterian (on the form). Actually, he was about as Jewish as the rest of us, so it was not a terrible deceit. He was accepted, won the scholarship, and went on to a spectacular academic career. Later, he repeated the same exercise and became a medical student at Johns Hopkins. It was retribution of a sort for me.

It was the Holocaust and my first wife that prompted my "conversion" to acknowledge that I was Jewish. Stella was a lovely blonde who always wore a giant silver Star of David. Again, we rarely went to temple even on high holidays, but we never denied our religion and our kids knew "what they were." The Holocaust caused me to rethink the whole business of religion. It was obvious that being born a Jew was an irrevocable fact. Whether you believed or not or converted or not, the bad guys would still try to turn you into a bar of soap when the chips were down. I never wore my religion on my sleeve, but I never denied it, and I did not [and do not] abide racial or religious jokes.

In all candor, I do not recall any time in my army career when my religion caused a problem. I was always promoted on time (even more rapidly to full colonel), and enjoyed superior assignments. In more reflective moments I have wondered: had I remained in the army,

being Jewish, paradoxically, might have been an asset. The army had become sensitive to criticism about the slow promotion of minorities, and I knew I had a fair shot at a star. This was not true of the line, where anti-Semitism and racial bias were unspoken ground rules. But in the medical corps things were more relaxed. And there had never been a Jewish surgeon general. So who knows...

But just a bit more about this Jewish business. I have never understood religion. That infamous Marxian quote, "religion is the opiate of the people" always impressed me as simplistic, socialist-atheist cant. Religion is a more profound and insidious phenomenon. An opiate is sedative in its effects, and that is what Marx meant. Dull the masses with doses of religion and they will not rise up to cast out their capitalist-imperialist oppressors. But that is far too ingenuous. Religion was invented because the world is so mysterious and incomprehensible, and at times so unspeakably cruel, that most people must believe that leading a "good life" and enduring earthly travails will earn a reward in a better hereafter. I cannot believe that; it seems a frightfully contrived sophism.

I have no quarrel with those who must abide faith to live in peace and with hope. Perhaps my life has been too easy and pleasurable to need to look "beyond" for greater fulfillment. I am an unabashed pragmatist, and I believe that we have one life here on earth, and when we die our good minerals replenish the soil. And that is that. This is your one shot; do the best you can with it.

But my real quarrel with religion (at least all religions that I have first-hand knowledge of; I have been told that Buddhists and Jains may be exceptions) is their intrinsic bias against all others. Of course, Jews are no exception. Our bias has always been less militant. That is, until the Hasidic fundamentalists began to deal with Palestinians in Israel at the end of Uzis. [I am inclined to believe that if the state of Israel ever falls, it will not be at the hands of Arabs, but from internal divisiveness created by the withering parochialism and arrogant prejudice of the Hasidim. Wandering again.]

"Goyem" and "shvartzeh" are words I learned as a child. My parents were not overtly prejudiced against other religions, but it would be false to suggest that such words do not bear demeaning overtones, an unpleasant aspect of Jewish culture. But we do not proselytize or persecute or kill people because they do not "see the light" of Judaism. In fact, as I indicated earlier, the arrogant Ashkenazi Hasidim in Israel want to deny Jewish identity to Conservative and (God forbid) Reform Jews. As for faith, which I have defined as belief without data, I find the burning bush and the parting of the Red Sea no more believable than virgin birth or attaining nirvana. How many millions of Muslims, Hindus, agnostics, atheists, and animists have been slain because they refused to embrace Christianity (or its different branches)? And then we have Northern Ireland and Pakistan/India. Some other religions (Jews, LDS, Adventists) may not kill, but they can also can demean, demonize and ostracize with unsubtle (or even subtle) rhetoric, often preached from the pulpit.

I was once told, with deadly seriousness and chilling intensity, by a roommate/friend who was a devout Catholic, that since I had been afforded the opportunity to learn about and convert to Catholicism and had opted not to do so, I was doomed to hell. I stared into his eyes in disbelief. He was an otherwise rational, intelligent human being, but he truly meant it! I suspect that in another place and time (Italy in 1232 or Spain in 1478) he would have felt compelled to save my soul, friendship notwithstanding, with fire and iron! It was my first revelation about where faith and rationality parted company.

What incredible presumptuousness to assume that your religion holds the "only answer," that those who fail to "believe" are doomed to eternal hellfire. From here it is an easy transition to hate, and then, the ultimate perversion of religion—to feel driven to kill all infidels.

So I think all religion is intrinsically evil—destructive and divisive. It separates people and sets them against each other. One need not ascribe to any faith to live a decent, humane life. One may find comfort in believing that the order of the universe is ordained by a superior

intelligence, but when one sees the chaos in society and the cruelty and misery of so many of "God's people" imposed by other of "God's people," acceptance of that reality requires a "leap of faith" that I cannot abide. I don't believe in antinomialism. But perhaps the problem of religion would be solved if we all believed in the same rules of humanity and decency—a single "God Plan." In an analogous thought, I feel that the problem of race would be solved if we all worked at becoming approximately the same shade of brown. I sort of wished one of my sons had married Halle Berry. And perhaps they do too.)

Having said all that, I must confess that we "joined a church." I remember attending services at a sort of "holy roller" place with lots of somewhat alarming people who were shouting, weeping and singing, while engaged in some startling acrobatic gestures. Mother said it was good for business and handed out dad's office cards to all the sweaty disciples. But there must have been significant ambivalence, because at the same time, she became very active with a lot of Jewish ladies in the Kirchoff-Ray Chapter of the Eastern Star.

Dad became a big wheel in the Masons (and a "Lion" and a leading member of the Greater Northeast Baltimore Businessmen's Association.) The apogee of his public service career came when he was the chairman of the Fourth of July celebration held at the old Baltimore Stadium on 33rd St. The grand old eyesore is gone now, but in its glory days it was the biggest stadium in Baltimore. We enjoyed ringside seats for the gaudy fireworks display and rata-tat-tat fife and drum corps parades over several memorable years.

We were closet Jews for a long time. My sister married a lapsed Catholic, and I know her kids belong to no church. My brother married a woman who was from a family that was very active in the early Zionist movement in Israel, but again, religion was never a big part of their lives. After my divorce from my first wife, I married a wonderful woman who had been raised amid Seventh Day Adventist beliefs. But she had long since rejected all religious foolishness before we met. We

share the belief that organized religion has caused more death and destruction than any other force on earth.

I will let go of this bone in my throat in a moment, but a final thought. I remain convinced that "even in America," if there is a significant prolonged downturn in the economy and average people become hungry and angry, the malignant Jerry FaIwells, Pat Robertsons and their mindless minions will turn on the minorities as scapegoats. And the white Christian middle and upper classes won't give a damn. Blacks, Latinos and Jews could be subjected to the same fate as the Jews "beyond the Pale" in Russia in the 1920's and the Jews and Gypsies and disabled of Germany in the 1930s. One hears that "it can't happen here." These are the same words uttered by the foolishly arrogant German Jews in the months before the Nazi pogroms (*krystallnacht*) that preceded Auschwitz and Bergen-Belsen. The disturbing popularity of groups such as Promise Keepers, the Christian Coalition, and other elements of the religious right, the growth of hate-militias, the groundswell to obliterate the traditional separation of church and state, and other signs that ranting about "Christian family values" has become an unfortunate touchstone for political success in America. All bespeak a tenuous state for minorities, if things ever get down and dirty in a chronically depression-riven America. I can never forget that the burning cross is the symbol of the Ku Klux Klan.

To a lesser extent, I feel the same way about national chauvinism. I cannot understand the psyche of two million Parisians going gaga on the Champs Elysees when their national team won the World Cup, or the wretched, near suicidal despair in Sao Paulo because their team lost. The wild fanaticism of some sports enthusiasts (soccer abroad, professional football in the U.S.) suggests to me a poverty of individual spirit, a woeful despair with one's day-to-day life, a personality vacuum that cries for fulfillment that can only be achieved vicariously and often irrationally, through the heroics of others. Pretty desperate stuff.

Maybe fierce dedication to "sports" is all just good clean fun, merely an innocent outlet to try to escape the boredom of daily living, but I

am doubtful. To me it might represent a less recognized form of mob psychology. I may be unduly worried, but I believe that the psyche that engenders fanatical clan-team loyalty is a merely the benign face of racism. I think it can flare into wild, social conflagration and that "it cannot happen here," is dangerously simple-minded. I am sufficiently paranoid that I am convinced that something insidious and restless lingers in the primitive hindbrain of many "average" men that predisposes them to being led down iniquitous paths by dangerously charismatic "heroes." I hope I am wrong.

# 3

## *Greenmount Avenue*

◆

### *(first groping adventures in sex and related foolishness...)*

When we lived on Greenmount Avenue in Baltimore, our house was directly adjacent to Oriole Park. Our yard was almost on a direct line from home plate over second base. What joy to watch the games from my back bedroom! From our two windows, without field glasses, I could watch balls curve and dip over the plate. The scoreboard was just to the right of our view of the field, and I watched with fascination as the two bustling scoreboard keepers deftly kept track of hits, runs, errors and, of course, the score. (It always seemed the Oriole's runs got slipped into the slot faster than those of the enemy team.) It was a completely manual operation. When compared to the electronic bells and whistles and fireworks and instant replay of today, it was primitive. But the operation had unmistakable charm. After I got over wanting to be a flyer, explorer, fireman, Marine (before doctor), I wanted to be a scoreboard-keeper. You could watch all the games free for life and be in total command of that magnificent facility!

Back in my grammar school years, the Orioles were in the old International League (Triple A). The other teams were Newark (a Yankee farm team that usually won the pennant), Jersey City, Rochester, Buffalo, Syracuse, Toronto and Montreal. It was perhaps a reflection of the national population distribution. Of course, Boston still had the Braves, Brooklyn, the Dodgers, St. Louis, the Browns. New York had

the glorious Yankees and Giants, and Washington had the feckless Senators. Baseball didn't really exist west of Chicago or south of St. Louis. It wasn't until Jackie Robinson broke into the Dodger line-up and that ageless wizard Satchel Paige pitched a few games for Cleveland that anyone ever heard of the great players in the black leagues. Our local hero for many years was "Pooch" Puccinelli, who hit 58 home-runs one year (a Triple A record). I got to see some of the great Yankee teams (in Spring exhibition) with Gehrig, Dickey, Lazzari, Crossetti and DiMaggio. We cheered the Birds for many seasons, and perhaps 30 home-run balls landed in our yard over the years.

One of the great delights of my kid years was the Saturday morning movie. The feature was always a cowboy epic with Hoot Gibson, Buck Jones, Bob Steele or Ken Maynard. No singing or kissing stuff. And then there was the serial. Always the heroine was precariously pitching off a cliff in the covered wagon or the mean Indian was taking dead aim at the unaware hero. But you knew, in your heart of hearts, that next week it would all be okay. It was a white and black world; the good guys and the bad guys were easily distinguished. Good always triumphed over evil. I can recall with remarkable clarity, leaving the darkened theater and emerging into the bright Saturday morning light, briefly elated by the wonderful escape into unreality. Then suddenly feeling guilty. I was having such a good time, and I hadn't done my homework. Honestly, that was the sensation; guilt in grammar school! Where did it come from? Certainly not parents or teachers. I began to do my homework on Friday nights; my Saturday movie adventures became guilt free. How early in life do we become chronic compulsives?

In earlier years we played a lot of roller hockey. A broad asphalt street about a block away became the arena for some ferocious pick-up games, almost every evening before dinner. Body checks and scuffed knees were just part of the rough and tumble. I could hear my mother call the "dinner cry" amidst the clatter and clang of sticks and skates.

We also played a two-man game that might have been idiosyncratic to Baltimore (as was lacrosse in those days). The batsman would wield a broom handle about four feet long and the pitcher would have a sackful of beercaps. Standing about 15 to 20 feet away, the pitcher would wing the caps (with the underhand-sidearm motion of today's Frisbee) into a liberal "strike zone." You could not develop much velocity, but a skilled pitcher could make the caps rise and dive as they approached the batter. "Hits" were score by nailing the cap squarely and hitting a particular level of the 12-foot wall behind the pitcher. I think we were allowed ten misses before we switched. It really helped to develop a batting eye. Simple tools; great two-man game.

I became a fairly good first baseman on our neighborhood teams and later graduated to "organized" sandlot ball in junior and senior high school. Organized meant you begged the local merchants for enough dough to buy uniforms and catcher's gear (we all owned our own gloves and a bat), and then passed the hat after the game. It may be an old man's lament, but I think our pick-up, strictly-merit team selection ("Tony can't hit, but he is a good right fielder; he'll bat ninth.") and financing techniques, were superior to the parent-dominated, often-combative, "win at all costs" Little League circus that exists today. It was unheard of for a parent to intervene in a game; it was an all-kids show. The recent murder by one parent of another over an ice-hockey game represents the ultimate tragic absurdity of vicarious parental involvement in kids' sports.

It was in my later grammar school years that I had my first date. Her name was Frances Hoffman, and she lived on the corner. Her father was a professional lamplighter. In the early 1930s a goodly portion of north Baltimore still employed gaslights for street illumination. Every evening before sundown, Mr. Hoffman would mount his bicycle, and with a kerosene lighter in his leather bag, pedal around the neighborhood, stop at each lamp post, stand on his pedals, turn up the gas in the lamp and ignite the wick. Once that kindly gentleman let me ride the bar of his bike while he made his rounds. He said he was a German

from "the old country." I had no idea what he meant, but he talked differently from my parents. He was a very gentle man. His son James ran a shave-ice business in the summer in their back yard. We called them snowballs, and for three cents you could get the most delicious concoction imaginable. They offered a variety of flavors, but root beer and chocolate were my favorites. Portions were most generous. I still salivate after 60 plus years at the thought. For an extra two cents they would add marshmallow or whipped cream. It was an extravagance I could rarely afford despite my recent attainment of affluence. This was related to acquisition of a *Saturday Evening Post* route. (My predecessor, Billy, had to move away and sold me his customer list for a dollar; my principal competition was some lout named Henry who was pushing *Liberty*.)

Frances and I started the first Baltimore chapter of the Junior Birdmen of America. We were crazy about airplanes and studied all the existing aircraft, obtained literature, and, on really special occasions, went out to the airport to watch take-offs and landings. To get a genuine "parchment" charter, you cut out a coupon from the Baltimore News (the local Hearst paper my father despised), and mailed it in with a quarter mounted in slots you cut out of thin cardboard. Within weeks you would receive a nifty certificate with your name printed on it and a neat set of gold-plated wings. After some heated dialogue, I became president and Frances agreed (with formidable reluctance) to be secretary-treasurer. I think Frances Hoffman preceded Gloria Steinem by forty years. We were able to recruit about three other birdmen, and we met weekly in our basement until my family moved away to Charles Street.

Our first date was an outing on the Tolchester Ferry. Our folks delivered us to the dock on Light Street with a picnic lunch in a wicker basket. We waved from the rail, wonderful breezes caressed our faces as we cleared the harbor and chugged across the bay. This was long before the elegant Chesapeake Bay Bridge leaped across the bay at Annapolis; the ferry was far more fun. We swam on the rocky beach on the east

side of the vast unpolluted bay and rode the roller coaster and bump cars. It was a grand adventure. I never kissed Frances; we were just best buddies.

During those Greenmount years, I was in grammar school (where the infamous denouement with Mrs. Townsend occurred). My very favorite was Mrs. Lottie Clark, my homeroom teacher who turned me on to good books. Under her guidance I devoured everything I could lay my hands on. It was here that I discovered Richard Halliburton. He influenced my life even more than Jack London, Zane Grey and Josef Conrad. His wonderful books whetted my appetite for travel and adventure more than anything else I ever encountered. That fever has never abated. I can still recall Halliburton's gutsy swims through the Panama Canal and across the Hellespont. I mourned his death at sea sailing a junk from Hong Kong to San Francisco. But what a way to go!

It was also in the sixth grade that I fell in love for the first time. Her name was Ellen, and she and I vied for the "first seat" (reserved for the best student). At first she wouldn't give me the time of day. She had many other more handsome and suitable admirers. Sweet Ellen was pretty and rich and lived in a classy section called Homewood, a considerable notch above humble Waverly. I thought she was way out of my league. But later, in high school she was always my date for proms and stuff. I kissed her only once, after a senior dance. I had just learned to drive and took the family car out to stretch of deserted road near Loch Raven. It was just before she went off to Goucher. I kept track of Ellen for about 30 years, long after she was married and divorced. I never really knew what she thought of me.

Looking back, my sexual development was painfully slow. When we still lived on Greenmount Avenue and I was a kid in grammar school, a part-time maid named Myrtle, worked at our house three days a week. She tried to seduce me. She was a rather narrow-bosomed, somewhat unattractive blonde with a bad overbite. I think she must have been 15 or 16, enormously mature to me. One day when the folks were busy in

my dad's basement office, I can recall her coming into my room, unzipping my trousers and touching my penis. She then pulled up her dress and pressed against me. I didn't know what to do! I had never seen a woman's genitals before (not even pictures). After a lot of squirming and rubbing against me with great writhing gusto, I had my first (daytime) orgasm. What a revelation! We carried on our "trysts" for some time, but we never got around to penetration (even after I figured it all out). I always vaguely worried about the possibility of fatherhood, so I was sort of relieved when Myrtle left our employ. My parents never knew of our "affair."

And then there was Henry (or "Hendry" as my mother called him; I think she thought it added a dimension of dignity). He was an dignified, elderly black man who lived in our basement and did chores. He was the only black person I had ever known. I was too young to wonder how he got to our basement, but I remember him for his wonderful smell more than anything else. It was a musty, sweat-tobacco aroma. He smoked an ancient briar and carved delicate little birds out of wood. After my licking in the schoolyard, Henry taught me the basic movements of boxing and even set up a light punching bag. I would like to say he told me fascinating stories and imparted great wisdom, but I don't think he did. In my mother's lexicon, Henry was a "good" *schvartze* or darkey. I didn't know much about black people except that we did not socialize with them, and they all lived below 27th street (three blocks south). Henry left us when we moved to Charles Street. I don't know what happened to him.

For some time there was an open-air produce market that operated directly across from our house. It was a Friday afternoon, all-day Saturday, spring and summer event. I got to know the owners, the Diskins, and they would let me wait on customers. I even got to work the cash register. I would weigh the tomatoes or potatoes, figure out the cost per pound, take the money and make change. It was better mathematics training than school, and I developed a love for fresh tomatoes and cucumbers.

# 4

## *Musings About Family*

◆

### *(you never really know your parents...)*

I have often reflected on my parents and their relationship to each other and to us kids. It was a time of financial travail. I was in grammar school during the Great Depression, but I knew nothing about that catastrophic phenomenon. We always had enough food to eat and warm clothes to wear. In retrospect I have come to realize that my father was struggling to make a living. He had been to chiropractic school before I was born. (He wanted to be a physician, but most poor, second-generation Russian Jewish kids didn't have much of a chance. Perhaps that is why both of his sons became doctors and his daughter a lawyer.) But he had a tough time getting started. As I described earlier, in the interval in Philadelphia, he was selling some strange stuff under the rubric "Approved Products." All I remember is that his most notorious approved product was a topical solution that was supposed to make dark skin lighter. It was purported to be a "boon to colored people." I was too young to be embarrassed. Perhaps my life of crime with the "Budd dime scam" came naturally.

When we moved to Baltimore, dad set up his office in our home, first on Monument Street then later on Greenmount Avenue. Mother always worked with him. His cranky brother, Boris, was also a chiropractor, living in a different section of Baltimore. He had a gawky wife named Florence, who used to tweak my cheek, and two daughters, one pretty, Beverly, and one plain, Rhoda. I really didn't like them much.

They always seemed to have more money than us. They also had a big car, and when I used to ask Aunt Florence where they were going as they began to drive away, she always said, "…to Europe." And for years I never knew where that exotic place was. When I found out, I disliked her even more. Several years later we acquired our first car, a 1935 Ford; we called it the "Green Hornet."

Mother ran our family. Dad was the dreamer, a very gentle man, madly in love with my mother. She did not reciprocate his passion and seemed to convey a sense that he was too soft, indecisive and less than practical. She managed the office and the money. I never really knew how bright they were. I learned that in his youth dad had a fling with a "Young Socialist" movement, but mother quickly disabused him of that politically disastrous course. He became a lifelong, very liberal Democrat, joined the Govans Democratic Club, and one year was elected president. He was active in local politics and very much immersed in Roosevelt's many campaigns. But I never recall political discussions at dinner, nor did we discuss books or music or art. Culture was not a big part of our lives. Mostly, dinnertime conversation was about practical, show and tell, domestic stuff. Perhaps my folks thought I was too young (certainly my siblings were), but we never engaged in anything that could be construed as philosophic discourse. (I never even received the traditional birds and bees lecture.) So I never really knew how smart or worldly my folks were. Life was simple and frugal, but I never recall wanting things.

My dad was a wonderful healer. He would have made a superb allopathic clinician. His patients adored him and he helped them. He was a thoughtful, gentle listener, and he had the strongest, softest hands I have ever encountered in man or woman. When he gave you a spinal "adjustment," well, you just felt relaxed and terrific. It was better than an hour in a Jacuzzi, almost as good as mediocre sex. Of course, he had all the conventional chiropractic nonsense equipment. I was never really convinced that he believed that any of the high colonics or galvanic stimulators or ultra-violet lights or other bell and whistle gadgets

ever did a damn bit of good. But he had great hands. Also, he never accepted a patient with a truly serious disease. He maintained a list of medical specialists to whom he referred such patients.

The contemporary fashion to legitimize "complementary and alternative" medicine (CAM—defined by me as mostly off-the-wall nonsense with no basis in physiologic reality—but with emphasis on attention and communication with the patient) has enabled me to appreciate the source of much of dad's success. It was his instinctive kindness and patience in listening to patients whose disabilities were real enough, but often caused by emotional (psychological) perturbations, with perhaps a modicum of physiologic dysfunction. I suspect that about 80% of patients who walk into any physician's office would fill this bill; now we now euphemize it as "somatization." No clinician worth his salt ever discounts the reality of such symptoms and their potentially debilitating impact on the patient. This powerful phenomenon is related to the mystery of positive and negative placebo effect that impacts all patients and all illnesses.

In some such individuals one can never find an explanation of symptoms by thorough and systematic exploration of traditional diagnostic logic. The classic example is Chronic Fatigue Syndrome (CFS). There is little doubt that CFS patients may be truly disabled by this impossible-to-characterize disorder. It has defied every investigation into its etiology and pathology. Perhaps our diagnostic capabilities are insufficiently sophisticated or refined to identify its underlying pathophysiology. But I suspect not.

I feel that we are at the primitive beginnings of understanding the enormous impact of emotion on physiology. I suspect that clinical depression can trigger unknown cytokines in the forebrain that are capable of causing subtle, long-term organic disruption of other organs. We have solid scientific data that chronic depression can inhibit the immune system and is related to poor survival in patients who have suffered a heart attack. So why not an effect on the kidney, liver, pancreas, *et al*? It will come in time.

I have a hunch that my dad had a feeling for this phenomenon. Maybe all his hokey gadgets were just props to help him in his quiet thoughtful approach to try to improve the quality of life of patients with severe psychosomatic disorders. And, after all, isn't that a large part of what medicine is all about?

When I became senior medical student (and he had retired from practice), I often wondered if his diagnostic skills were sufficient to prevent mistakes. On reflection, I think dad had superb clinical judgment. But my misgivings about many of his colleagues never abated. In my years in clinical practice, I learned of too many instances when chiropractors engaged in practices that I considered ill-advised, if not dangerous. Too-often they "treated" patients with "spinal adjustments" who had illnesses that required rational, traditional diagnosis and therapy. And many others engaged in high-pressure business tactics that trapped (intimidated?) patients into frequent return visits that were not necessary.

Today, I must confess that I am annoyed by the acceptance of CAM (e.g. chiropractic and all its equally unscientific cohort: herbalism, "therapeutic touch," crystal therapy, most acupuncture [*vide infra*], naturopathy, homeopathy and the rest)—as alternatives to rational, data-based allopathic medicine. I have no problem with meditation, yoga, relaxation, groups support or any other treatment that is harmless and relatively inexpensive. In the case of chiropractic, perhaps in the solitary instance of acute low back pain, chiropractic manipulation may be as effective (or ineffective) as any other form of treatment. Nothing works really well. And perhaps, there are many chiropractors who recognize their limitations (like my dad) and can help some not-too-ill patients.

But much I have read in recent years belies this assumption. In the prevailing climate of increasing "public enlightenment about medicine" (much of it facilitated by uncritical Internet information and florid disinformation), the public has unrealistic expectations ("If they can send men to the moon, why can't they cure cancer?") and con-

sumer empowerment. The latter has been bolstered by a litigious climate characterized by some outrageous pain and disability judgments.

The rising popularity of CAM (21.2 billion dollars was spent by patients—exceeding the cost of total visits to all U.S. primary care physicians in 1997, plus the 31 billion dollars spent each year on OTC drugs!) represents a backlash. So why do one in three patients in the U.S. seek CAM? The answers are not complex. First, there is disenchantment with conventional medicine. Patients often complain that doctors are too busy, too bossy, too insensitive; they do not take time to listen. Perhaps, more importantly, CAM is perceived as less authoritarian (our benign paternalism), and more in harmony with patients' personal values about health and illness. It is a matter of an individual trying to exercise some control over one's health destiny. And these are young-to middle-aged, reasonably sophisticated, well-educated folks. Clinicians are coming to learn that patients desire to **participate** in their management, not merely to be a **recipient**.

And having said all that, I am obliged to cite a paradox. Is it fair to wonder about the prevailing view that "good health" is a "right" (like life, liberty and the pursuit of happiness), while many of these same folks feel no moral or intellectual obligation to try to attenuate, delay or even prevent "self-inflicted diseases" (e.g. obesity, type II diabetes, coronary artery disease, lung cancer, venereal diseases, alcohol or drug addiction, hypertension, etc.), by adopting a lifestyle that incorporates rational diet, regular exercise, cigarette avoidance, alcohol moderation and stress control? Are these the same people who constitute the 61% of Americans who are overweight? Or those who never exercise? It is a puzzlement to me. I guess we all await the "magic bullet (pill)" that will ensure good health—while we continue to enjoy our pleasant lives of sloth and gluttony. But that is not the way of human biology.

I believe most earnestly that increased awareness by patients about what they can do to help themselves and general, realistic knowledge about medical capabilities and limitations is a good thing. It serves to keep doctors on their intellectual toes and facilitates the patient's moti-

vation to cooperate with sound management. Nonetheless, there is a mind-boggling paradox in medicine. Never has the capability to diagnose and treat disease been at a higher level; never has solid, evidence-based information been more easily accessible to every health care provider; never has the opportunity to truly help sick patients been more readily at hand. And we stand on the threshold of even greater progress as many aspects of genetic engineering and molecular biology promise to revolutionize medical diagnosis and treatment. Yet, public expectation remains largely unfulfilled; distrust of the profession is rampant. We have a lot of work to do.

And I have not even discussed the impact of profit-driven managed care (HMOs *et al*) on this equation. But these particular tea leaves are not at all felicitous. Certainly, medicine is not without sin in the genesis of the current chaos in health care. I am not sure how it will all come out.

I know my dad was a superb clinician and several generations of faithful patients adored him. In my years in practice I tried to emulate his thoughtfulness, his gentleness and kindness, his ability to listen respectfully without hurry or interruption, the therapeutic effect of his physical and psychological "laying on of hands." Quite a legacy.

It was a "given" in our household that academic success was a foregone conclusion for all us kids. Nor was there any doubt that I was going to be a doctor; it said so in my grammar school "yearbook." I always had medicine in the back of my mind and the cowboy, fireman, explorer, commando fantasies were never seriously entertained. This parental expectation of scholarly excellence was always disconcerting, especially later in medical school where the survival competition was particularly deadly. I came to appreciate my good fortune in having preceded my brother, Ken, by some six years through high school and college. I was a good student and I worked harder than most of my colleagues, but Ken was a whiz. As I have indicated, when Ken attended Baltimore City College (our singularly named high school), he was

graduated with the highest grade point average in the century-long history of that institution. He swept all honors at graduation.

When it came time for him to apply to college, I had learned a bit about higher education. No one in my family had ever been to college before me, so as mother said (more than often), "College is college." Loyola of Baltimore or Harvard University (shrug), what's the difference? But Loyola was decidedly cheaper and much closer to home. I didn't let that happen to Ken. He applied and was granted a four-year scholarship to Haverford College and several others. And, once again, my kid brother distinguished himself as a record-breaking scholar.

My sister Joan was six years behind Ken. I never knew her well in those early years. Twelve years kept us worlds apart. But she might have been the brightest of all. In later life when her kids had dropped off the family payroll, she went to Georgetown Law School and still practices. The unfortunate fact is that we kids never really got to know each other well. My recollections of Ken as a child were of a rather chubby little guy who followed me around a lot. And when I left home in 1942 for Villanova, we lost contact but for desultory visits. The same for Joan. We never really got to know each other well until much later in our lives. It is a regret that I bear to this day.

It must have been about the second year of junior high that we moved from Greenmount Avenue to North Charles Street, an important social upgrade. It was an elegant, three-story brick house with gleaming white marble steps (scrubbed by me at least once a week for two-bits a shot). My dad built a spacious office in the basement (with a separate entrance). Wyman Park was across the street with the art museum adjacent, and the Johns Hopkins University undergraduate campus was just a few blocks north. It was a very up-scale address for us. I was attending Roland Park Junior High School where all the rich kids went. The super-rich kids all went to posh Gilman School right next to Roland Park. It was a real kick when I discovered that Ellen, the unrequited love of my life, was also a student there.

Most memorable was my purchase of a first bicycle. It cost three bucks (earned by me), and I painted it green and black. Now I could bike to school instead of taking the lousy trolley car with all those silly, noisy kids. The trip must have been about two or three miles each way, and I savored every push of the pedals. That wonderful bicycle was the most liberating vehicle I have **ever** possessed. Richard Halliburton look out, a whole new world was unfolding! On week-ends I would ride for miles out into the countryside. Loch Raven dam was about 14 miles away. I would pedal out, lunch and nap by the reservoir, and then streak home. Even now I can still recall the joyous freedom, the exaltation of wind and rain in my face. I became a professional loner and relished every moment. Travel became a lifetime passion.

# 5

## *Junior High School*

◆

### *(first exposure to Maggie and Jiggs...)*

Junior high was the first time that I made some close friends (aside from my forlorn pursuit of the ever elusive Ellen). Fitzhugh (Fitz) Dodson was the son of a minister. He had access to dirty books and was a skillful master (and teacher) of foul language. He was also terribly smart. We became inseparable; he introduced me to Maggie and Jiggs (in brown cover) and Henry Miller (titillating but thoroughly obscure). I even started "Ulysses" but never made it past page ten. I think in college I got to page fifty; I still cannot grapple with Joycean rhetoric; "Finnegan's Rainbow" was equally arcane and obscure. Of course, all this exposure to Dodson-induced sexuality was many years before my Puerto Rican epiphany and my "night with Hester."

One of the more memorable "Dodson adventures" was his epochal fistfight with a kid named Weston. Fitz was a tall string bean and certainly no fighter. Weston was a small, wiry weasel who bullied Fitz mercilessly. I told my friend that he had to stand up and fight Weston to stop the harassment. So we arranged a bare knuckles battle to be held on Friday afternoon in the field behind Friends School (a rather ironic locale for fisticuffs). I would be Fitz's second and Weston would bring one of his own. For days after school, I "taught" Fitz a few basic boxing moves. He was slim and rangy but dreadfully floppy and unco-ordinated. We met at the appointed hour, but Weston had brought his older brother (a stocky sophomore at Maryland!) for a second. We

agreed the fight would last until one yelled "Uncle." So they started and Weston was more far more aggressive, faster and stronger. Soon he bloodied Fitz's nose and then knocked him down. I stepped in, pulled him off and yelled for a cease fire. Then Big Brother grabbed me and punched me in the ribs. He was about 30 pounds heavier and ever so much stronger. I could not outbox him, so I kicked him in the balls. And a battered Dodson and I scurried from the field. Weston never bothered Fitz again, but I'm not sure my friend ever forgave me for his bloody beating.

My other good friend was rich kid named Roland Adams. He was an athlete and we ran track and played basketball together. For two years I held the "bat the ball for distance" record (toss up a 12-inch soft ball and then smack it as far as you could). My name was up on the Roland Park record board for a while. As a senior I played on the varsity basketball team; I fear we were never very good. (But we did beat Gilman once.)

The only defection from my frustrating fascination with Ellen was my brief (but no less intense) adoration of a blonde girl named Beth. She was from a well-known Roland Park family, and I had no obvious way to get to know her. Then I heard that they were having try-outs for an operetta, "The Student Prince," and Beth was known to have a remarkably sweet voice. One day, I wandered down to the auditions, and Beth won the leading female role hands down. But there were no candidates for the male lead. Dare I? Why not? So I sang for the music teacher. I was really lousy but she hired me. Obviously, she was desperate. We actually began rehearsals every day after class. I practiced singing a lot; I thought I sounded terrific in the shower, but Morton Downey I was not. Nevertheless there were compensations. I got to hug Beth and even kissed her a few times (part of the libretto). But with about one week before Showtime I began to panic. How could I pull this thing off? I have always hated doing things that I wasn't good at, and Fitz was really on my case, despite his undisguised admiration for my insidiously clever scheme. "Got into her pants yet?" became the

Dodson mantra. But the gods were kind; my *deus ex machina* came in the form of the music teacher coming down with the flu. They had to call the whole thing off. The Beth interlude cooled off soon thereafter.

Another memorable junior high recollection was the 1934 World Series between Detroit and St. Louis. We prevailed on our homeroom teacher to let us listen to the seventh game on the radio in the school library. Dizzy Dean was pitching against Schoolboy Rowe. Detroit won. With some regret I must confess that none of the teachers encountered at Roland Park made a lasting impression.

# 6

## *High School*

◆

### *(continued adolescent awakenings…)*

**B**altimore City College was the rather pretentious name of our century-old high school ("third oldest in the country"). It was a noble looking building, with a splendid granite tower dominating a small hill. At that time it was an all-white, all-boys institution, some 3000 strong. Across the street was Eastern High School with about the same number of girls. Of course, sweet Ellen was there. "City" was a sports powerhouse during my four years. In 1937 we won 21 of 22 city championships in all sports. Our football team was made up of giants, even for those days. They scored 365 points and allowed zero! We were invited to play in the Little Orange Bowl in Miami for the mythical national high school championship. (*vide infra*)

My principal avocation was journalism. Our "Collegian" was a six-page weekly. I was feature editor as a freshman and became editor-in-chief as a junior. We swept all honors for schools our size (top rank) in the annual competition in New York for four straight years. It was a great high school newspaper. Fitz was sports editor and Gene Goodwin had been editor before me. The talent on the staff became evident over the years. Two of our colleagues, Lou Panos and Bill Miller, became reporters (later editors) for the Baltimore Sun. Gene subsequently went to journalism school and later became a most venerated chairman of the department of journalism at Penn State. Fitz wrote two best-selling books about parenting. He and his second wife ran a fancy school for

gifted kids at Palos Verdes, but he never sired children of his own. The "Collegian" staff was phenomenal.

One of the more noteworthy articles I wrote for The Collegian was based on an interview with Jim Thorpe, the great Native American athlete. He was one of my heroes and was still campaigning for return of his medals won at the 1912 Stockholm Olympic Games. He had been deprived of these honors because some jealous lout ratted that he once had received a few lousy bucks for playing semi-pro baseball. (How far we have come when sports millionaire professionals like Michael Jordan and Wayne Gretzky play for U.S. teams in these "modern" games.) Thorpe had his medals restored before he died. I thought seriously about pursuing a career in journalism, but then I began to read the really great writers. I could never become that good, so I thought I had better stick to something easier, like medicine.

I was a fairly good student, National Honor Society and all that, but I had a tough time with analytic geometry. I was great in languages and sciences, but the school paper was my joy. I played junior varsity basketball, but making any varsity team in those days at City required a level of muscle and coordination beyond my skinny capability. One of my classmates was Izzy Smelkinson. His father owned a kosher delicatessen on Lombard Street. They made the best horseradish and peppery mustard in the world. Izzy was a tall, husky guy, and he played forward for a team in the Junior Hebrew League. He asked me to join the team, and I played one season as guard. It was much faster than high school JVs.

During those tremendous sports years at City there was one team our varsity (and us JVs) could never beat on their home court. That was Southern High School; their basketball "court" (a converted cafeteria) gave fresh meaning to "home court advantage." It had an eight-foot ceiling and two structural pillars about 15 feet apart smack in the middle of the court. Naturally, they built all their plays around those damned pillars and learned to fire flat trajectory bullets at the basket. They also had a series of four or five brothers named Schuerholz who

came along about at two year intervals; all were basketball wizards. Southern was invincible at home for generations. They had to eat humble pie when they built a regulation gym and ran out of Schuerholzes.

During the professional basketball season I worked as an usher at the old Baltimore Coliseum. It was a great Saturday night job. It paid zilch, but once you had everyone seated you could stand in front of a pillar and watch the game free. In those days our home team was the Bullets, but the great team was the Philadelphia SPAHs (long before the Warriors and the 76ers). SPAH stood for South Philadelphia Hebrew Association, but they were so good they turned pro. They were all little guys, I mean five foot eight was **tall** for these guys. The SPAHs won by dazzling the opposition with fast, pin-point passing. They could always get a man free under the basket for an unobstructed lay-up. Also they had the best two-handed set-shot players in the league. Other teams hated to play them. The SPAHs wouldn't have a prayer against the skillful giants of today, but they still could give lessons in dexterous ball-handling and unselfish passing.

I also played sandlot baseball (as mentioned earlier) and Sunday football in a church league. I also boxed a little. I had three amateur fights, of course, all unknown to my mother. I won two and then (*mirabile dictu*) dad asked if I would like to box an "exhibition" at a Govans Democratic Club bull-roast/smoker and earn ten bucks. It was part of a four bout program. I always considered exhibitions as sort of fun things where you jabbed and danced around but no one really got hurt. I was wrong. My opponent was a wiry black kid a full head shorter than me. He didn't look too tough. I was calling myself "Johnny Waverly" (like my neighborhood), and it was terrific being introduced like a real fighter. The first round (of three) was a piece of cake. I had about four inches reach on the other guy, so I could keep him at bay with jabs. Toward the end of the round I got bolder and smacked him with a few classy combinations. I think that was a mistake. Round two started about the same as the first, but then the world

exploded. I never saw the punch. They said it was a right uppercut. I was knocked out! The brief career of young Johnny Waverly was over before it began.

All through high school I worked eight to five on Saturdays. I was a counterman at Schreiber's Meat Market, along with a handful of professional butchers and a legion of other high school kids. The market had three levels. Gourmet fare on the second floor, average stuff on the first, and then there was the raucous, swarming bargain basement with cheap cuts: pork liver, beef liver, ground beef and roasts. Of course, all the new kids worked in the dungeon. I learned to bone and roll a roast; I could guess the weight of a scupper full of slimy liver or fatty ground beef within an ounce. At times toward the end of the day, the crowds would get deeper and nastier, and we would respond in kind. "Yeah lady, pound and a half of pork liver?" "No, I said a pound and a quarter!" "OK lady, do you want me to wrap it or do you want to eat it here?" That was always worth a few growls and laughs.

It was a nine-hour day at thirty-five cents an hour, before the deduction for union dues. I was a proud card-carrying member of the Meat Cutters Union, Local 36. My dad thought it was terrific. Union forever! At the chopping block, one quickly learned prudence and caution. There could be three cleavers whistling through the air simultaneously. If my mother had known how "my son the doctor-to-be" was jeopardizing his precious digits...The great fringe benefit at Schreiber's was access to the best cheesecake south of Lindy's. If you could wangle a trip to the cold locker to pick up a side of beef, you could scoop a few handfuls of cheesecake and scarf it down before you kicked open the heavy door. On a good day you could make a whole two-pound cake vanish.

I learned to drive in the summer of 1939. Permit in hand, I worked for the U.S. Postal Service for the two weeks before Christmas, driving a delivery truck. It paid great money (three times Schreiber's and no union dues), and everyone loved me. I brought them presents. It was a

world of cookies and fruit cake and punch. I worked the whole area of northeast Baltimore using a city map and asking questions.

One of the more unusual experiences in high school was the "Mack Wilt" drama. Mack sat next to me in our sophomore homeroom, run by a chalk-tossing minor martinet, Mr.DeHaven. Mack was bigger and older than the rest of us but very quiet and unobtrusive. He played forward on our junior varsity basketball team, a talented athlete. Then he missed class for three straight days. Just about everyone (but goody-goody me) would "cut classes" for a day or half-day now and then. (Well, I did cut once with Fitz. We went down to the Gayety Theater to see the legendary baggy-pants burlesque comedian, Mike Sachs and the incredibly pneumatic stripper, Belle Starr. The place really smelled bad; the show was naughty but not very lubricous.)

But Mack had been absent for three days, and we began to worry that something had happened. The next morning the Baltimore Sun carried a headline, "Thieves Rob Westport Bank," and there was a picture of my classmate, Mack Wilt, glaring at the camera while two cops cuffed him! The story related that Mack was the leader and master-mind of a gang of young thugs who had successfully knocked off a half-dozen banks in the area. He was sent away for a long time. On careful reflection, I could never recall any incident, gesture, conversation or anything else that would have lead me to suspect Mack's "other life." I think it was the first time that I realized, one never really gets to know another human being from casual contact.

My first solo summer vacation (as a freshman) was spent working on a dairy farm in southern Maryland. Mr. Volland was a very satisfied patient of my father, and he agreed to take me on as a hired hand for room, board and a few bucks a week. I worked there for six weeks, learned to milk a cow (terrific for hand strength), run a tractor and hay baler (I was still too young to drive a car), pitch hay, weed, paint and string fence. I was even getting pretty good at plowing a straight furrow. It was up at 5:30 and in bed by eight. The work wasn't too hard, and I managed to put on about ten pounds of muscle and developed a

passion for fresh unpasteurized milk. The farm even had a swimming hole with the classic tire on a rope. It was a fine summer, but I soon realized that I didn't want to do that the rest of my life.

The high point of the following summer was my great Appalachian Trail Adventure. I had just made Life Scout, and our troop had done some wimpy weekend hiking and camping in the Catoctin mountains of western Maryland. Between my solo bike excursions and brief outings with the troop, I was ready for something more challenging. I wanted to hike the Appalachian Trail for three or four days. So I purchased some trail maps and plotted a course that would bring me out near Harper's Ferry. I figured it would be easy to hitch rides out and back. But all of my buddies begged off. I really wanted to make that hike; I had no fear of tackling it by myself. In fact, I actually preferred to hike and camp alone. But I thought my folks might not let me wander down the trail solo.

So I lied; I told my parents that a bunch of us senior scouts were going make the hike. I said that Billy's folks would drop us at the trailhead and pick us up in Harper's Ferry the evening of the third day. My folks were accustomed to my periodic biking and hiking excursions, so no one gave it a second thought. I loaded up my backpack with enough gear, food and water for a week and took off. I rode a city bus to the edge of town, and within minutes a Chevy pick-up loaded with bags of concrete and manure took me all the way to where my map indicated the Appalachian Trail crossed the highway near Hagerstown. I was heating up baked beans in a mountain glade by sundown.

It was a glorious three days; I saw only one other group of hikers coming north. The June foliage was delicate and soft, and the trail was overgrown and rough in spots after the winter. Too few campers had been abroad to tamp it down, but the hike was a piece of cake. I saw some deer and a skunk, but no copperheads. I stopped each day around four to find a stream and dig out hip holes cushioned with lots of pine needles. My air mattress and kapok bag kept me comfortable and snug. Food was simplicity itself; I must have roasted about a dozen

hot dogs and savored them along with baked beans laced with maple syrup. (I suspect my life long passion for beans and franks was born on this seminal expedition.) Dessert was a little can of fruit cocktail. I always doused crystalline stream water with halazone tablets (as a good scout should).

From the elevation of the trail and my trusty map and hand compass, I could identify small hamlets in the valleys. It took a bit longer than I anticipated. At about noon the third day, I spotted what I thought was the Potomac River configuration at Harper's Ferry. I came off the trail through some steep, unmarked, rocky scrabble down to what seemed to be an old wagon trail that ran beside the gleaming expanse of river. I knew there were noisy rapids at the Ferry, but I couldn't hear them. So I trekked southwest following the river trail. It turned out I had missed Harper's Ferry by about five miles. I was thoroughly exhausted since I must have covered about 10 miles of fairly unforgiving terrain seeking the elusive rapids. By sundown, I threw down my sleeping bag in a picnic area near John Brown's "fort" (where he had been captured). A Park Ranger awakened me about 5:00 A.M. and growled that it was illegal to camp there. He eased up when I zipped open my sleeping bag. The Scout uniform softened all hearts. I hitched a ride to Frederick with a family from Sacramento, and some college kids from Maryland dropped me at my front doorstep. My folks had been worried that I was a day late, ("Gee, no phones on the trail."), but they were only moderately interested in my adventures. I told them the other guys had a good time too. Over the next few years I must have hiked about 100 miles of the Appalachian Trail. Once I wandered south as far as the North Carolina border. Most of it I explored alone. I didn't get back to Harper's Ferry for another 20 years.

# 7

## *The Puerto Rico Adventure*

✦

### *(how I lost my virginity...)*

**M**y first experience with "real" intercourse (Myrtle really didn't count) came when I was 15 (1938). I was tall and skinny, about 5'-10" at 115 pounds. One of my father's patients was a venerable, portly, silver-maned sea captain named John Mumford. He was a skipper on the old Bull Line (later all its ships were sunk by German U boats in the Caribbean during World War II, and the company went belly up). The fleet consisted of dutiful, slow, small tubs (about 8000 tons) and shuttled farm equipment and a lot of other paraphernalia from Brooklyn to San Juan and then picked up raw sugar at Mayaguez and Ponce before laboring home. I shipped out as a cabin boy for one summer. It was the adventure of my young life. (As I have indicated my parents let me do a lot of wonderful, crazy things during my summers, and I've always marveled at their permissiveness.)

Captain John assured my folks that he would look out for me. So one hot June morning I took the huffy-puffy B & 0 railroad from Baltimore to New York, with my well-stocked backpack and first aid kit. With a hand-drawn map and detailed instructions ("Sure I know my way around New York. Remember, Gene and Fitz and I always went up for the interscholastic press award conferences.") I managed to switch subways several times, landed in Brooklyn and miraculously found the dock where the S.S. Emelia was berthed. I recall it being exhaustingly hot and sultry; I was wringing wet. The bustling commer-

cial dock area was adjacent to the Brooklyn Navy Yard, and a million intoxicating odors wafted from whining winches and steaming cargoes being loaded by burly glistening men. It was a scene of intense, intimidating, totally thrilling physical activity.

I climbed the gangway and was greeted by Mr. Bob Shockley, a very tall second mate, totally unprepared for my arrival, as was Mr. James Davis, the brawny first mate. After some cumbrous effort at explanation, they seemed less than enormously pleased at my presence. I was advised that my benefactor was asleep in his cabin. The mates were supervising the loading of cargo. I was led to a tiny cabin adjacent to the mates' quarters somewhere amidships. It looked wonderful to me. It even had a small electric fan above the bunk.

I soon discovered that the entire crew consisted of Puerto Rican sailors who spoke very little English. The chief boatswain's mate was a smallish, heavily muscled fellow with an elegant, toothy smile. I was told he had been bantam weight champion of Puerto Rico a few years back. In reasonably comprehensible English, he said to call him "Ricky". A deeper sense of prudence advised me to call him "Chief." He turned out to be my mentor, instructor and friend. About five o' clock (two bells, I was really getting into this nautical stuff), Captain John emerged resplendent in a sparking white uniform, brilliant gold-trimmed cap and four gleaming stripes on his shoulder boards. He was truly magnificent, if a trifle suffused. It all did ample justice to his very ample frame. The other officers wore white open-necked shirts and white ducks. I was allowed to stay on the bridge ("just don't get in the way") during the ceremonies of casting off.

I have been on many ships since, rusty old troop carriers, splendid white cruise giants, but the "setting sail" of the S.S. Emelia will live in my mind forever. It was spectacular! Captain John supervised, but Shockley, with his marvelous down east accent, ran the show. The ship's whistle blasted a few times (rather startling from the proximity of about 20 feet!) to alert the world that we were coming. Bow lines were cast off, we drifted a tad from the pier, then stern lines let go. A tena-

cious tug huffed us out of the berth, past the teeming wharves of Brooklyn (it must have been about 100 degrees), a few more blasts and we were under way. The tow boat cut us adrift, and we were under power just before we sighted the Statue of Liberty, some distance off our starboard bow. I can still feel the tingle of pride-discovery-awe as the Emelia saluted that Grand Lady. Soon we passed out of sight of land and encountered the Scotland Lightship.

After we cleared the harbor, Captain John retired to his cabin. Thereafter, I saw him for occasional meals. I think he enjoyed his grog. The ship was run by the mates and the Chief. The crew didn't quite know what to make of me. I was about a head taller than any of them and about 10 pounds lighter; I was all elbows and shins. My salvation came in a lovely way. The second day out I was chipping rust with two other crew members (chipping rust and repainting was a Sisyphean task), when one of them sliced his arm on a frayed steel cable. It was a fairly ugly and dirty wound. Shockley seemed to function as the ship's doctor, but I asked if I could help. So with my first-aid kit and some suture material unearthed from a battered medicine chest, I cleansed the wound and put in three sutures. (My "Personal Health" merit badge and some previous personal, painful experience with suturing was most helpful.) So I became the unofficial Doc for the crew; I was accepted. (In retrospect it might be the defining moment that confirmed my destiny as a physician. I loved the respect and the sense of being able to help people.) I frequently took meals with the crew in the forecastle (fo'c's'le), learned to sip good Ron Rico rum neat and shocked the crew with my confession of virginity..."*tiene quince anos?*"

My education (book stuff) was undertaken by Mr. Shockley. He taught me the rudiments of chart reading, how to use a sextant (not too well), navigation (equally iffy) and lots of seafaring lore. My lessons occupied about two hours in the afternoon, but I worked with the crew in the mornings always under the watchful eye of the Chief. I chipped, painted, swabbed acres of decks, polished a million brass fittings, helped remove and replace tarps during squalls. But mostly I chipped,

chipped, chipped. I was also the cheerfully naive recipient of a lot of greenhorn horseplay. I was advised to write to my folks every third day so we could drop off the mail at the various "mail buoys" that were staggered along all shipping routes. I marveled that we only seemed to pass them in the dead of night, but *c'est la vie au mer.* My dutifully written letters were, of course, all mailed from San Juan. The voyage south was uneventful but for a few heavy squalls. The Emelia did not cotton to rough weather; she pitched and rolled with the slightest encouragement. I only had one bad day of queasiness but never missed a meal. I saw dozens of dolphins and squadrons of silvery flying fish. A shark followed us for a few days. I worked hard, got almost as brown as the rest of the crew and loved it most of the time. But I decided the sea was not in my professional future (the same for dairy farming or meat cutting or truck driving). Perhaps there was some method in my folks' permissiveness about summer jobs?)

In 1938, San Juan was smaller, friendlier and more tractable than when I returned many, many years later. As we drew near the harbor entrance and the dear Emelia bellowed her hoarse greeting, I noted a four-masted schooner with its hull stove-in perched indecently on the shoals to the east. The Chief said it was a Norwegian school ship that had been driven on the reef during a terrible storm some months earlier. A squat, tenacious, all-business towboat nudged us into a pier adjacent to a troop ship. I think it was the President Wilson, unloading khaki-clad soldiers. I was reminded of pictures of Teddy Roosevelt and the Rough Riders. We maintained a large military presence in Puerto Rico. In those days there was considerable unrest with frequent violent outbreaks by rambunctious advocates seeking independence. During my visit, there was a bomb attack against Governor General Tugwell, and some folks were killed. Once ashore, I wandered the Old Town and toured the magnificent, decaying Spanish fortress, El Morro, but a large chunk of its real estate was off limits. Mysterious military business I was told.

When I returned to the ship in late afternoon, the crew assumed a very personal responsibility to correct one major deficiency in my life. They were going to sponsor me in getting properly laid. Apparently, they had all chipped in. They escorted me to the "best whore house in San Juan." It was an establishment of considerable grandeur (at least to a 15-year old) with rich carpets, damask drapes, plush maroon velvet furniture and dimly lit chandeliers. It could have been a Hollywood set for an Istanbul brothel. I was offered a few sips of good rum. (I was somewhat used to it from periodic after-work libation with the crew.) After a few minutes I was introduced to a perfectly gorgeous young brunette. She couldn't have been much older than I (we are speaking of chronology not experience). After a few words of whispered Spanish to my sponsors, she took my hand and very gently led me down a dim, heavily carpeted corridor to a wonderfully scented room dominated by a giant, pillow strewn four-poster brass bed. It was the Arabian Nights; the rum helped a lot.

Well, it was thoroughly spectacular, mostly *terra incognita,* for this dreadfully naive high school junior. But I have always been a fairly quick study, and I learned a great deal. I am not sure how many different positions or how many orgasms (lots), but it was all rather glorious. I seem to remember a trapeze playing a role sometime during the gymnastics. I did not wear a condom, but we "washed up" before and after each adventure. I didn't know then about STDs; I did know about pregnancy, but I had been assured that I was in "clean and safe hands." I was too enthralled to cogitate such details. Apparently, the report to my benefactors, who were anxiously clustered in the bar (I am not sure they could afford this place for themselves) was satisfactory. There was much back slapping as we wandered back to the ship with dawn breaking over a tranquil harbor. I never spoke about this experience to anyone back home. But when my high-school teammates chattered with their usual macho locker-room bravado about sex, I enjoyed a small, complacent smile.

At each stop around the island I managed to sneak ashore and explore. Once I had Mr. Davis' permission to hitchhike overland from Mayaguez to Ponce. It was my first exposure to the wonderment of steamy rain forests. I thumbed a ride with the son of a banker who was a few years older than I. He drove a sleek white Buick convertible, and he took me to his palatial family rancho outside of Ponce. We swam in his pool, and he "introduced" me to sickly-sweet Cuba Libras. (I didn't burst his bubble by telling him I had already met Mr. Ron Rico in the fo'c'sle with my shipmates.) It was all a bit rich and giddying, but I still beat the ship by one day. There was a problem with the ship's engine when we returned to San Juan, and we were delayed in sailing for home. It would have been too close to the start of school to chance a second voyage, so, reluctantly, I bid my shipmates farewell at dockside in Brooklyn. I shed my nobly tattered, proudly rust-stained dungarees and resumed life as just another high-school kid. But, oh, the memories...

# 8

## *Back to the Real World*

✦

*(prosaica—school days and the world of hard work...)*

The following year (1939) I turned 16 and managed to get a driver's license (and work that Christmas for the post office). I already could handle a tractor and operate a hay-bailer, from my summer on the Volland farm. At that time the Glenn L. Martin aircraft plant was in a hustle to construct flying boats, the glorious clippers that opened up the Atlantic and Pacific to air travel. They were building living quarters for workers down near the plant, and the call went out for "experienced truck drivers." I tore down to the hiring shack in the family car and was hired that same afternoon. They didn't even check my driver's license. The money was terrific and the overtime, magnificent. We were wildcatters (loved that sobriquet), so there were no union dues. A couple of ratty-looking teamster guys poked around and muttered darkly about "union busting," but the money was just too good for much recruiting. I thought it wise not to tell my old man; the ex-Young Socialist would not abide such traffic. The building went on at a furious pace, night and day. We kids only worked day shifts.

Friday afternoons some of the guys engaged in a most bizarre exercise. After the whistle blew at about five or six, a bunch of sweaty, grimy workers would hunker down, pass around a bottle of Calvert whiskey, and play "poker hands" with paycheck serial numbers! The highest hand scooped up **all** the other checks. I once saw a bald, snarly

truck driver collect 12 checks worth a few thousand dollars. These were older guys: tough truckers, rangy carpenters, white-powder-doused plasterers, mostly all family men. And they were blowing a whole week of wages. I never played that game. It was my first exposure to serious gambling, and to this day I cannot fathom the "fun" of gambling against enormous odds. At least those birds were playing six or 12 to one; but the lottery or Vegas? (I understand Americans blow 36 billion a year gambling; gimme a break!)

Well, after I had squirreled away about four hundred truck-driving dollars, plus another two hundred I had saved from Christmas (Post Office bonanza) and my slave labor at the meat market, I was loaded. I still had six weeks before school started so I prevailed on my folks to let me hitchhike the country. I told them I was tough (truck driver), smart (honor role), rich (money belt packed with 20s) and experienced in life (Puerto Rico and all that). To my amazement, once again, they let me pursue my heart's desire with the caveat that I call home collect every other night. I was to ask for "Mrs. Helena," mother's first name, and they would say no one by that name lived there. That was the signal that I was okay. Since I would be in a different locale every night, we figured Ma Bell would never catch on. If I was in trouble I would ask for "Dr. Moser," and they would pick up. It worked just fine; a few times I even paid for the call and chatted.

So I hit the road wearing a modified Boy Scout uniform. As I said, it had worked wonders in the past: khaki shirt and shorts, knee-high brown stockings and moccasins. On hot days I would abandon the socks and put on a white T-shirt, but always the broad-brimmed campaign hat. And my good luck held. My dad dropped me on the edge of town, and I began to walk. There were no super-highways in those days and traffic moved a lot more slowly. I always walked briskly between rides, unless I landed at a truck stop or some other strategic locale. But I always stopped to face the traffic, tried to look clean, interesting, pleasant, non-threatening and earnest. I always stuck up my

thumb like I meant it. I was carrying a large (about 40 pounds) back-pack adorned with a Maryland state flag.

After no more than 15 minutes a huge truck pulled over (I am not sure they had 18 wheelers in those days). The driver's name was Glenn. He was headed for Portland, Oregon, and he wanted company to help keep him awake. A home run! Glenn had a crude bunk set up in the back of the cab. He drove for 20 hours, stopping only to pee and grab a hamburger. Then he flaked out in the bunk for four hours while I slept on the seat. He drove another 18 hours; we had a big dinner at an all-night diner, and he slept in a motel cabin for about five hours. I hunkered down in the bunk. We rolled into the warehouse district in Portland after about four and a half grueling days. My first trip across the country was a hazy blur. It was an astonishing demonstration of endurance. Glenn never let me pick up a check. He wasn't exactly chatty, but he managed to tell me about his sexy wife and three little kids. He had been a red-hot halfback on a state championship high-school team in rural Virginia. His wife had been a cheer leader. They got married right out of high school. Kids came quickly, nice house, wanted to buy a farm. Owned his own rig, but he already had hemor-rhoids and hated being away from home so much. Story by Thornton Wilder!

Glenn chain-smoked for about 3000 miles, but he was wiry and tough, all 125 pounds of him. I have always appreciated the tough life of the independent trucker. I marvel at how they manage to stay alive with their wretched, all-fat, enormous-calorie diets and endless hyp-notic hours behind the wheel. I know Glenn did not pop bennies, at least on this trip, although he spoke candidly about their occasional benefit, "better than wheels up in a ditch." Long-haul truck driving was just one more occupation that I could scratch off my list.

I don't remember all the details of my magnificent odyssey, but I met dozens of kind and generous people, spent more than a few nights in spare rooms and was fed more free meals than I cooked or paid for. I visited Seattle, Los Angeles, San Francisco, Phoenix, the Grand Can-

yon (South Rim and hiked to Indian Springs), St. Louis (date with a girl I had known in Baltimore), and New Orleans. I slept in a fourth floor flop—two bits a night—with about 30 raggedy, stinking winos where the temperature hovered at 110 with unspeakable humidity. That was a bitch. These birds were all big boozers and mostly lived on the street. Aiming and flushing in the fetid latrine were unknown art forms. I did not make eye contact and kept to myself. My money belt never left my body. No one ever spoke to me, and that was okay. Slice of ugly life...

From there I landed a single hitch to Chicago along the Mississippi, then Boston, New York and home. At no time was I ever in peril, either from people or traffic. I encountered a few bad drivers, and one old lady in Arizona asked me to drive a few hundred miles. Most people were chatty, impressed with my independence, and curious about where I had been. Some were critical of my parents to "let you do such a dangerous thing," as one elderly gentleman said. When I counted my dough (which I did frequently in rest rooms), I still had about $ 270 in my belt.

(I have been asked if I would have allowed my sons to undertake such a hitchhiking trip when they were 14 or 15. Without question, I would **not**. Things began to change when superhighways were constructed, cars got faster and people seemed to get crazier. [Road rage is a relatively contemporary phenomenon.] Today when I see a young person, especially a girl, hitching along the highway, it floods me with apprehension. When I was practicing on Maui, virtually every few months it seemed, there were reports of pretty blonde girls from California being raped, even killed. I stopped picking up hitchhikers about 30 years ago when I pulled over for a pleasant-looking fellow with a cardboard suitcase. He pulled out a switchblade to clean his yellow fingernails and muttered, archly, that it would be "most kindly" if I could drop him at a town a few miles beyond my intended destination. He seemed to be responding to hallucinatory voices, but he did get out. I was damned lucky; many others have been far less fortunate. You hear

about them on the evening news. I know it is a cliche, but the 1930s were a gentler, less dangerous time. *Triste dictu*.)

When I returned to City after my wanderings, I started the "Travel Club." We would write to different states and countries (Chambers of Commerce and Bureaus of Tourism) for maps and brochures describing the charms and wonders of their environs. Each week a different club member was obliged to report on one of the states or countries that had responded. Within a few months we had over 100 members (all sort of nerdy Richard Halliburton wannabes). It was one of the most popular extra-curricular clubs in the school. We built up a tremendous library. The experience simply whetted my appetite to explore the world.

# 9

## College Years

✦

### (the intervention of war and things indirectly related...)

C ollege was a problem. As I have said, my folks had no experience with "college." No one in our family had ever been involved in higher education. My father had attended a chiropractic college in New York, but that was more of a trade school. We were still struggling financially (it seemed we always were), and "wasn't there a perfectly good college just up Charles Street?"—Loyola of Baltimore. So I could live at home and bike (or trolley) to class, and it was cheap. I think tuition was about $400 per year. Who knew from Harvard or Hopkins or Stanford. The fact was we just could not afford better, and besides "if you study, you learn, no matter where you are—right?"

So I was set to go to Loyola. It was 1940 and the desperate war in Europe was front page stuff. Our side was losing. The bad guys were blitzing London nightly, and Roosevelt had just "leased" some ancient destroyers to Britain over the howls of a Wheeler-dominated, ultra-conservative Congress. Lindbergh was extolling the virtues of the Third Reich and their invincible armed forces. The mood of the country was dark and distinctly isolationist. Some kids I knew had immigrated to Canada to join the RCAF or the RAF. They wanted to "fight Hitler." I muttered about it once or twice, but "such foolishness" was not open to discussion around our dinner table. It was before the Holocaust had

become a known entity, or my argument might have flashed a few more teeth.

For the summer, I was exiled to Mountain Lake Park, Maryland. I became a desk clerk-porter-bus boy-telephone operator-bookkeeper in a resort hotel for the summer. I don't remember how I got that job, but it was probably another satisfied patient of dad's. This was a rambling, clapboard place that had seen better days; it bore a redolence of long-past, aristocratic elegance. The hotel sat in a sun-dappled, sycamore grove in one of the loveliest forest settings I can ever remember. Mountain Lake Park was in extreme western Maryland; you could step into West Virginia. Two sweet old ladies owned and ran it. We had a flock of kids about my age doing all the chores.

One of the waitresses was a most comely young thing from a nearby town; she had been first runner-up in a Miss West Virginia contest. Her room was just down the hall from mine. (I had died and gone to heaven!) But she was "pledged" to a soon-to-be-sent-overseas soldier. We did a lot of very heavy petting, and I think she would have made "serious love" (her words) with me if I would "pledge" to her. The fiancée-soldier was safely sequestered in some remote camp and "besides he never writes." But West Virginia style pledging bore some overtones of commitment and raw-bone, shot-gun justice (Hatfields and McCoys and all that). Hardly a proper agenda for this up and coming college person. So we just spent the summer in tempestuous mutual frustration, just about everything but penetration.

I learned a lot that summer, even about the hotel business. Sleepy, seedy Mountain Lake saw a great deal of transient trade, especially on weekends. I became reasonably adept at keeping books (I hated it, remember analytic geometry?), clearing and setting tables (not as bad as keeping books), mixing exotic drinks (a Singapore what?), and smiling at fussy patrons whose hot water ran cold or encountered an itinerant cockroach exploring a closet. But it was a good summer. I knew I didn't want to become an innkeeper, bookkeeper, bar tender, or tourist flunky as a permanent career. I seemed to be running out of options.

Loyola College was a small Jesuit school with an undistinguished faculty, academically invisible in the world of higher education. It was hardly a place for intellectual awakening, but there were two teachers who were outstanding. One was Father McCarran, dedicated disciple of English literature. He was a noble chronic alcoholic who had the presence and bearing of a Shakespearean actor of the old school. He could have been trodding the boards at the Globe as he strode back and forth across the classroom, reciting Lear and Hamlet from memory. He was tall, gaunt, with a bald pate fringed with a silvery rim. Our class of boorish louts thought he was funny drunk ("he never flunks anyone"). But I loved him. For months he would vanish, banished to some isolated Jesuit retreat to dry out. But he turned me on to the classics. Many years later, when I was a medical resident at Georgetown, somehow I heard that Father McCarran was the priest of an impoverished parish somewhere in Foggy Bottom. I looked him up and took him to dinner. We had a pleasant but sad visit. He was no longer in the Order, and he seemed much smaller. I detected flagrant signs of hepatic cirrhosis. The old Shakespearean fire had long since been extinguished. He died a few months later.

The other teacher I remember was a brilliant, effeminate, painfully literate historian. I didn't know much about homosexuality in those days. "Gay" had not yet been co-opted as a non-toxic euphemism; it still meant "fun loving." But in retrospect, Mr. Wallace was unabashedly gay. Where Father McCarran excited my love of old books, Mr. Wallace introduced me to the exciting world of Joyce, Dos Passos, Saroyan, Conrad, Wolfe, Steinbeck, Hemingway, *et al.* He carried me far from the prescribed curriculum. Of course, I was one of those boring "premeds," hopelessly immersed in the doldrums of chemistry, biology, physics, mathematics and such. But my true loves were the classes with McCarran and Wallace.

The semi-monthly, four-page Loyola newspaper was a joke compared to our weekly, six-page high school "Collegian." It would have been a step down to work with those clods. I ran on the mile relay

team, but I never crackled 52 seconds, positively plodding by today's androgenic standards. But we placed second at the Penn Relays in our class two years in a row. I also played freshman football (right end—before wide receivers were invented). I enjoyed the body contact; tackling on defense and blocking on offense. Of course we played all 60 minutes with no change of wet uniforms at half time. Our version of macho. I must confess, I really did not enjoy or admire much of Loyola of Baltimore.

By 1942, we were well into the war. I told my folks I wanted to fly for the navy. Their enthusiasm surged to about the same titer as when I had suggested Canada and the RAF a few years earlier. Nada. But by the time I was completing my sophomore year, the navy had created the V-12 program. It enabled pre-med students to complete their training, go on to medical school (if they were accepted) and then serve as navy doctors. "But mom, it's all free, and I could be drafted into the army in a few months." I don't know which was the more compelling argument, but I was allowed to apply and was accepted. I raised my right hand on December 8,1942, one year and one day after Pearl Harbor. Somewhat to my surprise I was assigned to Villanova College not the University of Pennsylvania, as I had requested. The navy logic was soon obvious: I was attending a Catholic college, so I was assigned to an Augustinian analogue of Jesuit Loyola.

It was a tense, exciting time. Small, parochial Villanova had been invaded by 600 teen-aged sailors and marines. I think the total enrollment had been about 300 snobbish Main Line kids before we took over. We were all stacked six to a room with triple-tiered bunks. Study was a bitch. The library was always jammed and seating at one of the two desks in the room was tightly programmed. So we all bought reading lamps and studied mostly in our bunks. The college must have made a bundle from the military. The food was terrible: institutional starches and tasteless gray meat that challenged molars and mandibles. Everyone grumbled. We all policed our barracks, so there was no requirement for much janitorial help. They provided food, lodging,

laundry (starched unto death) and uninspired teaching. (I had occasion to visit St. Davids many years later and paused at Villanova. The campus was magnificently landscaped; they had about trebled the number of buildings and doubled the capacity of the stadium. Perhaps cynically, I mused that the good Fathers had been amply compensated for their contribution to the war effort.)

The war continued to rage all over the world. The Japanese had taken Singapore, but Jimmy Doolittle had fire-bombed Tokyo and the Brits were reciprocating the blitz by blasting Germany. At Villanova we were having a small conflict of our own. Everything was under forced draft. We were up at 5:30 for a three-mile run and serious calisthenics. We were taking all courses in concentrated form, trying to jam two years of pre-med into one. Every Friday afternoon the bulletin board would carry the names of students in the bottom 10% of the class. Those poor unlucky navy bastards were immediately shipped off to Bainbridge Naval Training Station. I think the washed-out marines went to Parris Island. The navy guys became "ninety-day wonder" ensigns, and most of them were assigned to rear deck gun crews on Kaiser-built freighters running the U-boat blockade to Murmansk. Or so went the prevailing scuttlebutt.

My life at Villanova was saved by dear Mary. Ironically, it was one of my roommates, Tom (who was convinced that my Jewish soul was condemned to hell, since I had been afforded a chance to see the light of Jesus and respectfully declined), who introduced me to sweet Mary. She was a very Catholic, very well-endowed honey blonde who went to Rosemont, a very Catholic girls college close by our campus. Mary had it all. Her father, "Call me Mac," was a well-heeled Philadelphia wholesale jeweler. They belonged to a three classy country clubs, and Mary drove her own bright red Pontiac convertible. On Saturday around noon, she would glide up to the edge of the parade ground, bemused at our sloppy drill. When we broke formation, I would race to the car, toss in my overnight bag, and we would zip off to the muttering envy of the other 599 grunts.

Some weekends I had to study, but most of the time we were off and running. Ice skating at Haverford Pond, dinner at the Ben Franklin (I paid), a weekend (with her folks) at Seaview Country Club near Atlantic City. Life at Villanova became thoroughly bearable. We only had one really bad time. One night after dinner at the Bellevue Stratford, Mary said she wanted to visit some bar on South Street that her friends at Rosemont had been whispering about. It had a naughty reputation as being "raunchy" (her word). It was a most un-Mary-like request. She had always been so lady-like, almost prissy (especially in public). But she was so sweet and compliant, how could I refuse? Besides how raunchy can a place be? Big mistake.

I was wearing summer whites, and she had some sort of beigy, lacy, clingy dress that did little to conceal her attributes. The bar was dark and smoky, filled with soldiers, sailors, bums and bimbos enjoying a typical Saturday night on South Street. We were interlopers, obviously in the wrong place. What happened in the next few minutes remains a blur. Almost as soon as we could find a place at the bar, I remember a very inebriated G.l. stumbling over, roughly shoving me aside, and wrapping his arm around Mary. He pushed a grungy face next to hers and murmured some obscenity. There have been perhaps three times in my life when I have lost complete control. It happens in a microsecond, a mindless reflex flash. In sudden fury, I tapped him on the shoulder with my left hand and when he turned, I hit him with my right. He must have had his mouth open because I felt a tooth snap. My third knuckle was laid open to the bone. Mary was drenched with blood on her bodice, and I was streaming crimson. Someone must have shoved us out of there, and we caught a cab to the Pennsylvania Hospital. My laceration took four sutures; the knuckle still aches on rainy days. We never spoke of the incident.

As had happened once before (and would again), Mary suggested we might get married before things got "really serious." It was a sort of Main Line version of the Mountain Lake scenario. A few times our sweaty hunger almost got out of hand, and I really never thought about

marriage. I didn't love Mary; I lusted after her. And I realized the difference.

(I think a little lust adds significant energy to "love," but it is just one dimension of a most complex, most-difficult-to-define human emotion. Love may be the most versatile (if not abused) word in our language. It moves with grammatical grace from noun to verb. It is used to express the perception of joy derived from every sense and much more. One might ask, what do these things have in common: Van Gogh's sunflowers, the scent of roses, Beethoven's Fifth, the feel of velvet, the Grand Canyon, the New York Times, the Green Bay Packers, your cat, your daughter, your spouse? We **love** them. Sometimes I think each type of "love" deserves its own word. But probably not; we know what each means. Love works. I don't think I really understood love of man and woman until I met my second wife. But that is a much later part of this story.

It may be appropriate to talk about concepts of sex in the forties. Before the sexual revolution that resulted from introduction of "the pill," penile-vaginal intercourse (it seems we are obliged to define what we mean these days) was a much more serious business. It had little (nothing?) to do with morality. It had to do with getting a woman pregnant. Even the threat of gonorrhea and syphilis (the dominant STDs) was less a worry. So one was obliged to use a condom. And we all had problems buying condoms. Usually pharmacists or the people [invariably women] who worked the drug store counter, kept the Trojans on a shelf accessible only to them. I am sure they did it on purpose. So you had to ask, and you knew that they knew, what you were about. So it was an embarrassing chore.

Also, it usually took a long time to "make the move," since first date sex was virtually unknown. I never had the occasion [opportunity?] to date an "easy girl." Most of the time after a few dates, most girls would allow just about everything but penetration. Oral sex was extremely rare, and I suspect much of the bragging about "blow jobs" was locker room bravado. And there was a lot of that. Occasionally girls would get

pregnant and that was a dreadful mess. Abortion was a sordid business you read about, performed in a dirty motel room by a pimply doctor with filthy fingernails who had lost his license. We knew very little about the tragedy of coat-hanger abortions and sepsis and death. As I said, we all knew about syphilis and gonorrhea, but pregnancy was the big no-no. I just never could bring myself to purchase condoms, so I confined myself to masturbation (especially before a hot date) and heavy petting. It was terribly unsatisfying.

From the comfortable retrospect of the "enlightened millennium" my attitude in the unenlightened 40s may seem anachronistic, a medieval throwback to chastity belts, knightly vows of eternal celibacy and all that rot. Probably. But I must admit a bias. The sexual revolution of the 60s that made a roll in the hay the emotional equivalent of a goodnight kiss never seemed all that liberating to me. And the legacy? Escalating rates of teen pregnancy [pill notwithstanding], a raft of unloved and unwanted kids, dead-beat dads, the alarming rising incidence of STDs [including AIDS] among adolescents and all the other dreadful baggage, have done little to enrich the soul, spirit and substance. And my timorous attitude about serious sex was common among those of my generation. Not that many would ever admit it.

But there is a reverse [perverse?] side to this coin. In retrospect, I will confess, not learning how to please a woman in bed was a big mistake. I should have bit the damn bullet, braved the smirking broad behind the cash register and bought the lousy rubbers. My lack of experience came to haunt me later in life.)

But back to sweet Mary. On several occasions I attended early mass with her, but the religion thing was just too heavy. I felt obliged to tell her that I was Jewish. She didn't blink an eye; Tom had already warned her months ago! She said I could "keep my religion" if I agreed to raise the kids Catholic. Well, at that time I wasn't much into Judaism, but I certainly wasn't into Catholicism or anything else. And even thinking about kids of my own was about as ethereal a concept as flying off to Mars. Our relationship just wasn't working, and we both knew it. We

parted friends. A few years later I heard that she married a nice Catholic stock broker and had a flock of handsome kids. I saw her once many years later. She still looked chic and appealing.

But I was having another more serious crisis of conscience. It was 1943 and our troops were catching hell in the froth and blood of the Pacific, Italy and North Africa. And here I was bitching about trivia and enjoying the high life on the Philadelphia Main Line. I felt guilty as hell. And the feeling never abated until I was immersed in the hot war in Korea in 1950. After about a year, I had enough credits for medical school. I applied to Johns Hopkins, Maryland and Georgetown. You know the "Hopkins Story," but I was accepted by Maryland and Georgetown. I was assured the navy would send me to one or the other. But the fall semester was to start in September and it was May or June. So I was placed on orders to the National Naval Medical Center at Bethesda for the interim.

Sometime before our "graduation" at Villanova, the navy announced the "V-5" preflight program. They called for volunteers from our V-12 (pre-med) program. Apparently the navy needed carrier pilots more than it needed doctors. About a dozen of us rushed to sign up, but parental consent was required. That weekend I wedged my way aboard a train at Penn Station packed with service men, wives, sweethearts. I felt like a skulking impostor in my dress blues. It exacerbated my guilt. Silently, I rehearsed the speech I had prepared for my folks. Well, you can guess the outcome. I think my dad might have relented, but mother (once again) was the alpha parent. After a few salvos from both sides, I retreated, stormed out of the house and slinked back to the train station.

In all probability they saved my life. Many of the kids who were flying off carriers in those early days perished. One of my friends from Villanova made it to the Pacific. Many years later, over some beers in a bar in Honolulu, when he was a commander-squadron leader at Barber's Point, he told me he had been forced on two occasions to ditch his Corsair after running out of fuel (when his carrier had been obliged

to take evasive action while under radio silence). By the grace of God, he had been spotted and picked up each time. Of course, after a few weeks I cooled down and made peace with my folks. But the guilt was unrelenting.

# 10

## *The Bethesda Interlude*

✦

### *(lots of opportunities, but no, dumbo…)*

Bethesda was a drag. I was an apprentice seaman, the lowest rank in the universe. I was assigned to the Streptococcal Typing Laboratory, and I washed lab glassware during the day and drove the ambulance every third night. Easy duty. I later discovered that the lieutenant commander-bacteriologist who ran the lab had spent the preceding ten years developing techniques to identify various strains of streptococcus and was creating specific vaccines. It was work worthy of consideration in Stockholm, but for one thing. Alexander Fleming had discovered penicillin! And that magical stuff killed **all** strains of Strep (and other gram-positive bacteria). No need to identify specific strains and develop vaccines. Ten years of hard work down the tubes. Perhaps with the emergence of resistant strains of many microorganisms in recent years, his work might be resurrected. He was a gentle man who always seemed a bit sad. He taught me a lot of bacteriology. And I sure could produce a spanking clean test tube.

It was during this time of "emotional dilemma" that I met Evelyn. She sorely challenged my resolve about casual sex and with malice aforethought. I don't recall how we met, but she was a tall, willowy blonde with a great body, a terrible tease. I was smitten early on; it was lust at first sight. She lived in Frederick and attended Hood College. I would take a bus or hitchhike up to that pleasant village on Friday nights and spend the weekend, often at her home. Her folks seemed to

like me. They were an old "first family;" a state park had been named after her grandfather. Before too long it all became quite serious; I even took Evvie home to meet my folks. They were enchanted with her family, smarts and obvious class. I wanted to take her to bed pretty badly, and she had expressed similar feelings. My resolve was fading fast.

But I was having problems sorting out emotions. Then we discovered a monumental stumbling block. Evvie knew I was due to start medical school in a few months, but she insisted that I volunteer for a "90-day wonder" OCS school, accept a commission as a line ensign, and "could get married right away." I was a trifle stunned, but reflected on it over a long, sleepless weekend. (An ensign is exactly what I would have been had I not kept up good grades at Villanova!) It just did not compute. If she really loved me, how could she ask me to give up my chance to become a doctor? I was so far down the track toward medical school that it seemed unfair. I argued that we could get married while I was in school. I had a few friends (perhaps two couples) who were fighting that battle. It was a rugged road, but then "true love would prevail." Well, soon it became evident, for reasons best known to Evvie, that she wanted to get married **now** and, preferably, to an officer. I began to realize that despite all the passion and promises, **that** officer was not necessarily me. It was a crushing blow, but I stopped hitchhiking to Frederick. About a year later, I heard that she married a local boy who had just been graduated from West Point. They did it right: stone chapel at the Point, arch of crossed sabers, colors, bugles—the whole nine yards. I never saw her again. There were many Waves and lady Marines at Bethesda. I dated, did a lot of heavy petting, but refrained from actual intercourse. Reflecting back on that time in my young life, I am at a loss…

My time at Bethesda passed slowly, awaiting September. Aside from the experience with microbiology, the only other notable event was my first exposure to death, up close and personal. Our ambulance team brought in a young Marine lance corporal who was comatose. He died within a few days of meningococcal meningitis. All those who had

come in contact were placed under quarantine for a week; there was no effective prophylaxis or treatment. It was a scary few days.

# 11

## *Medical School Years*

✦

### *(the work ethic and little else...)*

With no reluctance whatever, at long last I packed away my "swabbie suits" (bell bottoms and pull-over blouses) and splurged on winter and summer midshipman uniforms. I was an "officer candidate" now that medical school was imminent. I cannot deny the psychological boost of a simple change of uniform. Snobbishness? Guilty as charged. I found a rooming house within walking distance of the medical school at 35th street and Reservoir Road. Four other students shared adjacent rooms, three navy and one civilian. Dick DuPree had been one of my five roommates at Villanova, my dearest friend. Jock was a bright but painfully self-effacing soul, the living embodiment of self-fulfilling, dire prophecy. He was the product of an overbearing father, pallid mother and genius-like, elder, "already a doctor" sister. He washed out after the second year. George was a handsome, low-key workhorse who was bland, almost invisible. Joe was a trifle-too-cocky enigma, who had remained a civilian (under somewhat mysterious circumstances, no evident disability except for an unpleasant personality). I thought he was unrelentingly boring and cold and would not make a very good "people doctor." Except for Dick, I rarely socialized with the other guys. We all respected each other's time and space.

The first day, our noble dean (preceded by a formidable reputation as a petty tyrant who hated doctors—wonderful credential for the

leader of a medical school) strode to the lectern at the base of a cavernous amphitheater. It would be our lecture hall for the next two years. He was a stubby priest with butch-cut red hair. He postured shamelessly in stark silence, staring ominously at our terrified class: navy, army (ROTC) and a handful of civilian freshmen. Then he uttered the infamous words that came to epitomize our first years. They are etched into my memory. "Look to those on either side of you, because at the end of these four years only one of you will graduate." And that evil little man was almost correct. We started with 126; we were 76 upon graduation.

I did not enjoy the pre-clinical years. It was mostly rote memory, like parroting the lines of a bad play. It seemed irrelevant to our ultimate mission of learning enough about medicine to take care of sick people. I rationalized the enormous expenditure of time and intellectual energy by accepting that some wise men must have devised this system as some form of mental discipline, like studying calculus. The methodology must have been designed to exercise unchallenged areas of the brain. (From the advantage of 50 years of retrospect, most of the first two years was a waste of time, except for the development of lifelong habits of study discipline.)

I must admit, since my "being a doctor" was such a given in our family, I had not reflected much upon the deeper significance of dedicating my life to medicine. I am not given to lengthy introspection, and existentialist thought always seemed an intellectual indulgence in "how many angels..." I concede it is perhaps a failing, a fault line in the contour of my psychological development. Initially, I wanted to be a doctor because I enjoyed making people feel better (reinforced by my voyage as "ship's doctor" on the Emelia, where I first encountered the remarkable respect and admiration "doctoring" engendered). Later, it became obvious that I lacked the talent and imagination to become a great writer, although English and literature were my favorite subjects. In college, the life sciences came easier than mathematics and physical sciences. Finally, the study of medicine was comfortable, and once in

the clinical years, I began to relish the intellectual detective work of trying to sort out clues from history, physical examination and laboratory work to identify diagnostic possibilities and select appropriate treatment. To see the beneficial results of one's endeavors was an unsurpassing source of gratification.

I must confess no burning moment of epiphany about personal mission, no searing drive to save mankind ("Schweitzer" was a philosophic concept, not a career option to me.) Nor did I feel the urge to seek Nobel recognition. And in those days, clinical medicine was not a pathway to great fortune. Medicine promised an intellectually stimulating lifetime vocation with ample emotional and financial reward. I admit, it doesn't sound very ennobling, but to attribute my attitude to a "higher calling" would be sophistry.

Early on in medical school (1944), I was impressed about how **very little** we knew about human beings. Some bright person once said, "As the radius of our knowledge increases, the circumference of our ignorance expands even more." Perhaps a tiresome observation, but the amazing intricacy and complexity of the human organism continues to evolve, with almost daily revelations that were (and still are) beyond my imagination. One example: the lymphocyte. We were taught that this innocent, round blood cell with a large nucleus was somehow involved in fighting infection, but no one knew just how. Compared to the colorful and diverse polymorphonuclear leukocytes, the lowly lymphocyte was largely ignored. It sort of reminds me of today when geneticists speak of long segments of "useless DNA" that lie between the "active" genes.

Well, the simple "frog" lymphocyte has emerged as the "prince" of the immune system, in all its infinite complexity. And now when I try to comprehend the literature of immunology and genetic engineering (not to speak of arcane statistical analyses), I am always humbled by my own "expanding circumference of ignorance." As I have said before, the progressive evolution of knowledge in molecular biology and genetic engineering bears the promise of revolutionizing medicine

more than any other factors in the long history of our art/science. I wonder if physicians 50 years hence will feel the same way. Probably.

From the first day I became a Study Machine. I realized that there were perhaps, a half-dozen or more classmates who were as smart or smarter than I. The top handful emerged quickly from the pack. But I was determined to compensate by working harder. Dick DuPree, bless his lucky heart, had a photographic memory. One glance and he seemed to understand and remember. In college I had always studied about two hours a night; in medical school I upped this to five. Before major exams I would study entire weekends with time out only for a few hours to eat and sleep. It became an obsession. The kid who felt guilty (for not having done his homework) when he emerged into the sunlight after the Saturday matinee, had morphed into full-fledged compulsive.

Our routine was simple. After class about 4:00 p.m. we would dump our books home and troop over to a Greek restaurant on Wisconsin Avenue. The owner-cook was a huge, affable émigré from Thessalonica. By the grace of God he had a soft spot in his ample heart for medical students. For a few bucks one could assemble a vast array of tangy, steaming food. I am sure it was loaded with bountiful calories and lovely saturated fat, but I recall those meals with great affection. After the years of drab institutional fare at Villanova and Bethesda it was downright festive. If you were low on funds, Nick would allow you to run a tab until the end of the month. The same was true of the barbershop a few blocks further down Wisconsin. Two giant, coffee-colored brothers wearing sneakers with "bunion holes" snipped away ("What can you do for bunions, Doc?") clipped our hair military style. Again, they would carry you on the cuff; no one ever stiffed them. Years later I went back; both establishments had vanished, replaced by up-scale, cutesy boutiques. I'll bet **they** don't carry impecunious medical students till the end of the month. Great loss.

I would get back to my room by six, shut the door and study compulsively until eleven. Dick and Joe would usually stack the books

about nine-thirty and play double solitaire for an hour or so. Jock always seemed to be wandering from room to room. But after a few uninvited social diversions I declared my digs off-limits but for specific questions about the work. I don't know how George spent his time, except that he was in love with a childhood sweetheart and wrote to her a lot. Most weekends I remained in my cell and studied. Very rarely I would go out on a date. "Available" women were bountiful and hungry in D.C. during the war. But I had little time or inclination for more than heavy petting. Nothing ever got close to "serious." In retrospect it was a strange sort of mindless voluntary celibacy. About once a month I would take the train to Baltimore to visit the folks. I had my old room set up for study. The folks, brother Ken (now smashing academic records in high school) and sister Joan, who must have been seven or eight, honored the "rules of quiet when Bob is home."

The first major hurdle for Georgetown freshmen was the infamous anatomy "Head and Neck" examination. The folklore (from sophomores, always eager to exacerbate the terror) was that if you busted "Head and Neck," just forget it. You were out! It was accepted as gospel. The professor, Dr. Othmar Solnitzky, was a very short, stocky, completely bald gentleman who, in addition to being a dynamic, even dramatic, teacher of gross anatomy, nurtured a subtle streak of de Sade. For example, he scheduled the notorious make-or-break exam on the very day we were due to return from Christmas holiday. Of course, this meant that us obsessive-compulsives would consume about 90% of that festive season curled up with dreary anatomy texts and reams of notes.

The final manifestation of his peculiar sadistic demeanor came in distributing the grades. Would dear old Solly post them on the bulletin board (bad enough *deja vu* for those of us who had endured Fateful Friday afternoons at Villanova), like all other teachers? Oh no, we need a bit of theater here. We would be summoned in small clusters, and then called individually into his giant, potted palm cluttered sanctum. Our gnome-like Grand Inquisitor would be stationed behind an enor-

mous, paper-littered, book-strewn desk. Well, here it was, the ultimate challenge to my mantra. ("If you study earnestly and understand the material, the test is designed to be passed!") I recited that homily to myself every night before troubled sleep—until I almost believed it.

I remember the tableaux as though it were yesterday. Moment of truth: Moser at attention, Solly peering over his Ben Franklins. Deafening silence, interminable pause. He looks up. "You pass." No smile. No handshake. But I had just won the heavyweight championship of the whole damned world! That night we celebrated. All the roommates passed. We rarely drank beer, but that night we bought imported beer for the glorious Greek, the fabulous haircut brothers and our magnificent land lady, all of whom were absolutely wonderful and totally attuned to the *gravitas* of "Head and Neck." And, truth be told, those who failed seemed not to graduate. To this day I don't know if it was voodoo self-hypnosis, classic self-fulfilling prophecy, or if the test bore an unworldly prescience. It was not the most difficult exam we took from an intellectual aspect, but it was unsurpassed in its psychological power. I didn't sweat as much over my Internal Medicine specialty examinations.

Our other professors were more prosaic. "Histology" was distinguished by extraordinary ambidexterity; it enabled him to draw embryos on the black board with astonishing symmetry. At times I found myself more fascinated by his artistic virtuosity than the subject material. "Pathology" was an ancient retired army colonel (known, of course, as "The Colonel"), who drew the unfortunate assignment of lecturing at 1:00 P.M. The problem: most often lunchtime yielded to a quick sandwich and a rigorous session of touch football. At times in the depths of summer more than half the class was deep in sweaty somnolence as the crumbling Colonel droned on, oblivious to his semicomatose audience. "Physiology" was a mean-spirited, unusually seedy mutterer who suggested that we purchase his mimeographed "textbook." The rumor (once again spread by the ever-helpful upper classmen) was that despite being issued the classic, tried and true

physiology text, "Best and Taylor," most all examination information would come from his mimeographed notes. It was a scam, but we all played the game. The other teachers were even less exciting.

The summer of 1944 was also memorable in that the Redskins were using the Georgetown practice field for their pre-season workouts. I saw the legendary (even then) Sammy Baugh routinely toss the ball with pin point accuracy 70 yards. His perfect-spiral punts averaged 60 yards. He only ran often enough to keep the enemy honest. It was still single-wing offense, before Shaughnessy invented the T-formation. Most players went offense and defense. There were no androgenic steroids or weight-rooms (or selective breeding?) to produce 350 pound tackles, Olympic speed wide-receivers and kamikaze "special teams." It was undeniably a less spectacular game than today, but I haven't seen any Sammy Baughs in recent years.

The second year started a few weeks after the conclusion of the first, no summer vacation. On May 8,1945, the Allies had celebrated V-E Day. For us it was a day of joy and reflection. The war in the Pacific was still raging, and many combat-ravaged troops were being ferried from Europe to Asia. And here we sat on our safe, fat asses in classrooms griping about exams. Dick and I spoke of volunteering as navy corpsmen. They could really use us with our "medical knowledge" (of course we had never laid eyes on a patient). I spoke to our navy NCO commandant, a veteran of Midway; he was amused but indulgent. He said something like, "The navy has too much invested in you, for you to give it up now. Thanks but no thanks. Your turn will come." That did not assuage my guilt.

The navy allowance covered our basic needs (books, lab fees, tuition and some loose change). I considered it most generous, but it did not allow for much frivolous spending. So I began to work nights in the hospital clinical chemistry laboratory. The hottest item of equipment was the sexy new flame photometer. It enabled us to do serum sodium and potassium determinations, a great leap forward in managing many disorders characterized by electrolyte imbalances. The gadget was tem-

peramental and devilish to standardize. We were never certain of our results. We did blood (not serum) glucose, blood urea nitrogen and a few others by chemical means, painfully crude by modern standards. I did blood studies: hematocrit, hemoglobin, calculated indices and read morphology from smears. Also I typed and cross-matched for emergency transfusions. My previous Bethesda experience enabled me to work in the microbiology section. As the new hired hand I drew graveyard shift. That was okay; I could study between procedures. Mostly the lab work was boring and it consumed about three to four hours of sleep. But the boss said it was "invaluable experience," and it paid a few bucks.

We encountered our first patients in the middle of the second year (very progressive, in most other schools it was a third year experience). Dealing with sick people was traumatic for student and patient. We learned to do "histories and physicals," usually fourth hand after the intern, resident and attending physician. You may well imagine the delight of any patient, especially the sicker ones, when this amateur quasi-doctor came to ask the same questions and prod the same organs. It was part of the drill. But I seemed to have a facility for this. I enjoyed talking to patients and families. I always took too long, but it seemed important to really get to "know" the patient beyond the traditional signs and symptoms. Instinctively, I felt that factors such as family relationships, job satisfaction, income, past emotional experiences and other non-traditional phenomena, all contributed to signs and symptoms and could affect outcome and prognosis. I could never dissociate the person from the patient. I think it was a legacy from my father.

(Truthfully, as a student I actually spent **more** time with each patient than at any other time in my medical career. It is a sad commentary. It has only been in the past few decades that we have formally integrated "quality of life" into outcome evaluations. Even now it is difficult to educate some physicians that it is the **patient's** quality of life that we should be concerned about, not the physician's interpretation of that quality. But we have moved considerably beyond "morbid-

ity and mortality" as the principal criteria for judging the effectiveness of treatment. The outcome equation has become appropriately complex and comprehensive, sort of like people.

I have written in the past, many places and many times, about the problem of educating physicians and other "health care providers" [another unfortunate euphemism contributed by the new Centurions of medical management, along with "consumers" rather than patients] about how to be a human being. It still seems to me that sensitivity and compassion cannot be "taught." They are virtues that come from very early exposure as a small child, probably at mother's knee [assuming such tender anatomy is available these hurried days]. I think that by the time one gets to medical school it is often too late. And the experience in medical school often seems to exacerbate the problem. We seem to delight in leaching out the humanity from students and replacing it with data and statistics. We teach Oslerian detachment under the false rubric "equanimity," rather than personal involvement, advocacy and compassion. We have done [and still do] a lousy job in the creation of sensitive doctors. Sadly, it is a rare occurrence these days for students and house officers to come under the influence of a passionate, charismatic, scientifically solid teacher who stresses the virtues of "listening to the patient," thoughtfulness and concern for the total person bearing the illness(s). To add to the problem, with the finance-generated limitation on time allowed for patients to remain "in-hospital" these days—bedside teaching has taken another serious blow. There is too much haste; too much machinery; too few patients.

As a student I was appalled at the phenomenon of how we conducted "teaching bedside rounds." I speak of the habitual, callous indifference to the feelings of the patient. Here is some poor, frightened soul, desperately concerned about his/her illness. [Or else why would she be in a teaching hospital?] In my day, the bed was usually on an open ward or in a four-to six-bed bay. The thin cotton curtain was drawn and Herr Professor and his formidable flotilla of white coats would cluster in silence around the helpless, vastly outnumbered,

supine body. There might have been a cursory greeting from the *gehe-imrat*, most often not. One of the white coats would produce a chart and begin to recite to the assemblage, details of the most intimate aspects of the patient's history and physical examination. The terms could be terrifying, the words incomprehensible scientific jargon. Then the leader might perform a perfunctory examination while the other white coats watch. In those days, the entourage would usually be all male, and sensitivity to exposure of vital areas was rarely a high priority. Usually females got a better deal but not invariably.

Then there followed a Q and A dialogue that flowed over the inert form, also conducted in that foreign tongue. The patient might even be invited to speak, but rarely. The entire tableaux always bore a grotesque Kafkaesque aura; the patient did not exist. A few orders were usually barked, some notes scribbled in the chart, and, perhaps, a word or two of explanation or encouragement, but not always. Then the grand flotilla would drift downstream to the next bed. This may be somewhat of an exaggeration, but I have experienced teaching rounds conducted with insensitivity that bordered on cruelty.

I am told this bedside ritual no longer occurs. (Why do I doubt that?) In my years as a clinical teacher, l insisted that teaching rounds be conducted in a courteous, sensitive manner, ever mindful of the patient. Rounds can be a valuable exercise to help convince the patient that these white-coated geniuses gathered around the bed are devoting their enormous intellectual energy into solving **her** problem. They are seeking answers that might improve her life. The patient was always incorporated into the discussion, treated with respect and provided comprehensible explanations when such were known. My flotillas (some armadas) rarely left a bedside without the patient feeling that the encounter had been helpful and productive. It is an opportunity to combine the science and art of medicine. The patient who feels she is part of the team always does just a bit better. I was so impressed with this aspect of teaching that I wrote a book about the "proper" education of internal medicine house officers.

As a clinical student I came to realize that patients were [still] people. In all my years in teaching medicine I never allowed colleagues or students to refer to patients as though they were organs ("cardiac" or "cirrhotic" or "alcoholic"), or worse ("gomers" or "veggies"). Such demeaning language bespeaks a callousness and arrogance that has no place in medicine, especially in a dialogue with or about sick people. I purposefully cautioned thoughtless students, nurses and colleagues, always out of earshot of patients. I deplored and did not permit casual conversation (elevators and cafeteria) about patients within hearing range of other patients or staff. I know that many of my associates thought I was obsessive in conducting this idiosyncratic, Quixotic crusade against such semantic violence. They were wrong. I once wrote an angry column about a despicable book, "The House of God," that made a dark joke of such vulgar behavior.)

It was in my third year that I realized that internal medicine was to be my life's work. Initially I had been intrigued by neurology. The remarkable diagnostic detective work that was made possible by an intimate knowledge of neuroanatomy, and then conducting a meticulous neurological examination that could pinpoint the lesion, was fascinating. As a student, I was exposed to two great Boston neurologists (conducting Grand Rounds at Georgetown), Derek Denny-Brown and Raymond Adams. They were diagnostic wizards. But the inadequacy of treatments for so many dreadful neurological disorders (e.g. multiple sclerosis, stroke, Alzheimer's, Parkinson's, etc.) was discouraging. Internal medicine disorders seemed more amenable to treatment. You need an occasional victory.

For a time I thought about psychiatry. But I could never come to grips with the softness of the data base. I had read some of Freud and Jung and felt that application of their theories to management of patients with serious mental illness required a leap of non-scientific faith I could not abide. (In recent years, the emergence of drugs that can effect neurotransmitters and their receptors in the brain and actually help patients with schizophrenia, depression, obsessive-compulsive

disorder and attention deficit disorder, suggests that the previous efforts at long-term psychotherapy, (months-years on the couch) was a function of ignorance and frustration. Some psychiatrists have been loath to abandon their traditional practices and have been reluctant to accept the psycho-pharmaceutical revolution. And, in some instances, pharmacotherapy plus behavior modification seems to offer more than either alone. One might argue that conventional, months-on-the-couch Freudian deep analysis was better than nothing. Perhaps. One of my classmates is a practicing psychiatrist who still does analysis. He helps people, so who knows? Perhaps it depends on the therapist.

During my psych rotation at St. Elizabeth's Hospital, I had one unnerving experience. I was assigned to interview and conduct a physical examination on a schizophrenic navy pilot. A few weeks earlier he had been apprehended climbing the fence at the White House to "speak to Mr. Truman." He was a tall, rangy chap with a startling shock of positively crimson hair. He was in a padded cell. I was admitted, introduced and then summarily abandoned by the attendant. As he turned his key in the heavy lock (from the outside), he said he would be "just outside." I was instructed to knock on the mesh-reinforced window when I wanted to leave. The lieutenant was agitated from the outset. He paced the small room, intermittently looking up at me and muttering to himself. At first I was disconcerted but not alarmed. I asked how he felt, and without prelude, he began his story.

He had been at sea when he "heard" that President Truman had summoned his wife to the White House. He was convinced that sexual molestation had occurred, and when he returned from sea duty to San Diego, he flew immediately to Washington to confront the President. As he spoke the pacing accelerated, and he was becoming progressively louder and more agitated. I spoke to him quietly, seeking to calm him down; he ignored me. The disturbed guy was suffering his own private hell. I edged toward the door to see if the attendant was standing by. He could not be seen through the small window! The situation was deteriorating rapidly; pacing, gesturing, noisy exclamation and wild

excitement was approaching crescendo. I was beginning to consider how to defend myself. I tapped on the door window with the metal head of my stethoscope; no response! Finally, after an eternity, the door opened, and I beat a hasty, undignified retreat. The poor fellow was actively hallucinating. I found it difficult seeing myself dealing with that type of flagrant pathology for the rest of my professional life. Forget psychiatry; shrinks had to be made of sterner stuff than me.

It was during my junior year that I began to "moonlight" on weekends at the Casualty Hospital (now mercifully razed). The experience was extraordinary at the time. In retrospect, I must add the dimension of "occasionally horrible" to my description of that interlude in my nascent professional life. Let me hasten to explain. Casualty was aptly named; it was the repository for all emergencies that erupted in downtown DC. Although Georgetown, George Washington and Freedman's must have received their share, we fielded most of the violent trauma. I worked Saturday from early morning for 24 hours. I assisted at just about everything that was trundled through the door, and there were times when all other hands were busily occupied. I did everything from debriding and suturing horrendous knife wounds, probing for bullets, assisting at operations, resuscitating (CPR was in its infancy), helping salvage botched kitchen table abortions, dropping stomach tubes into would-be (and occasionally successful) suicides, starting IVs and drawing blood. All became familiar exercises. And I was a third year medical student! *Oy vey!*

But the *piece de resistance* came when a very distinguished, nationally recognized neurosurgeon on the faculty of a local medical school (not Georgetown), asked me if I could stay over Sunday morning and assist him in conducting a "neurosurgical procedure." In addition to the honor of working with this famous surgeon, I would earn $25! That's how I became a "head-holder." (There is no other way to describe it.) Bright and early the lightly sedated patient would be wheeled into the operating room. The neurosurgeon would place electrodes on his/her temples and promptly deliver an electroconvulsive shock. Then, while

the patient was unconscious, he would instruct me to hold the head "firm and steady." He would lift the eyelid (revealing the inner canthus), daub it with an antiseptic, and then take an icepick-like instrument that was notched in millimeters, apply the point to the inner canthus, aim it carefully upward and inward, and then with a little silver hammer tap through the thin bone of the inner orbit. He would reach an apparently pre-determined depth, move the pick laterally, back and forth, bang it in a little deeper, and repeat the lateral motion. I don't recall if this was done two or three times. Then he did it again on the opposite side. The patient would wake up about 30 to 45 minutes later—bereft of frontal lobes.

This was my introduction to pre-frontal lobotomy. I had read about it, and I knew it was a controversial procedure reserved for refractory (often violent) schizophrenia. But hell, I was a mere medical student, and he was the chief of neurosurgery at a major medical school. We did two or three procedures every Sunday morning for about a month before my ward rotations precluded further E.R. participation and head holding. I was too dumb (naive?) to realize that operating on Sunday morning in a "sweat shop" hospital with a third-year student for an assistant was all a trifle bizarre. Sometime later the good doctor became the center of a storm of vitriolic controversy. I think he was kicked out of the medical school and maybe even drummed out of the corps. Years later I encountered several patients who had been lobotomized. I don't know what they were like before the procedure, but now they were docile zombies.

Toward the end of the year, I was invited to become a preceptee at another non-academic institution, the Homeopathic Hospital. I looked up "homeopathy;" it sounded like the worse kind of medical voodoo. (In my opinion, it was and is.) The hospital administrator told me that the name was just a holdover from a past era; "no homeopathic physicians practice here anymore." During the two months I worked there I did not encounter any such alternative practitioners. I was told the name had been retained for "historic" reasons. I thought it was a

dreadful idea. Medical students from G.W. had worked there previously, and someone from the E.R at Casualty had recommended me. (I was beginning to envision a career of moving from one seedy hospital to another.) But I was offered room, board and about $35 a week. I would do emergency stuff: lab work and assist at surgery at night. It sounded pretty easy.

To try to put this "time in medicine" into appropriate context, I must relate an anecdote. Several of my classmates and I were invited to a lecture by Dr. Wallace Yater, an eminent cardiologist, who had been chairman of medicine at Georgetown, preceding Dr. Jeghers. The subject was "Contemporary Cardiac Surgery," an astonishing oxymoron at that time. It was "common knowledge" that one could operate on virtually any organ, including the brain, but not the heart. It was taught that an incision into the myocardium would cause immediate and irreversible ventricular fibrillation and death. Then Yater displayed some remarkable, grainy black and white motion picture films of a courageous military surgeon removing shell fragments from a beating heart. The patient did not fibrillate! Indeed, he survived. I recall gasps from the audience. Soon thereafter, bold surgeons began to incise the left atrium, and with a crude, serrated thimble-like device on the index finger, fracture (yes actually fracture along the cusp margins!) calcified stenotic mitral valves caused by rheumatic fever. The results were often dramatic. It was the birth of cardiac surgery.

It was 1946, and I wanted to buy a car in the worst way. I had my eye on a fairly decrepit but reasonably functional '39 Dodge coupe. So I quit my digs at 35$^{th}$ street and moved into Homeopathic. Dick DuPree had married his childhood sweetheart, Madeleine, and moved into an apartment. I was best man at their fancy wedding in Rochester. They had obtained special dispensation "from the Pope" for a Jew to participate in a Catholic ceremony replete with high mass. I already knew how to bob up and down with acceptable precision, a benefit of my catechismal apprenticeship with sweet Mary back in Villanova days. Thereafter, I frequently took the opportunity to remind Dick

that I was not sure that his marriage was ecclesiastically kosher. Probably all his kids would be bastards. Madeleine never thought that was particularly hilarious.

Back at Homeopathic, very quickly I made the acquaintance of a surgeon known locally as "Buttonhole" Cobb. Every abdominal procedure he did was executed through an incision that was just large enough to admit his right index finger. Most of the time he delivered an appendix (invariably gangrenous on the pathology report. "Ready to burst" was a notoriously familiar surgical mantra). And occasionally, Cobb did index finger "exploratories" (no kidding). The first time I worked with him he murmured that rarely he would be obliged (reluctantly) to "widen the field," but most often he could work through the initial incision. I must confess he had an extraordinarily long, prehensile index finger, and I hoped it was generously endowed with tactile sensory receptors.

After three or four of these anxious "assists," I checked with a senior surgical resident-friend at Gallinger Hospital (nee D.C. General). He knew of "Buttonhole." He said he was a very good technical surgeon, but his mini-incision procedure was outrageous and dangerous; I should "get the hell out of there." I went to the chief of staff at Homeopathic and growled that I did not want to assist Dr. Cobb any longer. Surprisingly he agreed without argument (I suspect he'd heard this lament before). But in passing, he mentioned almost casually, that good old "Buttonhole" contributed enormously to the solvency of the hospital. Apparently he was much sought after by well-heeled ladies who adored the minimal, often invisible spoor he left on their fair southerly terrain. I thought they were all pretty damned lucky that the magic finger had not missed an ovarian abscess or a tumor of some sort. I worked with several other surgeons on the staff who seemed fairly competent, but it was all straightforward emergency stuff. When I left at the beginning of summer, "Buttonhole" was still pleasing the ladies. I was pleased to be quit of Homeopathic.

It was 1947. The war was long-since over and the heat was off. I had not spent a day in the war, never heard a shot fired (in peace or anger). The old pangs of guilt returned to annoy at the edges. We were told that we could take a summer vacation, my first in about five years. It was to be a memorable summer, and it started well. I was asked if I would spend my fourth year as an "acting intern" on the highly desirable Georgetown Medical Service at the Gallinger. Only one other fellow in my class had been offered this chance, so I jumped. I had already had third-year rotations in ob-gyn, surgery and pediatrics, so I would work only internal medicine. In reality it would be a two-year straight medical internship, a unique clinical pathway that had been introduced by our new chief of medicine, Dr. Harold Jeghers. I was unofficially promised the second year (true internship).

This was before the introduction of the formal national matching (intern to hospital) program. In those more relaxed days, all the swapping of residents and fellows between medical school professors (the academic "good old boys" network) occurred in the delightfully informal environment of the Atlantic City boardwalk in front of the Haddon Hall Hotel at the time of the annual research society meetings. In this disarmingly benign environment many a career was launched or busted. It was a rare chance to see one's academic heroes up close and personal. For better (probably) or for worse, those days are long gone. Atlantic City has been captured by the "gaming" philistines, and the medical researchers have long since fled. But all of us old timers miss the camaraderie, informality and scintillating intellectual ambience.

So I bought the '39 Dodge and drove home to Baltimore. I had about $500 left from my extra-curricular moonlighting activities. I arrived in time to attend my brother's graduation from Baltimore City College. Once again I thanked the Almighty that Ken was six years my junior. He swept every scholarship award on the books! Highest grade point average ever attained, prizes in mathematics, English and a few others. He took home about $300 in prize money plus enough for a

scholarship to a college of his choice. He had already been accepted to Haverford, Franklin and Marshall and Oberlin.

So we put our heads together. At six years apart we really didn't know each other. So we made our folks a proposition. With our pooled $800 (a really hefty sum in those days), we wanted to make a grand automobile trip across the country. They had already let me hitchhike the country alone, so "with the two of us, it would be even safer. Right?" One problem: my old Dodge just wasn't up to a 6,000 plus mile excursion. Could we borrow their nifty '42 beige, Chevy sedan and let them putter around in the Dodge? I think the euphoria of Ken's dazzling graduation performance, plus the infinite logic of our plan carried the day.

Within a week we were loaded to the gunnels with camping gear, pots, pans, a ton of canned food, splendid new hiking boots, genuine L.L. Bean backpacks and a canvas briefcase full of maps. We divided our loot, now about $700, and sequestered it in macho leather money belts. We decided to make a trial run to Cape Cod, a sort of shake-down cruise, before heading west. I don't recall all the details, but the high points remain vivid. They have become a matter of family folk-lore. (My brother died in 1997, and *triste dictu,* this trip was the long-est interval we ever spent together. Our children and grandchildren always begged us for stories about the Grandpas' Great Adventure, which indeed it was.)

At Provincetown, we sought to pitch our tent on the beach. I drove the car too far into soft sand and we bogged down. Bad beginning! With driftwood boards, ripped up underbrush and a borrowed shovel, we dug our way out. Then we headed west. We roared through the dull Midwest, skirted blistering Chicago, camped two days in the lush Black Hills, got eaten alive by mosquitoes in the gaunt Dakota Bad-lands and saw a tourist-taunted black bear and up-close elk herds near the spectacular Grand Canyon of the Yellowstone. We drove "Going to the Sun" Highway at Glacier Park. It was in the days before they had invented guardrails. Glacier probably boasts the most magnificent

mountain scenery in the world. I have since toured the Alps and flown over the Andes, but the memory of vast carpets of multi-hued wild-flowers and pristine snow-capped mountains mirrored in motionless, Maxwell Parrish mountain lakes, remains forever bright in my mind.

The most memorable, scary experience of our odyssey occurred in Lake Louise National Park in Alberta. We planned to spend a few days camped in this idyllic spot within sight of the glacier. That first night we were sleeping side by side in our bags, head to toe. Something grabbed my toe in a sudden vice-like grip. I thought it was Ken fooling around so I yelled and punched him. I could tell he was dead asleep, and when I looked toward my aching toe there was the head of a giant black bear, filling the entrance to the tent! I screamed and thrashed my feet (my arms were trapped in the bag). The bear grunted and ambled off. Ken was jarred awake; we realized that the beast had been just a few inches from his head. We quaked in helpless terror. But the star-tled bear was gone. After a few more agonizing minutes, we screwed up enough courage to explore the area with flashlights.

We had committed the cardinal sin of the tenderfoot, left two baked potatoes in our cook fire. The bear must have thought the toe tucked into the corner of my kapok sleeping bag looked like a third. The can-vas was punctured, but the heavy down insulation had protected me from all but a mighty crunch. My foot turned the usual scenic purple to blue to yellow, and it ached like hell for days. A big lesson learned.

We enjoyed Banff and crossed back via Washington and Grand Coulee dam. We camped a day and took the tour of the facility. I have a problem recalling the events in the next few cities since I have visited them many times over the years, but some memories stand out. In Seattle we encountered a drenching downpour. We made a wet camp in a park adjacent to a series of giant totem poles, but we were flooded out and forced to sleep in the car. All our gear was soaked. I remember the waterfront area was clogged with huge log-rafts that had been floated down Puget Sound from British Columbia.

In San Francisco we camped in Golden Gate Park and were routed (not too gently) by park police in the early morning. We ate seafood at a curbside stand at Fisherman's Wharf. We turned east through Yosemite via Tioga Pass. The car over-heated before we reached the summit, and we had to gather water in our canteens from a stream. Somewhere in Mojave land between Bishop and Phoenix we stopped at night, exhausted and hungry. We pulled off the road and tossed our sleeping bags under a rare clump of dusty sage and sullen cottonwoods and fell asleep in minutes. I have no idea how much later it occurred, but we were awakened by the blast of a whistle from a diesel train in alarming proximity. To our horror we saw the bright swinging light of a locomotive bearing down on us! It was too late to move or run. The train thundered past about 10 feet from where we were lying rigid with fear. In the darkness we had thrown down our bags next to a railroad track. The only other time I have been that terrified was in Korea.

As many have said, the first sight of the Grand Canyon from the south rim is impossible to describe. We were awe-stricken, speechless for minutes. It was beyond mere spectacular—a sumptuous visual feast. I have revisited that glorious gorge many, many times, and I am still completely captivated on each occasion. Ken and I camped close to the head of Bright Angel trail at the south rim. It was an area that is now the parking lot of the rustic El Tovar Hotel or one of the other hostelries that now populate the lip of the south rim. At first light we watched fingers of sunlight transform the rich purples into golds and reds, trickling across the endless expanse, magically converting shadow to light. Then we hiked Bright Angel to the Colorado River. It took about two hours, a piece of cake even for two guys not in top physical condition. We lounged around Phantom Ranch, gobbled lunch, refilled our canteens and headed out—and up.

The trek out was an event to be remembered. It took about five hours. I can recall the agony of the last few miles, steep by any standard and hotter than the hinges. We staggered out, exhausted and dehy-drated. After about a half hour flaked out in the tent, I managed to

hobble on swollen, blistered feet to the general store. I bought us each a quart of vanilla ice cream. We were wiped out the whole next day, and it took almost a week for our blisters to heal. We felt like a couple of damned fools, but it made for one helluva yarn. Even the pack mules only go up or down once in a given day. (Many years later, I was stupid enough to accomplish a comparable feat of unintentional physical abuse, hiking the Kalalau trail on Kauai.)

I remember being awed by the anthropomorphic saguaro near Tucson and the coolness of the desert nights. We ate cabrito across the border in Nogales. In Miami Beach we camped unmolested on North Beach (try that today). It was there that we discovered we had almost run out of money, but we were too proud to call home for help. We spent two days gathering empty soft drink bottles and cashed in almost 500 at two cents apiece. We estimated that we had enough for gas and rare pretzel snacks if we drove straight through to Baltimore. We had not calculated the cost of the ferry across the James River. So we limped into Virginia Beach on the fumes and sought more discarded bottles. The pickings were not as lucrative as Miami Beach, but we gathered enough to make it back home hungry but happy. It was one glorious adventure; we'd had very few arguments and no pitched battles. Remarkable for brothers.

My final medical school year was spent at Gallinger. I had a room in the intern quarters and worked the wards and clinics. The only difference between my status and those of regular M.D. interns was that any orders I wrote had to be counter-signed by a resident. Quite often there was no resident available; I "expedited" and improvised a lot. Once again, in retrospect we did some awful things in ignorance. Drawing the "morning bloods" became a ritual. The open wards had some 40 beds with several bays of four to six beds. With a nurse at my elbow, I would check the order sheets for blood tests, select the proper tubes, and draw blood from almost every patient, carefully switching to a new sterile needle between each patient. But often we would just rinse out the glass syringe in sterile saline, and use the same syringe for

two or three patients, until the barrel got too sticky. I reflect on this now with considerable horror. God knows how many times we transmitted Hepatitis B or C or some other dreadful blood-borne virus between patients. Often "drawing the bloods" took an hour or longer before starting morning work rounds. Every good intern had his own whetstone; sharpening needles, and removing burrs once back in your digs became an evening rite. (I say "his" advisedly; in 1947 there were no women on the house staff at Gallinger Hospital.)

One of the major problems in those years was the risk to house officers of contracting tuberculosis. All patients with lobar pneumonic consolidation were suspect; they were highly contagious if the pneumonia was due to tuberculosis. Most often the chest radiograph was diagnostic and the patient could be isolated. But occasionally the diagnosis was not evident from radiographs or auscultation. Two interns developed active tuberculosis during the year. I suspect AIDS has replaced tuberculosis as the specter hanging over house staff today. But with the multi-drug resistant strains of tuberculosis abroad, it must remain a hazard.

One of my rotations was in the "Luetic Clinic" where we diagnosed and treated patients with venereal diseases. I recall that one of the senior staff members was conducting a clinical study on central nervous system syphilis, and we were doing lots of lumbar punctures on patients with primary and suspected secondary disease. On many occasions I would line up five or six patients in a seated position in the clinic, anesthetize the intervertebral space (usually L4—L5) and insert spinal needles in sequence, while nurses at my elbow would collect the spinal fluid. Then I would remove the needles and another nurse would cleanse the puncture site and place a dressing. It was an assembly line operation. All the interns became very adept at lumbar puncture. Most often patients did not know that the procedure had been completed until the needle was withdrawn.

Now I wonder about "informed consent." We were cavalier by today's ethical standards. It was not an issue we ever discussed. We

were just technicians gathering spinal fluid. No patient was ever injured, and central nervous system syphilis, almost impossible to detect clinically at an early stage, could be identified by examining the fluid. Treatment (albeit imperfect) could be administered before the dreadful, often irreversible signs and symptoms of tabes dorsalis or CNS syphilis developed. So it was a good deal for the patients in whom CNS involvement was detected. But I don't think an Institutional Review Board would sanction such a protocol today.

Then there was the "Rheumatic Fever Ward." In those days the relationship between Type A streptococcus and the occurrence of acute rheumatic fever (ARF) was just becoming established. The classical definitive work on air force personnel at Warren Air Force Base had recently been published. Criteria were still being evolved. Thus the kids we admitted usually had flagrant ARF manifested by low-grade fever, rash, arthritis, carditis (often with dreadful mitral and aortic murmurs) and occasionally demonstrating the peculiar choreiform movements of extremities. Our treatment: large doses of crystalline penicillin if the patient was still active with fever. But thereafter the only therapy was "rigorous" bed rest and enormous doses of aspirin. The "end-point" was sustained clinical improvement, but more often than not the tykes would first develop tinnitus (ringing of the ears) from salicylate intoxication. The aspirin dose was backed off but not stopped when this occurred. As with most of medical therapy in those days, data supporting such a thesis were woefully inadequate. Empiricism, anecdote and personal opinion (experience?) ruled the world of medicine.

So here was a ward with about 30 kids between about five and 12 who were supposed to lie in bed 24 hours a day, except to use the bedside commode and get washed. Some were so ill that the bed rest was all they could muster. But the others, especially the older ones without carditis or much joint pain were a "problem." I recall one night, for some reason, I visited the ARF ward late at night. The nurse had obviously left for a few minutes, and the kids were engaged in a wild pillow

fight with much shrieking and leaping up and down and romping from bed to bed. As soon as they caught sight of a white coat they immediately became subdued—supine and silent. They were part of a study on treatment. I often wonder about the "data" being collected on these kids, who were (supposedly) on "absolute bed rest." Of course, the concept of "controls," (allowing another group of kids randomized to normal activity) probably would have been considered unethical. Nevertheless treatment data from such studies were all but apocryphal. ARF is rare today in the U.S., perhaps one of the very few fringe benefits of our all-too liberal (some would say promiscuous) deployment of penicillin. ARF is still a problem in Third World countries where malnutrition and lack of medical care exacerbate the severity of all infections and their sequelae.

For exercise and entertainment, the staff played some 12-inch, fast-pitch softball during lunch breaks and after hours in the summer. We had a good intern team, and I was the long-ball, clean-up hitter. Our coach was "Nig" (her preferred nickname) Braxton who had played professional softball in North Carolina. She was a tough, wiry veteran psychiatric nurse, much adored by patients and staff. She was also our pitcher. We played in a local league but forfeited a lot of games because of staff being called off to the wards.

Our one game "World Series" was played against the inmates at the D.C. Jail, which was located next to the hospital. It had become an epochal annual struggle, sort of like our own little World Cup-along-the-Anacostia. The inmates cheering section was well organized and "beat the docs" was the centerpiece of an almost friendly and very raucous cheer. Enthusiastic off-duty nurses and staff watched from a special bleachers outside the double, chain-linked, barbed wire-topped, 15-foot fences that ran inside the stone walls. Escapes from the D.C. jail were not uncommon.

Of course, we played inside the jail perimeter while guards with rifles perched in the towers and strolled the high walls. The inmates played a very physical game but without rancor. Nevertheless, it was

somewhat disconcerting to slide hard into second base to blow the shortstop out of the play, when he just might be a convicted ax murderer. The inmates played sand-lot rough with a bit of an edge. But most often they would help you up with a smile, after they knocked you on your ass. I hit two homeruns (over the wall) that gave us a win. But no one was allowed to fetch the ball. Later Nig found out that their first baseman was a lifer (murder) and that all the infielders were hard-core felons. I think the series was about even over the years. I hope they still play that game.

About half way through my senior year I received a letter from an elderly man who had run a successful haberdashery in our neighborhood, another satisfied patient of my dad's. He had retired to Miami Beach to pursue his hobby of photography. The strange message told of a young photographer's model in Miami Beach who had expressed an interest in meeting me. (Who me?) The envelope contained a picture of perhaps the most gorgeous silver blonde I had ever seen. The letter went on to explain that he had obtained a picture of me from my parents (!), and he had "taken the liberty of showing it to Stella" with the suggestion that "if I was interested I should write to her." Wow! I was working in the E.R. and riding the ambulance, a tempestuous time, but I could not stop looking at that incredible face.

So I wrote and told her all about myself. Her letter in response was articulate, humorous and expressed appropriate embarrassment over the bizarre nature of our introduction. Our mutual friend fancied himself a matchmaker. Hell, the guy barely knew me, and he had met Stella (she preferred the nickname "Stevie") by photographing her on a shoot for a Miami department store. We exchanged a handful of letters, and I was impressed with her brightness and knowledge of classical literature (which far exceeded my own; I had barely read anything but medical books and journals for four years). I was intrigued and she seemed interested. She wrote that she was a "senior," and from the maturity of language and content of her letters, I assumed she was attending the University of Miami.

It wasn't easy, but I arranged to take a long weekend and challenged the old Dodge with a swift excursion to Miami Beach. (The "Dodge Story" is worth comment. Very few classmates could afford a car, so I had made the venerable Dodge available to any classmate who needed it. There was one major caveat. If **anything** went wrong or dropped off while you were using it, the unlucky offender had to pay for the repair. By this arrangement the ancient beauty acquired new brakes, rebuilt carburetor, a repaired right front fender ding and two new Firestones, at no cost to the owner. Not a bad deal.)

I had made this crazy trip to Miami once before. In 1939 our high school football team had been invited to play in the "Little Orange Bowl" for the mythical national high-school championship. We had a great undefeated and unscored-on team, as did Miami High. Two other guys and I took someone's old wreck and made the non-stop, hard charge down the coast, hit the beach for a few hours, saw the game (we lost) and then raced home. It had been exhausting but great fun. But now I was going to tackle it alone.

I remember driving along deserted southern highways that were often shrouded in light fog. I drank gallons of coffee and half a dozen egg salad sandwiches. It was about 1200 miles, and I made it in about 24 hours. I arrived before daylight and went to the beach near Stella's address. I fell asleep only to awaken under a blazing sun, with a badly sunburned face and overall body ache. Great way to meet a new girl. But it all worked out. She was even more lovely than her picture, a real head-turner. After a few moments of awkward introduction, I met mother, Sonya. Here was a real piece of work. She was also a blonde, in her 40s, over-dressed and over-made-up (by my stuffy standards). She spoke with a very thick Ukrainian accent, although she had been in this country ("from Hodessa") for over 20 years. It turned out she (deliberately) never lost the accent because "everyone thought it was charming." Perhaps. She had divorced her worthless, delivery-truck driver, German husband when Stella was three. She worked as a beautician-masseuse in Miami Beach solariums and was their sole source of

income. She regaled me with tales of her elite clientele and produced photographs of herself glowing with Zsa Zsa Gabor and Sophie Tucker. I learned all of this over bacon and eggs without asking a single question.

I soon discovered that Stella was 16 and, indeed, a senior—at Normandie Isle High School! I couldn't believe it; I had known many college women less sophisticated and literate. That first attenuated weekend we walked the beach and talked and talked. She was bright as hell. She had been "Miss Everything" in Miami Beach since she was 15 and read voluminously. She had been offered a screen test at Warner Brothers in Hollywood (her mother related with disturbing reiteration). The only irritant: they both smoked cigarettes, incessantly. I am not sure it was exactly love at first sight, but there was obvious chemistry. I kissed her goodbye, the limit of our physical contact. The eternal snake of highway heading north was as deadly boring and seductively soporific as before, but the radiant picture on the dashboard helped keep me awake.

During my senior year in medical school, I edited our class yearbook (a first). We took pictures of clusters of three classmates standing before various Washington landmarks. I wrote every word and did the complete layout. I took the liberty of writing a gushy "hail and farewell" editorial and capped it with a picture of myself studying, with a photograph of the beauteous Stevie gracing my desk as background. It was a helluva yearbook.

We corresponded almost weekly over the next few months. My family was appalled. "She hasn't even been graduated from high school!" But Stella had been invited to come to New York and do some modeling for John Powers. We arranged for Stella and Sonya to stop over and spend the night in Baltimore to "get acquainted with the folks." The event was a portend of bad things to come. I knew I was in trouble when they stepped off the train. They looked like the Gabor sisters (youngest and eldest). Matching sailor costumes with four-inch, screaming-scarlet platforms with wraparound straps, identical plati-

num hair done in Veronica Lake coifs. It was *haute couture*, Miami Beach style. I thought Stella looked terrific and Sonya looked, well, garish.

The tableaux did not play well in Baltimore. It never did. My parents were dead-set against any further relationship; brother and sister were silent and sullen. As ever, mother took the point on the charge. In private she was tearful, adamant, resentful. "All our hopes for you…" I thought it was all just too much. I admitted being embarrassed by Sonya's flamboyance, but I had to admire her guts and independence. And I wasn't interested in courting Sonya; I wanted Stella. And this time I thought I could tell the difference between lust and love.

I drove up to New York to meet her large, extended family. The matriarch was the magnificent Tanya, whose husband, Morris, was a furrier. They lived in a modest walk-up in the "Murder, Incorporated" neighborhood (announced with some pride) of Flatbush. They were all warm and wonderful. They were old-country Russian Jews who really loved bountiful America. There were countless aunts, uncles, cousins, friends. They stuffed me; we downed toasts of scalding straight schnapps: bourbon and vodka. (*l'chayim*!) I felt a sense of *gemutlich* that I had not experienced in years (ever?). And Stella was the star of the show.

Over the next months, we decided to get married after we were both graduated. Opposition was bilateral and fairly symmetrical. Sonya never liked me, and although I tried over the years, I could never really warm to her. She made no bones about my having derailed her daughter's predestined rise to Hollywood stardom. My mother never gave her blessing. Dad later relented when he was quite ill and faced with the inevitability of our marriage. Ken was always distant (I suspected some envy), and Joan never warmed to Stella ("too flashy for my taste"). The next months were painful. I made one more suicidal flying auto trip to Miami. This time it was very intimate, but we agreed not to have real intercourse until we were married. We almost fell off that wagon a few times, but never quite.

It was during this trip that Stella revealed another facet of her range of accomplishments. She asked me to "take a ride with her to Coral Gables." No further explanation. I would have jumped off a bridge had she asked. She directed me to a small private landing field on the edge of town. Here she gathered up her small carrying case, extracted a white cotton jumpsuit, and a matching cloth aviator's cap with pink-plastic rimmed goggles. I stood somewhat stunned as she said, "Wait here." and sauntered over to a guy standing next to a Piper cub. They chatted for a moment, then she climbed into the tiny cabin, quite alone! The guy grabbed the propeller, gave it a heavy push and the engine coughed into life. I couldn't believe my eyes. The plane trundled out to the runway, and in a few seconds my little blonde darling was airborne—alone. I walked over to the fellow still watching the tiny plane gain altitude. He didn't look away, "She is doing her solo flight today." Then he explained that she had been taking lessons for a few weeks, and "had the makings of a fine pilot." After vanishing over the ocean in the direction of Miami Beach, after about 15 minutes she returned circled the field, cleared some ugly looking telephone wires at the south end of the field and then landed with only one bump. She was aglow with triumph. And she could not yet drive a car!

Later in the year I drove up to New York once again. We went for dinner at the Starlight Roof at the old Astor Hotel just off Broadway. She was wearing a simple low-cut black silk dress, pearls and silver slippers. Literally, all conversation stopped when she entered the vast dining room. She was stunning; it was her most glorious moment.

A month before the scheduled graduations and wedding, she called it off. She was having second thoughts. I suspected (but could never prove) that my mother had somehow managed to toss a spanner in the works, but it could just as well have been Sonya. My mother had expressed concern about the "Jewish thing." It was no coincidence that just after one of these unpleasant, coldly polite "discussions," Stella began to wear an out-sized, silver Star of David around her neck on most all public occasions. "Religion" became a gnawing source of con-

tention. For Stella it was more a show of defiance and test of wills, than any sense of religious conviction. Stella and Sonya rarely went to temple, although the Brooklyn folks were Conservative. I decided to "become Jewish" to keep the peace with Stella, not from any shattering epiphany. The marriage situation was salvaged by compromise between the warring factions. Reluctantly, we agreed to get married twice. First in a dreary, cavernous Unitarian church by a very short preacher wearing a red bow tie, and the next day in a temple by the same pompous rabbi who had whispered the silly "words of wisdom" in my ear, years ago when I had been confirmed.

So we resolved the differences. Stella was graduated in early June; I tossed the tassel in mid-June. We were married (twice) two days later. After the first wedding, we had a rather joyless reception at some second-class restaurant with mediocre food and nothing to drink. The Hatfields and McCoys would probably have had a better time. My sister had been graduated from high school earlier that same day, and the reception was as much in her honor as ours. It was all strained with no semblance of joy or fun, a thoroughly inauspicious beginning. Stella and I escaped as quickly as was decent and fled to the old Southern Hotel in downtown Baltimore.

Our wedding night left something to be desired. Mutual expectations were soaring. We had waited an eternity. Stella was a virgin, and we were both inept and inexperienced. During my time in medical school and before, I had dated many girls. There had been dozens of sexual opportunities, but I had remained celibate. As I indicated earlier, this was a stupid decision. I should have learned much more about the art of making a woman happy in bed. We did consummate our marriage several times, but I don't think it was very pleasurable for Stella.

The "second marriage" was a ridiculous anti-climax. Once again she looked spectacular, but we had just spent the night making unskilled love. Besides, I was sure she had not felt "officially married" after the dreary Unitarian ceremony. So here it was the next morning, and

instead of languishing in bed enjoying oysters Rockefeller and sipping champagne cocktails, we had to contend with this sanctimonious rabbi. I crushed the traditional "glass." It was actually a disguised light bulb designed to keep the action moving. Later in private, I smashed a fine goblet to make it all official. So we escaped. My folks had given us a new Studebaker coupe as a wedding present. We spent the rest of our disjointed honeymoon roaming the beaches at Provincetown and exploring the narrow, cobbled streets of Quebec City, among other things.

# 12

## *Intern-Fellow-Resident Years*

◆

### *(blood, sweat and some tears...)*

**M**y "true" (second year) internship started on July 1, 1948, so we had about one week of physical intimacy. The sex got somewhat better, but we had a lot to learn. (I will never advise couples to "save themselves" until the knot is tied. I actually believe that couples seriously contemplating marriage should live together for at least six months, to see if there is true psychological and physical compatibility, to check out habits, hang-ups, biases, etc. before taking vows. It should be mandatory. With divorce rates in the U.S. hovering around 50%, it may not be such a crazy idea. Besides, I suspect "sex education" may be an anachronistic concept these days when thirteen years olds "make out" in junior high school corridors.)

We moved into a modest, badly furnished apartment in Anacostia, across the river from the hospital. We added a few critical items of furniture (decent mattress, TV set, a real luxury in those days) and basic household goods (utensils, frying pan and pressure cooker). My navy stipend had stopped on July 1, and I was placed on "inactive reserve." This meant that my monthly checks had ceased, and my intern take-home pay at Gallinger was about $25 a month. In those days all good teaching hospitals (from Boston to Chicago to New Orleans) paid a pittance, plus room, board and laundry. No allowance for married house staff; 90% of the interns and residents were single. We were slave

labor; medical penury was the accepted norm. We just didn't know any better.

Stella and I lived frugally on savings we both brought to the marriage, plus some money from wedding gifts. She tried to get a job as a fashion model at Garfinkel's and a few of the other better stores in town. No luck. Moonlighting was unheard-of in those days. Besides it would have been impossible; I was on call every other night and every other weekend. It was a very rough year for a 17-year old who had lived the fantasy of a fairy princess in a world created by the suffocatingly indulgent Sonya. Stella never complained, but her insomnia became a way of life. I suspected it was a manifestation of depression. It seemed to exacerbate during the intern year. Occasionally, I would sneak Stella into the intern quarters (my understanding roommate, Jim Fitzgerald, would disappear discreetly for the night), but such romantic interludes were infrequent. "On call" for an intern at Gallinger was a euphemism for "up all night."

As we approached serious insolvency, with great reluctance I contemplated hitting my folks up for a loan. Then I heard that the army was about to launch a program whereby they would sponsor selected interns and residents through their training period, in return for year-for-year pay back on active military duty. It was similar to the deal I had with the navy through Villanova and Georgetown. The remuneration? First lieutenant pay and allowances: a gold mine! But I was inactive-duty navy. Did the navy have such a plan?

I raced down to the old Navy Department Building and sought out a recruiting NCO. He said he heard "something about the navy starting such a program," but it was months away. I was devastated. As I was shuffling out, the same fellow sidled up to me and gestured to follow him outside. In *sotto voce* he muttered that he knew the army was just about to start such a program, and he could see no reason that I could not get an honorable discharge from the navy and be commissioned in the army. He was furious that the navy had been dragging its competitive feet. I could have kissed that rough old cheek.

I ran down the street, crossed Constitution Avenue to the Office of the Army Surgeon General. I found a friendly WAC sergeant who confirmed the story. She said they would be seeking candidates in about one week. I think my name must have been first on the list for the entire country. I filled out a million forms, applied for discharge from the navy (accepted), and the next day became a first lieutenant in the suddenly wonderful U.S. Army. By any standard it was a modest income, but for hungry kids like us it was a bonanza.

We left Anacostia after about six months and moved to a basement apartment near Children's Hospital. It was a terrible place. One night we heard scrabbling sounds in the kitchen and discovered a large, fearless Norway rat. A few weeks later someone tried to break in while I was on duty at the hospital. Within days we broke the lease and moved to an elegant, unfurnished, outrageously expensive apartment in a new complex in Falls Church, Virginia. We had to buy a batch of new furniture, and we were sorely strapped. Soon thereafter we discovered that Stella was pregnant.

My life at the hospital was typical of the times. House staff did everything. On our assigned patients we examined blood smears, spun hematocrits and read hemoglobins, red and white blood cell counts, blood smears, urine microscopic examinations and cerebrospinal fluid examinations. You name it, we did it. With one resident and one attending, we managed forty-bed, open wards. Each bed separated by a paper-thin cotton curtain; patients were packed in cheek-by-jowl. These were the sickest, poorest folks on earth. You had to be damned sick and dreadfully poor to qualify for admission. Most of our patients had multiple system diseases often compounded by malnutrition. It was Lambarene West.

In the withering heat and humidity of summer in Washington the toll on patients was often deadly. The wards were not air-conditioned, and the breeze from scattered electric fans was imperceptible. I can recall leaving the intern quarters after a quick midnight shower and walking out into that stifling heat and being drenched in sweat after

the 30-yard walk to the hospital. Our patients all were bedded on what were designated "general wards." An individual in diabetic acidosis might be next to a patient with myocardial infarction, next to a poor soul in sickle cell crisis. The sicker patients were kept in bays containing four or six beds. Patients with potentially communicable diseases were kept in isolation. There was no such thing as an ICU or CCU.

We saw a great many enigmatic patients with "fevers of undetermined origin" (FUO). This was one of the great clinical challenges; diagnosis could range from infective endocarditis to malaria to acute pyelonephritis; probably over 100 possibilities. There were published protocols for diagnosis and management of FUOs that would change with each new edition of a journal. These were early management algorithms. There was no consideration of "cost effectiveness," rather it was a matter of using your brain and the best tools available to help the individual patient.

(Rightly or wrongly, we were not considering the "greater good of mankind" in our zeal to help this one sick individual. It gets to the very heart of the present conundrum facing medicine: when does one's responsibility to the individual patient yield to the economic necessity of ensuring adequate medical care for **all** patients? In my opinion, there is no conflict. A physician **must** always be the advocate of the individual patient. Any interference with this sacred trust must come from an external, "higher authority" that bears responsibility for the health of the public-at-large. The physician must fight the good fight on behalf of his patient. That means seeking the best possible, medically rational care. If restrictions are imposed, they must come from a source beyond the power of the physician. Anything less, and no patient will ever trust the physician to be doing "all within his power" to help. It would deliver a death blow to the already faltering "patient-doctor" relationship.)

But back to Gallinger. One of my own personal triumphs occurred when I was caring for a winsome black prostitute heroin addict with FUO. I made a diagnosis of gonococcal tricuspid endocarditis (bacte-

rial vegetation growing on the valve) on the basis of a loud systolic murmur in an atypical location, plus several lung abscesses. She had used contaminated needles. (It was long before the era of AIDS.) We cured her with massive doses of penicillin, but the valve remained damaged. I never saw her again, but her prognosis was grim. She was hooked on heroin, and there was no such animal as a "needle exchange" program. She tatted some lace doilies as a gift to my wife.

On Christmas eve of 1948, Ken came down to spend a few days with me. He was on holiday as a freshman at Haverford. I worked Christmas and Easter holidays because I was Jewish, and I took off on Rosh Hashanah and Yom Kippur. Again, it was not a matter of religious conviction, but seemed a fair exchange. That night an eight-year-old black girl was admitted to our isolation unit. She was desperately ill with diphtheritic myocarditis (infection of the heart muscle). She had been seen earlier before I came on duty and given massive does of penicillin and diphtheria anti-toxin. Ken was horrified at the prospect of a child dying, especially on Christmas eve. I had seen a little boy die with diphtheria once before, and this situation was no less desperate. We stayed at the bedside all night; she died at dawn. Paradoxically, I think it was that shocking experience helped convince Ken to pursue a career in medicine. There was so much that needed to be learned; so many people that needed to be helped.

Again, in retrospect, we were practicing primitive medicine. Things had not changed a great deal since Florence Nightingale and the Crimean War. Our drug armamentarium was pathetically limited. Sulfa drugs were still our staple antibacterial agents. Penicillin (crystalline) was available but expensive. Dose schedules for most indicated infectious diseases were uncertain. I am sure we under-dosed and over-dosed many patients, as clinical experience expanded slowly. It was long before randomized controlled trials (RCT) brought some credibility to therapeutic decision-making. (The first published RCT appeared in 1951.) Thus, much of what we did was crude and not very helpful. And we knew it. But we attempted to compensate by **listening** to

patients. We spent many anxious, supportive hours at the bedside, never leaving a critically ill patient until the outcome was determined. A 24 to 36-hour continuous stint was not unusual. You can imagine what that did for home life. It seems to me that although we could do far less for patients than today, their expectations were lower and their gratitude for what we did seemed unbounded.

One of the elective intern rotations was ER-ambulance service. Our experience was quite different than of Anthony Edwards, TVs "ER" attending. We did not have the capability to do much except to try to salvage those desperately ill or injured. CPR was in its infancy. This was where I first encountered the brutality (and rare humanity) of city cops. More than once a shackled prisoner, usually black, who displayed arrogance or resistance or even pride, was beaten senseless behind a curtain. Always there were denials all around. You soon learned about the impenetrable "blue code of silence."

Riding the ambulance was another fear-inspiring event, more a psychosocial experience than medical. There were no EMTs; we were the ambulance doctors. We would work with a two-man crew, selected more for heft than brains. Frequently, we would call for a police escort into certain known-to-be-dangerous areas in town; sometimes the cops even showed up. I delivered babies in stinking beds in fourth floor walk-ups, almost got knifed by an irate boyfriend who had beaten his partner to a bloody mess (she wanted to hit me too!), helped schlep a litter down three flights of stairs, bearing a 275-pound woman in diabetic coma. I once encountered six winos sitting in a circle in an abandoned warehouse. Four were dead and two were blind and screaming. They had been drinking Chilean Riesling that (we later discovered) had been cut with methyl alcohol. I must have pronounced about a dozen people dead in bed. It was the seamiest side of medicine.

But the scariest aspect of ambulance duty was the all-too-frequent, purposeless, high-speed, siren-wailing race through downtown Washington. On a rainy summer night, one of our ambulances ran a red light, siren screaming, warning lights flashing, ostensibly en route to an

emergency. They smashed broadside into a city bus. The driver and his assistant were killed, and the intern in back and several bus passengers were badly injured. There was a brief outcry in the Washington Post, but it dissipated like smoke in a windstorm, yesterday's news. During my time they still drove like maniacs. The minutes saved were rarely worth the risk; it was a dangerous, useless macho drill.

The Georgetown Chief of Medicine at Gallinger was Dr. Hugh Hussey, a tall, lean, austere, laconic man with an encyclopedic knowledge of medicine. (I always thought he was cold and mirthless until I encountered Hugh Hussey much later in my career in a totally different context.) My other hero was Dr. Sol Katz, chief of the pulmonary disease service. He was already a legend; a perfect complement to Hussey. It was said their two-man journal club could have been recorded and published in any medical journal. They were intimidating and awe-inspiring teachers.

Gallinger Municipal Hospital was typical of the urban teaching hospitals in every major city (e.g. Boston City, Bellevue, Philadelphia General, Cook County in Chicago, Grady in Atlanta, Charity in New Orleans, etc.). To work in these prestigious places, one eagerly accepted a life of penurious servitude. It was work-work-work, but the house staff would encounter just about every malady known to man. At no time in my life thereafter, did I encounter any disease (with the exception of some exotica in Korea) that I had not seen before. In addition to work and teaching rounds, we had teaching conferences every day. Patient care always took precedence. If an intern or resident got too busy on the ward, he was obliged to miss the teaching session. It was medical education under forced draft, an unrelenting battleground. And it took its toll on families. Medical education did **not** have to be that unforgiving.

It was during this time that Dr. Harold Jeghers had come from Boston University Medical School to Georgetown as chief of medicine. He had done some seminal research in vitamin deficiencies and intestinal polyposis (Peutz-Jeghers Syndrome). He brought some of his young

stars from Boston and revitalized the department. He taught us how to create a personal file of the medical literature, modeled on his own 40 three-drawer cabinet system. We all started our own personal files, tearing and clipping articles from the medical journals that we all read (New England Journal of Medicine, American Journal of Medicine, JAMA, Annals of Internal Medicine and Archives of Internal Medicine.) We wrote penny postcards to authors of articles in other journals for reprints. We benefited from student rates, but for interns and residents journal subscriptions were still major budget items. I would also clip case summaries of patients with challenging illnesses that I had managed, personally, or had helped, to the pertinent journal article. Nothing jogs the memory like that difficult patient you sweated over in the wee small hours. Minute details stick in your mind the rest of your life.

Often I would earmark the articles for clipping in the journals and Stella would follow-up, clip and file them. She often read the articles and learned a lot of medicine. She became very adept at medical nomenclature. She would have made a fine medical student and doctor. Within one year, I had a dozen cardboard cartons filled with reprints. In my many years as a teacher, I transported my ever-expanding reprint file to every' assignment. When we moved to Walter Reed in 1968, the army had to move 20 four-drawer cabinets packed with medical literature. My interns and residents had open access to my files; I encouraged them to start their own.

During this year of every other night, every other weekend labor, I would return home exhausted to a young wife who had been alone during this interval. I would try to make conversation, but most often I would fall asleep early. It was a most difficult year, compounded by several other problems all related. Most importantly, our sex life was not very good. I have spoken of our mutual inexperience, but the fault was primarily mine. When lying next to Stella's lovely naked body, I simply became too aroused, too fast. We tried everything we could imagine or read about, but nothing seemed to help.

Another problem: Stella had been smoking cigarettes since she was 15. I occasionally smoked a pipe, but the odor of stale cigarette smoke permeating the apartment and rarely emptied ashtrays always annoyed me. We spoke of this in a non-confrontational way since I was also concerned about the long-term health implications of two packs a day (before the firm data on bronchogenic carcinoma and coronary heart disease had emerged). But she could not stop. I did not nag.

Then there was the almost intractable insomnia. I don't recall when it started or if it existed before our marriage, but it became exacerbated during this year. It never relented for the duration of our life together. She would frequently not fall asleep until two or three in the morning, unless she took a Nembutal or Seconal. I would fall into troubled sleep wearing a sleeping mask to block out her reading light. In the morning she was always in deep, much-needed slumber. We rarely had breakfast together; I got out of the breakfast habit.

Finally, Stella had no experience in doing dull, mindless but necessary domestic chores. I don't know who did such stuff when she lived with Sonya, but it was not a chore expected of blooming Hollywood starlets. She learned to cook simple things: splendid spaghetti with meat sauce, lots of hamburgers, meat loaf, chops, steaks, stews and such. On holidays she could turn out a fine turkey dinner with all the traditional fixings. Since my mother had been a disinterested and unskilled cook (we lived on chuck roast and "Mulligan stew"), and my experience with wretched institutional fare and four years of fat and calories at the glorious Greek's, *haute cuisine* never appeared on my gustatory radar screen. It was never a big issue in my life. (In reality I never really appreciated fine dining until I was remarried some 40 odd years later.)

Toward the end of my intern year, Dr Sol Katz invited me to become one of his two clinical fellows in pulmonary diseases. His unit occupied three floors of a separate building. I had never been particularly attracted to pulmonology, but an opportunity to work with the legendary Sol Katz was beyond expectation. Besides, I would be on-call

every third night and every third weekend. Stella and I discussed the implications of taking a year of fellowship. Among other things, it meant another year of military duty pay back.

We soon discovered that we had a problem in what now might be called "career goal identification." Her expectation (and that of the Brooklyn family and Sonya) was that a "doctor went into practice." Stella's vision had been that after my intern year we would set up practice in some felicitous place like Coral Gables or Grand Junction and live a quiet, productive, settled life. It seems strange in retrospect, but we had never really discussed my long-term career ambitions. I had been determined to become an internist since my third year of medical school. Stella was significantly disappointed, but played the good soldier. So I accepted the fellowship.

Sol Katz's assistant was another superb clinician, Dr. Nick Cotsonas, and the chief pulmonary resident was equally talented, Dr. Vernon Padgett. The only downside was my counterpart, the other clinical Fellow. He was arrogant, lazy and offensively "from that medical Mecca, Boston," as he never hesitated to remind all within earshot. Dr. Harry R (I will not use his real name) proved to be the bane of my existence. On too many occasions, he would fail to respond to a call ("I left my seat and row number at the symphony with the usher!"). Hence, I was often summoned from home to respond to emergencies that occurred on the ward, on my night off. Harry was reprimanded several times, but it never seemed to take. He made my life miserable. (I was to encounter Harry R much later in life, and he proved to be the same unreconstructed, wretched human being.)

On the pulmonary service we did a lot of things to patients that seem archaic, dangerous and downright bizarre by contemporary standards. About 90% of our patients suffered advanced states of tuberculosis. There was no drug treatment. Selman Waksman had discovered streptomycin in 1943, but clinical experience had revealed a severe problem with neurotoxicity (especially irreversible nerve deafness).

Treatment for tuberculosis had not progressed much beyond "The Magic Mountain."

Three days a week I would take a dozen patients to the fluoroscopy room, don a ponderous lead apron and bulky lead gloves, put on a double mask and then fluoroscope each patient in turn, making notes of progress (or deterioration). Every patient was scoped monthly. It must have been cheaper than chest radiographs, but the scatter radiation was horrendous. Also exposure to the ubiquitous bacillus, double masks notwithstanding, was frightening. My tuberculin skin test had already become positive from exposure during my intern years, but now it almost ulcerated. I was always concerned that radiation scatter might also perturb my gonads. It did not. All staff members had monthly chest radiographs. When Dr. Katz came in to read them, it was a tense few moments. Tuberculosis was a major occupational hazard. In the modern era, AIDS has replaced TB as the nemesis of medical students, nurses and house staff, but the nasty bacillus still remains a problem.

Treatment of tuberculosis consisted of pneumothorax (introducing air into the pleural space on the side involved, ostensibly to collapse cavities and "rest" the lung), and pneumoperitoneum (air under the diaphragm to collapse cavities in the lung bases.) I was never convinced of their effectiveness. And if those procedures failed, many patients received disfiguring Schede thoracoplasties (removing several ribs to collapse a lung permanently) to deal with unyielding tuberculous cavities. We had nothing to offer patients with disseminated tuberculosis or when the disease focused on an isolated organ (bone, brain, kidneys). That meant the disease had spread widely. All these options represented terrible, largely ineffectual therapies; we all hated it. But this was 1949; the therapeutic revolution that brought forth a host of potent anti-tuberculosis drugs was yet to occur.

Our year in Falls Church passed quickly for me; it was interminable for Stella. Her mother came for visits periodically, but bouts of depression were coming more often. The extra free time from the hospital

allowed for visits to Brooklyn, always warm and fun. I came to look forward to the ritual with Tanta Tanya. Lovingly, she would take me aside in the steaming, musky-fragrant kitchen as she stirred the kasha. "So tell me, Bobbila, when do you become a doctor and start practicing?" This conversation recurred even when I was chief medical resident at Georgetown in 1952. She meant well; I loved her.

Trips to Baltimore were never warm or fun. The mutual antagonism between Stella and my mother had matured into thinly disguised hatred. Mother was not subtle in her disapproval of Stella and Sonya. During her entire lifetime she was never reconciled to our marriage. In those years I was weak in the presence of my mother. I did not defend Stella with sufficient vigor and force. Sons have problems with mothers. In retrospect I have come to believe that if I had told her to be civil to Stella or go to hell, things might have straightened out between them. (But I am far from convinced that this action alone would have saved our marriage. There were many other intractable problems for us.) It was only after I came back from Korea in 1951 that I managed to gather up the gumption to tell my mother to back off. It didn't transmute hate to love, but her previously palpable animosity subsided considerably.

Our first child, Steven, was born in September at Georgetown. We had a fine obstetrician (chief of the service at Georgetown), and it was a relatively easy delivery. Months later we discovered that the baby had a mild congenital deformity of the tibiae. After a time, Steven had to be placed in leg braces to straighten them. It must have been painful; he cried a lot. Stella bore the brunt of this traumatic period since I was working so much. She did not complain, but the insomnia, cigarettes and bouts of depression were unrelenting. The year passed quickly, and I was accepted for a second year of residency at Georgetown University Hospital. My year of pulmonary fellowship counted as one of the three required for eligibility to sit for the American Board of Internal Medicine (ABIM) examination. I was also promoted to captain, a nice little boost in pay.

# 13

## *The Korean Experience*

◆

### *(from cloister to chaos...and back...)*

I started at Georgetown on July 1,1950; North Korean forces had crossed the 38th parallel on June 25th. Within days we heard President Truman's fulminations against the "unprovoked Communist aggression," and I knew what was coming. My Faustian bargain with the army was being called. (The gamble: if they pay rather handsomely during your training years, you will be lucky enough to pay back your time of indebtedness in some felicitous assignment, and that you will **not** encounter a war in the process.) I have already spoken of my guilt at having sat out World War II while friends were dying in Europe and the Pacific Islands. So I was ambivalent when the call finally came. It was wrenching to leave a young wife, now about to be left with a few-months old baby who cried because of leg braces. It also meant giving up a residency that I had anticipated with great eagerness. I had no fear about the war; what can happen to a doctor? And so it came.

The hospital intercom bleated my name. I was at the bedside of a sick, elderly man recovering from congestive heart failure. I did not respond until the fourth repeat.

Annoyed: "Hello, this is Dr. Moser. I hope this is important!"

Cool voice (he must have heard my tone before, this very day) "This is Major Winship in the Pentagon. Am I speaking to **Captain** Robert H. Moser?" I knew my goose was cooked and garnished.

Much less annoyed: "Yes...."

Cool voice: "Captain, it is my duty to inform you that you have orders to report to Fort Knox within 72 hours to join your unit."

Far less annoyed: "Am I going to Korea?"

Cool voice: "I don't know Captain. You will receive further instructions. You are being assigned to the Fourth Ordnance Battalion; you will report to Colonel Avon Bowman. Good luck, Captain." Click.

I turned to see a small circle of nurses, interns and aides who had somehow been alerted and eavesdropped on my end of the conversation. "I'm going to Korea." I think that is what I said, more than a trifle stunned. I like to think that I am rarely disconcerted, but suddenly I felt a strange, near-physical buffeting as waves of alien emotion washed over me—a million clashing thoughts. My immediate concern was for my little family. Where should they go? The big house in Baltimore with a vacant third floor would have been ideal, but I rejected the concept out of hand. I felt a flash of anger. Stella would never agree; my mother would devour her. How sad. Could they stay in that elegant but spare apartment in Virginia? No, she needed help with Steven. She should be near Sonya in Miami Beach, scene of her youthful triumphs. She should rent an apartment. I knew she still had friends there. I knew someone would cover my patients. But how long would I be away? Will my position be open when I return? Hell, I don't even have a uniform! Three days! I shook my head in confusion and disbelief—so much—so dreadfully fast! I felt depleted.

Dazed, I wandered down to the office of Dr. Jeghers. He knew that I was an "army resident," but he hadn't counted on losing one of his house staff so abruptly. He was kind and thoughtful; I could resume my residency whenever I returned. He even gave me a rare smile and a firm grab of a shoulder. Dear Sister Marie Antonio, chief nurse on my ward, was tearful when I returned to gather my tools and books. She said all the good sisters would pray for my safe return. It wasn't till I was driving home (too rapidly across the 14th Street bridge) that the full impact hit me. This would be the first time since kindergarten that I would wander, for any significant length of time, outside the protec-

tive cloister of academe! Ten thousand inchoate thoughts…I pulled into the parking lot of the apartment complex.

Stella met me at the door with Steven in her arms. It was an unlikely 10:00 A.M. One look and she said, "My God, they're sending you to Korea." We clung to each other, and little Steven obligingly joined in the tears. But we were cool; she had heard Truman too. After a brief discussion, Miami Beach it was. The army would pack up our meager possessions; she would find an apartment near her mother and await my return. Maybe she could get a part-time job or go back to school. It was settled in minutes. There was some worry about money; I would have to ensure that my army pay went to a bank in Miami Beach (a major hassle as it turned out). We sorted out all the other essential trivia that every other husband and wife have discussed since men began to trudge off to strange foreign places and try to kill each other.

We drove to Fort McNair, and I purchased winter and summer uniforms with appropriate insignia. The clerk was kind enough to indicate where the little brass ornaments were supposed to be affixed. When I indicated that I was on orders to Korea, she assured me that the army would issue boots, fatigues and outer garments. (She was wrong; we did not get winter boots and parkas until mid-October.) The next 48 hours were madness. We made lots of love and ate lots of expensive food in the best restaurants in northern Virginia. There was no talk of danger. ("Doctors don't get shot at. Geneva Convention and all that. Besides we wear helmets with big red crosses and travel in ambulances with bigger red crosses.") At National Airport, I took my first salute from a dapper navy NCO. I returned it awkwardly. (I had always initiated the salute in my navy enlisted days.) More hugs and tears at the gate. And so I took my first airplane ride, to Louisville to begin my Great Korean Adventure.

Fort Knox was pandemonium. The MPs at the gate were so harassed that I was not challenged for orders. I was overwhelmed by the turmoil. The area seethed and roared: jeeps, half-tracks, armored personnel carriers, every kind of truck imaginable. I even found row

upon row of ancient-looking tanks. The pungent dust was virtually impenetrable; hundreds of soldiers and civilians seemed to be milling about and yakking furiously. Everyone seemed confused. Is this the way we start every war, noisy chaos born of uncertainty and unanticipated crisis?

Ultimately I stumbled across the headquarters of the Fourth Ordnance Battalion, a very large, slightly sagging wall tent. Colonel Bowman turned out to be a reservist, Lieutenant Colonel Avon Bowman, a stocky, balding man who had run a repair garage in a small Georgia town until he was summoned for duty. He clutched an unlit, well-weathered briar between yellow teeth; he was pleasant and unprepossessing. I gained the impression he was a trifle more than surprised that a regular army doctor had been assigned to his headquarters. I felt obliged to tell him up front that I did not have **any** military experience (not even basic training, sir!), and my medical training had been in internal medicine. I omitted the pulmonary fellowship; somehow it seemed to lack pertinence. It all took a bit of explaining; Bowman was of the Aunt Tanya school of doctoring, "A doctor is a doctor, *nu?*" I explained that the difference was that I was **not** a surgeon. That did not seem to diminish his enthusiasm. I was introduced to the other officers and the chief warrant officer; they were less impressed.

That afternoon, I was joined by my sergeant, Tom Smith, who was to become my friend and counselor in the unfamiliar ways of the army in the field. He was a veteran corpsman, ever patient with my inexperience and naiveté. Smitty was unfailingly helpful and painfully respectful. (I had a rookie's ignorance of the difference between officers and men. I didn't like it, but soon came to realize why it was a military shibboleth. You cannot share all risks and tasks with your men, and you may be obliged to ask them to do dangerous things. But you can be a *mensch* about it.) Smitty and I shared a small-wall tent for eleven months in the field.

I inherited six other corpsmen of varying intelligence, experience and enthusiasm. They were all kids from the hinterlands of northern

Kentucky, dutifully respectful, but obviously wary of the "new Yankee doctor." Most of them had never worked with a physician before. In time, each proved remarkably distinct in skill and trustworthiness. Over the next year only one corporal proved to be a problem—a burgeoning sociopath. Permitting him contact with patients was against my better (clinical) judgment. Ultimately, once in the field, I had to "transfer him laterally" (the army finesse for getting rid of an undesirable without the fuss of a court martial).

Over the next hectic days we gathered our equipment. To my horror I discovered that the sum total of my medical supplies was contained in two hoary trunks. It was obvious from the contents that they were left over from World War II (**early** in WW II!): sulfadiazene tablets, sulfanilimide dusting powder (!), morphine tablets designed to be solubilized in sterile water over an alcohol burner and other archaic items that belonged in the Army Medical Museum, rather than in a 1950 field pack headed for a shooting war. Dressings and burn packs were sealed in olive drab packets of indeterminate age. (One wondered whether the equipment in combat units enjoyed the same venerable vintage. God help us.)

I dumped the lot. Smitty and I jumped into the jeep, already stenciled "Stevie" on the bumper, as was the prevailing fashion (I wound up with Stevie III by mid-1951.) We hustled over to the Fort Knox Army Hospital, where I introduced myself to Colonel Ryle Radke, chief of medicine. I commented that I had recognized his unusually alliterative name from some interesting work he had published on amoebiasis and amoebic hepatitis. This bit of intelligence seemed to engender immediate rapport as I explained my unhappy situation. He was warm and sympathetic and allowed me to raid his pharmacy and medical supply room. I was able to fill five bright new chests with just about everything I could envision that would be required in a battalion aid station in a combat zone. It turned out that many of my colleagues in Korea were less fortunate (no Ryle Radkes), and had shipped out

with their ancient supplies. I became a modest resupply depot for a few weeks in country.

Once you sorted out the chauvinist jingoism in the media, the news from Korea was dreadful. Already there had been some devastating defeats. At Taejon the 34th Regiment of the 24th Division had been overrun, lost its colors, the commander had been captured, and they had lost precious equipment and too many men. The ever-bountiful military grapevine was yielding some bitter wine. Apocryphal stories were circulating about how the troops coming from Japan had literally been rousted from their barracks (and some of the houses where they kept their local women), assembled half dressed and half asleep, issued some extra weapons and soon flung into battle. Some had never fired their new weapons. They were ill equipped physically, emotionally and materially to fight a tough, well-disciplined North Korean invading force. Our bazooka rounds were bouncing off the Russian T-34 tanks, and our poorly trained and ill-conditioned troops were getting clobbered.

Still many of the reports we read in the Louisville papers indicated that the "U.N. Korean intervention" (a detestable euphemism sanitizing an already dirty war) was still not being taken seriously by the American press and the general public. Our intelligence about the enemy was pathetic. The 24th Division troops had been told, in essence, that once the enemy realized that the invincible American army had joined the battle, it would soon be over. It was one of the most disastrous miscalculations in our military history, only to be exceeded by Viet Nam. Within weeks the beleaguered marines of the First Brigade, the 24th, the First Cavalry and several Republic of Korea (ROK) divisions had their backs to the wall in the infamous Pusan perimeter. It was highly problematic whether they could hold the line until significant reinforcements arrived. A Dunkirk-like evacuation was impossible; there were no instant, small boat fleets or white cliffs of Dover in the South China Sea.

Within days we were on a blacked-out troop train with several other units slowly snaking our way west. I am sure that army Intelligence, that wellspring of oxymoron jokes, suspected that legions of North Korean spies were watching our every move. So we chugged along, blindly, in a westerly direction. We would stop in unidentifiable remote areas for piss breaks. After a few dreary days of this nonsense, I peeked around the blackout drapes to be rewarded with my first glimpse of the magnificent Feather River Valley. I vowed to return one day and enjoy the scenic splendor at leisure. (I did.) Soon we arrived at Fort Mason near the San Francisco Presidio. We were all given two-day passes, and with a few other medical officers from different units, all raw as hell, fresh from walking the quiet halls of university hospitals, we explored San Francisco. It was my first return visit since Ken and I had camped in Golden Gate Park. (My God, that had been only a little over three years ago!)

Once the staff at the Top-of-the-Mark heard we were headed off to war, they gave us a great view table and provided a few good bottles of Napa Valley merlot. We had already called our wives and assured them of our safety and sobriety. It was a festive evening; no sense of impending disaster, nor fear of death or disability. We were young and foolish, invincible, invulnerable—convinced the Great American Army would end the war quickly and decisively. (How wrong can you get?)

Our intensely focused education in recent years (medicine, medicine, medicine) had not incorporated much political science. We did not realize that after every war since the Revolution, Congress and the American people assumed that there would never be another serious sustained conflict. Military budgets were slashed, the fleet put in mothballs, army and air force personnel chopped and R & D for next generation weaponry victimized. You might think we had learned a mean lesson in WW II when we almost let the allies diminish and die before we were able to tool up and join the battle. But this time the lack of preparation materially and spiritually was even worse. No one seemed to give a damn. The conflict was being softened and euphemized as a

"UN Police Action." Korea was some wretched hellhole half a world away. What was the threat to our national security? Truman was a good and honest man (hadn't he been with the field artillery in the Great War?). But he lacked the Roosevelt charisma. There was no patriotic rallying cry, no sense of national mission. It was a lugubrious, repetitious scenario, sadly destined for repetition less than a decade later, in Viet Nam.

We sailed on the C.C. Ballou, a tired, rusting, veteran troop ship that had seen its last action in 1945. You could almost smell the mothballs. There was a wonderful apocryphal story about this blue-collar transport. It was reputed to have perfected those key attributes of unseaworthiness: roll, pitch and yaw. The scuttlebutt was that it had served as an experimental platform to test Dramamine! But, by the grace of God the Pacific behaved like Walden Pond for the whole ten days of our transit. The legend remained unchallenged.

The ship was jammed to overflowing with about 3000 troops and every conceivable vehicle lashed on deck, including 105 and 155 howitzers and Sherman tanks. As officers we had a bit of a break on quarters and chow. The enlisted men stood almost continuously in line for the mess hall, latrines and bunks (two men were assigned to each of triple-tiered hammocks). Magically, the logistics worked out so that everyone had ample chance to eat, sleep and care for bodily functions. But there was a lot of time wasted twiddling thumbs in the next queue. There was insufficient deck space for exercise or calisthenics. A general sense of malaise and uncertainty permeated the bored, untested troops. News was sparse; we all had too much time to think. The politics seemed clear enough; a Communist aggressor had invaded a democratic republic. The U.N. opted to punish the renegade state, and we were the agent of the punitive action. Superficial analysis? Of course, but we were not privy to the machinations of international intrigue. Perhaps, it was better that way; it made life a lot simpler. Besides, I was a regular army doctor; no one had coerced me.

Major medical excitement occurred when a soldier developed a hot appendix in mid-Pacific. The only "real surgeon" on board happened to be a peppery, re-treaded ob-gyn type who admitted that he was "a little rusty on bellies." That might have been the understatement of the generation. The nasty appendix was buried in the retro-caecal area (tucked invisibly behind the caecum of the ascending colon). After an agonizing 45 minutes, our ambisinistral surgeon finally teased the recalcitrant, gangrenous organ into visibility. It promptly ruptured, spewing nasty, malodorous infection throughout the peritoneum.

As the "ranking internist," I assumed management of the post-op peritonitis; it was a thoroughgoing nightmare. If I could have air-evacuated the poor trooper to Tokyo or Honolulu, I would have done it in a New York minute. But we were smack in the middle of the largest body of water on earth. I administered unholy doses of intravenous penicillin (our only antibiotic), kept his two drainage tubes wide open, hydrated him, and kept him relatively free of pain. It was an exhausting 72 hours, my first exposure to "military medicine." And we were still a few thousand miles from the sounds of battle. There were a few other internist-residents aboard and we "consulted," but I hovered at the poor kid's bedside for the entire time. I almost lost him. He was still slightly febrile when we carried him off in Pusan, but he was taking fluids orally, and his abdomen was soft and less tender. It had been a sobering adventure.

The only other notable medical event while at sea was an epidemic of gonorrhea and chancroid (it was still a trifle early for syphilitic penile ulcers to surface). It began the third or fourth day at sea. I suspect it was wide-open, rip-roaring North Beach's major contribution to this largely invisible war. The thrill of inspecting the sheepishly exposed penises of 3000 troops by half a dozen pea-green medical officers (yet another queue) was one of the more daunting challenges of our young medical lives.

Finally, one day before our arrival, a scene from the Gregory Peck movie version of "Moby Dick" came to mind. Ahab was hypnotizing

the crew with his glistening silver dollar nailed to the mainmast as he described the great white whale. He snarled something like, "You will smell land where there is no land." He was describing the organic detritus and other debris that inhabited the harpoon-scarred hide of the monster. Well, our sea was shimmering in early July heat, and "there arose an aroma where there should have been no aroma." It defied description; nothing even close existed in my olfactory banks. It was an intoxicating blend of cinnamon, garlic, cloves, excrement, sweat and myriad other unidentifiable odors. It was The Orient. I loved it.

The ship came alive with excitement and subliminal anxiety. The radio reports had been uniformly grim. Our guys were hanging on to the perimeter by their fingernails. The weary old Ballou was driven through a sequence of "evasive maneuvers." With much horn bellowing, we began to swing in wide, ungainly, sweeping arcs. Surely such torpid gymnastics would have prompted any North Korean submarine commander to snicker into his periscope, as he fired torpedoes into our wallowing hulk. That night we were ominously blacked out—steaming silent and somber in stygian darkness. At dawn we sighted land or at least saw a mauve, sodden cloud that squatted heavily upon the land. Pusan.

As we disembarked, I noticed a British troop carrier just down the vast wharf, also off-loading troops. They looked tough and trim. They were the celebrated Gloucesters, the 27th Royal Regiment. I think they had come in from Hong Kong. Over the next months, they were one of the most decorated combat units in Korea, while suffering heavy casualties.

Within minutes, we were trucked to a racetrack where we set up camp in the infield, beside a tank outfit. At dusk we could see the flashes and hear the thunder of artillery to the west. The First Marine Brigade and the 25th Division were engaged in a life-death embrace with crack NK divisions. The previously amorphous "Pusan Perimeter" had taken on form and life; it was ominously close.

Little changed during the week we were hunkered down, organizing our equipment, preparing...for what? The hot rumor (of the hour) was that we were all going to bug out; the green troops grimly defending our toehold were fearfully out-gunned and out-manned. In this twilight zone, I was issued a .45 pistol. I had never fired a weapon in my life; I was inclined to forego the formidable, clumsy weapon. I recited to myself all the comforting aphorisms, "Doctors are non-combatants; big red crosses on helmets. Bigger red crosses on their ambulances. *N'est-ce pas?*" So Smitty took me aside. "I hear the NKs killed a few docs and corpsmen at Taejon. These gooks (I hated the word!) shoot at anything that moves. Geneva is just a city in Switzerland out here." So I test-fired the cumbersome thing. The kick was so bad and the explosion so loud that I couldn't have hit a bull elephant at five feet, and I couldn't I use my stethoscope for a few days. Smitty never even smirked, but suggested quietly that if it made me feel like John Wayne to have the comforting bulge on my hip, go for it. But we requisitioned a carbine and half a dozen clips of ammunition, never far out of reach. Fortunately, I had no occasion when I had to fire the weapon in fear or anger, but on several tense occasions I popped in a clip, chambered a round and fondled it a lot.

We painted out the big red crosses on our ambulance ("great sniper target"). My jeep was enhanced by an ugly fifty-caliber, air-cooled machine gun mounted in the space vacated by removal of the rear seat. That bit of nasty hardware made it impossible to enclose the vehicle and derive any slight benefit from our wimpy heater. But prudence took precedence over comfort. On many a day later in the dead of winter, we thought the reverse. But when General Matthew Ridgeway took over the sagging Eighth Army months later, he made all jeeps discard their canopies and mount 5Os. All jeeps were fitted with five-foot steel rods welded upright in the middle of the front bumper. Apparently one of the more vicious gambits, supposedly invented by the *wehrmacht* in WW II (and now enjoyed by all), was to string piano wire between two trees at neck level across a narrow road.

In the days before we decamped I got to know the other officers in headquarters. The G-2 (Intelligence), John Argue, was known affectionately as "The Judge." He was much too old and chubby to be a captain. I suspected he was more ancient than Bowman. I found him delightful. He had a favorite parlor trick that enjoyed wide notoriety among chums who had served with The Judge. He would deliberately provoke someone (anyone) into an argument to the point where they would challenge his sanity. Then with deliberate posturing, he would reach into his wallet and extract a yellowed, tightly folded document. He would unwind it with theatrical deliberation and hand it to the victim, "Here is a statement from the psychiatrist at Walter Reed attesting to **my** sanity...so where's yours?" I saw the "statement." It appeared to be genuine, dated several years earlier. The Judge never disclosed how he had obtained his treasure, but I saw him perform the ritual several times.

Our dentist, Charley Moore, was a very small, skinny guy who had been in practice in a small town in north Florida. He was a droll, taciturn chain-smoker. His equipment seemed even more antiquated than my original boxes of junk, and he had not sought to replace it. He did manage to obtain some Novocain. He actually had (and used!) a "field dental drill" that was operated by a foot pedal. His corporal would pump the pedal like mad while Charley drilled on some poor suffering soul. It would not have been out of place in Torquemada's inventory.

Charley's other singular skill was stealing my medical alcohol. Early in the war, rumor had it that the sanctimonious Women's Christian Temperance Union (WCTU) prevailed on the DOD to stop our beer ration ("fighting soldiers should not have alcohol"). Thus deprived, on occasion I would cut my pure medical ethyl alcohol about 50/50 with grapefruit juice, and we all would enjoy an occasional shooter. A far more sinister aspect of this ill-conceived, self-righteous contribution to the war effort surfaced when several soldiers turned up with methyl alcohol intoxication: blindness—acidosis—death. Unwittingly, some

enterprising locals had concocted a brand of white lightening blended with liberal dollops of deadly methanol. Very nasty business.

One day I noticed that my medical alcohol had begun to "evaporate" with unseeming rapidity. Smitty and I zealously guarded the only keys to the sturdy Yale. We secured a new lock, but the leakage continued. We watched, but never caught the skillful thief. A few days before I departed the peninsula, Charley confessed; he had swiped my key(s), had duplicates fabricated in one of our company machine shops, and helped himself in the wee small hours, or when Smitty and I were on the road. *C'est la guerre.*

Our adjutant was a malevolent first lieutenant who was responsible for the discipline and work assignments of our troops, including the ROK soldiers we had attached. I am convinced he was a psychopath. We had quite a few face-to-face confrontations when I called him out on disciplinary methods that were patently out of line. We developed an abiding mutual dislike, a dangerous situation in a combat environment. It all came to a climax one scorching August day when Lee Sam Hee, one of my two ROK corpsmen, came to me in uncharacteristic, hand wringing anguish. He insisted that I come with him. He led me to an open field a few hundred yards from our aid station. There was his colleague, Pak Chun Kee, arms and legs tied with four stakes, spread-eagled, stripped from the waist up! It was a scene from a bad spaghetti western. "The lieutenant did this," Pak whimpered through parched lips as I cut him loose. We carried him back to the tent, where I identified about 30% second-degree burns plus severe dehydration and shock. He had been lying there for at least four hours before Lee discovered him. We packed his burns in sterile Vaseline gauze, and I loaded him with saline fluids enriched with potassium.

I went hunting for the sadistic lieutenant, with blood in my eye and mayhem in my heart. He had left the company area. Lucky for both of us. I sought out Bowman and growled that I was going to press charges and get the sadist's ass court-martialed. Bowman knew of our previous clashes over lesser acts of cruelty. He said he would "take care of it." I

was not reassured. The good colonel was a wimp when it came to appropriate discipline. That night it was my turn to stand officer-of-the-guard watch. Whenever we were in hostile country, we posted walking guards and manned several air-cooled 50s on the perimeter. My task consisted of a four-hour stint of walking the area to ensure that no mischief was occurring and no guard fell asleep.

On this night my corpsmen came and told me that the lieutenant had boasted that he would "get me." I believed them. So two of my armed corpsmen kept an eye on that maniac through the night, while two others walked the perimeter with me. Nothing happened. In the morning the bastard had already been handed orders and schlepped off to a line unit. He was out of my reach; I hoped he would get killed before he could brutalize others. But I was always looking over my shoulder thereafter. He was a malignant son-of-a-bitch and should have been sent to Leavenworth. We found out later that Pak's capital crime had been stealing a small can of cherries from the headquarters pantry. Shades of Captain Qweeg! Happily, the other officers were far less colorful.

Back to Pusan and the "week of anxiety." Some inhabitants of the racetrack infield were less anxious (or more fatalistic) than others. After a few days I had another epidemic of venereal diseases on my hands. I soon discovered that despite our personnel being restricted to the race-track area, several shanties had materialized magically just outside the grandstand. They were populated by hordes of newly created prosti-tutes, mostly hungry women driven from the countryside by the NK invasion. I suspect that most women who become prostitutes in war-time follow the same tragic pathway. But despite my sympathy for these unfortunate women, when my V.D. rate approached 75% I went to Bowman. We created a hit squad, five men armed with rifles (no round in the chamber) and batons. We approached each of the shan-ties and, through an interpreter, strongly advised the pimps to vacate the premises within the hour, or we would level the hooches and call in the local cops.

Remarkably, they did not laugh in my face. Perhaps they thought it might be imprudent to sneer openly at armed men. Nor did they take my advice. Thus began the first campaign of "Moser's (silly, singularly unsuccessful) War." After two more unheeded warnings, on the third night we blew police whistles, scattered the pimps and women, and demolished the shacks. No one was injured. The next night all the hooches had miraculously reappeared about 20 feet away. This exercise was repeated twice again. Appeal to local police was useless. Those who were still around were either working the black market or running the whores.

So I launched Campaign Two, an equally ill-advised tactic. I sought out the Pusan Port Commander, a portly, slightly disheveled, light colonel inhabiting a dim corner of a sepulchral warehouse near the waterfront. Blood-shot eyes peered from between towering stacks of documents as he listened politely. I expressed my concern that every unit hunkered down inside the perimeter and not locked in hot combat was suffering an epidemic of venereal disease. I reckoned that our ability to fight was already compromised, and it could get worse. He stared at me morosely. My solution? "Sir, we can set up our own whorehouses. Our doctors and corpsmen can check the girls weekly. We treat those infected once. If they repeat, the MPs can put them in some temporary detention until the troops leave the city." I thought it was a very compelling speech.

I wasn't quite prepared for his reaction. He was a large man and he seemed to rise up like a balding grizzly. His face was suffused. He tried to speak, but only managed a sputter. I think he said something like, "Get the hell out of here, Captain, before I kill you." I suspected he might have had other things on his mind, like supplying a beleaguered army, rather than setting up whorehouses. But once again, fortune smiled. Two days later the First Cav broke out of the perimeter to the north. The now-blooded Eighth Army began to move. But an armada of traveling bordellos moved just a few days behind us. We did not

escape their bountiful microbiological contributions until we were many, many miles deep into the peninsula.

Our mission was to support the vehicles of the combat divisions in our Corps area. We had two companies assigned to our headquarters, rarely three. One was capable of repairing any wheeled vehicle in the military inventory. The guys were wizards with engines. I often marveled at the capability of those hardy mechanics who often worked in subzero weather battling grease and freezing metal with bare hands. The other unit was the famous 57th Tank Retriever Company. They were the troops who trundled out with their giant semis, winched up disabled tanks and other tracked vehicles that were considered salvable, and hauled them back for repair. Frequently the enemy would booby trap or zero-in with mortars and small arms, since they knew that we would try to retrieve and repair. The courage of the 57th in WW II was legendary, and these officers and men were continuing that fighting tradition. They were a wonderful source of anecdotes.

Once, while the company was still training at Fort Knox, they were far out in the Kentucky hinterlands running simulated rescues of disabled tanks. The retrieval vehicles were very large, with the cab roosting at about the level of the second story of a building. A rookie was driving one of the rigs, lumbering down a dusty country road when he rounded a sharp curve too fast. He plowed through a fence and brought the giant vehicle to a thunderous stop next to a farmhouse. The huge blinking red light mounted above the cab was aimed directly into a second story window, just like a winking bloodshot eye. The panicky driver swears he heard a female voice shrieking from the window. "Lawsy, lawsy, Billy, you gotta come here and see this thing! I ain't never seen nothin' like it, and I been to **Louisville!**"

Originally the 57th was an all-black outfit but gradually it was being integrated. Their commander was Captain Will Baker, undeniably the most charismatic leader I met in my career in the army. He was book smart and street wise, tough as a tank, and he inspired courage in his officers and men by example. Will became my best friend in Korea.

Very often our headquarters company camped with one or both assigned units; when Will was around, I always slept better. Many months into the campaign, I was called one night by a very apprehensive First Lieutenant Terry Brown, Will's number two. As we sped away he explained that their company had been engaged in continuous operations for weeks, and they had lost several men. Will had become frustrated and angry at the bad run of luck and the snail's pace rate of critical re-supply of engine parts, an eternal problem. He had gotten very drunk and was wearing four 45s; two in shoulder holsters and one on each hip. He had not eaten all day and was just sitting morose and silent in his tent, drinking Old Crow.

By this time, Will and I had spent many hours together. We had downed more than a few of my super-duper 50-50 ethyl alcohol and grapefruit concoctions. I didn't think he would shoot me, but I was not absolutely sure. I had never seen him angry and drunk. So I yelled out a cheery greeting. No warning shot across my bow. Still speaking loudly, I pulled back the tent flap and entered very slowly. No surprises. Will stared at me in sullen silence, a pistol in each fist. The scene was surreal, Stephen King stuff. Above the stove a single Coleman lantern swung in a light breeze making crazy shadows. "Can I come in and not get shot?" Slowly he smiled and holstered the pistols, shoved the bottle of Old Crow toward me. We talked and drank late into the night. He could not give a rational explanation for his bizarre behavior, but he thought that part of his brain told him that his whole company had been targeted by the NKs, and he had armed himself appropriately.

He admitted being depressed over recent personnel losses, inadequate resupply and the chronic overwork demanded of his men. I asked him if he would like to speak to a psychiatrist; one of my classmates was the shrink at the 10th Field Hospital. After a moment of reflection and another jolt of Old crow, he said yes, if we could keep it off the record. I knew he was indulging me, but I called Harold Kolansky and he agreed to see Will. The next day, we tooled back south

about 60 miles. Will visited with Harold for about 30 minutes, then we all chatted. All off the record. On the return trip Will said he felt better; Harold had slipped him a few Seconals to ensure a few precious intervals of nepenthe. Will later told me that he never used one. There was no recurrence of that bizarre night, despite the unrelenting pressure of his mission.

South of Taegu we stood just behind elements of the 25th Division, the 555 ("Triple Nickel") 105 Artillery Battalion and the 70th Tank Battalion. The fighting raging a scant few miles north was ferocious. A couple of times we were camped next to the 555, and the piercing, crack-crack-crack cacophony of an all-night barrage forced cotton into ears. No wonder most artillerymen become more than a little deaf. During these tense days we maintained an armed perimeter at all times since small guerrilla units formed by NK infiltrators were scattered throughout this area. I stood my watch with the other officers; it was a hairy time.

MacArthur's single stroke of genius occurred in September, 1950 with the invasion at Inchon. Whether it was dumb luck or inspired tactics (maybe a bit of both), this flanking operation broke the back of NK resistance. Soon thereafter the 25th spearheaded by the tanks of the 70$^{th}$, broke out of the perimeter and charged north racing to link up with the 7th Division. The First Marine Division and the 7th Infantry Division had spearheaded the Inchon attack, and the fighting to take Seoul was especially fierce and bloody. But soon thereafter, the army units linked up at Suwon and continued the attack against retreating NK regulars. In the mad, scrambling, Pattonesque race up the peninsula, the combat units destroyed and captured many enemy outfits. But they bypassed many other, often company-sized units that had shed their uniforms and melted into the torrent of refugees streaming south. Later they emerged and reformed into marauding guerrilla gangs. We followed hot on the heels of the fast-moving combat battalions. Often the front was so fluid that we had to pull back, or be pre-

pared to take the point! Not our cup of tea. But the NK spirit had been broken, at least for now.

It was a tumultuous, giddy time; crazy things happened. The adventures of the Turkish Brigade spring to mind. Some U.N. genius had dispatched the Turkish Brigade and the Greek Battalion on the same troop ship. I am told that only rigid, gun-barrel discipline kept another war from breaking out in the Aegean Sea. I came to really believe this; the enmity was ancient and unforgiving.

One day while we were in the north, a Turkish captain roared into our company area leading a very young soldier who was in obvious distress. The officer spoke little English, but anyone could tell the kid was in trouble. Questions were impossible, so I popped my stethoscope on his sweaty chest and discovered that he had a consolidated right lung. He produced some bloody sputum; his temperature was 103. He had lobar pneumonia, probably pneumococcal. I turned to the captain and indicated that this man needed immediate hospitalization. The 1055 MASH was a few miles back down the road. His English wasn't very good, but I got the message, "Turkish soldiers get wounded—not sick! Give penicillin and we go." I began to protest, but…He needed a week of penicillin, fluids and rest. The only "depot penicillin" I had was some vicious stuff called penicillin-in-oil-and-beeswax, guaranteed to cause a sterile abscess at the injection site 100% of the time. Procaine penicillin was available, but not to battalion aid stations until a few months later. So I gave the poor kid a killer shot into each gluteus and deltoid, some cough medicine, a dozen or so aspirin tablets ("no take all at once," plus gestures). He was dumped in the back seat and off they flew in a cloud of dust and anger. Tough army.

The Turks were insane, dangerous drivers. The narrow, twisty roads in most of Korea were mainly composed of fine-silted earth: choking dust in summer, pasty slick when it rained. The Turks were issued a batch of our two and a half ton (six by six) trucks, which they always drove pedal to metal. When a convoy of Turk-driven trucks was spotted, everyone hit the ditch. But as fighters they were unsurpassed. On

one occasion, they ran out of ammunition in a firefight with NKs and beat them back with gun butts and rocks. I was pleased they were on our side. But when the rumor started that they were to be issued tanks, I wasn't too sure. (To my knowledge they never were.)

By November, we were in Pyongyang, a burning wasteland of a city. We found an abandoned, firebombed school on the edge of town with one building relatively intact. By September, it had begun to get cold, but we were not issued parkas and winter boots until mid-October. By November it had turned bitter. It became evident that we were not far from Manchuria. Our sole source of heat was the infamous, treacherous gasoline stove. One unit would heat a wall tent effectively, but they were notoriously temperamental. Reports of explosions and deadly fires were not uncommon. We had just set up our dispensary in a large room with a single exit. We had placed six litters up on wooden horses. Four of us laid out our bags and were preparing for sleep. I recall Charley was already zipped up, Smitty was tidying up near the door, and one of my corpsmen was sitting on the edge of his litter-cot taking off his boots.

Suddenly there was a horrendous "varoom" in the far corner of the room. The gasoline stove had exploded. Sudden intense heat and flame were everywhere. I leaped from my litter, screamed for Charley and scrambled for the exit. I saw Smitty and the corpsman race out before me, but no Charley! He had been closest to the stove. I tried to reenter the room, but it was engulfed in flames, a sudden inferno—blistering, intense. I began to weep and tremble, a delayed reaction to the epinephrine surge that had probably saved my life. I thought Charley had been burned alive. Someone tapped my shoulder; it was Charley! The little bastard was still wearing his sleeping bag, singed and smoking. He had no recollection of how he had managed to jump or scramble from the deepest recess of that hellhole. We all suffered superficial burns, but had miraculously escaped. Those damned gasoline stoves had claimed more than a few lives, but often they were the only source of heat in that arctic, god-forsaken wasteland.

A few days later, the war stopped for about 24 hours. At least for our side. Ubiquitous Bob Hope, with Marilyn Maxwell in a shimmering scarlet gown that must have been painted on, choppered in to Pyongyang to entertain the victorious American Army. A few days later, MacArthur delivered his sonorous, dramatically cadenced "all troops home by Christmas" speech. I always have despised the pompous, imperious bastard; at least Patton made no pretense at not being an arrogant son of a bitch. We still have troops in Korea—50 years later.

We edged further north in pursuit of ragged fragments of the NK regulars. The Eighth Army was now well equipped and had acquired hard-wrought battle savvy. But when we set up camp near Anju, now deep in North Korea, my two ROK corpsmen sent a chill up my spine. They had chatted up some refugees who told them that hordes of Chinese regulars were poised, hidden along the north bank of the Yalu River. Will Baker and I hustled this bit of intelligence to Bowman who called Corps headquarters. He was informed that Eighth Army G-2 had "looked into those rumors" and there is nothing to them. "There were no vehicles massed, no bridges being built." Of course, the Chinese were building subsurface bridges at night, invisible to daytime aerial surveillance. (This was before sensitive satellites could read license plates from near-earth orbit.)

We were not reassured. I sometimes think that MacArthur simply could not accept the fact that a rag-tag army of communists supposedly exhausted from the long, bitter war with Chiang Kai-shek, might trump his brilliant coup at Inchon. I cannot believe that he did not know the Chinese were about to enter the war. I really think MacArthur intended to use tactical nuclear weapons once the Chinese provided an excuse by crossing the river. It would have been just another grandiose MacArthur stratagem. Who would be more worthy to start World War III than the Grand Old Soldier? But who the hell knew what was going on? Ground grunts are the last to hear anything.

A few days later we were still encamped near Anju. Will and I had climbed a hill just behind our encampment, just to chat and stoke our

pipes. We watched in silent fascination as a stream of vehicles surged west (on a road that turned to the south), rapidly was becoming a torrent. It was a gaggle of tanks, trucks, half-tracks, and self-propelled howitzers from different units moving with no apparent organization. Will drew on his pipe, "Looks like the victorious Eighth Army is buggin' out." Then our attention was drawn to explosions on a hill about a mile or two southeast. Navy and air force planes were dumping napalm! "Guerrillas?" I rasped. "No way, Doc, we don't bug out for guerrillas. Those bandits are Chinese, and they are turning our flank!"

We scrambled down the hill and grabbed Bowman and told him what we had seen. He chuntered, "We're trying to reach Corps for orders." Baker then uttered his deathless statement. "Colonel sir, Corps is probably already hightailing down the road. With all due respect, **Sir**, the 57th is taking off, and **we've got the guns**!" We were on the road in minutes. It was the beginning of the Great Retreat. The greater part of the Eighth Army was lined up bumper-to-bumper, many units were scrambled. No obvious panic, but fear was abroad, tension crackled like static electricity. There was little doubt in anyone's mind that if the Chinese could turn our eastern flank and cut the main escape route south, they could trap our entire western force. It would be Inchon in reverse.

But Dame Fortune was still smiling. There was a heavy overcast for the next few days. There is no question that if the enemy had been able to mount any significant air assault, they could have destroyed us. Hour after hour Smitty and I sat and slept in our jeep, wrapped in parkas and blankets to fight the penetrating cold, chomping on icy C rations as we inched back down the peninsula. During that fateful night I suffered my only "casualty" of the war. While asleep, my left hand mitten dropped off, and when I awakened my middle, fourth and pinkie fingers were blanched with frostbite. (It is a bit of curious physiology that some 50 years later I still get pain in those digits if the air-conditioning in a restaurant is just a trifle too enthusiastic. The cells in those vessels, nerves and skin must have been replaced a hundred

times, but the "tissue memory" of that 15 minutes of exposure has never abated.)

It was an endless night. Furtive glances always eastward, ever alert for telltale signs of rumble or fire. We moved in fits and starts with prolonged periods of helpless immobility. Sleep was hostage to apprehensive scanning of the black sky and straining for the drone of low-flying aircraft. Once back in Pyongyang, Will's outfit was tasked with the dangerous and onerous mission of blowing up batches of brand new Patton tanks still on flatcars, plus mountains of precious winter gear and other materiel, to prevent capture by the enemy.

By now the tactics of the People's Liberation Army were well known. They were not supermen, and they wore sneakers while carrying individual pouches of rice and crude water canteens. Not every man had a rifle until one was taken from a fallen enemy, but most carried grenades. They were swift and skillful in deploying small mortars. Attacks were sudden, preceded by blowing bugles, clashing cymbals, much screaming, and they attacked *en masse*. It was masterful psychological warfare, waged by hardy, seasoned combat troops. With small arms and mortars they were overwhelming U.N. units bearing superior weaponry. The Chinese suffered heavy casualties from cold and allied fire, but on they came.

About this same time the First Marine Division, Royal Marines, the Third and Seventh Army Divisions and two ROK Divisions were having their problems in extreme northeast Korea. MacArthur's master plan had been to have these units push north and west to link up with the rest of the Eighth Army, which he assumed would have stabilized the south shore of the Yalu. Neither prong of the pincers attained its objective. The marines managed to penetrate to the Chosin Reservoir, but had to fall back. "Chesty" Puller's heroic "attack to the rear" was more orderly, but suffered far more casualties than our inglorious escape from near the Yalu. The enemy took a very heavy pounding from cold and fire. It was a mean season for all involved. MacArthur's grand strategy had fallen on its ass.

We fled south of Seoul to Yongdongpo. In these chaotic weeks there occurred some of the inevitable incongruities of war. On December 30 we still held Seoul, but the Chinese who had streamed across the parallel had stopped their attack, apparently to resupply and regroup. At that time we did not know this vital fact. We thought they were determined to continue their sweep south to retake the capital and press their advance against our stumbling army. It could have been the Pusan Perimeter—revisited.

Through the mysterious military grapevine, I heard that some moonlighting G.l. in signal corps had concocted a Rube Goldberg ham radio operation that was still transmitting out of Seoul. Miraculously, he was able to make contact with families back in the States. Three of us leaped into my jeep and charged north, back across the Han River pontoon bridge, still jammed with troops and trucks streaming south. The terrified refugees were obliged to scramble across the river via the fragments of the old bridge that had been blown. They had jury-rigged planks and ropes between twisted girders. It reminded me of a single-file ant swarm over uneven terrain. Going against the surge of traffic was a challenge, but the MPs were disorganized and assumed that any vehicle crazy enough to be headed north must be on important business. Finally, with the aid of a crude, hand-drawn map, we located the partially burned-out warehouse.

The scraggly-haired, chain-smoking ham operator was still making contact! There were only a few guys ahead of Smitty and me. The operator was limiting calls to two minutes; it often took five or ten to patch into the local telephone system via a cooperative ham on the other end. Within a few minutes I was talking to my wife! I had lost track, but it was New Year's Eve in Miami Beach. We yelled scratchy excited greetings and hurried expressions of love. Before my two minutes were up, MPs were clubbing the door yelling that the city was to be evacuated. The pontoon bridge was being rigged for demolition. We piled into the jeep and raced south. I recall the shattered, smoldering capital building, blackened and skeletal. The streets were empty but for hus-

tling, whistle-blowing military police and clusters of soldiers. A few civilians were scuttling amidst the ruins. We had to dodge around hastily constructed tank traps and sandbag barricades. But soon we were back at our camp awaiting the next move. It was a tense, crazy night, but I was ecstatic. I had actually spoken to my wife!

The Chinese advance stopped just past the 38th parallel. With minimal logistical support, they could have pushed us into the sea with comparative ease. Those terrible weeks represented one of the darkest hours of American military history. Viet Nam might have been worse, but morale in Eighth Army was at its nadir. To make things worse, we heard that General Walker had been killed in a jeep accident just before Christmas. His replacement was Matthew Ridgeway, who had a reputation as a hard-nosed commander of the 82nd Airborne in WW II. Maybe weary Eighth Army needed another boot in the ass, but we had certainly already had our butt well kicked by the Chinese.

The fighting persisted into the new year and well beyond. Heartbreak Ridge on the central front was an especially deadly encounter. The NKs (backed by the People's Liberation Army) had retaken Seoul, then we took it back. The whole front was unstable, teetering. I don't exactly remember when the "peace talks" began in Panmunjon, but we moved up to Uijongbu just north of Seoul. The NKs postured and blustered as though they hadn't had the hell kicked out of them until they were rescued by the Chinese. So the process of wrangling over petty details (the shape of the conference table!), blustering walkouts, histrionic threats and cheeky 38th parallel violations, began to drag on. By now I was beginning to count down to June, and things settled into a tiresome routine. I had no complaints; it was a lot better than what had preceded. As someone else has said, war consists of periods of utter terror punctuated by intervals of interminable boredom. For now, the bad fighting had subsided all along the line. There were still some skirmishes, but it was mostly quiet.

The final "cease fire" treaty was signed in 1953, but "peace" has never been declared; both sides continue to brandish heavy concentra-

tions of troops and weaponry on either side of the infamous parallel. (Almost 50 years later, the bulk of the common people of the aptly named "hermit kingdom" still suffer outrageous, primitive living conditions, epitomized by privation and famine. But their irrational, unpredictable, Stalinist leaders still maintain a most formidable army, with advanced rocketry and a persistent hint of sequestering weapons of mass destruction. Frequent saber rattling (a small submarine hits the shoals in South Korean waters) has become the norm. In recent months, there seemed to be some indication that the "Rogue state" was willing to listen to some reason. But no significant progress has been made, and their invidious track record of past deceit and outrageous "ransom" demands (to act civilly) makes everyone wary.

Many curious things occurred during the preceding months, in venues peripheral to the main show. While we were moving rapidly through the north, my good friend, Captain John Ransier, an ordnance technical intelligence officer, was responsible for tracking down and identifying any enemy equipment that was new or different. John was a stocky, good-natured chap with a wonderfully contagious sense of humor and a dash of (at times unsettling) daring. His holy grail was the mythical Joseph Stalin III heavy tank. There were all sorts of rumors about the legendary monster. No one on our side had ever seen one, but the scuttlebutt was that the enemy had several JS IIIs, and they could tear up our new Pattons and the British Centurions.

One day John, his driver and his three ROKs popped up at my dispensary. Things were fairly quiet. He had "something" to show me. This was usually an invitation to eyeball some exotic enemy paraphernalia too clunky to move. But "this time was different." We drove about 20 miles into some forested hills. I became a bit edgy since this was known guerrilla country, and John was almost too jocular and reassuring. Nervous Nellie Doc with Big John Wayne. He led me into an abandoned lead mine that had been converted into a huge underground arsenal. We posted guards at the mouth and climbed down

into this subterranean powder keg. It was eerily silent, a soft earthen floor cushioned our footsteps.

There were some cavernous rooms that had been excavated and converted into a theater, kitchen and mess hall. Individual sleeping niches dotted the walls. Dozens of freshly carved-out areas still contained heavy machinery used to manufacture pistols, grenades and knee mortars. Thousands of rounds of live ammunition were neatly loaded into wooden cartridge boxes. We surmised that the enemy had been obliged to evacuate hurriedly; metal dishes with decaying food rested on some tables. Thankfully, there were no booby traps.

Then John revealed the jewel in this crown of caches: several boxes of NK cavalry sabers still encased in greasy cosmoline. (The NKs had cavalry with horses yet?) He had cleaned one off. It was rather crude with a mean-looking, two-foot curved blade and a hand-hewn wooden handle with a hammer and sickle carved on each side. Each had a heavy black plastic scabbard. Later John gifted every officer and non-com in the headquarters with a saber and kept half a dozen for himself. They were elegant war trophies. I kept one to take home, but it was confiscated by hard-assed MPs at the airport in Tokyo. Not a time to dicker. But the sabers became prime items for barter, mostly with air force jocks who had access to fairly decent Scotch from the Tokyo PX.

But that is not the important story. The day after our exploration, John returned to begin his inventory of the cave. At sundown, a gang of guerrillas attacked while his team was emerging from the mine. John's small group took shelter in an L-shaped trench adjacent to the mine entrance. A firefight ensued, and John's small detachment was pinned down. After nightfall, the enemy crept to one end of the L and began to pour gasoline into the trench. John knew they had only seconds to try to escape. He had no idea of the enemy strength, but it seemed like a handful. Quickly, he gathered his meager band and told them to scatter into the woods to regroup about half a mile away at a road junction they all knew. They bolted for the woods, firing as they scrambled. One of his ROKs was hit, a slight flesh wound in the arm.

They think they shot at least four attackers as they escaped. Subsequently an air strike sealed the mine entrance. John was awarded a Bronze Star for heroism.

In the field, personal hygiene was always a problem. Portable showers with immediate laundry capability arrived after we had settled down in Uijongbu. "Pit cleansing" via helmet or washbasin just did not suffice. I liberated a 50-gallon gasoline drum and had it acetylene-torched longitudinally into halves. Metal brackets were welded on each end of the bottom. I presented a twin to Will Baker ("Merry Christmas"). We enjoyed reasonable field cleanliness. I shared mine sparingly, and within a week copycats began to materialize. I should have patented "Doc's tub."

One day while we were still in Pyongyang an incident occurred that afforded me my first publication in a medical journal. Even in a grim war all is not unleavened dreariness. I must confess my maiden publication appeared in a section of the journal devoted to "medical humor," not exactly a venue guaranteed to land a trip to Stockholm.

One of the ROK soldiers (another Pak) assigned to our headquarters stopped me, and in his recently acquired English (far superior to my fumbling Korean), indicated that his grandfather lived in a village nearby. During a brief visit, Pak had discovered that the old man was ill and suffered rectal bleeding. Would I please see him? I told him that such a sign could indicate something serious, the old man should be seen in a hospital; he needed to be sigmoidoscoped. All I had was an ancient proctoscope that I had picked up in an abandoned North Korean hospital. But he pleaded, and the reality was that finding any hospital here in the war-ravaged north would be about impossible. So I agreed.

A few days later we were about to pack up and move when I spotted an old man squatting in front of the dispensary. I had forgotten my promise, but here he was. I called down to headquarters for Pak. He was not available, nor were my ROK aid men. The papasan spoke no English but smiled and gestured. And I was running out of time. So I

led him inside, had him roll over on his side, did a rectal examination, and then took a peek with the proctoscope. It was not very satisfactory, but what I could see appeared normal. Of course, I could not exclude some lesion higher in the colon beyond my range of vision. He needed to be advised. At that moment Pak materialized, and I explained the problem. There was a lot of animated chatter. Then Pak turned to me and spoke, in halting English, "This old man thanks you very much for all your trouble. But **now** can you tell him, which is the road to Seoul?" No wonder they call us barbarians!

The most significant medical event that occurred during my tour happened a few weeks before I was scheduled to depart. It was early June and the ever-choking dust was pervasive. The peace talks were stalled in uneasy limbo. About mid-morning an ambulance jeep with British markings skidded to a halt in front of my dispensary tent. Two British aide men eased off a litter bearing a comatose major. He was covered with petechiae (pin-point hemorrhages), some had coalesced into large bloody blebs. A raging fever was compounded by a weak, thready pulse driven by a racing heart and rapid shallow respirations. The sergeant said he had been ill for a few days and had refused evacuation. The major had been discovered in his present condition just a few hours earlier in his tent, and we were the nearest medical facility.

It did not require any diagnostic skill to recognize that this man was beyond the capability of my modest facility. I reverted to the traditional role of the battalion surgeon: stabilize and evacuate. I started plasma in each arm by rapid push, grabbed two more units and piled him into my ambulance for the 20-minute race to the 121st Evacuation Hospital. My dearest friend and medical school roommate, Dick DuPree, ran the medical service there. As the second two units of plasma were streaming in, my mind raced the gamut of diagnostic possibilities: fulminating typhus to meningococcemia to gonococcemia to thrombotic thrombocytopenic purpura, to God knows what? In 1951 we had not learned about disseminated coagulopathy (uncontrolled

clotting) or other cytokine-mediated (cellular hormones) perturbations related to overwhelming sepsis. It would have not made any difference.

My patient turned out to be one of the first cases of Epidemic Hemorrhagic Fever with Renal (failure) Syndrome. My colleagues at the 121st were equally baffled. Despite heroic doses of penicillin, vasopressor support, many units of whole blood and efforts to control his fever, he died within hours. Months later, after an alarming small epidemic had occurred, I was told that the disease had been identified by a former Japanese Army medical officer who was working at the Tokyo Army General Hospital. He had seen similar patients during the Imperial Army's occupation of Manchuria in the 1930s.

It was many years later that the microorganism (Hantaan virus) and the vector (Apodemus agrarius), a field mouse, were identified. At that time the military situation was so fluid that rumors of biological warfare were rampant. Over 3000 U.S. soldiers became ill with this vicious illness. Kidney shutdown was a common complication, and within weeks several hemodialysis units were operating on the peninsula. In recent years another variety has emerged, centered in the Four Corners area (Arizona, New Mexico, Utah and Colorado) in Navajo Nation country. This violent strain can kill within days with overwhelming, virtually irreversible pulmonary edema (fluid in the lungs). Mortality ranges around 40%, much higher than the Korean version. Rare isolated cases continue to pop-up, mostly in the southwest.

In the waning weeks of my tour I reflected on the past months. My war had been embarrassingly easy compared to those in active combat. Experience in war is largely a matter of where you are assigned. For me, it was the luck of the draw; I could have been assigned to a hot combat division at the whim of a pentagon bureaucrat. The attrition rate in line units was very high. We lost 56,000 soldiers, marines and sailors in Korea. Troops in areas behind the combat zone work hard, but rarely experience the mortal danger and physical discomfort that is the routine fare of infantrymen. In Korea, many of the officers and non-coms who lucked out with permanent assignments in the rear, lived with

full-time female companions. Theirs was a very different war. I suspect it has been the same in every major conflict.

Throughout the latter months of my time in country, I never ceased to be amazed at the venereal disease rate. Officers and men coming back from R and R leave in Japan seemed especially vulnerable. At one time when we were settled down in Uijongbu I noticed an inordinate number of soldiers coming from other national units (Brits, Belgiques, Turks) often from many miles distant, to have their STD treated in my dispensary. I was not convinced it was related to my superior medical acumen, and quite frankly, our bookkeeping was rather primitive—a large ledger with name, rank, serial number, diagnosis and treatment. Only much later was this formalized into accessible data and forwarded. My perplexity was answered by the taciturn Smitty, "If these guys get reported to their units as having VD, it means automatic reenlistment." Worth a few mile jeep ride.

My own celibacy was a combination of fear of VD plus a sense of the shabbiness of having intercourse with some hungry peasant girl for whom prostitution had become a necessity to survive. I never felt that deprived, and I never tempted fate by going to Japan.

We also saw the ugly face of what war did to men. On more than one occasion while in convoy, we heard shots fired and saw peasants fall. I was told that they probably were NK infiltrators, but they looked like ordinary country folk to me. The army had its share of psychopaths, and "shooting gooks" was one vicious manifestation of their sickness. Anyone can go a little mad when a comrade dies in battle, and there were atrocities on both sides. But there is another dimension to this pathology. It has to do with embedded racial prejudice, and it is not limited to "white supremacy." I have seen its venomous countenance in other races. It is the dehumanization of those who are "different," most often of a darker color, the concept of *untermenschen*, creatures that are "less than human." The Nazi Aryan super-race eugenic "cleansing" madness, the lynching of blacks by the KKK, the killing of "gooks" by white (and black) soldiers, are all related phenom-

ena. Perhaps it helps in war to demonize and dehumanize the enemy; it makes killing easier. But it is a most troublesome aspect of the human condition. And, it does not always stop when the "legal" shooting ceases.

In the maelstrom that is battle, courage and adrenaline-driven temporary insanity are often inseparable cohorts. We like to think we are more civilized than the enemy, but l am not sure. We encountered villages where napalm had been used; many civilian women, children and old people were horribly burned and murdered. I provided medical care for those we encountered. "NK sympathizers" was always the excuse for the carnage, but it rarely rang true. I can only hope my experience in Korea made me a better human being.

I have been asked about fear. The only moments that could be described as cold terror occurred during those interminable days and nights during the retreat on the road south of Anju. Also, on one bright day, deep in North Korea, our company area was actually strafed by three navy corsairs. They made two passes. They obviously had read the wrong coordinates or landmarks. We scurried into slit trenches, and I was badly frightened. But that was a matter of minutes. The retreat from Anju was endless.

No, I don't think fear builds character. I have heard the truism, "there are no atheists in foxholes," and maybe I was never frightened enough, but I experienced no epiphany. To pray for survival after a lifetime of agnosticism is unacceptably hypocritical. We know that both sides implore their separate gods for victory. God was not around when napalm wiped out villages and when soldiers on both sides died alone and in pain.

It is my firm conviction that after Viet Nam, the United States will **never** commit large armies to fight a long-term war on foreign terrain. As we have done in Libya, Bosnia, Somalia, Haiti, the Gulf, Kosovo and Afghanistan, we will strike by air and sea, commit small specialized units for intense, hit-and-run operations, and contribute some "peace-keeping" troops to U.N. ground action. I am opposed to the continu-

ous presence of U.S. troops in Germany, Saudi Arabia, Japan and South Korea. The time has long since passed when those countries (and the rest of the United Nations) should share the personnel and economic burden of policing the world. As we contemplate action in Iraq, I hope my "feeling" is correct.

When I am asked, "Was it worth it?" I am obliged to respond, by what measure? Do you mean in terms of men dead and disabled, national fortune expended, political gain, national honor upheld, world communism held at bay? I don't know. We did not "win" this war, just as we were denied victory in Viet Nam. So what have been the consequences? We did succeed in Korea in limiting the outlaw state of the north to the original border. But the much trumpeted "domino theory" of South East Asia was a fiction (the dominant *raison d'etre* for the Viet Nam war). No other country in the area has "gone Communist." Our rationale for Viet Nam (which was not a U.N. action and cost even more American lives than Korea) was completely unjustified, in my opinion. I think our foreign policy in these instances, was misguided; one can only hope that the UN will assume a greater role (political and military) in keeping world peace.

# 14

## *Changed World*

✦

### *(things would never be the same...)*

As my plane lifted off from Honeida Airport, I thanked God (or whatever divine providence had looked after me) that I had survived the mayhem alive and intact. I began to wonder if Stella would like the handsome handlebar mustache I had nurtured in the last dull months at Uijongbu. When I deplaned in Jacksonville, Stella was even more exquisite than I remembered, and a chubby Steven, now shorn of his dreadful leg braces, met me, joyously, on the tarmac. They had driven up from Miami Beach so that we could get a jump on the long trip to Washington. One look from Stella, and I scuttled my elegant handlebar before we went to bed. I think Jonathan was conceived on the slow drive north. We talked incessantly; she was radiant—so very bright and charming. She told me that times had been difficult.

The army paychecks had been delayed several months in the transition, despite dozens of calls to the Office of the Surgeon General. Sonya had been a great deal of comfort and help. My sister Joan had come for a visit, but she had acted like a surrogate of my mother. It had not been a pleasant time. Stella enjoyed a brief sojourn working as a social page reporter for the *Miami Daily News*. She showed me some of her stuff, and it was very good reporting, even if the subject matter was mundane. Laughingly, she told me that one of her old boyfriends had put moves on her. "You must miss making love, and he's probably

messing around over there." I had no problem accepting her words of fidelity, as she did mine.

Within two weeks after returning to the States, I was back on the wards at Georgetown, desperately trying to catch up with my peers. As with most Korean veterans, our return was anticlimactic; we drifted back into the mainstream trying to pick up the frayed threads of our lives. There was no victory, so no brass bands or tickertape parades, nor did we encounter the vilification and scorn that greeted many returning Viet Nam vets. We were just ignored, and that was okay. The experience was epitomized by my first encounter back in the hospital. I joined a group making teaching rounds at the bedside of a patient. The senior attending looked up, "Ah, Bob, I hear you've been away to the war. Nice to have you back. Now who has the lab data on this patient...?"

During my time in Korea, my brother Ken married. His wife was the delightful daughter of a much-venerated old Pittsburgh family. Stella and my parents attended the wedding at the family's fabled farm in upstate Pennsylvania. Ken had been graduated with honors from Johns Hopkins Medical School and was taking an internship-residency in medicine, to be followed by a pulmonary fellowship at Georgetown. I was very happy for them.

I was already late to resume my residency; somehow all of my colleagues seemed much brighter and younger than when I had left. Sister Marie Antonio greeted me with an uncharacteristic teary embrace. She told me that somehow the rumor was circulated that I had been killed during the Chinese invasion. We sat and chatted for an hour and the other Sisters drifted in and embraced me, a very heart-warming interlude. Obviously, many tears had been shed and novenas offered, predicated on my apocryphal demise. Good people. I figured every little bit had helped.

I remained on captain's pay while accumulating more army payback time for my residency years. We found a modest apartment proximate to the hospital, and soon things settled back to pre-Korea status. We

still had some inter-personal problems, but the ambiance was much better. We made friends with some neighbors. He was a virologist at Walter Reed, and his wife a voluble New Yorker who shared a lot of background with Stella. I found myself much more tolerant of trivial dissonance, less perturbed by minor annoyances. After the bliss of being reunited with my little family gradually subsided, I soon drifted back into my old, obsessive work habits. My assault on the certifying American Board of Internal Medicine (ABIM) examinations was a major agenda item. I began to keep a "hot file" consisting of articles and editorials clipped from the journals that I felt would be grist for potential ABIM questions.

Stella began to take a few courses at George Washington University in areas of her intellectual interest: philosophy, comparative religion, and psychology. She acquired a coterie of like-minded friends. These included a pair of *tres chic*, debonair Parisian exchange students named Robert ("*Robaire, s'il vous plait*") and Jean Louis. They spoke charmingly accented English and came over several times for martinis ("How the hell much vermouth do you add?") and dinner. I always thought they were a little light in the loafers, but they provided harmless diversion for Stella while I was studying. When she was about five months pregnant, Stella told me that the boys were going to take off for a week to visit Miami Beach. They had acquired a new Caddy convertible. She would like to go along to visit Sonya and her friends. I had no reason to balk. I had no thought of any sexual impropriety, nor do I today. They had a marvelous time. We were destined to meet these frivolous Frenchmen a few years later; it would be a less than felicitous reunion.

I was working a civilized every third night, every third weekend schedule. Our first visit to Baltimore was rough. My mother had offered **no** help to Stella during her difficult time in Miami Beach, despite one request for financial help (rent and food money!). It was as though the year in Korea-Miami Beach had not occurred. Mother was still maintained an unrelenting, rock-like indifference. Even the pres-

ence of little Steven failed to soften her unrelenting disdain of Stella and Sonya.

It all came to a boil over a characteristically tense dinner, pregnant with long intervals of unseemly silence. Stella had addressed an innocent question to my dad, who was already suffering oral difficulties, the dryness imposed by his Parkinsonism. (More on this in a moment.) He had some difficulty responding and suddenly began to weep! We were all taken aback. Mother lashed out at Stella for subjecting him to such "humiliation." It was an attack from left field, totally inappropriate—the final straw. I slammed down my utensils, "You will apologize to my wife!" Mother sat grim, unmoved. "Okay, we are leaving." I got up. "You are insufferable, and you are about to lose a son, grandson and daughter-in-law. How in the hell can you live with yourself." Mother was stunned. It was the first time I had ever raised my voice to her. I gathered up my little family, and we headed for the door. Finally mother stirred and managed a strangled, "I'm sorry." I turned and growled, "Well, that's a small enough start, but just a few years too late." We left. I had acquired a very low threshold for her petulance and intransigent behavior. I would like to say that the situation improved a great deal; it did not. Stella's tolerance had been tested beyond reasonable forbearance, and mother's future efforts at reconciliation never bore the ring of sincerity.

In the time I had been in Korea, my father had developed rapidly progressing Parkinsonism. I had noticed a slight intention tremor, some facial rigidity and skin waxiness when he attended my graduation in 1948. I had advised mother of my clinical suspicion at the time, but his signs and symptoms seemed to subside over the following year. But now he was much worse, compelled to stop practice because of problems with tremor, rigidity and unsteady gait. The drugs now available to ameliorate symptoms were not on the horizon in 1952.

Characteristic of the malady, his mind was as sharp as ever. Dad had always been volatile emotionally; frequently, he laughed until tears would flow. He was exquisitely sensitive to the feelings of others. But

now he often wept uncontrollably, expressing deep remorse at becoming such a burden to my mother. She had been caring for all his needs, and it was exacting a toll. It was my first personal encounter with the "love-hate relationship" experienced by all long-term caregivers. There are damned few Mother Theresa's around. After a time they had to hire a male nurse to do the heavy, unpleasant stuff. Undoubtedly, it contributed to mother's bitter outlook on life. We visited occasionally and, at long last, mother seemed to soften in her attitude toward Stella, but the emotional chasm was too deep.

The first month back on the wards at Georgetown was arduous. My late arrival put me considerably behind my peers, and I was really rusty. Every spare hour was spent in study. The visiting staff was indulgent, but for one key person, the staff endocrinologist. I tolerated his hostile behavior on rounds until one day when he deliberately made gratuitous, pointedly disparaging remarks about my general medical knowledge—at the bedside of a patient. I was very calm. I requested a private audience after hours in his office. He was a short, pugnacious bastard with a gray-white crew cut and a jutting jaw. Quietly I told him that if he ever embarrassed me in front of a patient, again, I would beat the piss out of him. I thought he would have a stroke. Before he could speak I turned and left. What a little exposure to war does to some people! I was sure that the Chief, Dr. Jeghers would probably ask for my badge and gun, but I never heard a word. And the little bully almost became a gentleman on rounds with all the house staff. No one could understand his Hyde unto Jekyll transformation. Three months later, I was caught up with my fellow residents, and one month after that Dr. Jeghers offered me the job of chief medical resident for my last year. Cloud nine!

My final year at Georgetown was only wonderful. I had my own little office, arranged all the resident and intern rotations, set up the teaching conferences, attended the teaching rounds of my choice and helped run the diagnostic clinic. Dr. Jeghers had assembled a fine faculty mostly looted from Tufts and Boston University. They were all

young, energetic and superb clinical teachers. The two outstanding, soon-to-be-national figures, were Proctor Harvey, the best clinical cardiologist-teacher I have ever known, and Charles Hufnagle, a pioneer cardiovascular surgeon (inventor of the Hufnagle prosthetic mitral valve). Proctor taught us how to master a stethoscope, converting it to an amazingly effective instrument. "It's like listening to a symphony orchestra. Every sound and interval must be separated. You listen to each instrument as though it were playing solo. Then you put it all together." Proctor could mimic every heart murmur and click with astonishing fidelity, and he taught us all the same magic. His "heart sounds" teaching tapes became standard fare for house staffers the world over.

As chief resident my hours were my own, but I felt obliged to set a tough standard for the staff. One night when I was on call, supervising the resident activity on all the medical wards, I was overcome with a wonderful, powerful sense of contentment. All our charges were tucked in, the wards were quiet but for the usual low ambient hum of machinery and the whispery susurration of restless patients. It was perhaps one of the more ennobling and humbling experiences in life. I am sure that every house officer has had the same feeling in those rare moments when you have a pause in the action long enough to catch your breath and reflect. What a great gift: being entrusted with the fate of your fellow human beings—granted the honor of being a physician.

One of the fringe benefits of being chief resident was the opportunity to spend a great deal of time with Dr. Jeghers. He was often invited to give guest lectures, conduct clinical pathologic conferences (CPCs) and chair Grand Rounds at other teaching hospitals. He was a remarkably astute clinician. In the areas of his greatest intellectual strength, especially leptospirosis, trichinosis, nutrition-vitamin disorders and metabolic perturbations, the old man handled CPCs like Mickey Mantle offered a fastball, waist high, down the middle.

His favorite story (that he told me at least twice a year) was about the orthodox rabbi who was admitted to Boston City Hospital with the

classic signs and symptoms of trichinosis. Impossible! You get trichinosis from eating undercooked pork. An astute intern checked out the
rabbi's eating habits. The wife said that whenever the holy man traveled he always carried a glass jar of kosher chicken. The intern checked
with the kosher butcher who prepared the rabbi's bottled chicken.
Angry denial that any contamination with pork was possible. But later
one of the employees took the intern aside and confided that occasionally the guys in the back room would run out of chicken and substitute
with pink pork. A terrific tale of medical detective work.
*Cherchez la histoire!*

We visited Johns Hopkins, Boston City, Massachusetts General,
Peter Bent Brigham, Yale, Western Reserve and Virginia. I had the
opportunity to spend a week as exchange resident at the Brigham in
Boston and the Osler at Hopkins. I stood in the shadows of the great
and the near great of internal medicine. Dr. Jeghers and I evolved a
sort of kabuki pantomime. It usually transpired on a Thursday afternoon but occasionally late Friday. He was a big, hulking man with the
body of a line backer. His shadow would cross the threshold of my tiny
office.

"Bob, What are y' doin' this week-end and Monday?"

"Well, not much."

"How would you like to visit New Haven?"

"Okay, I guess."

Invariably, he had already purchased tickets for a compartment.
After the first two surprise invitations, I alerted Stella to this possible
occurrence every Thursday or Friday, but it always came as a bit of a
jolt. She never complained; she appreciated the intellectual opportunities it provided me. She grew to love the old man as did I. He was deaf
in his left ear, and if some unknowing soul addressed him on that side
or spoke too softly, Jeghers often failed to respond. He acquired the
undeserved reputation of being aloof and distant. On all faculty social
occasions, Stella was always positioned to his right; Mrs. Jeghers rarely

attended such functions. Stella enjoyed chatting with the old man; they got on famously.

The first few trips I took with the Chief were unusually educational, more psychosocial than medical. We would be sitting in the train compartment facing each other and a conversation would start, usually about some medical subject. After a few minutes, he would simply stop speaking, often in mid-thought. After an awkward interval, I would try to revive the conversation, but often he would remain silent. Ultimately (it seemed like an eternity of 10 or 15 minutes), he would begin to chat again as though there had been no hiatus. I was never sure if he had *absence* seizures (*petit mal*) or just got lost in thought. It happened often enough that when the inevitable silence occurred, I would simply pick up a journal and read until he came back to life. He taught me that prolonged silence is okay; I never feel compelled to fill in the blanks when a conversation lags.

After the first few trips I came to realize that Dr. Jeghers was a terrible dresser, invariably unpressed and unmatched. I think he had two suits and three ties, maybe. Clothes simply never popped up on his radar screen, and, obviously, his good spouse had higher priorities (like raising five kids with minimal paternal assistance). In Hartford one time, the day preceding an award presentation and lecture, before the prestigious Hartford Medical Society, I made him buy two new, off-the-rack, dark suits, two white shirts and three conservative ties. For Christmas I bought him a classy white shirt with French cuffs and a set of cuff links bearing a gold caduceus. He wore the links whenever he lectured out of town. Thereafter I checked him out (always surreptitiously) before public appearances. I always showed his slides at meetings when he lectured; I carried spare bulbs and an extra pointer—as every chief resident does. After a while I could recite most of his stuff.

"Absent-minded" stories about Dr. Jeghers had become a part of Georgetown folklore. His forgetfulness-for-everything-but-medicine was legendary, mostly apocryphal. But I know one story to be true. One wintry night he brought his youngest son to the Georgetown

emergency room, howling with a hot otitis media. The Sister in the ER started to take a history, "What is the boy's name?"

"His name is Buzzy."

"No, I mean his Christian name."

Puzzled expression, pursed lips, awkward interval, "Well…anyway, Mrs. J will be along in a few minutes."

Add one more to the legend.

As chief resident I had the first "Master's Steps" constructed to begin to do cardiac stress (exercise) testing. It was many years before the treadmill and its accoutrements became the standard. Testing required the patient to step up two-steps and then back down at a rate of speed derived from a nomogram that incorporated height and weight (and I think age). The patient would have a resting electrocardiogram done, and leads would be unhooked from the machine. Holding the wires in hand, he would hike the steps and until he achieved a pre-determined duration of exercise, or target heart rate, or developed shortness of breath or anginal pain. Then the patient would lie back down, get quickly rehooked and the post-exercise ECG would be run. It was dreadfully cumbersome, and we only did it on patients suspected of having angina pectoris from coronary heart disease. It was long before angiography, echocardiograms or any of the many sophisticated diagnostic tools or surgical procedures available today. Our only treatment for unstable angina pectoris was drug therapy.

One of the more memorable patients I encountered in the diagnostic clinic was the ambassador from one of the Arab states. Our clinic attracted foreign diplomats referred by our own State Department and U.S. embassy officials from all over the world. It was one of the feathers in the Georgetown cap. On this occasion the senior resident called me in some despair. The patient was a distinguished ambassador from one of the "politically important" Middle Eastern countries. He was deeply jaundiced and had been losing weight for months. Carcinoma of the colon rated high on the differential diagnosis list. He had refused to

allow the resident to perform a rectal examination, an affront to his dignity.

I entered his room and was confronted by two very large, swarthy bodyguards. I spoke softly, "Sir, we are very concerned that you may have a cancer in your colon that has spread to your liver. You must let me see if I can detect a tumor in your rectal area." He rose up in the bed, weak, emaciated, deeply jaundiced. With consummate dignity, "No one has ever done that to me, and I have had a physical examination every year since I can remember." I told him that he had been deprived of one of the most important parts of the physical examination for a man over 50, and that his position as a high-ranking diplomat should not serve as an **impediment** to proper medical care. He blinked, dismissed his guards and nodded consent. I discovered a rocky hard tumor within easy reach of the probing finger. A few years earlier, it might have been diagnosed in time to do some good. Now it was far too late.

The lesson was a bitter one, to be repeated too many times in the annals of clinical medicine. The care of VIPs is often compromised due to the "intimidating" importance of the patient. They are "too busy" for thoroughness, or too arrogant to respond to your professional counsel, or (as in this instance) the procedure is viewed as demeaning, undignified. Every clinician can probably tell you VIP horror stories. It can be a deadly exercise in hubris. Throughout my career I never forgot my unfortunate diplomat. In the years that followed, I cared for ex-presidents of the United States, cabinet members, senators, congressmen, Supreme Court justices, astronauts, general officers and other "very important people." They never got less care than I would provide the common man. It was a lesson I taught every intern and resident on my service.

The only other unpleasant experience was related to the politics of medicine. As I have indicated, Georgetown was the hospital-of-choice for the State Department. And one of the nice things we did to encourage this relationship was to accept foreign fellows and residents for one

or two years of training. For the most part, they were carefully selected at home for their medical knowledge, English capability and (almost invariably) political connections. The only time this backfired was when a "senior resident" from the Philippines arrived, who had documentation indicating that he had been a medical resident in Manila for two years. So Dr. Jeghers assigned him to start as a second-year resident.

The guy was an unmitigated disaster. His English was fair, his knowledge of medicine about at a third year medical student level, and he was totally undisciplined. No concept of time or responsibility; work ethic was *terra incognita*. When supposedly "on call" he would simply disappear from the hospital. We later discovered that he was so fearful of responsibility that he just took off—and went to the movies! That might have been the only bit of clinical wisdom he demonstrated. I tried doubling him up with another second-year resident, but that began to work an unfair hardship on the staff. So after several weeks of this travail and countless heart-to-heart conversations and threats, I told Jeghers that he had to go. The guy could not even function as an intern.

For the first time I saw Jeghers perplexed. He asked that I "try harder." I told him that had already been done; the fellow was a menace to patients and an embarrassment to the staff. "But he is the nephew of President Magsaysay!" So we tried again, putting him in tandem with a first-year resident. It just did not work, and I told Jeghers that he was demoralizing the nurses and house staff, and presented a menace to patients. So the poor fellow was dispatched home with some face-saving explanation. I have no idea if there were any political repercussions, but many years later I heard the apocryphal story that our benighted nephew of the great man had later been made Secretary of Health of the Philippines! Must have been all that good Georgetown training.

Once again, gazing through my ever-handy retrospectoscope, the only quarrel I have with my residency years at Georgetown was the lack

of emphasis on clinical research. There had been many opportunities, but the clinical teachers at Georgetown and Gallinger simply did not engage in or stimulate their fellows and residents to conduct much clinical investigation. It was a singular aberration, since they had all come from Boston where clinical research was emphasized. I know that if Hussey, Katz, Harvey and the others had published more, they would have gained national stature much more rapidly. Jeghers did most all of his research before he came to Washington, very little thereafter. One cannot fault the clinical teaching; it was at the same superior level as I had encountered in Boston and Baltimore. By the end of my Chief Resident year I felt well qualified to organize and manage an internal medicine teaching program. It was a legacy I carried back to the army.

# 15

## *Austria-Germany Years*

✦

### *(among the best years of our lives...)*

Toward the end of 1952, we realized that the time was fast approaching when I would be obliged to pay back my years of "sponsored" education by returning to active duty in a military assignment. Jonathan had been born at Walter Reed—another delightfully uncomplicated parturition. He was a bit more fretful than Steven at a comparable age. We calculated that I had accumulated payback time that added up to two years of college, four years of medical school and three years of fellowship-residency. Korea counted for one year of payback. (It seemed like a year in a war should count at least two for one, but I didn't make the rules.) So I owed the army eight years. It seemed like a long time. At the Office of the Army Surgeon General they asked me to fill out an "assignment preference list" with the caveat that they would to "try to grant my requests," but the requirements of specific military units would take precedence. "Your record in Korea will be a factor." Thanks a whole bunch.

So Stella and I scoured maps. We thought we would like to live for a time in California, so we applied for Letterman Army Hospital (a prize assignment in San Francisco), and Camp Roberts (we could live in Paso Robles; it sounded romantic and wine-countryish.) As the days of June wound down, I received another call on the hospital paging system. A chilling bit of *deja vu* from 1950! Again the disembodied, pragmatic, official voice, but this time there was no ominous overtone. No

war was raging in some torpid alien jungle (at least none that I knew about).

"Captain Moser, would you be interested in an overseas assignment?"

"Perhaps...where?"

"Well, we need an internist to be chief of the medical service at the U.S. Army Hospital at Camp Truscott in Salzburg, Austria."

I knew Salzburg vaguely from the Mozart Music Festival, but otherwise it was an unknown. Stella and I had not even considered the possibility of an overseas assignment since I was so recently back from Korea. They needed a response in 24 hours, and there was one gigantic hitch. "No family housing would be available for at least four months." Another "unaccompanied tour!" We talked about it all night. Our neighbors who had lived abroad, said Salzburg was one of the loveliest places on earth, a "once in a lifetime" opportunity. I left the decision to Stella since, once again, she would be saddled with an infant plus a three-year old. She reckoned that if Sonya could come up from Miami Beach and stay with her for the four months, the opportunity to live in Salzburg and "experience Europe" would be worth it.

We accepted the assignment. I had two weeks before reporting to Fort Dix. We had traded in the old reliable '48 Studebaker for a flashy new '53 Studebaker coupe. We took off with Sonya and the kids for a cottage in the Catskills, a stone's throw from Grossingers. It was a fine vacation with many of Stella's *gemutlich* Brooklyn family already there.

Once home we salvaged my old uniforms from the mothballs and polished the brass (I had worn nothing but fatigues in Korea). Amazingly, everything still fit. So I took off for indoctrination at Fort Dix. Two pleasant events occurred during that week-of-purposeless-waiting. Stella drove up and we got Special Services tickets to "South Pacific" with Mary Martin and Ezio Pinza. We enjoyed a romantic weekend, late dinner and dancing in Manhattan. The other "event" was that I won the chocolate cake baked by the Colonel's lady, playing bingo at

the Officer's Club. (I mention this bit of trivia because the cake was the **only** prize I have ever won in any contest—in my entire life.)

I flew a low, slow, propeller-powered military transport to Frankfurt and took trains to Salzburg. In reflection, I cannot recall the time in Austria without a smile. It was thoroughly enjoyable from every aspect: professional, recreational and cultural. I arrived with a cadre of about half-dozen other officers. Junior grade (captain and below) were assigned small suites at the Bristol Hotel, facing the town square about a block from the Salzach River. Senior grade officers were quartered in the luxurious Osterreichischer Hof on the bank of the river. They were the two best hotels in town; both had been requisitioned by the army.

It soon dawned on me that we were an occupying army in a defeated country. The Austrians I met all seemed pleasant and gracious. It was difficult to realize that they had been among the most rabid Nazis in the Third Reich, eagerly embracing their native son, Hitler. During our entire three-year tour in Austria and Germany, I met perhaps a handful of honest people who admitted they had been party members, but the vast majority would not acknowledge they even heard of "National Socialists." I might have believed them sooner had they not said that all the nasty Nazis had fled to Argentina and Paraguay after the war. Probably not.

Allied bombers had spared Salzburg; it survived intact. Camp Truscott was located on the edge of town. It had been Luftwaffe headquarters and all the buildings were in superb shape. The Truscott Army Hospital was a little gem. The hospital commander was Colonel Eugene Jackson, a benign, uncomplicated old Internist whose principal achievement was that he had survived the Bataan Death March and the Japanese POW camps. No mean distinction.

Unfortunately, his wife turned out to be the first "war apologist" I encountered, but not the last. These were Americans who seemed a trifle **embarrassed** that we had defeated the Germans and won the war, and, in so doing, had wrought such "terrible havoc" upon Austria and Germany. (They always spoke feelingly of fire-bombed Dresden and

Leipzig; they conveniently failed to mention first-strike V-1 and V-2 ravages against London and Coventry.) Mrs. Jackson's had one other ingratiating attribute; she was an undisguised anti-Semite. I mused that Stella would really love this situation; the Star of David would get a nightly polish. But we never had a problem with the Jacksons; we kept our distance.

But the colonel was burned out. The hospital was run by his adjutant, an officious major. He was short, prematurely bald and ridiculously rank conscious. He made no bones about disliking medical corps officers (who were promoted to captain upon completion of medical school—speedy when compared to other branches). He was medical service corps, an administrative branch created specifically to support smart-asses like me. He was personally obnoxious, but he did his job well. The rest of the staff was about as interesting as the cast of MASH (the movie).

The chief of EENT (they did eyes as well as ear, nose and throat in those days) was Major Felix Hernando, Cuban-born, board-certified. His father had been a medical general in Batista's army, and Felix had never escaped that burdensome famous-father cloud, "Was your father, **the** Felix Hurtado?" He spoke with an engaging, heavy Cubano accent. I soon learned that he was living with a gorgeous redhead who had been a Viennese fashion model before she came to Salzburg. They could not get married because Felix was Catholic and his wife (who lived back in the States) refused him a divorce. So Felix and Elsa were the delicious scandal of Salzburg. They were delightful; she and Stella got along swimmingly.

The army had taken some pains to staff this place. The psychiatrist, Jim Dunlop, was a very warm, likable Freudian. His "cross" was a new arrival named Roy, heir apparent to the psychiatric throne of a well-known psych clinic in a large mid-western state. He seemed a bit smitten with his name and pedigree, but he was soon disabused of all that. Jim and Roy had a small personality clash; it happens even among psychiatrists. Jim won.

One of our weekly teaching conferences attracted some unanticipated interest. I asked each member of my staff to research the current literature seeking articles on the effects of cigarette smoking on different organ systems: heart, peripheral blood vessels, lungs, gastro-intestinal tract, genito-urinary tract, metabolic systems and whatever else they could find. At that time (1954) it was an established fact that cigarettes were related to Buerger's Disease (a mysterious and serious inflammation of peripheral blood vessels) and possibly, bronchogenic carcinoma, but not much else. However, a careful search of the literature indicated that a lot more mischief was occurring than anyone had realized. It was an exciting Grand Rounds.

There were perhaps 20 or 25 staff in attendance. Then came the broadside. The next week the overseas edition of the *Herald Tribune* carried a front page headline, "Army Doctors Condemn Cigarettes." It was a blow-by-blow description of our conference with the gratuitous editorial comment that we had recommended removing all cigarette-dispensing machines from barracks, post exchanges and other military facilities. We had not gone that far (although in retrospect perhaps we should have). Colonel Jackson called me in. He was catching heat from Heidelberg brass who were recipients of much static from the Pentagon. But Jackson had been at our conference and knew we had not "extrapolated conclusions beyond the data." Nor had anyone expressed the alleged "recommendations." I thought the article represented some good reporting but for the editorial fiction. We never knew who leaked the stuff and added the fluff, but we thought it might even do some good. It did not.

We were practicing excellent medicine and having a grand time. Well into the year, I was invited to give a guest lecture at the University of Bologna. Stella and the boys had long-since joined me. (More later.) She and I drove down through the Brenner Pass, Milan and Florence to Bologna and back through Verona and Venice via the fabulous, glacier-strewn Grosse Glockner mountain highway. It was a relaxed and leisurely trip but for "the car." The Camille-like, beautiful-but-chroni-

cally ill Studebaker stopped dead on the autostrada between Siena and Venice. It just quit. We happened to be about a mile from a Fiat assembly plant. I walked down and tried to explain our situation to a bunch of workers. The magic words (forget the Italian) were "1953 Studebaker." They dispatched a tow truck and hauled the inert hulk into the plant.

To our astonishment, they rigged a long 30-foot table and draped it with a white cloth. Then three mechanics tenderly disassembled the carburetor system and several other engine parts, piece by piece. We were invited out for espresso while they "try to fix." Several times I thought I saw flashes as from a flash camera. After about two hours we were invited back, the engine had been reassembled. It ran smoothly. They would accept no payment. I tried to figure out this amazing demonstration of Latin generosity. I suspected it was the unique fuel injection system, the first in any American car. I reckon Fiat could have purchased a '53 Studebaker and dissected it, but here was one delivered to their front door. I would like to say that we never had any further problems with that temperamental vehicle, but it would be a lie. It was the worst automobile I have ever owned. It suffered chronic maladies of many systems, sort of like systemic tuberculosis infecting an internal combustion engine. No wonder Studebaker later went belly up.

After the trip to Bologna, I invited American medical students to come to Truscott for two months of clinical preceptorship. It was their first experience with patients at the bedside. All in all we had about six bright young medical students make the tour. I kept track of some of them for many years. My guys loved the teaching.

Two officers with whom I had flown over from the States were Major Ernestine ("call me Ernie") Stevens, a witty, busty, 40ish California blonde who took over the WAC detachment (happily quartered at the OH), and dapper Lt. Col. Phil McMurphy, who was to become the command G-4 (supply). Mac was married, Ernie was not; I suspected they had something going but very discreetly. Since we were all "unaccompanied," when I wasn't holed up at the Bristol studying, we

hung out together. The OH had the best hotel kitchen in Austria (Vienna notwithstanding). I took breakfast at the hospital, never lunch, reveled in dinner, occasionally, at the OH. You could get a fantastic steak with decent wine for about seven bucks. Across the river was the Weisses Kreutz (Yugoslav food with zither music), the Goldener Hirsch (a five star Michelin delight, expensive even then), Paracelsus (best wiener schnitzel in town) and my very favorite, the Eulenspeigel (delicious everything, cheaper than the Hirsch). Dining in Salzburg was a joy. I began to learn about good food.

Part of the ambient charm of the OH was the band. Celso Lonzetti was an Italian national and his four bandsmen were expatriates from every corner of the continent. They made beautiful music. Celso had a teen-aged daughter with mitral stenosis (narrowing of the critical valve between left atrium and left ventricle) from old rheumatic fever. One day after dinner he told me she was in some difficulty. Of course, it was not kosher for a non-military patient to come to our hospital, but I sneaked her in the next evening, examined her, took ECGs and had some chest radiographs done. The child had mild mitral stenosis with some heart enlargement. I called an Austrian cardiologist-friend, who was chief at the Landes Krankenhaus, the main hospital in town, and asked him to undertake her management. He agreed and over the next few months helped the child a great deal. For the remainder of our tour in Austria, whenever I entered the OH dining room, Celso's melodious concertina would lead the quintet into a schmaltzy rendition of "San Antonio Rose," one of my C & W favorites. I loved being a minor celebrity.

About one month after I arrived in Salzburg, I was summoned to "the castle," as the elegant *schloss* occupied by our commanding three-star general was known. General William Arnold was the prevailing emperor of Austria and lived in appropriate style. He had an entourage of ancient retainers who sort of came with the place, plus a reinforced company of aides, drivers, MPs, etc. I was ushered into his presence while he was getting a haircut. He was small, trim, friendly and far less

imperious than most senior officers. Abruptly, the barber, a sergeant, concluded his exercise with a flourish, deftly snipping a presumptuous nasal hair. He was thanked and dismissed. The general glanced at his watch, "Four o'clock; sun must be well over the yardarm in Vladevostock, so how about a little single malt?" (Thankfully, Ernie had already taken pains to introduce me to the wonderful world of Macallan and Glenlivet). I was so relieved I almost grinned.

The last three-star general I had seen was Matthew Ridgeway flying down a dusty road in an open jeep near Suwon in Korea. And here I was, little old captain me, about to hoist one with General Arnold. Wow! As he moved to the bar, Mrs. Arnold entered, a striking, graying, aristocratic lady a few inches taller than the old man. She smiled and extended a brown gardener's hand, "Captain Moser, so pleased to meet you." I reckoned the accent was authentic FFV (First Family Virginia) from somewhere around Charlottesville. "We've heard so much about you from Colonel Jackson." It seemed that her elderly parents were coming for a visit, and her father had recently been advised that he suffered diabetes, "a tad difficult to control." Would I see him and look after him while they were visiting? Is the pope Catholic?

I stayed for dinner, as they say, "simple food, graciously served." Then we watched John Wayne doing "Rio Bravo" in the refurbished ballroom with a coterie of staff officers and their wives. My call to Stella was a winner that night. And that is how Captain Moser (soon to be Major Moser) came to take care of the Arnolds, their youngest kid Joe, their married daughter Emily, the staff, their guests and (even once) their lazy, long-haired dachshund, Schatzie. Later Stella would play Scrabble with the Great Lady, shop and gossip with Emily and enjoy many a dinner and movie (*immer nicht deutch*).

I soon learned that "the U.S. Army Austria" was in a ludicrously untenable position, militarily. We had one regiment (about 900 fighting men) backed up by a company of light tanks and a few platoons of heavy weapons. If you look at a map, you will see that the whole eastern half of Austria is a blunt nose sticking into Czechoslovakia, Hun-

gary and Yugoslavia. Everything east of Linz was Soviet Zone. By conservative estimate, we were facing about twelve enemy divisions. A MIG could fly from Budapest or Prague to Salzburg faster than I could walk to the river from my hotel. The "U.S. Air Force—Austria" consisted of one single-engine L-5 flown by a captain named Bud O'Bannion, who did weather reconnaissance whenever he was cold sober. (More about my "adventures flying with Bud" later.) Every family was provided detailed instructions and maps indicating evacuation routes in the event of enemy attack. It was a huge political joke. I hoped the Russians and their buddies behind the curtain found it equally amusing.

I got to meet the one-star commander of the regiment in a curious way. During the winter, Army Special Services would organize ski trains to take German and Austrian based U.S. troops (and families) on long week-ends to ghastly places like Kitzbuhel, Zurs, Lech, San Moritz, Cortina d'Ampezzo and the like. It was dirt cheap for the train, housing and food. Most of us owned our own boots and skis, but even these items could be rented. I think it was early in the season at Kitzbuhel, when I was just beginning to learn to turn and stop the long wooden monsters without flailing about like a demented windmill. I came over the brow of the hill and almost collided with a black-clad gentleman who was sitting on a log dabbing at a nasty cut on his left forehead with a red kerchief. I did not know him, but I had seen him on the train. "Can I help?" I pointed at the first-aid kit belted to my waist. He nodded yes. I introduced myself; he said "I'm General Kendall of the 21st." I indicated that normally his laceration (from a loose ski during a tumble) could use about two sutures. I cleaned the cut and bound the edges with a tight butterfly adhesive and dressed it.

As we sat there I said, "You know, General, we have already had three people turn up with fractures. It might be a good thing for these ski trains to have an army doctor and a few tools along to care for folks that get hurt or sick." I was only half facetious. Just about every one of these popular ski resort towns had an orthopedist super-skilled in man-

aging ski fractures. To my surprise and unalloyed delight he said, "You know, that's not a bad idea, I'll take it up with Special Services when we get back." I blurted, "I volunteer!" He laughed, but by God, I became the army "ski train doctor."

Several months after Stella and the boys arrived, she and I hit every resort on the circuit for two years, free as birds. I would pack a kit of medical goodies, announce that "sick call" would be in the lodge from 6 until 9 AM and 6 until 8 PM, and we'd ski all day. At lunchtime I would check in to minister to any sick or wounded. I always established contact with the local orthopedic surgeon, but I would provide "battalion aid" (stabilize and transport) for all injuries on the slopes. My clientele would show up with minor upper respiratory infections, upset stomachs, bruises, fevers and other lesser stuff. For busted tibias, I would splint, have it radiographed and checked by the local orthopod (who might cast it) and shuttle the patient back to Truscott. The skiers could have done perfectly well without me, but everyone said they were pleased that I was there. The perfect scam.

It was about one month before Stella and the boys were due to arrive. The life of a celibate bachelor had become boring, and I was tired of eating out all the time. I think I was drinking too much beer (some local *biergartens* served the magnificent local brews in two-liter steins). Government housing was still unavailable, and no one in authority could give me a definite time frame. So I got special permission to look "on the economy" for a dwelling for my little family. Someone told me that there was a quaint village called Obertrum nestled beside a charming lake about 17 kilometers out of Salzburg. I borrowed a car and took the drive. Obertrum turned out to be a pleasant, bucolic place nestled most amiably amidst gently rolling hills. The dominant building in the village was the Trommer Brewery that boasted (from a number painted on its tower) that it had been in continuous operation since 1492.

I stopped in at a local pub and sampled their brew; it was just as rich as Hofbrau or Wurzburger Hofbrau, my favorites, but it had an oddly

hospitable garlic flavor. The proprietor spoke a little English. It seemed the local hops were grown adjacent to garlic patches, an ancient local tradition. He knew of a furnished apartment in a house down near the lake. It was owned by a widow, Frau Heidi Triebel. She was fiftyish, well-groomed, and cheerful and spoke good English. Her second floor was available for long-term rental at a reasonable price. It was furnished in "Spartan rustic" fashion; a "central heating system" consisting of a seemingly over-matched coal stove in the basement fed a stout pipe that ran up the center of the house, feeding radiators in the middle corners of each of four rooms on each of the two floors. She assured me that a "reliable" man from the village would keep the furnace stoked. A spacious balcony that overlooked the lake sold the place. Nothing else in the village was more inviting.

Stella's last phone call had been disturbing. She had observed that Jonathan had been slow in motor development; he was reluctant to sit, stand and walk. Her pediatrician at Children's Hospital in D.C. said Jon was just a trifle behind the curve but not to worry. We were worried. They were due to arrive in Genoa sometime in early October, sailing on the S.S. Independence, a modified cruise liner. When the time arrived, I took the train to Genoa and met them dockside. They had enjoyed a wonderful passage. Stella had been elected Queen of the Independence, replete with glittering tiara. She was radiant. (Miss Miami Beach redux!) Jon did look small and was very restless, even in sleep. Steven was becoming tall and a trifle gangly, even at five. He was shy but curious about this strange new world. It was a wonderful reunion; it had been three months. Ernie and Mac and the Jacksons met us at the Salzburg bahnhof. I borrowed a sedan from the army motor pool and introduced my little family to our new life in Obertrum. Gradually we settled in. Our own vehicle was scheduled to arrive in Bremerhaven within ten days.

It proved a friendly village. We were the only Americans, the first they had seen since the war. Frau Triebel had lost her husband on the Eastern Front, but there was no sense of rancor. She was very kind and

helpful, breaking trail with the local butcher, baker and general store proprietor. Stella began to study German and was always testing her prowess on Heidi and the local folks. Our furnace man was an ancient relic named Joseph Kaiser. Of course, everyone called him Kaiser Joseph. One day Stella addressed him in her carefully articulated *neu deutch*. The old man shook his head solemnly and responded, "*Fraulein, bitte, ich nicht verstehen Englisch.*" On one other occasion she was shopping at the local butcher shop and proudly asked for "*Ein kilometer auf bratwurst.*" Frau Triebel threw her apron over her face amidst raucous but friendly laughter. So back to the books. Soon Stella became quite fluent.

Fresh cut flowers appeared in our rooms every day. Heidi told us of a 15-year girl from the village seeking employment as a cook-domestic. We agreed to interview her. Laura was a husky, fresh-cheeked farm girl with an external strabismus of her left eye; the pupil was deviated somewhat to the side. This was the source of some ridicule by boorish classmates, and she had become shy and withdrawn. We hired Laura on the spot; she remained with us the entire time we were in Europe. She was a simple cook, an adequate house cleaner, but she was terrific with the boys. (Later, after our tour in Salzburg, when we were ready to leave Wurzburg, our next duty station before heading home, Laura's conversational English was more than adequate. She married a staff sergeant and immigrated to the States.)

Stella and I made frequent forays into Salzburg for dinners at the Arnold's. We sampled all the good restaurants. She fell into the cycle of overseas army life quite easily and became a much sought after Scrabble partner. She charmed everyone, especially Celso. He always greeted us with his delightfully schmaltzy version of "San Antone" whenever we entered the dining room of the OH. It was delightful.

Trouble came with the first heavy snow. I had retrieved the car from Bremerhaven and the sleek, haughty bitch immediately decided to hate the winter. The first inkling of rebellion was a refusal to start in the cold. Stella had already experienced problems with car doors not fitted

well and sundry electrical malfunctions. In the ice and snow it had terrible traction, too much torque. But the biggest hassle was trying to negotiate snowdrifts on the narrow roads into Salzburg. I tried chains but it was on-again, off-again and finally I gave them up. On many occasions the local road crews and neighbors would help dig me out.

Then there was the local bus. On many a morning after a heavy snowfall, I would be skimming along a freshly plowed road only to run up behind the bus mired in a slushy bank. All the passengers and local farmers would be recruited to push the monster. I would always stop and help, but on too many mornings I was late arriving at the hospital. The snow problems happened often enough that I carried two shovels and a fifth of slivovitz to reward helpful shovelers and pushers.

There were winter compensations though. We all enjoyed the village, and on Christmas Eve we went to midnight services in Oberndorf where "*Stille Nicht*" had been written. It was a magical night; gentle flakes drifted down embracing the landscape with a coat of white down, an angelic children's choir with voices soft and soaring. I could never get over the Jekyll—Hyde paradox of Austrians and Germans, capable of such sensitivity and beauty and such cruelty and horror.

After about six months, Stella was taking German lessons from Frau Frankenstein, an austere, matronly, aristocrat whose fortunes had taken a bad turn. One did not inquire too deeply into causes; it was not politic. She was Catholic not Jewish, but it seemed her family had not enjoyed the favor of the Austrian Nazis. She was making her way by giving language lessons to army wives. But the linguistic champ of the family was Steven. He was now almost six, and all his playmates were Austrian kids. One weekend we had rented a cottage near Chiemsee, and Stella and I were sitting on the porch listening to a bunch of children chattering nearby. We recognized Steven's voice; his language and accent were indistinguishable from the others. Later I chided him, "You sound just like a little Austrian kid." He turned in anger, "I am not; I am an Americanischer!"

But the snow became too much. With considerable reluctance we found another rental apartment in a suburb of Salzburg and said farewell to our felicitous village. A few months later military housing became available. Laura had a room in the attic with her own bathroom, a luxury she never enjoyed at home. By now, my ABIM exam study had intensified; I was to take the written test in Heidelberg within a few weeks. Stella's insomnia was unrelenting, so we agreed that she should begin to see our army psychiatrist-friend for therapy sessions two to three times a week. I never asked him about her progress, but over the next few months Stella seemed better. I had the subliminal sense that he had developed "feelings" for her. He had a very sweet wife and a couple of little ones, and occasionally we shared dinner. I'm sure there was never any hanky-panky. We were to encounter quite a few men over the years who were attracted to the beauteous Stella.

We had Jon seen by the staff pediatrician, who had been on the faculty at USC. He ran some tests and said that Jon was just a little slow to mature, but not to worry. A pediatric consultant who came through on a visit also examined Jon and confirmed his opinion. We were still considerably disquieted.

We had quite a few visiting firemen wander through Salzburg. There were many air force and army hospitals in Germany, and these medical pedagogues never failed to include salubrious Salzburg in their Grand Consultant Tour. Some famous medical personalities rolled through. Most notable in my career was the 1955 visit by Dr. Dennette Adams, the celebrated internist/educator from Boston. In the process of studying for the ABIM examination, I had become impressed by the paucity of information in the medical literature about adverse reactions to common prescription drugs. I had seen quite a few patients with significant untoward responses to drugs over the years, so I began to keep track of them. I became fascinated, wrote a paper and submitted it for presentation at the annual U.S. Army Europe Medical-Surgical Conference to be held in Frankfurt. It was accepted. The

audience response indicated that I had stumbled upon something very intriguing, a largely unrecognized and unappreciated lacuna in medical knowledge. Later, Dr. Adams came to Salzburg to lecture and conduct teaching rounds. At dinner that evening he suggested I submit the paper to the "Medical Progress" section of the *New England Journal of Medicine*. Wow! The paper was published on September 27, 1956. It changed my life.

I continued to pursue my "hobby," and doctors from all around the world began to send me information about patients they had encountered with similar previously unknown adverse drug reactions. I was invited to give talks at military hospitals in Germany and at the *Landes Krankenhaus* in Salzburg. I published the first book called *"Diseases of Medical Progress: A Study of Iatrogenic Disease"* in 1959, revised DMP in 1964 and came out with an expanded, multi-authored version in 1969. For several years, I wrote a column analyzing articles that had appeared in the medical literature on the subject for the august journal, *Clinical Therapeutics and Pharmacology*. Dr. Walter Modell, the distinguished editor and doyen of clinical pharmacology, became a good friend. I was to lecture all over the country and in several foreign countries on the subject over the next ten years. It was my major contribution to the knowledge base of clinical medicine. I like to think I alerted the profession to a growing problem, as ever more potent therapeutic agents came to market. Physicians began to speak in terms of therapeutic/toxic ratios for all drugs. The army loved it.

Another consultant visit took quite a different turn. Sometime after Stella had arrived, we were scheduled for a consultant visit by the team of Dr. William Bean and Dr. Howard Rome. Bill Bean was one of my heroes in medicine—a legendary clinician-teacher-writer-raconteur. He was chairman of medicine at Iowa and editor of the *Archives of Internal Medicine*. Howard Rome had the reputation of being the sharpest clinical psychiatrist at the Mayo Clinic. They were fabulous consultants. We decided that they should have a "thank you banquet" at the OH.

It may be remembered as one of the most hilarious, completely delightful parties ever to reverberate through the hoary salons of the venerable OH. We had Celso and his troops to ourselves in a velvety dining room with baroque-ornate crystal chandeliers, the best house silver, heavy lead crystal and a delicious *haute cuisine* dinner, all lubricated with gallons of wine. After dinner, I asked Bill to recite his universally famous (at least in American medical academe) poem, "Omphalosophy, an Ode to the Belly Button." He was in fine fettle, not a dry eye in the house. The room was rocking with laughter. Then, to everyone's surprise, the very proper Howard Rome recited a rowdy limerick of his own. And then Bill, who was a master of this art form, began to regale us with selections from his enormous repertoire of dirty and near-dirty limericks. The ample flow of wine facilitated the boisterous hilarity; it was rollicking good fun. Of course, "you really had to be there."

Bill and I became fast friends thereafter. In later years, he invited me to give the DMP lecture at Iowa and asked me to be book review editor for the *Archives*, which I did for about three years. When I was editor of the *Journal of the American Medical Association* (*vide infra*), I put together a *festschrift* edition (selected writings of the honoree) of the *Archives* in honor of Bill Bean. Each year at the old Atlantic City meetings of the research societies, we would meet for breakfast at the Chalfonte and bring each other up to date. There will never be another Bill Bean.

One incident occurred during our time in Salzburg that carried me back to the dark days in Korea. Two black soldiers had confessed to the rape and murder of a seven-year-old Austrian child. The crime was so heinous that the defense counsel had asked for an evaluation of their sanity. I was appointed to a three medical officer panel (with two psychiatrists). Quickly the interview took on a surreal aspect. The soldiers were neither contrite nor frightened. The story: on a Sunday morning after a night of whoring and drinking, they found themselves in a wooded glade on the edge of town. They decided to play "chicken,"

daring each other to perform outlandish acts. As the madness of their horseplay escalated, one challenged the other to "rape the next woman that comes down the path." Within minutes a child wandered along coming home from church alone. She was raped by both men and then killed. The story was related in a flat monotone without a shadow of passion, no emotion, no remorse. They were not bright, nor were they imbeciles. In response to questions, it emerged that they really thought, "Austrians are not like us." I felt a chill as I recalled the "gook" phenomenon in Korea. They considered Austrians as *untermenschen*, not real people; one could take liberties. This dispassionate racial blast, from black soldiers who undoubtedly had suffered their own outrages of discrimination, caused me several sleepless nights. I will never forget that hideous descent into the heart of human darkness.

Salzburg was also the occasion for my first serious publication in the medical literature. It was late 1954 when we had three patients admitted within a few days; all suffered Infectious Hepatitis (as we called it in those days). We now know that it is Hepatitis A, one of a group of viruses that primarily involve the liver. The army had a great deal of experience with this disorder. In North Africa, portions of the German Afrika Korps were almost decimated with hepatitis A. We had seen a few cases before, but a cluster of three was unusual. We knew it was transmitted by fecal-oral contamination, but none of the patients was aware of exposure to possibly contaminated food, water or individuals who were ill. Detailed history taking by the staff revealed that all three had been on a Special Services train trip to Bad Gastein, a sophisticated resort town in the south of Austria, famous for its curative waters—an irony not immediately apparent. All three had been quartered in the same hotel.

I called Lt. Col. Al Peznik in the headquarters office; he was a crack epidemiologist. We obtained a list of all personnel who had been on the train. They hailed from units in Austria, Munich, and Frankfurt and beyond. Peznik's people managed to contact them all. As I recall, about 30% had come down with clinical disease and were in different

hospitals. We had another four or five admitted to Truscott. It was a nasty strain, and they all became very jaundiced and anorexic. In time, all recovered with no residual sequelae.

Peznik and I took a team of laboratory technicians to Bad Gastein. There were two adjacent hotels that were involved. We suspected that somehow they had cross-connected their sewage and drinking water systems, that someone on the staff (or another guest) had active hepatitis and had contaminated the system. The hotel officials were outraged. They "refused" to let us collect samples of their drinking water to test such a "preposterous hypothesis." They asserted (noisily and repeatedly) that Bad Gastein was a glorious health spa, and had been a thriving community for hundreds of years (before you *auslanders* were ever born—unspoken but distinctly implied). Nothing like this could possibly happen in their elegant, impeccable spa.

We sympathized with their situation, but we took samples from the drinking water of both hotels and half a dozen others. Back in Salzburg, the laboratory confirmed that the water from the two suspected hotels was contaminated with hepatitis virus. We relayed the bad news to the managers of both hotels. Somehow their sewage and drinking water systems had become connected and, indeed, someone in one of the hotels was shedding hepatitis virus at the time our troops were there. We were placing Bad Gastein "off limits" to all U.S. personnel until they found the plumbing glitch, corrected it and the water tested pure.

Pandemonium! Of course, we had no such authority, but it was a mandatory public health course of action. We went through the chain of command to get the order executed. The outcry from the good burghers of Bad Gastein was almost audible in Salzburg. Without the Americans, they would be out of business. It went all the way to top administration in the Austrian government and to General Arnold. Pecznik and I were hauled into the general's office. Here was a different person than the genial "Old Bill Arnold" of single-malt scotch and long-haired dachshunds. He paced back and forth while explaining the

enormous political repercussions of declaring Bad Gastein, perhaps the most famous health spa in Austria, off limits because "a few people got sick." We explained that more people would get sick. Anyone exposed to that contaminated water, Austrian, American or Zulu could get hepatitis. And it was a fairly nasty strain, and some American soldier might die. And wouldn't it be terrible if we had the power to prevent illness and possible death, and had failed to act?

So, the venerable watering hole was declared off limits to all U.S. personnel. Soon the moans from the south subsided, replaced by the growl of earth-moving equipment and lots of pipe hammering. They found the leak in the sewage system, and located the defective pipe that had linked the water systems of the two hotels. A cook was located who had been hospitalized with jaundice within the appropriate incubation period. All pieces of the epidemiological puzzle fit into place. A few weeks later, Pecznik was welcomed back (nicely) to the lovely mountain village with the magnificent in-town waterfall. The water tested normal. Back in business. Our paper, "Apparently Water-Borne Outbreak of Infectious Hepatitis" appeared in the *American Journal* of *Public Health* in 1956. The "apparently" was an editorial gratuity; if that had been the case, our report would never have been accepted for publication.

Soon after this episode, we experienced another fascinating medical challenge, but this time far more deadly. British troops occupied the sector of Austria in the southeast near Graz. They had been on maneuvers. Part of the British in-the-field training philosophy (as I had learned in Korea) was to simulate wartime conditions as much as possible. They lived "off the land" whenever feasible; this criterion often demanded considerable hardship. On this occasion, on a very cold and sleety night, one company (I think the Brits had one regiment in Austria—as did we) had sought refuge in the large, comfortable barn of a cooperative local farmer. It was a decidedly unfortunate bivouac.

They had their sleeping bags and personal gear scattered throughout the hay in the lofts and on the ground. Sometime after midnight, a

kerosene lantern was overturned and in minutes the barn was an inferno. In the chaos that followed several soldiers were badly burned and many others suffered severe hot smoke inhalation with serious damage to airways. The British had no hospital in Austria, and after considerable delay, they were air-evacuated to us.

Helicopters began to arrive in wind-blown, heavy snow about 3:00 am; the whole staff was standing by. We received about 30 critically ill young men over the next hour. While many of the burns were second and third degree, all had sustained lung damage. It was my first experience using large doses of steroids to suppress the immediate inflammation while caring for scalded airways with heat-moistened oxygen (positive pressure inhalation had not come to medicine yet). It was a difficult week, with extraordinary coordination between all departments. There is no medical situation more complicated and vexing than someone with severe surface and inhalation burns. But we did not lose a patient. Later, the British European Command sent the hospital a handsome plaque commending us for our effort.

About one month before Stella and the boys arrived, perhaps the most challenging patient I encountered was a Wall Street banker who had been touring with his wife. He was in his mid fifties and apparently enjoying good health. After dinner in downtown Salzburg, he complained of weakness in his left side and then collapsed, unconscious. I was in my room at the Bristol and on-call, but the phone message came from a very agitated Colonel Jackson. As I dressed hurriedly, I did not understand how a civilian had landed in an army hospital. It turned out that the banker was an ex-Marine corps bird colonel (WW II) highly connected in New York and Washington. He was a very sick cookie.

His wife was a handsome, stalwart, "take control" matron. She was stoic and dignified, albeit thoroughly distraught. My examination of the comatose gentleman revealed that not only had he suffered a partial stroke, but he also had sustained an anterior wall myocardial infarction and was in congestive heart failure. I thought he might die. I apprised

Colonel Jackson (who had raced into the hospital, reinforcing the heavyweight nature of the patient), about the gravity of the prognosis. The wife quietly asked about transporting him to a larger hospital (better-staffed and better-equipped was not mentioned, but implied). I told her quietly that I did not think he would survive immediate transportation.

In any event, management was a full court press. After tourniquet application to all four extremities and intravenous administration of digoxin failed to relieve the heart failure, I withdrew 500 ml. of blood, an ancient and dramatic gambit. (This was well before the availability of powerful oral diuretics or any effective drugs to combat CHF). He breathed a little better on his 100% oxygen. I treated him with a conventional regimen, but more vigorously and rapidly than usual. I stayed with him, more or less constantly, for four days. The third day his two sons and daughter arrived; all as bright, concerned and sophisticated as mama. They had sniffed out my credentials. They knew that I had not yet taken the ABIM examination. The eldest son all but challenged my competence. I sympathized with their concern and suggested they fly in any consultant in the world. But by day three, the mother had begun to gain some confidence in me.

After a tempestuous week, he had improved dramatically, even surprising me. It was a combination of solid DNA, attentive medical care, strong supporting family and more than a little damned good luck. His stroke was incomplete. With good physical therapy he would regain his speech and most of the use of his appendages. After about two weeks, he was ready to travel. The family was planning to fly in a cardiologist from Columbia-Presbyterian to escort him home. Mother said, "Dr. Moser will fly with us, if he is willing. He knows more about dad's condition than anyone." The family had bought out the whole first class section on a Pan Am clipper! We flew from Munich to JFK. By the grace of God, it was uneventful.

In the course of our days together, we had gotten to know each other. They were aware that my little family was still in Washington.

Upon landing at Kennedy, a waiting ambulance took us to Harkness Pavilion at Columbia-Presbyterian where I discussed the case with the chief of cardiology, whose reputation was known to me. He studied my notes, reams of ECGs, chest and abdominal radiographs. He smiled, "Good job" or something like that. I went to my patient's room; it looked like an over-endowed florist shop. His wife and daughter kissed me and said a car would take me to the hotel. This was the beginning of "Alice in Wonderland."

The hotel was the Plaza. Waiting in the suite, already loaded with flowers and fine champagne, was Stella! (They had even arranged for a baby sitter in Washington.) They had programmed us for a three-day second honeymoon: dinner at Twenty-one, ringside tickets to "Fiddler on the Roof," more flowers, more champagne, dinner with the whole Salzburg contingent in the Oak Room. It was spectacular. Stella flew back to National, first class; the tired but happy major returned to Frankfurt, first class. It was a "First Class" holiday. The rapidly recovering patient actually outlived his gracious wife. Somewhat later, the family offered to set me up in practice in Scarsdale. In fact, Stella and I visited there when we came back from Europe, but I was already committed to another life. The curious twists...

Another notable Salzburg event was the annual *fasching* ball, the Austro-German equivalent of Mardi Gras, but even more raucous and lascivious than New Orleans ever imagined. It was rumored that the birth rate trebled approximately nine months after the *fasching* season. We only went once. It was held in the building where the magnificent white Lippizaners performed their dressage. The affair was by invitation only, and everyone was masked and costumed. You and your companion were separated at the door. I have never enjoyed white wine; it does evil things to me. But it was the only beverage available, and it was flowing in enticing abundance. I soon began to feel the effects, and I recall dancing with an extremely well constructed young lady from Stuttgart who spoke no English. Her primary garment

seemed to be a sort of green-tinted, wide-mesh fishnet. But I was too looped to be a menace.

As the evening wore on, I sought to find Stella. There must have been several hundred (other) inebriated, confusingly costumed revelers. I found an unmasked friend dozing in a corner. He said he had last seen Stella out on the balcony with some fellow. In my state of sobriety it sounded like a call from a damsel in distress. After invading a few balconies and disrupting several amorous Cinderellas and Don Juans, I burst upon a golden witch (Stella) and some large harlequin joker standing much too close. So, naturally, I belted the guy. To my astonishment, he went tumbling over the railing of the balcony! Fortunately we were on the first floor, and he landed in a bale of the Lippizaners hay. It could have been ugly. Stella stormed out shrieking that I had just popped Joe Kirk, our chief of surgery, who had just gallantly rescued her from some mischief-bent Arthurian knight in pointy armor. Stella and I were gathered up and hauled off by several nurses from the hospital.

I awakened the next morning, still fully costumed in Ernie's room in the WAC quarters (off limits to all men!) at the OH. Stella cooled down after several weeks; Joe never knew that it was me who had nailed him. His recollection of the dreadful evening was as fragmented as mine. It took a while for all wounds to mend, and we avoided the grand event the following year. I swore off white wine forever.

So it came time to take the ABIM written examination in Heidelberg. I had been preparing for about four years. I was reasonably confident; I knew the current literature as well as anyone. But there is always that little demon-of-doubt whispering with menace and malice. My friend Captain Bud O'Bannion, the only air force officer in Austria, volunteered to fly me to Heidelberg in his little "weather plane." We agreed to meet at 0600 the day before the exam so I could do a bit of compulsive final brushing-up in my hotel room and get a good night's sleep. At the appointed hour, I was standing by at the deserted hangar at the airport. No Bud. At 0630 I called his home and a very sleepy,

somewhat smashed O'Bannion sputtered an apology. He would be right over. Before I could say, "Forget it; I'll take the train," he hung up. About 15 minutes later his mud-spattered Dodge coupe screeched up to the field and out he popped, cowboy boots, camouflage jacket, leather helmet and white scarf. He looked like a hung-over caricature of Smilin' Jack.

He hastened to assure me that the flight would be a piece of cake; he'd made it hundreds of times before, "You just follow the autobahn." He provided me with a jacket and goggles, and we rolled the astonishingly tiny plane out of the hangar. The U.S. Air Force Austria consisted of one refurbished single-engine L-5 artillery spotter. I had flown in bigger planes hauling medical supplies in Korea; Alaska had larger mosquitoes! But soon we were off. Yes, we were following an autobahn, but it looked unfamiliar. By now we should have raised Munich. After another minute, Bud threw the little plane into a sharp left bank, dove deep almost within 200 feet of the deck, and scared the living hell out of me. He came on the intercom, "Sorry, Doc. Wrong autobahn. We almost invaded Czech airspace!" I always wondered if we had managed to scramble a few MIGs.

The landing in Heidelberg was lumpy and bumpy; he was obliged to dodge between two abandoned flak towers to approach the runway. I had the feeling this was not the main airport since there were tufts of grass struggling out of the tarmac, and no other planes were in evidence. It was an abandoned WWII *lufthaven.* I think Bud was sober by now. I thanked him profusely for the adventure and gently rejected his offer to pick me up after the exam. I had to walk about a mile to hail a taxi.

The only other untoward event of this trip was that I had booked into a hotel that was directly across the street from a historical church with a historical clock that sounded on the quarter hour with a historical chime that could be heard back in Salzburg. It was like sleeping in the bell tower of Big Ben. I heard every single goddamn dong. The examination was tough but fair. I knew I had passed. In a few months,

I would have to fly back to Philadelphia to take the dreaded ABIM Orals, but for now a half dozen of us weary but relieved exam-takers celebrated in a few of the best *biergartens* and *weinstubes* in Heidelberg.

Salzburg was an ideal jumping off place for vacations in Europe. With Laura caring for Steven and Jon, we traveled at every opportunity. Soon after Stella arrived, we had an opportunity to attend the Swiss ski school in Arosa, Switzerland down near the Italian border. It was indeed a school, but it was where the Swiss instructors were observed and graded on their teaching ability. They needed students at all levels of skill. Tuition and lifts were free; hotel and food were a part of the incredibly reasonable package. By this time I was an "advanced intermediate" and Stella was an "intermediate." We had our own customized boots and skis. It was our first experience with the remarkable Swiss rail system, an adventure unto itself. Breath-taking, mind-blowing alpine scenery.

At Arosa, the snow was sparse and bare grassy spots conspired to make some courses hazardous. By the third day, we were both progressing nicely. Stella moved up to "advanced intermediate," and I was zinging along with my class. It was terrific! Just after noon on the fourth day, my group was practicing jump turns. I was second or third in line. The girl before me went charging down the slope and executed a sweet jump turn over a small ridge and disappeared on the lee side. I followed, came up to the ridge, jumped and could not avoid a large bare patch. I recall a hard bounce and landing on my left thigh. I next remember my classmates about a quarter of a mile away shouting up at me. I tried to get up, but the pain in my lateral thigh was excruciating. I felt my thigh; it had been augmented with a hematoma about the size of half a football. I managed to ski down, but I had to return to the hotel and pack the damned leg in ice. There was no point in Stella missing her ski instruction, so I holed up for a day and then tried it again. But the lousy thigh hurt too much. The hematoma needed aspiration.

When we got home, Joe Kirk drained about a pint of syrupy plasma and hemolyzed blood. I hobbled around on crutches. It took almost a year before my thigh was normal size. Some months later we had four staff doctors and two nurses all laid up with ski fractures or limping around the wards. The Colonel "forbade" any staff to ski until everyone was back to full-bodied duty. An exercise in frustration during ski season.

We visited Vienna twice. One was obliged to take the train, and from Linz to Vienna the swift diesel zipped through the ominous Russian (Red) Zone in eastern Austria. One needed a special pass to make this trip, and blinds were drawn while passing through the Red Zone (and no peeking; unsmiling Soviet guards with slung machine-pistols roamed the train). Vienna was divided into sections: American, British, French, Soviet and an international zone patrolled by all four occupying powers. The changing of the guard was a competition in spit and polish, precision military drilling and plain old posturing. It was silly and spooky; the Cold War at zenith.

Vienna was, well, ever-charming Vienna. We rented bikes at our modest pension and wandered the American, British and French zones freely. I seem to recall lunch *unter den linden* in the Vienna Woods in our zone, but the opera house was in the Russian sector. One needed some sort of permission (plus a ticket) to get in. We saw something boisterous and busy by Wagner. We had some problems negotiating trolley tracks with our bikes in the rain, but we saw a lot of the city. The bridge across the Danube was swathed in fog and mystery; the Iron Curtain loomed on the far bank. The "*Third Man*" had not been produced yet, but the rain-spattered, narrow, tortuous, cobble-stone streets with three-storied buildings looming like the walls of a steep valley, created a perfect venue for Orson Welles.

Our most memorable vacation trip carried us to Spain. The sick Studebaker was still giving us trouble, but I had it overhauled in the PX shop in Munich. They blessed it as "healed", and it decided to behave well on this trip. We crossed into Spain via San Sebastian from

Biarritz, a lovely, expensive swath of ermine beach. We arrived in Pamplona for the beginning of the Festival of San Fermin. We set up camp in a park on the edge of town and stashed air mattresses and sleeping bags in our small tent. Across the creek several families of Spanish gypsies had camped with their storybook wagons. We visited a swarthy, bespangled fortune teller right out of central casting. Her hushed advice was sort of like extracting a prognosis from a chiropractor, "Some good news; some bad news." The Gypsies never investigated our modest campsite.

The town was just as Hemingway had described (before it had been discovered by *Conde Nast*); a sleepy Basque village, quiet, indolent with a few dusty streets populated by farmers and goat herders. It was about to be transformed into a raucous, rowdy, wonderful Iberian version of Mardi Gras. I bought some light, white cotton trousers that tied at the waist, a few white blouses and some red neckerchiefs. The unofficial uniform was completed with a leather bota slung around my neck. I looked like a foot soldier in Pancho Villa's peasant infantry. Stella looked glorious in colorful native Basque blouses with flowing long skirts.

I don't think we paid for a bottle of wine the whole week. Soon after arrival in the square, we encountered a cluster of about a dozen American expatriates and their ladies. Matt lived in a garret in Montparnasse; his woman was a dark beauty from Tunisia (until she smiled—she lacked a few critical teeth). He introduced himself as the world's best, unpublished author and poet. Cliff was from Madrid; others were from Barcelona and Rome. The group was joined by one crazy Dane who spoke little English but would perform repetitive cartwheels with minimal encouragement. He could have been a model for Michelangelo's David. Mostly the expats were middle-aged ex-GIs left over from the war. Since we were the only other Americans in town, the group quickly forgave our military status.

By tradition the "day" started in mid-afternoon. Flute and drum dancing clubs began their performances, twirling and leaping in time

to the hypnotizing throb of the music as they pranced around the square. They reminded me of uninhibited New Year's Day Mummers in Philadelphia, sans feathers and spangles. These joyous folk represented dancing clubs from all the surrounding communities; they rehearsed all year for this grand week. We watched the endless show from the covered patio of a restaurant. It was hot as Hades, but the wine flowed all day. You could spot us amateurs by the expanding crimson splotches on our shirts as we tried to pour wine, goatskin-to-mouth at the challenging distance of several inches. On a few occasions, we felt obliged to dance with the clubs; they didn't seem to mind. There were a few stains on their blouses as well.

At five o'clock we all went to the corrida. The best matadors in Spain came to Pamplona. At that time the hero of Spain was El Cordobes, a tall, lean, elegant, darkly handsome athlete in his late twenties. Three matadors engaged two bulls each. I despised the picador attack but was advised by our ex-pat aficionados that without the lances into the shoulder muscles to bring the bull's head down, the matador would not stand a chance. Still it was a grisly business. The fighting bulls were all magnificent creatures with varying levels of enthusiasm to do battle. The adagio by a skillful torero is indeed a ballet of consummate agility, somewhat theatrical posturing and undeniable courage. We saw about a dozen clean, acrobatic, one-thrust kills, but some sword work was just terribly abortive butchery. One of the picadors had to leap out and sever the angry bull's cervical spinal cord with a close-up, short-knife coup.

These were the best bullfighters in the world, but a week of the spectacle was more than enough. I have never been to another corrida. El Cordobes won lots of ears and a tail. He was the toast of Pamplona. The second night we were having dinner (at the usual eleventh hour) and the Great Man and his entourage swept into our restaurant. He walked past our table and paused just a second too long when he saw Stella. His group drifted to the bar and later one of his flunkies brought a card to our table. It was an invitation for Stella to join his party later

at a private club. Our semi-drunk expatriate companions indicated that this was a singular honor, but the invitation did not include me. They said it was a traditional business for the matador to select a beautiful woman to spend the night. They also said that it would be lousy etiquette (and perhaps dangerous) for me to break the nose of Spain's handsome darling. So we demurred from both opportunities; Stella was infinitely flattered.

Each morning they held the encierra, when they release the fighting bulls to race through the narrow streets to the bullring. The police seemed to study all prospective runners to ensure that they were not too drunk (or perhaps too sober). I ran once, but I suspect I may hold the course record for wimpish velocity. The horns and hooves looked too real, and some foolhardy idiots ran too close or stumbled and got gored or trampled. In the bullring after the encierra sprint, they would release some ancient bulls with padded horns and let the wannabees swirl their veronicas and pirouette their fannies into harm's way. It was so damned crowded that some guys got trampled even here.

Each day was much like the next, and one soon fell into a routine of perpetual semi-drunkenness, dancing, singing and raising hell. I saw no evidence of hostility, until our flaxen-tressed Dane got into trouble. Apparently he was outraged at being grossly overcharged in a restaurant. (Routine gouging of non-Spaniards was the seasonal norm.) But our little David look-alike raised a ruckus, refused to pay and the local gendarmes were called. Also we were told he did his signature cartwheels before the magistrate, which did little to help his petition of innocence. So he was roughed up and tossed in the slammer, not a very good thing at all, especially in Spain. It was the not-necessarily-sober judgment of our group that, perhaps, since I was a major in the American army, I could bring the full weight of our military might to bear on behalf of our Danish ally.

So I gathered all my somewhat tattered dignity, stuffed my wine-stained shirt into my soil-stained trousers, tightened my sandals and led our indignant, semi-potted delegation trooping to the jailhouse. I

soon discovered that Spanish jails have probably not changed much since the Inquisition. Speaking through one of our group (fluent Cliff from Madrid), we explained my exalted status in the U.S. military establishment (Spain had been on our side in the war, hadn't it?) All we wanted was to liberate our exuberant but misguided friend from Copenhagen. It was soon established that the proprietor would settle for paying the bill, and the sergeant would settle for reasonable compensation for the inconvenience to him and his staff, plus the embarrassment wrought upon the good name of Pamplona. We took up a collection, and they fetched the storm-tossed Dane from some dark terrible place about three stories down. He was briefly furious that we had paid the usurious innkeeper, but soon he was cartwheeling merrily down the lane.

From Pamplona we drove down to Madrid where we stayed in Cliff's apartment. We did the Prado and other tourist things. Then Toledo ("a nice black-sequined mantilla for the signora, yes? And a desk set done in gold and silver inlay, of course.") In Barcelona we saw Gaudi's surreal ecclesiastical architecture. We landed in Perpignan in time for all-night fireworks and brass bandmanship on Bastille Day. And then scooted home, one helluva trip. But I fear *Conde Nast* has destroyed the ambience of San Fermin forever; it has been thoroughly and irrevocably discovered and converted to "tourist-friendly."

We made two and three day forays to Innsbruck, the Salzkammergut lake country (*die Weisses Rossel am Wolfgang See*) and Berchtesgarten (Hitler's eagle's nest). We visited Copenhagen (glorious Tivoli) and the low countries (acres of tulips in bloom). Stella made a pilgrimage to Rome with a Catholic tour group led by our chief chaplain (who had studied there for a few years). I was in the final stages of my board preparation and took a pass on this one. Stella had a grand time, waved at the Pope from Vatican Square and fell in love with Volterra in Tuscany.

Our trip to Paris might be worth a few lines. We drove the still recalcitrant Studebaker, and it only rebelled once in Metz (the fuel

injection system, again). We had contacted Matt, the self-avowed author and poet before we left, and he gave us the address of a hotel in Montparnasse. "A walk-up, but cheap and interesting." He was right. It was a steep four story climb and our neighbors were very successful Parisian ladies-of-the-night. Doors slammed and heels clacked all night. Much giggling and whispering and ohh-ohhing.

About two in the morning there was a new sound, this time some clanking from the street. I looked out the window and to my horror saw three Paris cops hooking our car up to a tow truck. I yelled at them, but soon they were hauling the vehicle away. I threw on some clothes and charged in the direction of the clinking caravan. After a desperate 30 minutes of running around Montparnasse, which was still a fairly busy neighborhood at two A.M., I spotted the tow truck still hooked to the sad-looking Stude. I raced into the police station up to a desk about 12 feet high with a Hercule Poirot double perched aloft. Having practically no *francaise*, I muttered and gestured toward the garroted vehicle. I fumbled out my military ID card.

American army majors in Paris carried even less firepower than in Pamplona. There ensued much sputtering back and forth in some mutually incomprehensible half-language. I managed to ascertain that while one could park on the north side of the street until midnight, it was off-limits after midnight. All clearly indicated by the street sign, of course, all *en francaise*. Looking back, I must have been a sight, disheveled, uncombed and still wearing my pajama top over rumpled fatigue pants. American army major indeed! The gendarmes finally agreed to liberate the car, and I discovered I had forgotten the keys! Ultimately, it all worked out; I think they were pleased to see the back of me. No fine, only a few fresh scratches on the forlorn beast.

Matt actually lived in a garret with his exotic Tunisian live-in. She was still missing those critical front teeth that made her radiant smile even more arresting. He explained that actually she had been sold to him in some village in the Atlas Mountains. He showed us his much-revised manuscript about a grasshopper plague in Morocco. The writ-

ing was awful. After a night wandering the bistros and bars of Montparnasse, we took "breakfast" in the morning produce market: onion soup. Fellow patrons were grizzled farmers, husky lorry drivers, leather-aproned greengrocers and weary hookers. Everyone smoked Lucky Strikes. We were right at home. It was undeniably the best onion soup in the universe. I had two giant bowls. We did all the other tourist stuff: Folies Bergere, boat ride down the Seine, Louvre, lunch atop the Eiffel Tower, superior curbside cuisine in half dozen restaurants, Notre Dame and Sacre Coeur. The whole nine yards.

The only untoward event was a visit with Stella's old chums from her G.W. days, Jean Louis and Robaire. They had a swanky address just off the Arc de Triomphe. The apartment was *haute decor*, their wives (acquired since the Cadillac odyssey to Miami Beach days) were *haute couture*. Our hosts were distinctly uncomfortable with us; it was my first taste of Gallic *hauteur*. We were offered tasteless canapés and a very pedestrian Chablis. Jean Louis attempted some conversation in halting English, but all languages apparently had forsaken the painfully silent Robaire. The wives chattered like jays between themselves, *au francaise,* of course. It was a transparent demonstration of deliberate bad manners. It really pissed me off, so we retreated before I embarrassed us.

Sometime in 1955, the word came down that the Russians wanted to say *fini* to their occupation of Austria. And within three months! Another manifestation of Soviet political gamesmanship. We were all asked to submit requests for reassignment. I had once made a consultant visit to the tiny, jewel-like army hospital in Livorno, and I had heard that the job as hospital commander was open. In that position, I figured I had a good shot at making light colonel within a year. We had already fallen in love with the Italian Riviera. Parenthetically, I think the men and women of northern Italy are the most graceful and handsome on the planet. They are even more beautiful than the Chinese-Hawaiian folks, who come very close. You don't see such magnificent

specimens in Cannes or the Costa Brava or even Redondo Beach. But Livorno was not to be; no *dolce vita* for us.

The Austrian command was rapidly winding down. Personnel were leaving, but no orders for Moser. Then I received word that I was being assigned to "temporary duty" in Geneva. "Geneva? Like in Switzerland?" Yes, the general's aide announced; I had been selected to provide medical support to the American delegation attending the Big Four Foreign Minister's Meeting. There were perhaps several hundred physicians in the army and air force in Europe. To this day I don't know how or why I got that job, but it was simply grand. My ego was in apogee.

I raided the hospital pharmacy ("Let me see those orders again, Doc"), and assembled three trunks full of tools, medicines, dressings, splints, everything I could imagine. (I harkened back to pre-Korea Fort Knox and those two archaic WW II trunks; never again!) So Stella and I took off for gorgeous Genf-by-the-lake. The trunks were to be shipped by "special (diplomatic priority) courier." They never made it. They were embargoed at the Swiss border, and despite all entreaties by the army and State Department, my magnificent trunks never made it to Geneva. But I didn't know that bit of intelligence until we had settled into our suite at the splendid Hotel Du Rhone. My medical sergeant from Truscott, Stella and I were the team. We used one room for living (the sergeant had a room of his own), and the other was set up as a clinic room.

At that time the Cold War was in full flower. The Russians were represented by no-nonsense Molotov; the English by wispy, angular McMillan; the French by short, raspy Bideax; the U.S. by hard-bitten, hard-nosed John Foster Dulles. After two days (one day before the first meeting), in response to frantic calls, word came from the border that no one knew **anything** about my three medical chests.

Shortly after banging down the phone on that futile call, an aide to Chip Bohlen knocked at the door. Bohlen was the U.S. ambassador to the USSR, a key player in the upcoming meetings. "Ambassador

Bohlen has a bad stye. Could you take care of it?" Without blinking I said, "Of course, just give us about ten minutes." I didn't even have a scalpel. The sergeant was off somewhere, so Stella was recruited to be my "head holder." We operated on Bohlen by draping his face with hotel towels (so he could not see what I was doing), and I lanced the stye with a double-edged Gillette blue blade sterilized over a candle. It was pure military "field expediency." It went well. I fabricated a dressing and eye patch from our first-aid kit, and removed it the next day. Clean wound. He never knew; Bohlen's office sent us flowers.

Within a few breathless minutes after the Bohlen adventure, I called for a car to take me to the University of Geneva Hospital. I sought out the chief of medicine and introduced myself. He spoke excellent English. I told him of my plight (the ghost of Colonel Ryle Radke must have been at my shoulder). This lovely man threw open his pharmacy and lent me some key items of equipment. It was difficult to read the medication labels in French, but the pharmacist also spoke English. I loaded up and hauled my stash back to the Du Rhone. They never sent us a bill. (I have never admired the Swiss politically. I consider their "neutrality" in WW II an unconscionable defection, and their bankers' stealing from Holocaust victims, beyond despicable.) But I could not fault the helpfulness and generosity of those Swiss professionals I encountered on this occasion.

The next few weeks were fascinating. Since none of the other national teams had brought a doctor, I opened my dispensary to members of all delegations and to the international press. We saw flocks of patients with a variety of problems: headache, nausea and vomiting, diarrhea, asthma. One ranking U.S. official who was obliged to make a presentation the next day developed intractable hiccups. After the usual "old wives" remedies failed, I sought a drug that I had read about called Largactil, precursor to chlorpromazine. It was available in Switzerland but not yet approved in the U.S. I asked my pharmacist friend at the Geneva Hospital for a few ampoules. I told the diplomat that it was a new drug, as yet unproved, but that it might stop his debilitating

hiccups. He was desperate, almost exhausted from the unrelenting diaphragmatic spasms. He stopped hiccupping after one shot, and then slept for a few precious hours. I was told he made a sterling presentation. Another batch of posies.

I have likened the experience in Geneva to practicing medicine in a combat situation. No bullets were flying, but everyone had to remain on "duty" all the time. In such situations, a physician is often obliged to shoot from the hip to "keep the troops on the firing line." One makes medical decisions that he would not consider under less arduous circumstances. Perhaps that is why the army sent me?

One day the word came down that Mr. Molotov was ill. Mr. Dulles had offered my services. We were to pack a kit and scoot over to the Russian embassy wearing civilian clothes. (Isn't that how spies get shot?) There was no clue as to the nature of his problem. A sleek black stretch limousine with U.S. flags aflutter picked me up with a very apprehensive diplomatic aide twitching in the back seat. He advised me of the delicacy of the situation, but that it could be a psychological coup for our side. (I thought, sure, if I don't screw up.) We arrived at the imposing gate of the Soviet embassy. Russian paratroopers with blunt-nosed carbines stood rigidly at attention. The attaché stepped out to a kiosk and picked up a phone. He talked for a few minutes and returned crestfallen, "Mr. Molotov is much better. We are not needed." I breathed a sigh of relief, but it would have been quite a kick.

Stella had a thrill. She got on an elevator at the Du Rhone and ran smack dab into the Israeli foreign minister (I think it was Moishe Sharon) and his Mossad bodyguards. He saw this pretty blonde lady wearing her giant Star of David. She recognized him and said, "Shalom." He invited her to his suite for tea. It made her day. Since I was offering care to all correspondents, we were invited to lunch with the members of the press corps on several occasions (always hunting for a hot tip I suspected). We met Marquis Childs, David Schonbrun and Walter Lippman. These were the doyens of print media. It was a heady time, and we loved every minute.

After two weeks we packed everything up and shipped it back to the university hospital. The original three embargoed trunks had been returned to Salzburg. I wrote a letter of thanks to the nice people at the Geneva hospital. The drive home was leisurely, via Lucerne, Liechtenstein and the Vorarlburg. We had a mixed greeting upon arrival. General Arnold requested that we remain in Salzburg, even as the hospital was closing down. We practically gift-wrapped our lovely institution, lock, stock and syringe, and handed it over to the gleeful Austrians. Then we gave them everything else in the military inventory but weaponry.

Still no orders to Livorno (to reward us for our heroic performance in Geneva, *n'est pas*)? Then, the general's aide materialized unannounced at our apartment. Sheepishly, "The general's folks are coming next week, and he wants you around to care for them. They like you." I soon discovered that the job as hospital commander at Livorno had gone to someone else. Later we received orders to gloomy Wurzburg. Thanks a lot, General Arnold.

Before we departed Salzburg, I flew home to take the ABIM oral examination. Military air (low, slow prop) took us to the Azores for refueling. The strip there was infamous for being short and bumpy. We came in very low over the water, and the props were reversed as soon as tires screeched. It seemed we shuddered to a halt a scant few feet of the other rock-strewn shore. It was after midnight, and we followed a grumpy, flashlight-bearing sergeant through a gale force wind up a goat path to the Officer's Club. We enjoyed hastily slung together hamburgers and fries and hoisted a few shooters of Macallan single malt, until the call came to depart. I sacked out all the way into Dover.

The exam was conducted at the V.A. hospital in Philadelphia. I was more relaxed than for the written; I felt confident with live patients. My senior examiner was Dr. Walter Snell from the Mayo Clinic. The patient had obvious cirrhosis and pursuing my diagnostic philosophy of always seeking out a second (usually more subtle) diagnosis, I discovered a faint diastolic murmur. It had been missed by the V.A. house

staff, but Snell could hear it. I also won his heart by slipping in that I was familiar with Witzell-Snell Syndrome (a bit of a stretch but the patient did have cirrhosis and **might** have had a palpable spleen). My junior examiner was a youngish, no-nonsense cardiologist. But the patient had a thyroid nodule, and the examiner knew less about lumpy thyroids than I. It was a sweep.

(In later years the ABIM abandoned the "oral boards" because they were "too subjective," and logistically very difficult to administer—too many candidates, too few reliable examiners. I still think it was an error. Perhaps they can do as well with a user-friendly, interactive computer system, but I don't think so. There is nothing quite like having a wise, seasoned examiner observe a candidate's performance at the bedside. From my technophobic aspect, the computer will never replace personal, one-on-one bedside dialogue. It seems to me that there are enough retired teacher-internists, with practical experience, who could be called upon to augment the "active duty" faculty—to ensure enough personnel to do the job. I would happily volunteer. But who's listening?)

Wurzburg! Everything that Salzburg was **not**; darkness had replaced light. We rarely saw the sun from September until April; it was gray from awakening until bedtime. The gloom was pervasive, a somber, bombed-out city that was about 50% rebuilt. *Kafka-burg am Main.* The hospital was nice enough, and the staff had a few stars. My assistant chief was Captain Arthur Haut who had completed a hematology fellowship with Dr. Max Wintrobe at Salt Lake City. Art was due to return as a faculty member. He was a remarkably talented clinician and resented the hell out of being displaced as chief of medicine by a regular army major. But he got over it. The chief of surgery was Lt. Col. Jim Hutchinson. We had met once before in Korea, very briefly under extraordinary circumstances. We recognized each other.

(It had been a very cold, rainy-snowy day in early winter, 1951. We were in a convoy creeping north following the 555 Field Artillery (lO5s). Suddenly there was a commotion up the road, and we watched

in disbelief as a 2 1/2 ton truck towing one of the field pieces lost a wheel over the edge of the narrow, slimy road. The heavy 105 slipped off as well, and the whole assembly began to slip and then tumble down the hill, gun-pulling-truck-pulling-gun. We watched in horror as the scene unfolded, seemingly in slow motion. The gun crew was trapped in the back of the covered truck. It came to rest at the bottom of a ravine about 50 feet below, upside down in a frigid, rushing mountain stream. Everyone scrambled down to help. I got there first and dove to pull one guy out. When I came up, a frosted, gray-haired guy surfaced beside me with another GI. It was Jim Hutchinson. We dove again and pulled out two more. The others had miraculously jumped or been thrown free. No one was hurt badly. It could have been a disaster. We were soaked and freezing and being deep in enemy country, we all scrambled back up to the road and took off. I never knew what happened to the tumbled truck and gun. There had been no time to exchange names with my fellow diver, and I never laid eyes on Jim again until we met in Wurzburg. Our families became very close.)

Wurzburg was the headquarters for the 10th Mountain Division. The commander was Major General Guy Meloy. The name was vaguely familiar; I was reminded that he had commanded the ill-fated 34$^{th}$ Regiment that had been badly mauled at Taejon in the early days of the Korean War. He had fought the T-34s in a valiant but futile effort, had been captured by the NKs and held prisoner for a long time. He was a much-decorated hero. He and his delightful wife became my patients, and we often chatted about Korea and WW II. I soon came to realize that Meloy and many other high-ranking officers seemed to have a Pattonesque philosophy. The Nazis were bad guys for sure, and we had to whip them. But we should not have stopped at the Oder. We should have advanced beyond and forced the war-weary Russians to yield the turf east of Berlin and return home. Ergo, no Cold War. I never heard this logic espoused in specific terms, but the

message was unmistakable. Turn on our allies, the Russians? It could have gone so terribly wrong.

Meloy was not a war-apologist, but more than a few officers and wives we encountered in Wurzburg were. I recall most vividly, one meeting of a joint German-American "friendship group," ostensibly designed to foster better relations between old enemies. Historically, Wurzburg, an ancient, walled town with many classic medieval buildings, had been declared an open city by the Allies because it was a major hospital center for the Wehrmacht. It was untouched until the last months of 1945. But then Allied intelligence received word that the German High Command was using Wurzburg also as a covert railroad marshaling yard to transfer troops and war materiel. The mayor was told to advise his military keepers to cease this violation of the "open city" agreement. Very foolishly, he responded negatively, with something abrasive and arrogant like, "We place our trust in God and the fuehrer..." The situation did not change. The Germans were warned twice again. No response. Then one morning a flight of Lancaster bombers firebombed the city through thick cloud cover. The raid lasted about 20 minutes; about 80% of the city was destroyed with heavy loss of life.

The bitterness against Americans in the town was palpable. You could feel it walking the streets of that desolate city. And here at this meeting the hostess, some colonel's inflated wife, rose to speak. She had the temerity to apologize for the "horror we had wrought upon the city" and topped it off with "...after all it was really the British..." Stella and I were thunderstruck! I felt hot words rising in my throat, but no one else seemed outraged. We rose from the half-eaten lunch and stalked out in fury. It wasn't the last time we heard such trash in Wurzburg.

One of the few bright lights of the Wurzburg experience was Stella's fling in little theater. She played the leading role in "Charley's Aunt," to crowds of appreciative GIs and officers at their clubs. She was

delightful and absolutely stunning. I took the kids to every performance. It was her finest moment in dreary Wurzburg.

We had less than six months to go, and the melancholy aura of the city was pervasive, taking its toll on everyone. Stella was driving to Augsberg twice a week to see an army psychiatrist. I would go with her whenever I could escape the wards. The insomnia was worse. She was taking secobarbital almost every night. We had a rash of suicides throughout the command. One of the staff wives who lived in our building killed herself, head in the oven. I was called; made a frantic abortive effort to resuscitate, but she already had beginning rigor. Ghastly bit.

During this time, Jon's slow growth and development became painfully evident. He was seen by military and civilian consultants. He was hospitalized, and a multitude of tests were done, requiring many blood samples. It was a pitiful, painful experience. Stella and I stood shifts at his bedside. It was decided that he lacked Growth Hormone (GH). But such a biological therapeutic agent was not available then. (Even when GH ultimately did come into clinical use, it was suspected of being contaminated with a "slow virus" [now called a prion] capable of causing a chronic ["spongiform"—as in Mad Cow Disease] encephalitis-like illness similar to Kuru. In recent years, the biological agent has been created in remarkably pure form by recombinant DNA technique. I only wish it had been available in 1956.) The consultants recommended a course of testosterone therapy. I was very ambivalent; there was pathetically little in the literature, and I was concerned about premature closure of the epiphyses that would limit longitudinal bone growth. But I trusted our staff pediatrician, Dr. Leonard Goldman, who had been on the clinical faculty at Baylor. Jon received the injections and seemed to perk up. Gradually he began to improve and over time he caught up with his peer group. Ultimately he attained height that landed him in the mid-percentile, and he was bright as hell.

Before we departed Wurzburg, the 10th Division was replaced by the Big Red One (First Division) out of Fort Riley. It was a monumen-

tal experiment in moving large units in and others out, on the same air-craft. Incoming transports brought Big Red One units; they departed with 10th Division men and equipment. It was declared a logistical success, setting a new precedent for shifting large numbers of men and equipment swiftly and expeditiously. We bade farewell to the Meloys.

Stella and I took enjoyed one more great European adventure. We flew to Glasgow and rented a car. It was our first experience with "wrong-side-of-road" driving from a right-sided driving position. I took a few spins around the parking lot; it seemed awkward but manageable. The true test came on the west side of Loch Ness, a narrow road with barreling lorries tearing down at us in the opposite direction. It was terrifying for Stella with a nervous novice at the wheel. It got easier after about an hour, but I don't think I made a right turn all day. The windshield wipers had a heavy workout since the lever was in the position usually reserved for the turn indicator. We stopped to make the traditional search for Nessie from a cafe on the left side of the road. Once off the main roads, driving became easier, never comfortable.

We went up the west coast and were enthralled by the classic green-clad mountains and crystalline lochs. The road was often single lane with turnouts. If you encountered another car, it seemed proper etiquette to pull over if you got to the turnout first. But some local drivers seemed to hesitate, so that I would be obliged to pull out first. Sort of a Scots version of reverse chicken. The Gulf Stream created a very temperate climate, and the forests looked semi-tropical.

We stayed in bed and breakfast places, but they were not to enjoy. The inevitable single bath and WC at the end of the corridor made for some tension. At one stop, Ballantrae on the Firth of Clyde, we landed in a B & B with an elderly couple from Delft on our right and newly-weds from Aberdeen to our left. The walls between must have been paper mache. Between snores and farts to starboard, and sighs, groans and squeaking springs to port, it was a night to remember. Most motels in the U.S. deploy unimaginative cinder block between the rooms, but here we encountered no motels. I have studiously avoided

B and Bs ever since. Sharing limited space with unknown others will never appeal. Nevertheless, our Scots hosts were uniformly felicitous, and the morning tea, scones and jam, always fantastic.

At Edinburgh castle, we watched the changing of the guard with pipes and drums, a colorful, uniquely Scots spectacle. We listened to whisky-husky Bobbie Burns recitations delivered in an undecipherable, basso highlands brogue in a wonderfully dark, ancient, smoky pub. Then we meandered south through the Lake country, Cotswold's, Stratford-on-Avon to London. We found a modest hotel just off Hyde Park, but Stella had a serious bout of G.I. upset compounded by depression and malaise. She insisted that I explore Westminster Abbey, the Tower, and parliament buildings alone. It was a doleful ending to a trip that had started so well.

Before we completed our Wurzburg tour, we visited Dachau. It was not easy to find. The map indicated that it was a few miles northwest of Munich but no natives ever heard of the infamous death camp, even in the town of Dachau! (All the Nazis had fled to Argentina and Paraguay remember.) We stumbled over that place of nightmares in the late afternoon. It was all there. An attempt had been made to sanitize it, but they could not disguise the gas chambers, incinerators, hanging trees, burial ditches, and the pervasive ambience of horror. I understand all the physical features have been preserved and, quite appropriately, the "new generation" of EU Germans has not tried to conceal the madness that seized Nazi Germany. We rode home in mournful silence.

(I acknowledge that the post-war generations of Germans have disavowed the barbarous Nazi phenomenon; they express outrage and shame. They seem to be in the vanguard of the European Union, despite its distinctly Francophile ambience. I am willing to concede that the skinheads and neo-Nazis probably represent a noisy (primarily former-East German) minority, more embarrassment than political threat. But the occurrence of the Holocaust in a civilized modern society, embraced ubiquitously at **all** social, professional, and political lev-

els, suggests to me that there may be some subtle, malicious aberration in the Teutonic gene pool. I admit my bias; I believe that under the proper conditions of poverty and hunger, the demon could emerge again. The next time there probably will be too few Jews to kill, so the Turks and anyone of less-than-Aryan coloring or less-than-physical "perfection" had best beware. And I'll repeat, under similar circumstances it could happen in America.)

A few months before we were scheduled to return to the States, we calculated that I still owed the army about two years. One more attenuated tour and then out. Then General Robert Blount, the USAREUR surgeon, called from Heidelberg. He offered me a one-year clinical fellowship in cardiology with Colonel Weldon Walker, one of the rising stars in the medical corps who had studied under the legendary Dr. Sam Levine at the Brigham. It was at Brooke Army Hospital in San Antonio. Another critical decision. I already had 13 years toward retirement and seven more would qualify me for a lifetime retirement pension at 3/4 base pay. So it would "only" add another two years, and I would be trained in pulmonary medicine and cardiology. Stella and I realized that the temptation to go for the 20 would be powerful. It would seem the Rubicon had several tricky branches. After much discussion, we agreed that it was probably a good deal. So we headed for Fort Sam Houston.

The voyage home was on the U.S.S. Constitution, sister ship of the Independence, source of Stella's triumphant west to east crossing. It was an easy north Atlantic crossing. We had a tidy cabin with two double-deck bunks. Two notable events occurred. First, Jon, who was about four went to a movie with Steven. "Village of the Damned" was a British production about children in a small rural town who became vehicles for an extra-terrestrial life-form. It manifested itself by creating a strange, brilliant green light that emanated from the eyes of afflicted children. Jon had nightmares about those luminous eyes intermittently for the next 20 years! He spoke of it frequently as an adolescent and young adult.

The other happening was no less spectacular. I was dozing in an upper bunk and sneezed. Your average simple, normal sneeze. I was stricken with sudden lancinating pain in my left sacroiliac that made it impossible for me to move. I was locked in a fetal position and could not scramble out of the bunk. An alarmed Stella called the ship's doctor. He gave me an injection of a "muscle relaxant" that had no effect. Finally, at my insistence, he gave me a shot of morphine. I was able to climb out of the bunk. I spent the remainder of the voyage lounging in the whirlpool in the ship's sick bay and taking aspirin until my ears were ringing. It took months for the pain to subside sufficiently to permit daily corrective exercise to strengthen my back muscles. I still have periodic twinges when I forget my infirmity and attempt to lift heavy things using my back rather than my legs. And I still do back exercises.

# 16

## *The Brooke Years*

✦

*(remarkable Weldon Walker—"take nothing for granted...")*

Colonel Weldon Walker was formidable: great bushy eyebrows, penetrating blue eyes and relentless intensity. He had been a professional boxer while in medical school, and his nose bore a slight residual asymmetry. Weldon was the best bedside pediatric cardiologist I have ever known. He and Proctor Harvey stand alone in my firmament of great heart doctors (and I have known a bunch). Dominating the wall above his desk was a hand-carved, oaken plaque bearing the maxim that characterized his life, "Take Nothing for Granted."

Weldon's philosophy and character were epitomized by a true story. He was absolutely intolerant of anecdote and hearsay; "They have no place in scientific discourse." He once ran an advertisement in the *New York Times* challenging **anyone** to produce "scientifically acceptable evidence" of the existence of extra-sensory perception. He offered to pay $10,000 to anyone who could satisfy a panel of scientists that ESP existed. He never had a single taker.

Walker was an enthusiastic hands-on teacher. There were two of us cardiology fellows, and he worked our tails off. Weldon was an expert in congenital heart disease, and he had written extensively about septal defects (primum and secundum of the ventricles and atrial defects). We did right heart catheterizations three mornings a week. Our equipment was primitive; jury rigged by Weldon with bits and pieces swiped

from radiology and Japanese "cardiac catheters" that showed opaque under the fluoroscope. I soon became reasonably adept at threading the sinuous, eel-like beasts into the right atrium, proximate to the tricuspid valve, and injecting dye while triggering the thunderous cassette changer to expose about half a dozen films, as the dye traversed the heart and lungs. By today's fully automated, user-friendly devices it was positively medieval. But it worked (most of the time). In the late mornings and afternoons we conducted clinics and rounded twice a day. In the latter part of the year, I did cardiac consultations, visiting other services.

A major flap occurred when the cardiovascular surgeon at Brooke, to whom we referred all our patients for repair of congenital defects, lost two young patients in rapid sequence. At post-mortem we discovered some very sloppy surgical work. An axiom in repair of congenital hearts in infants and children who are already severely compromised, is that you either make them **better** or they will not survive the trauma of surgery. It is simply life or death. Weldon spoke to the surgeon who denied having made technical errors even when confronted with his awful handiwork. Weldon went to the hospital commander and told him that in the future we would send all of our patients to the world-renowned cardiovascular surgeon, Dr. Denton Cooley in Houston, who was his personal friend. The general fumed, but Weldon's reputation in cardiology transcended the army, and when red-faced and adamant, he was *tres formidable*. So they compromised; the surgeon spent a month in Houston at the elbow of Cooley.

When he returned, the first child we sent for surgery died. At post-mortem it was the same story. The sorry surgeon had learned nothing. Again Weldon stormed up to the general's office and declared that Colonel X was totally incompetent to do reconstructive surgery on small congenital hearts. All our patients would be sent to Houston. It was a flap that went all the way to the Surgeon General. Indeed, Weldon prevailed; no more children died for lack of surgical skill. But after

my year in cardiology, the army exiled him to career Siberia—a consultant job in Europe.

A few years later Weldon resigned and became chief of cardiology at the White Memorial Hospital in Los Angeles, on the faculty at Loma Linda medical school. Ironically, in 1995 Weldon collapsed and died while taking his early morning jog, apparently succumbing to a fatal ventricular tachyarrhythmia. It was most sobering; he had never smoked, was tough and lean, no hypertension, no diabetes, ever watchful of his diet and religious in his exercise. No evident risk factors, but those damned genes! I will never forget him.

For the first time we were assigned quarters on a military post, Fort Sam Houston. Our home on old Infantry Post had been built in the 1870's, an official historic landmark. Two stories with wrap-around, screened verandas on each floor, 18-foot ceilings, and a cottage in the back that was an anachronism (quarters for the "batman"). In the old, pre-WW I army, this was usually an enlisted man who did chores for field grade officers. It made a nice garage. The house was an elegant, well-preserved relic, our first true home. Other wives on the post told Stella these homes were known as "wife killers." They required a lot of housework. Alas, when we departed Wurzburg, we had bid a reluctant farewell to sweet Laura. As I indicated, she had married a sergeant, and we lost track of her.

In San Antonio, Stella enrolled at Trinity College and took classes during the morning. She soon made a host of new friends, including a gorgeous Chinese-American girl named Priscilla. Jon was about four and attended a day nursery; Steven at seven began kindergarten on post. Jon was still small and poorly coordinated, but his intellectual development was ahead of the curve. He was still being followed by a pediatrician at regular intervals.

Stella's insomnia was unrelenting. The family began to attend weekly group sessions with a staff psychiatrist. It seemed to help. The year passed swiftly. We finally traded the sickly Studebaker for a very large, muscular Mercury station wagon. A WAC sergeant had fallen

behind on her payments, and the powerful beast was about to be repossessed. She offered it to me for a few hundred bucks if I would pick up the monthly payments. It was a good deal; the car was in top shape. We made trips to Yellowstone, Glacier, San Francisco, and Monterrey in old Mexico and it never flinched. Wondercar!

My parents came for an extended visit. Dad had become progressively more incapacitated. The drugs for Parkinsonism were primitive and ineffectual. He had become increasingly rigid with a very hesitant, unsteady gait, and his speech was severely impaired. Mother had some outside help while at home, but here at Fort Sam, he was completely dependent on her. We helped as much as we could. Dad would weep uncontrollably because he knew what a burden he had become. Mother was beginning to crack at the seams. We were watching a classic demonstration of the caregiver-patient, love-hate relationship.

To complicate matters the long-standing enmity between Stella and mother made the home situation even more difficult. They tried to make amends, but it never quite took. The folks stayed for about one month. Soon thereafter, dad had to be placed in a nursing home; he died within a year. His death caused me to reflect on our own lives. When he was well, he and mother had always spoken of those "great days that were coming"—when they would retire from practice, relax, enjoy life and travel. For dad, it never happened. And it never happens for too many who wait too long before illness or death overtake them. I began to understand the philosophy of "*carpe diem.*" I think it was my first true glimmer of personal mortality.

As my year of fellowship began to wind down, the chief of medicine, Colonel Dan Sheehan, asked me to stay on as his assistant. It would be the payback year for the cardiology fellowship, and a chance to get back into full-time clinical teaching. The old man was close to retirement, and he left the resident training largely to me. Over a few months, I installed a "Georgetown" type of program with 21 residents—a scintillating, provocative group. I brought in teaching consultants from the academic world: Leonard Berman, Don Seldin, Louis

Weinstein, Bill Crosby and many other teaching stars. We produced some superb young internists; our ABIM passage rate would have done credit to Harvard or Hopkins.

One of the great charms of Brooke and Fort Sam was the traffic in foreign medical officers. They came from virtually every country on earth friendly to the U.S. and hostile to the Russians. These seemed the only criteria. A few stand out. Major Alan Reay was a delightful Brit, a smashing David Niven look-alike sans moustache. He spent six months with us studying clinical cardiology. I was always amused at the British dress uniform, a sort of Gilbert and Sullivan color extravaganza, occasionally worn by the very proper Alan. It incorporated a giant, cumbersome saber. The monster device seemed programmed to engage someone's unsuspecting thigh each time he turned. Alan was very bright, personable, urbane and articulate. Many years later, I visited him at Sandhurst where he was chief of medicine in the hospital. He went on to become Surgeon General of the British army. It was almost predictable.

But the most memorable exchange fellow was Major Mohammed Abdullah of Pakistan. He spent a year with us in medicine, along with a colleague who was studying general surgery. Entertaining Abdullah and his friend was a delightful challenge. If you remembered that "nothing of the pig" nor fermented spirits were "kosher" (you should pardon the expression), it was okay. One night, just to be cute, I took a bottle of Glenfiddich and pasted over the label with one that read "non-alcoholic scotch." He said, "Do you approve that I drink this?" "Inshallah," I assured him, "let it be on my head; just read the label." Thus it was in San Antonio that Abdullah discovered the joys of single-malt scotch.

Years later when we visited him and his wife Zarina in Lahore, he took me aside, nervously, "You will not speak of non-alcoholic scotch to Zarina." I believe that Abdullah was a better Muslim than I was a Jew, but we both thought that religious dietary prohibitions were ridiculous. Occasionally, we shared the delights of single malt.

We went to the Texas State Fair and Abdullah was thrilled with the giant hogs, bronc-busting cowhands and horsy C and W milieu. He wore his 10-gallon Stetson and Spanish spurs. Our most hilarious experience occurred when Abdullah and his surgeon friend sought to repay our hospitality for all the dinners they had enjoyed in our capacious dining room on Infantry Post. They were going to cook "a genuine Pakistani dinner" for us. They gave Stella a list of ingredients including some spices that defied the inventory of the commissary and two supermarkets. They declared the kitchen off-limits for at least six hours while they toiled. The odors emanating were interesting, not exactly exotic, but notably dominated by pungent curry. Then we all sat down to relish this sumptuous repast.

It was inedible. Besides being chemically scalding, it clung tenaciously to each plate, a sullen, sodden gray lump. The kids were the first to bitch. They both loved Abdullah; he told them Arabian Nights stories, but this was too much. They bolted from the table. Abdullah and friend were mortified, "It is not very good." They took us to a Chinese restaurant. The cleanup was Augean; every pot, pan and dish in the kitchen had been pressed into service—none escaped char or blemish. In later years when we visited Lahore, Zarina heard the story with a great outburst of mirth, "No Pakistani man **ever** spends a moment in the kitchen. Abdullah must have lost his sense over there in America!"

It might be added that in those years we trained hundreds of Iranian officers and doctors. Virtually every civilian teaching hospital entertained Iranian fellows and residents, training them in all the specialties. (I recall one crestfallen chap who had just completed two years of cardiovascular surgery residency at Baylor and was about to head home. He lamented, "I can crack a mitral valve and repair a septal defect. When I go home they will send me to Ramar to treat wolf bites!"). Many managed to defect and remain in the States. At Brooke we always had a cadre of Iranian medical officers. And, of course, all branches of combat arms in the army and air force were involved in teaching Iranian officers and non-coms.

Our erstwhile friend, Shah Pahlavi, obviously had major problems with fair governance and respecting human rights, but he had the wisdom to educate a whole generation of physicians and army officers in the United States. I admit political naiveté, but it was difficult for me to comprehend the comparative ease of the coup by Ayatollah Khomeni in overthrowing the Shah. The subsequent demonizing of the U.S. (the Great Satan), and the taking of diplomatic hostages only meant that all of our medical and military friends must have been killed or imprisoned or expatriated or "converted" to the new militant Islam.

It was during this time that I became interested in kidney biopsies. Early reports by Bob Kark and others indicated that the technique was feasible and safe, with adequate precautions. It facilitated making definitive diagnoses of difficult renal disorders. I felt it was a procedure that we should master. No one in the army was performing kidney biopsies. With permission from Colonel Sheehan, I contacted Dr. Len Berman, who had been a resident with me at Georgetown. He was now the staff nephrologist at the Mt. Sinai Hospital in Cleveland. I knew that Len was doing renal biopsies. I spent a week at Sinai, and he demonstrated the technique, then let me perform six biopsies. (It was the "see one, do one, teach one" era.) I was introduced to the formidable eight-inch modified Vim-Silverman needle. One needed to identify the position of the lower pole of the kidney on an abdominal radiograph, mark out the coordinates on the patient's back, anesthetize locally and then perform the biopsy. I was rewarded with a nice sliver of tissue on four of the six attempts.

Brooke purchased four biopsy needles, and I devised a rigid protocol. The risk of hemorrhage was significant. Almost every biopsied patient would reveal some microscopic blood in the urine after the procedure, but the real hazard was excessive, largely uncontrollable bleeding that might require surgical intervention. My protocol ensured that: (1) a biopsy was indicated to determine the nature of the pathology of the suspected kidney disease when the clinical history and laboratory

examination were not definitive. (It is axiomatic in medicine that one does **not** perform a relatively risky or expensive invasive diagnostic procedure unless the result has a high probability of facilitating useful treatment), and (2) there were no contraindications such as a bleeding tendency, unusual position of the kidneys, or already significantly compromised renal function.

I taught all the Brooke internal medicine residents how to do the procedure and then traveled to Walter Reed and demonstrated the technique to their staff. This afforded me the opportunity to spend a day with Dr. Bill Manion, chief of the Walter Reed Institute of Pathology. Bill was one of the best renal pathologists in the country, and I was eager to become more adept at reading biopsy microscopic slides. We reviewed dozens of post-mortem kidney slides; he was delighted to get living biopsy material to study. Thus we added a diagnostic dimension to army medicine.

The only weakness in our Brooke teaching program was in hematology. We had no well-trained hematologist to take consultations and teach house staff. Army hematologists were in short supply. One day in mid-winter, the "eternal" Surgeon General, Leonard Heaton (he was SG for the entire time I was in the army!) visited Brooke. As part of his rah-rah program, he met with the staff of each department and asked the perfunctory question, "Do you have any problems?" Colonel Dan shook his head, smiled placidly and nodded at me. I said, "We need a hematologist." The Great Man acknowledged, "I'll see what I can do."

A very strange incident occurred while we were at Brooke. The family had taken a week of vacation in our newly acquired Mercury station wagon, visiting the north rim of the Grand Canyon. It was higher, wilder and less spectacular than the south rim, but we all enjoyed a little trail hiking. On the way home, we were traversing some narrow steep highways adjacent to some formidable drop-offs about 100 miles north of Flagstaff. The windows were open and the air was cool. Suddenly, Stella said, "I hear a car horn." We had not seen another vehicle in about an hour. So we stopped, and all of us could hear a distant car

horn, beeping erratically. We finally located the source; about 200 feet down one of the ravines we spotted an overturned pick-up truck with someone waving a red bandana from the window!

I told Stella to drive the wagon down to a place where the road had descended to the valley floor about a half a mile away. I scrambled down the rough scrabble of the ravine and reached the pick-up. The odor of gasoline was overpowering. I yelled to the person inside, "Turn off the ignition!" The truck was packed with ancient furniture (now scattered over the hillside and valley floor). It had obviously tumbled while negotiating a sharp bend in the road.

I crept to the window and saw a craggy old man still waving the bandana and still punching the damned horn. I said, "Are you okay? I'm going to try to pull you out." He muttered something incomprehensible. I had no idea of his condition except that he was able to speak and move his arms. I wasn't sure he had turned off the ignition; I could envision a horrendous gasoline explosion. The vehicle was tipped slightly, and I could reach through the driver's window and touch him. I repeated, "I'm going to pull you out!" I was concerned about head and back injury, possible fractures, but the immediate threat of igniting the gasoline was my dominant fear. So I reached in, grabbed him by his shirt and collar and began to pull, slowly. No seat belt.

Thankfully, he very slight and not wedged. I was able to slide him out through the window. I hauled him about 20 feet from the truck. He seemed stunned, shocky and did not speak. He reeked alcohol. His pulse was rapid but strong, he did not seem to have abdominal tenderness (no spleen rupture) and squeezing his extremities did not elicit a wince. It was a miracle that he was still alive and seemingly not badly injured after that dreadful tumble.

I could not see our wagon, but I knew the road leveled off at the valley floor about a quarter mile away. I could find nothing to use for a neck brace, so I used my heavy leather belt coiled gently around his thin neck. I found some old heavy curtains or such scattered around the truck, gently placed him in supine position and began to drag him,

head first, down to where I thought I would meet the car. It was a bitch. The ground was rocky and he moaned a lot, but after about 20 minutes (it seemed interminable), we came abreast of the wagon. I was a sweaty, exhausted wreck. Stella had already put down the back seats and laid out some blankets. All four of us placed him, delicately in the back of the wagon. His vital signs were still strong. He was able to drink some water. The boys were silent, white with apprehension. Stella sat beside him stroking his arm while I drove very slowly down the road. It was desolate mountain country we had never traversed before. After about 15 minutes we spotted a ramshackle gasoline station with a few crude cabins scattered in back.

The guy standing behind the counter was a monstrous Navajo. I quickly described the situation, "I need to call an ambulance." A thumb indicated a payphone on the wall in the corner. There was no book. So I dialed up the operator and asked her to connect me with the nearest state police barrack. Again, I described the situation. The desk sergeant said he would have to dispatch an ambulance from Flagstaff, but he would send a highway patrol vehicle immediately. I was obliged to pay one dollar for a pint of water; the giant proprietor took little interest in our travail. Geronimo's revenge! Within 10 minutes an Arizona patrol car zoomed up and out stepped a diminutive trooper, dark shades, giant .45 and all. He said it would take about an hour for the ambulance to arrive. I offered that it would not be advisable to move the old man without a proper neck brace. "You a doctor?" "Well, yes." Strangely, a faint grimace flashed and was gone. Then he bent over the old man. "How are you feeling Old Timer?"

The guy blinked, apparently recognizing the uniform. Then quite oddly, he looked over the trooper's shoulder at me and whispered, "Are you really a doctor?" These were his first words. Before I could answer, the trooper abruptly took my arm and pulled me away. "I think you'd best get out of here, doc. You probably saved the old bastard's life, but from now on you will be responsible for him—if he learns your name." I was flabbergasted, "But it really isn't safe to move him until the

ambulance gets here." The cop wiped his forehead, "OK, but go outside and have a coke; don't speak to the old man." The codger seemed stable for the moment so I left, completely perplexed.

After an eternity the "ambulance" arrived. It was just a beat-up, yellow van with an old army litter strapped to cleats in the floor. They had no cervical collar! By now, the patient was sitting up and talking. So they put him on the canvas litter, strapped him down and came over to speak to me. I told them all that had transpired. They asked for my name and address; the trooper stepped between us, "No need for that; just get on your way." And they did. As the van sped down the dusty road, the trooper came over to Stella and me. "Doc, you are a good person, and you did a very nice thing. But a month back, another Good Samaritan doctor, stopped at an accident up near Tuba City, helped an injured woman, and wound up getting his ass sued. So I don't want to know anything about you. Now, thanks, and beat it." Sobering lesson; litigious world—even in the Arizona outback. I still intend to stop for accidents, if I am first on the scene. But fortunately, I have not been so challenged. I will never forget the "North Rim Caper."

One month later I received a call from the Office of the Surgeon General. "Major Moser, General Heaton would like to know **where** you want to go for your hematology fellowship!" Astonished, I blurted something like, "What? But I have already done pulmonary and cardiology, and I don't even **like** hematology." But once again it was a rare opportunity: a year of hematology anywhere in the country! I talked it over with Stella; here was that infinite Rubicon again. This year of training, plus the payback, would put us at 17 years of service; three more to retire. The temptation was overwhelming. One of the best hematologists in the world was Colonel Bill Crosby at Walter Reed, but that would mean Washington again. I called my old Wurzburg colleague, Arthur Haut, who was now back in Salt Lake City on the faculty at the medical school. I asked him how it was to work with Dr.

Max Wintrobe, whose textbook was the hematology classic. He said it would be tough but terrific.

So we opted for Utah: hematology and the slopes of Alta and Brighton. I felt insecure and uneasy about another year of fellowship in a specialty I really didn't care much about. I asked if I could spend two weeks with a friend, who was a staff hematologist at the Mayo Clinic, to study blood and lymph node morphology, an area I hadn't visited in many years. So I flew to Rochester and spent the mornings participating in "slide rounds." About six fellows and six staff would gather around a large table with individual microscopes. The technicians would give each of us a box containing perhaps ten virtually identical slides: peripheral blood smears, bone marrow smears and lymph node tissue sections. With the chief at the head of the table and his senior technician beside him, we would review each slide: identify the tissue, describe the cells and try to make a diagnosis. We each took a turn and after the initial comment, everyone could critique. It was a very amiable, highly educational exercise. I would take my slides back to my hotel room and study them again, checking my notes, reading about various blood diseases.

In the afternoons, we would make rounds on hematology patients and attend clinics. I was ambivalent about the "Mayo System" of house officer education. Every patient was assigned to a staff physician, an expert in the area of concern. The fellows and residents could make recommendations, but the patient was managed (all orders were written) by the staff physician. Undeniably, this system was great for patients, but it seemed that Mayo fellows and residents failed to have a chance to develop that personal sense of patient responsibility and gratification that I consider a critical element in the education (and maturation) of house officers in clinical medicine. I thought our residents at Brooke were far more seasoned and confident than these chaps. It was a worthwhile two weeks. (Now that Mayo has a medical school, perhaps the situation has changed and house officers have more direct responsibility. I hope so.) When I left Rochester I had a nifty slide collection,

felt reinforced in morphology and was psyched up to tackle Wintrobe and Salt Lake.

Dining out in Rochester was fascinating if not conducive to *bon appetite.* The ambience was heavy with "pathology." The town was inundated with terribly ill patients and their worried families from every place on earth. Every conversation in every venue seemed infested with sad tales of some dreadful illness. It was impossible to escape. I tried a bar on the edge of town; an old, unshaven farmer type sidled up, "So what have **you** got?" I think Rochester, Minnesota may be the most depressing place in America.

Salt Lake City is the Mormon capital of the world. Folks at the medical school (still housed in the old Salt Lake City General Hospital) suggested we rent a house in the northwest section, just off the road to Bountiful. We found a pleasant, reasonable, two-story bungalow with a small yard for the kids. It was a mistake. We had landed in a solid, blue-collar Latter Day Saints (LDS) community. I suspect there was no neighborhood in the entire state that was not overwhelmingly Mormon. For the first few weeks Stella had frequent visits from pairs of "missionaries." She kept telling them we were Jewish, which didn't seem to diminish their evangelical ardor. Then they stopped coming, and the ambient temperature in the neighborhood dropped about 20 degrees. We were destined to learn a lot about the LDS mystique.

The only saving grace came in the form of our next door neighbors, Lyle and Susie Grainger. Lyle was a jack Mormon, Susie a defiant Catholic. Her mother-in-law was devout LDS, and there was open warfare for the souls of the three tow-headed kids. Lyle owned and ran the local supermarket, and he refused (wrongly) to take sides. Susie did battle with the whole Mormon community. Steven was nine and he caught a lot of flak in grammar school. Jon was still at home. We soon came to realize that the Stake, the local LDS "chapter," was the center of all cultural, business, social and political life. If you were not LDS, you did not "belong," and make no mistake about that. In Salt Lake City we encountered a unique, other-worldly, much-too-orderly,

"Stepford" atmosphere. I am told that for strangers, it was even worse in smaller, outlying communities such as Provo, Price, Bountiful, etc. Quite frankly, we found the pervasive clannishness oppressive and not a little intimidating.

Life at the hospital was much easier. I was one of three first-year clinical fellows and there were two second-year fellows. The fact that I was a few years older than my colleagues, board certified and "military," generated some amusing misapprehension. I suspected they anticipated I would show up in a dress uniform with glistening brass, a blaze of ribbons and a swagger stick. But I wore civvies and a white coat and avoided close-order drill in public places. "Uncle Max" Wintrobe was writing the next edition of his celebrated textbook, but he surfaced every day for the patient review conference. Most of our teaching came from Dr. George Cartwright, a smallish, twinkly, cheerful sort with a fringe of white surrounding a glowing bald spot. He was a superb hematology teacher and expert skier. My friend from Wurzburg, Arthur Haut was on the faculty, but we didn't see much of him. Each of the clinical fellows would take responsibility for a patient in rotation. Most of our patients came from afar with blood or lymph node disorders that had defied diagnosis or treatment back home.

The first four patients I acquired were children with acute leukemia, lymphoblastic and myeloblastic. In those days treatment was only occasionally effective in inducing temporary remission. All therapeutic modalities were painful and toxic. This was long before definitive cellular diagnosis, reasonably effective drug management and bone marrow transplantation were available. For the first time, I became aware of a singular clinical phenomenon: all of these children were undeniably charming and downright "angelic." Perhaps it was related to the life of unrelenting discomfort and pain, so that during periods of remission, they savored the pain-free respite. There was a fragile sweetness in these doomed tots that made their management even more heart rending. I went to four funerals within six months. I became seriously depressed, and for the first time in my life I pondered: had made the right career

decision? Thankfully my next few patients were adults with challenging varieties of anemia and thrombocytopenia (depletion of blood platelets). I began to feel better, but I never warmed up to hematology, especially the dreadful acute leukemias that plague little kids. I know there are more effective treatment modalities available today; some have even spoken of cure with marrow transplantation in acute lymphoblastic leukemia. But I much preferred cardiology.

Skiing was part of the Salt Lake culture. Every Wednesday afternoon the entire staff, but for one or two unfortunates on emergency call, hit the slopes. And that included Uncle Max and George. One day when I "had the duty" Stella was at Alta skiing with an old friend from Austria days. Chuck Welsh had been on the U.S. Olympic Ski Team and was a part-time instructor at White Pass in Washington. Chuck was Baryshnikov on skis. While he was zinging the upper runs, Stella was traversing an advanced intermediate slope when some jerk came whizzing down, flailing out of control and hit her. She fell hard. Something gave in her left tibial area. The ski patrol gave her a shot of morphine, splinted the leg, whisked her down the mountain on a toboggan and brought her to Salt Lake General.

By the time I was called, she was smiling (happily enveloped in the arms of Morpheus) and looked okay. I couldn't believe she had a fracture, maybe a bone bruise or bad sprain. The radiograph revealed a nasty spiral fracture of the left tibia and fibula! I insisted on having it reduced and casted by the chief of orthopedic surgery. He turned out to be a stolid, humorless chap (who had been grudgingly hauled off the slopes). I was concerned only with his clinical competence not his dour personality. He gave her another jolt of morphine, realigned the fracture and put poor Stella in a full-leg cast, hip to ankle. As he was completing the plaster application to a prone Stella, she turned to him and said, "Doctor, are you even remotely interested in the patient your broken leg has?" He had not even looked at her face, not uttered a single word to her. Cold silence; not amused much less chastened. I was pleased she took her shot **after** the fracture had been casted.

She had an *avante garde* floor lamp constructed out of her skis, poles and boots. I salted my gear away in the closet; we retired from the slopes. I had to call Sonya to come and help run the house and take care of the kids. She had a few interesting innings with the local LDS folks, but couldn't quite win them over to Judaism. Recovery was slow but complete. Stella was a good trooper; she learned to scoot around on crutches and do steps on her fanny.

Aside from the glorious Graingers, our only other friends were a couple from The Netherlands. Rob and Els Goudsmit. He was a clinical fellow like me, but he had been doing hematology at the university in Amsterdam and had come, specifically, to work with Wintrobe and Cartwright. Rob and Els had two children the same ages as Steven and Jon. We did quite a bit of home-and-home visiting. After a few months, we discovered that they were Jewish and were suffering the same unsubtle "shunning" as were we. On New Year's Eve we had a party with too much champagne, and we all wound up in the yard in a boisterous snowball fight. The next day we were visited by a delegation of neighbors who expressed their outrage at our wanton display of public drunkenness. I had to restrain Sonya; she did have her good points.

# 17

## *My Romance With Space*

✦

### *(enter the Magnificent Seven...)*

About halfway through the year an event occurred that had an enormous impact on our lives. I was in the clinic when I received a call from the Pentagon. Oh God, not again! Once more, there was no war (that I knew about) where American troops were in harm's way, but still...

Pentagon voice: "Major Moser? This is Captain Willis at the Office of the Surgeon General. You have been assigned to temporary duty at Patrick Air Force Base for training as a Medical Flight Controller for Project Mercury."

Stunned voice: "Would you repeat that please?" He did.

Still stunned voice: "But I am the middle of a one-year fellowship; surely you all know that."

Pentagon voice: "Sir, all I can tell you is that your orders are enroute. There will be a letter of explanation. You have to report on January 15." At least this time it wasn't 72 hours.

I scurried down to Dr. Wintrobe's office and rousted him out of his *sanctum sanctorum*—his hallowed medical file room. I explained what had happened. His response was simplicity itself. "You cannot go; you have a commitment here." Dr. Wintrobe had never dealt with the military in war or peace. I explained that failure to follow orders in the army was a court martial offense; I had little desire to finish my fellowship time weaving baskets at Leavenworth. If he had a problem, he

would have to take it up with the Army Surgeon General. Wintrobe was not a good sport, even after I assured him that I would make up the three weeks.

Thankfully, Sonya was still on board and Stella was getting around in a shorter cast. The day before I left for Patrick, I put on my green uniform with all brass gleaming, three decks of ribbons replete with Korean battle stars, and came to the hospital to say goodbye to the staff. It was a good move; the transformed image even impressed Uncle Max. He shook my hand gravely as though I were going off to war.

I flew to Cocoa Beach and then taxied to Patrick. The "letter of explanation" was about as cryptic as the voice from the Pentagon. I checked in at the BOQ and then went to the Officers Club for dinner. There I met three other U.S. Army Medical Corps majors who were as mystified as I. We all knew each other: Ed Overholt, Bill Hall and Doug Lawson. We compared notes. We were all board-certified with at least one year of sub-specialty training. We all had seen combat duty in Korea and were all in teaching assignments. So the great computer in the sky had spewed out our names to try to match this cockamamie requirement. We knew Project Mercury had something to do with the nascent manned space program. But where did we fit in? There was a rumor that the Soviets were about to launch a man into low earth orbit, and there was some urgency to "beat them." It seemed our virility as a nation was at stake.

The next morning we assembled in an auditorium on the base. We identified four navy doctors and five air force physicians. They were all flight surgeons, a designation that meant they had been dealing with military pilots. Several wore wings indicating that they were flight-trained as well. Two of the air force types, Chuck Berry and Bill Douglas, later became very important to NASA. Chuck became the NASA Chief Medical Officer and Bill became the fabled "physician to the astronauts." Very early in the indoctrination, it became evident that although remarkably little was known about man's psychological and physiological capability to endure and function in space, there was no

on-going clinical research program. Nor was NASA very much interested in establishing one, at any level. They were flying (in space) by the seat of their pants.

All early astronauts were died-in-the-wool, veteran fighter pilots. Any suggestion that they might become involved in any research effort to learn something about human reaction to space flight—was rejected out of hand. Anything that could possibly interfere with "the mission" (flying the spacecraft) was unacceptable. They were all volunteers, they had all been test pilots, they all accepted danger as "part of the job." And if they were willing to take risks, who the hell were the doctors to tell them otherwise? This became the mantra of the astronaut corps. Over the years, Bill Douglas, ever-rigorous as the astronaut advocate, did little to ameliorate this chronic intransigence. Life sciences has been the hat-in-hand stepchild of the space program ever since.

(The "we" [astronauts] versus "they" [doctors] philosophy was epitomized to me a few years later when Gus Grissom and I were deep in our cups at Louie's Bar in the old Kauai Surf Hotel in Nawiliwili on the bay in Kauai. We had become chums, and it was a rare down-time between simulated missions in preparation for the Wally Schirra six-orbit flight. Gus was capsule communicator (capcom). I asked him why flyers hated doctors. He straightened himself on the barstool and peered into my eyes. "I'll tell you, Doc, when you walk into the flight surgeon's office you **have** your ticket. When you walk out, you might **not**."

Later, under similar relaxed circumstances, I asked him, "Gus, if you were sitting on top of that big firecracker and the countdown got to about minus seven and suddenly you felt the worst sort of pain imaginable begin in your mid chest and radiate down the inside of your left arm, what would you do? Would you let us know?" Gus studied the bottom of his glass for a long few seconds. "Honestly?...Only if I thought I was going to die." That was in 1962.

The running battle to try to get meaningful information about physiological and psychological function during prolonged space flight

is still in progress. As I write this, the ancient and noble old Soviet Mir has already plunged into the South Pacific. So stay tuned for the evolving saga of the International Space Station—ISS Alpha—the latest and most elaborate NASA boondoggle—in my opinion. (More on this later.)

We were told that we were to be part of the American space endeavor: Project Mercury. We were introduced to the Magnificent Seven: John Glenn, Wally Schirra, Gus Grissom, Deke Slayton, Scott Carpenter, Gordon Cooper and Alan Shepherd. We were told that there would be two sub-orbital missions with Shepherd and Grissom, to be followed by the first orbital mission—pilot yet to be announced. Thereafter all the astronauts would fly orbital missions of varying duration. NASA was setting up tracking stations at positions on earth that would correspond to the orbital course: Cape Canaveral (it hadn't flip-flopped between Kennedy and Canaveral yet), Bermuda, Tenerife (Canary Islands), Atlantic Tracking Ship, Lagos, Madagascar, Indian Ocean Tracking Ship, Woomera (Australia), Pacific Tracking Ship, Canton Island, Kauai, Guaymas (Mexico), Vandenberg Air Force Base, White Sands Missile Test Range. A team of flight controllers (usually with an astronaut as capsule communicator), a few engineers and a doctor would be sent to each major site for every Mercury mission. Our task? To monitor the progress of the astronaut and spacecraft and be prepared to offer medical advice, if needed. Wow!

While in Florida, we went to the Cape, and in between indoctrination lectures we rode the crazy contraptions that were to be used to train the astronauts. They wanted us to get a feel of what the pilots were going to experience. The most fun was a Rube Goldberg gadget that simulated the interior of the Mercury spacecraft. It was fearfully tiny; obviously claustrophobia was not a problem for the Magnificent Seven. Once strapped in the seat, any movement of the stick would activate thrusters that could produce pitch, roll or yaw. The trick was to "fly" the rascal in the proper attitude while in orbit and for deploying the heat shield for reentry.

The training of the astronauts would include computer-driven "attitude problems" to be solved by manual manipulation of the thrusters (in the event the computer "fly by wire" failed). Later, even more sophisticated problems would be introduced (e.g., cabin fire, loss of oxygen pressure, carbon dioxide build-up, rising cabin temperature, inadvertent thruster firing, etc.) The engineers managed to cook up some realistic (and scary) possible in-flight disaster scenarios. Once in the field at the tracking stations, we all played the "simulated disaster game" with deadly seriousness.

There were several other gadgets designed to train in manual dexterity, rapid decision-making and hand-eye coordination. It soon became apparent that the only condition that would be encountered in space that could **not** be simulated on earth was prolonged exposure to microgravity. Putting a KC-135 into a steep climb and then nosing it over would provide about 30 plus seconds of near zero gravity (weightlessness), the same breath-taking phenomenon as when an elevator suddenly begins to descend in a tall building. All the movies of crews tumbling and gyrating were filmed in these specially tailored aircraft. It was too brief an interval for any physiological study of significant duration, more NASA photo-op stuff than serious science. Also SCUBA in swimming pools provided a "feel" for working in microgravity. In later weeks, all the doctors got to ride the human centrifuge at Johnsville, PA to experience the G load that Mercury would demand on launch and reentry (about 6 to 7 Gs). They called it the "eyeballs in" (positive—in your face—velocity) adventure. It was quite a kick.

We were advised that within the next few months, each flight controller-doctor would be assigned to join a team at one of the orbital tracking stations for several weeks of temporary duty. The first orbital mission was planned for early in 1962. But then I had to return to Salt Lake. It took a bit to readjust to terrestrial life.

Toward the end of the year, Dr. Wintrobe invited me to make general medical rounds with him. It was a throwback to the *herr geheimrat* days at Georgetown. He was a formidable bedside teacher. The house

staff was terrified when the boss made teaching rounds. (He was almost as brusque as my endocrinologist friend had been, but I never saw Wintrobe deliberately embarrass any house officer in front of a patient.) The prevailing philosophy: "What can the Old Man ask that we have not thought of?" It led to a lot of nonsensical, wasteful and expensive testing. (Years later, we would come to reap the bitter harvest of this folly; it contributed to the soaring cost of medical care, helping to open the Pandora's Box of the era of "managed care.")

Sometime in May I received orders for my next assignment. I couldn't believe it; I raced home with the telegram. "We're going to Honolulu! Tripler Army Medical Center." It was perhaps the choicest duty assignment in the medical corps. They needed an assistant chief and a hematologist. A marriage made in heaven.

# 18

## Our Hawaiian Holiday

✦

### (The Pink Palace…undeniably the best duty station in the army)

**W**ithout much reluctance, except to say goodbye to the Graingers and the Goudsmits, we piled into the Merc and drove to Oakland. We put the faithful beast on a transport and awaited our ship. And what a ship it was. The S.S. Lurline, sleek, white flagship of the Matson Line, luxury afloat. Four and a half days of undiminished delight, great food, well-stocked bar, orchestra, movies, baby sitters, the whole nine yards. (Several universes removed from the old Emelia or the Ballou.) Once again the Pacific was a docile pond.

Diamond Head, green and velvety, materialized from the shimmering deep blue, and we bellowed a hoarse greeting. Some nut-brown, daredevil kids swam out to the great white ship to dive for silver coins, the Royal Hawaiian Band umpah-pahed a brassy version of "Aloha Nui Loa" at the Aloha Tower, and ever-lovely hula maidens were twirling their sweet hips. We were all atwitter. A delegation from Tripler greeted us dockside and immersed us in fragrant garlands of leis. I mean they did it right, traditional aloha style. Alas, as I have said before, since United Air Lines discovered Hawaii (Captain Cook notwithstanding), and the swift, swooshing jets took over from the elegant, placid cruise ships, it has never been quite the same.

We found a home in a section just above Pearl Harbor called Foster Village. It was about 90% military. Pearl Harbor with CINCPACFLT

(Commander in Chief Pacific Fleet) was practically outside our gate, Hickam Air Force Base just about a mile down the road and Camp Smith (marines) just over the hill. The village was a perfect location. Tripler was about 10 minutes away. The house was single-story, typical island, single board construction on a small lot facing a pineapple field. Our neighbors were mostly navy with a few DOD civilians tossed in. Within a few weeks after I reported for duty, NASA called. I was assigned to be the medical flight controller at the Kokee Park Tracking Station on **Kauai**! Not Nigeria, not the Indian Ocean Tracking Ship, but on the loveliest of all the islands, a thirty minute hop from Honolulu. We were ecstatic. We settled in quickly; car and furniture arrived within ten days. Jon was now eight and Steven eleven. Schools were within walking distance.

The chief of medicine at Tripler was Colonel Bob Hoagland. I knew of him. He had been commander of the hospital at West Point, and while there, he identified the relationship between significant kissing (on the mouth) and the development of Infectious Mononucleosis (IM). This was long before the versatile Ebstein-Barr virus was discovered to be the etiological culprit. But Hoagland was a keen observer, and he tracked down cadets with IM and established the link between the last leave (lots of serious oscular exercise) and the development of symptoms. The media pounced on his original journal article. (They loved the "Kissing Disease.") Bob was still collecting cases. It became an inside joke; any young person admitted with a fever was fair game. The house staff became experts on IM.

Once again I was given, virtually, a free hand to beef up a sagging teaching program. I like to think that after setting up and running the program at Brooke, the Office of the Surgeon General was deploying me to shore-up ailing internal medicine residency programs. It was a labor of love. The Tripler house staff was almost as good as Brooke with just a few sour apples. One second-year resident was discovered to be incompetent, obsequious and dishonest (a deadly trilogy). He made egregious errors and tried to cover them up. I counseled him privately

on several occasions, yet he persisted in this unconscionable behavior. He was a menace to sick patients.

I told Hoagland that the guy had to go. "But he only has another year," was the wimpy response. But I was adamant. The flap went all the way to the commanding one-star, a foppish Southern gentleman of benign, "don't rock the boat" inclination. Finally, the lousy resident was "laterally transferred" to some unlucky station hospital. At least he was expunged from our program. Apparently it was unprecedented to bounce a second year resident. The incident was unsavory; it meant to me was that someone had not been paying attention to his performance (or lacked the *cojones*) to bounce him during his first year. The kid didn't go sour overnight. Relations were a bit rocky between Hoagland and me for a time, but he was too fine a clinician not to appreciate the reality of the situation. (The proper course of action would have been to kick the guy out of the army, if not medicine. But, under the circumstances, we did the best the system would allow.) You can't demand excellence from your staff when you tolerate lack of integrity. A little dumb I can handle, but intellectual dishonesty has no place in medicine. We ain't selling used cars.

I made teaching rounds on the general medical wards, did all the adult hematology consultations and saw pediatric blood problems in a special clinic once a week. Soon the teaching program was in high gear. It seemed I was flying back to the mainland about twice a month. I had been appointed to the AMA Council on Drugs in 1960, which meant that I flew into O'Hare for quarterly meetings. These were "out Friday evening, meet all day Saturday and half-day Sunday, then fly home" excursions. I usually drowsed across the Pacific. On one notable occasion, I boarded at O'Hare, exhausted as usual. The coach section was swarming with strange, boisterous people wearing New Year's Eve funny hats, blowing those paper things that unroll, blasting tin horns and drinking from brown paper-wrapped fifths. "These are McDonald store managers who have won a trip to Hawaii," moaned the distraught flight attendant. "Well, let me upgrade to first class; I'll pay cash," I

yelled above the din. Crinkly smile; "Sorry, that's filled with the **big** winners," she screamed. The tumult seemed to subside somewhere west of the Farallons.

The real kick was flying back for NASA briefing sessions at Cape Canaveral and Langley Air Force Base. This was always Pan Am (707) first class, before the intrusion of neither/nor business class, and cattle-car coach had become insufferably cheek-by-jowl. I adored the free Johnny Walker Black Label and the best food I have ever enjoyed on any airplane. (They really **can** do it! I suspect that monster planes and hordes of passengers have just made it too time-consuming and too expensive to carve up the side of rare beef or ladle out the ice cream sundaes with whipped cream, chocolate syrup and wet nuts. *Triste dictu.*)

I was in mission control at the Cape with a bunch of nervous people, standing uncomfortably close to Von Braun and Debus (the expatriate Nazi/Peenamunde V-2 geniuses), when Al Shepherd made his famous 15-minute suborbital, 115 mile dash in Freedom 7 on May 5, 1961. Fresh fingernails topped the menu that day. Yuri Gagarin had flown 23 days earlier, and the "great race" was on. I never did and still don't understand the urgency to "be the first," but I suspect that national chauvinism in the Cold War pissing contest was the major element. Really now, how could anyone "control space" with the other guys only 23 days ahead or behind?

A few months later, Gus Grissom repeated the suborbital flight in Liberty Bell 7, but he absorbed lots of flak when he blew the hatch and the spacecraft gurgled into the briny blue. I never believed that Gus panicked and hit the chicken switch. I got to know him very well on Kauai; he was just too cool for such foolishness. The ultimate bitter irony: after the Grissom episode, NASA decided to remove the skittish explosive hatch bolts on all future spacecraft. A few years later when the catastrophic Apollo fire occurred in the hangar at Kennedy, the crew could not blow the hatch. We lost Gus, Ed White, and Roger Chaffee.

I monitored four Mercury flights from Kokee: Glenn, Shepherd, Schirra and Cooper. Each was exciting in its own way. The epochal Glenn mission caused some terrible moments when it was discovered that he could not shed the package that contained the retro-rockets straddling his heat shield. There was grave concern that he would be unable to adjust the now-cumbersome capsule attitude. It had to be deployed at a precise angle to avoid incineration during the reentry burn. By the grace of God and a steady hand, John maneuvered the beast properly, the retro package burned off and the heat shield was in proper attitude. He landed a little further down range than anticipated, but all was well.

Scott Carpenter was "different." He seemed to be marching to some alien drummer. During his second orbit he had re-discovered John Glenn's "fireflies," and became fascinated. Too fascinated. By thumping the side of the Mercury spacecraft he could make the sparks appear. When he came over Kokee on his final orbit, he was obliged to review and confirm his retrosequence checklist with our capcom. Despite repeated, progressively more frantic calls, he failed to respond. In alarm our capcom recited the retrosequence list "blind," unsure that Shepherd had received and complied. The whole world held its breath. If he had failed to initiate the sequence, the heat shield might not be deployed properly, and he would reenter as a fireball. After an eternity, his chute was spotted about 100 miles downrange past his predicted impact point. At the private debriefing (press excluded), he was excoriated for his inattention. Yes, he had heard us, and yes, he had (finally) activated the sequence. But he had been diverted trying to identify the source of the goddamn fireflies. Carpenter never flew another mission for NASA. This was not the "right stuff."

During the many weeks I spent on Kauai, I always lived at the Smith cabin, just a few miles from the tracking station. On several occasions, Stella flew over with me. Her spaghetti and meatballs made a big hit with the Kokee crew. She was allowed to sit in on a few of the training sessions. During off duty times, I hiked most of the trails in

those magnificent mountains. One weekend, I met with some pig hunters, and they took me into the trackless Alakai swamp. It was a wild, primitive, bewildering place. The copious rain (about 465 inches a year) that fell on Mt. Waialiali mostly drained into Alakai. It was the source of all of the magnificent waterfalls that spilled into Waimea Canyon and off the cliffs of Na Pali.

One Sunday, I had been hiking the edges of the swamp, alone, and finally emerged from the brush, red bandana askew, sweaty, mud-spattered, with a three-day growth of beard. Around the bend near my cabin, a tour bus driven by one of my Kauai drinking buddies, a little guy named Elie, swung into view. He pulled the bus over and shouted, "Hey, look dere, a genuine peeg huntah!" Tourists streamed out of the bus and began to take my picture. I just happened to be carrying my old machete in a leather sheath across my back. (Okay, so I liked to play Great White Hunter and slash at an occasional vine.) So, of course, I whipped out the great blade and assumed an attack posture, as the Kodaks flailed away. It was very cool. Later Elie told me that I had saved the day; Kalalau Canyon had been fogged in and his disappointed clientele were grousing. Hapless tour guides always took the flak for bad weather.

But the real (mis?)adventure occurred just before the Gordon Cooper flight. For this final Mercury mission, NASA sent out Major Bill Hall to work with me. Bill was a class act, superb teaching internist who also was a sport parachute jumper. We decided to hike into Kalalau Valley from Haena. I was not sure exactly how far it was, but I figured if we left early, we could get in and out and still be on time for duty at the tracking station by 11:00 PM. We were up at first light with light packs, lunches, canteens and a dozen New England Journal of Medicine issues. I'd heard (apocryphally) that there was a hermit living in a sea cave at the mouth of the valley who had been an internist in Tennessee. At the trailhead, in semi-darkness, the sign was warped and difficult to read, but we interpreted it to indicate a 7.1-mile one-

way trek. Fourteen miles was a little more than we had bargained for, but here we were, so what the hell.

The trail was spectacular. It wound along the top of jagged Na Pali sea cliffs that rose hundreds of feet above rampaging surf. Then it would wind back into rain-forested valleys, across a surging stream and then back up the other side to the cliff edge. It was not an easy trail, overgrown in spots, very rock-strewn and muddy in the valleys. We forded a dozen streams and lost the trail several times. After about three hours, we thought we had gone about seven miles. But one valley was followed by the next, and none was the broad, deep Kalalau. But we decided to forge on. We **must** be close!

It took almost five hours to finally arrive at that magnificent valley. We flaked out, devoured our tuna sandwiches and refilled our canteens. We found a likely sea cave bearing a makeshift table, burned down candle nub and crude bed. But no hermit. We "hallooed" for a minute or so. No response. So we left a note, deposited the journals and began the trudge back. The return hike was pure hell. Soon Bill was limping on terrible blisters and pulled calf muscles. I developed traumatic arthritis in both knees (distinct painful swelling) and had to cut a crutch to hobble the last miles. Every step was agony for both of us. There was no moon, and we had no flashlight. The last few miles were treacherous, steep, rocky and forever muddy. We staggered out into the deserted parking lot at about 10:00 PM. Battered and bruised, we drove back to the cabin in mirthless silence, showered, drank a gallon of water and barely managed to report on time. It took days to recover. The next morning we were describing our ordeal to one of the local guys at the tracking station. He refused to believe that we had gone in and out in one day. "Bullshit, Doc, that's eleven miles one way!" We had hiked 22 miles in 15 hours over unforgiving terrain. A misstep could have brought disaster. I still get pain in my knees just thinking about it.

Tripler was idyllic. In Foster Village we befriended two wonderful families: the Omuras and the Smiths. Mildred and Kiyoshi Omura

were second generation Japanese who had suffered the indignities of all island Japanese in the infamous aftermath of Pearl Harbor. (Not internment, but ostracism, suspicion and hatred.) They grew exotic flowers in their extensive backyard and made glorious leis that they sold commercially, a true cottage industry. Kiyoshi had been a foreman at the Libby pineapple plant until retirement and Mildred had been an assembly line worker. Their magnificent leis could be found at the airport and half a dozen good flower shops in Waikiki. They seemed to toil endlessly and effortlessly, plucking and stringing as they chatted and "talked story."

The Smiths were pure Hawaiian (I never asked how musical Akana had become transmuted into blah "Smith," but I suspect it was a commercial decision.) They ran a sprawling household overflowing with handsome children and a thousand friendly in-laws. They introduced us to the "backyard luau," replete with imu pit, fireworks, slack key guitar and down-home traditional hula. Mae was a big, husky woman who could do the meanest, sexiest hula you can imagine. She taught a class three days a week. Stella got to do a reasonable version of "Little Brown Gal" and "Lovely Hula Hands." Mae said she had "good hands" but needed a little "more fluid" hip action. At every party the neighborhood girls gave wildly acclaimed recitals, but they never quite mastered the hip-twitching excitement of Tahitian hula. Too bad.

One memorable evening Smitty called and said that they wondered if Stella and I would like to join them for a "very interesting evening." So we piled into their old Oldsmobile and climbed the old Pali Highway (before the grand tunnel) to Kaneohe. We pulled up in front of a ramshackle, thatch-roofed bar with the name "Honey Ho's Place" adorning the front. From inside trickled the wonderful sound of vintage Hawaiian music and the murmur of myriad happy drinkers. It was a bar frequented by marines from the Kaneohe Marine Base and locals, mostly plantation workers. No visible tourists. Smitty said, "This is the best authentic Hawaiian music in the islands." He was right. It was the Don Ho band playing in his mother's bar. Don played a Moog synthe-

sizer, the lead slack key guitarist was Sonny Chillingsworth backed by Gabby Pahanui, and the singer was the fabulous (soon to be recognized) Marlene Sai. They also had drums, ukulele and another back-up guitar. Everyone could play everything. Don rarely sang, but his "Tiny Bubbles" got the whole crowd into the act. Honey's was small, noisy, and smoky. Fights and near fights between locals and marines was a nightly occurrence—part of the ambience. But for the most part the atmosphere was warm and felicitous.

If Mae and Stella wanted to go to the ladies' room the gauntlet was so formidable that Smitty and I took turns accompanying them. At six three and about 240, Smitty never encountered any rowdy behavior from the assembled ménage. We made the Kaneohe trip several times. Do Ho was a friend of the Smiths. He had recently left the air force and started his band. Sonny and Gabby were the best slack key artists the islands had ever known, and Marlene Sai was the Hawaiian version of Joan Baez. Her voice was crystalline—hypnotizing. One night I asked Don if they had made any records. He said they were contemplating it, but had not, as yet. So we brought a good tape recorder the following week and recorded the whole session. The background noise added to the authenticity, if not the purity of their sound. But the whole band gathered to listen, and we gave them their first tape.

A few months later the band was asked to fill-in at the Hilton Hawaiian Village in Waikiki. And that was the beginning of the "Don Ho Legend." They were "discovered." After that Don rose to national prominence, but Sonny, Gabby and Marlene and the other originals all went their separate ways. Don began to "please the tourists" with a lot of "modern" Hawaiian music, and he sang too often. His voice was whiskey charming, but he should have stuck to "Tiny Bubbles." Also he seemed to be drinking more on stage. Don got too busy to play at Honey's except rarely. About three years later Stella and I were in San Francisco for a meeting, and we saw a billboard advertising "Don Ho in Concert," in North Beach. We bought tickets and before the performance went back stage to say hello to our "old friend." He was half-

potted and did not recognize us. He appeared for his performance bearing his usual glass of clear liquid, and he was obviously half-drunk. It was an abysmal show. In later years he had a place in Waikiki called the "Ho House," but we never went to Oahu on subsequent visits to the Islands. I don't know what has become of him. But we caught him in his prime at that warm, wonderful dingy bar in Kaneohe.

The Smiths had family on Kauai; they ran the tourist river boats up to the Wailea Falls and fern grotto, taking off from a pier near the old Coco Palms Hotel (sadly wiped out in 1992 by hurricane Iniki). They also owned a cabin just down the road from the Kokee tracking station that they graciously offered for my use. It became my headquarters during all the subsequent Mercury missions. The Omuras and Smiths enriched our lives in Honolulu immeasurably.

The Tripler program in internal medicine was running smoothly. I had Captain Henry Mendez brought in as chief of general medical services; Hank had been a star resident at Brooke and was a natural teacher. I ran the hematology clinic for adults and children. Phil Fairchild was chief of pediatrics, a superb clinician, and his assistant was Bob Schlegel. We became fast friends with the Schlegels. Bob subsequently retired and became a much venerated chief of pediatrics at the Drew Medical School in Watts. One incident that cemented family relationships was a near-fatal surfing accident that occurred at the Banzai Pipeline, an expert surfing beach near Makaha on the west shore. Steven and Robbie, the eldest Schlegel son, were tackling some pretty big stuff on a Friday afternoon. The surf had come up to about 20 feet and became erratic and turbulent. Steven came ashore and was taking a breather while Robbie continued to stalk the big waves. After a moment, while Steven was half dozing, he heard a shout. Robbie had lost his board and was being carried north, out to sea by a heavy rip tide. Steven grabbed his board and paddled out to rescue a near-drowned Robbie. They got back to shore after a desperate struggle almost two miles up the coast near Kepuhi Point. It was a close call for

both kids. The Schlegels never forgot that Steven had probably saved Robbie's life.

One of the outstanding house officers we enjoyed was Adrian Edwards. He was one of the few black medical officers in the army at that time. He was married to Dolores, a strikingly gorgeous woman, who had been a fashion model in Manhattan. She became fast friends with Stella. I told Bob Hoagland that Adrian should be made chief resident. Bob was a Virginian of the old school and had not quite come to grips with the reality of an emerging cadre of astute, well-educated black physicians. But it was quite obvious that Adrian was head and shoulders above a group of very good residents. He made a terrific teaching chief resident. (Subsequently, Adrian became one of the most sought-after internists in New York City.)

After I had been at Tripler about one year, I received a call from a Dr. Quisenberry, the director of public health for the Islands. I knew him only casually and was surprised when he invited me for lunch at the old Pacific Club. After pleasantries, he asked if I would be interested in doing a *locum tenens* for the doctor who ran the hospital and clinic at mysterious Kalaupapa Settlement on Molokai. She was going on a two-week vacation, and they needed someone to cover her. I smiled and told him I knew nothing about Hansen's disease. I had seen one Hispanic patient at Brooke who had a peculiar "Sinaloa" variety of leprosy, but that was the pathetic limit of my experience. But was I interested? Of course. When I told Stella, she became excited, and we agreed she would come over for the week-end. Sonya, who was staying with us for an extended visit, was horrified. "Lepers" conjured up visions of unclean, "*trayf*" creatures with masks and bells and dangling body parts. No place for her beloved Stella.

So I obtained "emergency leave," scoured the library for information on Hansen's Disease (not much new stuff), and a few days later met a red-bearded, red-booted, cowboy-hatted bush pilot who "'lowed as how he made the run to Kalaupapa twice a week." He had a small single-engine, red, of course, Cessna (daintier than the artillery-spotter

L-5s I had hitched rides on back in Korea). We puttered across the Molokai channel at about 700 feet, raised Halawa Cape on the northeast shore, and then scooted along the magnificent pali, just about "within spitting distance" above the brow of a cliff that rose steadily from sea level to about 2000 feet. Soon we spotted the lighthouse at Kalaupapa and banked over the north-jutting peninsula. A rough, cow pasture landing strip materialized, and in a flash we were bouncing along with full reverse prop. We shuddered to a halt just a few feet from some completely unperturbed cows.

I clambered down to be greeted by four nuns in flowing white habits sporting those glorious airplane bonnets. We all piled into a rusted Dodge sedan of uncertain vintage but distinct personality. It lacked front fenders and about three functioning cylinders. Sister Wilma introduced her cheery entourage, all nursing sisters from the Third Order of St. Francis. This noble organization had been serving the patients of Kalaupapa since the desperate days of Mother Marianne, Brother Dutton and the fabled Father Damien.

The Red Baron help unload supplies onto another venerable, mud-spattered pick-up. With two other fellows we lifted the tail of the Cessna and aimed it back down the cow path. As we departed the field, the little plane charged bravely toward the lighthouse and then lifted clear in a swirling plume of dust, banking neatly abreast of the pali. So here was Kalaupapa.

I was taken to modest quarters adjacent to the hospital. It was still mid-morning, so I asked Sister Wilma if I could make rounds to examine the in-patients. I soon came to realize that her modest smile was a signal of approval. So I loaded my clothes into a dresser, pulled out my black bag, donned my white lab coat and trundled over to the hospital. It was a small, musty clapboard affair with an administration office off a four-step entrance. Sister Wilma had pulled the charts of a dozen patients and I began to read. The notes were brief but clear, written in concise Palmer script. But I could not ascertain the true nature of the various problems; these were progress notes, not histories and physi-

cals. Lab work was sparse or absent. Most patients had been admitted for dressing of wounds or fevers or physical therapy that, apparently, could not be managed on an out-patients basis.

I was not prepared for the physical devastation wrought by the notorious Hansen bacillus. Most of the patients were old, more than half were blind, and many had lost fingers and toes, even noses. Some bore tracheotomy tubes and spoke by occluding the orifice with a finger. Many had dreadful weeping wounds on extremities. I addressed each by name, introduced myself, apologized for my ignorance of their history, asked about complaints and listened attentively. Then I examined each with stethoscope, ophthalmoscope, otoscope, took blood pressures and listened again. It took three hours to visit 12 patients. I made notes on each patient and was pleased to see that Sister Wilma still bore her enigmatic smile.

The afternoon was to have been occupied with an out-patient clinic. Sister Wilma met me at one o'clock, but there were no patients. She was fidgety and notably embarrassed as we sat and waited. "They will come, perhaps tomorrow." I shrugged and explored the tiny hospital library. There were a few ancient, salt-rimed tomes, virtually useless as a resource to learn about leprosy, but I had brought a batch of photocopies of articles from reasonably current journal sources, gathered by the ever-helpful librarian at Tripler. Information about Hansen's disease was sparse. I spent the afternoon reading.

Then I wandered around the compound. I took the little hike over to Kalawao, site of the original settlement, and found the chapel where Father Damien was buried. It was quiet, appropriately modest and eerily reverential. I had seen the statue of the rugged, disfigured Damien in the capitol rotunda, and I could imagine him struggling to offer solace and succor in this lovely/terrible place. It had been well described in James Michener's "Hawaii." Kalawao had been a place of wild lawlessness ("in this place there is no law," was the watchword). Father Damien, Brother Dutton and Mother Marianne had managed to bring some semblance of civility and order to this infamous enclave

of outcasts. One could still feel the heavy hand of history brooding in that isolated, overgrown retreat.

Kalaupapa still lived with many strange taboos. In the dining room and theater, staff and patients were segregated. Staff did not enter patients' homes; all outgoing mail was "steam sterilized." People did not shake hands. I thought this was primitive, demeaning to patients and downright silly. Hansen's Disease was not transmitted by casual contact. No staff person had ever contracted the disease in the history of the peninsula. It was suspected that Father Damien brought his leprosy with him. I think I managed to break all the rules, some inadvertently, some very deliberately. I tried not to embarrass patients, but I did visit their homes, have coffee in their kitchens, shake their hands. I did wash up thoroughly after all encounters with patients, but I did that after examining any patient.

The next day Sister Wilma and I made rounds again; this time there was more conversational exchange with patients. That afternoon my clinic was filled with outpatients. "How come?" I asked. "Well, the Blinds have accepted you," Sister Wilma announced with a cheery, rosy-cheeked grin. It would seem that the "Blind Ones" were the conscience of the settlement. If the new doctor (or nurse) was "accepted" by them, the entire community would follow. Apparently my conversations, laying on of hands, changing dressings, etc. had indicated that I had no fear of the illness, and that I regarded all patients as worthy of dignity and thoughtfulness. The words of Sister Wilma. Quite a compliment for just doing my job.

I explored the peninsula with the younger sisters. We clambered up the treacherous footpath that clung to the sheer pali all the way to the top, some 2000 feet. Three sisters in full habits (but with Nikes!) scampered like mountain goats, giggling as the winded old doctor gasped and begged uncle, while gazing at the magnificent sweeps of sea and rain forest. Later, we crept through the sea caves and the volcano crater that a few thousand years earlier had spewed forth the lava that had formed the peninsula. The first weekend, despite the hand-wringing,

old world imprecations of Sonya, Stella flew in with the Red Baron. We picnicked above the sea caves, and enjoyed the movies in the "staff section" (a taboo I could not crack). The patients gave her some lovely, handcrafted doilies. Later Sonya discovered them and secretly boiled them (literally) into extinction. *Deja vu* from intern days at Gallinger.

The two weeks flew by. It was a soon obvious that much of the blindness and terrible extremity ulcers were caused by total loss of sensation. Corneal erosions and subsequent infections from foreign objects such as sand and dust traumatized eyes. Repeated injury to anesthetized feet with subsequent infection caused the chronic ulcerations, osteomyelitis and loss of digits. I had the carpenter shop fabricate sandals made from old worn auto tires with leather straps, and I had Stella purchase a few dozen cheap sunglasses with wide side flaps, to protect insensitive corneas from blowing sand. We later devised crude side flaps that could be affixed to conventional sunglasses. I don't know if all this helped, but it couldn't hurt.

I returned for three more "tours" to Molokai, and set up a system where my medical residents from Tripler could come over as a two-week elective. I felt it was a wonderful experience for my young people, far more valuable for its psychosocial, humanistic aspects than anything medical. I maintained desultory contact with Sister Wilma over the years. Kalaupapa now has very few resident patients (if any these days) and has become a national monument. In some aspects it is sort of sad to see that tempestuous cul de sac of history become sanitized, but far better than a sell-out to a flock of eager condo developers.

After a few months, Steven was having a problem in school. The local kids were giving him a very hard time; the "haoli" versus "local" conflicts made school a terrible daily ordeal. Jon was younger and seemed less subject to the ambient prejudice, but was not immune. We enrolled Steven in Iolani, a highly recommended private school in Waikiki, mostly attended by well-to-do, third generation island Japanese boys. He was a head taller than any other kid in his class. He soon became a "big man on campus," and we detected a new unseemly

hubris. The next year we decided to try to get him into Punahou, the classiest private school in the Islands, where the scions of kamaina families attended. He would have a struggle to become a BMOC there. Punahou had a fine reputation as a springboard to Stanford, Yale and Harvard. But there was a problem. As far as we knew, very few military kids had been accepted there. Steven was not happy with the idea of a move from Iolani. He was a star student-athlete-surfer. But he sort of knew he had gotten a bit too big for his britches.

So we arranged for an interview with the Punahou headmaster. I told Steven not to be intimidated, "just be polite and honest—be yourself." He had a fine academic record and was a nice looking (if gangly) kid. He came out about an hour later and was strangely silent. "So, how did it go?" "Okay, I guess." Silence. "So what did he ask you?" Long pause. "Well, he asked me why I was transferring from Iolani to Punahou." Dragging it out. "So?" Sheepish focus on the floor. "I said I was not sure, but I wondered if Punahou might be less expensive?" I suppressed a gasp and then a giggle. "But it's a helluva lot more expensive than Iolani! Why did you ever say that?" Big shrug—silence. I thought we were doomed. Well, candor (and perhaps a sense of humor) must be virtues; Steven was accepted within a week!

Much that happened at Tripler did not occur on the wards. I must describe my experience with the Loyal Order of the Boar (LOB—yes, that is what it was called). In all my years in the army I had never heard of this "secret military medical society" until Honolulu. As a matter of personal philosophy, I eschew all such "fraternal" organizations. My father's pragmatic, "business oriented" attitude toward the Masons, Eastern Star, Lions, etc. had soured me. Secrecy always suggested something clandestine and unsavory, stuff that could not bear the honest blaze of sunlight. I always wondered about the slippery slope from secret handshakes and "sacred" oaths to white hoods and burning crosses. But my friends all said the LOB was "not like that, just plain fun, even Leonard Heaton is a Boar."

So I went for the initiation. It was undeniably the most humiliating, demeaning, sophomoric exercise I had ever experienced. It was inconceivable to me that professional men could engage in such ribald, childish nonsense. We initiates were blindfolded, obliged to drink horrible-tasting concoctions, place hands in smelly, slimy stuff and assume ugly postures, while odors of excrement and alcohol wafted through eye-watering cigar and cigarette smoke. There was much more. I suffered through the evening, just to be a "nice guy."

Now, I can handle a bit of drunken revelry, but I have never enjoyed it. I never habituate bars, avoid stag parties and I don't enjoy nightclubs. So I'm a bit of a prude, but I hate dark corners, loud noise and cigarette smoke. But this incident was several dimensions beyond. I was so disturbed by the experience that I wrote a letter to the Surgeon General recommending that the LOB be disbanded. I realized that it was an "unofficial" organization, but I felt that it was tolerated, even encouraged, officially. Here we were trying to teach young physicians about human dignity, compassion and thoughtfulness, and then we expose them to this abyss of childish indignity. It was just not acceptable. (Years later, I could almost understand how the infamous "Tailhook" debacle could occur, although the LOB was strictly a stag affair. But the *gestalt* was similar.) Over the years I never heard of the Boars again. I hope I helped kill the beast.

Hawaii was a wonderful jumping off place for meandering around the Pacific on vacation. The Military Air Transport Service (MATS) operated out of Hickam Air Force Base—a link to all the exotic Orient. With a little time, a lot of luck and infinite patience you could go almost anywhere—for free. The most notable trip that Stella I took was in 1963 to Lahore. The big, spacious, slow-motion, piston transport (the Air Force did not have 707s yet) took us to Midway (goofy gooney birds dangerously stalking the runway), Wake (bleak remnants of that horrific Japanese invasion), Guam (Adana had just recovered from a typhoon), Clarke Air Force Base (now vanished beneath the ash

from the Pinatubo eruption in 1991), Saigon (steep dive in and steep climb out to avoid sniper fire) and Bangkok (our first tourist stop).

This was a more relaxed, less traffic-choked, less pollution-ridden Bangkok than I was to encounter some 25 years later. Stella and I were met at the airport by General Porn Piscanok of the Thai Army Medical Corps. The general had once been a student of Paul Dudley White, and an oversized black and white photograph of a younger and slimmer General Porn, smiling adoringly at the Great Man, graced the place of honor above his desk. He assigned a bright young captain to escort us during our three-day visit. Stella hit all the shops and gathered some lovely princess rings, Thai silk saris and other delicate treasures. We frequently passed saffron-robed Buddhist priests on the street with their omnipresent begging bowls. On one occasion, a priest stopped Stella, bowed and presented her with a small carved stone Buddha. Our captain-interpreter chatted with the priest; it was a good luck gift for the lovely lady with golden hair. Stella had it mounted in a gold case with a clear plastic face showing the small figure. It became her favorite bit of jewelry.

We toured all the wats and landmarks in military vehicles and private barges. I enjoyed an elegant, full-body, perfumed-lotion massage in the shadow of Wat Po. We visited the incredible giant Sleeping Buddha in Chiang Mai, close to the Golden Triangle. The U.S. Army Corps of Engineers had just cut and surfaced this critical military road through the rain forests to the north. We ate native Thai food every evening and enjoyed classic traditional dancing. I have always been amazed at the extraordinary hyperextension of the hands of these gracile, exquisite, lavishly-costumed beauties. We enjoyed every minute of Bangkok. Obviously, this was many years before the infamous "sex tours." We saw a few street hookers but no flamboyant, audaciously huckstered brothels. Or maybe our hosts were just protecting us.

I lectured at the Pramankatklu Army Hospital on "Renal Biopsy" and "Diseases of Medical Progress." The Thai Army Medical Corps, in conjunction with the Walter Reed Institute of Research, maintained a

top-notch tropical diseases unit in Bangkok. Some critical work in typhus fever and malaria had been done there. I enjoyed an extensive tour of the research facility.

We caught an MATS embassy flight to New Delhi and found a modest hotel near the center of town. The massive city was intimidating and overpowering; about six million people cheek-by-jowl. The pervasive evidence of poverty was awesome. Emaciated, threadbare beggars camped on the steps of mosques and temples; motorbikes, ancient cars, bicycles, carts and swarming hordes jammed the streets. In the early morning, we stalked the outdoor food markets before they came alive. The myriad pungent, exotic odors, dazzling sun-bright colors and ambient escalating cacophony were almost overwhelming. The juxtaposed beauty and ugliness of Delhi was always extravagantly on display. After three days of exhausting sight seeing, we hired a car and inherited a slightly surly, semi-English speaking Sikh driver to make the Grand Tour: Agra and Jaipur.

It was high adventure. We were completely enchanted by the simple elegance and magical simplicity of the Taj Mahal. We wandered the white-marble Taj under a full moon; it is perhaps the most romantic structure on earth. During the torrid heat of day swarms of boisterous, Kodak-crazy tourists tend to jostle any attempt at reverie and stifle any hope of contemplation. I am sure it is even worse now, but we did enjoy a few hours of unblemished moonlight dreaming.

On the road to Jaipur we stopped for lunch. I had observed that virtually all day the sky and the telephone wires seemed filled with big black birds. It looked like a scene from "The Birds." Later, we were eating sandwiches by the roadside when we were attacked by these powerful, crow-like beasts, ripping the food from our hands in swooping dive-bomb attacks! Stella's jacket was ripped, and my hand was gashed by beaks and claws. We dashed back to the car, arms protecting heads. The desperate bastards dove at the windows of the car. The driver sputtered as he kicked the sedan into gear. "They must be starving; we have had much drought." Those birds almost had us for lunch.

In Jaipur we rode the elephants up the great path to the maharajah's castle, explored the elegant rooms and marveled at the spectacular mountain views. It was a scene from "Gunga Din" in living color. One could almost feel the imperious arrogance of the British Raj and the sullen antipathy of the natives. I kept looking around for Sam Jaffe climbing the golden dome. It was a week to remember. From New Delhi we took Air India to Lahore. My friend Abdullah was to meet us at the airport, but he was not there. (We later discovered that we were one day early; a similar misfortune had occurred many years earlier in Amsterdam. It seemed to be a recurring Bob Moser blunder—the accidental tour guide.)

But this was a trifle different. Lahore was a smoky, spooky Asiatic city, and it was dusk. We had a four-year-old address, no phone number and everyone in Pakistan seemed to be named Mohammed Abdullah. Our taxi driver was a Pathan who spoke very halting English, but "I know every inch of the city; I will find your friends." We wandered up and down, large and small, ever-smokier streets and ever-eerier byways until dark. We were about to give up and cry, "Hilton," but, miraculously (*Allah akhbar!*), we found the right Abdullah house. If Mohammed and Zarina were unprepared for our arrival, they concealed it with thespian guile. Within minutes, tons of hot savory food and dozens of family members spilled out from every recess of the vast, sprawling house. In Lahore when children marry, the parents (I think it's a maternal thing) simply tack on an additional room or two, and the newlyweds hang around the homestead. Later they may depart for their own digs, but now we were greeted furiously by at least four generations.

We were given the "room of honor" with a bed featuring a heavy rope net "spring" covered by a thin straw mattress. It tended to get very crowded in the sagging middle, and after an hour of such suspension, one could distinguish every knot in the net. The toilet consisted of a very clean, small unisex room with an opening in the wall for reasonably accurate men and a slit trench with footprints for everything else.

The first night Stella and I had to suppress gales of giggles as we contemplated the suspension bridge-bed, the "need for excellent aim" latrine and the situation in general. Ah, Hilton! But the warmth of our hosts more than compensated for small un-Western discomforts. When in Pakistan...

Abdullah had left the army and was practicing cardiology in a government hospital. Zarina was publisher and owner of the first woman's magazine in Pakistan, a remarkable feat in a tough, male-dominated, quasi-fundamentalist, Muslim country. She was a small, sweet, robust, bright-as-hell, forthright lady. Her papa had been on the right hand of Jinnah, one of the grim Pakistani participants in the Great Partition. In the days that followed, we toured the city where former Hindu neighborhoods had been firebombed and the inhabitants viciously driven out. Abdullah and Zarina were obviously embarrassed. It was unspoken, but we knew that similar devastation of Muslim quarters had occurred in the dominantly Hindu cities of India. Two wars and the endless violent perturbations over Kashmir reflected the prevailing antipathy. Score another victory for religion. But we were unprepared for the endless blocks of destruction in Lahore.

Our first relatively sleepless night was punctuated by the shriek of air-raid sirens before first light. ("It is just a drill; the authorities are worried about air-raids from India. You know Kashmir and all that!") We settled back and just a few minutes later the silence was again shattered by the amplified wail of the muezzin calling the faithful to morning prayer. We had arrived just before the fast of Ramadan. It turned out to be a fascinating exercise in the world of Dr. Mohammed Abdullah. First, any family member who claimed to be ill was excused from the fast. Thus "ill" represented a major semantic (if not Koranic) challenge: pregnancy was ill; depression ("Why are you so sad, Kanu?") was ill; any random headache or URI or PMS was accepted as ill. So we seemed to be in the midst of a small, albeit diversely symptomatic, epidemic that allowed for quite a few fast-busters. Since we were hardly Muslim, we were also excused, but we demurred from daytime chow-

ing down just to be good guys. So everyone gorged before the morning muezzin reveille, and there was a grand feast after sunset. In this warm, wonderful home, I think people gained weight during Ramadan.

Abdullah asked if I would be willing to see "two problem patients," since I was the Great American Consultant who was his personal friend. The first was a "very important lady" who turned out to be a rather large, Reubenesque beauty of indeterminate age. She had simply taken to her chez in a state of chronic fatigue. We entered a large drawing room, and she was ensconced in layers of silk and lace, surrounded by some younger women, equally elegantly attired and obviously attentive. A large bowl of grapes graced a low table beside the lounge. She extended a surprisingly slender, much-bejeweled hand. But the most arresting item was a huge diamond that adorned the right side of her nose. I could hardly wrench my eyes away. Obviously our visit was anticipated, and Abdullah had explained that I could ask her clinical questions, but physical examination was out of the question. He was an excellent clinician and had explored all diagnostic possibilities. So we chatted for a few minutes, and my impression was that she was moderately depressed and was suffering a Pakistani version of Victorian "vapors." Abdullah was vastly relieved; he had arrived at the same conclusion.

The other patient was a different kettle of fish. This was an elderly gentleman who had been ill for about a year. He was a very wealthy person, and his two middle-aged sons had expressed some unhappiness with the medical care available in Pakistan. Before we saw the patient, Abdullah observed that that a diagnosis of very malignant Hodgkin's Lymphoma had been established on the basis of a lymph node biopsy. The diagnosis was absolute. He had received two courses of radiotherapy and chemotherapy, but had failed to respond. (Treatment for advanced stage Hodgkin's wasn't very effective in 1962; bone marrow transplantation was many years away.)

"So what is the problem?" I asked. Abdullah was slow to respond. "He does not know of his diagnosis. The sons fear that if he knows, he

will lose all hope." They had forbidden Abdullah (or anyone) to tell their father of his fatal diagnosis. So, I studied some of the biopsy sections in an office while the sons hovered over the microscope. One could see the characteristic chaotic cytology and occasional diagnostic "Reed-Sternberg cells." Then I examined the old man; he was a virtual skeleton with palpable liver, spleen and axillary lymph nodes. He said, "Doctor, no one knows what my illness is in this place. I fear I must go to London before it is too late." I was caught on the horns of the dilemma. One of my cardinal principles in medicine is that patients "have the right to know," especially when dealing with a life-limiting disease. The anxiety evident in the eyes of this sick old man was certainly exacerbating his clinical deterioration. I murmured that Abdullah was the best doctor I knew and "place your trust in him; you do not need to go to London." Out of earshot, I told the sons that they were adding the hardship of uncertainty to the physical travail in these last days. He should be told the truth, reassured that he was getting the best possible care and allowed to set his affairs in order. I reaffirmed my faith in Abdullah's clinical skill. One can never be sure of the "family agenda" in such situations. I had the sense that the sons meant well, but when there are significant assets involved, my natural skepticism makes me worry about wills, inheritance and such. We left and Abdullah thanked me profusely. I never knew what happened.

Lahore was the scene of one of my more memorable lecture experiences. My host had invited me to speak at the King Edward Medical College. I was still excited about renal biopsies. I had now done about 60 and owned a marvelous pack of highly transportable slides, including a sequence on technique. Abdullah advised me that no one in the medical department at King Edward (or perhaps in all of Pakistan) had ever done a percutaneous renal biopsy. That bit of intelligence inspired me to bring one of my prized, eight-inch, modified Vim-Silverman needle assemblies, with the anticipation of demonstrating my fabulous technique on a phantom patient.

I was scheduled for a Sunday morning. Although the temperature hovered around freezing, the lecture hall at King Edward was packed to the rafters with students and faculty, rosy-cheeked, smiling and half frost-bitten. Apparently the heat was turned off on weekends; obviously it had not been rekindled in time to honor the celebrated visitor from the west. It was a vast amphitheater; heroic-sized portraits of former deans and dons decorated the walls. It reminded me of descriptions of the frigid, breezy lecture halls of Edinburgh in the time of Osler. I became obsessed with the feeling that the bleak austerity in the portraits reflected years of exposure to countless weekends of this deep freeze. I felt my low-viscosity Honolulu blood sludging in all vessels.

In my turgid state, I pulled the long needle from its secure place, handed the slides to a bright young attendant, and put the naked needle with a cork protecting the tip, into in my back pocket. I strode to the front of the auditorium, and a bewhiskered elder embarrassingly and solemnly extolled my virtues and recited my pedigree. Then I sat down—right on my now mysteriously naked needle!

I don't recall all the details of the terrible scene that ensued, but it certainly broke the ice (sic), among other things. It was not a mortal wound, and I managed to deliver the lecture to a very attentive audience. I am sure, to this very day, there are still some silver-haired doctors in Lahore who reminisce about that cold day when a crazy lecturer from Honolulu skewered his right buttock by sitting on his own needle. Perhaps even the old deans and dons managed a sepulchral chuckle.

I wanted to rent a car and drive to Peshawar, walk to the Khyber Pass, and gaze into wild and wooly Afghanistan. But Abdullah said it was on the far side of the country, made much too dangerous by marauding bandit gangs who loved to kidnap or just terrorize rich, brash foreigners traveling in small groups. No sale.

On the return trip we detoured to Hong Kong to visit our friends, Priscilla and Bill Wong. Stella had been maid of honor at their classy wedding in San Antonio in 1957. Bill had become a highly successful,

much sought after architect, the toast of the Crown Colony. Along the way, he had designed and supervised construction of a magnificent home cantilevered over Repulse Bay. It was perhaps among the more expensive chunks of real estate in the colony. It had become a tour-bus landmark, since there was a local rumor (tourist hype) that William Holden owned the home.

Bill and Pris were very much caught up in the hectic fervor of the Hong Kong high life. Gleefully, we played the game: tea and croquet at Sir Arthur Wu's estate, betting (lightly) the ponies at the Jockey Club, gorging on dim sum and bird's nest soup at an infinity of sumptuous restaurants and sipping Singapore slings at the ever-posh Peninsula Hotel. It was a heady few days.

Pris and Bill had two very spoiled little boys who were vigilantly pursued by three indefatigable amahs. I could never figure out the intricate logistics, but every piece of laundry we placed in our hamper was returned washed and folded or pressed within hours. It was high-roller living on a scale of opulence completely unfamiliar to these military peasants, and we loved every minute. I gave the renal biopsy lecture (sans the cute needle trick) at the university hospital. After a whirlwind week, we were ferried back to Kai Tak, to catch a military flight to Honolulu.

That presented a problem. Military flights were dispatched from a small hangar on the edge of the airport. Before the new monster island skyport (Chek Lap Kok) was created, Kai Tak was jammed into an unbelievably small area, seemingly in the midst of downtown Kowloon. (The approach and take-off will always rank close to the top of "One's Greatest Air Travel Adventures." It reminded me of the old Kansas City and current San Diego flight paths, but even scarier; you zoomed in at penthouse level, eye-balling surrounding, not-too-tall office buildings.) Posted on the door of the military hangar was notice of a flight departing for Clarke Air Force Base that very afternoon. But it carried only one open seat. So we put Stella on that flight with

instructions to wait for me at the visiting officers quarters at the Clarke AFB Officer's Club.

For me it was slim pickin's. For two days I was hanging around the departure lounge (napping on the couch and feasting on crackers and Cokes at a depleted snack bar); no outbound flights were posted. I was wandering around the piers at the edge of the airport when I spotted a small navy amphib with two sweating and swearing guys loading rattan furniture into the small cabin. I introduced myself, offered them a couple of Cokes, and asked where they were headed. They were navy noncoms and they were taking a load of Hong Kong furniture back to Tainan (on the southwest coast of Taiwan) for their commander. I asked if I could hitch a ride. They looked uncomfortable (an army major might get fussed about a load of rattan being crammed into a navy amphib), but I told them of my sorry plight. They said if I could find a spot amidst the furniture I was welcome. So I wedged in. (In retrospect, it was a foretaste of my NASA Gemini days, when I flew in even smaller CODs [carrier-on-deck craft] sandwiched amidst tons of electronic gear.)

I had figured if I got to Tainan, I could take a commercial flight to Taipei and then hook up with a MATS connection to Clarke. It was a bit of a long shot, but I was running low on options (and leave time). I didn't have enough money to fly commercial from Hong Kong to Manila. (Poor planning, Bob. MATS axiom: never fly military air without a commercial option.) So I settled in amidst the bamboo jungle, and we freed up lines to taxi out into vast, teeming Hong Kong harbor. We labored out away from surface traffic. There was just a bit of wind and chop as we gunned along trying to get airborne. We screamed along at full throttle for what seemed like a mile, but the little plane couldn't break free. We were **very** heavy. I suspected that the very dispensable army major might get jettisoned before the commander's precious rockers and loungers. The pilot seemed a bit embarrassed as we taxied back. "We'll make it this time, Major!" I nodded smiling, but I had visions of another few nights on that cracked nauga-

hide bench. Since seaplanes can't lock wheels and rev up like land-based aircraft on short runways, we thundered along with twin engines straining, surf pounding hard at the undercarriage, an eternity of screaming, splashing, bump, bump, bump and we cleared the water! I think we flew the 500 odd miles at about 1000 feet. The furniture and I were happy shipmates.

We landed at a Republic of China air force base outside the city. It was late when I checked in at headquarters and identified myself. The sergeant spoke excellent English and gave me the key to a tiny, no-frills room in the BOQ. I was exhausted, but I tried to call Stella from a pay phone. (No mean feat at any time, but at 1:00 AM and trying to figure rate of exchange in Taiwanese coins made for a real challenge.) She should have been checked in at the Officer's Club at Clarke. By the grace of God, I got hooked up with a very helpful lady bartender who remembered the "pretty blonde army lady who kept asking if her husband had called." It was so late that I just left a message; I would get make it ASAP, but it might be a few more days.

Before dawn I was awakened by the thunder of a squadron of military jets. I leaped to the window and saw the ROC insignia on wave after wave of missile-laden fighter-bombers. Were they were going off to war or just some very serious maneuvers? All I needed was to be caught on a Chinese nationalist fighter base during a shooting war with the mainland communists; I had not seen a newspaper in days.

After a nervous-but-newsless breakfast at the officer's club, I took a taxi to the down-in-the mouth Tainan airport. I raced to nail down the "last reserved seat" on a local flight headed for Taipei. The plane was probably the last remaining DC-3 involved in commercial traffic in the universe. As it sputtered and wheezed down the runway, I reminded myself that these noble relics were noted for dogged durability and had "flown the hump" (India to Burma) in WW II. But that was over 20 years ago! I was not reassured. My fellow passengers were a diverse group, mostly farmers, laborers and guys in baggy, blue business suits, plus a few women herding lots of kids. There were a few scraggly

chickens in cages and one weather-beaten goat tethered just outside the john. It was more like a local Mexican bus than a plane. We must have hit every settlement in Taiwan; it took about six hours to travel some 200 miles. My "reserved seat" would have done our "no frills" airlines most proud. I shared it with many different folks, all generously offering chunks of very brown meat of dubious origin and vintage, plus other mysterious goodies lovingly sequestered in much recycled foil. Actually I enjoyed it. Being the only non-Chinese passenger, they all felt disposed to feed and chat with me. Of course, no one spoke English.

Once in Taipei, I managed to catch a MATS flight directly to Clarke. Stella and I enjoyed dinner together that same evening. It had been four days. Within two days we lucked into a new air force version of the 707 that went whoosh non-stop to Hickam. It was our first exposure to jet travel. A great way to end one helluva trip. I was only one week AWOL. (I had called to get an emergency extension; only moderate grumbling on the other end.)

I made one other trip to the Philippines about a year later. This was official since I had been invited to give another "Drug-Induced Diseases" lecture at the annual medical-surgical meeting run by the air force. It seemed the issue was still reasonably topical. The course director was one of my old residents, Dr. Preston Darby, who was chief of medicine at the hospital at Clarke Air Force Base. The three-day meeting was scheduled for the military rest camp (Camp John Hay) in Baguio in the mountains of northern Luzon. I do not recall the details, but Stella demurred. Nor did she want me to go. I think she thought that with the Mercury and AMA committee trips to the mainland, I had been traveling too much. But Darby pleaded that he wanted me to "anchor" his program by scheduling my "super special" lecture for the last hour of the last day. It was a big mistake, all around.

I flew MATS on a high "orders" priority, but it was still an iffy way to keep to a schedule. I landed at Clarke to link up with Darby and drive to Baguio the next day. He had given me instructions about how

to locate the hospital from the airfield. It was an "easy a 15-minute walk." It was dusk and the hot humid air swirled in little dust devils. Once the low-ranging cantonment-type hospital came into view, I realized I was not alone. I turned and striding behind me to the right was a pygmy bearing a slung bow, a quiver stuffed with arrows and a blowgun! I stopped to gaze in astonishment. He was right out of a grade B Tarzan movie. I smiled and gestured and pointed to my gold oak leaf. I muttered, "Army—major—come to see Captain Darby." No reaction. Then another Stone Age apparition appeared on my left. No one was smiling. Then this new guy gestured toward the hospital, and our little caravan meandered (one of us rather nervously) in the recommended direction. By the time I had covered the remaining 100 yards, four pygmies in full native battle regalia were trailing in my wake by about ten paces.

As I approached the entrance to the hospital, out popped a red-faced, hysterically guffawing Pres Darby. "I see you've met our Negritos!" I turned to "thank" my escort, but they had vanished. The ever-mischievous rascal had set the whole thing up. It turned out that these engaging chaps were, indeed, Negrito warriors, true aboriginal folk indigenous to the northern Luzon rain forests. The air force hired them as guards. During the Japanese occupation, they enjoyed a reputation among the invaders as ruthless, will-of-the-wisp warriors. Primarily, they served as scouts for allied guerrilla forces.

The next day we drove up to Baguio. We traversed some of the most beautiful mountains I had ever seen; some were terraced up several hundred feet with rice paddies. White hot morning sun on the gleaming fields created a delicate, lacy vision. Men with oxen lashed to wooden plows worked other fields, a scene from a thousand years ago. Travel poster stuff. Camp John Hay was a lovely bit of real estate tucked into a mountainside overlooking a verdant, steamy valley. The camp was swarming with perhaps 400 medical officers and nurses from all over the Pacific Rim representing all branches of service. The meeting content was fairly high-quality, practical, clinical stuff. I did notice

that on each of the succeeding days, attendance was beginning to diminish. It did not bode well for the last speaker at the last hour: me.

And so it came to pass. At 4:00 PM, when the distinguished clinician from Tripler rose to speak, the only people in attendance were my benefactor, Pres Darby, some poor soul who was obliged to introduce me, two chunky army nurses from Guam and one forlorn J.G. from Yokosuka. So I said, "Folks, I appreciate your dedication to the science of medicine. I will provide each of you with a copy of my speech. But now let me take you all to the club for a drink. We deserve it." I have never agreed to "anchor" another medical meeting.

Then another strange thing happened. When Pres called his office to check on things, he was advised that there had been an outbreak of cholera in Manila. The university hospital (Santo Tomas) at Quezon City had requested help from the air force: personnel, intravenous fluids, antibiotics. So we took the train to QC. I had never seen a case of cholera; it was a revelation. For three days we labored side-by-side with staff from the university and many others recruited from everywhere. These patients were the sickest I had ever seen. No antibiotic was effective against Vibrio cholerae. The liquid diarrhea was so profuse that the patients had to be placed on wooden troughs to collect and measure volume. Replacement IV fluids were poured wide open into four portals. In some cases we could not match the fluid lost and patients were dying. Mostly death came to those who were elderly, malnourished, or had some concomitant disease. By the grace of God, this epidemic was soon contained, but it turned out to be a new highly virulent strain, El Tor. I returned to Honolulu exhausted and with a new respect for an old disease.

Our time at Tripler was beginning to wind down, and we worried about our next assignment. I had been promoted to lieutenant colonel, and I still owed the army three years. I tried to extend in Hawaii and probably would have succeeded, but I was offered the chief of medicine job at William Beaumont Army Hospital in El Paso. This was what I had been waiting for: my own teaching department! It was a definite

coup for a lieutenant colonel. But the prospect of El Paso after Hono-lulu was not a popular subject at home that evening. Steven was now much invested in Punahou, but Jon was eager to try something new. Stella knew how much the teaching chief's job meant to me. She was supportive, but understandably ambivalent about swapping lush, green Hawaii for dusty, unpromising Tex/Mex border country.

We sailed on the Matsonia, sister ship to the Lurline. It was a very tearful occasion; we had come to love the Islands. Our leis floated back toward shore (a sure sign we would return), as we rounded Diamond Head. We landed in Oakland and our big Mercury wagon was already there. We loaded it with footlockers, suitcases, cooler and our vocifer-ous Indian Hill Mynah bird, Haoli. The trip was tiresome but uneventful, until Las Cruces. There we encountered the worst dust storm of our lives. It seemed almost as though all of southern New Mexico decided to move to Texas. The vista was an opaque yellow swirl and driving became dangerous to impossible. We pulled off into a dreadful motel and tried to sort things out. Everyone was furious with me; even Haoli was pissed. "We gave up Hawaii for this?" It was not a splendid night: gritty pizzas, deflated Coke and dish-water Coors light. By morning the Saharan sirocco had abated, and our sad little caravan chugged into El Paso. The desert sunlight was surprisingly bright and the atmosphere pleasantly crisp.

The commanding general at Beaumont was Bob Blount, the same one-star medical general who had advised me to take the year of cardi-ology with Weldon Walker and had assigned me to the Big Four For-eign Minister's meeting in Geneva. I think he liked me; he said he had asked for me, specifically. Bob Blount was sort of my guardian angel in the army (although I am not sure Stella quite agreed.) He was a slen-der, soft-spoken, unprepossessing Mississippian. His wife, Martha was a sweet woman. Alas, immediate post housing was not available for someone of my rank, so we searched off-post. We found a new one-story adobe within walking distance. The house was surrounded by a seven-foot wall, curiously punctuated by half-dozen apertures that

could best be described as "gunports." The kids immediately dubbed it Fort Apache. All our neighbors were retired army, and they literally "took us in." It was an auspicious, if short-lived, beginning.

I was just starting to acquaint myself with my new staff, when the fickle finger prodded yet again. Just about a week after our furniture had arrived from Hawaii, General Blount called me in. It was before people began to say, "I have good news and bad news," but his benign face bore a definite "bad news" message. "Bob, the Surgeon General has selected you to attend the Command and General Staff School at Fort Leavenworth." A bombshell! I was speechless. "But, Sir, this is my very first teaching service; I've been waiting for this for ten years. We have just arrived; Stella and the kids are barely settled. And I have never been to **any** army school in my life!" I sputtered in most un-officer-like fashion. He reached over and touched my shoulder, "I know, Bob, but this is only a four month tour. It **is** quite an honor. Very few medical officers are ever selected for Leavenworth."

I was tempted to say something ugly about the semantics involved in "only" four months, and the singular fact that four maximum-security prisons also shared the felicity of the Leavenworth environs. But I held my tongue despite a sense of deep chagrin. My military career aspirations had never included seeking "flag rank." It was a promise to Stella (and myself) that it would be "twenty and out." I knew that "maxing the course at Leavenworth" was a mandatory brownie point for every aspiring line officer seeking stars, but what did that have to do with me? It was a very bad night at Fort Apache; another "unaccompa-nied tour." Soon after arrival in El Paso, we had purchased a new Fiat Spyder, a tiny, hot convertible, ideal for tooling around the arid South-west. It was a real fun car, but it would almost cost me my life. I decided to take it to Leavenworth and leave the big station wagon with Stella and the kids.

And so began my adventure on the unpromising plains of Kansas. On the drive north I had time to contemplate the future. I was tor-mented and angry; I didn't give a damn about tactics and logistics and

all that military who-struck-john stuff. It would be a waste of four months of my life, away from my family. Also, I would be out of touch with medicine, suffering the same loss of edge that I had experienced when I came back from Korea in 1951. Only this time, I would be the "out of touch" **chief** of a teaching service! I rolled into the little town of Leavenworth in a foul state of mind. The base was just north of town. I had been told that the ill-starred George Armstrong Custer had led his brave Seventh Cavalry from this remote outpost to lose its colors and "last man" at the Little Big Horn. That dismal fact did not improve my mood; I might have even given a quiet cheer for Crazy Horse.

The "short course" class was divided into two sections, with about 100 officers each. All my classmates were majors with a few hotshot captains from infantry, armor, artillery, signal, engineers and ordnance. I was the only medical officer and I held rank. By virtue of this singular achievement, I was designated "class leader" of Section I. We had officers from Norway, Chile, Morocco, Great Britain and Turkey, as well as our own home bred star-seekers, all intense and eager. Olaf Breidlid, a handsome major from Norway, ultimately became the chief of staff of the Norwegian Army; Major Hassan from Morocco was reputed to be a member of the royal family. It was a fascinating bunch.

On the very first day, a grim reality settled upon me. We were given a two-hour written test designed to see "how much we know about the impending course material." It was an unmitigated disaster. I knew **nothing** about this stuff! "Calculate how many 155 mm rounds one should carry into the field for a three-gun firing mission, or delineate the fields of fire from the accompanying typographical map..." etc., etc. Two hours of frustrating madness. In my entire intellectual life, I had never felt so inadequate or unprepared. To add to my angst, one of my classmates, an engineer officer, later confided over bitter black coffee, that all the over-achieving officers enrolled in the "short course" had **already taken** the course in correspondence! It was a "given" that you take the course by mail (with correct answers returned) before you

ever set foot in Kansas. My erstwhile career benefactor, General Heaton, had never shared **that** bit of intelligence. Double whammy!

We were issued the first batch of course material: a giant stack of books and pamphlets. I began to study; it was like trying to learn hieroglyphics without a Rosetta Stone. The nomenclature was English, but it could have been Farsi or astrophysics. A few days later my phone rang; it was a Colonel Watson. He announced that he was my staff advisor, could I come for cocktails to his quarters "on the morrow?" He lived in an apartment on the post, so I polished my brass, straightened my ribbons and pushed his button at 1600. He was a smallish man, pencil mustache, painfully pressed khakis, West Point bird all the way to his cavalry jodhpurs. He stared at me. I wasn't sure whether he was waiting for a salute. I didn't salute. After an embarrassing too-long face-to-face interval in his doorway, he beckoned me in. "Sorry, Colonel, can I get you a drink?" I demurred but took an indicated seat across the coffee table.

"Colonel Moser, I don't mean to stare so impolitely, but I think you made the lowest pre-study score ever encountered in the long and noble history of Fort Leavenworth!" He did not smile; I did not smile. He continued, "Quite candidly, you really don't have much of a chance to pass this course." Then I smiled, slowly, "Colonel Watson, I have never failed a course in my entire life. As you probably know, I have never had occasion to need this sort of information before. My life has been dedicated to the study of medicine, where I have excelled. Now for the next four months, I have no need to study medicine; I will be devoting my full energy to studying this course material. With all due respect, Sir, I will **not** flunk this course." I was pompous, but pissed. Then we had a drink, Jim Beam on the rocks (first straight bourbon of my life, but it seemed appropriately macho as befitting my bluster). He gave me the traditional "my door is always open" bullshit as I departed. I swore I would fall on my sword before I called on this officiously honest little bastard again. But he probably spoke truth.

Well, the course was pure hell. I never studied harder or for more hours in my life. I got up every morning at 5:00 to run three miles and then study. I studied at lunch, over dinner and for five to six hours at night. I flunked the first test, but barely. Then I began to pass. The stuff was boring and difficult but not impossible. The course was divided into two units. I passed the first unit in the middle third. For the second session, my classmates elected me class leader (by acclamation, no less). I made a few friends, but I was a study machine, little time for fun and games. I went into Kansas City a few times with classmates to enjoy great stockyard steaks and Wurzburger hofbrau (not quite the same as in Germany but better than Coors). I visited Roy (the young psychiatrist from Salzburg) once at Topeka. He was now second in command of that world-famous psychiatric fiefdom. Stella and I had known his Salzburg wife, a handsome, aristocratic English blonde, studiously urbane and continental. His new wife was a pretty, ash blonde, but painfully obsequious around Roy. He was friendly but even more self-consumed, now truly sniffing his impending ascendancy to the throne.

For Thanksgiving, one of my classmates, an army artillery-spotter pilot from Fort Bliss, and I rented a spidery Piper to fly home for a few days of sex and turkey. En route, we were enjoying a full moon when we suffered a total electrical failure and had to land, sort of dead-stick, at a postage-sized, blacked-out strip somewhere in Oklahoma. It was after midnight. The field was conspicuously uninhabited, and I am not sure it had runway lights anyhow. I held the flashlight while Chuck made a few repairs with something like "baling wire and chewing gum" (standard equipment for all army spotter pilots), and we hurried on. All in a night's work; I think these guys are the best seat-of-the-pants pilots in the world.

I got pretty good at tactics, but I found some aspects disquieting. We were working out some field problems utilizing tactical **nuclear** weapons! It was a completely matter-of-fact drill. By 1964, the U.S. army had demystified tactical nuclear weapons; they could be delivered

by artillery, fighter-bomber, or possibly, a lone infantryman firing a modified, hand-held bazooka. This cunning device was still in proto-type configuration. They called it, disarmingly, the Davy Crockett. Atomic weapons available to infantrymen at squad level! I was chilled at the prospect. We studied "zones of destruction" (blast, fire, radia-tion); we predicted fall-out zones for devices of various sizes and differ-ent wind conditions. We calculated the destructive differences between ground, low-air and high-air bursts. We were told that orders to deploy nuclear weapons could come only from the President. (But it made lit-tle sense to me to place a nuclear weapon in the hands of an infantry-man locked into a hot firefight and tell him to **wait** for an order to filter down from the White House, before he could squeeze the trig-ger!)

I had a recurring daydream. I was an infantry battalion commander back in Korea. I have 1000 men dug into a low hill, cut off by devastat-ing Chinese mortar fire. We have lost communication with Division. Suddenly the mortar barrage stops; we hear gongs and bugles and a swarm of Chinese infantrymen, perhaps 3000 strong, begins to storm my position. I realize that within minutes I will lose a thousand men. At my side are two bazooka men with Davy Crocketts locked and loaded. I know I can stop the Chinese charge with two or three low air-bursts. I still cannot raise Division. The decision is mine. Do I start World War III or lose a thousand men? I spoke of this conundrum to several of my infantry classmates. They chided me, "What **is** your problem, Doc? You would be a lousy commander if you sacrificed your troops—when you had a weapon that could save them—while await-ing some order that might come too late or never come at all." Simple.

"Then what?" I said, "Let's play 'what if'? What if the Chinese turned out to be Russians, and they also had field nuclear weapons? And what if we had to drop ten or 20 "tactical nukes" on an advancing army of 300,000 or 400,000 about to overrun or outflank my 100,000? And **who** is keeping score in Moscow or Washington, calcu-lating how many kilotons of weapons are being deployed 5,000 miles

away? How will they know if the decision is 'tactical' or 'strategic'? And what magic number of megatons tips the balance to trigger a preemptive, now 'strategic' first strike? What are the parameters that define these limits? And does East agree with West about what constitutes a sufficient threat to launch a first strike?" I was pretty exercised; all conversation had stopped.

No response. These future generals had not even thought about it. Scary. Even back in 1964, I was convinced that the "tactical" use of nuclear weapons was a most dangerous fiction. My engineer friend, Bill was a hard-nosed West Pointer. We kicked this subject around over late-night beer and cigars. He was convinced that the smart folks at the Pentagon had "certainly thought about all of this, and had it all worked out." And besides, "If the Russians have tactical nukes, we've got to learn about them and not be afraid to counter them." I was hardly reassured.

(To this day I do not know the status of the Davy Crockett or its unholy contemporary brethren. But in my experience, once a weapon is developed, it may be moth-balled but never completely destroyed. I suspect they are no longer in the military inventory, since the new breed of international terrorists seems to have access to virtually every weapon of mass destruction. Do you really think Osama Bin Ladin would hesitate to employ such a nightmare device? Blueprints in computer memory can live forever. A few years back when the Russian, Alexander Lebed spoke of "unaccounted-for suitcase nukes," it gave me anxious pause. We live in a frightening world, full of conscienceless crazies. God knows we don't need to exacerbate the travail by stocking hand-held nuclear delivery systems. "OK, Bob," my dibbuk says, "so what if the bad guys have them?" It's the same circular argument that relates to world-wide destruction of remaining cultures of variola (smallpox) and all other weapons of mass destruction. There is no good answer.)

One of the final chores that faced everyone in the course was writing a thesis for grade. They handed out long lists of recommended subjects

to be researched in the ample military library on post. I could find nothing appealing. So for the second time, most reluctantly, I visited the ever-dapper Colonel Watson. By now he knew that I would be graduated, and he even expressed some wry admiration. I asked him for a favor. Would he intercede with the College powers and allow me write my thesis on a subject closer to my medical heart? I thought it might be fun to examine the impact of disease on the outcome of wars since the beginning of recorded history (Joshua at Jericho?). He was intrigued and obtained the permission. I called the thesis "Of Plagues and Pennants." A very helpful librarian at the National Library of Medicine became fascinated by my project. I never met her, but by phone and mail we selected a large, eclectic bibliography, mostly military history. She photocopied dozens of key articles. Once into the reading, I realized that I could only scratch the surface of this intriguing business. But my thesis won the first place award and was subsequently published in the journal, *Military Review* in 1965.

The final week of the course was devoted to computer war games. It was Section I (blue) versus Section II (red). I was commanding general of Blue team. I was given three divisions with all appropriate logistical and air support. Our War Room was very realistic; my senior-ranking classmates were my immediate staff. The battle raged for four exhausting days; we finally prevailed with an unconventional *tour de force*. We brought a company of Pattons through the "inaccessible" Pripet Marshes where eastern Poland abuts Ukraine and blasted crucial enemy supply dumps from the rear. My G-2 (Intelligence Officer) had obtained "critical information" from a Polish hunter who "knew the marshes", and he personally led the column through to the enemy rear. The referees allowed the ploy; we celebrated like it was V-E Day.

The final tribute from my classmates came on graduation day. When I sought to polish my brass, I discovered that not only had it all been burnished to a high (very infantry, not very medical) gloss, but the polish fairies had replaced my caduceus insignia with crossed infan-

try rifles. The ultimate accolade! So ended my adventure at Leavenworth. But the trip home was another story.

It was mid-December when I loaded up the Fiat convertible to charge home to El Paso. I filled a large thermos with scalding black coffee and prepared six fat tuna salad sandwiches. It had taken two and a half days coming north, but I decided to tackle the 1100 miles in one stretch, punctuated only by pit stops. I planned to pull off the highway to sleep a few hours if needed, but I was all fired up to get home. The heater in the Fiat did not cotton to the Kansas winter; it just couldn't forget it was born to languish near the Liguarian Sea. The wind tended to whistle through the canvas top, and I was obliged to wear longjohns, fatigues and a heavy army jacket even with the heater ratcheted up to "high."

The weather was definitely iffy, but I was going interstate (or what passed for interstates in those days) all the way. Emporia, Wichita, Tulsa, Oklahoma City zipped past, but there were some snow flurries. It was definitely colder. I was angling southwest toward Wichita Falls. About sundown, the sky turned gray with ominous, low-hanging, leaden clouds. I pulled up to a toll road; I think it was the Oklahoma Turnpike. The uniformed guy in the booth was occupied with a sloppy pizza dribbling over a comic book. "How's the weather further up the line?" A glint of anger at the disruption. "Traffic seems to be coming through from the south. Expect some snow but looks no sweat." I paid my few bucks and headed on down.

Now it was really cold, and the snow began to pick up. Large soggy flakes began to exceed the capacity of the wimpy Fiat wipers. I slowed down to 50 and tried reading the road from the open window. Not very helpful—too damned cold. After about 40 miles, the road became almost impossible to follow. I had passed a few trucks coming north earlier, but now nothing—it was pitch black. I was quite alone. I estimated the snow was about two to three inches deep. I slowed even more as the wind picked up and the snow was moving horizontally, almost an opaque whiteout. Then the infernal Fiat's engine began to

miss! I would throw it in neutral and rev it up; it would roar for a while but then spit and fuss. I was doing about 10; I just couldn't see.

Abruptly the snow stopped. I was under an overpass. I sputtered off the road swinging in as close to the bank as possible. I revved the engine, but in idle it still stuttered and then died. It would not start! For the first time I became alarmed. This is how people freeze to death! I calmed down, slowly downed some still-hot coffee, and tried to think. I could wait for a snowplow, but there had been no traffic for an hour. Perhaps the plows would wait until the snow stopped. But the storm could last for days; I could not. No, I had to keep moving to stay warm and try to find shelter. I drank the dregs of my coffee, ate the last two tuna sandwiches, rummaged through my duffel and suitcase. I found a heavy wool sweater, hiking boots, three flannel shirts and wool socks that would do for mittens. I put everything on, but the extra socks pinched my feet in the boots. I only had my military uniform hat, so I made a turban out of one of the flannel shirts to cover my ears. I fished a two-cell flashlight from the glove compartment (useless for vision in the blinding snow, but perhaps helpful to flag a passing truck). I felt like a sorry-assed version of the Michelin man. I stuck a note on the windshield indicating that I would be right back: "engine trouble." The only stuff of value in the car was my Remington typewriter, clothes, uniforms, books, papers, personal stuff, most of it locked in the trunk. Anyone could open the damn ragtop with a penknife, but theft was the least of my worries.

By now I knew I was locked into a full-scale Oklahoma blizzard—the white stuff was horizontal and blinding. I began to hike briskly down the highway seeking light. Any light—truck, plow, house. It was now about eight or nine; just a few feet past the flashlight beam it was pitch black. The wind chill must have been ten or 20 below. I could feel it in my "Korea damaged" fingers (despite the wool socks), but also in toes and nose. The wind died for a moment, and I saw a faint light—a house. I turned off the road and soon ran into a four-foot chain link fence. The Michelin man tumbled over the obsta-

cle. I walked up to a small, single-wide, mobile home with a tiny porch. I knocked. A light came on from inside. I brushed the snow from my face and tried to look pleasant. After a few minutes a shape appeared under the light; it was a spiky-haired, mountainous woman carrying a double-barreled shotgun! "Please help me, lady. My car broke down. I'm freezing!" A wide, scared face peered through the door window, "You git, no place here. Bar down the road. They got a room." I could hear the hammers click as she waved the barrel at me. I started to sputter, but realized that she was really frightened. The sudden appearance of Michelin man wearing a shirt for a hat in the midst of a dark snowy night was enough to terrify anyone. But to let someone freeze in the heart of the bible belt?

I staggered off in the direction she had indicated. It was a narrow road, rapidly disappearing under about four inches of snow. I walked about 100 feet. No light. I seemed to be having trouble cerebrating; I think I was delusional. I was certainly disoriented. I turned to look back; my benefactress had turned her light off. I stood there shivering and mused absently, "If I stay out here I will freeze; if I go back there she will probably shoot me. If it's in a leg, I could survive, but the range will be close, and she probably packs number 4 buckshot." I knew I was not thinking rationally. By now I was not sure where her house had been anyway. I stumbled on for another dozen or so yards and thought I saw another light. Yes, it must be the bar! I trudged, fell and ran until I reached a large house with a porch and sign: "Henrietta's." I pounded on the door. This time I **would** gain entry, shotguns be damned. I had already lost sensation in the frostbitten fingers of my left hand, and I could not feel the tip of my nose. The porch light came on. Another hairy harridan materialized along with a small bald man, but no visible weaponry. With half frozen lip and tongue I scream-grunted my terrible plight. There was some head bobbing conversation, larger and smaller silhouettes in intense dialogue. The door opened a crack, "Twenty-five bucks!" God had smiled. "Yes—yes, fine, **please** let me in." The door opened and blessed warmth swept over my

face. I fumbled beneath my layers for the wallet, handed it to her. She extracted some bills. "Behind the bar, room at the top." Mother Theresa in tattered chenille.

The room had a double bed with a heavy woolen coverlet. I tore off my jacket and fumbled with iced laces. I crawled under the blanket and shivered for about an hour. I awoke sometime later in pitch blackness, undressed to my underwear and fell into a dreamless coma. Many hours later, a gray finger of light crept through a tiny window above the bed. The house was silent; I remembered it was Sunday morning. God's day. I thanked Him for letting me live. There was no bathroom, just a sink, wicker chair and a three-drawer maple dresser. I crawled back into my rigid clothes. I detected an aroma, a mixture of Clorox and cheap perfume. I suspected my "little room over the bar" had served Henrietta well. It was certainly paradise for me. I left quietly.

The snow had stopped and there was no wind, but it was very cold. I began to retrace my steps through about six inches of snow, drifted to several feet in places. I realized that I had walked less than half a mile the preceding night; it had seemed like ten. I spotted the house of the shotgun bearer. I thought of perpetrating some act of malicious mischief, but the way my luck had been running, she probably would spot me and unload both barrels. I climbed the turnpike fence and walked back to my car, now buried under a ton of snow from a passing plow. I tried to dig it out, tough going, hopeless. The lock was frozen; I couldn't insert the key. I reached in through a loose attachment of the canopy (another classy Fiat Spyder feature) and popped the lock. I revised my windshield note to a hopeful, "Car will be picked up today," changed socks, stuffed my duffel with more possessions and began to hike toward Texas.

After a few minutes a red Datsun pick-up stopped. It was the first vehicle I had seen. It bore a Grant Wood Methodist minister and his very quiet son headed for Wichita Falls. After a too-profuse declaration of my renewed faith in God, I asked if they could drop me at the main gate at Fort Sill. I hoped the post garage might be open to provide

some help in trying to coerce the cachectic Fiat into running again. A frost-encrusted MP advised, "Sir, its Sunday; base is closed tighter than a drum. Blizzard last night got lines down." The good preacher carried me into Wichita Falls.

It was about ten o'clock; I found a V W showroom with a parts and repair department. An ever-eager salesman put me on the phone with a very sleepy parts manager. I gave him the short version and wrote down the number of the overpass where the only snowed-in, red Fiat Spyder convertible in Oklahoma might be found. He was very helpful. Blindly, I signed some papers for the salesman (he could have been selling me a VW bus), indicating that I would pay for towing and repairs. I suspect the proximity of Fort Sill and my exalted rank indicated that I was a serious, if shabby looking, customer. Besides, they could hold the Fiat hostage until I showed up and paid the tab. I was a dirty mess. I washed up in their lavatory and checked my wallet. I had about $25, not quite enough for a Greyhound ride to El Paso. So I called Stella and described Bob's Glorious Adventure. The Great Oklahoma Blizzard had not made the El Paso nightly news.

Then I called Pres Darby (of Clarke AFB, negritos and Baguio). He had left the air force, and I knew he was practicing in Big Spring. I knew Pres and Susie would be good for bacon and eggs, steaming shower, change of clothes, bus fare and some friendly chiding. He responded like the good old buddy he was, and offered to drive up to fetch me. Big Spring is a few hundred miles from Wichita Falls, but it is well on the road to El Paso. So I hopped a bus and told the driver to wake me in Big Spring. I had not eaten since the day before, so I had coffee and a cinnamon roll in Abilene and lapsed back into coma. Pres and Susie were vastly impressed with my "near-death experience." Their amusement at my lack of good sense was not too well concealed, "If it had been Texas that old broad would have shot you."

Once back in El Paso, I checked on the car. Miraculously, it had been picked up and was being repaired. Stella and I drove back up to Wichita Falls and retrieved it about three weeks and 350 bucks later.

Within a month I traded it in on a slick, new Thunderbird convertible (the practical kind with the rag roof that filled up the whole trunk). It wasn't a helluva lot more utilitarian than the Spyder, but it had a great heater.

It did not take long to get back into the swing of things; I hadn't dropped that far behind. I inherited a terrific staff. I soon discovered that I had two of the four best cardiologists in the army, Bill Nelson and Bob North. (The other two were Mel Cheitlin at Letterman and Bob Hall at Walter Reed.) But two for four ain't bad, and it took the army over a year to discover our good fortune. Soon our teaching program was rolling in high gear. While at Beaumont, I was still writing a monthly column for a medical newspaper directed to house officers (House Physician Reporter) edited by an old friend, Al Roller at $300 a pop. I was also writing a pungent monthly "book review/commentary" column about "medically-related books for the public" for another magazine (*Medical Opinion and Review*) at $350 a shot. Desultorily I was working on the next edition of "Diseases of Medical Progress." It was a very busy reading and writing period.

Soon after I returned from Kansas, an elegant old house on the post became available, so we retreated from Fort Apache. It was a grand old two-story just off the quadrangle, within walking distance to the hospital, PX and Commissary. Just by chance, one of my staff members, Major Jerry Twomey, a recent Irish émigré who had studied hematology at Baylor, came to me with a sad story. His father, a physician in Dublin, had died recently and his long-time housekeeper, Bridget, had no place to live. His dying father had exacted a promise from Jerry that he would look after "Biddie," and indeed, she was due to arrive in El Paso within the week, to work for the Twomeys.

One problem: Jerry's wife hated Biddie, and "I will not have her under our roof." Could I help? Probably. I called Stella and she was elated. We had not had a live-in housekeeper-cook since Laura in Wurzburg. And so within a few weeks, Biddie O'Leary came to the rambling Moser hacienda. She was a fair cook (her Irish stew was more

mulligatawny than mulligan and her Yorkshire pudding was more greasy than crispy), an indifferent duster-polisher, but a relentless laundress. She was small, plainly pretty, fortyish, almost wispy, but wiry and very Catholic. The church was her hobby and passion. Biddie seemed sexless; we never heard of a gentleman friend past, present or (apparently) future. She was a professional spinster. I was never sure of her immigration status, and, perhaps selfishly, did not inquire. It was never an issue; I have never sought a cabinet post.

One of my patients was Lieutenant Colonel Bill Higgins, an engineer officer at Fort Bliss. He soon retired and went to work as chief engineer for the Paradise Island Corporation in the Bahamas. One Saturday morning, Bill called; he had a job offer for me. No, he could not give details, but it was "right down my alley." The company would like Stella and me to come down to Paradise Island for an on-site interview and three-day vacation—all on the house! Well, why not? So we flew to Nassau, but not before the nasty "Return Trip Ticket Caper" transpired.

In the process of making a hasty departure from El Paso, I decided to shed my jacket (no need for a jacket in the tropics, right) and left it with my secretary at the airport. Unfortunately, It bore our return trip tickets in the inside pocket. I was holding the outbound boarding passes. All was well until we encountered customs at Nassau. A giant, uniformed passport official (he was at least seven feet tall, an overfed Masai) asked to see our return tickets. Apparently they had experienced a run of seedy folks who came, ostensibly, to visit, but decided to remain, uninvited.

I searched frantically but, of course, the tickets were in El Paso. He would not let us in. And that was that. I could see Bill Higgins on the other side of the customs area, but they would not allow communication. "But, if you just let me go to the ticket counter, I'll purchase return tickets right here and now." Giant, immobile Guardian of the Crown stood unmoved: Leonidas at Thermopylae. Finally, another airport official (fancier uniform) came along with Bill in tow. "Can't you

see these people are not riff-raff. He is a colonel in the U.S. Army!" I was sure that our monster impediment would mutter, "Just doing my duty, Sir." To his everlasting credit he did not; I planned to avoid his station upon departure.

Bill apologized, I apologized, and he piled us into his blue Mercedes 300 SL. He had not purchased this beast on army retirement pay! He buzzed over the new bridge (he built it) to Paradise Island (he was building it). We took up occupancy in a deluxe suite in the Ocean Club. Cut tropical flowers in dazzling array; mango, papaya, pineapple and kiwi graced crystal bowls, gourmet bar, open view to patio with private pool and beach beyond. Wow!

That very evening we had cocktails with Mr. John Crosby, boss of the Paradise Island "enterprise." His offer was simplicity itself. They had purchased the island from Mary Carter Paint, and they were putting the finishing touches on some five-star hotels, beach cottages, restaurants and, yes, a magnificent casino. We would tour the facility tomorrow. The job? It was almost, "Aw shucks. Well, we sort of figured that we could really attract a lot of Fortune 500 executives with a package that would include all of our better-than-superb amenities, plus a top-notch medical facility staffed by nationally-recognized specialists who could perform their corporate annual physical examinations, while the executives relaxed here, enjoying the delights of our little island paradise." He caught his breath. I took a gulp of my mai tai; Stella didn't gasp audibly. He continued, "Bill has told us about you. We've checked your credentials and made other inquiries. We think you are our man. You could design the facility, select your equipment, hire appropriate personnel. We want it to be a Mayo Clinic quality operation." He had gentle blue eyes and a low 80s golfer's tan, but he was a hard-nosed businessman making a hard-nosed pitch. I said we needed some time. He laughed softly and said everything on the Island was *carte blanche* but the gambling. "Take your time."

Stella and I discussed the proposition at length. First, in the spectacular restaurant (where Sean Connery escaped the Goldfinger assassin),

then in the awesome, Vegas-rococo gambling casino, later at poolside, in the markets and shops of Nassau, on the beach between snorkeling dives. The offer had an intriguing ring, but—it was out of the question, a career dead-end by every measure. The money offered was about three times what I was earning in the army, but that was the only positive. The intellectual challenge was nil. Besides, the Bahamas are not Hawaii; the tropical charm would wear thin rather quickly. And I was doing what I wanted, running an internal medicine teaching service and enjoying every minute. Even Stella felt that it was not for us. Mr. Crosby was gracious; "If you change your mind…" As he drove us to the airport, Bill said he thought it had been worth a shot. It had all been a trifle heady—a glimpse at a high-roller "quality of life," quite alien to anything we knew. It was just not for us.

Back in El Paso, another adventure was unfolding. The officers' wives from Fort Bliss and Beaumont often went on shopping forays to Juarez, a marvelous shopping town just across the Rio Grande. But you had to be a little careful. If your vehicle were involved in a fender-bender, the cops would physically remove your license plates, regardless of circumstances. It always took a lot of palm-greasing and frantic wheeling-dealing to square things away. So most people took the international trolley car or parked in El Paso and walked over the bustling bridge.

One day three officers' wives from our hospital parked and walked. They went to a very nice restaurant and had some very nice margaritas. As they were leaving, they decided to shop in the Mercado and took a short cut (one of them "knew the way"). Of course, they got lost and wandered into an unfamiliar section of town. Never a clever gambit in old Juarez. They were picked up by the cops and charged with "prostitution without a license." In the slammer with all the other "girls," they were allowed one phone call. Wisely, they called the Provost Marshall at Beaumont, a wily, tough MP with a pragmatic sense of humor. "Charged with operating without a license? Well hell, ladies, just **buy** licenses; they only cost about four bucks!" So three middle-aged ladies

from William Beaumont Army Medical Center now have framed licenses, testifying to their legitimate status as Juarez prostitutes, adorning their guest bathrooms.

Well, Stella didn't have such a distinguished trophy, but she did have Mauricio. He was a Polish Jew married to a Mexican wife. They ran a fabulous hole-in-the-wall shop in the seething heart of Juarez. Mauricio had a gold room, leather room, brass room and silver room. It was a labyrinthine warren of goodies. Every room was locked, and you gained entry only with a nod from the boss. Most guests were accompanied by a small army of sweaty kids. Mauricio and Juanita and Stella became good friends. There is little question that the "little blonde lady with the king-sized star of David" got some great deals in his shop. She also steered a lot of army trade toward Mauricio's emporium. Stella had a fine eye for jewelry; she could spot flaws in diamonds and estimate carats along with the experts. Her Mexican and Indian collection was all good stuff. We broke bread with Mauricio and Juanita on several occasions. I even wrote a letter to help one of their bright-eyed kids get into medical school at Tulane.

Steven was having a problem adjusting. Having been unceremoniously avulsed from his junior year at gentle Punahou and tossed into a mean milieu at El Paso High, was rough fare. He had forgotten the "haoli" versus "local" warfare in Honolulu, but now he was a gringo. It was *deja vu* for the poor kid. Jon was having less of a school problem, but both kids were learning hard lessons about bias against minorities. But possibly as a result of such experience, I know that neither of them has a prejudicial bone in his body.

Steven was applying to college. Stella and I agreed that a small liberal arts place would be good for him. We had brochures from St. Johns of Annapolis (they had just opened a campus in Santa Fe), Oberlin, William and Mary and a few others. I had met several undergrads from St. Johns and had been singularly impressed with their well-tempered demeanor, broad classical background and sensible, liberal view of the world. It was a Great Books college like Chicago. Stella eagerly

endorsed St. Johns; it was just the kind of environment where she would have thrived. My only caveat to Steven was that if he wanted to attend medical school, St. Johns would present a problem. He would have no grounding in basic "pre-med" biology, organic chemistry and physics. Studying Archimedes, Ptolemy, Plato, Newton, Darwin and friends was exciting and wonderful, but not terribly appealing to hard-nosed medical school admissions committees. He hastened to assure me that he was not interested in medicine. He was accepted at St. Johns in Santa Fe and William and Mary; New Mexico got the nod.

Jon's El Paso sagas became the stuff of legends. He was a diffident scholar; his talents lay elsewhere. For Christmas 1965 (he was 13), he asked for a Heath kit oscilloscope! I didn't even realize that he knew what that was, much less that he might be able to construct one from blueprints and a million parts. On Christmas morning, he gathered up his goodies, kissed Stella and me and disappeared into his bedroom. I knew he had all sorts of electronic sound equipment and strobes and such; he was doing "light shows" for classmates. About two, he emerged with his oscilloscope. With a shy grin he murmured, "Time for the smoke test." What? "You know, you plug it in and if it smokes, you made a mistake." He plugged; it smoked. Jon was crest-fallen. I said, "Tomorrow we'll take it over to Major Tom Binder, he runs the shop where they fix all the hospital medical equipment."

The next day, we hustled over with the wounded scope, and Tom inspected it with a magnifying lens. "Well, I'll be damned. It looks like the kid used a big old soldering iron!" Jon allowed as how that was the only tool he had. "Well, you missed one connection; everything else is perfect. Fantastic job. I'll give you a smaller, finer soldering tool for a Christmas present. If you ever want a job, look me up. Not too many guys in this shop could have done that assembly with the tool you had." Jon revised his connection, plugged it in. No smoke. Merry Christmas. What a kid!

Jon's other El Paso caper was less enchanting. Stella began to notice that several of her magazines had been embossed with what seemed to

be a Notary Public seal. Later there was word at hospital headquarters that the Provost Marshall's office had been vandalized and some small items of office equipment stolen. The military police were hot on the case. When I came home with the story, Stella put the facts together. We found the Notary seal device and several other bits of office hardware in Jon's drawer. He could not deny the facts. He admitted that another older boy and he had met late at night, picked the lock and swiped a few items they thought would "not be missed—nothing valuable." I knew the PM (the same wise person who gave such great advice to the Juarez wives) and explained the situation. He was very decent. On my recommendation, he showed Jon and the other kid what the Fort Bliss stockade looked like from the inside, a very unpleasant slammer. He did not pursue the matter. Jon was grounded for a month. Close call, federal property and all that.

I was still doing occasional chores for NASA via Gemini. The remote tracking system had been automated, and they no longer required crews at the global sites. I viewed this progress with some ambivalence. It had been a wonderful experience, probably never to be repeated in the annals of space faring. I was doing pre- and post-flight physical examinations on the first few Gemini crews. Most notable was the Gemini 4 mission of Ed White and Jim McDivitt. This was to be the first time an American astronaut "went EVA" (extravehicular activity—left the spacecraft while in orbit). About one week before launch we were all hunkered down at Cape Canaveral. I had performed the pre-flight physicals on the team. Both were in superb condition. Ed White was the best conditioned athlete I had ever encountered. He was a serious West Pointer who ran the sandy Florida beaches for miles on end. His resting heart rate was about 52; after exercise it soared to around 70. This was a well-known physiologic phenomenon among distance runners. Les Mac Mitchell, the world-record holder for the mile at that time, had a resting heart rate of 48.

But this caused a problem in headquarters. Chuck Berry, the ranking NASA physician (one of the air force original Mercury team) said

that they were worried that Ed might suffer a syncopal episode if his rate slowed too much. They were still snake-bit from the publicity surrounding the grounding of Deke Slayton for an entirely different cardiac-related problem. I assured Chuck and all the rest of the hand-wringers that Ed White was just demonstrating superb cardiovascular conditioning. They asked me to be "double sure." They had a lot riding on this EVA. They were already preparing Ed's back-up. He came to me in near panic. I told him I would reassure the brass upstairs, but that we would do some tests to prove the point. It was three days from launch.

The next morning we sneaked over to the dispensary at Patrick. I borrowed an ECG machine and we found a quiet room. I wired Ed and then ran several miles of ECG while he rested, ran in place, rested and then performed Valsalva maneuvers (strain with closed glottis). Then I gave him a 1/150 grain atropine sulfate tablet to swallow. Atropine is an ancient drug that is called a parasympatholytic in that it temporarily interferes with parasympathetic innervation. This causes acceleration of the heart rate. It is still used intramuscularly in cases of extreme bradycardia following myocardial infarction. After a few minutes Ed's heart rate rose from 56 to 64; his mouth became a little dry and his pupils slightly dilated. He could still see quite well, near and far. It all passed in about 20 minutes. I gave him three tablets. I told him that if I detected on the monitor at Houston that his rate had dropped to 50, I would ask the Capcom to query him, "How are you feeling?" That would be the signal to take one tablet. The mouth dryness and the slight pupil dilation were not enough to interfere with performance. It was our secret. If the guys upstairs even had a sniff of this scheme, they would crucify us both. As history recorded, Ed White did a masterful job. His heart cooperated. In the spacecraft his rate never went below 62; in EVA it rose to about 80. He never had to pop a pill. He was my friend for the remainder of his tragically short life. I have never told this story before.

After the impact point in the South Atlantic where Gemini 4 would land was computed, Chuck Berry and I hopped separate carrier-on-deck (COD) aircraft at Patrick. I recall being wedged in the tiny cabin with electronic equipment filling every space. (It was even tighter than the rattan furniture entrapment on the navy amphib in Hong Kong harbor.) I was wearing an orange life jacket and a helmet with earphones keyed to eavesdrop the conversation of the pilot chatting with the carrier buried somewhere in the blackness below. I fell asleep. Soon the pilot came on, "Doc, take a look out the window." I peered through the oval of glass and saw only absolute darkness. "No, look down—down!" I strained to get a better angle; I saw a dot of light a million miles below. That was the little carrier; I think it was the USS Kearsarge. It was designed to handle small propeller aircraft and helicopters. It now was the proud bearer of the crew of Gemini 4. We banked and dove for the light. We made one pass high over the now brilliantly illuminated flight deck, banked, came in lower, leveled off, smacked into the deck, caught the blessed hook and clattered to a breath-taking stop.

I was swept down to the tiny ship's dispensary. The old carrier was boiling along at flank speed headed for Jacksonville, every bolt and plate rattling. And I was supposed to listen to hearts and lungs, as well as draw blood! We were vibrating and bouncing. I shouted at the ship's surgeon, a lieutenant commander, "I can't hear a damned thing. And I can't draw blood. Please ask the skipper to give me about five minutes." He looked at me as though I were asking to run up a white flag during the Battle of Midway. Ed White said, "Give the Doc a break; he needs to do his stuff." Hero power. Magically, the giant bucket of bolts stopped rattling. It was not exactly silent, but I could hear hearts and lungs and draw blood without inducing traumatic exsanguination. Of course, Ed and Jim were fine, high with excitement. The President called soon thereafter, and within the hour we were all launched in CODs (another sudden "eyeballs-in" positive G load) to join the festiv-

ities back in Jacksonville. We spent a day reviewing all the in-flight medical data; everything was normal.

It was about one year later when Ed White, Gus Grissom and Roger Chaffee perished in that terrible fire in the Saturn mock-up at the Cape. As I have said before, the bitter irony was that after Gus' problem with the blown hatch, immediately following his suborbital flight the NASA engineers removed the skittish explosive bolts. Had the crew been able to blow the Saturn hatch at the first sign of fire, they probably would have survived. It was the last time 100% oxygen was ever used on a NASA manned vehicle. Ed and Gus had been the two astronauts I knew the best. They were true heroes.

It was in El Paso that Egon, Stella's pain-in-the-ass absentee father, entered our lives in a significant way. He had deserted Sonya and three year-old Stella over three decades ago. Stella rarely spoke of him in our early years together; Sonya referred to him with undisguised scorn. He had dumped them with family in Brooklyn, remarried and now had two truly ugly daughters and one truly ugly son. Stella's attitude toward him had softened over the years, and we actually visited him and his new family in Fort Lee once or twice. He was bald, gaunt, remarkably unattractive and an unabashed Germanophile. Bad enough in anyone, but unforgivable for a Jew, especially one whose family had been pauperized by the Nazis.

I despised Egon and all he stood for. His family had been rich merchants in Danzig, and it would seem he had been a much-indulged playboy. It was somewhat of a mystery how he had met Sonya. Her family had fled the pogroms in Kiev and had landed in Danzig. The Nazis drove Egon's father out of business, but they escaped the camps. According to some old photographs, Sonya had been quite a beauty, but young Egon always looked like "Egon." They met and married and soon immigrated to New York. The ex-playboy was suddenly reduced to driving a meat-delivery truck for a stern uncle, while Sonya studied "cosmetic chemistry" at NYU. Why he deserted Sonya and Stella was never explained, but I always suspected it had something to do with

Sonya's maniacal dedication to her child. But there had to be more. He left them high and dry, without resources, and never paid alimony or child support. Sonya had to tough it out on her own, with some help from her elder sisters. I thought Egon was a thoroughly despicable bastard, and I made no bones about my sentiment. I found it difficult to comprehend Stella's latter-day need to get to know him, despite the fact that "he is my father, after all."

Compounding this record of callous abandonment, Egon's unabashed admiration of Teutonic military "tradition and discipline" added to his enormous charm. I once felt compelled to play the "professional military officer" card. I told him, "In every war, gaggles of German soldiers have always acted like a colony of brain-washed ants. Kill the platoon leader, and they scatter in all directions. That's why we beat the hell out of them, every time. They are really lousy soldiers." His red-faced fuming was maliciously rewarding.

But he had acquired a bleeding peptic ulcer. His doctors in New Jersey had not been successful in treatment. Stella insisted that we invite him to El Paso, and since he was a veteran (he had been drafted late in World War II but never left the country), pleaded that we take care him in our hospital. We did accept occasional veterans, so I pulled a few strings and had him admitted. At that time we had two general officers from the West German army, who were learning about missile warfare at Fort Bliss, being treated in the surgical VIP area. So I pulled a few more strings and had Egon admitted to the suite. The little bastard was in hog Valhalla. I don't know what the two Deutscher brasshats thought about Egon (I suspect he did not tell them he was "Juden"), but they all chatted amicably in that thoroughly detestable guttural. Egon underwent major resectional surgery that solved his medical problem. I was pleased to see the back of him.

The war in Viet Nam was being felt in every military hospital. We received soldiers who required long-term care; we saw lots of patients with amoebic hepatic abscesses, chronic viral hepatitis, schistosomiasis and lots of orthopedic trauma. In the midst of all this, there was a very

scary outbreak of meningococcemia among recruits at Fort Bliss. No immunizing vaccine was available at that time, and treatment was rarely successful. Three soldiers from one barracks died. A team of epidemiologists from Walter Reed Research Institute and the CDC flew down. They set up a rigorous environmental cleansing operation, instituted isolation procedures and conducted classes for corpsmen aimed at early clinical detection.

Then the commanding general at Fort Bliss made an ass of himself. He declared, "There will be no more cases of meningococcus disease on this post!" He had given the malignant bug a direct order! He blabbed this bit of idiocy to the *El Paso Sun*, and then ordered the barracks building where the cases had occurred to be burned down! A singular act of stupidity. Within days three more patients turned up who were living in other barracks. We wondered if he would put the whole base to the torch. Tents were set up in the field and troops scattered. Within a week there were no more patients.

The war took on a tragic, personal note when Captain Howard Cohen, a young internist from New York, was assigned to my department as a general medical officer. Howie was savvy, personable, a very fine "people" doctor. He had a charming wife and two kids; they became our friends. After six months Howie was reassigned to Viet Nam. Within weeks he was killed when his ambulance helicopter landed to pick up wounded. His aid men had been pinned down and Howie went to help. They were all killed by small arms fire. Beaumont went into mourning. They gave him a Bronze Star; so hopeless, pointless, useless.

Well into the second year at Beaumont, I submitted a clinical research protocol to NASA. It was common knowledge that routine, regular exercise caused improvement in physical performance. But there were no data to establish exactly which physiological parameters were affected. I wanted to study two matched groups, before and after periods of sustained vigorous exercise versus usual physical activity. We wanted to gather data on ECG, blood pressure, pulmonary function

and various blood components. I enlisted the aid of two residents. NASA accepted the protocol, and we were rewarded with a modest but adequate grant. We recruited 20 officers and enlisted men between 19 and 44 (I was the eldest).

After gathering baseline data, we divided the group. Team A began to run three miles at least five days a week; Team B did whatever they always did (runners were excluded). It was to be a six-month study. We all started out with great enthusiasm, but week-by-week the levies for Viet Nam began to deplete our ranks. We lost twice as many runners as controls. After three months, we were obliged to abandon the project; our "n" had dropped to statistical insignificance. But most of the runners kept running. I continued until 1992 when I began to suffer bilateral traumatic arthritis of the knees. (I am convinced that long-distance running must begin when you are in your teens or twenties so that ligaments and tendons and muscles accommodate. Starting later in life seems to be an invitation to traumatic arthritis of the knees, but I know there are exceptions.)

Another interesting "research endeavor" occurred during my time in El Paso. Due to my interest in renal biopsies, I wondered if one could detect early changes in kidney histology that could facilitate diagnosis (and possible treatment) of disorders that were just beginning to become manifest by minimal dysfunction. I was especially interest in early effects of drugs that were often toxic to kidney tissue, or disorders such as diabetes mellitus (with minimal proteinuria) or hypertension of renal origin.

I realized that it would be impossible ethically, to perform biopsies on humans with such slight indication, but I had an idea. I had been lecturing at military installations all across the country about "space medicine," and most recently had been to Holloman Air Force Base, up near Alamogordo. While there I was taken on a tour of the Primate Research Facility, perhaps the largest collection of chimpanzees in the country. They had been used for the early space program; it was the home of the celebrated space pioneers, Ham and Enos. They were

enshrined in "early retirement." The chimps were being used for various types of "intellectual-performance research." Timorously, I asked the colonel-veterinarian, if he might be interested in a joint project in which we could study the effect of various putative "nephrotoxic" drugs on some old chimps that were not being used for the other projects. I wanted to do renal biopsies on them at baseline and then at various intervals after the drug(s) were introduced, while also testing renal function. I had access to an electron microscope at Walter Reed and thought we might be able to detect very early changes.

He nodded and smiled broadly, "To my knowledge, no one has ever done a percutaneous renal biopsy on a chimpanzee, but I'll check the literature." Indeed, no one had. Well, working with chimps is tough stuff. Pound for pound they are three times as strong as a human, and to try to stick a long needle…So, we anesthetized one old-timer, did an intravenous pyelogram, and lo and behold, the kidneys popped up in perfect position for biopsy. We did two more on other chimps, and the kidneys were always in the same position. In humans there can be considerable variation. So, I performed the first renal biopsy on a chimpanzee. We published in the *American Journal of Veterinary Research* in 1967. Alas, soon thereafter, I was placed on orders to leave Beaumont, and no one was left to push the project.

Sometime in mid-1967 we had another scare. General Blount called me into his office for a "chat." The memory of Leavenworth was still quite vivid; I wondered what new "honor" the Surgeon General had bestowed. Blount seemed dejected; I expected the worst. "The Surgeon General wants you to command a general hospital in Da Nang." I was not shocked; we had all been watching the gradual depletion of personnel of all ranks and skills to fill the ravenous demands of that mean, unpopular war. Everyone in the army knew that a tour in Viet Nam was always a possibility.

At that point the putative hospital was "on paper;" and consisted only of a batch of tents, vehicles and equipment stored at Fort Benning. The general told me that I had *carte blanche* to select staff from

any army installation not in Viet Nam. I thought of all my friends who would be somewhat less than ecstatic at being selected, uprooted from their comfortable teaching hospital assignments and dispatched to that nasty place. I began to compile lists of physicians and nurses that I would like to serve on my staff; it would be the hottest medical organization anyone had ever assembled in the army. In all seriousness, I knew that none of my old friends would be very happy, but they all knew the score.

I broke the news to Stella and the kids; they had sort of been expecting it too. By now they were familiar with the sudden demands of the army. But we all agreed that two wars in one career grossly exceeded our estimate of the risks of our Faustian pact. I was soon to be promoted to full colonel, but I knew that command of a general hospital in a combat zone would probably lead to a star, if I didn't screw up.

I bought new fatigues and boots and stripped down and oiled up my old 45 from Korea (happily, yet to be fired in anger). My indispensable departmental sergeant major (who made the top of my personnel list) and I were scheduled to fly to Fort Benning to survey our equipment. After my Korean experience, I was very worried about what some Pentagon bureaucrat might consider "essential equipment" to operate a general hospital in a combat zone. I was not about to head out "in harm's way" with less than a full complement of modern hospital goodies. No more mystery foot lockers. Orders were being cut to alert my new personnel. During sleepless nights, my head was boiling with ideas. I needed to get input from my new medical staff about their specific equipment needs and personnel requirements. I must take key staff on a preliminary trip to Viet Nam to inspect possible hospital sites, establish liaison with units we would support, etc., etc. There was so much about administration that I needed to learn. The challenge was daunting but undeniably stimulating. I admit it, I was brimming with confidence; my hubris was soaring.

The day before the sergeant and I were to leave for Benning, General Blount called me in. "Your orders have been cancelled. They will

not be sending a general hospital to Da Nang in the foreseeable future." I will confess I was deflated. From my initial surprise and ambivalence, I had developed a full head of steam and was looking forward to my first hospital command. To my knowledge a general hospital was never sent to Da Nang. Within weeks, I was on orders to become chief of medicine at Brooke Army Medical Center. Their internal medicine program was in trouble. We loved El Paso, but we also adored San Antonio and Fort Sam Houston. We knew them well.

# 19

## *Tour Two at Fort Sam*

◆

## *(...variations on the teaching theme)*

The move across Texas was our easiest. Steven was away at St. Johns and Jon was in high spirits. Biddie decided to come with us; El Paso held nothing for her. The Twomeys were out of her life. We moved into a fine old house on the edge of a golf course on "Colonel's Row" adjacent to the main hospital. The house was not as big as our Beaumont manse, but it was newer and brighter. My staff, once again, was excellent, a mix of seasoned old timers and whiz kids from university medical school faculties repaying their military obligation. Very soon the teaching program was sailing along. I was still making occasional forays to Houston and Cape Canaveral doing pre- and post flight physical examinations on Gemini crews. But participating in NASA programs was becoming more of a time problem as I became ever more deeply immersed in teaching and writing.

It was during one of my NASA trips to Bermuda awaiting the touchdown of Gemini 5 that Jon decided to expand his career as a budding delinquent. We had traded the magnificent (but aging) Merc wagon for a new Subaru station wagon. One night Jon, quite aware that Stella slept soundly after taking her now-customary secobarbital, slipped out his window and "borrowed" the Subaru. He was 15 and, of course, did not have a license; we had no idea that he could drive. With some friends he wandered about the area for several hours, and then managed to mire the car in deep mud trying to cross a stream on a

remote part of Fort Sam Houston. This time the MPs made a house call. This embarrassment was compounded by our discovery that Jon was either giving or selling prescription drugs, swiped from our medicine cabinet. Motive? To be "one of the guys." We had no indication that he was into hard drugs, but we suspected pot.

Summer was approaching and Stella and I decided to send Jon to a "boot camp" for some "tough love" discipline. We heard about a camp near Carlsbad in California run by a retired army colonel. They advertised that they offered remedial classes (Jon had flunked a course during the regular year) and a lot of physical activity. We were not sanguine about how it would play out, but we were more than a little desperate. We drove out, met the Colonel, who seemed a reasonable enough chap, and deposited Jon with much tearfulness and growling. We had a wretched ride home, replete with unalloyed parental guilt. We were soon to reap the whirlwind. About two weeks later, after many phone calls of dubious reassurance ("the food is lousy but the place is okay"), we received a late night call from the Colonel in a wild state of conflagration. "You had best come and get your little monster before I have him put in jail." Slam!

We fled to Carlsbad non-stop. The crime? Jon and a colleague had constructed a Molotov cocktail (Heathkit?) and fire-bombed a vacant tool shed. Jon admitted being the ringleader. It cost 100 bucks plus the lost tuition for the last four weeks. No charges were filed, but we were beginning to inch up on punishable crime. So I decided that we needed some one-on-one, father-son time. The summer was still young, so I took two weeks leave and bundled Jon and a stash of camping gear into the Subaru wagon. We took off for a "binding" adventure in Mexico. The trip got mixed reviews.

We camped all the way: the pleasant mountains near Horsetail Falls in Monterrey, beach at Vera Cruz, Chapultepec Park in Mexico City, Aztec pyramids, floating gardens at Xochimilco, park in Cuernavaca, beach at Acapulco. I let Jon drive part of the way. He grumbled a lot about the discomfort of camping. But I thought we were having fun.

After about 10 days his grousing became unrelenting and unpalatable. So from Acapulco, we streaked for home. I am not sure we "bonded" (whatever the hell that means), but we did a lot of campfire yakking and did get to know each other better. He was a complex bundle of intellectual energy; his compliment of skills resided in areas beyond my ken. After our "Mexican adventure" Jon seemed to stay out of trouble (at least it never came to our attention again). A few years later he told me that the trip to Mexico had been the "high point of his life." (Many years after that we rafted the Colorado River from below Lake Powell to Phantom Ranch—through the upper Grand Canyon. It was a better outing.) But several months post-Mexico, memories about bitching over gritty hamburgers, sand flies, belly cramps and sleeping on hard, lumpy deserted beaches, had subsided. Nice thing about the human brain; it tends to decant unpleasant memories.

One of the more engaging experiences at Brooke was the "Disaster Preparedness" exercise. These were periodic drills coordinated with the police and fire departments of San Antonio, designed to test our capability to handle a sudden influx of a horde of badly traumatized civilian patients. It had been done once previously, before my time, but on this occasion the simulation was an airplane crash at the airport. We had briefings on "mass casualty" procedures, and special equipment was pre-positioned for such an eventuality. Every member of the staff was trained for a specific task and assigned the "proper place to be" when the whistle blew.

We knew it would happen within the next few weeks, but the exact date and time were secret. As chief of medicine (and former battalion surgeon in Korea), I was designated "chief of triage." I had a team of three other physicians: two surgeons and a pediatrician who would make the critical "Immediate" (hustle to surgery), "Intermediate" (treat but delay surgery until the Immediates are cared for), or "Expectant" (a euphemism for little hope—relieve pain but survival is unlikely under the exigent circumstances). I oversaw all decisions.

The call came about 10:00 A.M. We were to receive 30 to 40 critically injured, burned and/or traumatized patients within 20 minutes. The "patients" had all been briefed on how to "act" and then "moulaged" with fake wounds reflecting varying degrees of horrific pathology. They were labeled with emergency medical tags, indicating what their condition had been and what treatment, if any, had been administered en route to the hospital. Soon the ambulances began wailing in, and the action rapidly became very realistic. The triage area was the scene of great drama. "Life and death" decision-making was organized but still frantic.

Apparently, one of the scenario writers had decided to interject a few "crazies;" passengers who were not badly injured but had become hysterical. These were handled with tender reassurance and "tranquilizers" (syringes filled with saline that had been designated as containing sedative drugs). But one large fellow was inconsolable; he refused to lie on a litter. He actually began to wrestle with attendants, shouting loudly and disrupting the triage process, interfering with the care of other patients. I thought he was flagrantly over-acting. But such *outré* behavior was always possible in a real situation.

I called for two burly attendants to pin him down and hit him with a large dose of fast-acting barbiturate. (All simulated, of course.) But the "script monitor" called for us to have exhausted our tranquilizer supply (a gratuitous touch of Hitchcock, I thought). Okay, so we had to be realistic. I called for two more corpsmen and the four of them put one litter fore and another aft (face and back), lashed with leather straps, and had them trundle the screaming, writhing bundle into a supply closet out of sight and sound.

The frenetic main exercise lasted for several more hours, and everyone was exhausted. Of course, our effort was being monitored and graded by a team of ubiquitous medical observers. Finally, about 5:00 PM, the drill was called. We all crashed and shared cokes and pizza. We did our own informal critique, and began to swap anecdotes. Sud-

denly, I remembered our "hysterical actor." He had been locked in the supply closet for about six hours! We all raced to fetch him with some fear that we might have precipitated some true disaster. But we found him quite asleep—still tightly bound between the canvas litters. We gave him the "best actor" award and broke out the beer. I don't think I earned too many points for that "field expedient" decision. (These days when the threat of chemical and/or biological and/or nuclear assault by small groups of ideological lunatics is quite real, it would seem the country is ill prepared. The national attention span seems to be dangerously short. I hope those who are tasked to try to prevent or manage domestic terror are being realistic. The tension between curtailing certain civil liberties and trying to protect us against violence is always a conundrum. I hope we have the wisdom to achieve a reasonable balance.)

As we were closing in on "retirement at 20" I investigated a few job offers. Both were intriguing (no seductive "Paradise Island" proposals). I was invited to Boston to be interviewed as a candidate for the job as editor of the *New England Journal of Medicine.* I knew that Dr. Joe Garland, the venerable clinician-editor, had announced his retirement. I was flattered and confused at the invitation, since I had always thought of the NEJM as a Boston "old boys" enclave, not likely to seriously entertain non-Boston clinicians as editors. Also, the only two physicians in Boston who really knew me were Denny Adams (who was so helpful in getting "Diseases of Medical Progress" published in NEJM) and Bill Crosby, the wonderful hematologist, who had recently joined the faculty at Tufts after retiring from Walter Reed. Neither had direct connections to the journal.

I was interviewed by a senior endocrinologist from Harvard who was very pleasant and impressively thorough. He knew of my teaching and writing. I think he liked me, but I didn't believe I had enough academic firepower to land such a prestigious job. That evening I had chowder and clams with Bill in the giant seafood amphitheater in Faneuil Hall. I didn't get the job; it went to Franz Ingelfinger, a distin-

guished Harvard gastroenterologist. If I had to get whupped, it could not have been by a more worthy physician. In later years we became good friends; Franz was most helpful to me in later years in another career—when I became editor of the *Journal of the American Medical Association* (JAMA).

Later in the year, Dr. Bill Levin a hematologist from the University of Texas Medical Branch at Galveston who was one of our teaching consultants at Brooke, sought me out. The medical school was seeking a new dean. "Would you be interested?" Of course. So Stella and I drove the T-bird down to Galveston Bay. I was interviewed by the president of the medical school, Dr. Truman Blocker. He bore a striking resemblance to his younger brother, Dan, of "Bonanza" fame. He was "Texas warm" and down-home friendly. We spoke for over an hour; I met with key staff and faculty; we toured the sprawling institution. I told him of my philosophy of education and my beliefs about running a medical school: hands-on all the way in faculty selection and promotion, student selection, curriculum revision when needed, imbuing students with the need to integrate compassion and caring into their professional lives, appropriate designation of authority but retaining ultimate decision-making power, etc., etc. I would participate in fund-raising, but that was not my primary interest (or skill.) I didn't say it, but I thought I would make one helluva dean. After all this he turned and looked me in the eye and said, "How soon **can** (not could) you come?" I told him within a few months, since the army would have to replace me at Brooke. I was elated; Stella and I celebrated at a seafood restaurant on the beach.

I never heard from Truman Blocker! After a month I called Bill Levin; he said the job had gone to some pediatrician from Los Angeles. He was unaware that I had not been notified. He also hinted that the decision probably was made **before** I had visited Galveston, unbeknownst to him. Shabby, shabby, shabby. I was sorely pissed. Galveston had missed its chance to become a great medical school. It is still second rate.

One of the more exciting events at Brooke was the arrival of LBJ for any one of several medical needs. During my tenure the Great Man's visits were the occasion of intensive preparation and universal anxiety. The roof of one of the wings of the main hospital building had been reinforced to handle the refurbished Huey chopper that was his Texas version of Air Force One. LBJ was known to be very consistent during his San Antonio sojourns—always in evil temper. And this annual physical visit was no exception. My staff had the unpleasant tasks of performing his general physical examination, drawing blood, taking his ECG and performing his sigmoidoscopic examination (there was an apocryphal family history of colon cancer). The ECG went reasonably well until someone handed the nervous nurse a too-hot towel to wipe the gooey ECG paste off the presidential chest. She dropped the towel directly on the hairy patch and the Great Man howled with imperial rage. The reverse happened with the carefully pre-warmed sigmoido-scope; it was still "too damned cold."

Then someone heard LBJ screaming at a Secret Service stalwart, "Git the chopper fueled up; we're headed for Llano." "Yessir." The burly agent must have been new; he dashed from the room. "Where the hell is Llano? Christ, it could be Llano, Nigeria or Llano, Bolivia! Somebody get a goddamn map." In the furor of milling aides, pilots and Secret Service agents, one of the corpsmen ventured, "Sir, its just north of Fredericksburg, up highway 16, right here in Texas up near LBJ's ranch." Silence, relief, backslaps; another national emergency quelled.

We had just about settled in for our final army tour at Brooke when the omniscient hand of General Leonard Heaton struck again. I was on orders to become chief of medicine at Walter Reed Army Medical Center, the most prestigious teaching assignment in the Army Medical Service! What a terrific climax to my military-medical career! The family was less than elated. But Jon would finish high school in Silver Spring at Montgomery-Blair, one of the best in the country. Steven was away at St. Johns. Stella could get another shot at college at George

Washington. But another move in such a short time was not easy. Biddie agreed to come to Washington with us. It was 1968.

# 20

## *Final Days at Walter Reed*

✦

### *(the Eisenhower et al experience…)*

Somewhat to our chagrin, we were ordered to live on-post in a very small house near the hospital. It was far below the standard we had come to expect at Brooke and Beaumont. I knew the commanding general, Fred Hughes, who had succeeded Bob Blount at Beaumont, so I made a friendly pitch to live off-post. His wife, Martha, had become close buddies with Stella during the latter days at Beaumont. But Hughes was insistent that all his principal staff members live close at hand. All the chiefs of service were housed in a tight circle of not-too-cute, diminutive cottages. We did manage to arrange for Biddie to have her own room and bath.

It was a turbulent time in the District (as in Watts and Detroit). The riots and burnings had occurred just a few blocks from the Walter Reed campus. But the chief reason for proximity of key staff was the presence of Ike and Mamie Eisenhower. I have often epitomized this year at Walter Reed as Julius Caesar had described Gaul. However, the medical center was not divided into "three parts", but rather two: Eisenhower and the other 950 patients. Staff, resources and energy were about equally divided.

It was an extraordinary situation. Ike and Mamie had moved into a modest suite just off Ward Eight, the "exclusive VIP medical facility," as the press liked to call it. Ike was suffering severe cardiac problems, most notably recurrent attacks of ventricular tachycardia, plus less fre-

quent flare-ups of his Crohn's Disease. His room was adjacent to a small suite occupied by Mamie. Vigilance was the watchword; Ike was monitored by ECG, 24 hours a day. There was always a nurse at his bedside and teams of three physicians just outside his door, observing the constantly-running electrocardiogram. Every physician on my staff stood an eight-hour watch. Those in specialties unfamiliar with electrocardiography were given a crash course, but every team was staffed by a cardiologist or a resident in cardiology or a resident in medicine. Ike's attacks would strike with frightening rapidity. He would be speaking to someone, the ECG would ignite with the rapid ventricular rate and within seconds he would be unconscious. At the first sign of a rhythm disturbance, most often before unconsciousness, the team would be at the bedside with defibrillation paddles at the ready. Once or twice Ike continued to speak for almost 30 seconds before the loss of cardiac output affected his brain. It would be too cruel to zap him while he was still awake and suffer the sudden jolt. Magically, within a few seconds of the defibrillation-cardioversion shock, he would be awake and alert. The conversation would continue. He always knew what had occurred, but it did not seem to depress this remarkable man. Astonishingly, over the course of the year he was defibrillated 72 times! I suspect those data belong in Guinness.

Senior staff all got to know The General (It seemed easier to call him "General" than "Mr. President;" he never expressed a preference). He was truly amazing, endowed with astonishing clarity of memory. Ike could recall the names of junior officers, even landing craft that had been involved in the Normandy invasion. Most of his conversation was military, very little political. He was always warm, magnanimous and appreciative of all the effort on his behalf. The media were in a constant froth for news about our celebrated patient. All major news networks had vans posted on the hospital grounds; some reporters had Ike as their sole "story." Each evening about 4:00, the Surgeon General, Leonard Heaton, would join Colonel Bob Hall, the Walter Reed cardiologist who was managing the case, General Hughes and me for a

briefing about the day's progress. Then we would craft a brief, buoyant news release.

Bob and his cardiology fellows did a superb job; he would often seek our counsel, and occasionally call on other army cardiologists for advice. But Bob Hall called the shots. Contrary to the circus that had ensued years earlier, when Eisenhower had been admitted to Fitzsimmons Army Medical Center with his original myocardial infarction, when foxy old Paul Dudley White and foxy old Brigadier Tom Mattingly squared off, we did not feel the need for outside experts. The medical problems were forthright, even if the management was difficult and the prognosis ominous.

Ike had many distinguished visitors, always limited to brief chats. Candidate Nixon came twice for "blessings," but I never felt he was "anointed." I had the impression (never expressed in words) that Ike regarded Dick as a slightly wifty child, who was nevertheless a member of the family. On one occasion, Nixon took several of us aside after visiting Ike and gave us a cheery little pep talk. He felt obliged to remind us that Ike was a great man and that we should do "everything in our power to keep him alive and comfortable. The country needs him." It was so god damned patronizing that I had to bite my tongue. Never voted for the smarmy bastard.

Mamie was in and out like a wraith. We were all impressed with her gentleness and total devotion. She always wanted to know what was going on, but she never questioned our judgment. She was aware and appreciative of the unprecedented care. Contrary to the asinine press, Mamie occasionally had a bit of wine with dinner or when a friends dropped in for a few hands of bridge, but no one ever saw her tipsy. If anyone had a reason for an occasional bender, it was she. But no one of my staff ever witnessed anything but a kindly, soft-spoken, always immaculately groomed First Lady.

Ward Eight, just down the corridor from the Eisenhower Suite was the personal fiefdom of Leonard Heaton. He kept a small office there. No one, regardless of rank or importance could be admitted without

the blessing of the Eternal Surgeon General. It was a symbol of some prestige for any congressman, even senator, to be admitted. Strangely, members of the Armed Forces Committee, appropriations committees and other key (to the army) legislators seemed to get the Heaton nod before all others. Supreme Court justices and cabinet members were always welcome. At one time, on this 10 bed enclave we had Justice W.O. Douglas, Senators Margaret Chase Smith (Maine), Jimmy Byrnes (Georgia), later to be Secretary of State and Everett Dickson (Illinois).

I performed annual physical examinations on Strom Thurman and his lovely wife-to-be. Also, my clientele included Senator Daniel Inouye ("so you were stationed at Tripler; you must come back to the Islands") and half a dozen "important" congressmen. All were seen at General Heaton's request. Security on Ward Eight was screwed down tightly; avaricious reporters were always hovering. We had armed MPs stationed at either end of the access corridors. I had full-time staff assigned and made personal rounds every day. We followed "Moser's Dictum" for the care of VIPs, "They will get the same superb treatment as any G.I. on the ward; rank or status does not disqualify anyone from any diagnostic or therapeutic procedure that is medically indicated."

One of our celebrated patients was a senior senator from a southern state (whose name I am disinclined to record). He caused me considerable grief, precipitating my only confrontation with Fred Hughes. The senator was a chronic alcoholic, a recurring visitor to Ward Eight. On this occasion he was flown in from Brussels on a military aircraft. He arrived in incipient DTs. Heaton, Hughes and I conferred outside his room. The wretched man was pleading for "just a little bourbon..." I felt he could be managed with chlordiazepoxide (Librium), multi-vitamins and ample fluids. There was pressure to "ease him down" with alcohol. (This was before we had diazepam [Valium].) My management plan drew some flack from "higher authorities," and we had a bit of a brouhaha. Gently, I said to the general, "Either I will manage him,

or you will manage him; we can't both do it, Sir!" He was my patient. It took a few stormy days but the tumult subsided and the good senator survived. Once sober, he was the personification of charm and gentility, a most endearing man. A few months later he was admitted to another private hospital in Bethesda, and the event was leaked, noisily. A field day for the heartless harpies of the media. I think it was my Walter Reed experience that initiated my life-long disdain of the media.

During this time Jon was putting on light shows at high school parties and dances for money. He had devised a system that caused multicolored lights to blink in synchrony with recorded music, throbbing tom-tom beats punctuated by flashing strobes. It was a surreal experience. In his room he had removed all furniture (clothes were stacked in the closet), and he covered every square inch with aluminum foil. In that environment his music-light shows were nothing short of apoplectic. Jon had extraordinary talent, and he stayed out of trouble. Steven was enjoying St. Johns; he was maturing into a thoughtful, reflective adult.

We did some fun things in the department. I established liaison with the Armed Forces Institute of Pathology (AFIP) and the Walter Reed Institute of Research (WRAIR). They had world-class researchers and teachers, but, strangely, they had been rarely invited to participate in the teaching program at the hospital, although we shared the same campus. They added a dimension of panache to our program; my residents and fellows were exposed to state-of-the-art information. I also expanded our external consulting staff: Louis Weinstein, Leonard Berman, Bob Petersdorf, Don Seldin, Harold Jeghers and star faculty from Georgetown, Howard and G.W. came out to make teaching rounds, lecture and conduct Grand Rounds. Most of my senior staff members were given clinical faculty appointments at Georgetown.

I established what I called the "Circuit Rider" program. Smaller Class II army hospitals were usually located at camps in remote areas. They had little opportunity for good medical education, and I felt it

was unfair for the teaching hospitals to hoard all the talent. So I set up three "teaching circuits;" we called them "Paul Revere" (army hospitals in New England and Mid-Atlantic states); "Robert E. Lee" (army hospitals in the southeast); "Daniel Boone" (reached out to the Mississippi). We coordinated with army air at Fort Meade to fly to some hospitals; often we would use army sedans or private vehicles. Teams of three specialists (selected from cardiology, gastroenterology, pulmonary, endocrinology, pediatrics, etc.) would visit three circuit hospitals on a given tour. They would lecture, make rounds and consult on problem patients.

Once we were up and rolling, the plan was joined by surgery and psychiatry. It required a sergeant and secretary full-time to administer the logistics. I even persuaded the hospital comptroller to augment my budget. At first there was some reticence by staff, but soon they began to enjoy it. There were a few "adventures" with missed connections, arrival on the wrong date, etc. But the program began to fly after a few months. I was very proud of this effort.

There is no doubt that my teaching career reached its apogee at Walter Reed. Those were halcyon years; our faculty of whiz kids represented the best and the brightest in the Army Medical Corps. I was brash enough to believe I could have taken my staff and transported them to Harvard or Hopkins and conducted the internal medicine training without the slightest blip in quality from aspects of teaching or clinical research. Most of that Walter Reed staff went on to distinguished academic careers in university academic health centers or other army teaching hospitals.

It was during this year that I had another memorable "podium experience." I was still lecturing around the country on adverse drug reactions. On this occasion, I had been invited to address a group with the formidable title of "International Association of Military Surgeons." The meeting was being held at the old Shoreham Hotel on the edge of Rock Creek Park. As usual, I underestimated the Connecticut Avenue traffic and arrived a trifle late. I flew into the auditorium, passed my

slide carousel to the sweating projectionist and strode to the podium. As I was being introduced, I noticed there were about 200 people crowded into the room, and the first row of seats was just a few feet from the speaker's lectern. The lights were dimmed, my first slide appeared and I began. About into the third slide two gentlemen in about the fourth row suddenly erupted into an animated, mumbling conversation.

Now I was an old veteran on the medical Chautaqua circuit, and I realized you don't charm all the customers all the time. There are always mutterers, coughers, snorers and intermittent *soto voce* commentators. But this was ridiculous. These two jabberers were almost as noisy as I was. Worse yet, perhaps they were even more entertaining! I persevered for a few more slides but the voices persisted. So I blew my usual good-natured, easy-going *savoir faire*. I stopped my monologue, cut the slides and called for lights. I glared in their direction, "Gentlemen, if what you have to say is more important than what I am saying, please share it with the rest of us. If not, please cease and desist." There was a pregnant silence. I called for lights out, slides on and resumed my lecture, feeling marvelously self-righteous. Just a few minutes later a disembodied hand reached over the lectern and placed a note before me. I have it to this day, framed on my wall. It said, "That is the Russian Surgeon General and his interpreter." I think I set glasnost back about five years!

At Christmas, Steven came home during his second year at St. Johns. In his characteristic low-key fashion, he dropped a bomb. "I think I want to go to medical school." He quickly acknowledged our previous conversation on the subject: the significant difficulty of getting into medical school with a "no pre-med courses, no-grades, St. Johns great books" pedigree. The situation was possibly more complicated than a simple change of heart. We all knew that Steven was vulnerable for the Viet Nam draft, but he had received no notification. I hated the war. I made no bones about it being a wrong war, against the wrong people and for the wrong reasons. And it was being directed by

the wrong crowd (mostly micromanaged [daily bombing targets, yet!] by ersatz civilian "tacticians" in the War Room at the White house, whose strategy and tactics were dominated by political considerations!) It was sure formula for military disaster.

Of course, I would go if called upon, but I was an officer in the regular army. But in my heart (and Stella's), we were adamantly against Steven going to Viet Nam, if he were threatened with call-up. Privately, Stella and I discussed advising him to make a prolonged visit to family in Canada or friends in Sweden, before the issue arose. I realized that such a decision could represent a major problem for the rest of his life, but we agreed to support whatever course he elected. At the time, we elected not discuss this with him; thankfully, we never had to. By the grace of God, soon thereafter, he was accepted to medical school.

But at the outset, acceptance to a medical school was a big problem. I spoke to his dean. I knew that other St. Johnnies had gone to medical school, but not very many. The dean was an impressive intellect; he offered his deeply felt belief that Steven had the unusual talent and the temperament to make a fine philosopher, perhaps even a teacher-scholar. He even alluded to the possibility of a future on the faculty at St. Johns. I was moved and thanked him for his endorsement of Steven's intellectual prowess, but I prevailed on him to arrange for the dons to create numerical grades for the benefit of stuffy medical school admissions committees. He complied with some reluctance.

That only left biology, organic chemistry, and physics (the heart and soul of the pre-med curriculum!) to be completed. A tall order. So after much scurrying we found that Steven could take summer courses at Stanford (designed primarily for undergrads who had flunked during the regular school year).

We had old army friends, the Schlegels (whose son Robbie had been Steven's surfing buddy on Oahu) living in Palo Alto. They were eager to have Steven as a houseguest for the summer. It turned out to be the toughest summer of his young life. The relaxed Socratic dialectic of St. Johns did not prepare him for the forced draft of organic chemistry

and physics. Later Steven said it was far more difficult than medical school. But he made it. The next summer he got his biology credits from a tutor on Maui (where we were living post-army). He was accepted at Southwestern and Georgetown. With Don Seldin holding forth in Dallas, solid academic virtue won over tenuous alma mater loyalty. No contest.

I could have stayed at Walter Reed for decades. But I had made a promise to Stella that I would get out after 20 years and fulfill her dream of settling down in private practice. We had been in for 22, and it had not been all fun and games for her. She still had problems with insomnia and depression; the cigarettes were unrelenting. The big question was what career path to follow. I had several offers from medical schools, but I would be the "new boy" faculty member at age 46. I would start as an associate professor, perhaps full professor at a lesser school. But after being chief of medicine at Walter Reed, I thought that would be too tough on my delicate ego. So we began to explore areas for private practice. We talked about it endlessly, exploring all options.

We had enjoyed Hawaii so much that we decided to explore opportunities in the Islands. The two major clinics in Honolulu were possibilities; I knew senior clinicians at each from our Tripler hospital days. But Honolulu we both agreed that it was just another urban sprawl with palm trees. Not our cup of tea. I flew out and visited Hilo; it rained for 48 hours. I had loved Kauai during my Mercury days at Kokee, but it was a general practice-oriented community with a one-horse hospital. Just too primitive, medically. On Maui, one of my old colleagues from Tripler, Dr. Bert Weeks, an internist who had run the out-patient service, belonged to the Maui Medical Group. It was a small multi-specialty group with two internists, two general surgeons, one Ob-Gyn, three family physicians, a pediatrician and an EENT physician. I would be the third internist. I would do cardiology, hematology, oncology and general internal medicine. The hospital was small but seemed adequate. We thought—this was the place.

The next hurdle was retiring. I was advised that "by tradition" any chief of department at Walter Reed who sought to retire, was obliged to pay his respects to Lieutenant General Leonard Heaton—in person. Of course, he knew me well from the Eisenhower experience, but it was a meeting I was not anticipating with any vestige of joy. Colonel Paul Teschan, chief at WRAIR, was also about to retire; we thought we should make our obeisance together. Strength in numbers and all that. Paul and I had known each other off and on for many years. We made an appointment and on the given day, polished our brass to high gleam, straightened our ribbons and sat, hats in hand, outside The Office. A crisp major-aide soon appeared and beckoned me, "Colonel Moser, General Heaton will see you now." As I entered the room, I was not sure whether I should salute, uncovered. So I saluted (better stupid than disrespectful). The great man acknowledged my salute. "Colonel Moser, so you're retiring?" He stood up and I muttered a faint yes. He extended his hand, "Good luck." It took about 30 seconds. I suspect I had expected (hoped for?) at least some minor expression of regret, or even the dangle of a star, or something. (After all he had dispatched me to Salt Lake for hematology, sent me to Command and General Staff school at Leavenworth and brought me to Walter Reed!) As the door closed behind me, Paul said, "How did it go?" I smiled, "Well, it was quick." Paul was out in about 35 seconds. We figured that the general had been down this road before. It's a big army. Welcome to the real world.

(I have often reflected upon our years in the army. While it was financial need that prompted our move into the army in 1948, I have never regretted a minute. Stella may have had other feelings, and perhaps the boys as well. But professionally it could not have been more rewarding. It was the "Golden Age" of army medicine. I like to think that by trouble-shooting ailing residency programs at Tripler, Beaumont, Brooke and Walter Reed, I brought university-quality internal medicine training to our programs. My staff and residents fanned out to other institutions and carried the educational message. The army

provided me the opportunity to take fellowships in pulmonary diseases, cardiology and hematology, thereby greatly expanding my teaching repertoire. What I learned as chief resident at Georgetown and participating in the programs at the Brigham in Boston, Osler at Hopkins, and Western Reserve, was carried directly into the army programs. By 1969, all army teaching hospitals had accredited internal medicine programs boasting ABIM passage rates as high as any good university teaching hospital.

Our assignments to felicitous places like Salzburg, San Antonio, Honolulu, El Paso and Washington, D.C. were some of the best the army had to offer. We opted for Salt Lake City, and in a perverse, retrospective way, even Korea was good for me—a maturing experience. The downside: frequent moves and social disruption. I know that Stella would have preferred settling down in one place, and I don't know what the boys' reaction has been. Certainly they gained in sophistication and appreciation of other cultures, races, climates and people. Military kids fall into two groups; either they mature, thrive and adapt to situations more easily than most, or they crash and burn emotionally. I have seen both phenomena. I like to think than Steven and Jon are better people for their military experience.

I have often wondered "what might have been" if we had remained for 30. I think I would have had a good chance for a star and even a shot at Surgeon General. Perhaps my hubris is showing. But there had never been a Jewish Surgeon General (perhaps it was high time). I had a combat tour in Korea; I went to Leavenworth C & G college; my professional credentials were as good or better than any other colonel in the medical corps. So…who knows? But then I would have never tasted so many other career delights, nor would I have met Linda. Better the way it happened.)

Within a few months of the farewell entreaty by General Heaton, we drove to the coast by way of Santa Fe to watch Steven gather up his B.A. He had a prissy new girl friend; she made no bones about her disdain for macho army types. It was not a comfortable time. I played

softball on a "fathers team" that whipped the pants off the graduating seniors. I hit a homerun. The kids were better at Plato and Pythagoras than Doubleday and DiMaggio.

# 21

## *Maui I*

✦

### *(culture shock like you would not believe...)*

S tella flew out to Maui in advance to house hunt. With Bert and Pat Weeks (my old army colleague from the Maui Medical Group), she found a place that seemed ideal. Breathless and excited over the phone, she described a bungalow "with great potential." It sat on about three and a half acres in a little town called Haiku on the old back road to Hana. It had been the home of the last Libby pineapple plantation "luna" (overseer), but had been vacant for some time. The back end of the property boasted a mature grove of eucalyptus and one could see a crescent of sea from the small front lanai. She said there was a competing bid and time was critical. The price was right; I told her I trusted her judgment. If she liked the place—close. It was the best real estate deal we ever made. Within months of moving in, we added a glorious bedroom with six ceiling skylights and windows on three sides, an elegant sunroom-library, a wrap-around deck and an oval, heated pool. Then we had the wood exterior sheathed in off-white vinyl and added a new shake-shingle roof. The little "luna" bungalow was transformed. God bless home-owner loans.

Within weeks we made the acquaintance of Mildred and Akira Ichikawa. Our name had been given to them by the lei-making Omuras, who had been our neighbors in Foster Village, back during our army days in Honolulu. The Ichikawas ran a modest plant nursery just around the bend of the road in Haiku. Aki was impressively handsome;

he had the mien of a traditional Samurai warrior. He had been a foreman for Libby for some 30 years and had recently retired to start the nursery. He was wise, thoughtful and close to the earth. Mildred was effervescent, cheerful; in Yiddish she would have been called a *baleboste*. It was rare for "haoli malahinis" (white newcomers) to receive such instant aloha from an island Japanese family. Our mutual affection was deep and enduring.

On many occasions Stella and I would return from town to find a new hibiscus plant or a young coconut palm artfully planted in our ample front lawn. They helped us create a most felicitous tropical landscape over the years. We enjoyed dinner at their home on many occasions; Mildred made the best *namasu* salad and pineapple upside-down cake in the world. We would reciprocate by taking them to Chinese dinners in Kahalui. But they far exceeded our efforts in generosity and hospitality.

Tragedy came to the Ichikawas when their youngest son, Ronald, was killed in a motorcycle accident. They never quite recovered. Aki, especially, was completely devastated unto long bouts of tearful silence. Their elder son was soon married and a lovely boy grandchild assuaged some of their anguish. Mildred and Aki had never been away from the Islands. Rare excursions to Honolulu had been their only adventures distant from Maui. Their dream was to tour the Mainland, but cost and some intimidation at the prospect, had precluded much beyond wishful thinking. Stella and I proposed that we pool our resources ("dollar for dollar") and make an automobile trip through the golden west. Together we planned to visit San Francisco (we had friends living in Piedmont who could put us up for a few days), ogle the Big Sur country, swing east though Paso Robles, cross over to Yosemite, climb Tioga Pass, gamble a bit in Las Vegas (Mildred almost swooned at the prospect of popping quarters into eager bandits), then gawk at the South Rim of Grand Canyon and return via Hollywood/Los Angeles.

Stella was appointed treasurer; every few days she would collect 50 bucks from me and Mildred for the pool. Actually, we (unobtrusively)

paid for the car rental, gasoline and whenever else we could avoid tapping into the "fund." It worked out wonderfully. They took a million pictures. For many years thereafter, the "Mainland Album" would be trotted out for guests to share the exciting odyssey. Small payment for their overwhelming kindness and generosity over the years.

Many years later, when Stella and I were living in Vorhees, New Jersey, Mildred called and said that Aki was very ill. We knew that he had sustained some sort of mysterious febrile disorder that had baffled his physicians. But now he was losing weight and was quite weak. Mildred was afraid he was going to die. I called his physician on Maui. Aki had a malignancy of the liver; it had been unresponsive to chemotherapy (all of them usually are). I flew to Maui and spent a few days with Aki and Mildred. He was agonal but still smiled, and we "talked story." He died a few weeks after I left. (Many years later, Linda and I visited Maui and spent an afternoon with Mildred. She was older and grayer, and she had returned to Las Vegas several times on gambling junkets. With a small tear or two she turned the pages of the well-worn "Mainland Album" for Linda.)

Private practice was true culture shock. At Walter Reed, I had been insulated from daily hands-on patient care by leagues of staff and house officers. I made rounds every day and saw a few VIP patients. But here on Maui I was one of three internists in a small clinic on a small island. It was the end of the pipeline; I was the "new boy from the big city." Within 48 hours of reporting to the office, I was called to see a patient in consultation. She was the 63-year-old wife of another physician. This poor soul had been in the hospital for several weeks and was in desperate condition from some "obscure cardiovascular condition." She was pathetically orthopneic (short of breath sitting up), cyanotic and edematous. It did not take any genius to detect rather quickly that she had a constrictive pericarditis with tamponade (fluid compressing her heart).

I called for a pericardiocentesis tray (to aspirate the fluid). The chief nurse said, "What is that?" I said, "Get me something to do a chest tap

with the largest bore spinal needle you can find." They delivered an ample 14 guage giant. As I assembled my tools, I realized that I had not tapped a pericardium since I had been a fellow in chest diseases. And that had been 21 years ago! To add to the melodrama, the chief nurse asked if the nursing students could watch, since, to her knowledge, no one had ever done a pericardiocentesis in that hospital before! It was a thoroughly hair-raising experience. By the grace of God, I tapped into the bulging sack on the second attempt. But the poor soul had pericardial effusion secondary to extensive metastases and died a few weeks later. Rough introduction!

I can best summarize my experience in private practice by saying that it was exhilarating and exhausting. As the "new guy from Walter Reed" (as I overheard in the doctor's lounge), I inherited a flock of tough patients. The consultation "ground rules" on Maui were somewhat bizarre. It seemed that if the patient was very ill (usually with something chronic and/or incurable), I inherited responsibility. If it was something acute and the patient would likely recover, the referring physician retained responsibility. It was somewhat frustrating, but I rolled with the punch.

Soon I realized that I had not worked so hard since I had been an intern. My patients were wonderful. They were mostly second and third generation Japanese with a scattering of haolis, Filipinos, Hawaiians and every conceivable cosmopolitan mix. They did everything I told them to do; trust was implicit. In return, they expected me to make them well or, at least, feel much better. I suspect that Maui in 1969 might have been one of the last bastions in America where physicians were honored and respected by patients. There had never been a malpractice suit. (There have been quite a few in recent years, *triste dictu*.)

Quite soon I ran into another curious but most vexing situation. For over 10 years I had been running internal medicine training programs in army teaching hospitals. Competence in house officers and fellows was easy to assess. We saw our charges at morning report and

on daily rounds, reviewed their charts, listened to their presentations. We lived medicine with them. The oversight of physicians in training stands in sharp contrast to the "policing" of physicians in private practice. I had never really thought much about it before. In theory, one could graduate from medical school, pass the state board examination and then practice for the rest of one's life—without ever being tested for clinical competence again! One might think that with residency training and specialty boards and all that, such a singular escape from any future "test of competence" would be rare. It is not, and this deficiency came to my attention in a dramatic way.

I encountered a distinguished, elderly, silver-haired general practitioner, disarmingly charming and much beloved by his patients. Yet he was frankly incompetent. My concerns about this physician were widely shared by the nurses and other doctors. This gentle old man was a menace to very sick patients. Yet, he was strangely tolerated. After about a dozen "around 2:00 AM" frantic, almost-too-late emergency consultations, I sought out the department chief and indicated that something had to be done.

The response was stony silence. Here is the short version of what transpired. I was advised by a lawyer on retainer by the hospital, that "old Bill" was very much venerated in the community, and everyone knew "he had a few problems," but no one had ever complained about him. I became an instant pariah—the uppity, smart-alecky new kid on the block—the whistle-blower. But I was so alarmed for his patients that I persisted. With the begrudging consent of the lawyer, the chief of staff authorized **me** to review his situation. I studied some 30 randomly selected charts going back five years. They were replete (when legible) with too-many egregious errors of commission and omission. I presented the data to a rather hostile *ad hoc* committee of peers. I "succeeded," insofar that his privileges were "limited" (not defined), but all patients he admitted were to be seen in consultation for the next three months. It was a cautionary slap on the wrist. It had been an emotional ordeal for me, but quite a lesson. Yes, I would do it again, but I can

understand the ambient reticence of most physicians to "become involved."

(The cold fact is that the civilized western concept of "due process" requires an inordinate dedication of time and effort by those willing [morally compelled?] to make the accusation. In medicine, as in other arenas, there is also the threat of embarrassing and costly litigation to individual whistle-blowers and institutions. It is a challenge that American medicine has failed to tackle since it will require a sea-change in physician attitudes ("don't we already have enough problems from the lawyers and bureaucrats...?") and a major overhaul of tort law. Certainly fear of litigation and some social isolation by colleagues are mitigating factors, but they are not an excuse to tolerate the flagrantly incompetent.

I have advocated [in my active years in medicine] that we must install formal mechanisms to protect those moved to take action and investigate their allegations. Of course, due process must be honored, but we must provide legal immunity for the investigators while ensuring that bias, frivolous claims, or personal vendettas are never factors. Tall order? Of course. But similar mechanisms are already in place in several institutions. They must become universal.

While on my soapbox, I feel obliged to comment on the "marginally incompetent" clinicians, the largest group and perhaps the most difficult to identify and help. Evaluating the clinical competence of practicing physicians is as difficult as assessment of "quality" in medical management. We do neither very well, but we are learning. Bravely, the American Board of Internal Medicine has floated a revolutionary new plan to try to assess (for purposes of periodic recertification) the clinical competence (intellectually and psychologically) of all ABIM internists. The program is still in painful evolution, and, thus far, most internists have greeted the early version with considerable skepticism.

One of the great ironies in contemporary medicine is the phenomenon that reliable, practical clinical information has never been more readily accessible, yet is far from broad application at the bedside and

clinic. The concept of "evidence-based medicine" derived from carefully designed randomized-controlled trials, objective reviews of peer-reviewed medical literature, even meta-analysis [of many related randomized studies] has placed clinical information at the fingers of every physician in the country through books, journals and the Internet. Yet periodic surveys indicate that too many of our colleagues do not take advantage of this capability. By way of example, quite recently I read that despite guidelines issued by the NIH in **1997** about management of asthma [which has undergone an unprecedented increase in mortality among children in recent years—5000 deaths per year, accounting for a third of all lost school days by children], 80% of doctors were **not** performing any type of lung function assessment [in asthmatic children]—a critical step in management, and only 25% knew that inhaled corticosteroids were recommended as first-line treatment for moderate to severe asthma. Astonishing! I could cite dozens of similar examples of failure to provide well-established diagnostic and therapeutic care by working practitioners.

How to translate the achievements of clinical research into reality in the trenches remains elusive. But now in the computer age, "real time" information based on solid clinical information [several new websites] is at the fingertips of every clinician who owns a computer. Of course, I realize that we cannot begin to test those other terribly important intangibles of medical care: taking time to listen, kindness, compassion, attention to detail, follow up, etc. But a fundamental knowledge of contemporary diagnostic and therapeutic information is an absolute prerequisite. Perhaps the new ABIM "recertification" experiment will evolve to a point where it is accepted by the profession. Certainly, we must do something about the "good old Bills" still flailing about out there. Let us hope so.)

But back to Maui. To keep my hand in teaching, I ran the professional program for the hospital. Not quite Walter Reed, but rather a breakfast meeting with a guest lecturer once a week. I began to give Wednesday night lectures for the non-physician staff of the hospital

(nurses, aides, dietitians, pharmacists, technicians). I spoke about common illnesses: coronary heart disease, hypertension, breast cancer, etc. We usually had 30 to 40 in attendance. Later we gave a recurring course in CPR in association with the local Red Cross. The staff elected me chief of the medical department at the hospital.

I arranged with Bob Petersdorf, then chief of medicine at Washington in Seattle, to have fourth-year medical students (one or two at a time) spend four weeks with me in preceptorship. For brief periods, I took students from the University of Hawaii medical school, and occasionally, second-year internal medicine residents from Tripler. Every two weeks I would make teaching rounds at Tripler. I learned a lot about being a preceptor in the private practice milieu. It required an astonishing amount of time to do it right. Hospital rounds demanded an extra hour or two, twice each day. My colleagues tolerated my slight decline in dollar productivity, but I partially compensated by working 12 to 14 hour days. I must confess that after about 18 months, I began to wither. I took fewer and fewer preceptees, until finally, I quit. I did enjoy the one-on-one teaching, but the effort was wearing me down.

After a few months of preparing lecture notes for the Wednesday night sessions, I asked the managing editor of the *Maui News*, the island weekly, if she would be interested in a medical column tailored to the Maui audience. I spoke to Nora Cooper, the ebullient publisher-owner, who was enthusiastic. It was all *pro bono*; I accepted a check for one dollar a year. The lecture notes could easily be cobbled into a medical column. Later, Nora asked me to do a 15 minute taped radio presentation of the column; the newspaper and radio station belonged to her. It all turned out to be pleasantly successful; Stella and I became minor local celebrities. Big fish, little pond and all that.

Undeniably these were the happiest years of Stella's married life. She enjoyed her status in the community; she began to play duplicate bridge once a week and enjoyed a new circle of friends. We joined the Maui Country Club, a very kamaiina (old timers) place. Soon Sonya came over, stayed with us a few months and then took an apartment in

Lahaina. She plied her trade with facials and massages and selling her (secret ingredient) face and body creams. She was a superb masseuse. "Madam Sonya" soon became a well-known Lahaina personality. She was still a pain in the ass to me, but you had to hand it to the old girl. Sonya never lacked *chutzpah*.

It was during this time that Stella developed abdominal pain and menstrual irregularity. She was 39, and women in her family usually began menopause quite a few years later. It turned out that she had uterine fibroids, and her Ob-Gyn man, who had excellent credentials and superb rapport, recommended hysterectomy. We had no further interest in having children, so it was no big deal. She tolerated the procedure well. Soon thereafter she began to suffer severe hot flashes with sudden intense perspiration and palpitations. She had to increase her dose of Premarin and the symptoms eased off. Once again she was urged to stop smoking, tried and failed. She was visiting Dick Auerswald, a heavy-set, full bearded Freudian psychiatrist and dear friend (whose wife was my patient). But Stella's insomnia was unrelenting. Her nocturnal habits had not changed despite the felicitous Maui ambience.

After about three years, I must confess I became restless, for lack of a better descriptor. I remained very busy; the work pace was unrelenting full-court press. There were no physicians staffing the hospital emergency room in those days, and quite frequently I would make the mad 17-mile dash from home to hospital in the wee small hours. One night I was driving the big T-bird too fast on a wet road near Hookipa Beach and spun-out in a 360. The car was unwieldy and top heavy. Within a month I traded it on a new Shelby-Cobra 500 convertible, the hottest wheels on the island. It cornered like a Formula 1; it was my "mid-life" toy. One night on the stretch between Wailuku and Lahaina, the neck of the island, I topped 135. A few early mornings, I made the run to the top of Haleakala, 10,000 feet in about 30 miles, swinging the S curves—just for the sheer hell of it. The Shelby was a crazy outlet for a lot of emotional steam. Back and forth from home to office, the cops

hit me with three speed warnings, never a ticket. I took care of most of the cops and their families.

Jon had graduated from Baldwin High School and was enrolled at the University of Hawaii taking classes in communications. He was in his element. He shared an apartment with a sweet Japanese-Hawaiian girl (an unusual combination), and he had a part-time job. He was a little mysterious about his new avocation. Once Stella and I were visiting, and he took us to his workplace. It was a cavernous room crammed to the ceiling with sophisticated communications gear. It could have been an FBI or CIA surveillance operation. TV monitors flashed simultaneous programs from all three major networks; Jon was monitoring and recording selected programs (or portions). Why? "Well, these guys sell these program tapes to stations all over the South Pacific." Next question: Is that legal? "Hell, I'm not the business manager; I just make the tapes and hand them over every evening." I am sure it was a pirate operation, but he was happy as a jaybird and making enough money to enjoy life. Jon was on his way.

Steven was deeply immersed in medical school in Dallas and working very hard. As I have said, the free-wheeling, logical disputation method at St. Johns was hardly preparation for the hard-nosed, rote memory required in the first two years of medical school. He was not happy, but he was hanging in. "It will get better when you get into the clinics in your junior year." My occasional elder medical statesman pontificals were received with long-distance grunts.

People often sigh when I tell them I practiced on Maui. They recall their two weeks of sublime vacation, enjoying sun and surf and slack key. My recollections of Maui are quite different. My life was office, hospital, emergency room and the snaky blacktop to and from hospital. I seemed to have rare opportunities to immerse myself in the charms of island living. In retrospect I realize I could have created more free time, but the demands of private practice were enormous. My compulsive nature had taken control.

As I have said, I encountered few medical challenges in practice. My time in the army and in university hospitals had exposed me to a vast spectrum of illness. But there were exceptions. One night I admitted a 35-year old Japanese insurance executive with precordial chest pain. Coronary heart disease was virtually unknown in young Japanese males. He denied any history of hypertension and diabetes; tests were negative. But he had characteristic pain, sweating and was shocky. He had a gallop rhythm—characteristic of a damaged myocardium. I still suspected acute pericarditis or a dissecting aortic aneurysm or a pneumothorax (collapsed lung). But, of course, I ran an ECG. I was astonished when it revealed a whopping anterior wall myocardial infarction! He died within hours despite heroic recussitative and supportive efforts. At post-mortem he had a classical thrombosis of the left anterior descending coronary artery. The myocardial damage was just too extensive. It was the first (not the last) young, second-generation, Japanese man to be seen on Maui with a killer heart attack. In retrospect, he was obese, never exercised and had been consuming a typical "western" high-fat, high-calorie diet. He had overwhelmed the "good genes" that protect most Japanese men against coronary disease, until they began to adopt western sloth and diet. It was a scenario to be repeated with breast cancer in second and third generation Japanese women.

Another bizarre "local" illness phenomenon was the high incidence of systemic lupus erythematosus in young Japanese and Hawaiian girls. At one time I was caring for about ten—extraordinary. I also cared for dozens of young people of all races and mixes with type 1 diabetes mellitus; many others had severe asthma. They were quite a handful to manage.

Sometime in early 1973, I was attending a medical meeting in Honolulu, and I had a message waiting in my room at the Royal Hawaiian Hotel. It was from Dr. Malcolm Todd, president of the AMA; could we meet for a drink in the bar? I had no idea how he got my name. I had never belonged to the AMA and, certainly, had never met Dr. Todd. He was fiftyish, chubby, cheerful and direct. "We are

hunting for a new editor for JAMA; would you be interested?" I was flabbergasted! He went on to say that "they" knew about my editing, writing and teaching background; I had made their short list. Since my abortive shot at the NEJM, I had always fantasized about that job—editor of a weekly medical journal. Here was another chance. But it was far from an easy decision.

I knew that Stella would hate the idea of moving back to the Mainland. And not without justification. We had arrived at the ultimate (penultimate, as it turned out) branch of the Rubicon. I promised that in the unlikely event that I got the job, I would sign on for only three years. She was quietly livid. She would **not** go to Chicago with me, but might come later. I was already welshing on my "settle down in private practice" agreement. I think it was a combination of some boredom (and fatigue) with practice, not being terribly happy at home (our sex life still left a lot to be desired—for both of us) and the prospect of an exciting new challenge. In retrospect it was s singularly selfish decision. I think I would not have liked being married to me.

I flew to Chicago to be interviewed. I met the EVP, soft-spoken, smooth, urbane Dr. Bert Howard, and some of his key staff. Not only would I be editor-in-chief of JAMA but director of the division of scientific publications that produced monthly specialty journals in internal medicine, pulmonary medicine, public health, ob-gyn, psychiatry, neurology, pediatrics and surgery. Each had a distinguished editor who would report to me. In reality they were virtually autonomous, as indeed they should have been. Salary was better than the clinic. I asked for one morning a week free time, to make teaching rounds at Illinois. I was hired on the spot. And so started my third career.

# 22

## *The Chicago Adventure*

◆

### *(JAMA and Dee...)*

I think the watershed in our marriage occurred around the time of my fiftieth birthday (our 25$^{th}$ year of marriage). I was due to depart for Chicago in a few weeks, and we decided on a poolside party. We invited "everyone who had been nice to us" and a few dozen others—perhaps about 70 to 80 people. We settled on a late Sunday morning Mexican-fare brunch. We hired the "Maui Mariachis" and had it catered with huevos rancheros, tacos, enchiladas—all liberally lubricated with margaritas, Tecate, Carta Blanca and Dos XXs. By one o'clock everyone was blasted, and we all wound up in the pool. Great party. The last truly good time Stella and I ever shared. We should have separated and divorced after 25; the marriage went all downhill after that.

In preparation for the sojourn in Chicago, reluctantly, I sold the Shelby beast. It got about 12 miles to the gallon, and I thought it had just too much firepower for urban puttering. (It was a great mistake; today it is listed as a rare classic car worth about $100,000. But who knew?) I bought a new Datsun 240-Z and shipped it to Oakland. The next few weeks were the nadir of my life. (Worse was to come.) I drove to Chicago stopping only to catnap along the way. The Z was lovely; not the powerful Shelby-500 but smooth and fun. I stopped at Fort Sheridan, just north of Chicago on the west shore of Lake Michigan and called Stella. It was a mutually tearful conversation, but she

remained adamant about not coming "for a while." After a few days I found a furnished efficiency apartment (why do they call them that?) in a rather shabby, yuppie high-rise about six blocks from the office. The bed was a hideaway couch. The space was tiny and gloomy. That first night, after cooking my own hot dogs and beans, I was wallowing in self-pity. I questioned my sanity.

The job was **not** a piece of cake. The Journal had fallen on hard times. It was not attracting topnotch clinical articles, and the advertising revenue had fallen off drastically. Then to my astonishment, I discovered that the interim editor was Dr. Hugh H. Hussey, who had been one of my idols during residency days. I would be replacing the incomparable Hugh Hussey! It was even more intimidating than I had anticipated. What to do?

I plunged into the job. My day began at 5:15, jogging two to three miles. I got to know the early morning clientele of Clarke Street (blonde black hookers returning from a tough night at the Congress Hotel, sleepy-eyed shop keepers sweeping the place out, waiters coming or going, newspaper deliverers, embarrassed "suits" furtively slinking from squalid all-night porno peep show joints). We got to "know" each other in passing. In winter I would bundle up in Gore-Tex ski mask and wool mittens against the cruel, snow-flecked wind whipping off Lake Michigan. I always hoped that no major crimes occurred in the vicinity while I was jogging; a runner in a ski mask. Yikes!

I got to my desk by seven. I inherited four seasoned senior editors and a hard-working staff of about 40 others. The first day Hugh Hussey welcomed me. He was the same lean, tall, taciturn clinician I remembered. As ever, he spoke with perfect syntax and a polished vocabulary that I admired. Always complete sentences. Warmth was never apparent, but this time he startled me with his sensitivity and candor. If he could remain a senior editor for another six months, he would acquire enough tenure for full retirement benefits. He realized this situation might be awkward for me but "he would never interfere." Hussey was a superb, analytic clinician who wrote with crisp precision;

his editorials were thoughtful; his semantics impeccable. I told him I was deeply moved that he would be willing to remain on board as advisor, senior editor and editorialist. He turned out to be the best senior editor on staff; he certainly never "interfered." I hated to lose him.

So, I didn't know a damned thing about being the editor of the largest circulation, **weekly** medical publication in the world. Of course, it helped that all members of the AMA received our book as a "benefit of membership." I went up to Wisconsin to the paper mills and spent a few days learning about paper. I went to the printer and studied inks and type and layout. With the staff artist, I redesigned the JAMA logo (*sans serif*) for the first time since the legendary Morris Fishbein held sway in the 30s. Within a few weeks I selected new, clean type for body and headlines. I revised the format for publishing articles—to make them appealing to busy physician-scanners.

My abiding philosophy was that JAMA should become a vehicle for topnotch clinical articles. I felt that every faithful reader of our publication should be kept abreast of every important medical, social and political development, plus every new physiologic and therapeutic innovation that had been reasonably well-established as worthwhile. (It was before "evidence-based" became a cliché.) My purpose: to facilitate the enlightened practice of medicine. For generalists, it should be the **only** journal they ever had to read. For specialists, it should provide information about all the rest of medicine, beyond their immediate specialty. It was my firm intention to challenge the *New England Journal of Medicine* (now being edited by my friend, Franz Ingelfinger) as the best medical weekly in the world.

Well, I didn't quite make it, but we had one helluva run. I might add that I had absolutely no interest in charming the *New York Times* or the *Washington Post* or "*60 Minutes*" into selecting our articles as "newsworthy" front-page fare. Our audience was working doctors. Our mission: to educate those professionals working in offices, wards and clinics who were seeing patients every day. Entertaining, perhaps even educating, the public was not my concern. Sexy, provocative "break-

throughs" had to be justified on the basis of hard-nosed scientific evidence. Perhaps the more exiting, topical stuff should have been more visible on my radar screen, but the task at hand seemed daunting unto itself.

I decided that to capture more attention from front-line clinical investigators and clinicians, we had to show more class. So I established an editorial advisory board. There had never been one before in the long history of JAMA. I selected judiciously from among my more scholarly and literate friends. Then I wrote letters to just about everyone I knew in academic medicine; every chairman of every department of medicine, inviting them to encourage their staff members to submit their first-line clinical research articles to JAMA, always citing our eclectic mission and broad circulation.

Then I did a most outrageous thing to attract attention. To jump start interest in JAMA, I used full-blown, full-color, dramatic photographs, a la *Life* magazine, (usually related to some article inside) on the front covers of occasional issues to lure readers inside. Soon, I was working 16 to 18 hours a day, taking manuscripts home to my dingy apartment, reading and writing between pizza and hamburgers and Chinese take-out. The pressure was intense but very different from practice. I was not involved in life and death decisions. In large measure it was sublimation for all that was missing in my emotional life. But I will confess, I reveled in the sense of power and the feeling that one might, just might, bring some new light to the medical masses.

Gradually, we moved into more social, economic and political areas, but never at the expense of practical, scientific medicine. And we began to attract better manuscripts. I started several new features that served to review specific areas: proper laboratory use, physiologic reviews, old and new treatments. The intention was to balance the heavier original clinical research material. I think we achieved a reasonable equity. After every issue was published, the staff would meet to critique every article that had appeared. These were frank, knock down, drag-out sessions; every editor was assigned an article that he or she had not seen before. I

felt these were critical meetings to establish a sense of "team" while seeking constantly to improve our Journal. Esprit was high.

One of my more adventuresome ideas was to coordinate an article in the Journal with the production of an audio-visual tape on the same subject. I planned to take an AMA audio-visual crew to clinics and medical schools that had super-specialists on the staff, stars who were well-known to all physicians for their expertise in a particular illness. For my trial run, I selected "Hemochromatosis," a serious, genetic disease related to disordered iron metabolism. It was often overlooked in differential diagnosis, and such an error could lead to severe complications if untreated. Yet it was amenable to treatment if caught early enough. The world expert was my old friend Bill Crosby, who was now at the Scripps Clinic in La Jolla.

So I took the team to California, and we taped a clinical conference devoted to hemochromatosis. It was all orchestrated by Bill and me, employing volunteer patients and the clinical staff at Scripps. It was a superb, state-of-the-art teaching session. The taped "program" included some spectacular shots of roiling surf caressing the elegant beaches of La Jolla, preceding and following the scientific presentation. The next issue of the Journal had a full-blown cover of the beach scene and contained a tightly edited version of the conference. The plan was to make the videotape and reprints of the JAMA article available (at nominal cost) to community hospitals for teaching conferences. Response to the initial offering was tepid at best. I was chagrined. We repeated the process, utilizing the same dramatic format, with "Diabetes Mellitus" at the Straub Clinic of Honolulu. Response from community hospitals was still lukewarm. It was an expensive, labor-intensive effort, and the result was less than wonderful. In my workbook, I had plans to go to Mayo, Harvard, Stanford and Phipps during the first year.

But after two productions I abandoned the project. The teaching vehicle was superb; I would have loved such tapes and reprints when I was running the physician education at the Maui Memorial Hospital.

But I had not anticipated the dreary apathy in the majority of community hospitals for clinical teaching material. I should have learned a lesson, but I must not have. (*vide infra*)

Within weeks after I settled in, I visited the advertising people. I had discovered that for every two pages of advertising, I could add one page of editorial material. "So how can we increase our advertising revenue?" They seemed astonished. Apparently no editor had ever deigned to concern himself with revenue. They described how half a dozen big ad agencies controlled the adverts in medical journals. It was a serious business based on a rigorous, multi-faceted formula that included data on circulation ("epidemiology of the readership"—generalists, specialists, hospital-based, practice-based, etc.), readership exposure (was the journal read cover-to-cover or just selected articles or rarely or never), physical placement of ads within the publication and the actual impact of art and words within the ad. It represented a complex, arcane commercial discipline, a universe of data and statistics designed to provide pharmaceutical companies a detailed roadmap of where their dollars went and what yield they could expect.

I spent a few fascinating hours learning about this extraordinarily competitive world. I volunteered to go with our sales reps to the leading agencies in New York, Philadelphia and Chicago to make a "sales pitch" on behalf of JAMA and the specialty journals. Once again all jaws dropped. "Listen, I am willing to take my coat off and pitch to these guys, if it means I can get a dozen more editorial pages per issue!" And so I worked up a flip chart presentation, and we pounded on tables at about ten agencies. Again, the execs at the agencies were flabbergasted that the editor of JAMA was standing there making a "sales pitch." Actually, I sort of enjoyed it. After a few months, we had promises of ads that would increase our annual revenue from 7.4 to 9.2 million dollars a year. I also mastered a few peripheral skills: how to calculate expense accounts (creatively, but not too), the infamous three-martini lunch (not for me, thank you) and other high-living tips from the wonderful world of advertising.

After a few months I moved to a terrific (by contrast) one-bedroom apartment on the 48$^{th}$ floor of the west Marina Tower. It was two blocks from the AMA building. After my tenement existence, it was just marvelous to sit out on my tiny, private balcony and gaze down at the busy barge traffic negotiating the Chicago canal, opening on to Lake Michigan. The "twin corncobs" of Marina were a remarkably self-contained community. In the basement were restaurants, grocery store, liquor store, barber shop, theaters, florist, shoe repair, tailor, etc. It was said that some old-timers never left the complex; I believed it. The orbit of my morning jog just moved a few blocks south.

After a few months, Stella came to Chicago. It was not an easy time; she disliked the confinement of the apartment. We spent some time looking in the suburbs for a house, but that would mean a lengthy train and cab commute for me. I must confess, I did not shop for a new residence with much enthusiasm. I thought we could enjoy Chicago from center city for a few years. We were within easy walking distance of art museums, the planetarium, symphony hall, great shops and stores, movie theaters, superb restaurants. I argued that we could vacation on Maui during the next few years; she could return to visit her mother at any time. But it was unavailing. Stella was inconsolably miserable, rarely leaving the apartment.

We did make two trips abroad. The Parisian Bureau of Tourism invited editors of dozens of American magazines to come to Paris to celebrate the opening of a new *tres moderne* exhibition hall. It was an all-expense trip for two; the gala was to be a three-day international film festival. We flew to Charles de Gaulle Airport on Air France. I was seated next to Judy Wax, wife of Shelley Wax, managing editor of *Playboy*. Judy was a published poet, totally charming, disarmingly literate, a rare unprepossessing intellectual. Shelley was quiet with a droll sense of humor, the perfect complement to effervescent Judy. We became good friends during the hectic time in Paris. Upon return, Stella and I saw them often; they introduced us to the splendid ethnic restaurants of Chicago, and often Judy cooked for us at home. (Two years after I had

left Chicago, they were on an ill-fated United DC-10 that lost an engine on take-off at O'Hare. They perished along with several hundred other passengers. I discovered their names quite by accident in reading an account of the crash. They were a wonderful couple. The world lost two brilliant lights of the literary world, and we lost two treasured friends.)

Our second trip was related to my intention to launch foreign language editions of JAMA. My plan was to start modestly with a monthly Spanish language edition and then move into French, Italian, German, Japanese...I planned to establish editorial advisory boards in each country consisting of distinguished, widely-recognized clinicians who would select articles from the weekly issues of JAMA to incorporate into the monthly foreign language edition. Spain was to be the prototype; lessons learned here would pave the way elsewhere. By mail, I contacted publishers in Barcelona and Madrid who had experience in scientific publication. I set up a schedule of interviews in each city.

It was a phenomenal expedition. The three publishing houses in Barcelona vied with each other in wining and dining; Stella was taken on shopping tours. I visited each publishing house, and spoke to the editors and publishers. The same occurred in Madrid; our visit seemed as much social as business. It was quite a bit different than our previous foray into Pamplona in 1955. It had been more fun the first time.

I selected a publisher in Barcelona, and the first Spanish language edition appeared on March 4, 1974. One of the caveats I insisted upon was that any pharmaceutical advertising had to be approved by me; some of the drugs employed abroad had no track record of clinical studies and were, by any standard, risky. This caused some problems since many of the most popular drugs had been employed for a long time and were "known to be safe", albeit of unproved clinical effectiveness. Some were utter junk. I was accused of imposing U.S. standards, a sort of ugly-American medical arrogance. I compromised to the extent that the primary criterion became some historical proof of safety; I gave up on effectiveness. It soon became a status symbol for a

pharmaceutical to be advertised in *JAMA en Espanol*. I planned to visit Paris and Rome after ironing out the kinks, but circumstances prevented this occurrence during my tenure. Today, there are half-dozen foreign language editions of JAMA.

Sometime later Stella returned to the Islands for an indefinite period. I was invited to be a "visiting professor" for one week at the Autonomous University of Guadalajara Medical School. One of the students who had come up to Salzburg from Bologna in 1952 was Bill D'Angelo, now a rheumatologist in New York. He had developed an interest in American students studying abroad. He told me of the plight of American kids down in Mexico from the aspect of lack of clinical teaching. He had initiated a program to bring teachers from the U.S. to spend a week with the students in Guadalajara. So I flew down and was met at the airport by a stretch limo and taken to a classy hotel. I discovered the school was "owned" by a very rich *patron* who was interested, ostensibly, in improving the quality of education.

The next day, I was taken to the medical school, and I asked if I could make teaching rounds. Embarrassment and confusion. One of the American students said there was no facility for visiting in-hospital patients. All teaching was didactic: lectures and demonstrations. There was no hands-on exposure to patients, even for junior and senior students! I was amazed. I had several lectures prepared, but that was not why I had made the trip. Later I learned that upon completion of the fourth year, before they would be awarded the medical degree, all students were obliged to "serve in the countryside" in an area designated as underserved, for a period of two years. A most admirable plan. But most all American students would try to avoid this obligation by applying for admission to a U.S. medical school. Hopefully, they would be allowed to complete the last two years of clinical training and qualify for a degree from the latter institution. (This was called the "Fifth Pathway.") In many instances, however, students from abroad were obliged to take all four years over again. The experience in Mexico

often served to fortify their credentials for admission in venues where they had been rejected before.

I was determined to try to provide some clinical orientation, so I tried an experiment. I gathered all the English-speaking students (and anyone else who wished to attend) in a large auditorium and we had a "phantom CPC." I would introduce a fictitious patient: "A 45-year-old carpenter walks into your office complaining of chest pain. What is the first question you would ask him?" Silence; no response. "Well, what would you be thinking of as possible differential diagnoses?" Still silence. "Look, this is not an examination; I am not giving grades. This is a game—a clinical game. So play along with me."

Gradually there was some relaxation. In response to a few more questions, timorous hands went up. As we got deeper into the creation of a scenario of coronary heart disease, interest gathered. We started with key points in history, then physical examination. ("The patient has an S-3 gallop. What does that mean? Heart failure—correct!") Then we "did" laboratory tests and discussed management options. Within half an hour audience participation was brisk and enthusiastic. It was fun.

The next day we played "cirrhosis," with more audience participation. I noted a few Mexican students had filtered into the auditorium. On each succeeding day we did another patient-illness; by Friday the 250 seats were all filled. It was an exhilarating five days. I was impressed that the kids had a decent background in basic sciences, but an appalling lack of knowledge about clinical medicine. After my final morning session, the gleaming limo picked me up once again, for a farewell lunch with the invisible *patron*. With a little arithmetic, I figured that the tuition being paid by the American students was netting this man close to a million dollars (not pesos) a year. I had no idea what the Mexican students were paying, but they all seemed well dressed and probably were from wealthy families. The guy had a money machine.

I was whisked to an elegant estancia some distance from the bustling, dusty city. My host was a plumpish, fiftyish, slightly unctuous, Panama-suited gentleman attended by two beefy, thug-like brutes. It had a Mafioso feeling. He offered some bottled Coca Cola (I declined the ice), and he began to question me in fractured English. I gathered that he wanted a critique of his medical school. OK, fair enough, but I wondered to myself, did he want honesty or a courteous confection? Brashly, I asked if he really wanted a candid response. I said it twice using different words. He smiled wanly and dismissed his two comrades with a barely perceptible gesture. Then he nodded and said something like, "Yes, tell me truth." And I did. I told him the lack of clinical training—the failure to see actual patients was an educational nightmare for students of medicine. He blinked enigmatic, frog-like eyes. I couldn't tell whether he was offended or curious or would summon his hoods to come hurt me.

After a too-long pause, "How would you like to become dean of our medical school and teach our students?" (in flawless, accentless English!) Stunned, I smiled inappropriately and shook my head in disbelief. Finally, I managed, "I am flattered, Senor, but I must decline your kind invitation. I have just taken on my new position, and I couldn't possibly leave for several years. You need a seasoned clinical educator who must be prepared to dedicate many years to the task. I am not your man."

He did not protest. Then he asked if I would like a massage! No kidding, a massage? So much for context. I was so taken aback that I muttered a yes. I was escorted to a locker room adjacent to a gymnasium some distance from the main house. Soon there appeared a very muscular, midget-sized chap who delivered the best Swedish massage with some shiatsu flourishes I have ever received. I flew out the next morning. Strange place Guadalajara.

For several years I had been enjoying a rather desultory correspondence with Dr. Walter Alvarez, a legendary clinician who had been one of the pioneers at Mayo. He wrote a widely-acclaimed, syndicated

newspaper column on medical subjects. One day I had a call from one of his two assistants; they wanted a "favor." They came over to my office; one was a dazzling young blonde, the other a charming older woman who was married to the famous portrait photographer, Josef Karsh. They were Walter's staff, responsible for all the research to respond to readers' questions. I had the sense they mostly wrote the column, and Walter sort of edited and signed-off. He was approaching 90. The favor: they wanted me to be master of ceremonies for a gala party celebrating his up-coming birthday. They planned to invite about 100 of the outstanding clinicians in the U.S and abroad who had been students or colleagues of Alvarez.

"Why me?" Walter had read some of my editorials, liked my letters, heard me speak once and thought I would "do a good job." I was flattered so I met with the splendid old man and was easily persuaded. The staff women provided notes on all the guests. Some 30 were to be invited to comment, relating anecdotes about their adventures with the honoree. The guest list was a Who's Who of contemporary medicine. I broke out my old tuxedo and made personal notes about all of the commentators. The event lasted over three hours, and everyone had a fine old time. But I discovered that being an M.C. was exhausting work. One had to be constantly alert, reasonably witty, maintain the flow of events and retain command of the situation, without boring everyone unto terminal somnolence. Tough job; Georgie Jessel I am not.

Stella and I made the acquaintance of another columnist-celebrity, Eppie Lederer, (aka Ann Landers). One of her staff (of about six) called for some advice about a medical question they had received from a reader. I began to respond, and Eppie picked up the phone and invited me to lunch. I thought Stella might enjoy meeting the Grand Lady, so we joined her in a swish Michigan Avenue French restaurant. Eppie was (always) groomed to the nines, direct, no-nonsense with a sharp, incisive mind. But her appearance and her opinions always seemed a trifle brittle to me. We soon learned that she had a cadre of world-class

medical specialists representing every discipline, stashed in her computer-rolodex. They were eager to respond to readers' questions. When Ann Landers provided medical advice, it came from the top drawer. Staff drafted responses, but she edited, revised and signed-off on every one. She was syndicated worldwide, lectured everywhere and her office walls were plastered with honorary degrees. Eppie Lederer was a class act. I had lunch with her a few times after Stella went back to Hawaii.

Stella's departure came after a very rough time between us. She planned to rent an apartment in Honolulu and take some classes at the university until I came home. Our "time table" for Chicago called for about another two years, but our relationship was on very rocky terrain. Jon had been graduated from the university, but left before the formal exercises. He headed for Los Angeles to pound the pavement in search of a job suited to his considerable talents. The kid had *cojones*.

Soon after arriving in Chicago, I had made contact with Dr. Mort Bogdonoff, chairman of medicine at Illinois. He had been one of Dr. Gene Stead's whiz kids from Duke. Several generations of that talented cadre had fanned out to bring high-class teaching talent to dozens of medical schools scattered across the country. Mort gave me an appointment as a clinical professor, and once a week I took the morning report from the house staff and then made teaching rounds. Mort and his wife, Mary, became good friends.

The other intellectual task that I undertook was the first ABIM rectification examination. I figured that if I had the temerity to edit a medical journal, the least I could do was to maintain my credentials as a clinician. I studied at home, between reading manuscripts. I was a little nervous when the big day came, but the exam was fair and reasonable. I was pleased that I passed.

Then there was Dee. She was a senior copy editor, a striking brunette. Dee was small, slender, always tastefully groomed, with a disarmingly brilliant smile. She had the carriage and grace of a ballerina. Several months after Stella departed, I found myself watching Dee at staff meetings. Occasionally she caught my glance, and I felt a flicker of

interest. One day she brought some copy into my office and suddenly I blurted, "I have a meeting in Madison next week-end, how would you like to go with me?" She appeared stunned for a moment, but demurely dropped her head and then nodded. We became lovers. She was married to a nice man who suffered severe diabetes and had "lost all interest" in sex. My situation was little better. Dee had a daughter in her 20s so I estimated her age to be mid-forties.

I had worked in close proximity to some beautiful women before, but had never had an affair. This relationship was idyllic, torrid and mutually fulfilling from the beginning. Dee was a voracious and imaginative sexual partner. About every other week she would arrive at my apartment on Friday evening loaded with edible goodies. We would spend almost the entire weekend making love, with occasional excursions to walk beside the lake or sneak out to a distant restaurant. She would always prepare a superb meal Saturday night; I would provide good champagne, candles and Roberta Flack. Dee was a delight; I cannot recall a serious argument. We would discuss books and movies and aspects of work, but rarely wander into politics or culture or philosophy. She was bright, frank and ever cheerful, a perfect lover. We were painfully discreet. Dee was the eager agent of my sexual epiphany.

I entered this relationship with some trepidation about my ability to please a woman. My experience with Stella had been hardly reassuring. Dee quickly disabused me of this fear. We were very good for each other. From the outset we agreed that it was, indeed, an "affair." I had no intention of leaving Stella; Dee felt an obligation to care for her husband. I think she fell in love with me, and I came very close to loving her. But at that time I was not prepared to give up on my relationship with Stella. Dee accepted this without tears or recrimination. She was wonderful for my ego. I saw her a few times after I left Chicago, but only for dinner. By a sort of unspoken mutual understanding, we did not sleep together again. We remained good friends. For many years, thereafter, she would call occasionally wherever I was working, and we would chat about life and times.

Well into my second year in Chicago, Dr. Jack McGovern, an ENT specialist from Houston and a prime mover in the American Osler Society, proposed that we dedicate a *festschrift* issue of the *Archives of Internal Medicine* to Bill Bean on the occasion of his (I think) 70th birthday. I had continued my desultory correspondence with Bill, although since the research societies had abandoned Atlantic City as their ritual meeting place, we no longer met for breakfast at the old Chalfonte. (This was just another bit of evidence that Donald Trump and the "casino Mafia" had destroyed the ambience of that quasi-magical or frankly tawdry [depending on what you were seeking] watering hole.) I set up the plan for the *festschrift* and selected papers from the enormous repertoire of Bill Bean. Some were classic examples of medical literacy. We augmented the volume with a few contemporary papers by his disciples. Then we set up a dinner-presentation meeting at the Drake. We invited Jim Clifton, Frank Aboud, and half a dozen other Bean friends and aficionados. McGovern lured Bill and his wife to Chicago on some elaborate pretense, and when they entered the banquet room they were delightfully surprised. It was a grand evening; Bill's celebrated "omphalosophy" once again echoed through the night and was enjoyed universally. Shades of Salzberg and the grand old O.H. hotel. All we lacked was Celso Lonzetti and his melodious concertina.

One of the other delights of the new job was the opportunity to become close friends with Lois DeBakey. She was the sister of the famous surgeon, Mike DeBakey. Lois and her sister, Selma, were the medical librarians at Baylor. I met Lois at the Council of Biology Editors, a formidable clutch of science editors from all across the country. She invited me, along with Franz Ingelfinger and a few others, to help conduct her annual course on "medical writing." It was here that I first met Rollo Hanlon, the scholarly EVP of the American College of Surgeons, who has become a life-long friend. We all gave lectures and conducted seminars. Lois was the acknowledged "conscience of American medical letters." She had written extensively about the crying need for

literacy in medical writing. Lois and Selma were marvelous old-fashioned "Southern belles:" slight, graceful, whispery, soft-spoken, shy, almost courtly. But Lois was a tiger when it came to violations of her sacred medical English. Proper spelling, punctuation, semantics and clarity in medical literature represented her personal holy grail. When you wrote a letter to Lois DeBakey you double-checked every word to ensure conformity to her soaring literary standards. You could not help but love the woman.

Our friendship was sealed when the Council of Biology Editors asked her to create a book on "How to be a Medical Editor." She asked four of her friends to write chapters and assist in editing. Franz and I were invited to participate. Over the course of several months, we all wrote chapters, exchanged them with comments and Lois made the ultimate edits. The final manuscript was approved by all of us. It was a crisp, tidy, helpful book. Then the stodgy executive committee of the Council asked Lois to submit the final manuscript for **their** edits and approval. She was outraged. "Who would be qualified to pass judgment on the work of these distinguished editors and myself!" The Council insisted; she refused. It was a standoff. Lois called all her co-authors to enlist their support; she wanted to publish the book without the blessing of the Council. I don't know how my colleagues "voted," but Franz and I backed her stand. Ultimately the book was published without the stamp of approval of the Council. There was much vitriol and anger; Lois, Franz and I resigned from the Council. She was a close friend forever after. We still exchange occasional letters, share things that we publish and exchange outrageous neologisms, usually verbalized nouns that tend to exacerbate the mongrelization of the language. She is a grand lady.

I also continued my friendship with Franz. I visited him in Boston on several occasions, and he taught me a great deal about the art of medical editing. I had lunch with Franz and his wife in San Francisco many years later, when he was in brief remission from his ultimately

fatal carcinoma of the esophagus. In my opinion he was the best editor the NEJM ever had, and that includes some very talented folks.

My experience at Dearborn Street can be epitomized by quoting a paragraph I wrote that appeared in every issue: "The mission of this journal is education: to inform its readership of progress in clinical medicine, pertinent research and landmark developments in the political and social interfaces of medicine. It is a forum for open and responsible discussion. In consonance with this concept, all articles published in The Journal, including editorials, letters to the editor, and book reviews are signed (or authorship is otherwise indicated clearly). These represent the opinions of the author and do not reflect the official policy of the American Medical Association or the institution with which the author is affiliated, unless this is clearly specified." JAMA no longer carries my beloved paragraph. But when it did, the infamous "Dear Debbie" letter (about assisted suicide) by an anonymous author would never have seen the light of day. I have always despised the cowardice implicit in anonymity.

The only real clash I experienced with AMA hierarchy occurred soon after my arrival. It was a copy of a speech by President Malcolm Todd (who had first contacted me in Honolulu about the job) that he was about to deliver at the annual meeting. In my opinion it was bland and boring fluff, typical medical-political rhetoric. The manuscript had come from the "front office." I sent it back to the front office with a note that it was best suited for the association newspaper, the *AMA News*. I was summoned to Bert Howard's office; my second visit to that august chamber. He explained that by tradition the farewell speech of the outgoing president "was always published in JAMA." I said that I could not honor that tradition. Dr. Todd could submit an editorial with the same content as his speech for peer-review "like every other manuscript." It would be given serious consideration. Bert did not push the issue.

My next encounter came just a few weeks later, a far more serious challenge to my editorial autonomy (which had been a condition of my

acceptance of the position). We received a fine manuscript from Henry Simmons and Bob Stolley at the University of Pennsylvania medical school. It was the first paper to cite the overuse (abuse) of antibiotics by working practitioners. They discussed the prospect of the emergence of antibiotic-resistant microorganisms many years before it became a major international problem. It had been refereed, vetted and was due to be published in two weeks. I considered it a landmark article.

Another call from Bert. This time three of my old chums from the advertising department were in attendance. Bert said, "That Simmons and Stolley article will cause a lot of our advertisers great unhappiness. After all the effort you have invested to build up your advertising revenue, this article may well cause problems." The advertising guys, my old three-martini-lunch buddies, were all studying the parquet floor. I sputtered, "How the hell did you learn about Simmons and Stolley?" Nervous glances flashed one to the other. Someone said, "We're only thinking of the good of the Journal." I gulped and then growled, "Bullshit—this is censorship. If the drug companies have a problem with the article, let them submit a letter to the editor and I'll publish it. But if you force me to pull the article you can get another goddamn editor!"

I stormed out and called an immediate meeting of my entire staff. "I'm only going to say this once. Someone on this staff is leaking articles that have been accepted for publication to the advertising people. This will stop right now. If I ever hear of it again, and I do not discover the source of the leak, I will fire everyone who had access to that article. And I mean **everyone** regardless of rank. You are dismissed." I was never sure about the culprit; it could have been anyone from a senior editor to a copy boy. We published Simmons and Stolley; there were several moderately unhappy responses from the drug industry, all published in "Letters". There was no withholding of advertising. The issue of censorship never arose again.

About halfway through my tour, the gentlemanly, urbane, rational Bert Howard retired and was replaced by Jim Sammons. The contrast

was extraordinary. Sammons was a short, brash, loud, bombastic, medical street-fighter fresh from Texas City. He was just what the Board of Trustees wanted, a feisty political road warrior. He left me alone for a while. Then, out of the blue, word came down that Sammons was about to decree that **all** pharmaceutical advertising in AMA publications would cease! I was speechless. It was common knowledge that it was the advertising revenue that allowed us to "give" the journal to AMA members and keep subscription costs within reason for non-members. My business people calculated that without income from advertisements, the membership dues allocated to publications would have to be about tripled. If not the journals would all go belly up. It was a preposterous and irresponsible dictum, a unilateral decision without consultation with those who would be involved.

I rushed to speak to Sammons. He had no idea of the cost implications of his fantasy. He "allowed as how" it would be great for the always penumbral AMA image to be "free of any suggestion that our publications were hostage to the pharmaceutical companies." I spoke in language that I knew bantam rooster Jimbo would comprehend. "That is pure bullshit. (It seemed to be a word that came to mind only in the office of the EVP.) You haven't done your homework; this would kill us. You must be out of your mind!" The Texas tornado asked me to leave. When the word leaked, I saw my advertising pledges begin to vanish. A few weeks later at the annual meeting, the ever-pragmatic Board of Trustees told Jim to cease and desist. It was a crazy idea. After a flock of embarrassing, apologetic phone calls, I managed to salvage most of my advertising. But the unpredictable stupidity of the front office caused a roiling in the medical advertising community that persisted for several years. This was only prelude.

Within months of Sammons arrival the Great Financial Disaster descended upon 535 North Dearborn. It would seem that Jim had inherited a "financial nightmare." It was never clear to me why we were in such tough shape since the AMA owned a large chunk of priceless real estate in downtown Chicago and an office building in the District

of Columbia. But it was announced that **all** AMA divisions would be obliged to take a 20% budget cut. (Of course, the sacrosanct propaganda-lobby-PAC operation never took a hit during this bad time.) Once again, I sought an appointment with the EVP. The wounds had not healed from our previous joust. I explained that my division was the **only** one in the organization that was actually making money. The cut would cause me to reduce my pages per issue ("we'll become a goddamn pamphlet"), delay publication time of all articles (already a problem) and prevent me from adding a batch of planned new features. Jim said that all divisions would have to "share the pain." Once again he "'lowed as how" (that irritating south Texas drawl) the cut would be temporary. "Define temporary," I growled. He said, "about three months." I cogitated silently. That would make it tough, but I could live with it. I nodded and left.

After eight weeks I saw him again, "When can I resume my pre-cut status?" He stood up; his rumpled black and white checked suit and sloppy tattersall were fussed at and straightened. "We're still in trouble; I can't give you a specific time." I lost my cool. "Jim, that is not acceptable. I'm giving you six weeks notice! I will not preside over a dying journal." I left and went back to the apartment. I knew that a large part of my action had been prompted by my unhappiness over the Stella situation. Had that not been a factor, I might have attempted to live through the frugal period, but I am not sure. I was never convinced that there was a legitimate financial crisis. It was common knowledge that there was a lot of high-on-the-hog living by the Trustees and Uncle Jim. (He was later accused of some financial shenanigans before he resigned.)

I really loved the job, but I felt angry, betrayed and frustrated. Later in the week, Jim called me in. He said that there were great opportunities for me at AMA; he suggested that I could join his executive staff in another capacity at a higher level. I told him that was not my cup of tea. I was not cut out to be an AMA politico. I called a meeting of my staff and told them of my decision. Most of my loyal senior editors said

they would submit their resignations too. I thanked them all, but advised that my decision should not influence them. They were mostly older men and women who did not have the advantage of the career options still open to me.

That weekend Dee was tearful but resigned. She knew the score. For several years after I departed Chicago, the JAMA was, indeed, little thicker than a pamphlet. The vital juice had ebbed from the publication; the content was weak. Years later, It took a new editor and a new budget to resurrect JAMA. I am pleased that it is flourishing once again. (I always suspected that the unspoken war that existed between Jerry Kassirer of the NEJM and George Lundberg of JAMA to see how many hits they could achieve in the *New York Times* and network nightly news had somewhat distorted the educational mission of both journals. JAMA more than NEJM. I wondered how many manuscripts were considered for publication based on their "newsworthiness" (sensationalism?), in addition to scientific merit and value to working practitioners. A few years ago, Lundberg was fired for publishing an outrageous article that had no scientific merit, but attracted much media attention. Some of the medical-editorial community screamed "censorship," but those who know Lundberg realized that he had overstepped the bounds of rational editorial responsibility. There had been other manifestations of arrogance that had been ignored by the front office. Apparently, this was the final straw. Even later, Kassirer resigned because the Massachusetts Medical Society sought to use the NEJM panache to promote other less scientifically rigorous publications. Jerry was on the side of the angels.)

# 23

## *Return to Maui*

◆

### *(another joust with private practice and ennui...)*

**M**y trip back across the country took four days. I was depressed and ambivalent about recent events and not at all sanguine about what loomed ahead. Stella had returned to Maui, but our relationship was still in limbo. My experience with Dee just exacerbated my anxiety about my life with Stella. In reflection, I came to realize that I had forced the issue with Jim Sammons. A "good soldier" would probably have toughed it out, and I did not like myself for that. But the chapter was closed, so what the hell. I would just revisit my old formula for getting over rough patches—"*Labor Omnia Vincit.*"

And I did. It seemed that within days my practice resumed the old furious pace. I started up the lectures, *Maui News* column, radio spiel, the whole *megillah*. But I did not take any more students in preceptorship; enough was enough. I told my group that I felt we should begin to do treadmill stress tests (TST). We purchased a gadget with all the appropriate bells and whistles, and I established a working protocol. Within weeks I was inundated with referrals. I was doing two to three TSTs two mornings a week and soon built up a significant backlog. I soon discovered that most of the requests were not justified on the basis of clinical indications; the TST procedure was so *au courant* that my colleagues were unduly charmed. So I stiffened the protocol. All candidates would be submitted for cardiac consultation, and I would make

the determination about the indication for a TST. My group was not pleased, since the new machine had become a bloody gold mine. (It was my first experience with "how a doctor can get rich in medicine." Just become the first kid on your block with a shiny new gadget and "they will come.")

Later, I had a similar experience with flexible bronchoscopy. Previously we had to send anyone who needed bronchoscopy to Honolulu. I had done about a dozen bronchoscopies with the old rigid scope during my fellowship at Gallinger (in 1949!). With the flexible scope, it should be a piece of cake. So the group invested in two state-of-the-art Japanese scopes, and I went over to Tripler and spent a week on the pulmonary service learning the new technique. When I set up shop one morning a week at the hospital, the TST phenomenon recurred. Once again I established a protocol whereby all candidates would be seen in consultation before I would accept them for bronchoscopy. It turned out to be a rather limited clientele, as indeed, it should have been.

I also introduced peritoneal dialysis to Maui. We had no hemodialysis capability on the Island; it was a periodic Honolulu trip for patients for all end-stage renal disease (ESRD) patients. (Coincidentally, these days my son Steven, who is a fine nephrologist, does all the hemodialysis on Maui.) But back then I did not want to become a "service" for the unfortunate ESRD folks. For quite a few I was able to decrease the number of visits they had to make. I also managed a few barbiturate overdoses with peritoneal dialysis. From my experience with TST and bronchoscopy, I could see how physicians could be seduced into becoming "proceduralists." The irrational Medicare and private insurance reimbursement systems encouraged the use of instruments; it was a prelude to escalating costs (and physician incomes). I also pioneered in inserting emergency pacemaker catheters into the base of the right atrium. It was a primitive operation in a radiology department ill equipped for such a procedure. I did this for two or three patients who developed heart block with a very slow ventricular rhythm. It was far

from ideal, but they all made it to Honolulu for permanent implantation.

Then I did chemotherapy for a few breast cancer patients. I accepted only those who had been diagnosed, staged, operated, required chemotherapy and did not want to hop on a plane ride every time they needed treatment. I followed the Italian (Bonadonna) protocol that had been accepted by the National Cancer Institute at that time. In reality, I only treated three patients; each of them ill with metastases. It so reminded me of the bad old days in Salt Lake City when I buried those kids with acute leukemia, that I stopped being a part-time oncologist. I felt guilty, but it was an emotional load I was unwilling to bear. Perhaps I became too emotionally involved with my patients. No other physician on the island was treating with chemotherapy. It was just another serious flaw in our ability to provide proper care for patients. The island was not "paradise" for some patients with serious illness.

I also took care of chronic alcoholics, again by default. No other physicians would accept them. I had a very simple rule, stated very candidly at the first visit. "I will take care of you, but only if you will attend Alcoholics Anonymous, faithfully." I always took new patients for their first visit to AA. There were two chapters, one in Kahalui, the other in Lahaina. I attended so many meetings that I am sure many people thought I was an alcoholic on the wagon. And I kept tabs on who attended and who did not. My success rate (or recidivism rate; glass half full...) was about 50%. Not bad for alcoholic patients. But left to their own devices they would break your heart.

Most of my time was spent with sick patients in the CCU and ICU. Too many nights my phone would cry out after midnight, and I would race the Z into the hospital to meet the ambulance. If I finished after 2:00 AM, I would spend the night on a cot in the ER. I was doing that too often, and I felt that I was rapidly getting too old and tired for such nocturnal gymnastics. My reaction to private practice was the same as before. The intellectual challenges were minimal; I loved the personal, one-on-one contact with patients and their families. I enjoyed the

occasional sense of accomplishment and the joy of truly helping sick people feel well (or at least better). And (hubris notwithstanding) I enjoyed the "big fish in little pond", minor celebrity status for Stella and me. But I could feel that I was getting bored again, *deja vu*. I began to take half-day Friday's off, then full days. So it was not a matter of "burn out;" other physicians were working just as hard. It was a combination of circumstances, personal and professional that made me restless.

In reflecting on those days, I fear I could not practice under the restraints imposed by "managed care" these days. I could not tolerate having my professional decisions second-guessed by some bureaucrat flipping an algorithm chart and pushing buttons on a computer. I could not manage to see more than 30 patients a day. My patient schedule allowed 15 minutes for follow-up visits and 30 minutes for new patients. (I am told that the average time for an HMO doctor to see a patient is eight minutes! Preposterous!) I had to **talk** to patients and their families. I made rounds at the hospital starting at seven and tried to be in the office by about nine. I jogged at lunch and that would consume an hour. I saw new patients in the afternoon, left the office at four, and made rounds until about six. Thus I would see about 12 old patients and four to six new ones each day. But this schedule was very flexible; some days I would have to see more old patients, fewer new ones. After a few months I could accept only a few new patients; my cup had runneth over. Or I would get called to the hospital during the day, not infrequently, and have to reschedule office patients. I just could not adhere to a formula imposed from a third party.

Also, I used generic drugs whenever I was convinced the generic had the same quality, potency and delivery characteristics as the proprietary drug. I would not have tolerated an arbitrary switch (by the pharmacist or the HMO overseer) to a "similar" drug because it was in the "HMO Formulary," without receiving my blessing. I believe I practiced thoughtful, rational, cost-effective medicine, and I would not abide interference from someone less qualified, when it came to caring for

my patients. I think I would have received a bad report card from my HMO keepers. I realize that I am probably a hopeless anachronism; my intellectual drummer is not in sync with the realities of contemporary medicine. But I think there are a lot of "us." And I feel there is a quiet revolution in the wind.

I realize that too-often decisions by hubris-laden physicians are not based on solid reasoning or appropriate knowledge, and in the past we were often profligate in our "leave no stone unturned" approach to patients. But the solution is not third party oversight by less qualified individuals. We need to teach rigor and discipline in decision-making by practitioners. As I have said before, the capability for real-time access to patient records and the ability to obtain superb, current, information—via Internet—is already a reality. It will take some time to educate physicians and other health-care providers in the wonders of this remarkable new dimension in information retrieval. But it is in the wind.

Life at home was not wonderful. Our sex life had devolved into a strange, almost formalized ritual. Details would serve no useful purpose. But the dissatisfaction and unhappiness was mutual. I admit that on more than one night, I would lie there under my sleeping mask thinking about Dee, while Stella played computer bridge or chess well into the night. It was a thoroughly bad scene.

After about one year back on Maui, I wanted to fulfill a life-long dream: to raft the Colorado River through the Grand Canyon. It was not Stella's cup of tea; Steven was in medical school and Jon was already working in Los Angeles. So I went alone. I flew to Flagstaff and joined a group called OARS. We were bused to Lee's Ferry a few miles south of the Glen Canyon Dam. It was a 224-mile river voyage that would take about 10 days. There were four five-person rafts with a professional oar person doing the tough rowing. It was paradise. At Marble Canyon the sheer walls rose a few thousand feet until the perfect, Maxwell Parrish sky was just a streak of sapphire soaring high above. We body surfed where the ebullient Little Colorado thrust its way into

the main river. We were allowed to row during calm transits, and we held on or bailed like hell during the great sallies through raging rapids of varying levels of difficulty. But the hours of virtual silence and the embracing sense of peace were therapeutic. Everyone shared the emotion; one could get rhapsodic under such conditions.

I think it was about the fifth day out, before we arrived at Phantom Ranch, that all hell broke loose. We had stopped for the evening, and I was setting up my air mattress and sleeping bag on a sandy beach upstream from the main group. Suddenly a red helicopter came blasting down the river from the north, no more than 30 feet aloft. This was as illegal as it was hazardous. We had commented on the noisy, sightseeing choppers, fixed-wing aircraft and giant, motorized tour rafts that too-frequently disrupted the soft susurration of wind and water. Planes were not allowed to fly below the rim of the valley. This guy was way off limits; he disappeared around a bend of the river.

A few minutes later the tour leader appeared with a fellow wearing yellow coveralls. "Bob, you have an emergency back home. Your wife is sick. They've come to take you to the airport at Tusayan." No further information. I gathered my gear and clambered into the chopper. We swept up the canyon, strained over the rim and eased down at the tiny airfield. Frantically, I called the hospital; Stella had been admitted with a heart attack! She was stable at the moment and being attended by Bert Weeks. I chartered another helicopter to take me to the motel in Flagstaff, landing on the front lawn. I gathered my gear, taxied to the airport and caught a flight to LAX. I fretted at the terminal through the night and caught the first flight out to Maui.

I was still wearing my river clothes when I arrived at the CCU. Stella had sustained a myocardial infarction involving the inferior wall. It was causing some frightening rhythm disturbances; her blood pressure had to be maintained with pressor drugs. Bert had not left her bedside, but he was obviously way in over his head. I was too emotionally distraught to take over the management. I called the best cardiologist in Honolulu, Al Morris at Straub. I knew him from Tripler days, and bless his

heart, he flew over that night. Bert acted miffed, but I think he was relieved. Either way I didn't give a damn. Steven was interning at the University of Illinois hospital in Chicago and flew in the next day. For about three more days, it was touch and go—very scary. Stella's ectopic ventricular rhythm was difficult to control, but the infarct did not extend. At length everything calmed down and she recovered slowly.

At home Sonya, Stella's favorite cousin from New York, Esther, and a friend, Emily, the wife of a patient of mine, stayed at the house. They took turns tending to Stella for a few weeks. A myocardial infarction in a 45-year-old, non-diabetic woman was unusual. It later became known that the combination of estrogen treatment plus cigarette smoking predisposed middle-aged women to coronary disease. She exercised by swimming in the pool, but could not relinquish the cigarettes. Stella's recovery was steady; she had no angina or any myocardial failure.

I had already organized a rehabilitation program called "Run for Your Life" for my patients who had sustained myocardial infarcts. It was before angiography had become almost routine for post-myocardial infarction patients and coronary by-pass grafting had yet to achieve true clinical legitimacy. Angioplasty and stenting were to come much later. But there was strong suggestive clinical evidence in the literature that a low fat diet and a regular, graded exercise program were beneficial to prevent second attacks.

My program was free, available to all patients if their physician agreed for them to participate. Once discharged from the hospital, each patient would be given a treadmill stress test. There were nomograms, based on age, height and weight, to indicate the ideal exercise heart rate to achieve and sustain during the 15 to 30 minutes of exercise. The hope was to encourage coronary arteries to remain open and collateral vessels to grow and supply more blood to the damaged heart muscle. A low-fat, reasonable caloric diet was part of the program to decrease cholesterol deposition on coronary arteries. Of course, cigarettes were verboten, and one was advised to learn to "cope with stressors" (I never

knew how to deal with that.) There were no excellent drugs to reduce serum cholesterol levels as there are today; nor did we know about the "anti-platelet stickiness" advantages (in preventing cholesterol plaque deposition) of aspirin.

I began my patients with much softer criteria than was published, sort of flying by the seat of my clinical pants. Each patient was individualized. We set up the gym at Maui High to serve as an exercise area. We started patients walking increasing distances: half mile, one mile, two miles. Later they graduated to jogging, again gradually increasing the distance. They learned to check their own pulse rates while sustaining their "ideal exercise heart rate" for the duration of the exercise or until they became fatigued or developed angina. Only one patient ever experienced significant angina. The four internists on the island took turns observing the exercisers. We ran the "clinic" one evening a week, but the patients were advised to exercise five days a week and keep diaries of minutes exercised and heart rates. Later when I was running in the mornings in Haiku, some of my patients would join me for a jog through the pineapple fields. Of course, this was many years before the "exercise/diet clinics" became so popular in Houston and elsewhere. They were (and are) expensive and beyond the reach of most patients. We started perhaps 40 patients on a lifetime program of diet, exercise and cigarette avoidance. I collected no formal data on follow-up (only hearsay from other doctors), but I heard of no recurrences. So I have no idea if we were successful. But the program could not hurt.

I soon became aware of two autochthonous syndromes that seemed almost "Maui idiosyncratic." The first was a form of acute mountain sickness that occurred when tourists from the mainland would land at Kahalui airport (sea level), leap into a rental car, race to the top of 10,000 foot Haleakala, step out to view the crater and collapse with acute shortness of breathe, dizziness and, occasionally, syncope. It was acute altitude sickness, pulmonary edema induced by sudden decrease in the oxygen content of the atmosphere, exacerbated by sudden physical activity. This was thoroughly frightening, but easily curable by

rapid transit back to sea level. But in situations where rapid return to sea level is not possible and medical therapy not immediately available (as in some remote ski areas), it can be fatal.

A cardiovascular variation was the tourist who would sustain a true heart attack while lugging heavy suitcases across the airport after the long-flight from the mainland. Some tourists would suffer angina (or sustain an actual myocardial infarction) while walking too rapidly in the suddenly decreased oxygen saturation at the peak atop Haleakala. We all saw many patients with these problems.

The other syndrome was called "Global Amnesia." The flight from the mainland to Honolulu consumed at least five hours (from the West Coast). Often there was an hour or so on the ground before the short flight to Maui. (Later there were non-stops from the Coast to Maui and Kauai.) Our tourist, usually a middle-aged or older man, would hustle the family into a rented car, drive to the hotel in Lahaina or Kaanapali, eagerly jump into his swimming trunks and leap into the pool. When he surfaced he would have total amnesia! Absolute disorientation. He would not even know his name, where he was, or recognize his wife. A thoroughly terrifying experience. When I encountered the first patient with this syndrome, I suspected he had suffered a mild stroke, not involving motor areas. But physical examination was entirely normal. I did a spinal aspiration: normal. I called Fred Plum, my favorite neurologist, in New York and described the clinical situation.

He said it sounded like "Global Amnesia." I said, "What the hell is that?" He responded that the etiology was unknown, but prognosis for full recovery was excellent. He was correct. "Skillful neglect" (no procedures) and reassurance about full recovery represented the best treatment. But sometimes it took weeks for all the data to be restored in the memory banks. I saw about four patients with this exotic psychological perturbation. It is well documented in the psychiatric literature. Apparently the lack of sleep and time zone shifts disrupt the wiring in the cerebral switchboard for a time.

There were a few other medical curiosities that occurred on Maui. First I encountered some patients that had all the signs and symptoms of a mild form of typhus fever. On the island paradise? Well, after the second patient, I sent serum to the state laboratory in Honolulu and asked for specific antibody tests for typhus. It came back positive for "endemic typhus fever." We had our own home grown variety of typhus. We began to recognize more patients.

Then there were the hippies. During these years, Maui became the Pacific Mecca for gentle young people seeking respite from overwhelming earthly travail. This *angst* often seemed to include the work ethic. That may be a trifle harsh, but these shaggy folk eagerly partook of the welfare system (food stamps, welfare checks) while they castigated the bureaucratic enterprise that provided their largesse. They also had some bad habits. Quite a few purposely scorned all aspects of unnatural (AKA "civilized") living. Many seemed to eschew cleanliness, and they wanted their babies to be born "naturally." Often these infants were delivered in hovels under conditions I had not seen since intern days in the depths of Foggy Bottom. Most often the "natural mid-wives" managed the delivery quite handily, but too often a complication would arise and a badly bleeding teen-ager would be rushed frantically into the emergency room or a nasty post-partum sepsis would develop.

But mostly I saw heptatitis A from fecal-oral contamination. The only treatment we could offer was bed-rest, parenteral B vitamins and IV glucose in water (to provide calories while they were anorectic). I was never sure that any of it made any difference, but it was all we had. And more than once, the glucose would be refused (once the needle was viciously extracted by a furious, bearded, red-faced idiot because he would not "contaminate my body with any substance that was not natural.") I always reminded such folks that glucose is produced in the liver, but that bit of intelligence was dismissed as "organized medicine" cant. And, of course, failure to pay the hospital or physician bill was just another defiant, anti-establishment gesture. Frustrating folks; I felt sorry for their little kids.

It was during these years that I became involved in the "Andromeda Phenomenon." As a result of my time with NASA during Mercury and Gemini, I was asked to chair a committee with the formidable handle, "Committee to Prevent the Back Contamination of the Terrestrial Biosphere." (honestly) NASA life science folks asked me to offer names of other possible committee members, and I selected a half dozen of the best infectious diseases specialists, a few epidemiologists, statisticians and ecologists. Our mission seemed disarmingly simple, but actually it was insidiously complex. We were tasked to devise a scheme to ensure that some exotic microorganism (Crichton's "Andromeda") would not invade and depopulate Mother Earth, when the Apollo astronauts brought back their (possibly contaminated) samples of rocks, earth or whatever!

We met six times. From knowledge gained from previous unmanned lunar explorers, it was generally accepted that the unforgiving environment of the moon surface would be hostile to any living organism: man, microbe, plant or beast. "But, doctor, how can you be **positive** that there is not some life form that employs a metabolic system that is alien to us earthlings? Perhaps something completely unknown and exotic beyond imagination?" Well, of course, there was no facile answer; it was the null hypothesis with a new spin. Convince me that something that has never happened, will **not** happen!

I was on the deck of the carrier when we ran mock exercises with the "recovered Apollo spacecraft and crew." The decontamination precautions were extraordinary. Perhaps "theatrical" would be too heavy, but it was close. The spacecraft was lifted from the sea by a derrick and submerged in a giant vat of antiseptic (I think it was merthiolate!) on the storage deck. The crew disembarked, was sprayed with more antiseptic and immediately stepped into sterile plastic suits and hustled to an isolation area below deck. They were to remain there for a week. It was all very arbitrary, because no one could state with any assurance that what we were doing was right or wrong. "Better safe that sorry" (terribly disastrously sorry!) was the NASA anthem.

In Houston, the Lunar Receiving Laboratory was built to accept the moon specimens. It was entirely automated and built to "implode" contaminants. Air was sucked into the building, sterilized (according to the best earthly standard), circulated and then resterilzed before being allowed to escape into the atmosphere. After the Apollo specimens were finally returned, studied unto exhaustion and then studied longer, it was agreed: there was no life form, known or unknown that existed on the lunar surface. The moon surface was sterile. It was a thoroughly fascinating exercise, and I am sure it will all be repeated when specimens are fetched from Mars. There is a similar reverse argument about man transplanting earthly contaminants to the planets and moons of the near solar system ("forward contamination"). It is "assumed" that the surface environment of moon or Mars would not sustain any form of earth life, but there are some respected scientists who are not completely convinced.

It was early 1976 when the fickle finger beckoned again. Stella was well recovered, at least physically. But our psycho-social-sexual life remained unsatisfactory for both of us. She had become a first-rate duplicate bridge player and competed in tournaments in Honolulu, accumulating lots of red points. When it came to games, she was a *nonpareil*. She would whip me in Scrabble four times out of five, and she loved chess. I was lousy at parlor games, and I never learned to enjoy things I am not very good at.

I realize that I have not addressed the subject of Stella in sufficient depth. Each time I contemplate her I am beset with ambivalence. She was the most complicated woman I have ever known, a cauldron of paradoxes. She had retained much of her remarkable youthful beauty and was extremely bright. Her IQ was in the genius category. Yet she was an intellectual dilettante, incapable of perseverance. Her primary interests were philosophy and religion, although she was neither very philosophical nor at all religious. She was almost a speed reader with remarkable capacity for retention. She was an excellent writer and editor with a formidable vocabulary. She had learned enough medicine to

be able to proofread my medical writings. Stella enjoyed an incredible facility with most light manual things; she could knit the most complex patterns (I still have two of her Aran-knit, fisherman sweaters that defy age and wear). As I have indicated her ability to master chess, duplicate bridge, Scrabble, anagrams and any other word game was phenomenal. She could have been a master cryptographer.

She had never harangued me to "make money," and she endured some frugal, lonely times without complaint. In the army she rarely entertained, but, ironically, considering our personal situation, she was very good at helping young wives of house staff deal with emotional problems. She could best be described as a "reluctant" army wife, but she never interfered with my career aspirations, until she called my hand at Walter Reed. She once wrote a very perceptive piece for one of my *House Physician Reporter* columns called "The Reluctant Acolyte" about the life of an army physician's wife. It was insightful and articulate. In all fairness, I had made every career decision before the final departure from the army. She tolerated these moves with good grace for the most part, but there is no question that our life was far removed from the quiet, settled, private practice milieu that Stella had anticipated when we married. And in all honesty, at the time we married, I had no idea about my professional future, except that I was attracted to internal medicine as a medical student. I could never have anticipated the labyrinthine path of my subsequent life in medicine.

Later, during our time in Uxbridge and Vorhees (New Jersey) Stella developed a pathologic fear of being alone at night. It was a time when I was obliged to travel quite a bit. We hired the elder daughters of neighbors or Stella slept at a friend's home, or Sonya would be living with us. I never understood the genesis of this fear, but it was real—a considerable source of distress. With the boys, during their younger years when I was either working or studying Stella would engage them in friendly quasi-philosophic discourse. In retrospect there was some lack of maternal (and paternal) warmth. Stella was in her twenties and her primary concern was for their intellectual development. Of course,

I was virtually the "invisible father" like so many other workaholic physicians of my generation. In retrospect, we were far from ideal parents; I don't think there was enough hugging, horse play and emotional support from either of us. I think in Stella's case she just had received too much smothering affection from Sonya during her childhood, and my parents had just been too busy making a living to spend a great deal of time with any of the children. I believe our parental inadequacies exacted a toll on the boys' psychological maturation.

For Stella there were only rare times when she was totally free of insomnia and periodic depression. Through the years she wore her considerable beauty well, and she was not vain. She never pressured me for more financial or social "success." We always lived comfortably, but only on Maui did she truly enjoy her life. I suspect our major problem was a divergence of views about what we expected of life and marriage. It is probably simplistic, but I think the ultimate cause of the demise of our marriage was a shared disappointment in what each expected of the other.

After the first year back on Maui we had an unexpected bonanza. One of my patients was Cecil Horowitz, a retired multi-millionaire from Newport Beach. Cecil had suffered a stroke that left him with severe left-sided weakness and slurred speech. It also seemed to affect his behavior; at times he was gratuitously gross. His wife, Emily, was an accomplished artist. Some of her paintings enjoyed permanent status in small museums in southern California. She was a connoisseur of modern art. I managed Cecil's hypertension and mild diabetes. The families became close. We spent many happy hours in their luxury condo in Kaanapali. One day Cecil asked if we would be interested in being their guests on a Baltic cruise! Due to his physical condition the Holland-American Line would not accept him as a passenger unless accompanied by a doctor. This seemed a bit extreme, and I was never quite convinced that this caveat was true. But we never questioned it. So the four of us flew to Copenhagen, boarded a luxurious cruise ship and toured the Baltic. It was a delightful, relaxing vacation. I jogged

the top deck of the ship every morning. When we were in port I ran the streets of Amsterdam, Helsinki, Stockholm and Leningrad as dawn was breaking. The Horowitz's were marvelous hosts. Cecil and Stella played hours of Scrabble and chess. They remained our very dear friends.

Back on Maui, I was drifting into the same state of professional ennui that had occurred in 1973, but I was resigned to spend the rest of my life on the island. Then I received a portentous letter from Bob Petersdorf. My last contact with him had occurred when I decided not to accept any more students from Washington. He was the current president of the American College of Physicians and chairman of a search committee seeking a new executive vice president. He called to say that I had made the short list! (I didn't even know I had been on the long list.) So, we had come to another treacherous fork in the road. This time I realized that I could not take leave of my group, once again abandon my patients, and ever hope to return to clinical practice on Maui. The bridges would really be burned. I knew Stella would hate the idea of living in Philadelphia even worse than Chicago. I was right.

The ACP represented a totally new type of professional challenge. My contact with the organization had been minimal. I had been elected to fellowship way back in 1960, had lectured at regional meetings, attended a few annual sessions and studied their journal, *Annals of Internal Medicine*, religiously. My impression of the College was of a hoary, scholarly organization run by a handful of academic bluebloods from Eastern establishment medical schools. This perception was shared by about 90% of my colleagues in internal medicine. For every aspiring young internist, fellowship in the ACP was a requisite punch in your "credentials card," much like passage of the ABIM examination. I knew precious little about the ACP.

In the subsequent weeks while I ruminated, Stella fumed, "You know I hate the East. I made my mother take me away from Brooklyn when I was three! Now you want to schlep me back. I have roots here, and you want to rip them up—again. You are violating your bar-

gain—again!" I had no effective counter argument. After a while she stopped boiling, but settled on permanent simmer.

# 24

## *The American College of Physicians*

♦

### *(prelude to the denouement...)*

I agreed to let the Search Committee toss my hat in the "short list" ring. At the invitation of the College, Stella and I flew to Philadelphia to be interviewed and reconnoiter. Friends on Maui had relatives, older folks who lived in Vorhees Township in New Jersey, just across the Delaware River from Philadelphia. They had decided to sell their home and retire to Florida. In the days before my fateful meeting with the Search Committee, we did some pre-emptive (just in case) house hunting. We explored the Main Line (elegant but frightfully expensive, a train-ride to work) and Bucks County (trendy, pleasant, just too far). The home in Vorhees rested in a pleasant deciduous forest on the edge of the Jersey Pine Barrens. It was a modest, rustic bungalow set on four acres. It was seemingly isolated, but actually was surrounded by a rapidly growing, upper middle-class bedroom community. The price was a little beyond our projection, but negotiable. We told them of our situation—all was contingent upon landing the job. So we asked for a few weeks to let things settle, We wandered around the greater Philadelphia area for another day and then offered a reasonable counter bid with the "just in case" caveat. They wanted to think about it, but the vibes were good. If I got the job we would take the house; I thought "the little cottage in the forest" was ideal.

The members of he search committee were a formidable group. Chairman Bob Petersdorf knew me well. He had been an army consultant, who knew me from my days as chief at Brooke and Walter Reed, as a preceptor of his medical students on Maui and as editor of JAMA (I had appointed him to my editorial board). I suspected that it was Bob who had proposed my name. Jim Clifton was chairman of medicine at Iowa, successor to Bill Bean and a member of the "*Archives of Internal Medicine festschrift* banquet" group. I knew Jerry Barondess only by reputation as an erudite, literate clinician and educator. Jack Myers was chairman of medicine at Pittsburgh, better known as Black Jack, the legendary terror of the oral ABIM examinations. He was reputed to be the toughest senior examiner in the Board stable. Every candidate's nightmare was to draw Black Jack (or Red Butt of Mayo). The other committee members were unknown to me.

For the preceding month I had been contemplating this meeting. The College was the second largest medical organization in the world, after the AMA. It enjoyed a marvelous reputation as a venerable institution, a pioneer in innovative medical education. And there were many fine internists, some wiser, more literate and articulate than I, who could lead the College into new educational endeavors. But the world of medicine was beginning to roil. From my experience in practice, I had experienced the first *frisson* of the impending sea change. "Cost containment" had never been a consideration in all my years of teaching; a foolishly cavalier attitude in retrospect. I had worried about the implications of lack of access to proper medical care for millions who had no health insurance or marginal coverage. I was concerned about the escalating, near astronomical "pain and suffering" awards handed out by juries in medical litigation, escalating malpractice insurance premiums, and a dozen other "non-scientific" problems that were beginning to encroach on the professional lives of all physicians. But during my time in private practice these issues had been vaguely irksome, but always peripheral. They were the stuff of occasional editori-

als in medical journals. Concerns about economics and politics had never been important to me, professionally or personally.

I knew the College hierarchy had traditionally eschewed such mundane, "practice-related" problems, viewing them with some disdain. Many years earlier, the august Board of Regents had elected to remain "above the (political) battle." This attitude caused some members to feel that the "academic elitists" governing the ACP had lost contact with the day-to-day realities facing its constituents. They felt disenfranchised, their concerned voices unheeded by the Regents. A group of these dissident rank and file members responded by creating the American Society of Internal Medicine in 1956. Thus, internal medicine became the only specialty to have two organizations, quite disparate in orientation and philosophy. The Regents had made a miscalculation of historical proportion. (It took until 1998 for the two organizations to reunite.)

I had no experience in medical politics. From my hands-on experience at AMA, I learned to deplore the rough and tumble tactics of AMA-oriented lobbying, the detestable PACs and the whole "inside-the-beltway" mentality. I also felt that the AMA was viewed by most lawmakers as little more than a noisy, partisan, self-serving trade union that cared more about preserving the cushy financial *status quo* of doctors than serving as advocates for patients. The AMA track record in hysterically opposing Medicare in 1965, as "the camel's nose of socialized medicine under the tent wall," had sorely compromised any hope of political effectiveness. (Paradoxically, it was Medicare that began to make doctors rich. Bills to old folks that traditionally just gathered dust, began to get paid. Reimbursement for whatever a doctor thought his services were worth was paid—no questions asked. Indeed, you could get rich with a treadmill or a flexible sigmoidoscope.) That foolish AMA miscalculation about Medicare betrayed a mind-blowing lack of vision and exposed a level of venality that seemed to confirm public perceptions about greedy doctors.

I wondered if, perhaps, the ancient and honorable ACP, currently invisible in this turbulent arena, could change that image of avaricious, self-serving medical organizations. I wondered if the search committee representing the Board of Regents was ready for such a dramatic new philosophic adventure. I also wondered if I was the proper person to lead the charge down that dangerous road. I was far from convinced that I had the inclination or the *chutzpah*. I said all that during the interview. It lasted over two hours.

Afterward, I wandered through the elegant old mansion that housed the headquarters, somewhat dazed. I was convinced that my unseeming candor had been counter-productive. Who the hell was I to tell these distinguished medical "masters of the universe" how to run their shop? I came back to the hotel to tell Stella that I had self-destructed. Soon after we returned to Maui the phone rang; I got the job.

I still had two months before I was obliged to report in late 1976. Back on Maui we decided to rent the house rather than close it up and risk vandalism. The rental agent assured us that she would rent only to those with "proper references" who could prove they had the means to pay rent and maintain the house and land. We had poured thousands of dollars into the property. It was a delightful domicile, and we had every intention of coming back—after the Philadelphia intermission. The decision to rent turned out to be an unmitigated disaster. (*vide infra*)

Stella decided to spend the last weeks with the Horowitz's in Newport Beach. Cecil had struck it rich in post-war California by inventing and manufacturing "ready mix" concrete. It revolutionized the building industry overnight. Their home on Linda Isle in Newport Beach was a tribute to Emily's exquisite taste, a veritable museum of modern art. Emily was one of the cadre who came to help at home after Stella had sustained her myocardial infarction. So, after Stella departed Maui, I had the furniture shipped to storage in the mainland, pending settlement on a home in the greater Philadelphia area. I was camped in the Haiku house on an air mattress and sleeping bag. I was cooking for

myself, back to baked beans, hamburgers and hot dogs. It bore an uncomfortable redolence of the mean days when I first had landed in Chicago.

Then a strange thing happened. I was running in the Maui Marathon for charity. Three friends and I had formed a relay team, and we each ran three two-mile legs from Kahalui to Hana. It was a great fun event; we came in about the middle of the pack. And there was a beer bust afterward on the beach park at Hana. Somehow I found myself talking with a young female reporter from the *Maui News*. She said she knew of me, admired my column. She drove me back to her apartment in Wailuku, and we made love. She was a very sexy lady, and I was pretty hungry. For about a week we saw a great deal of each other. She knew that Stella had left the island, was not happy about the move to Philadelphia and I am sure that I expressed my ambivalence about our domestic situation. Suddenly, she became very possessive, insisting that I separate from Stella. She would "come to Philadelphia and live with me!" I was appalled. I avoided seeing her for my remaining time on Maui, but she would show up at odd places unannounced and uninvited. This harassment persisted for many months by phone after I was working in Philadelphia. She was a very scary lady.

I flew to Los Angeles, picked up the Z (a newly acquired VW Rabbit was being shipped) and drove to Newport Beach. Stella was already in a terrible snit; her angst over the move East had been on low boil for months. Our trip across the country was an unrelenting nightmare. On three occasions Stella insisted that I take her to an airport so she could fly back to Maui. In Salt Lake City she actually had purchased a one-way ticket. But we thrashed it out, and she decided to give Philadelphia a chance. We drove directly to the cottage in Vorhees to close the deal.

It was evening and the quarter-mile driveway through the pines and oak was already in heavy shadow. Out of the blue, Stella said, "I couldn't stay here alone when you are traveling. It's too isolated." I was stunned; it was the first time that issue had surfaced. We both knew that the EVP job would require considerable travel. I said we would try

to get someone to stay with her, but I did not suggest that Sonya come from Maui. The "little cottage in the woods" was dead. The conversation with the older couple (who had accepted our compromise offer by phone and had the papers to be signed spread out on the desk) was strained, surreal. They had been counting on the sale of the house to help finance their impending move to West Palm Beach. I was virtually speechless. After about 15 dreadfully awkward minutes, we departed. We had no place to live! I was due to report to ACP in about one week.

For two days we wandered around the area from Camden to Cherry Hill to Paulsboro (where my old classmate Dick Dupree was practicing); everything we saw was either too shabby or too expensive. Finally, we found a condominium development near Haddonfield, called Uxbridge that seemed promising. They had several buildings that were already occupied and half dozen others under construction. The dwellings seemed a trifle dark but reasonably spacious for two people. There was one drawback; the waiting list would make it impossible to move into a new place for a month.

We decided to tough it out. We rented two adjoining rooms in a motel near Moorestown, smuggled in two illegal hot plates and camped uncomfortably for the duration. It was not a happy time, but Stella took it with remarkable grace. For the first few months Uxbridge was wonderful. We made friends with a lovely older couple, Ruth and Sherman Rose. He was chairman of the board of Subaru of America, and they chose to live in this modest condo "to be close to my office." Sherman was a very wise businessman who helped me understand some of the intricacies of corporate finance. The families became close. Later after we moved to Vorhees (ironically about half a mile from the "cottage in the woods"), Sherman became ill. He had been a chain smoker for 50 years and died rapidly from carcinoma of the lung. I had friends working in oncology at Penn look after him. Sherman had been asymptomatic until he began to lose weight. A chest radiograph revealed extensive disease. Radiation therapy was unavailing; death

occurred within six weeks. (It was a terrible scenario that was to be repeated with my brother Ken many years later.)

During our time at Uxbridge, Steven, who was now taking his internship at the University of Illinois Hospital, had met a sweet blonde nurse from Dallas named Kathy. They had been living together for a few months and decided to get married. We offered to have the ceremony in the pleasant club that served the folks in our condo. Stella took a dislike to Kathy. For her part, Kathy took few pains to cultivate Stella. But they suppressed their mutual antipathy, and Stella helped her select a trousseau and made all arrangements for the modest wedding. Kathy's parents flew up from Dallas; they were a pleasant, unprepossessing couple. The wedding was simple reformed Jewish, even though Kathy was an unenthusiastic southern Baptist. Soon thereafter, Steven accepted a fellowship in nephrology at UCLA (L.A. County Hospital) and they headed west.

In the meantime Jon had been graduated from the University of Hawaii and took off to try his luck job-hunting in the rough and tumble Los Angeles media market. With the money earned "free-booting" in Honolulu, he rented a small apartment and then really pounded the pavements. Jon did not lack *chutzpah* and soon landed a job editing news videotape for one of the large LA television stations. Quite rapidly, he earned a reputation as one of the best editors in the city. Over the years, he became the chief editor for "Eye on LA," the top-rated news-feature "magazine" program in the area. He won three California Emmys for videotape editing, a singular feat in that most competitive environment. We were very proud of our sons.

While we were living in the condo, Stella had a close call on the interstate when the brand new VW Rabbit just quit at 65 miles an hour. We had it checked out at the dealership; of course, they could find no problem. Then it happened to me on my way to work. Within a week we traded it for a new Mercedes 300-D, a superior and thoroughly dependable beast. Our relationship hit a new nadir (still not the lowest perigee we were to endure), when Stella "discovered" shreds of a

letter that Dee had written to me a few months earlier. She would write to me at work occasionally, nothing sexy or even suggestive, but there was a tone of intimacy that was unmistakable. When I discovered the old letter in the pocket of a jacket, I (stupidly) tore it up and tossed the bits into a bathroom wastebasket. Stella went ballistic. I didn't deny the affair that had occurred while I had been in Chicago—living alone. But I spoke truth when I said it had long since been over. Of course, that did not matter; Stella was shattered.

To escape the acrimony, tears and threats, I threw some clothes into a bag and headed out. I landed in a grungy fleabag motel run by a couple of smarmy, pizza-munching ("you pay cash up front") Pakistanis, and spent three sleepless, guilt-ridden nights in that wretched place. Ultimately, I was "let back into the house," but our life was downhill thereafter. Stella became acutely depressed, threatened suicide. Empathetic intercession by a woman neighbor with whom she had become friendly, offered brief respite. But I think we were saved, temporarily, by the trip to China.

# 25

## *The Trip to China*

✦

### *(a nation in a time warp...)*

In December 1974 when I was editing JAMA, I wrote an editorial called "Message from China." It started as a "go with" piece in comment upon a thoughtful paper written by a young hematologist. He had been concerned about the failure in many developing countries to come to grips with the tough problems related to the inadequate preparation of indigenous medical professionals to meet the practical health needs of their people.

In seeking new insights to a discussion that I felt was already trailworn, I began to read about medicine in China. I wrote of "...the ruminations, pseudo-scientific and scientific, from a new generation of China watchers..." Some of the writings were annoyingly obsequious and uncritical, but some few of the papers expressed wonderment and admiration. Several of the authors were distinguished investigator-clinicians, and what they described tweaked the curiosity and challenged the imagination. I recall that E. Grey Diamond of Kansas City had written so glowingly of medicine in China, that I took it *cum granum salum*. I wrote, "We cannot be bulldozed or embarrassed into accepting anecdote and casual observation as scientific fact. We must weigh carefully the potential value of Chinese contributions against all other scientific pursuits. All ventures in investigative medicine must be scrutinized with steely-eyed impartiality. There is a limit to the talent, funds, and time available for research. All protocols must compete in

the market place of science." On rereading several years later, this essay comes off more than a trifle pompous. But I believe in the essence it expressed to this day. (I feel that the current attempts to legitimize "alternative" medicine and its multiple euphemisms, "complementary," or "traditional," or "new wave," by short-circuiting the scientific method and elevating hearsay, anecdote and "personal experience" to the level of scientific acceptability is wrong-headed, counter-productive, expensive and dangerous. More of this later.)

Quite out of the blue, Stella and I were invited to visit the People's Republic of China by Dr. T.O. Cheng, a fine cardiologist on the faculty of George Washington Medical School. TO had been graduated from the old St. John's Medical College of Shanghai. He emigrated to the U.S in 1949 and completed his education here. He had been back to China several times and was well known and widely respected by Chinese medical educators and administrators. This was a most unusual situation since relations between the PRC and the U.S. had been hostile since the Communist defeat of Chiang Kai Shek in 1949. The war in Korea had greatly exacerbated the political enmity. The Nixon visit of a few months earlier had been the first sign of a thaw. Thus TO's invitation was extraordinary. The trip was "all expense paid" by the Chinese Medical Association (CMA), including air and surface travel, food and housing. It seemed too good to be true, but it was real.

The CMA had asked Cheng to suggest candidates for a small medical delegation whose members might serve as contact points for future medical professional exchanges. He selected me because he had read my cheeky editorial (back in 1974!) indicating my "interest in traditional medicine" plus the fact that I was now the EVP of the College. Thus we were invited to submit CVs and reprints of our writings for perusal by the CMA. I was a little nervous about my time in Korea when the Chinese and I had been trying to kill each other, plus the JAMA editorial, "Message from China," a candid expression of my curiosity and reservations about non-allopathic medical practices. But I

had described my admiration for the major public health accomplishments of the health officials of the PRC.

In any event, our stuff must have been OK, and I was invited as the representative of the American College of Physicians. Accepting the invitation was sticky politically, since I had only been "in the saddle" at the College for a few months. But the Regents approved. It was one of those rare *carpe diem* situations. It seems I have had quite a few in my life.

Stella and I were invited to meet the PRC embassy staff in Washington. There we met the other members of our delegation. Dr. Sam Rosen was a venerable ENT surgeon of international reputation. Sam had invented the "stapes mobilization" procedure and had brought auditory relief to hundreds of poor people in Third World countries. He had been to China on several previous visits. His wife, Helen, was a strident liberal activist, supporting Sam's efforts, but officiously and aggressively "seeking help for all oppressed peoples." (Most of the time she was a major pain in the ass.) Dr. Victor Sidel was a noted community medicine specialist who had written the best book I had seen on medical care in China, "Serve the People." His son, Mark, was a rather pleasant nerd, a student of political science with two years of Mandarin tucked under his belt. The team was rounded out by Marie Cheng, an American nurse and wife of our group leader. (Ruth Sidel, Victor's wife, had been to China very recently; she was co-author of "Serve the People" and had written two other books about urban life and childcare in China.) All had been to China several times.

Let me say that from a political aspect, our little group could not be construed, by any possible standard, as being anything but openly sympathetic to the communist Chinese. They all leaned so far to the left that, on many occasions, it was patently annoying. Stella and I were the newcomers, certainly not great China aficionados, nor were we America apologists.

(I could never abide the basic philosophy of communism. From my earliest studies of Marx and Lenin I felt that any political thesis predi-

cated on suppression of individual initiative, call it capitalism, entre-preneurialism, or democracy, in the hope that the "people" would benefit before the "individual," was doomed. Alas, all men are **not** created equal; some are born rich, some smart, some black, some in Bangladesh or Grosse Pointe. All should be afforded the opportunity to rise to the station in life they can achieve by hard work, education and good luck. Every civilized society must ensure that no citizen regardless of genetic inheritance or affluence, is denied the basic needs of life: food, shelter, health care, education. As has been said many times, the measure of a civilized society is how it cares for its poor, ill and aged. But this can be accomplished without stifling the basic human drive to achieve and prosper, the essence of freedom. Of course, our system is admittedly imperfect, but thus far it is the most successful man has yet devised. Any student of human nature could have guessed that within time the Soviet system would implode. This is the same fate that occurs in fascist states or any other system of governance that is based on denial of individual freedom. Although I deplored communism as a political philosophy and the repressive way of life it imposed on its subjects, I planned to be open-minded and quietly observant while in China. I had never walked in the shoes of a Mao Tse Tung.)

The meeting at the PRC embassy was prelude to what we would encounter in China. Tea and cigarettes were in abundance. Initial stiff formality, bows and handshakes all around, attended by rare smiles; It was all very business-like. Monitoring cameras ogled from every corner. The décor was a study in austerity—Spartan furnishings and wall hangings. Apparently not too many westerners had been within these grim walls. (Curiously, this grave building was just a few blocks from the Australian embassy where I had attended more than one raucous, classic Aussie beer bust after Mercury mission briefings at Langley. Two of our medical flight controllers were from Down Under. The contrast in atmosphere was striking.) Our hosts outlined the itinerary of our visit; it was breathtaking in scope. After a few mai tai toasts, the

too-serious Chinese loosened up a tad, a few more smiles. More importantly, we all passed muster.

I prepared three large foot-lockers filled with a year's worth of back issues of *Annals of Internal Medicine*, audio cassettes of teaching sessions, dozens of complete copies of the most recent ACP Medical Knowledge Self Assessment Program (MKSAP). I had them sent to the Chinese Medical Society for distribution to medical schools. We were asked to prepare three lectures to be delivered to faculty and students in Peking (now Beijing), Shanghai, Chenyang, Sian and Harbin. The only problem with all this was that English had not been used in the PRC for the past ten years. It had not been taught, and those who knew English were forbidden to speak the language. We were told this was changing, but at the present time very few Chinese had any familiarity with English. I prepared lectures and slides on "Viral Hepatitis," "Coronary Heart Disease," and "Diabetes Mellitus." Good luck!

We departed on June 21, 1977 for a tightly orchestrated 28-day visit. We flew Air France from JFK to Charles de Gaulle in Paris. There we spent a dreary evening at the Jacques Borel Hotel at Roissy near the airport. It was one of those super-sleek European hostelries—all chrome and glass splashed with decorator orange. The tiny rooms were reminiscent of Pullman compartments or Tokyo "bureau drawer" airport facilities. The waiters in the mawkishly baroque, out-priced dining salon worked diligently to preserve and embellish the traditional *soupcon* of disdain and arrogance that has come to characterize generations of Gallic soufflé servers. (shades of Robert and Jean Louis; it must be in the genes) I expressed my ugly American displeasure at their slow service and officious attitude by leaving the traditional U.S. copper penny under the plate. Stella was horrified, but I felt vindicated. They can shove the Jacques Borel. The only good thing that has come out of France since Lafayette was Edith Piaf.

The next morning we flew CAAC (Civil Aeronautics Authority of China), a people-packed 707 to Karachi. Passenger nationality reflected the prevailing political preference of the PRC, a marvelous

spectrum of color, costumes and babble: Mali, Mexico, Albania, North Korea and Chile. (Chile? Yes, Chinese recognition of Chile followed swiftly upon the retreat of Soviet "technicians" after the CIA-assisted demise of Allende. Sino-Soviet antipathy was rapidly displacing Sino-American antipathy. Siberia was uncomfortably closer than California.)

We caught shrouded glimpses of the Golden Horn of the Bosporus as we swept over the uneven, barren plains of the Middle East (the long-since gone "Fertile Crescent"). In Karachi we tumbled sleepily into buses and were trundled past machine-pistol laden guards into the terminal waiting room. We stretched muscle-knotted legs as we prowled the exotic shops adjacent to the terminal: camel saddles, marble chess sets, brasses, bronzes, rugs and myriad intriguing trinkets. It was the usual tourist-oriented oriental bazaar *chazerai*. We noted the prominent, larger-than-life-sized photos and heroic portraits of Bhutto and his current henchmen. (On our return trip the pictures had all been replaced by large clean empty rectangles; Bhutto and company had tumbled from grace. *Sic semper tyrannus.*)

Soon we were smoothly airborne again. The food was rice with some mysterious brown meat. (I though it might be some kin of the same strange beast I had eaten in Manila, or was it Lahore, or Tainan?) We drowsed across the top of the subcontinent; cloud-covered Tibet slid below and someone said we were over China. Glimpses of the land revealed an unchanged landscape—no Great Wall rose to challenge the morning sky—no tinkling caravans from Gobi. Just low-ranging, parched, dun-colored, rough-hewn hills. It could have been Nevada. Abruptly, the mauve land turned splotchy green with patch-quilt farmlands, aggressively irrigated.

Our faithful workhorse slanted in and settled gently on the tarmac. We emerged squinting, pleased, hungry, sleep-frazzled. The Beijing airport serves over seven million people, a population about the size of Chicago. But this was no O'Hare; I counted four planes in the unloading area. A giant, two-story portrait of a benevolently smiling Chair-

man Mao dominated the front of the terminal building, flanked by cryptic quotations in Chinese and English, warmly welcoming all friends of the revolution. We had arrived in China.

We were not prepared for what came next. Over the years Stella and I had been peripatetic wanderers into some rather remote corners of the planet. Such exposure should endow one with some sophistication in handling abrasive encounters with strange people in unlikely places and alien cultures. The special tyrannies of petty officials at dozens of international borders were nothing new to us. But we were not prepared for the Chinese version.

In the noisy turmoil of the Beijing Airport there was a some minor hassling with very young, very grim, sloppily-uniformed immigration officials (all wearing the distinctive arm band of the Red Guard). Obviously, they did not like round-eyed, imperialist devils; tourism had not yet come to China. The problem? Evidently some bored clod back in 1974 had neglected to stamp Stella's yellow immunization record, after she had received her required shots. That bureaucratic sin had remained undetected in countless countries—until now. After over an hour of inter-lingual wrangling with neither team understanding a word spoken by the other, we were rescued by our embarrassed hosts from the Chinese Medical Association.

Their leader was deputy secretary-general of the CMA, a lean, handsome, chap who spoke little English but soon became a dear friend. (He also had a delicious sense of humor and a devastating table tennis backhand; he and Stella had some spirited matches.) The chief interpreter was a charming, effervescent young man, veteran survivor of several previous English-speaking delegations. The second interpreter was an affable, reflective gentleman. These three were to shepherd us on our four-week exploration of China. We all became close "comrades." They were unfailingly cheerful and helpful, courteous and thoughtful. After the airport unpleasantness, we never had the sense that we were unwelcome interlopers, never suffered that eerie feeling that we were being spied upon (even after anticipating such stuff).

Our delegation was a mixed bag: individuals with vastly different temperaments, personalities and, as we were to discover, agendas. To accommodate our individual needs and desires required monumental patience and consummate malleability by our hosts. Their equanimity was awe-inspiring. Stella and I were the least demanding of our fussy group. After determining that my four crates of educational goodies had arrived, but that our personal luggage had not (!) but was "being traced" (it arrived two days later, having "detoured" mysteriously to Moscow), we were whisked away in the sanctuary of "Car #4" (out of five). As the new people in the expedition, our ranking was appropriate. Each couple in our party had been assigned a gray, six-cylinder, Chinese-made sedan. It reminded one of a forties Chevy, reasonably spacious, with curtained rear windows, unpretentious in appointments, but comfortable. Stick shift and static-haunted radio tuned to commercial channels were standard.

Car #4 seemed to be miraculously transported to every city we visited; obviously it had many siblings. Chinese chauffeurs were hand picked. They were compulsive about maintaining formation despite traffic conditions. This necessitated occasional, sudden dashes attended by much frantic horn blowing. Chinese pedestrians, cyclists and ox-cart drivers seemed "traffic naïve" to the point of suicidal nonchalance in the presence of our raging vehicles. I knew our car enjoyed three speeds forward, but third gear became the hands-down favorite, regardless of traffic conditions. It was sort of like driving in Tokyo or Rome, but the enemies were pedestrians and bikes instead of Toyotas and Fiats.

At that time there were no privately owned automobiles in China. Later we caught glimpses of another type of sedan—a long, black, more elegantly appointed model—obviously reserved for very VIP types. We saw trucks of every size and description all painted olive drab, some with camouflage designs. There were hundreds of tough, jeep-like vehicles seen on every road, all spotlessly maintained. None had military markings. But the capability of pressing several thousand

such vehicles into use for mass military transport in the event of "national emergency" was unmistakable. Our cavalcade swept through the tree-lined outskirts of Beijing and came to city center. Bicycles were the obvious mode of private transportation; they swarmed like locusts. (I noted to Stella that this was in marked contrast to Leningrad, where despite the paucity of private automobiles and desultory public transportation, there had been few bicycles. We reckoned that Russians walked a lot.)

Most of the new construction in Beijing was solid, cinder-blockish, certainly unpretentious (an apt word to describe much of what we saw in China). However, we did see thousands of crude, hastily knocked-together shacks cheek-by-jowl, jammed into almost every parkway and open lot. Our interpreter said these were "temporary" shelters that had been erected soon after the terrible earthquake that devastated much of central China in 1976. Millions of displaced homeless people were still living in these wretched hovels.

Soon we swung onto a broad thoroughfare that was truly gridlocked with bicycles. The din of horns was cacophonous. Incongruously ornate street lamps that we had observed on peripheral streets had been replaced by even more elaborate, baroque multi-globed creations. The contrast with the painfully functional design of everything else we had seen was striking. Was there some streetlight "status" symbolism at work, or had some enterprising Viennese streetlight huckster given the mayor of Beijing a great sales pitch?

Everywhere people bustled. One could easily believe "a billion or so," and it would seem that most of them were clustered in downtown Beijing. Clothing was austere and simple: adults wore black, white or gray. Rare flashes of color came from small children. At length, we pulled into the driveway of the Peking Hotel. Visitors from every Third World country swarmed the entrance and lobby. The hotel was a vast, impressive structure with a "Woolworth building-like" facade. It was a landmark reminder of the profound Russian influence on everything Chinese, a dreary relic of the preceding decade of paper-thin

Sino-Soviet felicity. Clunky Muscovite-style architecture was among the Soviet's less memorable cultural contributions. The hotel rose about 20 stories and must have contained a thousand rooms. The lobby was adorned with giant frescoes and posters fervently extolling the virtues of the socialist revolution and "hard work in factory and farm." The cliché came in many languages, but Spanish was notably absent. The Sino-Chilean reconciliation had been too recent for the fresco painters.

Once in our spacious, adequate (and unpretentious) room, we were advised that there would be a briefing in 30 minutes. Since we had no clothing for changing, we splashed water on dusty faces and were properly prompt. We were greeted by high-ranking members of the CMA and the Peking Medical Association. After the amenities of dutifully translated, overly-effusive introductions, tea was served (a delicate, marvelous beverage served from large two-quart thermos dispensers stationed at intervals along the long table), and cigarettes (ubiquitous, plentiful, sans filters) were offered. Then we got down to business. We were to visit eight cities: Ta Ching (the red banner petroleum city). Harbin, Dairen, Shenyang, Yenan, Ta Chai (the red banner agricultural city) and Shanghai. We were to spend five days in Beijing before departing.

Lunch was our first exposure to the magnificent cuisine we were to enjoy throughout our time in China. (Often during these sumptuous repasts, I reflected, guiltily, on the skinny displaced peasants we had seen in their pathetic "temporary" shelters. One of our meals could have fed a village.)

Our first orientation tour was to the amazing Beijing underground system. Access was available through unobtrusive stores in many different neighborhoods via sliding floor panels that exposed long ladders. One descended about 30 feet into an endless labyrinth of corridors punctuated by large rooms. It reminded me of what underground Winnipeg must have been like during excavation, and the dank atmo-

sphere jolted me back to the underground arms factory I had explored in Korea.

We were given an extensive, top-of-the-lungs briefing by a very proud, very young engineer, always through the political filter of our interpreters. In walking the vast damp corridors, one encountered the aroma of incense while the giant catacombs reverberated with eerie, piped-in Chinese opera music. I assumed this extraordinary audio-olfactory experience was designed to lessen the sense of claustrophobia and isolation, if and when the areas ever swelled with habitation. It did not succeed for our small group; the scent and sound merely exacerbated a sense of the surreal. The tunnels all connected to amphitheater-like rooms that had been designated for power generation, grain storage, cafeterias, sleeping areas, hospital, etc. At this moment they were all just capacious, empty caverns with ghostly reverberations and flickering low amperage illumination. In every sense the tunnel system was being prepared as an underground, nuclear-escape warren for the luckier citizens of Beijing.

But why? They made no bones about it; the Chinese felt vulnerable to a missile attack with nuclear warheads. With a curious pride and some element of defiance, the officials displayed this and similar areas under other major cities to all VIP foreign visitors to indicate that they are "ready" for such an eventuality. I did not ask the obvious question, attack from whom? But it was common knowledge that tension along the wild and barren Sino-Soviet border in Siberia was an everyday fact of life. Clashes between battalion-sized units had occurred in Sinkiang. And, of course, the U.S. and the Soviets both had ICBMs that could reach China. The chief engineer spent considerable time discussing the threat of the "socialist imperialists," which we soon came to recognize as the official euphemism for the Russians. The U.S. was called the "capitalist imperialist," but we were spared that lecture. (I suspected the Cubans and other "friends of China" got the expanded, unexpurgated version.)

Aside from the sheer magnitude of the engineering undertaking, we were impressed that the labor for this "work in progress" was being done by "volunteers" from neighborhood groups: children, retired people, workers from every aspect of life. They would dedicate days to work on the underground project. As with all other public works in China, this was a communal, people-powered endeavor. Picks and shovels and lots of sweat, not giant earth-moving equipment, were the vehicles. Volunteerism in communist China had a different definition than in the democratic West. It was simply accepted that as a citizen you would pitch-in and do these good works for the benefit of **all** the people. The sense of personal sacrifice that might arise in the mind of someone in the West and result in grudging compliance with this "obligated volunteerism" did not seem to exist here. I could have been wrong, and perhaps there was some resentment at the quasi-forced labor, but I think not. There was a different mind-set at work here, quite alien to free-wheeling Westerners. And from what we saw there was an enormous amount of work yet to be done to convert these monstrous caves into habitable living space. I only hope that the easing of world tensions that has resulted in the markedly diminished threat of nuclear holocaust has resulted in a retrofitting of these monuments to national paranoia, into curious anachronisms or tourist attractions. But I am far from sure.

The remainder of this first afternoon was spent exploring the Forbidden City. It would be difficult to describe the dazzling splendor of these grounds and buildings that had been the abode and playground of imperial dynasties for centuries. Now they had become political symbols. Score another one for the revolution. In the past, direct eye-contact by commoners with any members of the court was forbidden under penalty of torture or death. The People's Revolution had thrown open the gates to everyone and invited the people to enjoy, even touch, the priceless statuary and wall hangings. Uniformed guides described the incredible delicacy of craftsmanship, always emphasizing that the work represented the labor of peasant-artisans cruelly exploited by the

ruling classes. As we soon discovered in modern China, the exquisite artifacts of the imperial past were preserved for their intrinsic beauty, but also to serve as object lessons of past oppression, especially for the young. We all reveled in the beauty of the trees of jade and precious stones, and I saw once again some of the fabulous T'ang flying horses I had been privileged to admire during the PRC exhibit that had toured the U.S. in1975. At every opportunity the cadres of official guides rhapsodized about their newfound freedom and the benevolent release from the bad old, kowtow days of subjugation by the imperial dynasties.

(I have often pondered over the fact that most of the great enduring monuments of the past, the pyramids of Egypt and Mexico, the Great Wall, the inspired cathedrals and castles of Europe, were mostly constructed by "involuntary" labor (or something worse) and paid for by "involuntary" taxation of common people. Does that mean that voluntary labor and non-coerced finance **cannot** create such deathless structures? Were these eternal monuments worth the insufferable hardship endured by the workers and their families? Probably not.)

We returned to the hotel in the early evening, fatigued but exhilarated. Dinner was a festive event with much all-around toasting (mai tai and plum brandy that had the kick of Yugo slivovitz). The alcohol exacerbated our considerable jet lag, and I have dim recollections of endless expressions of undying international friendship and everlasting personal felicity. "Gam bei" (bottoms up) took on several new dimensions; either our Chinese hosts had prodigious ethanol tolerance or they were faking it. We all got very clever at raising our glasses often but taking small sips.

The most memorable event of the day was our meeting with the legendary Dr. George Ma Hatem. He was an American dermatologist, trained in the U.S., who had come to China in 1933. He was the most venerated and respected American in China. He strode beside Chairman Mao on the Long March and was an adviser and confidant during the time of reorganization in the caves of Yenan. He had been an active

leader in the reconstruction of China, especially tackling the over-whelming problems of public health. He was personally credited with the virtual elimination of widespread malnutrition, schistosomiasis, venereal disease (he shuttered all the infamous brothels of Shanghai and other cities) and was working on Hansen's disease (he was intrigued by my stories of Kalaupapa) and tuberculosis. George radi-ated wisdom and charm; the affection of his co-workers was palpable. I use the word "charisma" very selectively; George Hatem had charisma. We saw a great deal more of him. (In 1988 I brought George to an ACP annual session where he gave a guest lecture on "Medicine in China." He received a standing ovation. For many months after our China visit I tried to persuade George to record his memoirs. I offered to send him a tape recorder, provide secretarial support and serve as his editor. He thought this was much too hubristic, not in consonance with his modest, socialist "all for the masses" philosophy. He died a few years later, his experiences unrecorded. A great cultural and histor-ical loss. Few individuals have had a greater impact on the health of millions of people than George Hatem.)

It was powerfully evident that politics in the PRC was a paramount force. It permeated every aspect of life: medicine, industry, agriculture, education. Our delegation was one of the first to enter China since the fall of the Gang of Four and the Cultural Revolution that inspired Mao to create the infamous Red Guard. That terrible political aberration was the darkest era in modern Chinese history. Several generations of intellectuals were systematically humiliated and their minds and spirits virtually destroyed. The saga of "a thousand flowers..." will forever remain an enigma to me; it set all progress in China back 20 years. In some cities, notably Shanghai, there was still some episodic violence from remnants of "Gang" adherents. The propaganda barrage was unrelenting. We became inured to the constant repetition of the axiom, "To believe what has happened in China, you must see it." Indeed we did, for the next 27 days.

Our third day in Beijing brought our luggage (the story of its bizarre migration was never revealed) and a torrential downpour. I had made a special request to our Chinese hosts that Stella and I wanted to visit the Great Wall. All the others in our party had performed this ritual before and were not particularly interested in a fairly long and soggy auto trip. So Car #4 made the pilgrimage with our translator. Ever since I was a small boy and devoured the tales of Richard Halliburton, I had sworn to visit three places before I departed this wondrous planet: the Taj Mahal, the pyramids of Giza, the Great Wall of China. We had already been to Agra, and Egypt was to come later, but here we were! The trip through the rain-spattered countryside was uneventful, and we were afforded a running commentary on the history of the Cultural Revolution. By the time the first distant fairy towers came into view, we had received a detailed accounting of the life and times of the Great Hero and the miraculous transformation he had wrought in the wretched lives of the people (suffered under the heel of the Kuomintang and the despot Chiang Kai-shek). It was classic dialectic cant; our enthusiastic young translator had memorized the Little Red Book. But his sincerity was endearing.

The Wall was all that I had envisioned. I climbed to the "Fourth Tower," a traditional up-hill hike for all reasonably well-conditioned tourists. Beyond this point the Wall had crumbled for several hundred feet before it rose once again. Mist drifted eerily to obscure distant battlements, but it merely added to the mystique. The driving rain ensured that I was quite alone; I explored the tower for half an hour. Enemies have breached the Wall several times, but it had repelled Mongol tribesmen from medieval times. Most recently in the 17th century, a scurrilous Ming general turned traitor and enabled Manchu invaders to breach the barricade, and the Manchus established the last imperial dynasty to rule the Central Kingdom from Beijing.

It would seem that all great walls and battlements and forts serve only to challenge invaders to attack and breach. The history of warfare is an endless repetition of new weaponry conquering old weaponry. I

gazed into the swirling fog banks and could almost hear the clash of arms, the chaos and tumult of ancient battles. The magnificent Wall weaves its way across 2400 kilometers from Kansu Province to the Yellow Sea north of Beijing. I left reluctantly. I am told that today the Wall has been besieged once again; it has been "commercialized" with motels, shops, McDonalds and swarming herds of "marauding" tourists. I have no desire to go back; I'll keep my magic.

From the Wall we went to see the Ming tombs. One must pass down a wide road flanked by greater-than-life-sized carvings of real and mythical creatures to reach the Great Tomb, where we were allowed to wander freely amidst the crypts. The Ming Dynasty ruled from 1360 to 1644—almost contemporary by traditional Chinese standards. Its last "partisans," clinging to the dynastic heritage, held out on Taiwan after they had been driven from the Mainland. I think the magnificent movie, "The Last Emperor," related to these few sad, deposed and degenerate folk.

From the tombs we went to the Summer Palace of the Dowager Empress. We had lunch in a marvelous "audience room" that bore the most elaborate, intricately designed (and magnificently preserved) ceiling we had ever seen. The Summer Palace area is a favorite resort stop for the citizens of Beijing. Of course, it has been propagandized as another benefit of the Revolution; previously off-limits to common people, now open to all. It is an enchanting park; the palace languishes beside a vast, lily-padded lake with fairy-tale arched bridges linking small islands where ancient pagodas seem to float in the distance. All the covered walkways were intricately and ornately carved and painted. Various treasures from the imperial past, jewels and carvings, were kept under glass. I marveled at the lack of security, but theft of such treasures was not a consideration. All the ancient statuary (as in the Forbidden City) is exposed, but seems to have withstood the vicissitudes of nature and the curious hands of "commoners" remarkably well. One can only wonder how long before such exposure to the polluted atmosphere and public pawing will exact a toll.

In Shenyang we were taken to the Hospital of Traditional Medicine. After the now well-established ritual of tea (accepted eagerly) and cigarettes (refused smilingly) and an orientation by a Leading Member of the hospital's Revolutionary Party Committee, we were taken to the radiology department. There we were introduced to a 15-year-old boy who had suffered a fracture of the left lower leg. The radiograph revealed a comminuted tibial fracture with moderately displaced fragments and a simple fracture of the fibula. The translator told us that the patient had been receiving galvanic stimulation for 15 minutes through two "negative electrodes" (acupuncture needles) inserted just above the lateral malleolus of the fractured leg with a "positive" acupuncture needle inserted just below the lateral tibial tuberosity. The boy's ankle twitched rhythmically with the surges in current. We were told he had received no previous medication. He was alert, somewhat apprehensive (perhaps due more to the presence of Western strangers than his fracture), but he responded to questions with an eager smile.

After 30 minutes of galvanic stimulation, three husky fellows came into the room. One gently took hold of the ankle, another grasped the thigh above the knee. They pulled with considerable, though controlled, force, while the third chap reduced the fracture manually, apparently massaging the fragments into proper alignment. I watched the boy's eyes and demeanor throughout the procedure; there was no wince, no dilatation of pupils, no indication of pain. Soon after the reduction, the ecchymotic fracture site was wrapped in cloth impregnated with a blackish, sticky ointment. Some thin padding and five splints, about one inch wide and six inches long, made of dried wood pulp (bamboo is also used) were placed longitudinally around the circumference of the leg and held in place with Velcro strips. We were told that the splints would be adjusted periodically, tightened or loosened according to edema and the alignment of the fragments as seen on radiograph. The middle straps were tightened first, then the distal and finally the proximal. Post-reduction films revealed the tibial fracture to be in excellent alignment.

The child left the "operating room" smiling and posing for pictures by his appropriately astonished Western visitors. The physician who had directed the procedure said that the boy would remain immobile with the limb elevated for two weeks while the edema subsided. (What would an HMO administrator have to say about that?) During this interval he would have passive manipulation of knee and ankle joints by gentle massage. By the third or fourth week he would have exercise with passive joint flexion; regular active exercise would begin at five to seven weeks when callus formation had taken place. At seven to ten weeks local external fixation would be removed and weight-bearing begun, then walking exercise would start. We were told that no one could recall the last open (surgical) fracture reduction that had been done in that hospital. However the doctors advised that they have employed regional Novocain block (local anesthesia) and even general anesthesia for more difficult fractures.

Plaster of Paris and joint fixation were anathema on Chinese orthopedic wards. I had spoken to several American orthopedic surgeons who had visited China; they were uniformly impressed. Admittedly, one child, one procedure, no chance for long term follow-up, but…it was a unique experience. Orthopedics (known as traumatolgy in China) has a 3000 year heritage. It reached a zenith during the Yuan Dynasty (1271-1368). Kublai Khan, the first Yuan ruler, invited Arab "traumatologists" skilled in fracture management to the kingdom. It was he who greeted Marco Polo. Yuan descendants included Genghis Khan, the leader of the aggressive "Mongol horde" that swept across Europe. The Khans were overthrown by the Mings who built the Wall. All of this was part of our indoctrination in Shenyang. In the weeks that followed we were to witness a variety of surgical procedures conducted under herbal and acupuncture analgesia that were frankly astonishing to Western eyes.

Ta Ching was a state of mind, as well as a wind-swept outpost on the vast Manchurian plain. It epitomized the much publicized "spirit of China" in 1977. From our very first briefing in Beijing, we heard,

"in industry we learn from Ta Ching; in agriculture we learn from Ta Chai." It was one of those eternal mantras—repeated endlessly. (I began to think of the "Manchurian Candidate" with the hypnotic, drum-beat repetition.)

And so we were in Ta Ching—after a relaxed overnight train ride from Beijing. The rain was unrelenting; ashen sky matched the unsmiling countenance of the beige countryside. No nonsense here. No dogs or cats either. At least we had some respite from the pervasive, choking smog of the big city. In every urban area we visited, even without significant motor traffic, the ambient irritating atmosphere came from domestic cooking fires and industrial effluent. Smokestacks belched furiously, reminiscent of the ugly glory days of Pittsburgh and Birmingham. Everyone in our party developed laryngitis and itching conjunctivae. I mused about the synergistic effect of epidemic cigarette smoking plus the chronic, pervasive, toxic atmospheric exposure, on respiratory and cardiovascular systems. I did not know our physician hosts well enough, yet, to broach the subject of potential long-term health effects.

In late afternoon we pulled into Ta Ching station. It was bedecked with large-character, white-on-red (always) posters flanked by huge portraits of Marx, Engels, Stalin (long dead, now vilified in the Soviet, but not forgotten in Stalinist China; a statement about current Russo-Sino relations) and Mao. "Leading Members" of the Ta Ching Revolutionary Committee greeted us formally, and we were escorted to the Ta Ching Industrial Museum. This was a monument to the spirit and energy of one man, the late "Iron Man" Wang Chin-His, a popular legend—exemplar of Chinese bootstrap operations.

Ta Ching was the place of oil fields. Progress in this area had been slow. The years of war against the Japanese and the revolution to oust Chiang Kai-shek and his minions, had exhausted China. There was little skill and fewer resources to develop the vast fields and compel them to yield the black gold. Merciless storms sweeping in from Siberia made work in this unfriendly tundra arduous even for the most hardy.

When the era of Sino-Soviet cooperation was in full flower, engineers from the lush oil fields of Baku swarmed Ta Ching, helping eager but inexperienced local workers extract the treasures that lay below the forbidding land. But when the era of fragile political friendship ended, with astonishing suddenness, several thousand Soviet technicians departed from all parts of China. The Russian oil field engineers and roustabouts soon vanished, lock, stock and barrel (including drilling teams, heavy equipment and even blueprints). China was left with little but enormous pride, ferocious anger and legions of idle people. It could have meant disaster for Ta Ching.

Into the breach stepped "Iron Man" Wang, "vanguard fighter of the Chinese working class." (It had a nice ring.) He rallied his amateur oilmen and set about to wrest their rightful prize from the reluctant earth. Where scarce equipment was needed, he had it fabricated from existing bits and pieces. Cannibalization became a way of life. When a new oil rig had to be hauled miles across the tundra with no bulldozers or trucks, he put thousands of callused hands on long cables—and the derricks were moved and erected manually. He was the Paul Bunyan of the oil fields, but indeed no fictional character. I suspect the tales of his feats became magnified as the legend grew, but the documented stories of his personal bravery and charismatic presence, his singular devotion to the "teachings of Mao Tse-tung" were preserved in heroic-sized paintings, photographs and dioramas in the museum. Wang Chin-His was a true folk hero. We were told that China was approaching self-sufficiency in oil production and was soon to begin export to Third World friends. I suspected that this was optimistic propaganda, but Ta Ching made one helluva story.

As we walked from the museum, we encountered several hundred People's Liberation Army (PLA) soldiers. It is remarkable that personnel of the PLA wear no insignia. I learned that one could distinguish an enlisted man from an officer by counting tunic pockets; officers had four, EM just two. Otherwise rank was impossible to delineate. They all looked like kids just off the farm. (They had not looked like that

when their daddies came roaring over the ridge with bugles and cymbals and grenades in 1951. Time and tide and all that...) As we approached they broke into spontaneous applause (typical of other crowds we encountered in China). We bowed and responded in kind.

We visited a model drilling rig and watched a team go through its paces with the precision of a ballet troupe. It was just a trifle stagy. I had seen drilling teams operating near Odessa in the Permian Basin. These Chinese roustabouts seemed just as tough but worked with a precision and confidence around the powerful equipment that made their performance seem almost choreographed. In Ta Ching the "lesson" is simple: China must be independent and self-sufficient. The "proper line of Chairman Mao" dictated that China must learn from the West, master the nuts and bolts of technology, but not be seduced by the negative Western ethos. They made no bones; they would "go it alone"—operation bootstrap—if necessary, rather than succumb to the sloth and corruption of the imperialist capitalist West. This was never, never spoken, but one could feel it in every nuance.

During a briefing session we were informed of the impressive productivity of the Ta Ching fields. But even to the inexperienced eye there was no active drilling. We saw no pumping stations, no overland pipelines or tanker trucks. We were told it was all occurring underground. We could not assess the efficiency or productivity of these oil fields, but obviously the PRC did not consume petroleum products with the same gargantuan gulps as the West. One could only wonder about the future of world pollution and global warming when a billion plus Chinese all own automobiles!

Ta Ching served a purpose: dramatic, pragmatic "proof" of the toughness and resilience of Chinese workers and the virtue of self-reliance. As we were to observe in Ta Chai, workers arrived daily by the busload from all parts of China to "learn the lesson" of "Iron Man" Wang.

The Revolutionary Committee treated us to a banquet with the usual sumptuous, multi-course cuisine. This was followed by a two and

a half hour full-color film depicting the life and struggle of "Iron Man." The Chinese dialogue bereft of any English was mercilessly boring, but the message was clear (once again). Wang's difficult youth as a poor peasant in Kansu was the product of "ruthless exploitation and oppression by imperialism, feudalism and bureaucratic capitalism." We saw his melodramatic struggle against the Kuomintang and his heroic battles with hostile natural elements. Ultimately he overcame all adversity and led his singing comrades out to tame the oil fields.

It was a super-heroic movie done with the exaggerated expressions and gestures that reminded one of the silent films of the '20s. We were told that the production had been the brain child of Chiang Ch'ing (Mao's widow—now deposed and disgraced along with her other "Gang of Four" henchmen). On every side, in every brigade, hospital, factory and schoolroom we were regaled with tales of the evil and nefarious influence of Li Shao Chi, Lin Piao and the "Gang." It became a familiar litany; even the words changed very little from one corner of China to the next. Obviously, the country was still reeling under the impact of the 11th of October "revolution" (it had been a scant eight months earlier!)

In the blustering wind of another driving rainstorm, we visited a nearby "small parts depot." I wondered why this expensive delegation of doctors was being taken to this obviously humble facility. It soon became evident. We were treated to an amazing demonstration. Individual employees proudly displayed their ability to identify and locate various items of equipment in their particular warehouse, while blindfolded. Not only could they identify the weight, material, diameter, etc., but also the exact location of every nut, bolt, washer, spigot and widget. We were told that there were 150 such human "locators" in the warehouse area. But why? "To keep the warehouses operational in the event of a power blackout." It was the Beijing Underground Syndrome again. Was something rumbling in Sinkiang?

We saw a district hospital. Similar to all others: stark, functional, Spartan in equipment by any standard. But the stated mortality statis-

tics were astonishing: 159 deaths over a four-year period from a population of 25,000 served. Of course, such statistics are difficult to sort out: Were they truthful? What were the admission criteria? How many of the 25,000 died out of hospital? I did not ask. Most admissions were due to accidents, a few to stroke and the rest from cardiovascular disease and cancer. They attributed the low death rate to the fact that in Ta Ching only six percent of the population was over 65. But this was not unusual in a country where it was estimated that 50% of the population was under 30. One wonders about average life expectancy when confronted with such figures, and/or perhaps the birth rate?

In the afternoon we visited an agricultural brigade that raised corn, millet and a dozen other crops. We saw a fish hatchery and several cottage industries, including a modest distillery for the manufacture (and largely local consumption) of a particularly fiery, proudly-extolled brand of mai tai. This rugged beverage was guaranteed to keep any oil field roustabout feeling warm in his innards despite any arctic ambience. It would have done very well in Midland or San Angelo.

Our quarters in Ta Ching (you might guess) were spare, but clean and adequate. (As we were soon to realize, China had not yet discovered the wonderful world of tourism. In most places accommodations were not designed for western concepts of comfort. Actually, it was rather refreshing.) We shared the quarters with a colorful, chatty delegation from the Philippines (very little English). I wondered if they were from the communist (Moro) enclaves on Mindanao and northern Luzon that continued to terrorize local militias. I didn't ask. We did share the local beer, which was—as all the beer we sampled in China—robust and excellent even by European standards. (In my "post-holocaust bias," I have always suspected that the major contribution the Germans have made to world culture was their beer—Bach, Schiller, Leica and BMW notwithstanding. Sorry.)

Later I commented to one of our translators that I had seen no cats or dogs in China. This prompted a slightly embarrassed smile and shrug. But later someone told us that all non-working domestic ani-

mals had been eliminated by "popular consent." There had been no formal government edict. It would seem that (non-working) pets have little status in a pragmatic society where human competition for food is critical.

Despite the rain we sloshed to a farm brigade kindergarten where we were entranced by tiny tots who danced and sang delightfully. They were all decked out in gaily colored costumes in stark contrast to the somber grays and blacks of the adults. All the songs, plays and pantomimes had social-political themes: glorification of the worker, peasant and soldier. In Ta Ching, as everywhere else in China, the ethic of hard work was a constant drum beat. (Now I could understand the "Chinese water torture.") We never heard anything of the virtues of art, science, philosophy. Perhaps these were still considered bourgeois frivolities in the face of the practical problems of survival for a billion plus people. Or perhaps the decimation of the intellectuals by the Red Brigades made such thoughts politically incorrect—even now. Perhaps...

That evening Stella and I discussed the events of the day. The people all live hard; they lack material things. But we could sense no feeling of antipathy or envy for our obvious opulence. We could not escape the feeling that the "good of the majority" had superseded the aspirations and needs of the individual—on a universal scale. This was a difficult philosophy for Westerners to comprehend. It was the ultimate demonstration of pragmatism. Politics permeated every aspect of life. In one room of a factory where young women were repairing the rough, tattered clothing of oil field workers, one woman was reading aloud to the group from the fifth book of Chairman Mao. We were to see this tableau reenacted with different players many times. We conceded that our knowledge of ancient and contemporary China was painfully inadequate; it was impossible to place what we were witnessing into any realistic context based on our personal experience. But "the lesson of Ta Ching" embodied a graphic demonstration of the toughness and resilience of the people. Or were we being spoon fed?

(Let me wander for a moment. I have been hesitant to tackle the subject of traditional Chinese medicine—acupuncture and herbal medicine. Much has been written about traditional medicine that is anecdotal, laced with emotion, or frankly bad medical science. [Have you ever seen a report by an acupuncturist that was not positive? Talk about publication bias!] In the U.S. today, the subject has been politicized to the extent that there is a section of the NIH devoted to "investigation" of varieties of traditional medicine, most medical schools offer "alternative medicine" courses to students, health plans reimburse for many types of "complementary care" and conventional medicine has been driven [by threat of litigation] to grant legitimacy to practices that have never been subjected to the rigors of randomized controlled trials.

It is apparent that in America public disenchantment with conventional scientific medicine, as experienced via contact with many of its dispassionate practitioners, has driven many patients to seek help from the "traditionalists." The causes of this defection are legion. But most can be related to patient perceptions of arrogance and cavalier attitudes by physicians, an irrational escalation of public expectation for relief and cure that is beyond current medical capability, and a desire by many patients to "participate" in their management, rather than be passive "recipients" from paternalistic practitioners.

There is no doubt that allopathic medicine lacks many answers, and each day new discoveries (or review of old existing data) cause us to delete long-accepted concepts and/or expand our inventory of new "evidence-based" ideas. I hasten to concede that many of the successes of traditional medicine may well have roots in undiscovered physiological truth. Such things demand exploration by tough scientific methodology. If they withstand such scrutiny, each new procedure or therapy will be embraced eagerly, by us "traditionalists." And there are many precedents.

But, having said that, in my opinion (bias?) we have entered a dangerous arena where anecdote and hearsay threaten to gain status com-

parable to scientific rigor, in the public mind. Widespread scientific illiteracy, innumeracy and unrealistic expectation have all contributed to this mess. Unfortunately, publicity and politics have emerged as dark figures to challenge scientific truth. I don't know how it will end, but I am increasingly worried.)

Much that we witnessed in China was frankly amazing: acupuncture (with or without galvanic stimulation), acupressure (for dental extractions), moxibustion (in its infinite varieties—burning herbs on needles), cupping. I could not begin to evaluate all of this from a therapeutic aspect while on the scene. The patients all seemed satisfied and certainly "compliant," but there were no obvious options. One could argue that economics, expediency and availability dictated mode of therapy; one cannot deny the necessity for pragmatism in such a poor populous society. Wherever we went, quite frequently herbal medicines were in evidence, but no "western" drugs were ever seen.

Diagnostic studies had little place in this system. I am sure that the "barefoot doctors" spoke to patients and assessed symptoms, but I saw no physical examinations or laboratory procedures in this outpatient environment where the bulk of traditional medicine is practiced. Hospitalization is reserved for severe trauma or life-threatening illness. Our exposure was hurried, but it seems we saw a great deal of joint disease—all lumped into one diagnostic pot. For example, in Ta Chai I saw one girl with a swollen, tender knee who had been receiving local acupuncture for several weeks with no perceptible benefit. I examined the knee; it was impossible to distinguish a septic arthritis from trauma, rheumatoid, rheumatic fever or acute gout. There were no diagnostic data.

In common with other medical tourists, I saw legions of patients with all sorts of needles poking out of every conceivable anatomic site. Impossible to evaluate. Aside from some concern about HIV, hepatitis B and C transmission (the needles were usually "sterilized" by immersion in some sort of antiseptic solution), I suspect the incidence of adverse reactions from acupuncture and moxibustion is comparable to

over-the-counter and prescription drugs in the U.S. It would seem that three main factors dominate the system: (1) patient expectation is far lower than in the West (the mere fact of having a "health care professional" fussing over you must have a salutary positive placebo effect); (2) the basic tranquillity (and faith in the wisdom of Chairman Mao—as we shall see) of the people; and (3) lack of resources. China is poor; western medicine is expensive. But for an American medical scientist trying to determine effectiveness of specific treatments by our tough-minded, evidence-based, outcome standards, was just not possible. So much for acupuncture therapy.

Acupuncture and herbs for **analgesia** were a different story. I have already described the smiling 15-year old boy with a comminuted fracture of the tibia and simple fracture of fibula, reduced under galvanic acupuncture. Undeniably the most dramatic operative procedure we were privileged to witness was a young woman doctor who was undergoing repair of a ruptured Sinus of Valsalva (the area above the aortic valve). Her surgeon spoke fair English. He advised that she had been premedicated with 0.1 gram of sodium phenobarbital intravenously while still on the ward. In the operating room she was given acetyl chlorpromazine, 20 mgm., promethazine (Phenergan) 50 mgm. and meperidine (Demerol), 50 mgm. intravenously. She was receiving nasal oxygen at a flow rate estimated to be about four liters per minute.

Six acupuncture needles were symmetrically distributed, three on each side. One pair was inserted just below the clavicle in the midline, another on the median aspect of the flexor surfaces of each wrist, and a third pair on the ulnar aspects of each wrist, parallel to the others. All were connected to low amplitude galvanic generators. The adjacent muscle groups twitched rhythmically. This process continued for 30 minutes preoperatively and throughout the operative procedure. Two nurse "anesthetists" were stationed beside the patient's head. They administered no medications but whispered reassuring words and read from the Little Red Book throughout the procedure. We were told she

had been taught "diaphragmatic" respiration to minimize thoracic excursions during the operation.

During the operation there was no naso-tracheal intubation, and she received 10% glucose in normal saline IV, throughout. And aside from what I have reported, the remainder of the procedure was virtually identical to that of any major cardiovascular surgical center in the West. We watched with mounting interest during the sternum splitting and spreading. The patient did not wince, nor did her pupils dilate. She had been given an additional 50 mgm. of promethazine just before the rib spreaders were inserted. Coronary perfusion was started while on partial by-pass and at the proper moment the surgeon indicated a shift to complete by-pass. Cardiac arrest was achieved with a cold saline flush.

The surgeons worked with skill and dexterity. At the moment before suturing the perforation in the Sinus, the surgeon signaled for complete pulmonary arrest and the patient was given a drug "similar to tubocurarine." For this few second interval the patient became unconscious and her eyes rolled up. However, soon thereafter, an analeptic drug was administered (type unknown), and the patient resumed breathing. Soon she returned to consciousness. The patient was carried through the entire procedure with no apparent pain or difficulty. Blood gases were collected twice during the procedure; levels were not known to us. She left the operating room smiling. The entire procedure took 45 minutes. It was a thoroughly remarkable demonstration. In all candor I, would never have believed this demonstration had I not seen it with my own eyes!

During subsequent weeks we saw a medial lemniscus (knee) repaired, a partial lobectomy (lung) (this patient was intubated) and a thyroidectomy—all done under acupuncture with galvanic stimulation and premedication similar to our young lady of the Sinus of Valsalva. Of equal interest was a 20-year-old woman who had a tubo-ovarian mass removed while under **herbal** anesthesia. She also received an herbal "relaxant" called *hansugchi,* plus the usual minimal premedica-

tion. She was awake throughout the operation and carried on a hushed conversation with two anesthetists. We were told an anesthesiologist was available in the event his services were needed. They were not. Once again, she left the OR with a benevolent smile (perhaps standard procedure when Western observers were in attendance).

During those years just about everyone who had been to China commented on the remarkable phenomenon of major surgery under acupuncture and herbal analgesia. In China there was a significant research effort on-going to try to understand the physiology and pharmacology of these modalities. On the last day of our visit we attended the First Medical College of Shanghai. Among many fascinating things we heard was a detailed discussion of the changes in medical education that were occurring subsequent to the fall of the Gang of Four. Most notable was a resurgence of research into acupuncture that had been suppressed during the "infamous reign of the Gang." A bright young physiologist who spoke excellent English (a rarity) told us about the isolation of a polypeptide from the cerebrospinal fluid of acupunctured rabbits that had opiate-like qualities (when tested in rabbits). Chinese researchers suspected the peptide was a product of the caudate nucleus of the lower brain, elaborated in response to stimulation of the traditional acupuncture "hoku" points. They said that obliteration of the nucleus eliminated production of the peptide, and placing a microelectrode in the caudate nucleus and stimulating it galvanically, seemed to eliminate pain in rabbits. This was being tried in some terminal cancer patients.

The study of pain was very big in China. They conceded the major problem was the subjectivity that haunts all such research. One is tempted to speculate on the meaning of what we witnessed. In anticipation of questions about "hypnosis," our friends assured us that surgical procedures on animals under acupuncture were just as effective as on humans. Nevertheless, I had a distinct impression that "faith" played a major role (the belief that Chairman Mao had **faith** that acupuncture will work), plus some significant level of stoicism. However,

our hosts said that less than 20% of patients could tolerate surgery under acupuncture (had we witnessed a selected group?), and no one was compelled to accept acupuncture analgesia. Certainly I cannot explain the psycho-physiologic phenomena involved. Nor can I understand fire-walkers, voodoo deaths, mothers lifting autos from trapped children, or soldiers charging a hill under enemy fire and suffering wounds that prove mortal, only after gaining the crest. Obviously there is much to be learned here.

Today (2002) I wonder if one would see these phenomena in China, now that the cult of Mao is passé and exposure to the influence of the West is so much greater? I still feel that "traditional medicine" must stand in the queue of medical scientific endeavor. It cannot be granted "political immunity" from the rigors of the scientific method for establishing medical truth, despite some "acceptance" by the public. But I still must shake my head when I recall that young doctor with her sternum split asunder, still awake and whispering.

We went to China with the usual cold-war Western preconceptions. China had been demonized ever since they whipped our tails in 1951 in Korea. We anticipated a rigid, monolithic, Stalinist-Maoist political system that immersed its people in jingoist slogans. We anticipated a down-trodden, hard-working, poor-unto-hunger, compliant people who were pathetically "orderly." Indeed, China had many of these elements, but there was much more. We found people who were friendly, perhaps a bit guarded, but rapidly—through daily conversation and proximity—acquaintances became friends and a spirit of comradeship developed. Our hosts were warm, sensitive, good-humored and hospitable beyond expectation. Coming from our free-wheeling society with our proud tradition of virtually unshackled human rights, to another where survival of the masses largely preempted individual freedom—was a shock. It took time to understand and tolerate the psychological differences that had been translated into political reality.

(The judgment of history indicates that the pragmatism of Mao had gone too far. Even the desperate plight of the Chinese people could not

justify the Draconian measures he felt obliged to employ. It is estimated that when Mao ordered mass mobilization of the rural labor force to build dams, irrigation projects and other infrastructure, too few workers were left to tend the fields, and too much grain was taken from rural areas to feed those in cities. This resulted in famine that claimed 30 million lives. Another million were lost during the rampages of the Cultural Revolution, with another 100 million left scarred physically and emotionally. It is estimated that Mao caused the death of over 35 million people over a period of 30 years. And this came on top of the 1.5 to 6.0 million soldiers and civilians killed by the Japanese army and another 10 to 15 million who starved under the Japanese occupation. Then the Kuomintang caused the death of perhaps another 10 million by killing and famine. There is little experience in the West, excepting perhaps the Holocaust and the Stalin killings in the Gulag, to enable us to begin to contemplate human disasters of such magnitude).

Indeed, we experienced annoyances, most notably the sheer repetition of jingoist slogans. In every briefing we heard almost identical, word-for-word, party-line rhetoric—until we could repeat the phrases to each other. It took on a tragicomic aspect; any possible impact was diluted. After a few days we began to realize that the barrage of slogans was not directed at us specifically; that was how the Chinese cadres addressed everyone in public (and I even suspected they did it in private!). I tried to go through the mental gymnastics of placing the ceaseless propaganda barrage into some rational context. ("Just remember the hell that was a tragically ravaged China in 1949, and look about you now. Indeed, it is the worker's paradise—almost.")

Edgar Snow, one of the few Western patron-saints of China, once said, "China has emerged from a state of misery to a condition of poverty." I think that was a fair commentary, perhaps understated. But a brief look back revealed the flames of Nanking subsiding in 1949 as Chiang Kai-shek and his beaten nationalist armies slinked off to Taiwan. The rag-tag army of revolutionaries surveyed their ravaged land.

It was a sad inventory. Mao Tse-tung saw 600 million people sick and starving, modest hovels destroyed or crumbling, clothing in tatters. Food was scarce. It was said that there was "not a tree left in China"—all had been consumed for firewood. Generations of famine, flood, drought, disease, western exploiters, indigenous bandits, Japanese invaders and Kuomintang imperialists had exacted their toll. The Chinese people were weary, worn down, hoping for little beyond immediate survival.

Mao moved with a rare ruthlessness. First, he set about to consolidate his power base. He knew his people; they were beset with hopelessness and despair. His immediate followers were a hardy cadre—survivors of the Long March—resilient and faithful. They were dedicated to the land and sought salvation in the strident, egalitarian syllogisms of Karl Marx. While holed up in the cold caves of Yenan they had regained their pride and gathered strength to win the civil war.

The various accounts of the upheavals that marked the turbulent Japanese-Kuomintang-Communist relationships in the chaotic 1944–1945 period will never be understood fully. Even the inner circle in Beijing did not know how many "unreconstructable" Kuomintang supporters and "refractory" political dissidents had been killed or jailed or turned over the "Lao Dong Gai Zao" (reform through labor) penal system. Uncertainty bred ruthlessness. This was translated into zero tolerance for dissent. All hands were obliged to work for the survival of the masses. Mao read the situation as most desperate; he silenced any voices that he felt could disrupt his quest. As I have indicated, we now know that over 35 million died, by killing or famine. In 2002, world judgment has been harsh; even the current Chinese leaders have tried to dispel the myth of Mao and disavow his ruthless policies. But it would seem they still have limited tolerance for any dissonant voices. Significant endeavors to shore up "human rights" do not enjoy very high priority on the Chinese politburo agenda.

Historically, when Mao looked upon his world in 1949, he found hostility on all sides. After a few years of uneasy political romance with Stalin, the end came suddenly and bitterly. Soviet "socialist-imperialists" emerged as the greatest threat to China. (Hence the underground cities beneath Beijing, Sian, etc.). The bitter border at Sinkiang bristled with battalion-sized troop concentrations. And Mao also distrusted the West. The brief interlude of warmth for the U.S. that existed after the common effort to defeat the Japanese in 1945 was shattered by our unabashed political and military support for Chiang Kai-shek. This antipathy was exacerbated by the U.N. adventure in Korea in 1950 and the subsequent Chinese intervention. Then the Chinese turned inward, convinced that they stood alone in the world, to rise or fall by their own efforts, pulling on "their own bootstraps." The history of China's dealings with the West engendered an abiding distrust and pervasive national paranoia.

Mao felt the people needed to move as one body with one voice; he considered any means to accomplish this goal justifiable—and to hell with world opinion. The philosophy of dialectic materialism—"continuing revolution" permeated the political process. The life of every citizen was touched. The Cultural Revolution of 1966, the fall of Lin Piao and Lin Shao-chi and finally in 1976, the "Gang of Four," were all very visible manifestations of continuing revolution. It may be the ultimate modern example of evil, brutal means employed to achieve the ends sought by a handful of powerful old men.

The infamous Cultural Revolution has been viewed by many as a prime example of Mao's concept that long periods of political tranquility breed an intellectual and political elite, and that the "purity" of the revolutionary spirit can only be maintained by recurring revolutionary upheaval. Again I have great difficulty weighing means and ends. As I have indicated, the ridicule and torture of intellectuals, artists and any suspected dissidents, by workers and peasants had a devastating effect on the political and intellectual viability of the country. It ranks as modern China's darkest hour. To me it represented inconceivable

political myopia, the irrational product of fear and paranoia. The "proper line of Chairman Mao"—any deviation is not acceptable—is impossible for any rational human being to comprehend. It is the stuff of oligarchy and repression. It is akin to interpreting the bible literally—political fundamentalism.

In China today, following the dictates of Deng and his successors, only the naïve and foolish interpret the words of the Little Red Book as dogma. But the crushing of dissidents, exemplified by the Tiananmen Square massacre and the recent 10-year prison terms for "anarchists," and the ruthless repression of the Falun Gong indicates that any deviation from "the line" still will not be tolerated. Jiang has made smiling conciliatory gestures for international consumption, but the rigid political pragmatism of the communist hard-liners indicates that little has changed since Mao. The next revolution in China will be quiet and bloodless. When the monolithic octogenarians all die off and a new breed of executors takes control, China will move into the millennium as a formidable economic and political force. Let us all hope the old guard will all die off before any outrageous military adventures are launched to bring Taiwan "back into the fold."

While one cannot set aside the bloody history, the Chinese effort to improve the health and welfare of their people remains one of the remarkable public health success stories of our century. Over a period of 15 years (from 1950 to 1965) the major pestilences: cholera, plague and smallpox were eradicated for all practical purposes. Adequate nutrition became a reality for most of the people; nutritional illnesses (scurvy, beriberi) virtually disappeared. Opium addiction and rampant venereal disease were eliminated through massive social and medical efforts. Alcoholism, while never a major epidemiological threat, was no longer a "social problem" by 1977.

I don't know if any of these illnesses has reemerged in China today. Mao organized "great patriotic health movements" in which the masses were mobilized against the "four pests." At first these were flies, mosquitoes, rats and sparrows. After the conquest of the sparrows they

were replaced as "public enemies" by bedbugs. Rampant schistosomiasis was almost completely eliminated by mass action. Entire villages were mobilized to eradicate the snail vectors, time and again by thousands of feet stamping the banks and shallow areas of creeks to crush crustacean shells, until the disease was no longer a national menace. But, as I have indicated, the price for all this might have been the loss of farming manpower that resulted in famine and mass starvation.

Proper personal hygiene became a part of political ideology. Good health habits became a source of personal and national pride. Personal cleanliness, physical exercise and modest but adequate diet became a part of the national psyche. A sense of frugality, toughness—a Spartan attitude—struck every visitor especially in places like Ta Ching and Ta Chai (the agricultural showplace). Life was hard, and I am sure there were pockets of malnutrition and terrible living conditions in China. But we saw no evidence of this in the hundreds of miles we traveled, and I cannot believe that all of our vistas were manicured to hide such things. I suspect that today with over 1.3 billion people and the unprecedented floods and droughts of the past decade, China may be facing a recurrence of disease and famine. Even in the age of communications enlightenment, bad news is slow to emanate from China.

I must return again to a major paradox that existed amidst all the public health fervor and enthusiasm: the omnipresent cigarette. As I have mentioned, cigarettes were as ubiquitous as tea at every briefing, gathering, dinner and social occasion. Later in our visit, I felt sufficiently comfortable to question our doctor-hosts. Apparently they felt the symbolism was more important than the menace. In old China, cigarettes were a luxury available only to the affluent, far too expensive for the masses. Today the cigarette is available to all—another "highly visible reminder of the improvement in the quality of life since the revolution." Wow! I told our hosts that this was a terrible mistake and tolled off the list of diseases caused and/or exacerbated by cigarette smoking. They were not convinced that cigarettes contributed to coronary heart disease.

I suspected that the general populace had not been smoking for enough years to see an escalation of bronchogenic carcinoma, chronic obstructive airways disease and coronary heart disease. They did admit to a high incidence of chronic bronchitis. I thought this was the tip of the iceberg, especially in the northern cities where the environmental miasma was suffocatingly pervasive. I think Beijing may be the most heavily polluted city on earth.

I felt obliged to warn that the combination of heavy ambient industrial pollution and the expanding legions of cigarette smokers would result in epidemics of coronary heart disease (especially with the impending McDonalds invasion when they also adopt a western diet), but certainly more COPD and bronchogenic carcinoma within about 15 to 20 years. I had never experienced an instance before where "political correctness" took precedence over common-sense public health.

(Although, one might make a rough parallel between this situation and what exists in America today. Our high-calorie, high-fat, no-exercise lifestyle has become synonymous with the "affluent lifestyle." The attendant obesity, Type II diabetes and coronary heart disease suggests an analogy to Chinese cigarettes and bronchogenic carcinoma. But at least our government is not espousing this madness. And quite recently [it has now been 24 years], my Cassandra-like predictions seem to be coming true. There have been a spate of recent articles indicating that coronary heart disease, bronchogenic carcinoma and COPD have begun to emerge as major public health problems in China. This has resulted in a curious conundrum. Ostensibly, the government of China is seeking to curb the consumption of cigarettes, although that nation is the world's largest producer of cigarettes, and tobacco represents a major source of income in their nascent, slowly emerging, quasi-free-market economy. *Triste dictu.*)

In the early 1960s the first barefoot doctors (*giaiao yisheng*) emerged in rural areas around Shanghai. They differed remarkably from the Soviet *feldshers*. Barefoot doctors were peasants (or workers or soldiers)

first, and "doctors" second. *Feldshers* are primarily health care workers. I considered the barefoot doctors one of the strengths of the Chinese health care system. First, the *giaiao yisheng* was a worker in the same brigade or "guild" as his/her neighbors, completely immersed in the lives and problems of the patients. This level of intimacy must have a therapeutic effect. The *feldsher* (like the western physician) is from a different guild, set apart from the working lives of his/her patients.

During our visit we often had difficulty understanding what our hosts meant by "doctors." We would ask about the number of doctors in a specific institution and be given a specific number. But on closer inspection we would find that some were graduates of conventional three-year "western-type" medical schools, while others came from the secondary schools. Still others might be barefoot doctors. This was not due to any artifice or intention to deceive, but indicated a genuine lack of distinction between types of medical personnel. Many times we found conventional (three-year) doctors working side-by-side with *giaiao yisheng*. We were advised that the latter would refer more difficult patients to the conventional doctors, but most often they worked closely together. It reminded me of my days in Korea working with my corpsmen.

This blurred distinction is purposeful since all medical personnel are trained in both "Western" (to some extent) and traditional (to a greater extent) medicine. In most medical schools in China, at least in 1977, a significant portion of each class was made up of former health workers from the farm brigades, factories, or the army. As I have mentioned, in the aftermath of the Cultural Revolution, a wave of anti-intellectual hysteria swept over China. Entrance examinations were abolished as a manifestation of "bourgeois intellectualism." Admission into professional school was determined on purely political grounds: party loyalty, recommendations of peers (farm, factory, army) and some "evidence of intellectual aptitude." But no formal examinations.

Several of our hosts timorously ventured the opinion that the quality of students and the entire process of education had suffered as the

result of this "Gang of Four" political correctness policy. They said the "new line" of Chairman Hua (who preceded Deng) and his associates of the politburo indicated a shift toward a demand for more realistic academic requirements. Party loyalty and the recommendation of fellow workers "would remain important, of course," but examinations were to be reinstituted. The professional schools would have something to say about acceptance or rejection of candidates. I wondered if the ambient political climate would ever permit a professional school to reject a candidate that came with strong party endorsement. Probably not.

One cannot pass judgment on the matter of public acceptance of the medical system in China. As I have suggested, "public acceptance" is not the same in China as in the West. But we saw no indication that the patients we saw were unhappy. Other visitors to China had similar experience. "Happiness" is relative and must be placed in context with the past. Medical care (or food or shelter) could only be considered "excellent" when compared with the recent past, when universal poverty and famine and lack of housing had been the norm for decades. In 1977 every individual in the brigade, factory, or neighborhood could identify a person, usually someone who lived nearby, who was his/her "doctor." This could be a brand-new *giaiao yisheng* with scant training, but that mattered little—he or she was **concerned** about the health and welfare of his/her colleagues and patients. The health care worker provided immediate help in the areas of immunization, personal health advice, distribution of pills to prevent pregnancy, management to any minor health problems and provided an avenue of entry into the health care system for more serious problems. The system was not infallible, but it was not a casual achievement in a nation of over one billion people. The barefoot doctor was depicted as a noble figure, like the worker, farmer or soldier. We saw half-dozen skits by pre-school tots glorifying the *giaiao yisheng*.

Thus the Chinese had recognized the importance of "concern and availability" in trying to create a workable health care system. One may

wonder if these intangible factors were merely an effort to compensate for such things as lack of sophisticated diagnostic equipment, paucity of modern medication, professional competence—all the things we use to measure health care success in the West. Probably. But in our country one often hears a lament for the days of "thoughtful and caring" professionals. We live in a climate of far greater sophistication and expectation, but I suspect there is a lesson to be learned from the Chinese system. I am willing to bet that within the decade or two in this country we will arrive at some happy compromise. Most all out-patient care will be conducted by nurse practitioners, physician assistants and nurse midwives (our sophisticated version of *giaiao yisheng*) supervised by primary care MDs. Hospital care will be delivered by "hospitalists"—internists and specialists.

During the rest of our trip, we visited Shanghai, Sian, Ta Chai and perhaps dozens of factories, farm communes and hospitals. We all lectured to stoic audiences of Chinese "doctors" via interpreters with limited skill in basic English and no experience with scientific lingo. No one fell asleep; I suspect they dared not. Remember, English had been not been spoken (much less taught) officially, for at least a decade. All of our audiences applauded politely. I think they would have done the same had we been speaking in Urdu.

We had quite a few "adventures." One notable morning I was jogging near our compound on the outskirts of Harbin. Suddenly, I was confronted by a soldier with a very long rifle with a very long fixed bayonet. Apparently I had startled him, and he pointed the damned thing at me. He looked to be about twelve, but the weapon was old and serious. I smiled vigorously, waved (hands above head), and gestured at my shorts and (fortunately) red, white and blue bandana. After a tense mini-second he smiled wanly and raised the rifle. I jogged backwards until he was out of sight. There was still some "Gang of Four" turbulence abroad, and I suspect our hosts were concerned about our safety. But an armed military guard?

On the morning of the Fourth of July, I went jogging around the central square in Sian. I was wearing a red headband, blue shorts and a white T-shirt. Of course, no one in the gathering market place crowd knew what it represented, but I suspect few will forget the strange-looking foreigner with the pale face and the outrageously brief costume, loping cheerfully and amicably through their town, waving a small U.S. flag.

The China we visited was not at all prepared for tourists. We stayed in ancient hotels that obviously had been reopened for our benefit, some military barracks and even some private homes. Everywhere we went we were a great source of curiosity. Stella's blonde hair caused some children to cry in alarm; bolder adults reached out to touch it. But we saw no unfriendly faces, and it could not all have been "arranged." In several towns I wandered the streets alone, never too far from our "headquarters," but never did I have a sense of fear or being watched.

I understand that much has changed, and most for the better. In recent years there has been some effort at openness, but it is not easy to shake off years of centralized decision-making, ruthless suppression of dissent and national paranoia about the motives of the "capitalist imperialists." The tragedy of Tiananmen Square and the recent jailing of Falun Gong dissidents for long prison terms indicates that China has a long way to go. But they seem to have solved the "population explosion" (by means not entirely palatable to some Western minds). It would appear that the rigid control of birth rate has resulted in a proliferation of males. Now there is concern that lack of females could have unfortunate long-range effects on future generations; the population is growing older. But the situation is far from as serious as in some western Europe countries where declining birth rates threaten to have profound future economic implications.

But the quality of life for most of the people has improved significantly. The next few years will be critical in the determination of the economic salvation of this nation. The great expectation is that when

the octogenarians are all finally gone, a new generation (50 year olds?) will take over and move the slumbering giant into the new millennium with less anger, paranoia and a desire to compete peaceably in the economy and politics of the new world. Some pundits are not sanguine; there is so much "history" to overcome. Nevertheless, China will be a force to be reckoned with for everyone on the planet in the next century.

# 26

## *Meanwhile…back at the ACP*

✦

### *(return to reality…)*

To pick up the story at the College, in 1987 I wrote a book, "Decade of Decision," describing in some detail my ten years at the College. I will not repeat all of that here, but will try to chronicle events that seem most pertinent and interesting. From the very outset, the decision by the Search Committee to appoint me was not universally applauded. I was replacing Dr. Ed Rosenow, a good old boy who had been in the job for 18 years. He did not want to leave. In a rare lapse of his usually sound judgment, Bob Petersdorf, the ACP president, thought it would be helpful to me if Rosenow and I were to "overlap for a few months so he could show me the ropes." I arrived in late December, 1976, and the "few months" (of hell) lasted until the annual session in Dallas in April. Rosenow had a vast office that could easily have accommodated another desk, but he exiled me to a dark, damp room in the basement. His "briefings" consisted of airy hand waves in hallways. I soon realized that Rosenow and two chief cronies were also less than charmed with my presence. They were all firm believers in "*apres moi le deluge.*" So I had to "learn the College" on my own.

I read the history of the first 45 years, "Gateway of Honor," by Dr. George M. Piersoll. I called for all the minutes of the Board of Regents, Governors and key committees for the past two years. I was appalled at the poor quality and paucity of information. I was told that minutes

were kept by secretaries who attended the meetings, took notes and then made drafts immediately after the meetings. Many seemed incomplete, others were ungrammatical. At times they were incomprehensible, almost illiterate. I could not vouch for accuracy. It bespoke a "mom and pop" operation run by the tight triumvirate. One of my first acts was to invest in quality recording equipment to document every word spoken at every meeting. The rough drafts would be reviewed by responsible staff, the chairman of the committee and then finally edited for semantic clarity and then distributed to every member of the committee and key staff.

But I spent most of my time interviewing every member of the staff, reviewing personnel records, attending all meetings and wandering and chatting my way around the building. When I questioned Rosenow about budget and finances, he smiled his smile of infinite wisdom and told me that he "left everything in Fred's capable hands." I never saw a balance sheet in those three months. In reviewing the Treasurer's Report summarizing 1976, I discovered a deficit from the Annual Session of $261,000. Rosenow Crony #2, the chief financial officer, told me this was "sort of a tradition around here—a loss leader." It didn't make much sense.

From the outset I found it extraordinarily difficult to assess the financial status of the College. There were no monthly variance reports. In fact all budgeting was done centrally, in the College Finance Office, with arbitrary allocations distributed to each department at the beginning of the fiscal year. There was no requirement for each manager to submit annual budget projections and no method to monitor expenditures. It was, indeed, "mom and pop," but with no balance sheet! There was no mechanism to encourage staff to assume any fiscal responsibility and participate in the budgeting process.

From my experience running medical departments in army hospitals and a major division at AMA, I knew this was crazy bookkeeping. No wonder the Annual Session was always in the red. There was no incentive to make it (or any other College activity) solvent, much less

profitable. However I was the "new boy," and the Regents' Finance Committee seemed satisfied with the system. Careful scrutiny of their minutes covering the preceding few years revealed no indication of concern. No red flags. So I put College finances on my back burner. It turned out to be a colossal error, almost my undoing.

As a result of my informal basement interviews, I grew to learn about the staff. There were some high-ranking folks who had difficulty actually describing how they spent their day. Others were obviously bright and competent. Rosenow's hostility towards me was reflected in the dour attitude of his principle acolytes, the Terrible Two, but no one else. I am not a Machiavellian manager by nature; I do not believe in firing all the old guard and bringing in all my own people, up front. Soon after I moved upstairs, I gathered the entire staff and told them of my philosophy of management. All those who could handle the change to a new boss, who could establish their competence to perform their assigned tasks and could work for the "good of the order" as a team player, would be retained on board. Those who could not should leave. I encouraged initiative and innovation; I was open to ideas. I did not expect love, but insisted on respect, integrity and loyalty. Not exactly Vince Lombardi stuff.

I made no distinction based on rank. It took about a year to establish my own frame of reference to judge what people really did. I fired about five of the "old guard" (including the Terrible Two) who simply could not accommodate to my "tough" management style (demanding accountability and loyalty and all that), or who were obviously dead weight. I promoted from within and hired carefully from outside. After some exploration, I discovered that the ACP overall pay scale was distressingly lower than any comparable medical organization. I convinced the Finance Committee to grant about a 20% raise in pay for all staff members. It was long overdue; it didn't hurt my popularity.

Soon after my arrival, I discovered that the Regents had decided (previous to hiring me) to establish a high-level committee tasked to explore the "mission of the College" and make recommendations for

structural revisions. I was appalled. Why hire a brand new EVP and then hand him a report (that would be a literal mandate from the Regents) on how to do his job? What ever happened to initiative and innovation? I spoke of this to Jim Clifton, the amiable new president. Jim had been on the Search Committee, and I expressed my confusion and concern in very candid terms. If Rosenow had been kept on as EVP, I could understand a move to revisit the fundamental underpinnings of the College. But I felt this undertaking, at this time, was tantamount to a vote of "no confidence" before I even got off the Philadelphia tarmac. Jim hastened to assure me that this was not the case. Dan Federman, chairman of the committee (and perhaps the wisest Regent I encountered), also assured me that their mission was to help me in "leading the College into the future." With some reluctance I accepted all this and urged my staff to cooperate with the task force. But I was not pleased. As it all turned out, the need for revision of structure and function was so obvious that by the time the task force submitted its formal report, I had already implemented most of their recommendations, plus many of my own.

The most impressive and enjoyable aspect of the job was getting to know just about all the major players in American medicine. The Regents and Governors represented the best of teachers, investigators and practitioners internal medicine had to offer. Of course, some turned out to have clay feet, but by and large they were dedicated to the high road. I think that my naiveté in ACP politics served me well. I had not been "conditioned" by working my way through the ranks—governor—regent—officer. From my vantage point as a fellow in the ranks, I saw the College from a fresh vantage point. I was concerned about the elitism that seemed an intrinsic characteristic of the organization. A prime example: the criteria for advancement from member to fellow were unfair to working internists, weighted heavily in favor of academics.

In my first few meetings of the Credentials Committee, where advancement decisions were made, I felt the unduly heavy reliance on

review of published papers did not make for a level playing field. There were many distinguished, scholarly, hard-working practitioners who simply did not have the time or opportunity to demonstrate "scholarly achievement" by writing basic research or clinical papers. Any young person who moved from residency to a junior faculty position in a medical school was obliged to write papers. "Publish or perish" was a reality. There was virtually no consideration given to "other scholarly achievements" such as teaching as a clinical faculty member, serving on hospital committees, working with health officials in the community, etc. Without a batch of papers to your credit (often quantity seemed more important than quality), the committee usually gave the candidate a rapid pass. There were exceptions, but I felt the hoary system was grossly out of balance. I did battle on this matter for about five years, until I finally persuaded the Regents that I was not seeking to trivialize the traditional "advancement to fellowship" standards. Ultimately, the requirements were revised to allow greater consideration of "non-paper" scholarly attainment. We still considered published papers, but they were no longer the *sine qua non*. We began to bring some very worthy, long-ignored gray heads into fellowship; it strengthened the College. It was a significant step in the democratization of the grand old club.

For many years I had been concerned that many of the things we did each day in the clinical practice of medicine seemed to have little basis in scientific reality. In truth, the randomized controlled trial (RCT), the backbone of scientific medicine, was less than 30 years old. (Austin Bradford Hill's seminal publication of a trial testing streptomycin on patients with tuberculosis appeared on October 30, 1948.) All clinical practice that preceded the arrival of the RCT was predicated on empiricism, instinct, anecdote and personal experience. This non-data-based approach frequently resulted in the perseverance of egregious error. Even now most surgical procedures are tested by "trial and error." Of course, it is extremely difficult to have a realistic "control" group to study a new surgical procedure. (Sham operations are

not popular with institutional review boards, volunteers and lawyers). But even here some headway was being made.

So I thought the College should embark on a program to investigate the scientific merit of many of the drugs, tests and procedures that had long-since been accepted, unchallenged in clinical practice; the euphemism was "routine." It would require committees of seasoned clinicians, clinical investigators and medical statisticians to study the world literature, conduct internal debate, derive data-based conclusions and then publish the results for the benefit of our members and all other interested practicing physicians.

It was a bold step; no other organization within or outside of the government was involved in such a program. I received approval from the Regents to attempt to obtain a grant for seed money to explore feasibility. I called it the "Medical Necessity Project." I went to Blue Shield/Blue Cross in Chicago and made a presentation. They listened thoughtfully, but felt this project was not within their area of interest. They suggested I speak to the grant folks at the Hartford Foundation. It took almost a year to get an audience, but finally, I went to New York and made my pitch to Hartford. They awarded us a three-year grant of $650,000! It was one of my proudest moments.

The project became the "Clinical Efficacy Assessment Program" (CEAP). I tried to entice my good friend, the wise and scholarly Rollo Hanlon, EVP of the American College of Surgeons to join us, to begin a similar review of surgical procedures. He demurred. CEAP became the flagship of an ACP flotilla of projects. Over the years scores of drugs, tests and procedures were reviewed by committees of academics and practitioners. Position papers, approved by the Regents, were published in the *Annals of Internal Medicine*. Today there is a quasi-federal agency (Agency for Health Care Policy and Research—AHCPR) involved in such evaluations in a vastly expanded fashion. But CEAP was the pioneer; it is still very active.

During the final months of my tenure, I hoped to expand the CEAP concept to set up a mechanism whereby ACP fellows would serve as

members of a post-marketing surveillance network, to evaluate important new drugs. They would be alerted to detect adverse reactions (AR) and evaluate effectiveness, once they were in widespread clinical use, immediately following approval by the FDA. It seemed like a worthwhile extension of CEAP. I proposed that the ACP and FDA, working jointly, could devise protocols that would be followed by selected ACP practitioners in the field. (Every ACP fellow could become potential clinical investigator.) We could stratify by specialty, geography, practice mode, etc. and gain practical experience as new drugs came to the market place.

It is an old axiom in drug research that clinical trials quite often miss serious but rare ARs. The numbers of volunteer subjects available for most trials is often just too small. For example, a drug that causes severe liver damage in 1:1000 patients will require many thousands of patients to be treated before the liver damage becomes recognized. If you had 100 internists tuned into looking for adverse reactions from a specific drug, the rare but important AR could be detected much earlier than by the existing, largely insensitive, FDA passive surveillance mechanism.

To my chagrin. there was little enthusiasm for the idea either within the ACP hierarchy or the FDA. I still think it is a viable concept, certainly better than the voluntary, non-system that the FDA relies on today. (I once chaired the FDA Advisory Committee on Adverse Drug Reactions. We dissolved ourselves after two meetings because the data that came in from the field were too sporadic, incomplete, even misleading. Dr. Herschel Jick was on that committee, and he devised a pro-active, nurse-involved, chart-review-in-real-time mechanism in several Boston hospitals (later in Britain) that resulted in much earlier detection of adverse drug reactions. Herschel has published extensively, making significant contributions.)

I spent a lot of time on the road. The College was divided into "regions:" larger states (Texas, New York, and California had several regions). I felt obliged to visit each of them perhaps on a three-year

rotational basis. Of course, Stella was encouraged to travel with me (at College expense) and, wisely, she opted to visit the more felicitous areas. But these were always very busy social affairs. It was my only opportunity to get to the "grass roots" feelings of College members. Stella and I also traveled rather extensively: Australia (adding two weeks of just plain touring), Egypt, Canada, Mexico and Chile. We also took a "luxury" vacation cruise to the North Cape (of Norway).

I confess that part of the charm of the travel was to escape escalating domestic unpleasantness. After the "Dee discovery," Stella fell into a sustained depression. I felt that part of this was related to the smallness and darkness of the Uxbridge condo. We took out a mortgage and bought a lovely new house in Vorhees Township (ironically about two miles from the "cottage-in-the-woods" we had rejected). It was bright and cheery with a large yard where our wonderful German shepherd, Amy, could run and explore. But the change of venue made scant difference in our relationship.

One of the more exciting events of my ACP tenure occurred during the 1978 annual session in Boston. Someone called into our headquarters office and said a bomb had been planted in the convention center. I notified the Boston Police and their initial response was a distressingly cavalier, "We get lots of bomb threats." I refused to accept this unseemly "reassurance" and insisted that we clear the entire building and have the Boston Police bomb squad do their thing. The exhibit area and the lecture rooms were evacuated in a swift and orderly fashion. With a somewhat reluctant bomb squad we conducted a detailed sweep. I insisted that we empty all waste cans, examine all boxes and closed cabinets. The squad chief and I followed the team through the abandoned exhibition hall and lecture rooms. The entire drill consumed about one hour. No bomb was discovered. The teaching sessions reconvened, and those people whose exercises had been canceled were given refunds.

These were very busy and productive years at work, but always under the cloud of unhappiness at home. One of my proudest accom-

plishments was "railroading" the College into its new permanent location. There are few times in life when one is so convinced of being "right" that one becomes unrealistically intolerant of others who fail to share this viewpoint. I realize that such hubris invites obvious, glaring pitfalls. (Hitler had a similar, albeit malignant, vision.) But rarely am I **that** certain about anything; this time I was unabashedly guilty.

It had become obvious that the rapid expansion of College activities over the years, with many more committees requiring much more staff and space, that the gracious old former cigar baron's (Bayuk Phillies) mansion at 4200 Pine was just too small. We had expanded into every conceivable nook and cranny. It was still not enough. There was insufficient room on the existing property to build, and, besides, the graceful old manse would not lend itself to architecturally inelegant appendages. It was an historic landmark. For a time I had to move several divisions to rented space in an office building in town—a dreadful expense and inconvenience. It was a logistical and morale nightmare. The Regents established a committee to explore potential venues for construction of a new headquarters building. Indeed, it became a long and tedious process. We explored sites in Philadelphia, Wilmington, Washington, Bethesda and northern Virginia. I felt that a move from Philadelphia would be very ill advised, politically and financially. But the committee felt obliged to "explore all possibilities."

The Regent-chairman of the committee was a dogged, part-time lay minister from Tulsa, who had his cap set on becoming ACP president. He was a black-suit, thin-dark-tie preacher right out of central casting. He was determined that this committee would a vehicle to help him achieve that exalted goal. I found him irascible and difficult. After about a year of frustrating searching, I was adamantly vocal in my opposition to a move to Washington. We had already established an office in downtown D.C., but moving the headquarters within the benighted Beltway would send an ugly, political signal, in antithesis to our historically scholarly approach to the world of medicine. My bull-

dog position was not popular with several politically oriented Regents and staff.

Then I heard that the city of Philadelphia was considering building on the last remaining site available on Independence Mall. I sought out the Mayor (Wilson Goode) and established contact with him and his city planners, led by Mr. Craig Schelter. The proposed site was on Independence Mall West, a stone's throw from the Liberty Bell, at the opposite end of the Mall from Independence Hall. The property sat on the corner of Sixth Street and Race, adjacent to a TV station. I thought it was a gift from heaven. Once the city fathers learned who we were, they were sympathetic to our cause. And the price was right—a virtual gift. How could anyone (including my Tulsa nemesis) be anything but delighted? Wrong!

First, I had a staff insurrection. Led by John Ball, whom I had hired to head up our Health and Public Policy Division (in downtown Washington) and the editor of the *Annals* (who had hated me, gratuitously, from my first day—I never knew why). They gathered several key staff to "confront me." The grievance? They had not been "allowed to participate in the new site selection process." Loyalty, or even an open, amicable, face-to-face, intra-staff discussion was not in their repertoire. Ball and his chief co-conspirator had been holding clandestine meetings to push for the move to D.C. It was a tempestuous session; it was obvious that there was a larger, unspoken agenda. I told them that my door was always open; the Site Committee had never met behind closed doors. Staff had been free to speak out on dozens of occasions, but they never had. After our little conflagration, they complained to the president, Dan Federman, about my "intransigence." He told them to back off. This incident really raised my hackles; it was a crude attempt at a "palace coup." It failed; I could never trust John Ball again.

But my biggest problem was the man from Tulsa. In our very first meeting with the city planning board, his boorish arrogance ("gotta play hard-ball—we would be doing the city a favor") almost torpedoed

the whole deal. Talk about looking a gift-horse in the mouth! A few days later I made a special trip, alone, to speak to the mayor and Mr. Schelter to try to iron things out. It was not easy, but they were reasonable men. Ultimately, the chair of the committee passed to a more tractable human being and common sense prevailed. The new College building was completed in 1989. It is a permanent, elegant anchor to splendid Independence Mall, a worthy neighbor to its illustrious, historic antecedents.

One of the least desirable adventures during my time in Philadelphia occurred during a visit to a regional meeting in Panama City, Panama. Dr. Ed Hook, his wife Jessie, Stella and I were the guests of the Central American chapter. As part of our entertainment, the College Governor asked if we would like to see the famous canal. So on a bright, hot, mid-morning we all piled into his large Buick. Stella sat in the rear right seat, Ed Hook next to her, Jessie in the rear left and I sat in front next to the Governor. We were driving with all the windows down, and I had assumed that the vehicle lacked air-conditioning. We were stopped for a red light in a rather grungy section of town when suddenly some street thug reached into the rear window and grabbed Stella's purse. Unfortunately she had the thong handles wrapped around her right wrist, and she was pulled roughly into the window when the purse failed to come loose. She shrieked, and I turned immediately as did Ed Hook, and we both tried to grab the arm of the assailant. In the next instant my arm and Ed's were both streaming with blood, as the attacker cut the thongs with a knife and fled into the crowd.

Ed was bleeding profusely from a stiletto wound through the fleshy part of his forearm. I was bleeding from a small gash in the middle of my right hand just below the proximal joint. I could not extend my middle finger; the extensor tendon had been severed. Stella had not been cut, but her wrist had been badly traumatized. We managed to rip up my shirt and stop the bleeding. The Governor was mortified and immobile, behind the wheel. I said, "How close are we to the near-

est hospital?" "Gorgas is just about a mile." "So let's go there—now." So we fled to the army hospital.

As we entered, I told the first sergeant I saw that I was a retired army colonel and that we needed immediate help. The staff responded quickly. Soon they learned that one of the patients was Dr. Ed Hook, a world-famous infectious disease expert. His wound was clean with no major vessel damaged. Outside my curtain I heard two young medical captains arguing, "But I think he should get prophylactic antibiotics!" "No," the other voice, "He has written about the overuse of antibiotics and resistance and all that." "But this is a dirty knife wound!" Then I heard Ed Hook's voice, "For goodness sake, you're the doctor. It certainly bled a lot, but I think I could use some oral amoxacillin."

I was lucky enough to find an orthopedic surgeon, who did a clean tendon repair. I was placed in a hand cast with my middle finger held in permanent extension with other fingers moderately flexed. (For the next two weeks my disability facilitated my ability to express displeasure at anyone foolish enough to run afoul of my foreshortened temper.) Poor Stella was hurting worse than any of us, but had only a badly bruised wrist to show for it, was given aspirin. Then we debated: Should we go to the gala reception that had been planned for the evening. If we failed to show up, the poor Governor would lose even more face. So we all gathered ourselves together, replete with splints and dressings and arrived looking like the "Spirit of 76." Margueritas helped ease the discomfort.

But the denouement did not occur until the following morning. The crestfallen Governor was taking us to the airport in the now infamous, blood-cleansed Buick. As we pulled away from the hotel, he said, "Would you like the air-conditioning?" We looked at each other in silent astonishment. "...yes, that would be nice."

I had a few other frustrations as you might imagine. From my past experience trying to bring some form of continuing medical education to the doctors at the Maui Memorial Hospital (and despite my bad experience in trying to bring CME to community hospitals while at

AMA), I still felt that the College could help non-university-affiliated community hospitals achieve worthwhile teaching programs. Here in Philadelphia we had five excellent medical schools, and I thought the College could act as a "broker" to have faculty from one or more of the schools make teaching visits to some of the community hospitals in nearby Jersey and greater Philadelphia. (It would be a civilian version of my Walter Reed Circuit Rider program.) I spoke to the chairmen of medicine at Penn and Jefferson. They were willing to explore the possibility. I then visited the chiefs of medicine at two hospitals in New Jersey and one near Wilmington. To my astonishment, they were very cool to the idea! I said that outstanding clinical and research teachers from the faculties at Penn and Jeff could come and lecture, make teaching rounds, deliver a clinical pathological conference, even see problem cases. There would be no cost to the community hospitals; ACP would do all the paper work, scheduling, etc. I planned to try to get a grant and hire new staff to run the logistics, just as I had done for CEAP.

My "Community Hospital Project" never got off the runway. I still do not understand the grumbling apathy that I encountered. I suspect the golf-tanned practitioners in the community hospitals were just too busy with their bustling private practices, making gobs of money, with no time or disposition for fancy "medical education" from academics. It was another discouraging glimpse of my colleagues in practice. Later I will speak more of this deplorable (and potentially dangerous) tendency to self-imposed clinical ignorance, exhibited by far too many practicing physicians.

My other major "failure" was what I called the "electronic text book of medicine." Lord knows I am no computer maven, but back in the late '80's it seemed to me that the future of electronic communication as a practical, realistic, affordable means for gathering real-time medical information for working clinicians was just a matter of time. It seemed that if we could provide such a worthwhile service to our members, it would represent a tremendous benefit-of-membership. Dr.

Hack Schoolman, who was second in command at the National Library of Medicine (NLM), had been one of the creators of their "Viral Hepatitis Knowledge Base" (VHKB). Hack was also chairman of our Telecommunications Committee. Through him, I met Dr. Lionel Bernstein, who ran the NLM-VHKB. I took key staff to Bethesda to learn about the unique project first hand. NLM had launched an ambitious enterprise. It was far from being user-friendly, but the concept was brilliant. The possibilities were unlimited.

NLM had assembled a panel of experts representing all fields related to viral hepatitis: virologists, hepatologists, epidemiologists, working clinicians, all were linked via electronic communication. The NLM had always been in the forefront of electronic information systems in medicine, and they had established a network that facilitated easy intra-committee member dialogue. As new information about viral hepatitis became available, panel members would submit it (via modem to the central data base) for consideration for incorporation into the final VHKB. The data were updated via consensus meetings every three months. Thus the information was far more current and critically reviewed than what appeared in journals.

The unsolved problem was getting the database to respond to specific questions from working practitioners or researchers who logged onto the NLM-VHKB. The NLM system would select key words from the question and then respond with paragraphs selected from the database. It was slow and excruciatingly clumsy, often regurgitating reams of irrelevant information. Dr. Bernstein said it was "in early evolution." It was during this time that Dr. Jack Myers, chairman of medicine at Pittsburgh and former ACP president, was deep into the evolution of his own electronic textbook, called "Internist." Jack was having some problems with continued funding and privately indicated to me that he would be more than pleased if, within a few years, the College would accept his data base as a gift with the promise to continue and expand it. He also admitted similar problems of access and pertinent response.

I thought the VHKB and Myers' "textbook" represented pioneering efforts that could ultimately be combined and refined to become a realistic information source. It was all prelude (by over a decade) to the excellent sources of medical data currently accessible via various websites on the Internet. The College could have been a pioneer in this endeavor.

I also thought that the College could come close to providing a "real time" source of medical information by establishing an "immediate telephonic response" capability. We had the intellectual resources to designate teams of experts in every subspecialty, who could come "on service" for a week, once every few months, to be available 24 hours a day (just as they go "on service" in teaching hospitals). They would be available to respond by telephone to questions from ACP members about specific patients. The College would serve as the "switchboard." There would be sufficient numbers of panel members "on call" so as not to over-burden any one particular individual. Liability would not be a factor, since every ACP member would have signed a "release form" excluding the College or the panel member offering advice, from liability. Also, the final decision about accepting or rejecting the advice of the consultant would remain the prerogative of the primary physician. Obviously, there were many logistical bugs to be worked out, but I knew I could get a grant to conduct a pilot study. It would be a sort of prelude and complement to my "electronic text book." To my chagrin, I could never convince the Regents of the virtue of this idea.

Dr. Lionel Bernstein was intrigued by the prospect of refining the VHKB into a much broader, more user-friendly mechanism. He was rather frustrated at the slow pace of the NLM and was ready to come to work for ACP to expedite his research in this area. His salary request was reasonable. He and I knew we could get grant funds to support the project. With great eagerness, I made the proposal to the Medical Education Committee. I never knew why, but it never got out of committee. The "electronic textbook of medicine" and the "real-time telephonic response" program both died abornin'.

Over the years, many organizations have attempted to create such a resource. Some have come very close, but to my knowledge, there is no authoritative resource that can answer a clinician's patient-related questions, 24/7 by phone or Internet in real time. I can think of no way to improve the general quality of care than to create such a mechanism. The ACP could have launched a pilot program for internal medicine; the other specialty colleges would have soon followed. Another Moser pipe dream bit the now-familiar dust. (Quite recently, I have been advised that the College is in the process of setting up an electronic data base available for subscribers to obtain information in "real time"—called PIER, and there are other similar systems from other organizations in the electronic wings. It is now 15 years later!)

I must speak of my two wonderful administrative assistants: Alice Porter and Pat Carter. I inherited them from Rosenow, although neither had much status under the previously autocratic regime. They were remarkably different yet remarkably similar. Both were extraordinarily bright, loyal, competent and devoted to me. Alice was warm, eternally cheery and had a marvelous wry sense of humor. We soon developed a close, almost brother-sister relationship. Alice was my confidante, and she, above all others, knew what was happening in my life.

Pat was the acme of efficiency; she was a handsome, aggressive, driving woman who brooked no nonsense from anyone. Her warmth became apparent only to those close to her. She was politically astute and a rare judge of people. Pat made no bones, she wanted to "move up" in the organization (and indeed she did). Alice had no desire for upward mobility. In time, Alice became my personal assistant; Pat had obvious administrative skills and became my administrative assistant with wider duties. She also became my close friend. Pat and Alice worked well together, but there was always an element of competition. Toward the end of my tenure they had a falling out. Pat had no desire to leave the College and (in Alice's opinion) did not stand by me firmly enough during some tempestuous later days. I had no sense of this. Pat was a hard-nosed pragmatist. Alice retired when I did; she did not like

the decision of the Board to replace me with the colorless John Ball. I thought the Regents had made a terrible decision too. Pat figured she could accommodate and survive. Indeed she did. Pat is now a high-ranking executive staff member at ACP; she is the corporate memory and conscience. Linda and I still maintain frequent, home-to-home contact with both, and we love them dearly and equally.

There were two other women in my "ACP life." One was a striking blonde who reminded me of Candice Bergen. She was bright, shrewd and aggressive with well-honed Machiavellian instincts. Indeed, about half the Regents and Governors cast covetous glances at her. The other woman, Linda Salsinger is now my wonderful wife. The former had just undergone a painful divorce, and was not "permanently affiliated" with anyone. I don't know exactly how it started, but I was smitten with her, and she returned my affection. We enjoyed a very careful affair for about a year. I had never had a sexual liaison with any of the women with whom I had worked, before Dee. This time it was always less than comfortable. From the very outset we knew that the liaison was not going to be permanent. She was wonderfully alluring and sexy, but I soon realized she was the most manipulative woman I had ever encountered.

Linda Salsinger was a different person. She was a tall, elegant brunette with the most spectacular body on the planet. She had been divorced for some time and was living with a handsome, young staff person. Quite often the four of us would have dinner together. I had always been aware of her brightness and beauty, but never considered her in a romantic context. In time Linda became my director of medical education. I became impressed with her remarkable competence, initiative and leadership ability. She was a superb executive.

Shortly after Stella and I moved into the Vorhees house, Sonya came for an extended visit. She remained with us for almost one year, but could not ply her trade of mixing and selling her magical face and body creams and giving massages. Occasionally a few neighbors came to the house for massage, but it always made me feel uncomfortable.

When she returned to Lahaina, Stella often went to Maui for extended visits, up to three or four weeks. I was left alone a great deal, and my quiet affair occupied most of my "social time." Our most memorable romantic interlude occurred when I managed to take advantage of the rain check I had received from OARS (the river running outfit) after my first aborted Colorado River rafting effort, when Stella had suffered her myocardial infarction. This time I completed the breath-taking 227-mile trip, and when they brought us back to the motel in Flagstaff, my friend was waiting for me. I was deeply tanned, tough and grungy; she was deliciously beautiful and inviting. We spent three glorious days in Flagstaff and at Camelback in Scottsdale. It was a languorous time. But even in this idyllic, romantic environment, it was evident that we were winding down. When we both realized that our relationship was going nowhere, she offered some sage advice, "You have a lot in common with Linda Salsinger; you would be perfect together." She was right.

Months after the liaison had subsided, Linda and I made a business day-trip to Baltimore to discuss a joint venture with the American Psychiatric Society. I had recently purchased a flashy red '76 Mercedes 450-SL. Another supercar. We drove down together. Linda made me feel boyish and happy. I had never so much as touched her, yet I felt a powerful excitement. On the way home, we stopped at the Dupont Hotel in Wilmington for an early dinner; we had the elegant, high-tiered baroque dining room to ourselves. There was a sweet lady playing a harp. For some reason (dinner wine helped) this struck us as hilariously funny, and we were convulsed with inappropriate (but fairly discreet) laughter. The poor soul was not a very inspired harpist. I believe that if Linda had not been still living with her young man, I would have asked her to spend the night with me. I suspect she would have gently demurred, but there was unmistakable magnetism. I think she felt it too, because within a few weeks she broke up with her boyfriend and rented a house near Society Hill. Soon thereafter, while Stella was still in Hawaii, I told Linda that I wanted to make love with

her. To my amazement she agreed! It was an epiphany for both of us. I had never experienced such complete melding with any other woman. She whispered the same. We knew that we had "a problem."

My life with Stella had deteriorated to the point where we were both so miserable that I had broached divorce. This was "not acceptable." She had been going to a psychologist, ostensibly for her chronic problems of depression, insomnia and my "forcing her to live my life." She persuaded me to see a psychiatrist (the husband of her psychologist), and for several months I "bared my soul" to this pleasant, non-confrontational therapist. Once we had laid out the whole problem, he told me that the only solution was divorce. But in his conversations with his psychologist-wife they agreed that Stella was "not prepared" to accept this solution. They suggested joint sessions, so the four of us met half a dozen times. The whole business came to naught except to cost several thousand dollars. There was a brief time when things were so dismal that I became clinically depressed. It was the only time in my life when I ever reflected, seriously, on suicide.

I began to see Linda at every possible occasion. I discovered that I had fallen in love. I laughed at myself, "…at your age, gimme a break—you're a goddamn cliché." But this was the first time in my life, including all the good early years with Stella, that I was totally immersed in an all-encompassing relationship with a complete and mature woman. Even with sweet Dee it had never been this wonderful. I knew that I was skating on very thin ice. One more blow to Stella's fragile ego could be catastrophic. At least that is what I thought at the time. But we were both beyond wretched, and since I had begun to see Linda my unhappiness at home was exacerbated. "Sex" (now a euphemism) with Stella consisted of rare episodes of complex, convoluted game playing, rarely yielding any satisfaction for either of us. It was unmitigated hell.

Ultimately, word came that Sonya was ill. Stella flew out to Maui, and it was discovered that her mother had carcinoma of the lung. Stella remained on Maui for about six weeks until Sonya died, and then she

decided to remain longer. During this time another extraordinary event occurred. I wanted Linda to share the "Colorado River-Grand Canyon" experience with me. She was a kindred spirit in our mutual love of the outdoors. After making reservations to meet a river raft expedition at Phantom Ranch at the bottom of the Grand Canyon, we flew to Flagstaff and rented a car. We drove to the South Rim and turned the car over to the expedition folks who were to transport it to the take-out point.

The next morning we hiked down the Bright Angel Trail, an exhausting, dehydrating experience in mid-August. Linda was wearing running shoes with no socks and by the time we arrived at Indian Gardens (about 1/3 of the distance to the river) she had rubbed painful blisters on both feet. I cleaned and bandaged them with stuff from our first aid kit, but the remainder of the hike was hell for her. Even my whistling of "Colonel Bogey's March" failed to succor her pain.

At Phantom Ranch we each drank a half-gallon of lemonade, dangled our battered feet in the delightfully icy Colorado, and then wandered to the bank to await the rafts. Despite such an inglorious beginning the expedition was truly glorious. We hiked all the side trails, took turns rowing on quiet, placid stretches, shrieked through the wild cascades and were captivated by the stunning beauty of the Canyon. On our last scheduled day we were advised that a flash flood had wiped out the take-out beach and trail. We would be obliged to hook on to a power boat and get towed across Lake Mead to another beaching site.

As we were passing down the river a few miles from the lake, we saw a crude, block-lettered sign on the west side of the river. Astonishingly, it read, "Dr. Moser, your wife is ill. Call hospital at once." I was flabbergasted; oh my God, *deja vu*! After an eternal haul across Lake Mead, we hired a light plane that dropped us in Williams, where the rental cars had been deposited. I called the hospital. Stella had been admitted with chest pain; she was in the Maui Memorial Coronary Care Unit. We picked up the rental car and sped to Flagstaff. Linda flew back to

Philadelphia, and I went to Maui. This time the situation was far less grim than previously. Stella did not suffer any new myocardial damage, but her sustained anginal episode had frightened everyone.

Once back in Philadelphia I arranged for Stella to be seen by Dr. Leonard Dreyfus, the best cardiologist in the area. He felt that her past history and current symptoms indicated a need for a coronary angiogram. The radiographs revealed narrowing of three vessels; she was a candidate for by-pass surgery. She had obvious residual damage to her left ventricle, but no heart failure. She was placed on conventional anti-anginal therapy and urged (once again) to stop smoking. She tried again, but could not. Things had been bad enough, now Stella's illness served only to sharpen the needles of her unhappiness.

I called Lois DeBakey, my friend from JAMA days, with whom I had maintained desultory correspondence. I asked if she could prevail on Mike, her illustrious brother whom I had met only once, to perform the operation on Stella. Mike DeBakey was the best cardiovascular surgeon in the world. Within days Mike called. He would be pleased to place Stella on his schedule. Soon thereafter, we went to a College meeting of the Governors in San Antonio and then flew to Houston where Stella was admitted. Mike conferred with his chief of cardiology, Tony Gotto, and we reviewed the angiograms from Len Dreyfus. It was agreed that triple-vessel by-pass was indeed indicated.

Mimi, our gracious neighbor from Vorhees, who had become Stella's closest friend, came down to Houston. The operation went well, and I took Stella back home in a wheel chair within a few days. Her incisional pain largely subsided in about two weeks, and she joined Smoke Enders. The promising results were only temporary. Our relationship continued to deteriorate. Every evening saw continuous combat. The "Dee episode" seemed to surface in every conversation despite the original context. God knows what would have happened had she known about my involvement with Linda. Again I broached the subject of separation; no dice. To say we were both utterly wretched would have been the understatement of the generation.

Linda and I had truly fallen in love. We shared a love of the out-doors: camping, hiking and just getting away from people and things. We both loved to drive, fast and long; exploring new mountain roads was sheer joy. We took top-down, hair-flying runs in the 450 at every opportunity. Linda had been married twice. First, when she was very young, and that union produced her only son, Von. Her second mar-riage was to a very smart, charming scoundrel and habitual gambler. She had endured six years of his shameless promiscuity and inveterate gambling. She finally left him after he actually stole money from her.

As we discovered during our discreet "courtship," we were both the products of experience with unhappy marriages. We had been trauma-tized and were wary. We danced a very careful adagio, exploring every aspect of the other's personality. Bitter experience taught us what we wanted in a lifetime mate; we thought we had found it. But I could not find it in myself to leave Stella, especially now, so soon after her heart surgery. Stella continued to visit Maui, and Linda and I saw more and more of each other. We would spend weekends at Cape May, making love and walking the beach with our wonderful shepherd, Amy.

The situation came to crisis around Christmas 1985. Linda had gone on a vacation trip, crewmate on a felucca down the Nile. Before she left, I had agreed that I would leave Stella. The week before Christ-mas was dreadful, perhaps the ultimate depths of our relationship. I felt that I just could not leave her. I genuinely thought she was potentially self-destructive. I could never reconcile the bitter realities: we were totally miserable together, yet she would never consider separation. I wrote a note to Linda who was due to return in a few days from Egypt, telling her that I loved her dearly, but I could not leave Stella. I remem-ber pushing the 450 down Interstate 295 on a Sunday morning with tears streaming down my face until I was pulled over by a highway patrolman. He told me I was clocked at 110. The ticket cost over $300.

Later I learned that Linda became profoundly depressed after receiv-ing my note. She saw a psychiatrist and was placed on anti-depressants.

She was preparing to leave the College and disappear somewhere in the Southwest. After a few weeks I realized that I had come to the ultimate branch of my personal Rubicon. I had to leave Stella or lose Linda. Stella seemed to have recovered from her operation physically, but was unchanged emotionally. Every day was unrelenting hell for both of us. I was desperate. I knew Linda was within days of resigning and disappearing from my life forever. I knew she meant it. So I bit the bullet. One afternoon I packed a bag and told Stella I was leaving. And I left a stunned Stella standing in the living room, speechless. I moved into a spare room at my secretary Alice's house. (She had long since married a very nice insurance executive.)

At first Stella did not think I was serious. But after several caustic, stormy sessions, she realized that I was determined. I did not tell her about Linda. I told her that she could have everything in the house but for a few odd pieces that I cherished (an ancient grandfather's clock, an original etching given by the College, a temple rubbing from Chaing Mai, and several other odd pieces). She returned to the home on Maui, and, subsequently I shipped about 90% of the household furnishings, including a complete Jensen silver service, fine Bavarian lead crystal, all kitchen utensils, chandeliers, furniture, etc, etc. Of course, she kept all her nice jewelry.

Within a few weeks I moved in with Linda. She had rented an apartment on Queen Street in a gentrified section of downtown Philadelphia. It was a new life. I felt that an enormous burden had been lifted from my shoulders. Linda and I were totally compatible; it was a revelation living with a loving, worldly, mature woman with whom I shared everything, intellectually, culturally and emotionally. It has not changed in almost two decades. Neither of us has ever even looked at another possible lover. We know life just can't get any better.

During the College years, my son Jon had married a sweet girl named Carole. They lived in Sherman Oaks and later Granada Hills. Jon continued to do videotape editing, but longed to become a producer. He was acknowledged to be the best editor in Los Angeles and

won several California Emmys. They had two children, Melanie and Jordan. Stella and I had visited them several times. As I said earlier, Steven had married Kathy while we were still in Uxbridge. He completed his internal medicine residency at Illinois and had gone to LA County for a fellowship in renal diseases. His preceptor was a world-recognized clinical nephrologist. However Steven soon realized that his boss was more interested in publication volume than scientific integrity; he suggested to Steven that he "even out" some data from an experiment. Steven left after a year and decided to practice general internal medicine and nephrology on Maui. In the interim, my mother who was living in Washington, D.C. and had begun to travel and enjoy life, became ill. Sister Joan lived nearby and saw her frequently. I visited twice over the year. Mother died in 1982.

During these years my brother Ken had settled into La Jolla, California and soon became chief of pulmonary diseases at U.C. San Diego Medical School. He and Sara had four children, three daughters and a son. Ken's interest in clotting disorders and pulmonary embolism became the central theme of his professional life. He published extensively and developed an international reputation. He was invited to lectureships all over the world. He soon had one of the best regarded fellowship programs in the country. He identified a new syndrome: pulmonary hypertension secondary to chronic pulmonary emboli. It should have been called "Ken Moser Disease." With a team of surgeons, he devised an operative procedure to remove offending emboli and relieve the pulmonary hypertension. He attracted patients from all over the planet and soon became known as one of the finest pulmonologists in the world. I was exceedingly proud of him, although our disparate professional lives made for very rare visits. We never really knew each other well. It is one of my greatest regrets. In his early 60s he became ill, first with coronary heart disease, then with bronchogenic carcinoma. He died in 1997. We had shared only the "great western trip."

My sister, Joan and husband Gerry settled in at Bethesda and had two children, Leslie and Keith. Gerry was an assistant professor of anatomy at Georgetown Medical School. He was a superb teacher and talented investigator in anatomy and histopathology. Joan was a Goucher graduate and later went to law school at Georgetown. She established a solo family-law practice. Leslie proved to be a handful as a rebellious adolescent. She later matured into a fine young woman while living at home and worked as a successful manager at a Holiday Inn. Keith turned out to be a language maven. At Georgetown and U.C. Berkeley, he became proficient in a dozen languages. His relaxed pursuit of his Ph.D. became almost a family joke. It took almost 10 years. Leslie and Keith are both bright as hell and delightful.

I always thought Joan was the brightest of all us siblings. Mother had given her a pretty tough time throughout her youth, and I always had the feeling (shared by Linda) that Joan never had a chance to fulfill the promise of her enormous intellectual capability. Gerry had a marvelous, subtle sense of humor, but he could be stubborn and rather truculent at times. I thought he was pretty tough on the kids as they were growing up. But that is all ancient history; we have become much closer to Joan, Gerry and the kids in recent years.

My final year at the College was spent predominantly in securing the Independence Mall site. As I have indicated in "Decade..." I feel we accomplished a great deal. In essence we moved the doughty old College from the Mom and Pop management operation (Rosenow's "good old boys club") into the next century. I enjoyed rubbing elbows and sharing ideas with the best and brightest in medicine. I cherished my relationship with Rollo Hanlon of the ACS, John Benson of the ABIM and the dozens of Regents and Governors. The last few months were less than wonderful. One politically oriented Regent faction was determined to make John Ball my successor. Another group wanted a more clinically oriented, scholarly leader. I suggested to the Search Committee that either Norton Greenberger or Bob Kreisberg would make a fine EVP. I thought Ball lacked the personality, clinical back-

ground or academic credentials; he was a thoroughgoing political animal. The Ball faction prevailed; he turned out to be a poor choice.

In April 1986, shortly before I left the College, Linda and I took one of our most exciting trips. I had been invited by the army to lecture at the annual U.S. Army Europe Medical-Surgical Conference in Garmisch-Partenkirchen. This was memorable from several aspects; it was in 1956 that I had delivered my first lecture on "Diseases of Medical Progress" to this very same conference in Frankfurt. The current invitation was a distinct honor. After the ACP annual session in San Francisco, Linda and I flew back to Philadelphia and then boarded Alitalia for Rome.

While we were airborne over the North Atlantic, the pilot came on the intercom. "NBC news just carried the flash that U.S. warplanes have bombed the headquarters of General Muammar Qaddafi in Tripoli, Libya." There was a lot of anxious chuntering as everyone digested the information, contemplating what effect it would have on their time in Europe. I did not think it would impact our visit, but I was very wrong.

We landed in Rome and everything seemed completely normal. We promptly forgot about the bombing incident. Thus began a thoroughly delightful tour of southern Europe. We rented an Opel sedan (with Swiss plates) and immediately plunged into the bustling Roman traffic. Our hotel was near the Via Venito overlooking the fascinating Villa de Borghese. Driving in Rome proved to be high adventure. Traffic is ferociously aggressive. Where one might consider near misses of a few inches the norm in New York, in Rome it was a matter of millimeters. Always such encounters were attended by much horn blowing and out-of-window shouting, obscene gesturing and door pounding. But no one ever became sufficiently vexed to leave the vehicle; road rage was not a Roman thing. It was a top-of-the-lungs, semi-civilized, nonviolent game.

Of course, it did not help matters when once or twice I was seduced by invisible street signs onto a one-way street, heading in the less con-

ventional direction. We subsequently learned that having a vehicle with Swiss plates made us the object of universal scorn by all non-Schweiz drivers. Once I got the hang of being appropriately obnoxious and aggressive, things seemed to go more smoothly (but for Linda's chronically blanched knuckles). We did all the proper Rome things at delightful leisure. We wandered the Forum at dusk, prowled the Coliseum, explored the baths of Caracalla, ogled at St. Peters and the Sistine Chapel, walked the cobbled Via Appia, crept through the catacombs and reveled in the marvelous cuisine of half dozen bistros. We "did" Palatine Hill, San Pietre in Vincoli, St. Maria Maggiore, etc. We purposefully eschewed the infamous Roman nightlife.

Then we headed south to Naples. Driving on the "speed limitless" *autostrada* was more challenging than tooling down the *autobahns* I remembered in Bavaria. Italian drivers are no less swift, but far less disciplined. Cruising speeds of 90 mph keep you in the slow lane. Our little Opel was obviously engineered to handle such velocity. About 50 kilometers south of Rome we encountered a horrendous accident scene; about 30 battered vehicles were scattered over about a half-mile of roadway. It looked like a combat zone with wailing sirens and flashing lights. Ambulances and police vehicles were already on the scene. We were waved ahead to weave slowly through the nightmarish scene. Later we were told that such events were rare, but when such occurred, they were terrible.

North of Naples we turned east seeking a road that would take us to the western slope of Vesuvius. We thought it would be romantic to spend the night overlooking the Bay of Naples, intending to ascend to the crater the next day. As we climbed it became apparent that motels and hotels were notable by their absence. About two thirds to the crest it was now dusk, and we were about to retreat back to Naples when we saw an ancient stone edifice, "Hotel Eremo." We drove into the courtyard, ominously devoid of vehicles. The old graystone darling had seen better days, but beggars…We climbed up to the first floor veranda and cautiously entered what appeared to be an open entryway. We shouted

greetings—into silence. Soon a profusely apologetic, somewhat corpulent Italian gentleman emerged, buttoning a tattersall vest under a ratty tweed coat. He spoke no English but indicated that we were vastly welcome. In a very dimly lit lobby we signed a battle-scarred, well-thumbed registry. I could not discern the dates of entry of previous guests, but I was certain they were not of this century.

Dinner "would not be a problem" I think he said. Our room was on the third floor off a corridor that had ceiling and floors in exquisite black and white Volterra marble. Our leather heels clacked, reverberating rather alarmingly—accentuating the vast emptiness of the milieu. The suite was also a marvel of marble with a delicious balcony where we could see the romantic lights of Naples and the bay. A storm seemed to be brewing in the south. After a wondrous hot bath, we descended to the dining room. Again our smiling, paunchy, one-person welcoming party materialized. There was no apparent menu, but we managed to convey, "specialty of the house." Dinner was inauspicious calamari and spaghetti, but we were starved. We suspected that tattersall vest was also the cook.

The night was incredible. A vicious storm swept in from the bay with spectacular lightening, thunder, rain and hail, escorted by near-hurricane force winds. The horrendous noise seemed exacerbated by the stone and marble of the old hotel. Soon after the storm subsided, just as sleep beckoned, a new sound emerged. "Click-click-click, tee-hee-hee, door slam, (muffled *sotto voce*) tee-hee-hee." An all-night sound show! Terrific! I looked out the window and saw half a dozen vehicles in the previously deserted courtyard. Linda and I had a fit of uncontrollable giggles. The good old Eremo was the clandestine trysting spot for young Neopolitans. We departed early; the ever-pleasant owner presented us with a most modest bill. We will never forget the Eremo.

We climbed to the smoking crater (cinder cones and smoldering fumaroles) of Vesuvius and hiked a greater part of the rim. One could see the ancient lava flows that had consumed Pompeii and Hercu-

laneum in 79 AD. We drove down the mountain to Naples, a sprawling, dusty, undistinguished port city. We were not disposed to tarry and fled on to Pompeii. We spent the rest of the day wandering the ruins: mosaics ("*cave canum*"), wall paintings, graffiti (plenty "dirty pictures"), pottery shards, encrusted furniture, even some lava-embalmed bodies of (unsuccessfully) fleeing inhabitants. It was unique, but strangely unmoving—considering the nature of the disaster. Perhaps it was just too ancient.

By evening we were in Sorrento and found a lovely seaside hotel, the Bristol. The next day we ferried across to Capri. These were perhaps the most enchanting few days of our trip. We taxied (exorbitant fare) to a modest hotel in Anacapri overlooking the town square. The manager at the Sorrento Bristol had made reservations. We were astonished that a Dutch couple were the only other occupants of the hotel. We inquired of the maitre d'. "Oh, signor, it is the Americans and Colonel Quaddafi; no tourists in Italy!" I turned to Linda, "For God's sake, that's why we had no problem with a hotel in Rome!" She smiled archly, "Probably explains the Eremo, too." Cute.

And it was true. Europe was devoid of tourists. What an extraordinary time to travel! We did everything in Capri; buses and taxis and Adidas opened the whole island. We did the Blue Grotto, hiked to the Faraglioni Rocks, trudged through narrow, wisteria-gushing walkways and explored breath-taking cliff-side vistas hundreds of feet down to a turquoise Mediterranean. We have been to many islands on this earth, but none bears the historical fascination and physical beauty of Capri. All the Caesars, from Augustus to Tiberius, benign and cruel, knew a good thing, when they built their summer palaces on the island of the Blue Grotto.

Reluctantly, we returned to Sorrento and headed down the Amalfi drive through Positano to Amalfi. These magnificent, snow-white cities seemed to cling perilously to the cliffs, overhanging a spectacular azure Gulf of Salerno. Amalfi was the scene of our most magical night in Europe. Once again our hotel, the Santa Caterina, was practically

empty, but still expensive. We wandered hand in hand through the leafy town square, a gentle, balmy evening with flowering trees, soft music wafting from restaurants. We discovered an open-air restaurant overlooking the sea decorated by a glorious full moon. It was almost stagy. We were the only patrons, swarmed by waiters. The meal: grilled fresh sardines (nothing like canned sardines), sliced fresh tomatoes with mozzarella sprinkled with freshly shredded basil, boiled baby new potatoes, and tiramisu for dessert. The headwaiter selected the red wine. We have never had a better meal, simply yet so elegantly served.

At Salerno we headed north, bypassing Rome (not easy, "all roads...") and, en route to Siena, discovered some charming mountain villages in Tuscany. We wandered those ancient streets, dined in an open-air restaurant on the square where they ran the colorful Palio each year. We got thoroughly lost afoot in the maze of tiny streets of Siena and had one helluva time finding the trail back to our hotel. Back on the road we sought the by-ways and found Montereggione and incredible Volterra (the walled city). It was easy to fall in love with Tuscany.

The next day we landed in Florence, along with a million school children on "annual holiday." The town was packed. Our hotel overlooked a square that was swarming with shrieking kids, not exactly a "room with a view." We did walk the Arno and its mystical bridges, pushed our way through a packed Uffizi, paid our respects to Michelangelo's David (magnificent beyond belief), and elbowed our way through throngs of midgets to ogle fire-eaters, jugglers and magicians (with frequent patting of money belts to frustrate the inevitable pickpockets). We vowed to return to Firenze under less tempestuous circumstances.

I wanted to visit Bologna, scene of one of my great teaching triumphs in 1954, but we had "many miles to go" before Garmisch. So we headed to Ravenna. We found the mosaics intriguing. The town was in celebration with colorful parades and lots of brassy bands. Our "speaka no English" pension proprietor tried to cheat us out of 50,000

lira, but we were not that gullible. We raced up the coast to Venice, passing a motorcycle cavalcade en-route to a jamboree in San Marino—miles and miles of the snorting, burbling beasts.

Linda and I had a minor squabble near Venice when I became confused about parking and how to get across the canal. ("But, dear, you **have** been here before!"). We had a thoroughly dreadful hour. In desperation, we took a "taxi-ferry" that cost 60,000 lira—ripped off again. The regular ferry was about 2000 lira. We had a reservation in a much-touted "romantic" hotel (the Bisanzio), just off St. Mark's Square. Problem: our tiny veranda overlooked a walkway that was inhabited by noisy revelers enjoying the night, all night. The weather was a trifle dodgy. Linda balked at the outrageous "tourist prices" for a gondola ride, so we walked the bridges, toured the museums, churches and palaces, enjoyed the fine restaurants, and soaked up the unique atmosphere of that decaying, charming city for two days.

From Venice, we headed north into the Dolomites. I had wanted to enter Austria via the Gross Glockner Highway, famed for its glaciers and snowy alpine vistas. But we were warned off: the road was still blocked with ice and snow. So we went to Cortina D'Ampezzo. I had been skiing there during my Austrian days and recalled the wondrous open slopes. We found an alpine restaurant with the best bread we had ever eaten; we bought three extra loaves. It was just prior to crossing the border into Austria that I got a ticket for speeding—or something. It had to do with a misread sign. But I paid the cop on the spot (another 12,000 lira!). We came into Lienz and promptly found an open-air *biergarten,* and I had my first 1986 taste of genuine Hofbrau, true love revisited. Linda caught a picture of my unmitigated bliss as I savored a one-liter stein. She was captivated as well, although she is not a beer aficionado, more a wine person.

We had to backtrack through the mountains to get to Bad Gastein. My last visit, in 1954, had been less than felicitous; it was when Al Pezcenic and I closed down the town after the Hepatitis A outbreak. It was even more charming than I remembered; thundering waterfalls

tumbled through the center of town, quaint with old watering places, old-fashioned hotel-spas and multicolored-umbrellas gracing outdoors cafes.

We were in Salzburg by evening. We found a fine old pension on the edge of town. I remembered the narrow streets and medieval squares well. We enjoyed the colorful shops and elaborately ornate, overhanging signage on the Getriedegasse, climbed the walkway to the towering Obersalzburg that looms so dominantly over the valley, and lunched at the deserted Winkler restaurant on top. That evening we dined in elegant luxury at the Goldener Hirsch (still too expensive for most humans, but undeniably superb) and later enjoyed the Eulenspiegel (still wonderfully quaint). Alas, the Paracelcus (best schnitzel in town) and the Weisses Creuz (Yugoslavian with zithers) were no longer extant. We visited all the old buildings, Mozarteum and even saw a movie with English subtitles. ("Hi Ho, Silver, *vie gehts* Tonto?")

We spent a day at the Weisses Rossl (am Wolfgangsee) in the lovely Salzkammergut lake district and took a lunch basket in an electric-powered boat onto the placid *see*. We were overcome with the joy of it all (*und bier und wurst und brot*) and barely made it back to shore. Dinner on the veranda was wiener schnitzel and kartoffeln, but what the hell. Linda thought the "genuine Bavarian" zitherers and *shue plottlers* were enthusiastic but graceless. We really enjoyed our few days in Austria. It is still hard for me to grasp the hard fact: the "light-hearted Austrians" were among the most virulent of the Nazis. And then there is Mr. Haider.

We were closing in on Garmisch. We stopped in Berchtesgarten, drove to Hitler's mountain lair and stopped in the Walker Army Rest Camp. For the first time, we learned that all U.S. military installations in Europe had been on high alert since the bombing in Libya. They expected reprisals. In addition the Chernobyl catastrophe near Kiev had just occurred. Everyone was very uptight. So we retreated in some disarray. To clear our minds, we took a towering gondola lift to the top

of the spectacular Unterberg. We landed in Garmisch by late afternoon.

We were one day early. We checked in at the U.S. Army Headquarters, following the directions in my letter of invitation. "I'm Colonel Moser; we're here for the medical surgical conference." Silence. The duty sergeant was completely perplexed. He read my letter several times and then, after a respectful excuse, retreated to an inner office. Something was wrong; the place looked terribly dead to be the site of an upcoming meeting of several hundred doctors and nurses. The sergeant materialized, "Sir, could you please speak to the captain; he's in Heidelberg."

In the next room he handed me a phone; it could have been a sizzling potato. "Colonel Moser here." A twangy Tennessee voice, "Colonel, we have been trying to contact you for the past two weeks. The conference was cancelled since the alert was called. Every installation in Europe is on high alert; all leaves have been cancelled." I might have guessed, but we had been having such a good time enjoying an empty Europe that I hadn't thought to check in. It was a just as well; we would never have done all those delicious things."

"Well, Captain," I said cheerily, "we're here; what would you like to do with us?" Long pause. "Sir, I'll have to check with the USAREAUR surgeon's office. Let me speak to Sergeant Willis." There was more chit chat, then he replaced the phone. "Sir, it may take a few days to sort this out, but we'll put you in the General Abrams suite. I think you will like it. I'll get back to you."

Oh boy, did we like it! It was strictly general officer country. We were in no hurry to scramble for home. We wandered the rustic ancient Bavarian village, drove to Oberammergau (the wood carvings were about 100 times more expensive than when I had bought my wonderful Don Quixote in 1955). The Zugspitz tramway was not running because of intense fog half way to the top. The restaurants were not exciting but adequate. We did not push Sergeant Willis. About the third day we had about "done" Garmisch, when a call came from

Heidelberg, "Sir, the general would like to take some advantage of your being here in Germany. He would like you to give your lecture to some of our hospitals. Would you prefer Frankfurt or Berlin?" I grinned over the phone at Linda, "We're going to West Berlin!"

So we drove to Munich, visited the site of the Oktoberfest bash and flew commercial to West Berlin. It was still a divided city with the infamous "Wall" very much intact. We stayed in a hotel reserved for field grade officers and for the next three days explored the town. I lectured at the Berlin Army Hospital to a pack of nervous doctors and nurses. It was only a few weeks since a bomb had destroyed a nightclub killing about a dozen GIs. Some thought the attack on Qaddafi had been in reprisal. Linda toured the fabulous Berlin zoo. We took a bus tour of East Berlin via Checkpoint Charley. The Wall was all they had said. You could see the Soviet tower guards peering through binoculars at the U.S., French and British tower guards, who were gazing back over the killing fields of the intra-wall no man's land. It was the Cold War up close and personal.

The contrast, west versus east was startling: Soviet style tenements, terrible, raucous, fume-spewing Ladas, shabbily-dressed "Easties." There was an undeniable sense of near-poverty, tension and despair. At Charley we were joined by a dour East Berlin "tour guide" who escorted us to the Soviet War Memorial. This was a much-larger-than-life edifice with heroic statuary, dedicated to Russian soldiers who had fallen during the capture of Berlin. It was profoundly moving and unsettling. We were advised that some 20 million Soviet soldiers and civilians had perished in World War II. We all filed back on the bus in pregnant silence. One could understand some of the bitterness of Moscow, if not the persisting national paranoia and Stalin-era mass murders. The highlight of the tour was the visit to the People's Museum where we gazed in awe at the painted limestone bust of Nefertiti. If this is a true likeness, she possessed the most beautiful face I have ever seen. It rotated slowly, positively hypnotic.

We were embarrassed by the burgeoning ostentation of West Berlin. The stores adjacent to the Kurfurstendam were bulging with every imaginable comestible and consumer good. It was almost as though the Westies were going overboard to demonstrate their opulence, flouting the success of their free-market economy and democratic political system, compared to the flinty communist East. There was talk, even then, about Soviet withdrawal from Berlin. (The implosion of the Soviet Union and destruction of the Wall was still three years away.) Linda and I discussed the tremendous economic burden that would befall the West if and when they brought their eastern brethren into the fold.

(I was not entirely thrilled at the prospect of unification. As I have said, I distrust the Germans. There was nothing in their entire history to inspire confidence that a more powerful, unified Germany facing another major economic down turn would not produce another Hitler, another scapegoat race. They have about run out of Jews to kill, so the Turks had better be wary. I still feel that way; it is just too soon since the horror.)

All in all it was a glorious trip. To travel through a Europe virtually devoid of swarming crowds of tourists, was an unanticipated delight—probably never to be repeated. This trip may represent the only fleeting vibration of pleasure I derive when I think of that awful, enduring despot, Qaddafi or the horror of Chernobyl.

When we returned to earth, back in Philadelphia, we began to contemplate what to do with the rest of our life. The new location for the College on Independence Mall was settled. I traveled a lot to Regional Meetings, still went to meetings of the Residency Review Committee, the Joint Commission on Accreditation of Hospitals, the Federated Council of Internal Medicine. But my days were numbered; I was a lame duck.

I had been asked to chair the NASA Life Sciences Committee. I did this for three years, even after I left the College. It was frustrating but fascinating. NASA really didn't know what to do about manned space

flight. Life sciences had a minuscule budget compared with the other space science disciplines, and after the glorious Apollo adventure the manned program practically vanished. There was scant interest in Congress or by the average citizen to commit significant public moneys into "exploration of the near universe by man." There was no public sentiment to try to send crews to Mars.

We already knew that man could withstand the vicissitudes of microgravity for periods up to one year. But for a two-plus-year Mars mission it was physiologic, psychological and radiological *terra incognita*. We needed a space station that could remain in near earth orbit for years on end to study the chronic effects of microgravity, isolation and survival in the closed, easily-contaminated (chemically and biologically) environment of a spacecraft. And there was no national commitment to pay for such an adventure. The shuttle flights were too brief and too limited to provide the kind of long-term data that would be required before rational scientific folks could sanction a mission that would launch a crew to Mars.

I felt there was no ratiocination, no scientific justification for the enormous expense of a space station unless it were dedicated, primarily, to study man. Everything else, astronomy, planetary sampling, earth observation, deployment of communication satellites, could be done better and cheaper with unmanned spacecraft. It became my mantra. I managed to have my opinion inserted into several official documents. Those "station advocates" at NASA (and in industry), who were deeply invested, financially and politically, in "crewed space flight," were hardly objective. They did not like my cant. I was not surprised. (More of this later.)

Within another six months, I was on terminal leave from the College, and Linda had submitted her resignation. We bought a little Nissan Stanza and took a leisurely stroll through the Maritimes. Gorging on lobster in PEI, witnessing the rolling tidal Bore in Nova Scotia and cycling the by-roads of Newfoundland. They all had unmistakable charm. We adored each other's company and chatted endlessly about

our future. About a year earlier, we had moved into a delightful rented house in Medford Lakes, N.J. (which we adored, despite a long commute for both of us, in separate cars). No one except Alice and Pat knew we were living together. (I think!) I know my productivity at work had increased substantially. For the first time in many years I was truly happy. I looked forward with childlike eagerness to coming home to Linda; she felt the same. We enjoyed a lot of mundane things together: shopping for food, bicycling, eating out, still walking the beach at Cape May.

I had begun to explore job offers. Ed Stemmler, the thoughtful, low-key dean at Penn Medical School, offered me a position as an assistant dean. He needed someone to coordinate his faculty clinic and teaching time, plus other administrative chores. I liked Ed, but the job had the scent of bureaucratic ennui.

I had an offer from Smith, Kline and Beecham to coordinate their clinical research programs. It was intriguing and the pay was superb. I was dubious about my qualifications for this job, but they said, "We think it is a good match." Then there was a sudden change in top administration at Smith Kline, and the new people put me on hold "until we can sort things out." No time limit; no thanks.

I was invited to New York to meet with the folks at MetLife. They needed someone to help establish criteria for hospitals and physicians to qualify for their burgeoning health insurance program. This was a most challenging opportunity, and I was sorely tempted. The salary was extraordinary. Linda and I spent a weekend in New York actually exploring places to live. We decided that the urban milieu of New York was not what we had in mind for our "proximate-to-retirement" years. I had an offer from Medical Economics to head up one of their publication divisions in northern New Jersey; it did not sound exciting.

Then, as usual in my life, fickle Fate interposed her whimsy. I was in Chicago for a meeting and ran into an old friend, Dr. Dan Azarnoff, whom I had known when he was chairman of the pharmacology department at Kansas. Over lunch, Dan brought me up to date; he had

been director of research at Searle Pharmaceuticals for the past five years. He said he heard that I was retiring from the College; "So what are you going to do?" I explained my various offers. He said, "You should talk to Bob Shapiro." Dan explained that quite recently Monsanto had bought Searle and spun off their NutraSweet Division as a wholly—owned subsidiary. They were hunting for a medical director. Might I be interested?

Well, here was something really new, totally alien to any of my previous careers. But I was intrigued; Linda thought it worthy of exploration. A few days later back in Philadelphia, I received a call from Mr. Shapiro himself. Dan had spoken to him; could I come to Skokie and chat with him and some of his key staff? He said they would all be gathered there next Friday. I told him I had a long-standing speaking engagement in Hamilton, Bermuda on Saturday afternoon, and I was not sure about connections from O'Hare. He said, "Not to worry." So I met with the CEO of NutraSweet. As they say, he was a "piece of work": 49, distinguished lawyer who had been in government for a few years, charming to his toenails, articulate, an aficionado of classic literature and an acknowledged business genius. He had studied my CV. I asked, "What is it you want of me?"

He paused and began to pace around the room. Head down, tie askew, hands in pockets, gaunt, angular, intense. (It was to become known as the "Bob Shapiro Shuffle.") He said, "I want you to win the hearts and minds of health care professionals on behalf of our product." I confessed I did not know a damned thing about the world of business, much less anything about the company's **sole** product—aspartame. (Nor did I know about the storm if controversy it had provoked!)

Later, I met with several other key executives; they were impressive and very different than most of the medical people I had known. I was intrigued by their single-minded dedication to this mystical white powder! About three o'clock I was getting very nervous about Bermuda; Shapiro reiterated, "Not to worry." We had a light repast at a

nearby bistro, and about five, we bundled into his Mitsubishi convertible and tore off to a small private airport a few miles from Skokie.

Casually, he told me that the corporate jet would take me to Hamilton, and "…let me know your decision about the job, as soon as possible." As soon as I regained my composure, I told him I would have to do some research on aspartame before I could make **any** decision. He drove up to the lip of the tarmac in the shadow of a sleek Jetstream. The landing stairs eased down and Shapiro shook my hand, "Have a pleasant trip." I was appropriately dazzled. I was the sole passenger with a crew of three; the male flight attendant served up a marvelous dry Rob Roy and a delicious meal of lamb chops and boiled baby potatoes. It was just like uptown; I could get used to this. We refueled in Charleston and eased into Hamilton before nine. A taxi was waiting and whisked me to the Bermuda Princess. I was dead asleep before eleven. It was an impressive performance. Yes, I could get used to this—obvious seduction be damned. (In the next five years I rode the corporate jet only one other time, but *c'est la vie*.)

# 27

## *The NutraSweet Years*

◆

### *(how sweet it was...)*

Since Linda and I had left the College, I had some time on my hands. So I went to Bethesda, visited my sister and haunted the National Library of Medicine for a few days. I ran a Medline scan on "Aspartame." To my astonishment it printed over 100 articles and listed a book. I selected about 60 of what appeared to be key references and had them photocopied. I called Shapiro's office and had them send me a copy of the "big white book" (that described all the animal studies done on aspartame). Off and on for the next few weeks, I studied aspartame. The data spoke for themselves. It was abundantly evident that this simple dipeptide molecule had been studied to death. It was obviously quite safe. Then why over 100 studies and a book? I would soon find out.

I called Shapiro and after some discussion with his associates about salary (most generous) and staff (seemingly adequate), I accepted the "still somewhat nebulously defined" job (Director of Medical Affairs). But I had come to believe that one creates and redefines every new position. I agreed to a five-year contract. Intellectually, I had already accepted the fact that I would no longer be my own boss, and that in entering the world of corporate business, I would be a greenhorn, surrounded by much younger people, all of whom were far more experienced in this profession and lifestyle. But for the superb salary and an

opportunity to try something radically different for a final career, I was willing to accept the compromise, foregoing status and power.

Linda was excited about moving to Chicago, and we did some intense house hunting before my start date. Having danced our cautious, exploratory, living together "courting minuet" for a few months, we were both convinced that we should get married. It was decidedly awkward, even in this *avant garde* era, for a somewhat-less-than young couple, to check into hotels (always awkward) and meet old friends on social occasions (always strained). Besides, I have always felt that these *au courant* "significant other", so-called permanent liaisons sans marriage ventures, plus "foolproof" pre-nuptial agreement arrangements, were sure-fire indicators of impermanence. To me they represented admissions of insecurity and a lack of mutual commitment and trust. All are flagrant harbingers of a doomed marriage. Linda never pressured me to get a divorce, and I was still apprehensive about the psychological effect it would have on Stella. I was a damned fool. However I was coming closer to facing the inevitable.

The company set us up for a house-hunting visit, and we drove out to Skokie. We were placed in contact with a most pleasant, non-pushy real estate person, and we must have stomped through about 20 to 30 residences in the northwest suburbs. As usual, what we adored was too expensive; what we could afford we did not adore. Finally on the last day, we were taken to a charming Dutch Colonial off the beaten track in Barrington. We wondered why it had not been shown to us previously. (Later we found out.) It was isolated, surrounded by three acres of luxurious old oak and sycamore adjacent to the Lake Barrington golf course. It was about a 30-minute commute to my office in Skokie. It needed some work, but we both fell in love with it. As would happen many times in our life together, there was immediate congruence, a simultaneous, unspoken recognition that "this is the place" (or car or dog or restaurant or rug).

The owners were a very weird couple. He, quite obviously, was a dedicated aficionado of Old Granddad; she was tiny, feisty and talk-

ative, the obvious alpha person. And, among other *outré* things, they raised yappy, show-class West Highland Terriers. The house was alive with ribbons and trophies. The asking price was far more than we could afford, and we departed for Philadelphia in heavy-hearted silence. After about an hour on the road, Linda suggested we talk about "making them an offer." We paused in a roadside truck stop and chatted over coffee and cherry pie. We did a bit of "back of the envelope" calculation and determined what might constitute a reasonable offer. We called the real estate lady despite the rather late hour. She agreed to contact the owners "right now." We were to call her back in about an hour. We drove on in thoughtful silence, stopped, called. Yes, they had accepted our bid! It was a bubbly, joyous drive home.

We were obliged to move to Chicago before the house would be available for occupancy. The company put us up in an apartment in a small residential hotel in Evanston. It was modest, but the hotel dining room had made Michelin. It was also sufficiently expensive that we indulged only rarely. One evening, after we closed the house deal, we drove out to Barrington to take another look at our new digs. As we crossed the threshold, we both noted the heavy aroma of—yes, it was oranges! Not unpleasant, but certainly remarkable.

Weeks later, after the house had been vacant a few days and deprived of its generous dollops of orange-doused disinfectant, we finally moved in. We were floored by an overwhelming, unpleasant odor. It permeated the house. Brief olfactory exploration revealed the source: a room adjacent to the kitchen that opened onto an enclosed "patio." Obviously it had been the happy hunting ground where countless generations of frisky Westies had romped and done their business.

Linda attacked the area with relentless vigor, scouring and scrubbing with a dozen powerful disinfectants and deodorants. Lots of red knuckles but no enduring success. We sealed off the dog exits to the enclosed runs outside, removed the fence, added a truckload of topsoil and layered it with rich sod. Still no luck. The hapless Bermuda grass

was overmatched; it gasped, withered and gave up the ghost. Nothing worked to dissipate the stench. Finally I had an inspiration. We had the "dog-room" lined (walls and ceiling) with cedar. We placed flagstones over the outside run area (where the sod had been defeated). The odor abated immediately, but on hot humid days the room still bore a ghostly redolence of habitation by legions of Westies. After a few months either our olfactory bulbs accommodated or the aroma finally relented. In retrospect, I think we could have offered a few thousand dollars less and still carried the day. Aside from this flaw, the house and land were terrific, an enclave of serene green sequestered within the raging development and roiling traffic of the exploding surrounding Barrington suburb. (Gathering itinerant golf balls sliced over the fence into our dense woods from the $16^{th}$ hole became a modest weekend diversion.)

So I started to work in "industry." The first day I drove the 450 to the company garage arriving at 6:30 AM. I wanted to get a little work done before the crowd arrived. It had been my habit at ACP for years. I was astonished to discover the garage half filled with cars. It turned out that early arrival was just a part of the NutraSweet "corporate culture." These upwardly mobile MBAs were just as eager and compulsive as young doctors. I was reporting to a youngish lawyer-politico, Charlie Maculae, a handsome, articulate Down Easter, who also was brandnew to the world of commerce. He had earned a fine reputation as a key staff member in Ed Muskie's ill-starred presidential run. Charley lasted only a few months after I arrived. Later, I discovered that the long knives had been out for him; the old timers, mostly rethreaded hard-cases from Searle days, had taken a dim view of Shapiro hiring a brash outsider upstart to head up the communications-PR operation. Charley was commuting weekends between Skokie and his home and family in Portland, Maine. This odd arrangement was interpreted as a lack of ferocious commitment to the job (another shibboleth of the local culture). But Charley was a *mensch*; he was very good to me and allowed me to build my small department.

I inherited a nurse-dietitian, two ADA dietitians and a food scientist. But I needed to hire an executive secretary. While I was still trying to learn the capabilities of my small (all female) staff, I began to interview candidates. It was a thoroughly distressing experience. In all my previous careers I had been blessed with smart, dedicated support personnel. All contenders for this job were obliged to come from within the organization (house rule). Uniformly, they bore enthusiastic recommendations from other departments (so why is she leaving?). But each, in turn, failed to meet the even the most rudimentary requirements of the craft. They were fair typists (word processor, of course), none could take direct verbal dictation (fair from tape), telephone communication seemed an occult art and there was uncertain awareness of basic English, spelling and forget grammar. I suddenly realized I had been thoroughly spoiled in the army, at AMA and ACP. I would never find another star in the class of a Pat or Alice or Adie or Gretchen or Vincent or Thelma (the marvelous women administrative assistants of my other career incarnations).

Finally, I hired a sweet young thing a notch above the pack. She was a whiz with computers, but her lack of knowledge of the world was astonishing. Her dim awareness of history began a few years post Viet Nam. She was raising two small kids alone, so reading books or newspapers was a rarity. The *coup de grace* occurred early on, when I gave her a tape containing several business letters and asked for drafts. In one of the letters I used the expression, "I hesitate to insinuate myself into this situation..." To my horror the "final" draft ("...ready for your signature, Dr. Moser") read, "I hesitate to **inseminate** myself..."). I triple checked every draft thereafter. But she was always prompt, pleasant, loyal and earnest. Beside with a couple of little kids and no visible husband, she was really trying. Besides my stuff was not exactly rocket science. We struggled on together for five years; she improved to a tolerable level of competence.

In order to try to fulfill my "mission" ("to win the hearts and minds"), I embarked on an ambitious program. But within weeks I

came to realize that aspartame and The NutraSweet Company, were under siege! Apparently, there were some neuroscientists of significant repute, who were far from convinced about the safety of the product. They had been joined by a group of noisy, non-scientist zealots, who had attracted considerable media attention by insisting that they had developed myriad dire symptoms as the result of aspartame ingestion. It was an unholy and unlikely alliance. The attitudes of some of the neuroscientists were perplexing to me. The data on aspartame were quite clear with regard to the characterization of the molecule, its digestion and metabolism. Even at grossly abusive test doses in human volunteers, it was remarkably benign. And the amounts used by consumers were physiologically insignificant. I continued to find the data sufficiently compelling that I had no problem defending the product.

Now for a bit of historical irony. You may remember my introducing Dr. Harry R, the terrible man who had been my nemesis when we were pulmonary fellows together back in 1949 at the old D.C. General Hospital. Well, now he had resurfaced with a new name, and he was now sporting a very bad, Sam Donaldson-type hairpiece. After some god-awful publications on "chronic hypoglycemia" (a factitious illness featuring ephemeral symptoms and no signs), seemingly endemic among rich, blue-haired, mostly West Palm Beach widows, he had taken on aspartame as his *cause celebre*. He had no controlled data, merely an undocumentable cadre of "aspartame victims," with anecdotal complaints (notably unshared with the FDA Adverse Reaction Data System [ARDS]). He became the darling of the army of anti-aspartame loonies. The reincarnated Harry R was to become a royal pain in the butt (once again) for the next decade.

Before I arrived in Skokie, one national TV news magazine had produced a rather disastrous segment on aspartame. The reluctant "corporate spokesperson," a distinguished pediatrician-nutritionist who had been my predecessor (and was still on board), had projected an image best described as pompous and pedantic. I reviewed the tape of the broadcast; he was frankly awful. (I often wondered if that had been the

crowning incident that prompted Shapiro's ultra-cunning Bermuda seduction of Moser.) So I inherited this dubious chore from a much-relieved colleague. This "corporate spokesperson" business had **not** been discussed during my job interviews; it soon became a principal responsibility.

My very first encounter with the media came in the form of a very hostile interview (on subsequently edited tape) by a Danish TV "Mike Wallace" wannabe. He was a blond weasel with a phony Oxford accent. I was given a crash course in "media training" by a wily, grizzled, former network newscaster from Burson-Marsteller (New York). I found the whole procedure annoying, degrading and demeaning. "Remember, Doc, it's all show biz. The '**facts**' really don't matter; what you **say** really doesn't matter; success is measured by public perception—your appearance and how you come across." And, *triste dictu,* that old hack was right. So with malice aforethought, even under the most arduous and provocative situations, I tried to look sincere, never (obviously) lose my cool, always act (apparently) friendly, seem appropriately (never pompously) authoritative, but always avuncular—avuncular—avuncular. A tall order for a professional curmudgeon.

Over the next few years I must have achieved some measure of success. After numerous TV and radio appearances, I did not get canned or sued or assassinated. Among my "credits" were appearances on "Regis and Kathy," "Gary Collins," "Phil Donahue," "Hard Copy," "60 Minutes-Australia," a BBC—TV "investigative reporter" show and numerous local TV and call-in radio shows in Los Angeles, Chicago, Philadelphia, Anchorage, Dallas, Toronto and Monterrey (old Mexico). I might have missed a few. All were unpleasant and anxiety-provoking experiences. Most often the hosts were glib, superficial, loquacious, Armani-armored airheads (especially Regis Philbin, Kathy Gifford and Gary Collins). The sweaty, officious, barely pubescent producers always lined up an assortment of uniformly obese, ill-mannered, loquacious "talk show" types who gloried in describing personal,

always unverifiable, horror stories. This "15 minutes of Warhol fame" played to an eager national audience of idiots like themselves, who had nothing better to do with their daylight hours than watch insipid television. I was obliged to respond to these offensive twits on the basis of hard-wrought medical science, while playing "Marcus Welby." It was "talk show" hell. I always hated it; I earned my pay. I learned a lot about the avaricious media. "Sweeps Week" periods always brought out the worst.

But it was the occasion to meet the most charismatic person I encountered during my tenure at NutraSweet. Darrald Donnell was responsible for sales (and such) in Central and South America. I met him on the plane to Monterrey, old Mexico. We had received word that a Mexican TV station was about to run a call-in program dedicated to "Aspartame Problems." So Darrald who was fluent in Spanish (and Portuguese and French) was shanghaied to translate. My CV had been faxed in advance, and the host was intrigued by my time with NASA. So, after a few benign questions from the unseen audience about the product, the rest of the hour was occupied with a discussion of "space medicine." I loved it. Darrald (and Ann, his accomplished wife) have been dear friends ever since.

To try to educate the health professionals, I recruited about 20 consultants from across the country. Most were ADA registered dietitians ("ambassadors"), two were dentists; one was a pharmacist and one a nurse—to round out the team. All had nutritional and "media" experience. We gathered them in Skokie twice a year for social-scientific training. Soon they all became well-informed, reasonably articulate spokespersons, responding to aspartame-related issues that arose in their localities. With the help of some outside experts we designed an exhibit (with two duplicates) that simulated an old apothecary shop with a garden. It carried the message of "aspartame safety" in a low-key, data-based format to health care professionals. Each exhibit was staffed by three dietitians (staff and consultants), and they toured the annual meetings of the American College of Pediatrics, American Col-

lege of Physicians, American Academy of Family Physicians, American College of Ob-Gyn, American Diabetes Association, American Dietetic Association and American Dental Association. We also made the nurse midwives and physicians' assistants annual meetings. We often exhibited at two meetings occurring simultaneously. I frequently attended to "oversee" the operation, but the ADA consultants were all professionals, well-versed in the clinical research on aspartame. The exhibits constituted my biggest budgetary allocation aside from salaries.

We did this for about three years, and gradually the anti-aspartame noise level diminished. In all fairness the appearance of half a dozen excellent, randomized controlled trials published in peer-reviewed journals, provided added impetus to the message of aspartame safety. By the time I left the organization in 1991, there were no serious medical scientists who were taking shots at NutraSweet. (Harry R did not count as a "serious" scientist.) Only the lunatic fringe continued the drumbeat of negative propaganda. But aspartame sales were never better; obviously, the public enjoyed the product, and the customers (Coke, Pepsi, General Foods, *et al*) loved it. Most all "low calorie" products in the marketplace contained aspartame.

Later I recruited consultants from other countries where NutraSweet was moving into the market. I personally interviewed physicians with a background in nutrition, in U.K., South Africa, Canada, Mexico, Costa Rica, Jamaica, Panama, Colombia, Argentina, Brazil, Chile, Uruguay, Australia, Indonesia, Singapore, Hong Kong, Taiwan and the Philippines. We already had consultants in Germany, France and Italy. It made for a great deal of fascinating international travel. Linda accompanied me to Southeast Asia and Australia, and we usually managed to tack on a few weeks of vacation. These were marvelous outings.

In Australia I interviewed potential consultants in Sydney, Melbourne, Canberra, Adelaide, Perth and Brisbane. We enjoyed the best hotels and superb ethnic cuisine. Then we rented a car at Alice Springs

and did Uluru (Ayer's Rock) and the Great Barrier Reef (Heron Island). In Hong Kong we languished in the elegance of the Peninsula (perhaps the world's classiest hotel), and in Singapore we did Raffles. Those were the golden days at NutraSweet; the molecule was still under patent protection, and we enjoyed a virtual monopoly on the artificial sweetener market.

I met with the Latin American consultants for annual three-day refresher courses in Aruba, Cuernavaca and Iguazu Falls. We did the same with the consultants in the Orient in Cebu (Philippines). We published a newsletter every other month that up-dated all consultants on newly published papers and other corporate news. It was a highly successful operation. In my trips out of country our local PR folks always arranged for me to lecture to healthcare professional groups about nutrition, healthful lifestyle, obesity and, of course, aspartame safety. I gave a zillion interviews to local TV and radio stations, news-papers and magazines.

Despite this enormous exposure, I never became comfortable with reporters. Some few were very bright, reasonably literate in science (could tell the difference between a randomized controlled trial and anecdotal hearsay), and actually "listened" to presentation of data in the interest of fairness. But the vast majority were barely post-pubes-cent, densely scientifically illiterate and innumerate, and had already made up their minds about the "story." They greeted any offering from the "corporate hired gun" with ill-disguised skepticism. I didn't win many of these encounters.

In addition during my first two years, the director of public rela-tions, Thym Smith, and I visited reporters for TV stations, newspapers and magazines who had produced uncomplimentary and usually inac-curate programs and articles about aspartame. They most often quoted each other—reverberating misinformation. We visited Toronto, Bos-ton, New York, Philadelphia, Atlanta, Cleveland, Los Angeles, Phoenix and Anchorage. It was during a visit to Los Angeles that I met Dr. Art Ulene, who had said some things on "Good Morning America" that

were simply ill informed. He was thoroughly rational and could recognize the credibility of the published safety data. We had a pleasant hour together; he was most gracious. We became friends, and we still communicate at frequent intervals.

The personnel turnover at NutraSweet was an unending source of anxiety for everyone. It seemed that every few months there was a painful reorganization, sometimes attended by "downsizing," a thoroughly dreadful corporate euphemism. At periodic intervals we would all be hauled off to a "retreat" at some remote spa. Here we would be regaled by a trendy, psychobabble-spouting group of frightfully expensive gurus (who had invariably written a dull, incomprehensible book that had wowed upper-level management). They conducted insipid mind games. Their mission seemed to be: convince we middle management and lower level clods that it is okay to lose your job. It was very Esselenesque, with usually sensible people being required to participate in asinine, demeaning group exercises. I went to one such seance, walked out after the first day and refused to participate thereafter. Corporate America had been hornswoggled by these psycho-trendy charlatans, and I was just too old for such silly parlor games.

Charley was soon riffed and replaced by a pretty, tough corporate woman lawyer. She had been a member of Shapiro's ivory tower "in-group." My new boss was young enough to be my daughter, and I had never worked for a woman before. But I was not anticipating a problem.

(I was at peace with my new job. As I indicated earlier, I had long-since agreed to play the cards I was dealt when I joined corporate America. I'd "had my turn" at playing the Big Shot: army colonel, chief of major teaching services, independent practitioner, editor-in-chief of JAMA and CEO of a large medical association. Admittedly, the job was not very challenging, intellectually. But I was comfortable; the product was safe. I was not compromising my scientific integrity. In all candor, I was working for income, seeking to ensure financial security for Linda and myself for the rest of our lives. NutraSweet was

the vehicle. So I became a serious member of the team. The job did offer many new challenges far removed from anything I had ever done. I confess that I did not love some of the stuff I was obliged to do, but I was not intimidated. It was the easiest, best-paying job I'd ever had—an appropriate final career.)

With the change in bosses, my only concern was that I might have less freedom than I had enjoyed under the free wheeling Charley. But that was not the case. My new chief became a friend, never second-guessing my operations. We only had one semi-serious confrontation. She had been a long-time disciple of another "inspirational guru who changed my life." He and his team had conducted seminars for a dozen of the Fortune 100 companies. Their (ostensible) mission: to teach individuals how to develop "inner strength", a sense of "self worth" and imbue them with a "spirit to compete successfully in the rough and tumble world of business." I read some of their literature that the chief provided. It was the same old tired hogwash in a slicker wrapper. But in a weak, "nice-guy" moment, I agreed to attend a five-day seminar in Santa Clara. The tuition would come from our departmental budget. My boss would be attending as well; it would be her fifth course!

We were sequestered in a rustic resort surrounded by a gracious cypress forest overlooking the coastal mountains. I admit, I entered the soiree encumbered by considerable bias; I left unrepentant. The audience consisted of about 200 mostly young, eager, earnest, obviously "exceedingly upwardly mobile" junior executives from well-known corporations. I seemed to be the eldest in the room by about 20 years. (It brought back uncomfortable memories of the first day of the "short course" at Fort Leavenworth.) The first hour our "inspirational leader," a fortyish, darkly handsome, slightly paunchy, sonorously voiced individual, materialized. He came on as an L. Ron Hubbard wannabe.

But after observing a few performances, he was more like a psychological Torquemada in tailored slacks. He singled out individuals who had attended previous classes and viciously tongue-lashed them before

the group. He attacked their abysmally dismal progress in achieving maturity, lack of intelligence, poverty of insight, abundance of sloth-fulness, etc. It was a verbal blood bath; it had me squirming. But, to my astonishment, his audience was completely captivated! Beatific smiles on all sides; the same bland, self-satisfied, sheep-like expression appeared on every face. They were enjoying the spectacle! It could have been Jonestown transported to southern California or an audience at Jerry Springer!

The *coup de grace* was a withering verbal broadside directed at my hapless boss, his most faithful disciple. She was reduced to tears. I almost raised my voice in protest, but, hell, this was **her** snake pit. That evening I expressed my outrage at the gratuitous obloquy at dinner with a half dozen classmates. They were all still smiling blandly, were disgustingly indulgent and said I needed to give it more time. I found their docile, blissful tolerance of my strident apostasy downright obscene. If this wasn't Jonestown or Heaven's Gate, it was probably Stepford. Was there something weird in the Santa Clara water?

The next day was more of the same. At the break, I told my col-league that I could not abide this nonsense. I was wasting my time and the company's money. She was disappointed, but I was adamant. Her mindset was beyond my comprehension. I sought out the guru and told him (privately and calmly) that his course and his methodology were not my cup of tea. With a half-bitten tongue I refrained from say-ing bullshit. I told him I was bailing out, but I wanted him to know that I thought his methods were reprehensible, demeaning and counter-productive, if not downright evil. He stared blankly and said nothing. Obviously, I was not promising convert material. Once back home, the matter was never discussed, but she remained supportive and helpful.

Soon after we arrived in Barrington, I began the process of seeking a divorce. It was a thoroughly traumatic experience. (Isn't it always?) Stella had secured the services of a law firm that had an unsavory repu-tation, well known in Chicago for their shark-like, "take no prisoners"

demeanor. My law firm (recommended by my lawyer-boss) was a "distinguished and well-respected-in-the-Loop" outfit. I could have used a little more feist and a little less "old school tie" dignity. And the lawyer assigned to my case turned out to be a not-too-bright pussycat. It was no contest; we were badly out-lawyered (but not out-spent).

After 34 years as an itinerant army wife, Stella had few wage-earning skills. The alimony settlement has been characterized as "appropriately generous." Some 13 years later that observation would seem a significant understatement. But such things are always in the eye of the beholder. Certainly, Linda and I do not begrudge Stella's comfortable quality of life. At the time I was eager to stop the ambient unpleasantness. Also, I wanted to marry Linda as soon as possible. The divorce became official on March 15, 1989; at least the Ides were somewhat kinder to me than Caesar.

On March 18, we both dressed up in our finest (she in her "pre-Bob" $7000 Japanese tanuki fur coat), me in my best dark suit and raging violet silk tie (contributed by niece, Leslie), and we drove to Waukegan. We had scouted it out and had been informed that we could get hitched expeditiously, by a judge in the city court. We arrived about ten in the morning and were ushered into a waiting room with a large glass panel looking out on a courtroom. A mirthless, overweight clerk advised that the judge would marry us after he had concluded his morning business.

His "business" turned out to be the sentencing of some heavyweight prisoners. Some of our fellow observers in the viewing room (connected to the court by a one-way speaker system) were scowling, milling, muttering family and friends of the unsavory chaps handcuffed on the other side of the glass partition. I think we looked a trifle out of place. After about an hour, the judge seemed to figure out what the strange, overly dressed, somewhat older couple, staring open-mouthed at him, were up to. He interrupted the sentencing process long enough to smile benignly and say the magic words. It seemed a trifle frivolous to kiss in the midst of so much heavy-duty law and order traffic. So we

smiled blandly, escaped and kissed on the courthouse steps. I don't think we giggled too much.

Sometime after we settled into life at NutraSweet and Barrington, we received a distressing message from my younger son, Jon. It seemed that he had developed some deafness and tinnitus (ringing) in his left ear. He was seen by an ENT physician, and after a "too long" interval (in my opinion), a diagnosis of an acoustic neuroma was established. Jon had "researched" the Internet and learned a great deal about this tumor. I made some inquiries and identified a neurosurgeon at the Massachusetts General in Boston, who was reputed to have the best track record in the country as measured in "excellent outcomes" after surgical excision of such tumors. The surgeon was much sought after, and we were advised that we would be obliged to accommodate to his schedule. But I prevailed on a few old ACP chums from Boston (who rounded at the MGH), and we arranged for Jon to be operated a bit ahead of the queue.

Jon called and asked if he could come and spend a week with me before his operation. He arrived at O'Hare, spent a few days in Barrington, and then we flew to Boston and rented a car. We toured the coast of Maine. It was the first time we had been together since our raft trip down the Colorado many years earlier. It was a very warm and intimate time; we were both very concerned. The probability that Jon would lose hearing in his left ear was very real. And since his job of videotape editing required good hearing, he was depressed and worried. I was equally concerned about facial nerve palsy and the overall risk of the procedure. From Maine, we went to Boston where Jon was admitted to the MGH.

Stella and Carole were to join us, but I elected to stay in a different hotel. The first time I encountered Stella (since the divorce in Chicago) was the day before the operation. I extended my hand. She scowled, turned on her heel and stalked away in white-faced silence. I could not believe it! Even in the presence of a serious threat to the well-being, perhaps even the life of our son, she could not set aside her rage for a

moment of shared anguish. At that moment I decided that any effort to maintain any sort of amicable relationship with Stella would be futile. This sorry situation has not changed over the years.

Jon came through the procedure rather well; the tumor was resected completely. But he did lose hearing in his left ear and suffered a slight left facial weakness. He soon overcame some residual vertigo, but was otherwise free of symptoms. He learned to compensate for the loss of bilateral hearing with an electronic device that picked up sound in his dead ear and transported it to the right. Soon he was able to sort out the direction of sound. The versatility and adaptability (they now call it "plasticity") of the brain has always amazed me. Jon showed lots of courage and determination. He has suffered no recurrence.

I feel it is about time I write about Linda. I have already spoken of the remarkable compatibility that we share, but there is so much more. At first I was concerned about the 19 years that separated us chronologically, but (thus far) the age difference has not been a problem. We are classic examples of an old aphorism: each of us is the product of all previous experience. She had a rough young life. Her parents were rigid Seventh Day Adventists, and she was reared in that parched environment. She rebelled as a teenager, even ran away from home several times. Her intellectual endowment simply did not allow her to embrace that doctrinaire religion and lifestyle. As I have indicated earlier, her first husband was a nice young man who simply lacked the intellectual firepower to provide her with sustenance. Her son, Von, was born of that marriage, her only child. Linda's second husband was a charming salesman-entrepreneur, who suffered the misfortune of being an inveterate gambler. He led her into a life of fantastic highs and dreadful lows. He was very exciting but flagrantly profligate. He broke her heart. She endured seven, kaleidoscopic years.

When Linda worked at the College she was living with a handsome, bright younger man, who was also on the staff. She was quiet and unobtrusive. I knew Linda was bright and competent in addition to being sexy and beautiful, but I knew little else about her. When she

took over the ACP Department of Education, I came to realize that her capabilities included warmth, imagination, initiative, star leadership qualities and incredible organizational ability. Besides, her troops loved her. She could have run a large corporation. I had vastly underestimated her from every aspect. Over the years (some 17 plus now) that we have been together, my affection and admiration has only expanded. I am continuously amazed at her intellectual virtuosity, an incredible capacity to master new disciplines. My love and devotion have become the dominant forces in my life. She is still the most desirable woman on earth.

Linda is constantly seeking new intellectual challenges. She is the consummate "finisher." Her sense of humor is droll, and she has a marvelous belly laugh that always invites a smiling, "What was that?" She is kind (we tend to collect and nurture abandoned creatures, large and small), and she is earthy in the best sense. Linda has become a master weaver, superb "high-altitude—short growing season" gardener, creative, imaginative cook (featuring low-calorie, low-fat foods—each dinner a gourmet delight) and has become a student of the stock market. She manages our portfolio with imagination, verve and rare skill. I have never seen her fail to excel in any endeavor she tackles. It is all done with boundless, contagious enthusiasm.

And to top it all, she walks in grace—an enduring natural beauty. How could I not be totally captivated by such a woman? We share so many common interests that we enjoy just about everything together, yet we have enough differences so that life is never boring. We give each other time and space without comment or reflection.

We made two remarkable trips in these early years that deserve comment. In 1987 I was invited to give an orientation lecture to the NutraSweet team in Zug, Switzerland, our European headquarters. We coordinated this with an invitation I had received to deliver the annual General Leonard D. Heaton (you remember the "eternal surgeon general"—he had passed on a few years earlier) lecture at the U.S. Army Europe Medical-Surgical Conference in Garmisch-Partenkirchen. So

Linda and I decided to tack on a visit to Portugal and Spain. We flew Swissair to Zurich and took the super-swift express to Zug. Linda made the acquaintance of Teutonic *spargel* (a delightfully sweet asparagus) and started a diary documenting where we wandered and what we ate. When we concluded the company business in Zug, were driven back to Zurich, and then flew Lufthansa to Munich. We drove to Garmisch by way of Oberammergau and Gstadt. I gave the Heaton lecture, and we enjoyed the army's hospitality as well-wined guests of honor at the formal banquet. We knew Garmisch from our previous visit (during the Khadaffi and Chernobyl unpleasantnesses), so we only stayed one day. Then we flew Air Portugal to Lisbon.

Again, we rented a compact Opel. I gave our hotel name (Tivoli Jardin) and the address to the agent, and she provided me with a city map (not very detailed), and in heavily Portuguese-inflected English, offered directions. So we took off with Linda poring over the map and me squinting at street signs. It did not go well. Lisbon is an ancient, leafy, sprawling city with a few broad avenues and circular plazas, but mostly it is a warren of narrow, tortuous streets. To make it even more exciting the street signs are tiny, virtually invisible. It is one of those quaint places that seems to chide, "If you don't know your way around, buster, you don't belong here." After about half an hour of futile exploration, we gave up and felt our way back to the airport.

This time Linda joined me to audit the florid hand-waving directions and finger-jabbing (purple polish, yet) at the map. We tried again; we failed. Back to the airport. So I hailed a cab, gave him the name of the hotel and indicated that we would follow. That worked. We had not even been close on our two pioneering forays. Not a great start in the town that launched Magellan and Vasco Da Gama.

Lisbon was delightful. For three days we walked the town. We spent hours haunting the shops and bistros of the ancient alfama, explored the colorful harbor where fabled Portuguese adventurers set sail on their epochal voyages, and picnicked in the verdant parks that seemed most-artfully dispersed in congested areas. The prices in Portugal were

the most reasonable in western Europe. Then we took off for the Algarve, the Portuguese version of the Spanish Costa Brava or the French-Italian Riviera. But the Algarve is far more rural, less sophisticated, no Ferraris or Porches cluttering the landscape. But driving in Portugal is a very serious challenge. The rural roads are narrow, much-divoted with frequent deep *vados*; every contour of the land is followed with fastidious, nerve-wracking fidelity. Curves and dips are rarely signed. The drivers are macho fast and even crazier than Italians. The traffic accident death rate is the highest in Europe. (I wonder if they get as fascinated by the working cork trees as we were?) But we were rationally prudent, non-confrontational and confined our ohhs and ahhs to reasonable straight-aways.

We found an amazing "genuinely unspoiled" fishing village, Salema, (aptly described in Linda's Michelin). It was nestled in the heart of the Algarve close to the "end of Europe" (Cape St. Vincent is the farthest west place on the continent). There were no obvious tourist facilities, but after a few cervezas in a local tavern, we made inquiries. The bartender was a friendly, rotund, retired fisherman who had passable English. He spoke of an apartment nearby whose owner rented, occasionally. It turned out to be a gem, at about eight dollars a day. A sun-drenched patio smiled out at picture-postcard fishing boats hauled up on the beach of a dazzling blue-green Mediterranean. That first evening in a modest, four-table family restaurant, perched on a rickety balcony swung over the shoreline, we discovered the joys of freshly caught tuna (about 30 minutes out of the sea). It was spectacular. We tried for "fresh tuna" again every night but none approached that first offering.

We headed east along the coast, but when we tried to cross into Spain we ran into big trouble. We did not have a carnet (my error), but we finally pleaded our way across the border. In lovely downtown Seville, our car was ransacked (window smashed while parked adjacent to hotel). But most of our stuff was inside with us. We spent the better part of the next day filing an accident report at the local cop station

(boring "old hat stuff"—unsympathetic unto hostile) and wrangled another car from the local Hertz folks (ungracious unto hostile). We did Granada and strolled the glorious Alhambra for half a day. Then Romanesque Toledo, Salamanca, Nazere (charming fishing village but poisonous clams), Guincha and back to Lisbon. It was 27 days of a thoroughly relaxed and memorable excursion; I don't think we ate meat twice.

One year later, in May, I was invited to give a paper at a nutrition conference in Greece. It was a new part of the world for us. Linda had once been on an archeological dig at Cyprus, and we had both been to Egypt (with previous companions). But neither of us had been to Greece. So we flew British Airways to London and then on to Athens. For two days we enjoyed the Hotel Intercontinental, walked the old city: acropolis, agora, Temple of Hephaistas, Synagogue Square, National Gardens, Parliament and changing of the guard (as rigid and rigorous as Buckingham Palace). We were met by tour people who drove us to the meeting site in Olympia in the southwest, past the Corinth Canal. They provided pleasant bus tours, and we trudged through a dozen ancient ruins. After a while they tended to some similitude.

To our astonishment, the meeting was held in seaside Club Med (non-topless variety), but with the same programmed, "entertainment to suit every taste," tour-group mentality. All "activities" were delineated by age and slothful preference. Effusively amiable hard-bodies ("My name is Jane; let's introduce ourselves") joined every table. The food was "institutional awful," especially after the savory cuisine of working-class tavernas and bistros in Athens.

After the dull conference, we fled to Piraeus and hopped a ferry to Crete. In a tiny, rental rattletrap, we toured that marvelous island from Khania to Iraklion. We did the "Minotaur" tour, stalked the Minoan architectural remnants, admired the working windmills and visited Knossos. We beached a lot and savored the native red wines. Linda wallowed in the incredible fresh seafood: taramasalata, courgettes, tons

of exquisitely-rendered calamari, flounder, pork shish kebobs—just for me—and the inevitable giant Greek salad laced with mountains of feta and kalamata olives. Then we ferried to Paros (toured via bicycles and boots), Santorini (heavenly bleached terraces magnificent beyond belief, a white stucco fairyland—while blasting about on rambunctious motor scooters), and then Rhodes. There we rented another venerable vehicle and drove the fabulous coast to spend the day exploring Lindos. The Greek Islands are all that Byron said.

We returned to Athens and spent another two days wandering the acropolis. The High Adventure (always one per trip—we could not handle more) occurred on a boiling, typically-summer-in-Athens afternoon of the second day. We had to accept a hotel fancier than the Intercontinental (which was fully booked), since the town was packed. It was the day before our departure for the States. For some obscure reason they upgraded us to a penthouse suite about eight floors above the din of the city. The day was deadly hot, and the air-conditioning was barely up to the challenge. Linda stripped to panties and bra; I was in boxer shorts. I went to explore our patio that boasted a dramatic panoramic sweep of the distant acropolis and the roiling city below. I was quietly absorbing the sights when Linda stepped through the door. I said, "Don't..." I never had a chance to finish. In order to preserve the anemic air conditioning from the blistering external heat, she shut the sliding glass door. There was an ominous **snap**. We were trapped!

So what does one do isolated on a torrid patio eight stories above noisy, teeming Athens? The walls on either side were six feet high to preserve privacy of adjoining suites. So I shouted, "Hello," first to port then to starboard. No response. What other idiots would be stewing on their patios at 1:00 PM? There was no phone, no water. We would get dehydrated and probably perish as smoky crisps before the maid arrived for "turn down." But that would never happen, since I had been clever enough to put out the "Privacy Please" sign and chain-lock the door. Obviously, we were doomed.

So after another abortive bout of loud yelling, I scrambled over the starboard-side six-foot wall and landed in the next patio. I prayed that our neighbors had not bolted the patio door. They had not. So, again, hallooing loudly, I strode (creeping could be hazardous to your health) into the alien suite. I had visions of a mountainous naked Turk boiling out of the bedroom, scimitar at the ready. I was in luck; the apartment was obviously inhabited, but presently empty. I snatched a bath towel and wrapped it over my sweaty boxer shorts and slinked to the elevator. Thankfully, I was the sole passenger. I gained the lobby (crowded of course) and sidled nervously up to the desk clerk. Before I could even speak, the officious bastard said, "Sir, we do not allow bathing attire in the lobby." I tried to explain my unusual predicament, but either language difficulty or the intrinsic arrogance of all desk clerks precluded communication. He repeated his admonition. Then I yelled, "Listen, buster, I am locked out of my room, my wife is trapped on the balcony, and the chain is barring the door." A flash of recognition. "But, how…?"

"That doesn't matter, I need a maintenance person with a bolt cutter!" We had gathered a considerable and attentive crowd. Finally, after an unseemly interval, a large swarthy man bearing a leather, tool-laden apron materialized. I waved cheerily to the vast international assemblage as we boarded the elevator. When we reached the door, naturally he rang. I said, "For Christ sake, my wife is still trapped on the patio. She can't answer the door." Mercifully, he understood. Then he did a very disconcerting thing. He leaned heavily against the door, the lock went snap, the door budged open a crack, and he **reached** inside and flipped off the chain. So much for security. After I admitted the bedraggled, parboiled Linda, I slipped the guy a twenty (U.S.). It was one helluva few hours, but it made a wonderful story. *Zito Helas.*

But back to Barrington. While I was working in Skokie and later in Deerfield, Shapiro and later Bob Flynn (who replaced him as CEO when Shapiro moved up to Monsanto), encouraged me to continue my other professional pursuits. Dr. Arnold Nicagossian, the chief med-

ical officer at NASA, had asked me to chair the NASA Life Sciences Committee during my years at ACP. Probably on the basis of this experience, I was asked by the National Research Council to join the Space Studies Board. I served as a member for four years. It was a unique intellectual experience; I was the only physician. Other members were physicists, astronomers, agronomists, earth scientists, materiel experts, former astronauts, biologists and mathematicians. Brilliant people; it was all a trifle over-powering. They were all so damned bright.

(My chief contribution during those years was to bring some semblance of reality to considerations about manned exploration of the near solar system. It was [and still is] my conviction that the International Space Station—Alpha [in its tumultuous evolution and infinite permutations] could **only** be justified if the nation had made a firm commitment to explore the near solar system, which was not the case. In April 1992, I represented the National Research Council-SSB in testifying before the "Task Force on Defense, Foreign Policy and Space of the Committee on the Budget of the House of Representatives." Representative (now senator) Richard Durbin (Illinois) was chairman. I followed a very dynamic, very positive female astronaut and an aging but still eloquent, James Michener, both of whom were ardent supporters of Station. Among other things I said, "The primary purpose of physiological, psychological and radiation-effect research in space, is to learn enough to provide some reasonable assurance that crews can survive and function in this most unforgiving of environments. Prolonged space-faring, as would be involved in any human mission to Mars, remains *terra incognita*...Without prolonged human space flight remaining as a high priority on the American agenda, I can find no compelling reason to continue the space station."

It was remarkable that the NRC-SSB allowed me to make such a statement; it was totally antithetical to the NASA party line. But I had been hammering away for four years. There was no presidential, congressional or public mandate to send a crew to Mars. Without this rea-

son, there was no justification for the expense and danger of creating and building a space station. Aside from testing humans in the microgravity environment for prolonged periods in low earth orbit, any other research could be done more cheaply and safely on unmanned or man-tended vehicles. Aside from the exploration of physiological modifications in microgravity (and developing rational countermeasures), I was also concerned about the inevitable heavy particle radiation exposure that would be encountered on a trip to and from Mars [exposure that cannot be replicated in low earth orbit]. And, perhaps, even more risky than any other aspect, the **psychological** effect of crews sequestered in the Mars Transfer Vehicle [MTV] for periods of up to three years, with no means of escape, was absolutely untested and, therefore, unknown.

In various SSB reports, I had written that the experience in nuclear submarines and Antarctic crews [both of which **might** allow for possible escape in emergency situations] raised many questions. I felt that NASA had not explored this avenue. I proposed that if ever there were a national mandate to have man explore the near universe, crew selection would be a critical factor. I proposed selecting several candidate crews [after meticulous psychological profiling and psychiatric interviewing], sequestering them in terrestrial mock-ups of the Mars Transfer Vehicle for periods up to six months. "Escape" would not be allowed [of course, life and death illness would permit exceptions—an option that would **not** be possible on the voyage to Mars]. Those individuals who passed this test would then have the experience repeated in an MTV mock-up that was incorporated as part of the International Space Station, in low earth orbit, perhaps for four to six month tours. Again, "escape" would be discouraged except for life or death situations. Then, and only then, would one have some assurance that the crew would be sufficiently psychologically compatible to justify reasonable confidence that they would not kill each other during the three-year Mars mission.

I raised questions about crew composition: all male? all female? if mixed, what would be the sexual arrangements? Married? Paired? Any switching allowed? The history of NASA in sending "politically correct" crews on shuttle flights [rich Saudis, aged senators] would not be acceptable for the Mars mission. Could they exclude political considerations? What would be the command structure: military with chain of command, or more "democratic" with majority rule? How would we handle severe illness [heart attack, stroke] or death? I was the first to acknowledge that all crews would be obliged to sign extensive waivers. God knows "the right stuff" has so permeated the astronaut corps that they would be willing to accept **any** unknown risk. But this is not the way of science and exploration.

I have often cited the fallacy, especially perpetuated by the astronauts, that as "volunteers," they alone are responsible for their fate. It is not that simple. When I was chief at Walter Reed, during the last days of Eisenhower, the newspapers carried a story that only a heart transplant could save the great man. Dr. Christian Bernaard in South Africa had recently been lionized by performing the first successful—for a time—transplant. I had two soldiers on the staff at Reed come to me to "volunteer" their hearts to "save this great American." I explained that it was a little different from kidney donation; there you had two such organs and would survive, quite satisfactorily, with just one. "But you only have one heart; give it up and, well, you die." They both agreed that they would be willing to make the ultimate sacrifice! So much for volunteering. The risks of prolonged space flight would be high enough, without introducing unknowns that, with sufficient time and ingenuity, could be learned and probably [not absolutely] solved.

As it has evolved, the International Space Station is a textbook political football. The "international" adjective is a joke. Russia has agreed to contribute virtually nothing but manpower, and the other national partners have contributed tokens. It is a 99% U.S. effort, and NASA has been sufficiently clever to ensure that about 90% of congressional districts have a piece of the "construction pie." This means jobs, jobs,

jobs, a surefire way to assure congressional and senatorial support. When you ask NASA **why** they are building the ISS, they say, "science." Then they mutter about cures for osteoporosis, heart disease, discovering new pharmaceuticals, unique crystals, etc.

The bottom line: NASA is so consumed with **building** the Station, and everyone in aerospace is so **invested** in the Station, that everyone has lost sight of the **mission** of the Station. I am not even sure that the ISS-Alpha will be equipped to perform the research needed to study man's physiological and psychological performance in microgravity for prolonged periods. As I have indicated, the radiation problem is still unresolved; the psychological problems will need more than the ISS.

Finally, there is the cost: 60 billion is a conservative estimate. Now I am told that NASA is trying to interest private investors. Good luck. My ever-unpopular observation is that once the damn thing is in orbit, someone will look aloft and say, "Well, that was fun, now what are they doing up there?" And NASA will say, "Science, dummy." It could be the biggest, most expensive, dysfunctional white elephant ever fired into low earth orbit. Of course, everything I have said would be moot if the engineers manage to invent a propulsion system that would achieve the voyage in weeks or months, rather than years. That may happen, but thus far it has not. And besides, no one has even estimated the diversion of funds from other worthy unmanned NASA science projects. In the NASA lexicon, "fungible" does not exist; it is a zero sum game with Alpha gobbling up most of the zeroes)

So back to earth. I have not mentioned my attempt to "change the spin" of the NutraSweet corporate mission. During the Shapiro years, all employees were exposed to a rather hyperbolic "mission statement" that adorned every bulletin board; it was typical human resources, rah-rah blather. I thought it was inflated and obtuse, crying out for simplification and realism. Not an easy undertaking. In efforts to expand on the aspartame "miracle," the R&D folks were seeking products and services to fulfill that ambition. In consonance with this effort, I soon became aware of a cloak and dagger enterprise called "Beta," that was

being conducted behind locked doors in a separate building. The inevitable, coffee-room grapevine murmured something about a "fat substitute" that would be as "big as aspartame."

In time, I was invited to some clandestine briefings and discovered that "Beta" (later to be named Simplesse) was a microparticulated protein produced by a multi-patented process devised by a bright-but-wifty food-scientist. (At times the secretive Beta people acted like they were involved in a resurrected Manhattan Project.) The product was derived initially from a combination of milk whey and egg white; later, whey was used alone. The product had all the organoleptic (taste and mouth feel) qualities of animal fat. It sounded impressive. The Simplesse propaganda blitz was launched in New York at the Plaza by Bob Shapiro. It was a glitzy champagne and hors d'ouerves extravaganza, featuring cheeses and ice cream made with Simplesse. It seemed as though all the food and beverage editors in the universe were in attendance. (Incidentally, the trip to and from NYC was the only other time I was privileged to ride the corporate jet!) Simplesse received incredible media coverage. The Simplesse inventor and I answered dozens of thoughtful, friendly questions from reporters; it was a love fest. All reporters love free food; food reporters especially love low-fat food.

The first Simplesse-containing products to hit the marketplace were ice creams and cheeses. They tasted okay to me (and Linda), but the ice cream was being touted as a fat-free Haagen-Dazs. Alas, it was not. It just might have the taste and texture of a Meadow gold, but rich, butterfat laden super premiums it wasn't. In a stunning corporate decision that none of us peons could fathom, Shapiro and cohort bought an ice cream plant, drafted some ice cream "experts" and began to produce "Simple Pleasures." It appeared in a few test markets and did not do well. It was too expensive; they priced it with the super premiums, where it could not begin to compete. Also the problem of squeezing out shelf space in super-markets was another arcane business-art form that the company had failed to master. Finally, the inventor and his team could never create a "good" vanilla. Apparently, it is axiomatic in

the ice cream business: you cannot hope for a winner without a solid vanilla. The things we learn!

In the meantime, a team of dietitians from the now-expanded, no-longer-clandestine Simplesse operation, plus the inventor and me, launched an all-out effort to educate health-care professionals and nutritionists about the virtues of the product. For months we hit the hustings making presentations to colleges of agriculture, boards of directors of AAFP, American Dietetic Association, American College of Cardiology and even the executive committee of the AMA. I used some of my ACP IOUs to generate invitations. It was a fairly elaborate dog and pony show. Simplesse was an easy sell; everyone wanted low-calorie dairy products that tasted like they contained savory animal fat, but did not.

But the product never flew. Soon Simple Pleasures disappeared from the few supermarket shelves where it had managed to elbow some space in this most cutthroat of commercial worlds. A few cheeses continued to appear, and The NutraSweet Company (in another unfathomable demonstration of market naiveté), opened a few specialty "dessert shoppes" in suburban Chicago shopping malls, featuring Simplesse-bearing pastries. The goodies were actually quite tasty, but patronage was sparse. After a few months the shops all died.

Of course, all of this occurred over a few years. In theory, Simplesse could have been a notable addition to the food chain, but there were problems. It could not be heated to extreme levels without special precautions (the protein would coagulate). Then it was discovered that commercial-volume production was far more expensive than anticipated, while market demand was far less than predicted. There were other problems: transport fragility, iffy product shelf life, the need to educate customers about manufacturing intricacies, etc. Also competitive fat substitutes were beginning to appear.

Finally, the public seemed to be losing interest in all low-fat foods that failed to taste as good as the real thing. Disenchantment with the whole concept of "healthful foods" was becoming a national phenome-

non, as the "obesity epidemic" of the American population became a growing and visible manifestation of affluence and self-indulgence. The whole Simplesse project became a monumental production-market research debacle. Later the inventor got fired; Simplesse became the Edsel of NutraSweet. All of this history is a matter of public information.

The other ill-conceived commercial adventure was "Wellbridge." Someone had the bright idea that there was a vast untapped market for upscale, programmed exercise facilities, tailored to the needs of affluent senior citizens. They planned to purchase an exercise center in a suburb outside of Boston, refurbish it with classy, "geriatric-oriented" exercise hardware, staff it with some hard-body types, teach something about nutrition (with the expert help of the Jean Mayer School of Nutrition at Tufts) and then sell memberships. A sleek blonde marketeer came to my office and made an articulate, Madison Avenue presentation to me and my staff. (Perhaps because I was the only senior citizen in the building?) Then she said, "What do you think?" It was pure rhetoric, of course; this presentation was all after the fact. The pilot facility was already in operation; they just wanted my blessing.

I reflected for a few moments, asked a few clarifying questions and then told her (in my best avuncular, elder-statesman style) that such a concept would fly **only** if it were completely "user-friendly" and offered a variety of services that were unique to the population they were seeking to attract. The affluent elderly would sign up only if the place provided "one-stop shopping" for most of their physical, nutritional, psychological and other needs. I suggested that they ensure that some older folks were employed beside the impossible-to-emulate hard-bodies. They needed some staff that could really empathize with their customers' lifestyle problems.

Aside from the "elder-tailored" exercise programs, they would need to provide pragmatic nutritional counseling. Only older individuals on staff could provide realistic, believable advice about sex, social problems, financial questions and other things that concern the rapidly

expanding population of "well elderly." Perhaps a retired clinical psychologist could be hired to help with problems of depression and loneliness. To cover other areas of concern and interest, they should have a referral list of seasoned experts, and the Wellbridge staff should facilitate making contact. Finally, the place had to be "fun," a center of social activity in addition to the physical and nutritional stuff. It had to offer more than the country club or neighborhood gym. I realized this was a tall order, but the plan, as presented, seemed doomed to failure. Just another expensive designer gym. I predicted that with the elderly population expanding so remarkably over the next few decades, facilities such as I described, would be popping up all over the country. It could become a most lucrative franchise, if it were done right from the outset.

The talky marketer seemed to listen, even made a few notes and said "these are great ideas." A few weeks later, I visited the facility. As anticipated, it was a very fancy gym and swimming pool, staffed with a batch of young, exuberantly healthy, overly-friendly, hard-bodies. No one on the staff was over 25. There were three "paid-up members" using the facility. None of the things I had suggested was ever implemented. Wellbridge was petering out after about one year. *Sic simper* Cassandra.

Once Bob Shapiro had ascended into higher orbit in St. Louis, his replacement was a lanky, down-to-earth mechanical engineer who had run one of Monsanto's equipment production companies. He was a pleasant, folksy, unprepossessing fellow and soon after arrival called me in to chat. He took me by surprise by asking what I thought about the future of the company. At that time, the Simplesse episode was still unfolding and Wellbridge had just been launched. Both held promise. After I ascertained that his question was not just a courtesy to my gray hair, I told him that I thought the American public (at least the "enlightened" aspartame-consuming 10%) had demonstrated concern about adopting a "healthful lifestyle." But many folks were becoming disenchanted by conflicting messages from the nutritional and medical

gurus. (The epidemic of public disaffection with "diet-exercise" I spoke of earlier, had not yet become overtly manifest.) Most average folk were eager for simple, clear-cut, authoritative advice that could be implemented without a major upheaval in their daily lives. I thought that goal was achievable. I said our company now had three products (aspartame, Simplesse and Wellbridge) that fit neatly into the nutrition-exercise part of this equation. And this made the NutraSweet Company unique.

I suggested that our advertising pitch should move away from "diet" (It has always been my contention that the very word "diet" defines a limited, short-term, unpleasant program that is usually foredoomed to rampant recidivism.) We should begin to advocate (publicly and in our advertisements) a corporate dedication to a life-long program that would include: nutritionally-balanced, low-fat, high-fiber, calorically-appropriate-to-your-energy expenditure **diet**; reasonable, regular, fun **exercise;** cigarette **avoidance**; alcohol **moderation; stressor** management; domestic **hazard** avoidance (auto seat belts, removal of low stools, etc.) The boss became very excited. For the remainder of my time in Deerfield, he often spoke of me (often embarrassingly) as a "visionary." He even tried to implement such a program, but I could see little objective change except for "chit-chat around the water cooler" sort of stuff. I heard a lot about the new "lifestyle pitch" in the men's locker room as I prepared for my noon jog, but that was the extent of my impact on corporate philosophy. Well, I had made my pitch.

In later years, Monsanto assumed the configuration of a "health sciences" company. They sold off the chemical and other divisions and concentrated on pharmaceuticals (Searle) and invested heavily into research on bio-engineered (genetically-modified—GM) foods. A waning aspartame market resulted in an ultimate sell off of that company. Despite initial Wall Street optimism in the wisdom of Shapiro in reconfiguring the company to embrace health sciences, over the next few years many converging negative vectors (the Mad Cow [BSE} meat

scare in Europe that precipitated an irrational backlash against all GM food products). The rabid antipathy was focused on Monsanto, and the future of all GM foods was thrown into serious question. American consumers were far less concerned. Europeans are a different species when it comes to food. The heat was just too intense, and Monsanto ultimately capitulated. The world has eagerly embraced genetically-modified biologicals, that have already revolutionized much of medical therapy. But when it comes to food—in the creation of novel, highly nutritious products that could help solve Third World malnutrition and starvation, the crazies have mounted the barricades. Within a decade GM foods will become as widely accepted as GM biological drugs. Shapiro and Monsanto were 10 years ahead of their time; stay tuned.

The tour at NutraSweet made for some fascinating international travel. As I have indicated, in my job as an "international fireman" on behalf of aspartame, I went to places where the media had gotten hold of some unfortunate misinformation and was exploiting it. I made several quick trips to London to put out fires ignited by the BBC. On one occasion I was sitting before the ravenous eye of a TV camera within an hour after making a rain-swept, hairy cab ride from Heathrow. Later, after another dreadful broadcast, we decided to challenge the BBC, and brought the case before the very august, very British (and very fair) Broadcast Complaint Commission, charging the network with making untrue and damaging statements. I testified at the hearing; we won and BBC made a public retraction.

I lectured periodically to "concerned customers" (Coca-Cola, General Foods, etc.) in London, Frankfurt and Johannesburg. Once when I was in Jakarta recruiting a consultant and lecturing to a nutrition congress, my hotel (Borobadur) room phone rang at 2:00 AM. It was a near hysterical NutraSweet PR person in London. *The Guardian* was about to publish a god-awful article about aspartame, but at the last minute, they had called to get a "response from the company." Undoubtedly, some editor had reviewed the copy at the last minute.

Within a short time, I was hooked up to a very hostile reporter who apparently had been chided; he really didn't give a damn about what I had to say. Obviously, his story was already completed with "information derived from impeccable sources" (the usual assortment of noisy malcontents).

When it appeared, the story was incorrect, alarming and mean-spirited. It confirmed my long-standing bias that most "investigative reporters" were not Woodward and Bernstein, but overheated "anti-big corporation" zealots who rarely took time to do proper homework. It seemed that shooting from the hip was a journalistic malady that transcended international borders. Anything for a splashy story. We sued *The Guardian* for damages. The case took over a year and, once again I flew to London to testify. We won again, and *The* (doughty) *Guardian* published a front-page apology. Since then the British media has treated us with circumspection.

Another somewhat distressing adventure occurred during my stay in Jakarta. I was ensconced in the elegant hotel with a Sunday to kill before my plane departed. The local aspartame-product distributor, a very well-heeled Indonesian business man, who had been my host, called and invited me to spend the day on his "private island", just off the coast in the Java Sea. With his handsome wife and teen-aged daughter, we tooled out in his sleek motor launch to a very small island a few miles from the homeport. They had a modest bungalow on the beach; it was the only structure. The wife said they needed to get some supplies from another island nearby and that I should just relax and take a swim. So they puttered off, and I climbed into some borrowed trunks, and quite alone, swam from their dock into the seductively warm, salty water.

I must have been about 200 yards from shore when I realized that I was being carried by a tide that was both strong and subtle. And I was being moved rather swiftly past the island! I knew from my time in Hawaii that one cannot fight against a rip tide; you let it carry you while you try to escape its grip. But there was no other island in sight; I

was being swept along into the Java Sea on my way to Borneo! So I began to swim slowly, husbanding my energy, angling toward the island. I think I was in the water for over an hour, and finally made it to shore on the far side of the island. I was exhausted and trekked my way back to the bungalow along the beach. My friends had returned. "Did you enjoy your swim?" "Yes," I managed, "it was very invigorating." And I did not even mention my fear of becoming shark fodder. It was a close call.

During the last few months in Illinois, Linda and I began to reflect on our future. I was tired of working and, frankly, the "aspartame wars" had become boring. Linda had expressed no desire to return to the labor force. She had been working since she was 16 and was enjoying being a full-time homemaker-hobbyist-retiree. We had been making very good money during our five years with NutraSweet, and Linda had been investing prudently in mutual funds and selected stocks and bonds. Despite what I was paying out to Stella each month, we thought we could get by on our military and ACP retirement incomes (half of which went to Stella), if we were reasonably prudent. We loved our house-in-the-woods, but the winters were cold and gray, and the traffic once outside our felicitous cloister was becoming increasingly horrendous. The population in and around Barrington was escalating at an alarming rate, far outstripping the capacity of the archaic road network.

So we decided to explore the Great Southwest—seeking our future home. Independently, we had done some hiking and camping in Arizona and New Mexico, and it seemed to be our kind of country, relatively unspoiled and undiscovered by Eastern standards. In anticipation of our "great retirement adventure," we sold the flashy, slightly wifty Mercedes (more like gave it away!) and bought a new Nissan SUV Pathfinder. We figured we would need something a bit more robust than the rain-snow-ice-skittish 450SL. Then we rented a 25-foot class C motor home and headed west. Over a period of about three weeks, we wandered the countryside from the arid wastelands

near the Mexican border at Nogales to the magnificent mountains of southern Colorado. We visited Tucson, Scottsdale, Prescott, Sedona, rustic towns dotting the Mogollon Rim, Flagstaff, Albuquerque, Santa Fe, Taos and all points in between. Many were inviting; some were reasonable; none were ideal.

Then we labored over the mountain pass between Taos and Tierra Amarilla (Route 64 in New Mexico) and stopped for a picnic overlooking the Chama Valley. Linda gazed over the awesome panorama and murmured, "Wow, imagine living **there!**" Snow-capped San Juan Rockies framed the distant horizon and the wide valley spread before us, lush and vibrant. We swung through the switchbacks down from the pass and stopped at a real estate office. A very pleasant young man decked out in snakeskin cowboy boots and ten-gallon hat sporting an eagle feather, listened patiently. "We just want a few acres with an unobstructed view of the mountains, appropriate for building a modest home." We spent the better part of the next two days stomping across the countryside. Again, some sites were just what we wanted, but too expensive and vice versa. We were running out of time and patience.

Then he said, "I know you're are not looking for a house, but there is one you should really see. It's really something unusual, and has been on the market for some time." We loaded back into his jeep, and he hauled us a few miles south of town, up a long, twisty gravel road. The house was a two-story, double-walled adobe sitting on a hill with a 360 view of coniferous forest and mountains. Linda and I looked at each other, and, as often in the past, we read each other's eyes, "This is the place." The house had many imperfections (some immediately evident, some not). The heating was "passive solar" backed up by a cumbersome wood-burning furnace; kitchen was a trifle dark and the guest room and kitchen were Lilliputian. There were tasteless color schemes in bathrooms. But—all in all—we were enchanted. The two-story galleria was elegant and the view from every aspect was glorious. It still takes our breath away.

The owners were an elderly couple. They had built the place in 1979, and George, a retired Marine Corps officer and mechanical-electrical engineer, had done "a lot of the work myself." (We later came to appreciate—often ruefully—the creative plumbing and ingenious electrical contrivances that George had devised. We still have not sorted out some of the Rube Goldberg wiring configurations that haunt the place, nor have a few electricians.) The owners wanted to sell the house and 103 acres. Alas, the asking price was way beyond our reach. We turned toward home crest-fallen. As with the Barrington experience, ever-thoughtful Linda suggested that we "make an offer on the house and 25 adjacent acres," with an option to buy the other land at some later date. Our proposal was snapped-up (perhaps too eagerly). In retrospect, once again, we probably could have succeeded with a lesser offer. But at the time we were dancing with delight.

One of the less memorable events that marred our departure from Barrington was our first (and only!) yard sale. We had closets stacked with clothes, shoes, books, dishes, pots and assorted *tsatskes* that we decided not to schlep to the mountains. So we carefully tagged every item. Some of Linda's ACP-vintage work and play dresses were very expensive *haut couture* stuff, and she priced them at a fraction of value. About 5:30 AM on Yard Sale Day, I took about a dozen of my artfully handcrafted signs announcing the time (eight o'clock) and location. I began to distribute them around the neighborhood. To my astonishment, two vehicles followed me home; it was about 6:00 AM. And that set the tempo for the day.

With few exceptions these people were voracious, boorish, selfish, cheap and often ugly. They haggled over every item despite the pittance being asked. They swarmed like locusts, and we were virtually stripped clean by early afternoon. All rooms except the bathrooms were clearly marked "Off Limits." Yet, strangers wandered throughout the house, and some tried to "bargain" about *in-situ* furniture, pictures on the wall, plugged-in kitchen appliances—none of it tagged. It was the sweaty Kasbah transported to Illinois! We were too exhausted to be

furious—a thoroughly dreadful experience. We will never do such a crazy thing again; the Salvation Army will be the recipient of any future such largesse.

# 28

## *Chama and Retirement*

◆

### *(sort of...)*

We drove both cars, Stanza and Pathfinder, each loaded to the gunnels with kitchen essentials and both dogs, through some very cold November weather from Barrington to Chama. Household furniture and stuff would follow in a few weeks. Once the boring plains faded into the rear-view mirror and the true west emerged, the golden aspen and rusty mountain oak were breathtaking. The view from the house was even more spectacular than we recalled. But life on the mountain took some major accommodation. Within a few weeks, we replaced the garishly papered (silver and orange!) bathrooms and had the too-dark (true adobe) two-story galleria repainted a felicitous lighter cream color.

We endured first two winters with the wood-burning furnace as our principal source of heat. I cut some oak and pine from the adjacent forest, bought aspen and juniper, split the lot and enjoyed every minute. Linda became the principal "fire-tender." After a few misadventures, when the temperamental flame expired sometime in the dead of night, we learned how to stack properly to ensure survival of a bed of coals until frigid morning. But the stove was a pain in the butt: labor-intensive, bothersome and dirty (soot seemed to permeate the ground floor). We replaced it with a propane system and wondered why the previous owners had lived with such a wretched furnace for so many years. Propane was not that expensive.

Then there was the driveway and the snow. It was long (0.7 miles), tortuous and climbed about 300 feet from the county road. George had sold me a beat-up old Chevy truck with an ancient detachable snowplow and a menacing little yellow bulldozer. (Did that provide a clue, Bob?) We knew that we would have lots of snow, and I even looked forward to the macho excitement of plowing with the truck. George said (too casually in retrospect) he only used the dozer when the "walls got too high," and the truck-plow was unable to budge the frozen high banks. Thoughtfully, he provided three single-spaced pages of instructions on how to start and operate the beast. It was a joke! The Cat was an ancient diesel that had a gasoline driven "donkey engine" (started with a lanyard!), that would provide the power to kick over the big diesel. Well, I never could get the recalcitrant monster started. Nor could a few other local, heavy-equipment "old hands." I finally gave up and sold it to a gnarly old retired cowhand for a few bucks. After a dozen or so abortive tries (and little tricks with spanners, combustible sprays, cussing and praying), he finally coaxed the tired old Cat to sputter and kick over long enough to back it onto a truck. We wished him Godspeed.

We have only had to call on a bulldozer (someone else's) twice over the years to push back the snow wall I created with the truck-plow. The dozer business was typical of the "tough life" the previous folks imposed on themselves. It might have been economy driven, but we suspect George liked the rugged "do-it-yourself" aspect of life on the mountain. After two years, we practically gave away the wheezy, old truck and plow and bought a new, fire-engine red Ford 250 and a shiny red Western plow.

After a month or so we had plans to build a large deck and make other changes in the place to make it more compatible with civilized living. But we were a little shy on liquid capital. So I had a great idea. I wrote to Rich Nelson, director of public affairs back at NutraSweet, who had been my last boss (after the petite lawyer had departed). I offered my services (and that of my Linda) as "media consultants." We

knew the company was still being blitzed by the relentless lunatic fringe, especially during Sweeps weeks. Rich had not hired anyone to replace me, and out-sourcing was *au courant*. I suggested that for starters, Linda would answer media stuff after it was written and edited by me. (Later she would learn enough to do 90% of the work.) I would continue to do media interviews, train other consultants, etc. To our delight, Rich quickly accepted our offer.

We created the Canyon Consulting Corporation ("embracing the spectrum of medical communications"—perhaps a trifle florid, but what the hell...). The brightly lit den became our beehive office. Over time we acquired an answering machine, FAX, computer-modem and photocopier. Linda and I drafted a library of "responses," since 90% of the aspartame criticism stuff was old hat, boringly predictable. She would read the media clips sent to us by an agency and draft the response. I would edit, she would send it to NutraSweet for vetting, and then fire off a final letter with my signature. It took a few hours a week, but it augmented our income handsomely.

Linda became fascinated with three new hobbies. As I indicated earlier, she became a skillful weaver; took classes in Rio Grande style (old Northern New Mexico) weaving at the community college in El Rito (south of Ghost Ranch). We had a local craftsman build her a four-harness, cherry wood loom that dominated our loft area. So she weaves in the winter. Some of her rugs have been exhibited at Ghost Ranch. She has even sold a few (like selling a child!). In the spring and summer she becomes an avid gardener despite caliche-ridden soil, a growing season of about six weeks and hordes of grasshoppers in dry season. She has our mountaintop glowing with flowers.

Her third passion became the stock market. She read everything (Wall Street Journal, Money, Forbes, Value Line) and became quite adept. Our modest portfolio has flourished under her vigilant guidance. (A buoyant market soon after retirement didn't hurt.) She also developed a passion for hummingbirds. During the height of the season she has ten feeders that often demand replenishment several times

a day. Come evening in summer, the voracious little buzzers swarm like bees. Linda is the original "hummingbird lady." As I have said this bright, cheery woman has that remarkable capacity to bring unbridled enthusiasm and consummate skill to any undertaking that captures her fancy. And, happily, that includes me.

Our life on the mountain gradually took shape. We would make periodic forays to Santa Fe, Taos, Albuquerque, Pagosa Springs, Durango, Silverton, Ouray, Telluride and Alamosa. We have scrambled through just about all the mountain back roads of Rio Arriba county. Our trips to Albuquerque are facilitated by being able to stay at the Distinguished Visitors Quarters at Kirtland Air Force Base, enjoy the hospitality of the officer's club and load up on groceries at the commissary and goodies at the base exchange. We have sampled all the good (and fair) restaurants within a hundred miles. Then we made some memorable foreign trips.

While I had been full-time at NutraSweet, we made a business-vacation trip to Australia and Southeast Asia. I mentioned this earlier very briefly. Australia was a place Linda had always wanted to visit. Since I had been there before, I charted our itinerary and Linda made all reservations. Once we had completed our business, we flew to Alice Springs and rented a car. After some exciting reorientation to "wrong side" driving, we charged down the red-dust roads. We drove to mystical Ululru (Ayer's Rock) and the crimson-tinged Olgas, in the heart of the Outback. I had "climbed the rope" at Ayer's Rock once before, so we decided to forego that particular pleasure. We hiked around the base visiting some of the sacred caves and pools enshrined by the Aborigines. The next day we explored the blood red Olgas. We donned bush hats (with protective netting to discourage rapacious flies and midges), doused ourselves with malodorous repellent and took a long trek through the eerily unearthly, glaringly bright, low red hills. We saw only one other couple on the entire 12-mile hike. It was hot and dry and wonderful.

That evening we were staying at a ramshackle motel proximate to a site where we could drive out and gawk at the fairy-tale colors that transformed Ayer's Rock at sunset. It was unlike anything we had ever seen. Every imaginable variation of the infra-red end of the spectrum was on display, flamboyant, evanescent, shifting in hue and intensity minute-by-minute. Even sunset at the pyramids at Giza or White Sands in New Mexico could not match the mystique. It was easy to understand how primitive people could attach metaphysical significance to Uluru. It lent credence to animism as a viable religious option. Late that night just before midnight, we walked to an isolated, low hill adjacent to the motel and witnessed a total lunar eclipse. We sprawled on a grassy knoll, head-to-head and absorbed the phenomenon in absolute silence. All in all, it was quite a day.

From Alice Springs we took the Ghan, the overnight sleeper train to Adelaide, past the vast underground digs of Goober Peedy, where they mine most of the Aussie opals. Then we flew to Rockport and took a delightfully drenchy catamaran ride to Heron Island, a lush green coral speck in the midst of the Great Barrier Reef. It was a little bit of paradise. We had a cottage by the beach, and each night we would await the few giant Green turtles that swam ashore to scramble up on the sand spit, dig out a small pit and deposit their precious eggs. There were perhaps 20 or 30 couples sharing our small island; it became a nocturnal ritual to watch for turtles waddling ashore. The ponderous beasts left a very distinctive track. But it was a desultory business; many nights none of the big guys showed up.

The other tourists maintained an eternally hopeful vigil, often dismayed at not finding any telltale tracks. So one night just after sunset, I went to the water's edge and dug out "turtle tracks" by hand, leading to a strip of dense vegetation adjacent to our cottage, where we actually **had** discovered a turtle doing her business a few days earlier. We retreated to the darkness of our veranda and sipped long, tall, cool ones and watched the tableaux unfold. I think my ersatz tracks thrilled about a dozen very excited tourists that night. Of course, the "turtles"

had returned to the sea long since, after leaving their "spoor." Linda and I enjoyed the "ohhs and ahhs" of every group of lucky track discoverers.

We loved Sydney. One could walk or take public transportation anywhere. The seafood and ethnic restaurants were as good as San Francisco. We wandered all over the harbor area, stalked the shops of "The Rocks," walked the great bridge, ogled the botanical gardens and enjoyed a Spanish dance troop with their clap-stomp-twirl in a flamboyant musical show in the Sydney Opera House.

We returned several years later and stayed in an apartment in The Rocks, bussed and hiked all over town, and then did Brampton Island. It was not quite as idyllic as Heron. Once again we reveled in Sydney and almost enjoyed Melbourne. Linda picked up some mysterious gastro-intestinal virus and had a dreadful time. I nourished her on egg-drop soup from the best restaurant in Chinatown. She recovered sufficiently that we were able to stroll around that elegant, Victorian city and ride the venerable trolley to Geelong by the sea.

We then flew to New Zealand and drove North and South Islands, visited Auckland, Wellington, Christchurch and Milford Sound. We took a cruise on the sound and enjoyed porpoises showing off, acrobatically rollicking and leaping beside the boat. A few dramatic waterfalls enlivened the rugged coastline. The countryside was delightfully green with gently rolling hills and some formidable mountains (on South Island). Of course, sheep were ubiquitous, gently softening every Turneresque landscape. All very bucolic, mindful of the Cotswalds. The weather was overcast in the south, and we could not take full advantage of the mountain scenery. All in all, we enjoyed New Zealand, a most pleasant visit.

Winters in Chama can be challenging. Our first serious snow usually arrives in late October and hunkers down on the northern slopes and in the sun-deprived "chute" (the shadow draped part of our upper driveway) until late April. We are not winter sports enthusiasts; we have done some snow shoeing (mostly to brush snow off our satellite

dish), and some cross-country skiing ("some" is a lie; we don't enjoy it—very hard work uphill, lack of control downhill) and we despise noisy, smelly snowmobiles. All of our neighbors have them, and perhaps one day we will be compelled to get one of the growling beasts. If a very serious snowfall closes down automobile access to the highway, it may become a necessity. But as I write (after nine winters in Chama), we have not been driven to this extremity.

But we do escape part of the winter. The first year we went to Belize in January. It rained for ten straight days, and we saw very little of the countryside, jungle or reef. The next year we went to Southeast Asia and had a ball. We started in Hong Kong. We could not afford the luxury of the forever-splendid Peninsula (the super posh hotel that we had enjoyed enormously on our previous visit, sponsored by NutraSweet), but we had cocktails in the leather and crystal bar. We did all the Hong Kong things: clams and black bean sauce on Lamma Island (discovered by Linda on her previous visit), rode the front-seat of double-decker buses (cheapest and best show in town), took the tram to Victoria for lunch and gorged in superb restaurants. The most expensive meal occurred in a Japanese restaurant. Quite unexpectedly we ran up bill of over $150 (U.S.) It was not a billing error; the place was ridiculously overpriced. And we didn't even order fugu.

Then we made another mistake. We visited my old friend Bill Wong. Bill was the bright young architect who married the beauteous Priscilla Wu back in 1956 in San Antonio. Stella had been the maid-of-honor. Stella and I had visited them many years ago. Bill had become an enormously rich and successful businessman-architect. Priscilla had long since divorced him and moved on (something about an excess of mistresses). I had not seen him in about 25 years. I called Bill and he invited Linda and me to join him for a late breakfast at his tennis club tucked away in Victoria Heights. A few days later, we took a long taxi ride to his reclusive lair. Bill arrived late, sweaty and distraught from his match. We suspected he had been trounced. Alas, Bill had simply become older and foolish. He was ridiculously obsessed

with his health and diminished physical appearance (shorter and fatter), impressed with his wealth and suffused with self-importance. He had not aged well; the adjective "insufferable" came to mind. Breakfast was no fun at all. Goodbye Bill; no wonder that Pris took off.

We visited Kuala Lumpur (good native Malaysian restaurants, wonderful open-air bazaars), Singapore (still too hot and sterile), Bangkok (more crowded and polluted than Jakarta or Mexico City). Dutifully we visited all the deteriorating wats and boated the stinking klongs; the ambience was just awful. (*Triste dictu*. When Stella and I had visited in 1963, Bangkok had been engaging and delightful.) Then we went to Bali. Here I almost lost my life.

I made the classic stupid American blunder. I failed to look right when crossing a street. I walked directly into the path of a moped bearing a small Balinese man carrying an enormous sack of French bread. All combatants were flung violently in all directions; chunks of bread littered the impact site. We both escaped with minor injuries, mostly to dignity. The bread was a total loss. Had it been a car rather than a bike, I would have been history.

The beaches of Bali were pleasant but infested with swarms of aggressive, unrelenting vendors and raucous, blue-collar, beer-swilling Aussies on holiday. Denpasar was a sweaty, bustling oriental city with wonderful shops and so-so restaurants. The best part of Bali was our trip to Ubud in the highlands. We stayed at a wonderful, old-fashioned hotel that sprawled over a terraced hillside. We were assigned to a suite called, "puri-one-down." (No idea what it meant, but we loved it.) We purchased a large, carved, garishly painted garuda (sort of a devil-dog), that still guards our living room with ferocious devotion. Except for the antiquities, Bali comes in a distant second to Kauai in the "island paradise" category, at least in our reckoning.

But for the past nine years, we have been blessed with the opportunity to escape to Kauai. (I acquired quite a few United Airlines Award miles over the years. We always splurge on First Class, since we were obliged to use miles before they expire—changed in 1999).) As "retired

military" we are able to compete ("space available") for one of the cottages that grace the wide swath of pristine beach at the Pacific Missile Range Facility (PMRF) at Barking Sands, just across the channel from mystery-shrouded Niihau. During my Mercury days, I had become familiar with the magnificent, snowy beaches at Barking Sands (but I had not known about the beachside cottages).

Linda and I were staying in a rental apartment about ten miles east of the base near Kekaha, when we decided to "take a look" at PMRF. We were astonished; ten gracious, two-bedroom cottages plunked right on the beach, modest but perfect. So the next year we applied (six months in advance) and were accepted for a two-week interval. We have been back each year since. In 2000 and 2001 we were able to stay for one month. In the past we were obliged to spend the second two weeks in an expensive condo in Poipu. Kauai makes for a relaxed "annual honeymoon" interlude, and it breaks the back of winter in Chama. (This handy *raison d'etre* has changed in recent years, as I will describe.)

The only bit of unscheduled excitement during a visit to Kauai occurred a few years back. NutraSweet got wind of an upcoming "60 Minutes-Australia" program that promised to be exceedingly ugly. Chicago called and asked if I could "fly to Sydney and defend the product." I was not carrying my passport and, certainly, did not have an Australian visa. The PR folks were desperate; the Monsanto office in Sydney gravely predicted that the program could bring disaster to our corporate reputation in all Southeast Asia (and knock the hell out of sales). I thought this was a bit overblown. But I flew over to Honolulu, begged the U.S. Passport Office for an emergency passport. ("...only for life or death situations, Sir"). I asked to speak to the Consul, pleaded my singular case and was issued a temporary passport. I jogged down the street to the Australian Consular office and prevailed on them to issue me a visa.

I flew to Sydney on Qantas that evening. I slept poorly, was rushed off the plane by anxious, hot-breathed NutraSweet locals, whisked to a

hotel, allowed to shower, shave, then hustled off to the TV station. Within 10 minutes, I was facing the most hostile "vintage Mike Wallace" clone I had ever met. The interview went as well (or as badly) as could be expected. My Inquisitor had his mind closed; consideration of any scientific proof of aspartame safety was not on his agenda. (So what else is new?) With considerable effort, I managed to retain my ever-charming, avuncular facade. En route to the airport the following morning, my cabbie turned to stare at me, "Ain't you the American bloke what was on "60 Minutes" last night?" I nodded weakly. Cabbie smiled, "Miserable SOB ain't he?" I felt much better, slept most of the way to Honolulu. All in a day's work.

On Kauai we lead a very simple life. We have been blessed with marvelous weather on each visit, and we usually hit the beach (or pool in Poipu) in the morning and read Kellerman, Crichton, Wambaugh stuff. We play Trivial Pursuit (relaxed rules with helpful pantomime permitted) or somewhat-less-than-rigorous Scrabble in the afternoons. We do a lot of hiking in the mountains around Kokee. I think we have explored every trail, some many times. A few are frankly arduous, down-down-down (into the upper valleys), picnic, then up-up-up, as much as 1000 feet of difference. I usually stagger out gasping and wheezing a few hundred feet behind gazelle-like Linda. But the scenery is beyond spectacular. Lush "Bali Hai" valleys and sweeping, multi-hued landscapes characterize Waimea ("Grand Canyon of the Pacific," sort of).

We always pay homage to tropical-lavish Kalalau valley, and about half the time the sea mists dissipate long enough for a breathtaking sweep of narrow, plunging waterfalls and succulent rainforests to sparkling beach. We never fail to make a pilgrimage Haena, clamber over the giant sea-swept boulders nestled at the foot of the brooding Na Pali cliffs that grace the north side. Occasionally we will do sushi in colorful-but-crowded Hanalei. We once stayed a week there in an oversized beachside house. But it rains too much on that side, and the proximity

of swish Princeville, awash in hordes of too-cunningly-attired, too-evenly-tanned golf aficionados, is off-putting to us.

We have come to love the non-tourist-discovered, slightly shabby west side just past Waimea and Kekaha. In the evenings, Linda prepares sashimi and sushi with tall, cool libation, and we relax on the lanai, field glasses trained on the humpbacks at play in the Niihau channel. Then we pause to inhale the passionate sunsets. We eat out rarely, but few of the islands have restaurants that would titillate a serious gourmet. If God is good and the market does not founder, we plan to continue to visit Kauai until we are very old folks. (After our Mileage Plus miles expire we plan to fly space-A military air transport from Travis to Hickam; not First Class, but what the hell—it's free!)

Life in Chama evolved into a simple, pleasant routine. I have published a few papers (in *The Pharos* and *Annals of Internal Medicine*) about retirement, primarily for medical colleagues. My central thesis is simple: have a game plan worked out many years in advance of the Great Day. I will not rewrite the paper here, but three cardinal aspects bear repetition. Good health is first and foremost; this involves far more than the blessing of sound genes. Early in life there is much one can do to help oneself (and spouse) avoid or delay serious illness. It is related to a common-sense quality of living: balanced, calorically appropriate **eating**; reasonable, regular, serious sweat-inducing **exercise**; cigarette avoidance and making some peace with your inevitable demons (stressors?).

Next is **financial security**. It would seem obvious, but far too many of my clinically sophisticated, high-earner colleagues vastly underestimate the cost of "living in the manner to which they have become accustomed" during their later, less financially productive years. And finally, one must have a **plan:** how you will spend your day. Implicit in this planning process is thoughtful, penetrating, frank discussions with your spouse. And this may be the most difficult task of all: golf, fishing and reading good books simply won't cut it over the long haul. Retirement must be regarded as a final career—contemplated as carefully as

any other in your lives. There are many options, all dependent on the desires and resources of the individual couple. But if you have made adequate preparation and are reasonably lucky, it may well be your longest and most enjoyable time of life. It has been for us.

This may well read like a poor man's Baedeker's, but travel is a very important part of our *carpe diem* philosophy of retirement. We wander around quite a bit. At least once a week, and perhaps twice a month, we made an afternoon trip to Pagosa Springs in nearby Colorado (for food shopping and barbeque at the Ye Olde Hog's Breath Saloon) or zing east over the Tres Piedras pass to Taos (for lunch at Doc Martin's). Occasionally we wandered to Durango or Alamosa or Santa Fe. About once a month we made a weekend foray to Albuquerque and catch up on movies, Chinese and Indian food or prime rib at the Kirtland Officers' Club. We have hiked most of the trails in the area (Abiquiu and Heron Lake).

When the extravagant fall colors bless our aspen and oak, we take visiting friends up into Colorado to Ouray and Silverton, by way of Telluride and Mesa Verde, a singularly glorious loop. A few years back, we discovered one of the best kept secrets in the country: the breathtaking Black Canyon of the Gunnison, just east of Montrose, Colorado. It is wild and exciting, an extravagance of tumbled black rock and sheer cliffs, unlike any other national park in the country.

For the past four years we have established a "Christmas ritual." It may sound a trifle misanthropic, but we struggle to avoid the tourist swarms that now invade all national parks in most seasons. On December 23, we head out for Monument Valley to stay at (miraculously still undiscovered) Gouldings motel, just over the Utah border north of Kayenta. It is owned and operated by Navajos, and the bookkeeping is charmingly informal (inchoate?). The next morning we wander through the fabulous, usually deserted, marvelously grotesque, windetched sandstone monoliths. (The valley has been immortalized by the likes of John Ford in dozens of westerns. It is now background for more TV auto ads than any other real estate on the planet.)

Then we spend Christmas Eve at the rustic old El Tovar Hotel on the brink of the South Rim (reservations one year in advance). Margueritas in the friendly bar on arrival, and then we revel in the festive, tastefully garlanded, *gemutlich* dining room. In the morning we enjoy a full breakfast in the room, unwrap gifts, hike part of the rim trail (snow and slipperiness permitting) and then repeat libation in the bar, before another sumptuous repast. It makes for a wondrous holiday.

About once a year, we make a pilgrimage East to visit Linda's aging mother, middle-aged son and family, my sister and kin, and old friends in the Maryland, Philadelphia, New Jersey area. We call it our "Annual Crab Cake Run." We always escape to the Eastern Shore of Maryland to gorge on seafood. Our favorite restaurant is Hemingway's. They have a great deck perched on the east side of the Chesapeake Bay bridge, and offer the best crab cakes and crisp fries we have been able to find (and our quest has ranged as far as Crisfield and Pocomoke City).

After our first year in Chama, we decided to buy a 25-foot, Hitch-Hiker II fifth wheel trailer. As I indicated earlier, we had already acquired a new Ford F-250 truck (primarily for plowing the driveway), but we had it outfitted with a fifth-wheel attachment and a rear axle, heavyweight "haul package." We have always wanted to cruise the inland waterway to Alaska. So we signed up for a USAA cruise package out of Vancouver. What better way to take a "shake-down" trip in the trailer than to meander leisurely up to Vancouver? We picked up the giant (to us) vehicle in Albuquerque. It was considerably different than the handy, manueverable17-foot Class C we had driven a few years earlier. (But how hard could it be? One always sees craggy 90 year-olds and their blue-haired spouses tooling down the highway in giant RVs.) So we began our westward trek.

Linda had never seen Rocky Mountain National Park, so we headed north from Albuquerque, where we had picked up our "rig." Late that evening, we wheezed into Leadville, Colorado (about 10,000 feet), and found a pull-through (thank God!) RV park. We disembarked, hitched up the myriad, medusa-like umbilicals ("which is gray water and black

water?"), and Linda cooked her first meal. It was very cozy and roomy. We had a queen-sized bed and enjoyed our first night. The next day was cold, but we savored coffee and rolls, unhitched the life-support systems and rolled north toward the park. By now I had some sense of confidence in driving the beast, but as we began to ascend in the park we both noted an alarming paucity of similar vehicles—rolling in either direction.

Well, traversing Rocky Mountain was a true-blue, white-knuckle odyssey. The road was damn narrow (at least it seemed such to me) and very demanding. The highway engineers had outdone themselves in imaginative corkscrewing. In some spots the drop-offs were steep and forever. Linda soon discovered that gazing out the window was an invitation to vertigo—down about 2,000 feet on some formidable curves over an invisible shoulder. She spent most of the voyage studying her palmer creases. For me the problem was keeping the rig moving at some reasonable speed and, of course, on the road. At times, I had to drop into first gear utilizing four-wheel drive to maintain up-hill speeds up to 10 miles an hour! On the downhill I dropped into second to keep from burning brake linings, but the stench of hot asbestos permeated the cab. There were very few places to pull out and release the endless snake of fuming sedans that tailed behind. I was the innocent recipient of many and varied digital gestures whenever the angry serpent managed to sneak past.

But we survived, now well blooded. From here on all driving challenges **had** to be less arduous. We wheezed into an RV park in Estes Park and collapsed over stiff drinks. We were soon besieged by a host "old timers" who felt disposed to chat. We swapped pedigrees, admired work histories ("24 years selling' for Sears..."), listed geographical conquests, sniffed at each other's rigs, boots, etc.—all the good-old-boy RV fraternity chit-chat. They asked where we "came in from." When we said over Rocky Mountain National Park, a look of frank disbelief. "Only a darn fool would take them mountains in a big rig!" Now they tell me.

So we continued our trip; the driving was all anti-climax after that. I would not be so cavalier as to brag that it was a piece of cake. I never became comfortable backing the damned thing, and we both hated negotiating city traffic. It was most pleasant when we stopped (after wrestling the wires and tubes). We decided that RV travel was just not for us. We parked the fifth-wheeler at the Whidbey Island Naval Air Station, unhitched the RV and drove the truck to Vancouver to meet the cruise ship. It was not an uneventful excursion.

Linda was driving, and we anticipated swift transit across the "friendliest border in the world." This did not happen. We found ourselves in an endless parking lot of barely-moving vehicles; two lines snaked for over a mile back into Washington. I could see Linda beginning to unravel at the tedious process. Fractious Canadian border guards seemed to challenge every vehicle. She had arrived at full boil by the time a cheerless, green-clad chap leaned into the window and said, "Any alcohol?" She replied, "No," but it had a palpable edge, and it made me very nervous. Never get snippy with cops or border guards is an ancient and much-honored traveler's shibboleth.

Then, "Any firearms?" To my astonishment, "We have a shotgun, but it's back in the RV." Her voice had acquired the friendliness of a scalpel. I was aghast. It was true, but the weapon was about 60 miles back in the U.S. "Please pull over to the building there and step out of the vehicle." I sputtered, "But it's back in our trailer." He stepped back and indicated, with stony countenance, that we honor his recommendation. They explored every inch of the truck and consumed a deliberate 45 minutes. As we finally pulled away, "Why did you say that?" Still simmering, "He just pissed me off!" My ever loving wife of the short fuse.

The USAA cruise (Holland-America Line) from Vancouver to Alaska was a mixed bag. I think we were the youngest couple on board. We estimated average age at about 82. And the "entertainment menu" was appropriately geriatrically-adjusted: bingo, Lawrence Welkian evening dances, parties with funny hats and blowy things. Lots of

gaily-colored, polyester jump suits, radiant checked sports coats and cunning ties. The food was superb but seductively abundant and all-hours available. One could easily consume 8000 calories every 24 hours, and some folks did.

Soon we discovered a wonderful bar on the top-most deck that had plush leather chairs overlooking the bow. We took the early (less popular) feeding and then retired to our favorite chairs in the almost deserted bar. The waiters got to know us and anticipated our drink requests (and at what pace). We were fascinated by the hypnotic play of light and shadow in the narrow passages as evening crept abroad. The sunsets were often dazzling. Once deep into fjord country it became an extravaganza of shifting color. We went ashore at Ketchikan and Sitka and took little hikes through crisp pine forests. We made the traditional helicopter ride to the glaciers and enjoyed lunch amidst the icy blue, snow-laced glacial tundra. It was a very relaxed cruise but not exactly our cup of tea. I don't think we are chronologically or psychologically old enough to really savor such luxurious sloth, yet.

We only made two other forays in the Hitchhiker, and they confirmed our suspicion that RV travel was not destined to become our preferred mode. We were never completely relaxed while driving, and it was an unrelenting pain in the butt to have to hitch and unhitch every day. Also one has to be "mechanically handy" to correct a million little, measly-but-crucial widgets that get bent or busted. I am now and always have been mechanically challenged. And in too many camps, nice, overly friendly folks from Chattanooga and Council Bluffs want to share their dreary life's story and hear about yours. All we wanted to do, after an exhausting day of herding the monster, was to flake out and relax with a little wine and cheese. I concede we are anti-social, but what-the-hey, it's our life.

So we sold the trailer (at a 50% loss) and decided to splurge on a new Range Rover. We had come to realize that we wanted to travel faster, further and to more remote sites than the RV would allow. (On some rough roads, despite turtle-like speeds, the crockery and books in

the RV always seemed to gravitate to the floor—in pieces and tatters.) Also we wanted to start later, stop earlier, find a comfortable motel, seek out a decent restaurant, belt down a few cocktails and catch a little cable before sacking out. Linda didn't mind cooking in the RV, but I always felt guilty. Rompin' and ragin' in the Rover was far more attuned to our style than trailer travel.

But Range Rovers were expensive, so Linda wrote to about half a dozen dealerships across the country to compare prices. We had been assured by the starchy Albuquerque Rover folks that prices were pretty much fixed across all dealerships. ("Land Rover does not bargain!") They were wrong. The best offer came from Wilmington, Delaware. So we closed the deal by phone and drove east in our sturdy Pathfinder. We picked up the Rover and drove both vehicles to Edgewood and presented the ever-faithful Nissan (it had racked up about 110,000 well-tended miles) to Linda's son and family as a "nothing" present. They desperately needed another vehicle and were delighted. We took off in the Rover to revisit the Maritimes, a sort of shakedown, re-familiarization-with-PEI-lobster trip.

We visited an old friend, a former teacher from Maui (Seabury Hall) named Snooker (really) Hamilton, living in Chester, southern Vermont. Then we took off for Maine. Suddenly, the brand spanking new, top-of-the-line Rover (it had logged about 400 miles) developed a terrible shuddering sound that seemed to emanate from the windshield. At first it sounded like something had shaken loose but frantic inspection revealed nothing visibly amiss. The noise escalated at about 60 mph and became so loud at 70 that we could not speak to each other. But it was capriciously intermittent. We were sorely disconcerted. After one more day of this nonsense, I called the Land Rover emergency number just south of the Canadian border and was referred to the nearest dealership—in Boston! I spoke to a pleasant mechanic who said that one other owner had made a similar complaint, but the cause had not been identified. He suggested we bring the vehicle to Boston. That was just too far. He assured me that the noise, although

obviously troublesome, did not seem to threaten function or longevity. How could he be so damn sure?

Linda and I pondered the situation. We had planned to return to the States via Michigan, and we figured we probably could survive the decibels until we landed at a dealership we knew was in Barrington. We decided to persevere. I won't say we accommodated to the persisting auditory assault, but we tried not to allow the shudder inhibit our fun. We drove to Halifax, wandered the coast of Nova Scotia, took the ferry to Prince Edward Island (the new bridge was under construction) and gorged on lobster for a few days. We biked the wind-swept northern beaches and then drove the Gaspe peninsula (not very exciting).

Somewhere before we arrived in Quebec City, we received word from NutraSweet (we kept in contact every few days by phone) that the infamous TV magazine *Hard Copy* was preparing a very nasty piece on aspartame. They wanted to send a crew up to Quebec and tape an interview with me. And, indeed, we did. In a shabby suite in some nondescript hotel, a surprisingly friendly, distinctly Francophile TV crew flew in from Montreal. We taped an on-camera interview with a mean-spirited, invisible reporter firing questions from Los Angeles. I responded by speaking to an uncommunicative red eye mounted on a camera, most disconcerting. It lasted about 20 deadly minutes. As usual, when the edited version was aired, I appeared for about 30 seconds. *Hard Copy* had pursued their traditional, sensation-oriented editing. I was interspersed inopportunely, amidst the usual assortment of garrulous, obese, dysfunctional "victims of aspartame."

We enjoyed Quebec City from the vantage of a pleasant apartment in the shadow of the Frontenac (where we could not get a room). Then we drove the trans-Canadian Highway to Sault Ste. Marie and spent a day bicycling quaint Mackinaw Island. We skirted the east side of Lake Michigan, spent a night in Green Bay, then on to Barrington and the Land Rover dealership. I took a mechanic for a ride, and, naturally, the Great Shudder (which had always been unpredictable) refused to perform, at any speed! Neither he nor any of his compatriots had ever

heard of a Range Rover committing such an egregious, undignified sin. But he said he "believed us, but..." Of course, 20 miles out of Chicago, the malevolent rascal gave a wonderful, shuddering performance.

Once back home we took the vehicle to a dealership in Albuquerque, and this time I succeeded in reproducing the noise in all its full-throated glory. Redemption! The mechanic said it was coming from the seal around the windshield. Apparently there was one small segment that had not been glued (or whatever) properly and wind would cause it to vibrate at high speed. The ever-skeptical mechanics were appropriately embarrassed and had it repaired within hours. We have never had the problem since.

Within three years we laid on over 100,000 tough miles. (Our country road in Chama is a five-mile stretch of gravel torment that we drove about every day. But our noble Rover handled it with reasonable grace. Perhaps it bore some residual guilt for its indecent lapse.) But the vehicle was very temperamental, with too-frequent minor problems for a putative ultra-tough, safari-qualified SUV. And every time the irksome warning light went on, it cost a flaming fortune. We were tempted to trade it in on something less expensive and less fragile. (As I edit this, a few months later, we have done just that.)

Our most recent adventure was the building of a second home in Madera Reserve, Arizona, a small community about 30 miles south of Tucson. As I get older there is little question that the cold weather and snow that shares our wonderful mountain, has become less fun and more physically challenging. So we purchased a four-acre lot that is relatively isolated from adjacent homes, but will provide the amenities of "city" sewage (no leach field and septic system), faithful electricity (no outages when snow and wind conspire) and city water (no well and pump with a half-mile uphill pipeline).

We opted for more civility, yielding some obvious freedom and solitude as we enter the millennium (and I approach 80). We have enjoyed dreaming with a reasonably compliant architect and created a modest, one-story home wrapped around an oval pool and spa, with

two guest rooms in a wing distant from the master bedroom. The kitchen is a "heart's desire" affair engineered by Linda, who once again had become a student. This time her subject was "kitchen stuff" (and she created a reference book of appliances and other accouterments thicker than the New York City yellow pages).

Thus I am writing these lines from the den of our new home. We moved in on November 3, 1999 and enjoyed a high desert Christmas on the patio. We toasted the Millennium from our spa. At present, we plan to spend six months here (early November to early May) and the rest up in Chama. If God is good and the Dow Jones does not tank, we hope to enjoy the best of both worlds.

As is obvious, travel has become an important part of our life in retirement. It adds just a bit of spice to our otherwise quiet life. And since we have just returned home from another terrific automobile "walkabout," I would like to talk about it. Relaxed auto travel is a thing we love, one of our much-preferred hobbies. By the grace of good fortune (and some sustained effort) we are both in good physical condition, have a respectable retirement income (we worked for it), and we share a joy of the open road, good food, a little liquid libation come sundown and occasional forays with boots and backpacks to places reasonably accessible in our Rover (and now our Volvos).

Over the years we have wandered every quadrant of the country (plus the Canadian Maritimes, Baja Sur, the Alaskan outback and far-flung points along the Alcan Highway). Of course, this preferred mode of travel is a more expensive way to wander about than hauling a fifth-wheeler. But, after all, it is cheaper than megabuck fat cat cruises (been there—done that—not again), and far less stifling than organized tours with blandly smiling shepherds waving little flags and blowing whistles, with one eye on the watch. Besides, it represents our principal form of self-indulgence.

We have evolved a few simple rules of the road. We are not early risers, so we hit the trail about 9:00 am. We carry our own coffee maker, so we do a few cups and perhaps a croissant or a banana. A giant break-

fast of pancakes and poachies is a rare (and much savored) treat. We carry an ample ice chest loaded with diet soft drinks and some good cheeses, fruit and crusty bread (Jewish corn rye preferred). We grab a light lunch on the fly, unless we encounter a particularly breathtaking vista where we pull over, picnic and sniff the flowers.

Our Rover, once cured of its pediatric malady, did all the "car things" in superb fashion: autobahn cruising speed all day; rock solid traction in snow; took to rocky terrain like a homesick mountain goat; sound system as good as our home. But, as I have indicated, it had so many electronic bells and whistles that it came off a trifle delicate (daily charges up and down our lumpy, dusty road did not help).

In mid-May 1998, we loaded up and headed off to New Orleans. (Linda and I planned to write a travel-food article for *Sunset* or *Conde Nast*) Fresh seafood has not come to Chama this century, and it is our number one gustatory pleasure. As I have said, we have been known to make near desperate "crab cake runs" to the Eastern Shore of Maryland We are unabashed "blue road" junkies. Whenever possible we eschew the interstates and seek out roads with dotted lines. We even do gravel if the scenery is very promising and the distance less than about 100 miles.

From Chama it was about two and a half days of pleasant cruising to the Big Easy. The first night we landed in Memphis, TX (southeast of Amarillo in the neck of the panhandle). We stumbled across terrific T-bones and chicken fajitas. Even the refried beans were memorable. Linda suspected their "secret ingredient" was liberal dollops of lard but was too timid to ask. The next night we had a stroke of good luck in Bossier City, LA. Since, we are retired military, whenever possible we try for DV (distinguished visitor) quarters, if space for itinerant retirees is available. We lucked out into some elegant digs at Barksdale AFB.

We landed in New Orleans the next afternoon (reservations at the modest but adequate Comfort Suites on Baronne Street). It was the "wrong side" of Canal, but just a short (swift and ever alert) walk to the Quarter. It was early so we strolled the Riverwalk for a few hours. We

each had our first dozen oysters on the half shell at the French Market Restaurant and Bar, ogled the bright lights and brazen "beauties" on Bourbon Street (even at this hour), and then consumed another batch of oysters and crawfish *toffee* at the Market Café on the edge of the Quarter. We were early enough to land a balcony table in range of a jazz quintet belting it out next door. One of the delightful aspects of wandering the Quarter is that you never quite escape the joyous sound of good jazz. It permeates the atmosphere like no other place on earth.

Later that evening we crowded in with a million other stand-ups at Preservation Hall for about two hours of jazz. None of those seated seemed disposed to play by the house rules and vacate after each stand, so we just shifted our feet, leaned against each other and absorbed. We ended up roaming the strip and nursed some over-priced, under-sexed drinks so we could soak up some down-home, eardrum-busting' Zydeco.

The next day we drove to Biloxi for crab cakes (not quite Hemingway's-on-the-Chesapeake but adequate for the seriously crab-deprived). The profusion of "river-boat-like" casinos tethered along the shore was impressive. (I always wonder what this importation of "the gaming crowd" does to the local quality of life. I am not sure it does much to enrich.) We took the great causeway back across Lake Ponchartrain and were thrilled by a spectacular lightning show that played across the city. That night it was The Great Splurge—at the Court of the Two Sisters. Thank heaven some good things survive the blessings of modernity. We relished the splendid food: more oysters (of course), crawfish bisque, *etouffee* (of course) and lobster-stuffed sea bass. The rain had passed, so we ate in the garden—lovely ambience and sparkling service.

(In reading this over I think it is appropriate to say some nice things about oysters. There has been a lot of doomsaying in the media, and I feel our bivalve buddies have gotten a bum rap. Obviously, Linda and I are hooked on raw oysters, and, yes we know that some oystermen have been known to exercise reprehensible personal hygiene habits, and

some unfortunate folks have acquired some ugly diseases. But we prefer to place our faith in restaurants that would never risk their reputations by dealing with unreliable suppliers. So we consumed tons of oysters in New Orleans, Galveston, Corpus Christi and San Antonio. We had nary a gurgle. Okay, we were lucky, but one cannot live in fear.)

The next day we dutifully plodded to the Café Du Monde for *café-au-lait* and *beignets*; it was aswarm with tourists (just like us). Lunch was boiled crawfish and, yes, oysters, at the Acme Oyster House. Their superior chow was matched only by the ambient noise level. It must be the superdome of decibels. The sun stopped smiling temporarily as we drove out of town, but we found a friendly blue road that hugged the south levee along the river to Donaldsville in Cajun Country. Why Donaldsville? Well, there is a **must** dining place just north of the town. You really have to stumble around to find it when driving in from the East, but every native will give directions, proudly. Lafitte's Landing has been a landmark for many years. We first sought it out after Linda encountered a mouth-watering piece in *Gourmet* in 1990. We always seem to arrive in good restaurants a little before a civilized lunch hour, but the service is always gracious. Lafitte's seafood bisque will give Bookbinder's (Original) in Philadelphia a mighty good run. We had sautéed soft-shell crayfish (the only place we had ever seen this on a menu) and a seafood platter, which included oysters, catfish, shrimp and calamari. It was "over-abundance" Cajun style. So we stashed the overage in a "go box" that became lunch the next day.

As our visit to Lafitte's will attest, Linda is an inveterate article clipper. She keeps a file, state-by-state of maps, motels, drives, hikes, and, best of all, general food reviews. Sometimes this obsession has curious consequences. In a November 1997 issue of the *Wall Street Journal*, she saw a piece about Hebert's Specialty Meats, a "fabulous" place stashed away in Maurice, LA (not on every map). They had created the "turducken," a culinary chimera consisting of boned turkey, stuffed with boned duck, stuffed with boned chicken. Layered between each "bird" is your choice of stuffing—crawfish, cornbread, rice, alligator meat,

shrimp or *andouille* sausage. We had elaborate plans to ship several frozen birds home to friends, but *triste dictu,* they did not freeze or ship! Since we had no friends of kinfolk residing in Maurice who could overnight an insulated care package, we departed down hearted and empty-handed. Our "Great Turducken Quest" was a bust. (In December 2000—garrulous John Madden introduced turducken to the American NFL faithful. So it was "discovered." We had one shipped for Christmas dinner 2001; It was over-priced and not wonderful.)

However, we made up for the Maurice misadventure in spades. We bedded down near Lafayette, and reveled in an absolutely wondrous dinner at Enola Prudhomme's Cajun Kitchen in Carencro. Enola is the "mother of all cooks," the actual mama who taught all the other perhaps more-famous Prudhommes how to find their way around a kitchen. As with Lafitte's Landing, Prudhomme's is not easy to find. It is an unpretentious, not-too-well-marked, low building sort of near Carencro. We enjoyed another treat: typical Cajun crawfish bisque, shrimp and blackened catfish.

The next day we charged west on I-10 (famous only for state cops whose principal hobby is issuing frivolous tickets to foreign, "out-of-Louisiana" vehicles, especially those from New York). Western Louisiana and eastern Texas are flat and dreary. We picked up a blue road just west of Beaumont and drove the coastal Bolivar Peninsula to Galveston. Wide stretches of deserted beach invited some serious leg stretching. Later, in Galveston we explored the tastefully restored Strand area. It had really been done well, revitalized since my last visit in 1968. The downtown had been recreated with meticulous historical accuracy over many years, following the disastrous hurricane of 1900 that leveled just about every structure on the island and killed thousands. Then we hiked a few miles of the broad beach adjacent to an endless protective seawall.

That night we broke one of our cardinal travel rules. We asked our desk clerk to recommend a good seafood restaurant. From past experience desk clerks rank about one notch above 18-wheeler jockeys as

connoisseurs of good road food. But our man was right on target. His recommendation of Gaido's Seafood Restaurant was outstanding (even by New Orleans standards).

We approached Corpus Christie by tracking down Padre Island from Port Aransas. Barrier Islands have always fascinated us. Long Beach off Barnegat in New Jersey and Hatteras from Whalebone to Okracoke (wonderful names!) off the Carolina coast are familiar stomping grounds from our years of living in the East. As they say, lovely places to visit but maddening for dwelling—unless you can tolerate hurricanes in your face every other year. Padre Island presented a redolent, enchanting vista: vast uncluttered sweeps of sea, sand and billowing clutches of sea grass, punctuated by occasional, well-weathered clapboard-house villages. In Corpus we were lucky again: modest quarters at the Naval Air Station, just a few miles down the strand, isolated from the bustle of town. We watched a glorious crimson sunset and did our seafood thing at Landry's (a chain but not bad) perched on the edge of the marina.

The following day we drove the South Padre Island. Friends had advised that South Padre was the "coming place" for snowbirds seeking barrier island respite. We were disappointed. Dozens of new, architecturally uninspired condos stood shoulder-to-shoulder obscuring any view of the Gulf. It lacked the grace of a Nag's Head or the folksy atmosphere of an Okracoke. It was a long drive for a visit we could have omitted. Back in town dinner was at the Lighthouse, one pier down from Landry's. The menu was less versatile than its competitor. All-in-all a less than a wonderful day.

Then it was on to San Antonio and Fort Sam Houston. I barely recognized the place; bright new edifices had sprouted all over the venerable campus. I felt as ancient as some of the grand old buildings that were now museums. We did get fair lodging on post and immediately headed for town. We had not paid our respects to the Alamo for many years. It remained an icon of quiet dignity, a place for thoughtful

reflection. In the warm, benevolent afternoon sunlight it was difficult to conceive of the violent 13 days of 1836.

(Always in the garden of the Alamo, I have wondered if post-Vietnam American men and women could galvanize **that** depth of patriotic fervor, to face certain death voluntarily, because they believe in a cause. I am far from sure. But even so, is it worth the ultimate sacrifice? What would have been the fate of Texas had it remained part of Mexico? Would the quality of life for its citizens have been worse? Probably. A visit to any town just across the border would seem to indicate so. How can just a few hundred yards make such a difference in people so similar in ethnicity? The American dream.)

We walked the full extent of Riverwalk beside the born-again San Antonio River (in 1955 it had been a trashy, polluted eyesore, resurrected a few years later to celebrate Hemisfair). Now it is a mid-city masterpiece of urban revitalization, populated by inviting waterside restaurants and fascinating shops. Mariachi music and down-home jazz wafted from a dozen hidden courts. Motorized launches with pleasantly hushed outboards murmured down the winding canals. Linda said all it needed were a couple of gondolas and a soprano aria from Rossini. It was just a stone's throw from La Villita (a kitsch replica of old San Antonio) and the Four Seasons Hotel. Lunch was double-dip Haagen-Dazs (one of our few dessert falls-from-grace on the trip). Dinner was chili rellenos and chicken fajitas with splendid margaritas at Casa Rio on the canal. We think it would be difficult to get bad Tex-Mex on the Riverwalk.

The next day was glorious. We headed for the fabled Hill Country north of San Antonio. Our mission was two-fold: bluebonnets and barbeque. We first landed in Johnson City and ran into Ronnie Weyerhaeuser, the owner and first (only) pit cook at Ronnie's Pit Barbeque. He makes the best barbecue brisket and smoked sausage on the planet. It was barely lunchtime, but we could not resist. Two succulent slices each of mesquite-smoked brisket smothered in sauce, onions and pickles, totally spectacular.

Later we sought dinner at the much-touted, pride of Llano, Cooper's Old Time Pit Bar-B-Q. But it came in a dim second to Ronnie's stuff. The cabrito was tough as rawhide, ribs were okay, brisket only middlin'. The pinto beans were good, as was coleslaw and potato salad. But the overall *gestalt* was, well, just blah. Also, the accouterments left us cold. Okay, maybe we are just finicky, big-city wimps, but we have never been kvetchy about good finger lickin' fare. However, a paper plate (instead of a square of butcher paper) would not get old man Cooper run out of Texas. (But we're not sure.) Maybe we just caught Coop on a bad day.

To get from Johnson City to Llano we took the 20-mile plus Willow City Loop. The scenery was so astonishing that we drove it twice. It is bluebonnet, coreopsis paradise, the Yellow Brick Road of Texas. Linda and I have logged more than a few miles but never have we experienced the magnificent sweeps of blue with scattered clusters of purple, yellow, orange and white flowers that brought charm to every bend of the road. We shot two rolls of 35 mm.

We eased along County 965 to Fredericksburg, another Hill Country gem. The old town was settled by a handful of Germans immigrants in 1846 and still retains some Old West charm, with a teutonic twist. You can hear occasional *deutchsprech* in the shops. We loaded up on sour cream and apple strudel (tucked into our trusty ice chest) from George's Old German Bakery and Restaurant. So we blew our breakfast discipline for the next few days. Back to San Antonio and then to Del Rio, when Dame Fortune smiled again. We were provided plush VIP quarters at a seemingly deserted Laughlin Air Force Base. At Don Marcelleno's #1 in lovely downtown Del Rio, the guacamole was very good, chili rellenos and chicken enchiladas were B plus.

Just west of Del Rio we encountered the vast Amistad International Reservoir, fed predominantly by our own Rio Grande. When you cross that gentle river at Espanola or El Paso, you cannot believe it could fill such an enormous watery domain (in addition to Elephant Butte lake in New Mexico). But aside from the Pecos and a few other piddlin west

Texas creeks, it does the job. You begin to appreciate the grandeur of the Grande. We detoured a few miles to walk into Seminole Canyon. This is a strange cul de sac of southwestern history related to the migration of Seminole Indians from Florida who met up with slaves from Texas. They became the original Buffalo "scouts" (not soldiers), legendary trackers for the frontier army.

That night we landed in Presidio in anticipation of our trek into Big Bend National Park. En route we encountered an eerie ghost town, Shafter, populated by a few hardy residents. Its intriguing story included a major silver strike, boom and bust, the Mexican War (Pancho Villa rampaged nearby) and then decline. This was all related by old pictures and letters contained in a wood frame exhibit in the marvelous old-town boot hill. We took some extraordinary pictures, tottering gravestones decorated by brilliant blooming ocotillo.

Presidio was a let down. We anticipated a quiet picturesque border town, but it had seen better days. Too late, we discovered that Ojinada in Chihuahua just across the river would have been a more intriguing watering hole. In the morning we realized that we should have done more homework; if we had hung on a few more miles east we'd have landed in Terlingua or Lajitas. The latter bills itself as "the Palm Springs of Texas." We were not convinced that selection of that particular sobriquet would ensure invasion by the rich and famous, but the village seemed to attract lots of shaggy Big Bend camper-hiker types. Lajitas was low key and tastefully put together. State 120 romps playfully through the hills and washes beside the Rio Grande. It earns high marks in our Blue Roads hierarchy.

Inside the park we took the Ross Maxwell Scenic Mountain route through the western reaches to Santa Elena Canyon. Then we hauled on boots and daypacks and hiked the gentle trail into that magnificent canyon. Lunch was under the towering basalt cliffs where the unique topography creates an optical illusion—the great river seems to run uphill. Then we made the dumbest mistake of the trip.

Indicated on the park map was a primitive road ("four wheel drive, high clearance vehicles only"). Just the kind of stuff for our hardy Rover, right? **Wrong**! It looked like about 50 miles, and it explored the south part of Big Bend where we (and now we suspect untold thousands of others) had never been. Well, it was one helluva challenge for man and machine. "Not maintained" (a favorite road sign) became the euphemism of the century. One ten-mile stretch, aptly and ominously named "Black Gap" was so boulder strewn and steeply angled with nasty drop-offs, that it demanded our lowest range four-wheel drive and the vehicle raised to its maximum clearance, to barely crawl up and over and down. We felt like a Range Rover advertisement. That "50 miles of bad road" took three and a half hours to traverse, and the scenery was not all that great, unless you adore acres of scrub cactus and a surfeit of boulders. We passed one other poor fool laboring along in a battered pick-up. But we suspected he **had** to be there. So forget River Road West (and East).

Thus we staggered into the remote Chisos Mountain Lodge. We had made reservations months in advance. Dinner at the lodge restaurant (the only show in town) was solid south Texas fare. The next morning we hiked to The Window. It was 5.2 miles of well-manicured mountain trail. Just as I have described the trails in Kokee on Kauai, it was all down then all up. We lunched at the base between sheer black basalt walls polished to a fine gloss by generations of roaring "pour-off."

The return trail up would rate about a "5." (In my personal mountain trail rating system; a "10" [tops] would be the 9.5 mile Milolii Ridge trail on Kauai—it almost killed me; a "9" would be the Peek-a-Boo Loop with its awesome 29 switchbacks in magnificent Bryce Canyon. Mountain goat Linda thinks I'm a wimp.)

The following day we stayed in great bungalow-quarters at the White Sands Missile Range (a plaque indicated that Werner Von Braun lived there during some of the early Redstone firings). In nearby Alamogordo we toured the strip seeking a likely dinner candidate. We

were disheartened by miles of unrelenting, uniformly dismal, fast-food dives. In desperation we made a swing through secondary streets and encountered Le Montchiari. The cuisine was northern Italian, a thoroughly delightful surprise. Very high marks.

Sunset was a magic time in the surreal splendor of the White Sands National Monument. It is unique and unsurpassed in our experience. We doubt if there is another place on the planet that hypnotizes all witnesses unto spectral silence. It is an ethereal spectacle, subdued colors dancing on dunes of dazzling white gypsum stretching to the limits of vision. It ranks with Uluru in the Australian Outback.

We took an old friend home. A winding blue road meanders from Ancho to Tijeras via Gran Quivera National Monument. Tijeras Canyon is an elegant passage to the foot of towering Sandia Peak, forever guarding the eastern approach to Albuquerque. For our final gustatory fling we returned to our favorite "local" restaurant, Yen Ching. We shared our traditional sizzling rice soup, special fried rice, lobster with spicy garlic sauce (Linda) and moo shoo pork (me). All washed down with Tsing Tao beer.

And so we returned to Chama via our final slender road, winding through the Jemez mountains to Cuba, then Coyote, Tierra Amarilla and home. We had been gone about three weeks; we had explored some dramatic blue roads; we each gained about five pounds, a tribute to our delicious sloth and unrestrained caloric indulgence. But now we were ready to return to our "post vacation" regime of rational diet and reasonable exercise.

As I make these "final edits" much has occurred since I began this story four years ago. Son Jonathan resides in Ridgefield, Connecticut with wife, Carole and two children, Jordan and Melanie. He has been and editor-producer for NBC, but recently began to work for a small TV production company where he has more opportunity to exercise his creative skills. I feel than Jon has never been properly appreciated by his industry; he has a rare talent. Steven still lives on Maui where he practices internal medicine and nephrology. He is a widely respected

clinician with a fierce dedication to environmental preservation. His daughter, Lauren, is an "island beauty" who now attends St. Johns College of Santa Fe. She has been to visit us in Chama and here in our new residence in Madera Reserve. Lauren is a thoroughly delightful, intellectually disciplined young woman. A "chip off the old block." Steven visits Stella, my former wife, who still resides on Maui, quite frequently. I am pleased with my offspring and their progeny.

We have come to love the high desert, and, in all probability, ultimately, we will sell our home in New Mexico (with great reluctance) and spend the rest of our days here in Arizona. Yes, we sold the Range Rover. We flew to Gothenburg about a year back and picked up a sleek Volvo convertible at the factory. We "did" Scandinavia and northern Europe for five weeks (5000 miles). We loved the little beast so much that we recently bought a 2001 Cross Country Volvo station wagon. Super vehicles!

Linda and I still are blessed with reasonable good health. I have taken to bicycling in the mornings for exercise. The road to Madera Canyon wanders past our little development. So I bike for about six or seven miles gently up-hill, which is a decent, sweat-provoking ritual and then glide back down. I do this for three days and relax the fourth.

Linda walks our Aussie Shepherd, Boomer, for about a vigorous mile each day. She has found a delightful trail through the pecan groves that avoid the cactus and scrub of the desert that surrounds us. We still plan to travel quite a bit. (We "did" Alaska and the Canadian parks in 2000 and last year tooled down to dramatic "Copper Canyon" in Sinaloa, Old Mexico to ride the train).

I still do some *pro bono* committee work, edit and write an occasional article/editorial for medical publications. I took on being book review editor for *The Pharos,* the Alpha Omega Alpha quarterly, and that is sort of fun. We still read a great deal. Linda has taken up "desert gardening," but if and when we finally sell the Chama house we will bring her loom down here, and she will resume her first love, creative

weaving. In her gleaming "personalized" kitchen she still produces magical dinners each night. So our life remains close to ideal.

In July 1998, I wrote a somewhat facetious piece called, "Some Insouciant Reflections on Approaching Age 75" (*Southern Medical Journal*). I will borrow from it since I feel it may be an appropriate way to end this meandering opus. I described the fact that more and more of us Medicare and Social Security "entitlees" plan to be hale, heart and sexy well past 65. (And with sildenafil [Viagra]—the latter delight may persist for another score or more. We can only hope.) Most of my generation who have been blessed with less-than-awful genes and having paid our dues with 50-plus years of reasonable diet and exercise discipline, have become progressively more circumspect. No, change that to **selfish**.

We really do care about the threat to our national security posed by international terrorism and the impact of increased surveillance on individual freedom and privacy. But I don't mind cameras in the supermarket; we have nothing to hide. We worry about the Bush-Cheney-Wolfowitz militancy. We worry about escalating national indebtedness (and the enormous credit card debt of too many people) that some economists say will threaten the financial and physical security (Social Security and Medicare) of our grandchildren. And we also vaguely wonder about depletion of the ozone layer (but aren't they saving the rain forests, preparing to build "fuel-cell" autos, and burying old spray cans?). Global warming appears to be a real threat (but would it be so terrible if ugly L.A. and concretized Manhattan got a bit submerged; they might become as charming as Venice—only kidding). Disappearance of endangered species is more than bothersome, but hasn't that been happening for centuries? But aren't we saving the manatees, Mexican gray wolves, swordfish, condors, and aren't there more elephants in Kruger and koalas in Australia than ever before? I understand that cloning techniques may provide a method of saving endangered species.

I don't intend to trivialize such stuff; we do have some enormous global problems. One can only hope that the terribly bright young people who are bringing us dramatic adventures in biotechnology, genetic engineering, metallurgy and electronic communications will take time off to come to grips with these vexing social, political and economic challenges. But can we hope to maintain our national intellectual viability and creativity by relying on 0.01% of the population? Perhaps we must.

But we worry, even more, about the not-too-subtle "meaning down" of America. This was dramatized by the recent effort by some pop-psychologists to justify rampaging road rage in America as just another contemporary expression of the rugged, old-fashioned competitive spirit. When the trip to the ATM becomes an exercise in evading a minefield of muggers, and when I begin to suspect that our elk-hunting neighbors are refugees from Ruby Ridge, things are really getting out of whack.

Finally, we are concerned about the well-intended-but-potentially disastrous "dumbing down" and "ego amplification" of our kids. Schools seem to be teaching them that its "OK to fail" as long as you have "pride in yourself," while their SAT score sag to Third World levels. I am not at all reassured; this a new definition of "pride."

So okay, life has always been filled with such worrisome clutter. But most of us pre-yuppie types have managed to thrash our way though much of this chaos—realizing our impotence at solutions—and get on with our retirement lives. We figure that we gave life our best shot (at whatever we were doing) for 50 or 60 years, and now we have passed on the sputtering torch. Our primary concern has become the maintenance of a reasonable quality of life. This includes sustaining our blessed good health (or however much of it is left), ensuring continuing financial security (after a lifetime of reasonable frugality, while squirreling away some modest investments and other assets], and retaining sufficient intellectual juice to enjoy a few good friends, occasional grandchildren, thoughtful books, stimulating conversation, non-

rap music, delectable food and drink, and the infinite joy of tooling down a deserted western highway with the top down.

It has required a little work over the past seven plus decades to get to this point, and we are not about to relinquish it easily. As one of my older friends once said, "When you begin to think more about your bowels than Bosnia, you are over the hill." But more seriously, the greatest fears of those of my generation are poverty, loneliness and irreversibly poor health. When life comes to the dismal nadir of failing to enjoy each day, and then becoming a burden to those we love, most folks I know would prefer to toss in the towel than endure life without joy. One should not have to move to gloomy but enlightened Oregon or cultivate jailbird Kervorkian to be master of one's fate. One should certainly retain the choice of "the final option," with or without legalized professional assistance.

And a final reflection. I have always wondered about the one major glitch that occurred during the wondrous process of evolution that created this marvelously complex, incredibly efficient (yet imperfect) maze of DNA coils we call *Homo sapiens*. We should have been programmed with a "universal apoptosis" gene. Yes, a sort of Faustian arrangement. We should have been designed to generate a protein that would allow us to live to be 90, but during that time we would be impervious to disease, hip fractures, suicide and homicide, with all of our arteries, and most of our teeth and critical synapses intact.

The "pact" would be invalidated (another enemy protein activated) if we consistently abused our robust homeostatic mechanisms. Then, at the proper time, the apoptosis gene would activate the "death protein" and it would allow us to just peter out in deep and restful sleep. I could easily accept that Faustian fate. Perhaps, when I am 85 I will change my mind, but I think not. It has been a terrific life, and I have enjoyed almost every minute, but enough will have been enough. I hesitate to contemplate a future where life expectancy has expanded to about 150, and there will be many more old people than young people—world-

wide. It represents a potential reality that the world has not come to grapple with.

I often suspect the Grand Planner didn't do His/Her long-term genetic homework too carefully. The GP did not count on our stubborn species solving most of the problems that for many centuries knocked most of us off at a much earlier age. As I have indicated, it seems there already may be too many of us now for our resources to accommodate. And it promises to get worse: Malthus may yet be vindicated. It will require a unique economic, political and social paradigm. I know the eternal optimists tell us that human ingenuity will solve all of our problems for food, energy and space, but I am not so sure. Even if the whiz kids can be persuaded to look up from their electrons and genes for a moment to see that the world is disappearing, that too few people are working and producing, and too many people are just living and consuming, I am not sanguine.

I suspect this is the time when I am allowed to look back on my life and wonder, "What was that all about?" Was I put here to accomplish something? Or, more likely, was it a chance biological phenomenon—a "luck of the genetic draw" that I was not born a titmouse or an eagle. I thank God that I was born me and not some other species in some other terrible place in some other terrible time. I really appreciate that. So, what did I "accomplish" during my tour of duty? If I had been da Vinci or Einstein or Gandhi, or even Napoleon or Stalin, I might be able to indicate how my presence on earth had altered the fate of mankind. But those kinds of folks are most rare. Most of us are obliged to settle for something far less grand.

In moments of quiet reflection, I think I am reasonably satisfied with my life. I did no particular wonderful or awful things. For better or worse, some of my genes helped produce some fairly good offspring, and a few very nice grandkids. They are good people—not perfect, but I like them most of the time. I have helped educate a batch of doctors and nurses, made a lot of patients feel better and even cured a few. I have written no deathless prose or poetry or created any notable works

of art or music. But some folks enjoyed some of my stuff. I have led no earth-shaking political or social revolutions, but then, I have not caused anyone pain (knowingly) or deprived anyone of justice or dignity.

My contributions have all been sort of nice and small. So, on balance it has been a good life, not particularly distinguished or memorable, but how many truly "important" human beings have there been? Yes, I would be willing to vote for the "universal apoptosis" gene.

But I reserve the right to change my mind.

# About the Author

Robert H. Moser is a retired internist-cardiologist with an eclectic career background. He has been an educator of young internists, a battlefield surgeon during the Korean War, his 22-year medical military career culminated as chief of medicine at Walter Reed Army Medical Center. Subsequently, he was a practicing general internist in a small group on Maui, editor-in chief of the *Journal of the American Medical Association*, CEO of the American College of Physicians, and medical director of The NutraSweet Company. He was one of the original medical flight controllers for NASA's Projects Mercury and Gemini. He has published extensively in the scientific medical literature, and written newspaper and magazine columns about medicine for the laity. He has published three books related to adverse reactions to drugs, training of internal medicine residents, and a history of the American College of Physicians. He is a Master of the American College of Physicians and a member of the Institute of Medicine.

0-595-26388-7

18231563R00313

Made in the USA
San Bernardino, CA
05 January 2015